MEMORIES OF LOVE, TEARS OF SADNESS

Louisa opened her eyes and looked at him tenderly. Oh God, you look so familiar, yet I don't know you, she thought as he stared into her eyes, filling himself with their blueness.

Like the sky on a cloudless day, he reflected silently, wondering if her eyes promised the same freedom and joy he felt when he looked up into such a sky.

Before either of them realized it consciously, he began to caress her cheek, kissing her mouth to find her yielding softly to him.

Then he kissed her deeply, gathering her urgently into his arms, his desire for her obvious and unrelenting. And Louisa met his warm mouth as if she were coming in from the cold, unable to deny the warmth that surged in her body or her desire to respond to him for, though nothing else was certain, she knew their coming together was inevitable.

LOVE, REMEMBER ME

JESSIE FORD

BALLANTINE BOOKS • NEW YORK

Library of Congress Catalog Card Number: 79-91714

ISBN 0-345-28533-6

Manufactured in the United States of America

First Edition: March 1980

Chapter One

LOUISA Boyd Hudson had not yet grown used to this desolate coastline. San Diego, the southernmost town in California, was very different from the tropical Louisiana parish she had come from, and she wondered if she would ever get used to the drab vegetation scattered randomly over the thin soil ledges above the beach. But Louisa had readily grown used to the area's drier climate, to the seemingly endless spring, to the seasons of early fog.

She had spent the past four months in this unfamiliar place collecting her sanity and strength, preparing for childbirth, growing fond of the comfortable house that had been built for her use within the Hudson Compound, which lay at the ocean's edge, some distance from the small cluster of dwellings at the town's center. She filled it with her possessions, many of them gifts from Marshall, and she planned for the arrival of their baby, settling herself slowly and peacefully into the house. She had come to accept her situation and attempted to put the incidents of the past behind her, knowing she had courage enough to live beyond the past and, she believed, love enough to build herself and her child a future. She reasoned anyone who had traveled as far and as hard as she, had many more and better roads to see. In fact, she promised herself nothing less.

During these four months, Louisa felt she'd walked enough miles along the beach to equal the physical distance separating her from the man she was trying desperately to forget. Though she hated the early morning more than any other time of day, she would often wake even before the gulls descended on the beach. Then, in her drowsiness, in the softness of her bed and the stillness of the hour, she would lie beneath the covers to feel the warmth of her blood course through her veins, and ache with longing for Marshall's touch, and the fulfillment his love had given her.

To compose herself, Louisa made a ritual of going into the morning, greeting it face to face, defying her instinctual fears, challenging her ghosts. Covered by darkness, she would slip out of the compound to walk for as long as was necessary, and soon she grew intimate with the gray mornings and with the restive shore. She would walk, shivering in the dampness, never quite stepping into the tide as it inched slowly up the sand. Often she was engulfed in the silver fog that wound its glistening mist around her. But the chill she felt was not merely physical, and even the heavy wool shawl she clutched around herself could not protect her. She paced the wide, seemingly endless beach like a delicate, weary shore bird, her blue dressing gown as pale as the morning, wondering if she would ever be completely free from the ice-cold grip of pain and sorrow.

Now, suddenly, those months of waiting, those moments that were often tortured and lonely and passed so slowly were erased by the news that Marshall Hudson would soon disembark from the *Golden Lady*. The ship had been due, but Marshall's appearance was totally unexpected. Louisa was eager to welcome him into her life again, but only under the right circumstances. She swore this to herself even in the confusion of his sudden arrival. Yet, she was joyous because this must mean he was coming for her, otherwise why would he come at all? Their parting had been so final, and, even in her desire for him, she had not entertained the slightest hope that their separation was not permanent.

While Louisa tried to rest after the exhausting day, she found herself restless and eager in spite of her weariness. Her contractions had begun in the early afternoon, and she'd welcomed them, her labor progressing normally until shortly before dusk. Then, the pain stopped. Louisa was full term, but Carmen assured her, "Sometimes first babies are a little slow." She had only Carmen to rely on, and she'd come to trust her in all matters. "I have no choice but to trust you now," Louisa said wearily. The sturdy, dark Mexican woman saw herself as much a mother as a servant to Louisa, and Louisa had bonded herself to Carmen like countless other sea-swept creatures had. At times Carmen was as volatile as her mixture of Spanish and Indian blood might suggest, but to Louisa she was as gentle and protective as the silent morning fog that crept along the coast.

And when Louisa asked for the carriage to be brought for her so she could meet Marshall at the harbor, Carmen exploded, horrified by her request. "No, señora!" Carmen gasped. "Your pains stopped for now but that don't mean you not having a baby!"

Louisa knew Carmen thought she had completely lost her mind, but Carmen could not know the joy she felt, or her longing to touch Marshall again. Though he was partially responsible for her banishment to California, he had loved her, and she had loved him, beyond all redemption she knew. He had known her all of her life, and had interceded for her soul when she had felt most desolate. He had loved her when she was certain there was no hope for her and, in a way, had abandoned her only to save her. Marshall had been the source of all light in Louisa's life for as long as she could recall, so it did not seem so strange to her that she would go to meet him at this odd time.

Carmen did not know the full history of Louisa's relocation to California, but she recognized simple insanity when she saw it. Her face livid, she yelled at Louisa, "Now, you listen to Carmen! You soon gonna need all your strength. Señor Hudson can get here without your help. Back to bed, *niña!*"

"All right, Carmen," Louisa obeyed reluctantly. "But send the carriage on immediately. I want someone there the minute he gets ashore."

"*Sí,* señora," Carmen said, hastening from the room before her mistress could reconsider.

Louisa settled back into the pillows, wondering what the night would hold. The priest should be summoned, she thought suddenly. "Surely, Marshall will want the union sanctified *before* the birth." She was elated to think he would be with her for the delivery of their baby. It would help erase the endless months she had waited totally alone. But Marshall had not known of the pregnancy, and neither had she when she left Louisiana. She only learned she was "with child," as the "doctor" had advised her, aboard ship.

She had been so incredibly ill by the time the *Winged Horse* left its last American port that Captain Tomas Sebastian had said, "You're in my charge, Miz Hudson. I can't have you waste away before we even lose sight of land. You've traveled with me before and you never paled so."

Ordinarily, Louisa came alive aboard ship, the sea air only enhancing her delicate appearance. She usually looked like fine porcelain, fragile and beautifully feminine, slender with shining blue eyes, and long honey-blond hair left free to fly in the breezes. But, in fact, it was a false appearance, for beneath the fragility lay a reserve of strength that surprised even Louisa.

Now, she appeared gaunt, rather than slim, weak rather than delicate, and she couldn't conceal her increasing illnesses. She and the captain often took meals together. Lately she ate sparingly, or not at all. And, what she ate usually did not stay with her for long. Finally, one morning while she was retching before she even touched food, the captain came to her door with Doc Ellis.

"Doc is not a regular physician," he apologized, "but he's seen his share, and he's helped us through many a rough spot. Besides, he's the best nursemaid you'll find aboard this ship. Tell him your troubles and he'll do what he can for ya."

Louisa stared at both men with glassy eyes, not caring whether she lived or died. But in her present state she could hardly protest, and Captain Tomas left Ellis and his skeptical patient alone to discuss her ailments. If anything, Doc Ellis was sure of himself and not the least bit reticent. "You pregnant?" was his first question. Louisa started, then retched again, feeling more miserable than she had thought possible. She had been steadfastly forcing the possibility of pregnancy from her mind. Oh, God, she thought, and vomited again.

Doc Ellis went to her and felt her forehead. "No fever?"

"No fever," Louisa replied as she sank onto her soft bunk.

"Any aching, thirst, or dizziness?"

"None, just weakness and nausea."

"Weakness is 'cause you're not eating proper. You bleed regular?"

Louisa colored at his bluntness, shaking her head in answer.

"Well, seems a damned good possibility to me. When'd you bleed last?"

"I've only missed once," she said quietly.

"I take it you're not going to insist you're a virgin," he said matter-of-factly.

By that point, Louisa had somewhat recovered her stomach, and her tongue. She looked Doc Ellis full in the face. "Nor do I claim to have been ravished, beaten, and mistreated! You've merely pointed out what I chose to deny for convenience and peace of mind. Thank you for your diagnosis. You can assure the captain I'll no doubt survive this ailment!"

Doc was unmoved by her heated outburst, and continued almost as if it hadn't occurred. "I'll see Cook sends you broth and bread until you can manage. Get some fresh air when you can. I'll report to the captain you are with child." He paused to look at the very pale young woman. "Think he was suspicious anyway." He went to the door. "Your first?"

"Yes, my first," she said drily.

"You seem fit enough otherwise. Best you're going by sea, though. This voyage will be fair enough. We're traveling at a good time of year."

Some weeks later, she wondered at his prediction. The trip had been unremarkable after she recovered her appetite, but it certainly was not mild by her standards. As the ship struggled around Cape Horn, Louisa did not consider the storms in any respect close to mild, although Captain Tomas said he'd seen much worse. It would take two months of further traveling to reach her destination, and by the time she was settled in the California compound, she would be into her fifth month of pregnancy. She traveled alone, with adequate provisions for establishing a respectable household at the end of the California coast. She would be expected at her destination if overland messages had preceded her as planned, and she presumed correctly that all would be ready for her. Her guardian Simon Hudson was renowned for efficiency, so she felt certain her needs would be well met. Recently, Louisa had been a severe disruption to Simon Hudson's orderly household, but he did not begin to know the extent. What would the outcome have been, she wondered, if her pregnancy had been known before she left Louisiana?

Perhaps she should have been more suspicious of her physical condition as her slender body filled out almost voluptuously, and she shone like a jewel despite everything that seemed to be crashing down around her. But she had not noticed the changes in herself as much as had Marshall who watched her bloom even amid the destruction of their private dreams. He wondered at the sudden fullness of her breasts and the tautness of her belly, but he never questioned her as he caressed her silken body. In their passion, neither could believe the arrangements to which they had both given their consent. And they stole what time they could together, unable to change their fate which seemed irrevocably sealed.

Chapter Two

AFTER what seemed an undue length of time, Louisa heard the carriage returning to the compound. She had waited, resting as quietly as possible, trying to order her tumbling thoughts, and now she excitedly lifted her awkward form from the bed. Her labor pains had not returned, and she assumed her earlier pain was only a false beginning, just as Carmen said.

Anticipating Marshall's arrival, Louisa had dressed carefully in an emerald green dress with an appealing low neckline that distracted the eye from her very obvious condition. As the carriage pulled to a stop in front of the house, Louisa rushed from her room, nearly stepping on Carmen in her haste to greet Marshall.

But the carriage was empty.

Louisa was frightened by the driver's worried look. He spoke excitedly to Carmen in Spanish, glancing anxiously at the woman's mistress. Carmen's sob and *"Dios mio!"* accompanied by the sign of the cross made Louisa turn to ice.

"Tell me, tell me!" she cried, caught up in Carmen's excitement.

"A terrible fire on *Golden Lady,* señora. There is much excitement in the harbor. Some men died."

"Where is Señor Hudson, Manuel?" Louisa demanded directly of the driver. "Why have you returned without him?"

Carmen shuddered. The driver did not answer, refusing to look her in the eye.

"Well?" Louisa shrieked.

"Señor Hudson is missing," whispered Carmen.

Louisa thought she would faint, but instead she

7

stumbled into the house for her cloak, and returned
demanding Manuel drive her back to the harbor.

"But, señora, you cannot go in your condition!"
Carmen exclaimed.

"Damned if I can't," retorted Louisa. "It doesn't
seem this baby will be born tonight, and I can't sit here
wondering. Are you coming with me, Carmen? If so,
let's go—*now!*"

The driver assisted the women into the carriage.
"Hurry!" Louisa called after him. From Carmen's anxious look, Louisa was well aware that the woman was
holding her tongue in face of her ferocity. "If necessary, I'll whelp at the pier, but I won't stay here,"
Louisa snapped as the carriage turned back to the harbor.

The short trip took longer than usual because of
darkness and, measured only by Louisa's heartbeats,
seemed interminable. She did not dare consider anything but a natural delay due to the confusion of the
fire. But if that's so, why am I rushing to the scene in
this state? she asked herself.

Carmen appeared to be praying "for us all," Louisa
suspected, yet she couldn't pray herself, feeling suddenly drained. No rational thought entered her head,
no utterable prayer. She felt wild, as if she were about
to explode. And she felt gigantic, like a balloon, she
thought as she pressed her arms around her inflated
body. A balloon released to the elements and out of
control in the battering wind. God, where will I come
down? she wondered.

When they arrived at the dock, the harbor was exceptionally quiet considering a fire had been reported
aboard the latest ship to arrive. There was a lot of activity, but nothing resembling the panic a fire could
produce. Everything seemed relatively calm, and, in
turn, Louisa calmed herself while she waited in the
carriage for Manuel to find Luther Dobson. "He will
know. He knows everything about the port," she reassured herself in the seemingly calm night.

It took some time for Manuel to reappear, and
Louisa felt a hard contraction which, with enormous
control, she concealed from Carmen. Perspiration

beaded her forehead, and Carmen suspected instantly when Louisa's face was reflected in the glow of a passing torch. Then, Luther Dobson approached the carriage, looking none too pleased to see Louisa. "Mrs. Hudson, you shouldn't have come. This is no time for you to be out."

"Luther, I'm looking for a passenger from the *Golden Lady,* a . . ." she stammered, "Marshall— Marshall Hudson. He was aboard—I just received word today. I couldn't wait at the compound after I heard about the fire. I understand there have been deaths. Have you seen him?"

Luther Dobson sighed, and reached to assist Louisa from the carriage. He said nothing further, but ushered her into his cluttered office at the foot of the dock. "You rest here, Mrs. Hudson, and I'll be back momentarily. Are you sure you're all right?" he demanded when she took in a deep breath and closed her eyes, steadying herself against the edge of his desk. "Yes. Yes," she said hastily, then sat down behind a stack of documents and ledgers piled on Luther's desk.

Louisa waited, counting the minutes, and paced the tiny office. Her contractions were now mild and irregular, and her mind raced over memories of the past and her sudden hopes for the future.

Luther returned shortly. "Don't ask questions. Just come with me," he said quietly, taking her arm, helping her in the darkness. He carried a lantern, and they walked a short distance to a small storage shed which he unlocked and quickly ushered her into.

Heavy coils of rope hung down the walls and barrels were stacked everywhere, covering most of the floor space. But immediately Louisa saw the draped plank set on a cleared space on the floor. Her heart lurched, and she leaned against Luther. "He died of smoke. Wasn't touched by the flames. It was an accident. Fire in a passageway. Trapped him in his cabin. Got the fire out before it got to him, but the smoke . . . you can look at him, if you want." He hesitated then, touching her trembling arm. "Maybe you shouldn't."

"Leave us alone, Luther," Louisa commanded in a whisper.

"But Mrs. Hudson?"

"Please! I don't have much time!" she cried urgently.

Luther placed the lantern securely on one of the barrels, and retreated reluctantly, turning to look at the young woman who stood immobile in the close shed. Then he shut the door to stand impatiently before it. The bustle in the port had declined to nothing, and he felt certain, with the other deaths, that this body could be concealed easily. "Damn the fire," he grumbled under his breath.

Marshall Hudson's death was a tragic accident, certainly uncalled for. He was thought to be an innocent party in the affairs under investigation. It definitely was not part of the plan, yet perhaps it would facilitate matters. "God, poor Louisa Hudson!" intoned Luther, not one to be easily moved.

When Luther left her alone with the body, Louisa stood frozen for a few moments. She felt as if she had crawled into a crypt, possibly her own. Certainly, if what she feared was true, she might very well die. She was weary and her whole body felt weighted down as she moved slowly to the covered form and crouched beside it.

Tears spilled from her eyes as she remembered Marshall's almost beautiful face, his wonderful deep-brown eyes, the warmth of his dark olive skin against hers. "God, I've tried to forget you," she sighed, choking on her tears. Carefully, dreading what she would see, Louisa pulled away the sheeting. "Oh, Marshall, Marshall," she whispered, leaning against his body. For several minutes, she cried shamelessly, quietly choking her sobs for fear Luther would rush in after her. Then she looked again at Marshall's face. His eyes were closed, but otherwise he looked perfect, as if he were asleep. She brushed his lean face with her fingertips, stroked his shining black hair, and took his cold hands in hers. "How can it be we're separated again? And by another fire!" she cried in an anguished whisper. "Oh, why did you come here? It was all right. You knew that. I came here, even though I loved you. Because I loved you." She felt she was drowning in her own tears as she knelt beside him, clutching him to her as if he could surely hear and feel her.

Suddenly. gripped by an even deeper chill, she stopped crying. Louisa sensed she was being watched, and as she held Marshall, she raised her eyes. A dark figure was standing, watching her from the shadows. Louisa shrank from the body and from the other dark figure. She was transfixed, unable to sort out what she saw. What did she see?

Louisa knew her whole being wished to deny the inexorable loss of the man she loved so desperately, the man she had given up hope of ever having by her side again. She could barely comprehend his death. But who was this other man, who, though still and silent, was very much alive? She wanted to run in terror, but, just as in some of her worst dreams, she could not move. She could only stare helplessly.

Shock covered her and she slipped into an almost dreamlike state where reality and fantasy were not easily distinguishable. It was a hazy, oddly familiar place she had been many times before. Louisa swayed slightly, and the man who stood before her crouched quickly, steadying her with warm strong hands. She looked into his face, overwhelmed by its familiarity, his touching her too much to bear, and she collapsed against him, succumbing to a contraction that seemed to crush her. Gasping for breath, she closed her eyes tightly against the intense pain, struggling to keep from screaming. When the wave of pain released her, she opened her eyes and looked down, again to see a man's body. "Marshall?" she questioned as the next contraction overcame her.

Then her rescuer lifted her gently into his arms and carried her from the dimly lit room into the cool night air. With a nod to Luther Dobson, he placed Louisa in her waiting carriage, and climbed in next to her, pulling her against him. "Go on carefully, but swiftly," he demanded in a voice she recognized, and the driver obeyed instantly.

Louisa clutched frantically at the man she thought she knew, feeling her nerves stretched beyond endurance. Carmen watched her with alarm and listened with great concern to Louisa's cries of misery. She noted Louisa's unmistakable pain, but saw the agony in her face was not merely physical. At first, Louisa cried uncontrollably, calling out with each of the contractions that now seemed very intense and more closely spaced than Carmen would have liked.

As they traveled cautiously toward home, Louisa's crying soon stopped. She had no more tears to shed. She was too exhausted and filled with despair. She was comforted, yet confused by the man who held her firmly in his arms. "Who are you?" she asked almost silently, turning her face up to his as she nestled against him in a respite from pain. He put his cheek against hers and gathered her closer to him. "I'm who you think I am. I'm here to be with you," he whispered for only her to hear, and he raised his head to smile down at her. Louisa closed her eyes and rested quietly against him, now bearing her pain quietly until weariness overcame her and she slept between contractions. He held her, and when she needed him to comfort her, he stroked her, moving his hands surely against her back as she arched her body toward him.

Carmen could only worry over Louisa's state, realizing the struggle yet to come. Louisa seemed already spent, yet the birth was probably many hours away, and the greatest test still to be met. Carmen would assist Louisa as best she could, having attended many a birth as well as bearing five children of her own. None had survived and she prayed desperately that Louisa would be spared such grief. Louisa had captured Carmen's heart, and had responded openly to her mothering, seeming to have a deep need also unfulfilled. But there was little comfort or aid for Carmen to give on the journey home. As much as could be given was offered by someone else. She only hoped this darkly handsome man, who seemed remarkably in control, could lend Louisa courage and strength, and when they arrived at the compound, Carmen led the way to Louisa's room, then rushed off to complete her earlier preparations.

Louisa felt herself lowered onto her bed, and he sat with her, holding her hands while she grasped at him. "I'm here now. I won't leave you. Trust me," he said.

God, who are you? Louisa asked silently. Why didn't he tell her what she longed to hear? Hadn't the words always come easily?

"I love you, Marshall. My God, I've ached for you! Where have you been? You've been away a long time, haven't you? Why can't I remember?" It seemed his presence and her pain were all she could attend to.

Carmen interrupted them and all but threw him out of the room amid Louisa's hysterical protests. She undressed Louisa and forced her to drink a small cup of warm bittersweet liquid. "This will help. You won't take till morning, just do as I say."

Thereafter, everything became even more dreamlike. Louisa only vaguely recalled the priest, but she remembered Marshall and the sense of strength she felt in him when she grasped his hands trying to survive her pain, and also his gentleness whenever he touched her swollen belly between contractions. She recalled her incredible urge to push down, to finally free the captive within her, and then see her gorgeous baby, Rachel, perfect in every detail, miraculous and fat and crying vigorously. But, most of all, she would never forget Marshall, and how he seemed to be as awed and as joyful over their wonderful creation as she was.

Chapter Three

After the birth, Louisa slept peacefully for several hours, waking to nurse her eager infant, and then sleeping soundly again. Carmen hovered over both mother and child. She was confident the sturdy-looking baby would fare well. However, her concern for Louisa only increased. The delivery had gone well enough, but all that preceded the birth seemed to have left Louisa unsettled. Maybe she just needs rest, Carmen thought. I've forgotten how it is. Been a long time since I had a baby. At least her appetite was reassuring. "If you keep on, no one will notice your baby was born," Carmen laughed as Louisa ate double her usual portions that evening.

Over the next week a routine was established under Carmen's watchful eye. The man who identified himself as Marshall Hudson reappeared at intervals, made his requirements known, and established himself in the house. He said he had come to oversee the family's shipping affairs in California. He was solicitous of Louisa's well-being, but Carmen noticed Louisa was surprisingly cautious with him. From what she'd seen on the night of his arrival, Carmen had expected more than polite indifference to pass between the couple. He was quite indifferent to Rachel, yet Carmen thought she could understand that. He didn't seem the kind of man to be preoccupied with anyone's children, even his own. So, Carmen concerned herself exclusively with getting Louisa fit again.

For her part, Louisa seemed to be fully occupied with the euphoria of successful childbirth. She spent hours mindlessly looking after herself and Rachel, with Carmen interceding as often as she was allowed.

Louisa had little time or inclination to dwell on the man who called himself Marshall Hudson, never once thinking of the day preceding Rachel's arrival.

As the days wore on, Carmen sensed a hollowness about Louisa, but she couldn't pin down her uneasiness. The young mother was cheerful and attentive with her new baby, not seeming to overlook the slightest of Rachel's needs. Louisa also seemed to be regaining her strength, eating well and providing plentifully for her infant. But there was a blandness, a flatness, in her responses that concerned Carmen. Señora Hudson has always been moody, reflected Carmen, but not empty. Yet beyond Rachel's needs, Louisa now lacked vitality. "Oh, well," sighed Carmen, "it will take time."

Louisa also felt empty. On the one hand she was pleased with herself; Rachel was a fine baby, a child to please even the most exacting parent. And physically, Louisa had come through the birth with relative ease, giving her a sense of strength and hope. But slowly a deep loneliness invaded her, and by the time Rachel was six weeks old, Louisa was very restless and discontent. She saw Marshall only briefly during the course of her day, merely accepting his presence, exchanging few words with him.

Then, one morning Marshall left the compound abruptly, saying he was going north to inspect mining properties. Louisa thought his leaving would matter very little to her, but she found herself thinking of him constantly. His absence gnawed at her. Gradually she began to recall the recent events, and the past, and her nights became unbearable as her dreams once again became haunted. For several nights she woke screaming, sweating, almost choking, believing the house was on fire. Carmen was quite alarmed because each time Louisa seemed more distraught, increasingly unable to realize she'd only had a nightmare.

He's murdered Marshall, she thought. But the idea made no sense in the light of day.

Louisa began to let Carmen take greater care of Rachel. She resumed her walks along the beach, rested, read, and oversaw the small household. It seemed to her all she was urgently needed for was to nurse the hungry infant. She had little else to concern herself with, for she had been nearly reclusive since her arrival in San Diego.

Often her mornings began just before light when she woke to the mewing of gulls circling above the beach. She listened to the thundering waves, puzzling over her thoughts and dreams, and by the time Marshall had been absent three weeks, she had recalled fully the events of the past and the present. Louisa knew who she was, but not who he was. He was not Marshall, of that she was certain, but she said nothing to anyone. Who would I tell? In this country, who else cares? But what can he want? And though she had regained her sense of reality, her dreams grew more distorted.

She began staying up later each night to avoid closing her eyes in the darkness. One night she stayed up until Rachel's last night feeding, propping herself in the bedside rocking chair, leaning a familiar book on the night table. Soon the lateness of the hour found her nodding. She too quickly started up from her dozing, knocking the lamp off its perch. Instantly the glass shattered, spilling oil and flames on the lace draperies, and on the carpet. This time Louisa woke to a living fire, not merely one from her memories, and she was paralyzed, mesmerized before the flames.

Reflected in the windowpanes, doubling their visual effect, the flames slithered quickly. Louisa tried to call out, but she was transfixed and transported in time. Suddenly she started to laugh wildly, tipping the table with its lace cloth into the leaping flames. She reached for the bedding to throw it into the growing conflagration, but as she moved, she was caught forcibly by Marshall, who dragged her out of the way. "God damn! Are you crazy?" he shouted and thrust her at Carmen, rushing to beat the flames with the same comforter with which she would have fueled the fire.

Louisa looked stunned, coming quickly to her senses. She ran to Rachel's room, and Carmen's screeching alerted men from the compound to help.

Quickly the fire was smothered or drowned, and with it Louisa's room.

When the house was empty of helpers, Carmen looked wildly at Louisa, snatching an unhappy Rachel away from her mother. "What is the matter with you, señora?" she demanded. Her heart was pounding wildly, her night clothes and hair in great disarray. "I know you are not yourself, but are you completely *loca*? You could have killed yourself, all of us, your precious baby! Is that what you meant?"

"Carmen," Marshall interrupted. "Take Rachel back to bed." Turning to Louisa, he added, "I'll see to the señora. It's time we understood each other."

"This isn't your house to set in order," she flashed as Carmen disappeared.

"You're mistaken. I'm legally your husband and Rachel's father. You may not recall the priest, but he was here, and our union has been formally acknowledged, señora." He moved toward her, taking her arm brusquely, forcing her to sit next to him on a small settee. "And, it will be my pleasure to consummate our union at some appropriate time."

"You admit you're not Marshall," Louisa said, choosing to ignore his last comment. "I wondered how much longer you'd pretend. But your resemblance is breathtaking. How can it be? And, why?" Her eyes filled with tears. "Did you kill him?" she whispered, finally voicing her dread, and any fierceness she felt vanished. Louisa put her hands over her face and cried softly, but deeply.

"My name is Aaron Sumner," he said quietly, taking her hands from her face. "Look at me!" he said sternly. "To the world, I am Marshall Hudson, a man who has joined his lover and made her his wife." He stared deeply at Louisa as she watched him silently. "Marshall's death was unnecessary. He was to have been held secretly until the investigation was concluded, and I was to take his place. My resemblance to him *is* remarkable, isn't it?" he asked in a voice discouraging an answer.

"What investigation? Marshall was never involved in anything needing investigation. I can vouch for it."

"I won't explain. Let me just remind you, there are things in your past that would best not be investigated in any depth." His voice was threatening and Louisa sucked in her breath, paling visibly even in the dimness of the room.

"Who are you? You've given me your name, but that hardly explains anything. How can you possibly know the things you allude to? And if you know everything you say, how can you mention Marshall in the same breath with 'investigation'? You couldn't have known him!"

"All I say is strictly a warning. I speak to you now because, as long as you're sober and rational, I know you couldn't fool yourself about my being Marshall. You were a little too familiar with him, and for too long," he grinned. Then his voice hardened and his body stiffened. "Make no mistake. This is very serious business, and its gravity puts you in a precarious position should you think of not cooperating." He gripped both her arms tightly above the elbows, and turned her forcibly to him, putting his face very close to hers. "Do not fool yourself that you are indispensable. I would just as soon you cooperate in the masquerade," he said, taking a long look at the fullness of her breasts. "But you are, despite your beauty, nonessential. Don't forget it," he whispered with a murderous look that communicated all he intended.

Louisa had no reply. Her mouth was dry, and her blood cold. She was frozen, looking into a face that was both handsome and deadly. How odd, she thought, that Marshall's apparent double was so unlike her memories. It was confusing. Her recollection of Marshall was of warmth and light, but the reality of the face before her was dangerous, cold and on the edge of final darkness. Aaron Sumner looked exhausted, but vitally alert. He must have been traveling long and hard, she remembered. His clothing was well cut and covered his lean, muscular body perfectly. He was obviously playing Marshall's part well, both men careful of detail.

In answer to her utter silence, he continued, releasing his grip on her. "In view of the little bonfire tonight, now is as good a time as any for us to begin sharing the same bed. And now that you're well recovered, it will be my pleasure, Mrs. Hudson."

Louisa only stared.

"You needn't be demure, Mrs. Hudson. I know too much about you," he said as he stood up and turned to leave the room, obviously expecting her to follow him. When she did not, he faced her again and commanded, "Now!"

Chapter Four

LOUISA reflected on her options. Aaron Sumner had left her very few. In fact, none. She sat motionless at his command, fatigued and beaten, and he sensed her immobility was defeat, not defiance. Her paleness and fragility was cast against the dimly lit room, her honey-blond hair enfolding her body as it cascaded down her shoulders and back. She sat amid a few of her treasured and carefully transported possessions, and despite her simple bedclothes, she was unmistakably elegant, like the French furnishings in the room. Aaron thought of her as a possible bonus in this assignment, yet an unpredictable one. He knew a great deal about her past, and even more about her present. He knew he'd made his point with her, but from tonight's events, he wondered if she might again be treading the fine line of madness.

After several moments, Louisa stood to follow him. Silently she put out the lamp and, pausing, looked hard at the man waiting for her. He seemed wonderfully familiar, but she had only to reflect on his recent words to remember this was a different man from the one with whom she had been so intimate. She knew she could linger no longer without provoking his anger, so she moved quietly to face him.

Aaron took her hand, and led her to his room. He did not light the lamp, but opened the draperies, letting in the bright moonlight. Pulling back the bedcovers, he motioned to Louisa, who hesitated, then slipped off her dressing gown, pulling her soft nightgown closely around her, as if to conceal herself. She climbed into the narrow bed, feeling incredibly cold and tense, and stared mutely out at him, watching him carelessly discard his clothing. He put a loaded gun on the table beside the bed, and turned to face her. He took a long look at Louisa who at first returned his gaze, but not for long. She rolled over, turning her back to him, grasping for the covers, feeling herself go rigid as he moved next to her.

Louisa felt trapped, certain some dreadful blow would fall on her. Instead, she felt warm hands gently stroking her soft hair as it cascaded over her body. He pulled some of it to his face, and inhaled its fragrance while Louisa stiffened and turned herself nearly onto her stomach. But again she felt Aaron's hands on her. He touched her hair and caressed her slowly, moving a hand down her back, over her buttocks and thighs. His breathing became slow and heavy, and he drew her against him, reaching for her breasts, rubbing their fullness in his hands. He put his mouth against her ear and sighed deeply, eagerly kissing the curve of her neck. His hands moved down her body, pressing her urgently to him. He stroked her thighs which she only pressed more tightly together and he pulled her gown to her waist, pushing his hands against her belly. She arched her back and stiffened even more. "No!" she cried hoarsely.

Aaron was still for a moment, then pressed his body heavily against her. His breathing was strained; his body taut and eager for hers. He clutched her to him in an almost crushing grip, and nestled his mouth below her ear, gently stroking her throat with his tongue. "I won't rape you, Louisa. But I will have you one day."

Louisa lay very still, barely breathing. At length, he gradually relaxed and she knew he was asleep. At first, Louisa thought her body and its various limbs would snap under the tension she felt. Then, very slowly, she let herself go, and relaxed under his weight, feeling some warmth return to her, and by early morning, she, too, was sleeping soundly. In their slumbering, they shifted their bodies in the narrow bed, alternately moving close and away. They drew warmth from each other and their dreams were familiar and gentle.

But just as the sun came up, a knock at the door woke them both. Immediately Aaron was alert. When he heard Carmen's voice, he relaxed. "Señora, baby needs feeding." Hearing an angry baby in another room, Louisa turned to face Aaron and started to rise, but he put his arm over her.

"Bring her here, Carmen," he called. Louisa just stared at him, too exhausted to dispute him but very uncomfortable in the small bed, and again she tried to get up. This time, Aaron put a leg over her hip, pinning her down.

"I have to nurse my child," Louisa frowned.

"What better place than in her mother's warm bed," smiled Aaron.

"It's too crowded here," she glared.

"We'll make room." He touched her bursting breasts. "Just what I like," he grinned.

Louisa's face reddened, her whole body flashed with heat, and her milk began to drip relentlessly. "You're crude," she said, gritting her teeth, not believing her position.

"And you're beautiful, and a little overmatched," he laughed, slapping her bare bottom soundly. She lurched up under his hand, inadvertently thrusting her breasts into his face. "Mmm," he groaned, and laughed loudly. Louisa struggled as he pushed her down, his hands seeking her furiously, but they were interrupted again by Carmen's loud rapping on the door. "Come in," he called, releasing Louisa.

In her rumpled state, Louisa's face colored as she stared wildly at Carmen. Carmen was nonplused, and quickly entered the room, handing Rachel over Aaron's half-covered body to Louisa. "I'll be back for her," she said, excusing herself from the room. Rachel was furiously hungry and Louisa turned her back to Aaron and snuggled the eager infant, meeting her anxious mouth with her breast. Quickly, Louisa and Rachel were soothed, and not disturbed even when Aaron pressed himself against Louisa, putting his arm around her and the infant.

Louisa was very weary and dozed intermittently.

She felt oddly comfortable in the warm bed. Soon Rachel was satiated, and the three of them slept peacefully in the early-morning quiet.

Later Carmen rapped discreetly on the door, hesitating when there was no response. She rapped again and still there was no response. She fumbled at the door and entered the room to stare pensively at the quiet threesome. She was struck by the handsome little family nestled together, but suspected the tranquility was somehow an illusion.

Aaron soon sensed someone was in the room and woke with a sudden tenseness which also disturbed Louisa. Aaron realized instantly he was in a safe place and relaxed, turning over leisurely.

"Sorry, señor. I worried. Nobody answered. I'll take baby back to her bed," she offered nervously.

Aaron nodded. "Breakfast later, Carmen? But leave us alone for now," he said as he gently lifted the sleeping infant from Louisa's arms, and gave her over to the older woman.

When Carmen left the room, Aaron closed his eyes again and lay back in the bed. He stretched and sighed, then turned his head to look at Louisa. She seemed relaxed and half asleep as she lay on her back, eyes closed. He smiled at her and turned on his side to face her. Pushing wisps of soft, golden hair from her face, he gently ran a finger over her profile, lingering at her mouth whose soft fullness he slowly outlined.

Louisa opened her eyes and looked at him tenderly. Oh God, you look so familiar, yet I don't know you, she thought as he stared into her eyes, filling himself with their blueness.

Like the sky on a cloudless day, he reflected silently, wondering if her eyes promised the same freedom and joy he felt when he looked up into such a day, and before either of them realized it consciously, he began to caress her cheek, kissing her mouth to find her yielding softly to him.

Then he kissed her deeply, gathering her urgently

into his arms, his desire for her obvious and unrelenting. And Louisa met his warm mouth as if she were coming in from the cold, unable to deny the warmth that surged in her body or her desire to respond to him for, though nothing else was certain, she knew their coming together was inevitable.

Chapter Five

RECONSTRUCTION of what had been Louisa's room began late that same morning. Surveying the damages, she found very little needed to be done. It would be easily restored. There seemed to be more water than fire damage, and in this dry climate, repairs could be made easily: new draperies, a few panes of glass, new carpet, paint, and all would be fresh.

But now Louisa had little inclination to re-establish herself in this lonely room where she had spent long haunted hours trying to settle herself on this coast. Perhaps she would make it a sitting room, or Rachel might use it as a playroom one day soon. Yes, that was it. "But we'll want my bed. It's larger, and we could use a bit more space to sleep in," she mused. How quickly she'd adjusted to the new arrangement! Especially after this morning.

Her body became flushed when she thought about Aaron. She had spent months forgetting the pleasures her body had to offer, thinking its joys might well have been lost to her past. She'd thought the passion she'd felt for Marshall certainly was for him alone. But incredibly she'd discovered life still had lessons for her to learn. Aaron had rekindled a fire in her she only wished to fan. Even now she thought she could still feel the heat of Aaron's body, his mouth seeking every part of her, the warmth that flowed from her, and the eagerness with which she accepted his thrusting body into hers. She had made this disturbingly familiar stranger a welcomed part of her, a stranger no more. At last she had taken the man with the familiar face and met him, separate from the other's identity.

The familiar face was one thing, his body another. Louisa's memory of Marshall was one of love and tenderness and an incredible sweetness. But Aaron wanted more from her, and would exact nothing less. There was a fierceness in his lovemaking, an urgency in him, an almost dreadful need she could only wonder at. Marshall had only fleetingly exposed her to that side of him, so these experiences were new to her. Aaron made her want more than she could recall. And she knew she wanted more of him. Louisa had yet to know him fully, she realized, remembering his threats of the night before, weighing them against the wonderful tenderness he'd shown her. And she also wondered over the flashes of violence he'd shown. Perhaps he wanted more from her than she wanted to give, more darkness than she cared to summon.

Facing the thoughts among the debris of the night's fire, Louisa looked back to other fires. She sat down in her old rocking chair and began to rock gently, closing her arms around herself, as if to hug a needy child. She wondered why she'd salvaged the chair at all, or the faded baby doll. These things may have held some pleasant memories, but certainly the majority of the thoughts they summoned were nightmarish. In fact, why did I bring any of these things with me to my new life? she thought. They came from an unclean past. But these objects were surely guiltless, like she was, after all. They would remind her, not damn her. And she didn't want to forget entirely, or else she might not be able to salvage anything good of herself. . . .

Fire, always fire. Like the flames of Hell, she thought.

The first fire she remembered was accidental enough. A servant had failed to tend a cooking fire properly. Afterward the girl had been publicly beaten within an inch of her life. Just punishment, it was said. Louisa couldn't comprehend it all. The only thing she'd salvaged from her pretty room that night was a china baby doll, and she had barely escaped with that. The flames had traveled fast. The wind was up, and in the dry spell, they were lucky, everyone said, to have lost

only the main house. It was then that Louisa began to
have nightmares, dreaming of the fire and the face of
her china doll, Tessa being consumed in flames. In her
dreams, Louisa mourned Tessa as if she were a real
person: except for Nanny, she had only her baby doll.
Momma belonged to Papa, if she belonged to anyone,
certainly she hadn't belonged to Louisa. Momma was
so frail, Louisa thought. "Momma is not well today.
Go with Nanny. Don't disturb me now. That's a good
girl."

But how Momma glittered on special occasions, if
not for Louisa. Everyone raved about her. Her beautiful clothes, her jewels and perfumes, her gay manners.
Surely she was lost in this barbarian country, some
said. Perhaps she would have been happier in her native France. Papa was gone a lot, which seemed to
weigh on Momma, too. But when he returned, he
would bring back such wonderful things, not the least
of which were the decanters of special liquid Momma
was so fond of.

Louisa recalled Momma's glitter but also her tarnish. After those gala parties they seemed to have
whenever Papa's ships came back, Momma would dis-
integrate. How Louisa worried! Sometimes Momma
would seem at death's door, at other times frighteningly agitated; she would laugh and cry and scream
until something would calm her. What, Louisa never
knew.

Often, when one of these gala events was planned,
Louisa would be packed up with Nanny and sent off to
the Hudsons', which certainly suited her, because she
would see Marshall Hudson and Andrew Sutton again.
She dearly loved those "dreadful boys" as Momma
called them. They introduced her to all sorts of things
she'd never have learned about if she'd had to stay in
Momma's house. Momma failed to understand how
Emma Hudson allowed Marshall such freedom, but
when it suited her convenience she never failed to
send Louisa off to the Hudsons' hospitality And Louisa joyfully shared the boys' freedom. "That child is
too confined," said Emma Hudson firmly.

Then after the fire, they all stayed with the

Hudsons while their house was rebuilt. Louisa had
never known such delicious, seemingly endless freedom. Momma fretted some, but the fire had left her
even more distraught, and she had less inclination than
usual to worry after Louisa. Occasionally, she'd warn
Louisa about being too friendly with Andrew Sutton
because he wasn't "high-born" like she and Marshall,
but that made little sense to her. Nanny, dear Nanny,
covered up as best she could for Louisa, who guile-
lessly followed Marshall and Andrew into the swamps
and into any mischief they could invent.

What Louisa loved best was frog-hunting. Momma
often expounded on the wonderful delicacy of frog's
legs, but Louisa was sure Momma would perish instantly if she knew Louisa, Marshall, and Andrew
were regularly catching and feasting on swamp frogs.
What enormous fun she had bounding after those creatures, giggling wildly, turning over each of the few
she captured to Marshall or Andrew to stash safely
until enough were caught for a proper feast.

Then Louisa busied herself getting fuel for the fire
while the boys prepared the frogs for cooking, something she steadfastly refused to have anything to do
with, in spite of their insistence that cleaning the
"game" was something a girl ought to tend to. She
preferred setting up and lighting the fire. It was
almost a ritual of absolution for her, but she hardly
recognized it as such. She was always totally transported in the act of preparing the fire. Marshall and
Andrew merely got used to her fascination with that
aspect of their outing, and they paid little attention to
the solemnity with which she accomplished her task.
After all, Louisa took some getting used to anyway. At
eight years of age, Louisa Boyd was a skinny wisp of a
girl, taken in hand reluctantly by the boys simply
because she refused to leave them. And she never
cowered, no matter what death-defying stunt they in-
vented. She merely wore them down, and finally they
accepted her.

The threesome became infamous around the plantation, among the hands as well as the family. For the
most part, their mischief was innocent enough, but one

night they decided to aid a runaway slave and succeeded in effecting his escape. Infamy and acceptance spread rapidly among local slaves, and, at the same time, sealed the fate of their eventual separation.

They made a curious trio: one fair fairylike imp of a girl whose nerve was undisputed; two handsome boys, oddly similar in character and alike as brothers in appearance, except that one was blond, one dark. Louisa loved them both, desperately drawn to them as her mother's behavior grew increasingly strange, and as her own dreams grew worse. Often, if they stopped to doze in an afternoon, one of the boys would spend some time comforting Louisa in the timeless way of sheltering a frightened animal in one's arms. But they forgave her her terrors, as children do if they remember the horror dreams can sometimes hold, and the boys' compassion essentially saved the child.

Chapter Six

EMMA Hudson was nearly beside herself. Ordinarily she was hard to ruffle, but the strain of the Boyds' lengthy visit in her home was telling on her usually calm nature. Claudia Boyd was increasingly difficult and demanding; "ill" as often as not. "Drunk," Emma pointed out to her husband, Simon.

Emma was an odd match for Simon, but a lucky one. She had propriety. He had flamboyance. And their match suited his purposes well. She also had enormous wealth, as well as self-respect. And being a man of vision, Simon acepted her worth and her rules, straying only until it was no longer profitable. Perhaps he should have seen the handwriting on the wall even then, he reflected later, but fortunately, for him, Emma had forgiven his transgressions. She knew her power, and his financial position at the time was precarious. His assets were primarily tied up in land and slaves, with very little liquidity for schemes just beginning to prosper. So, when she agreed to graciously overlook his blatant infidelity, exacting his promise of future fidelity or utter ruin, he acquiesced, knowing he'd made a good bargain—a few petty dalliances were not worth the loss of Emma Hudson with her many assets; after all, she adequately warmed his bed, as well as filled his coffers.

Other financial considerations had prompted the appointment of Simon Hudson as Louisa Boyd's guardian. Since Louisa's father, Justin Boyd, and Simon were often involved in joint business ventures, and Justin was frequently away from home, it seemed a logical designation in view of Claudia Boyd's increasingly precarious health. And so, the families inter-

twined from the beginning. The guardianship made
sense, but, as much as she dearly loved the child,
Emma worried over the possible burden of taking her
into their home. Louisa often woke the household, not
to be consoled when she stirred from her dreams, and
Emma wondered if insanity lurked in Claudia's family
background. Little was known of Claudia, except that
she was French. A born courtesan, thought Emma.
She fascinated men and enhanced any entertainments
her husband deemed lucrative enough for his attention. These attributes seemed to be credential enough
in this society, thought Emma.

Between mother and child, the Hudson household
seemed permanently unsettled. Even Justin Boyd was
more than a little annoyed with Claudia's consumption
of alcohol and concerned by the effects of quantities
secretly consumed over the years, readily visible to
anyone who cared to look and comprehend. And the
fire, and its destruction of the things Claudia regarded
as irreplaceable, had not enhanced her disposition.
Nor had the fire quenched her thirst. Justin had
married Claudia when she was young and beautiful,
he recalled. He couldn't quite forget her seductiveness,
but it had somehow blurred. Louisa echoed little of her
mother's allure, especially in the Hudson household,
and Justin grew quite restless as he found himself even
temporarily forced to remain in the home, often patron, it seemed, to lunatics. Overseeing the reconstruction of the household was something Claudia would
have been responsible for, had she not been floating
in a crystal decanter, hour after hour.

Justin found planning the minor details of restoring
furniture and possessions to the household to be beyond his patience and attention span. He increasingly
relied on Emma, and whenever possible his principal
servants made choices they would never make in another household. He found it almost amusing that one
of the highlights of his recent weeks was planning
Louisa's new room.

"I saw some pale blue silk on one of my trips which
I think would make a lovely canopy and cover for
your new bed, Louisa."

"Can't it be pink, Papa?"

"I suppose it could be any color you choose."

"And I think a wood rocker, like Marshall has, would please me."

"Like Marshall's?"

"Yes. And he has a toy cannon. I think I'll need one, too."

"What about dolls, Louisa?"

"I have my baby," she said firmly.

"The one from the fire? She's a dreadful mess. We'll have to replace her. In fact, didn't Emma give you an elegant doll to start a new collection?"

"She's too prissy to go out with the boys and me."

"I'm afraid you'll miss the boys when we go home again, Louisa. In fact, I'm sure you will." And he wondered what point there was in sending the child home with Claudia. He would be gone soon—the instant it was possible.

By the time the house was barely ready for occupation, the Boyd family moved in, and only Marshall and Andrew regretted their departure from the Hudson household. Justin grew increasingly agitated over Claudia's dependence, and her condition deteriorated to the point where she required nearly constant supervision. Justin was aware that he was consoling himself a little too liberally with alcohol, but he kept drinking and between the three of them, the Boyds began to haunt the new house.

Justin was an interesting man with remarkable good looks. He had both the influence and the appearance to move in whatever circles he chose. By preference he chose the darker ones, but carefully maintained his respectability where he considered it necessary. He traveled the world and partook of its various pleasures and entertainments, taking a wife as it suited his purposes. He had learned early in life that fortunes often were to be made if one chose the right company. And Justin rarely did anything in public that would not in some way enhance his political or economic position.

Yet even from his private point of view, he'd married carefully. He'd chosen a woman thoroughly acquainted with his needs, and one not loath to meet them; and her background, based on manners alone, looked good. She would not have stood up under close scrutiny, it was certain, but few questions were asked when he'd arrived with his blushing bride, convincingly demure and impressed by her new surroundings. He'd had his pleasures with her, and had she kept away from the bottle, they might have been a life-long match. But no man is a match for alcohol, reflected Justin. He wondered how long she'd last. Or, if he drank enough, would he kill her first?

He felt increasingly tied to the household, disbelieving its frequent moments of sheer madness: between Claudia's hallucinations and Louisa's nightmares, Justin listed darkly. In the past he'd often been charmed by Louisa, as any father might be. Recently, between her bouts of night terror, she'd been an enigma, moody and doelike. Away from the boys, she was definitely more appealing and she hesitantly drew closer to him as Claudia's behavior became even more unnerving in the incomplete, meagerly furnished mansion. They had retreated from the Hudsons before they might have, because of Claudia, and father and daughter came closer to each other as a haven from too-close association with a woman they loved for different and, at times, unfathomable reasons.

At first, Justin sought only to calm his terrified child when she woke from one of her nightmares. "Louisa, Louisa, it's only a dream," he said taking the distraught child from Nanny's arms. But, as he retreated more deeply into alcohol, as his own loneliness overwhelmed him, the blackest side of his nature readily surfaced. Initially, he managed to exert self-control, but years of willful catering to whatever need struck him eventually won out. He was a man of worldly and varied desires, and with his wealth, his pleasures were readily sated. He'd traveled the world and had been unsatisfied by the ordinary splendors, seeking and finding darker revels, tasting everything that surfaced.

Louisa was easy prey as she lay in Justin's darkened room, terrified of her dreams. She clung eagerly to her fascinating, consoling Papa, and he took her soothingly in his arms, slowly easing her terror, slowly seducing her to his own needs. "I can help you feel much better, Louisa," he courted. Louisa trusted this man with her whole being. He was, after all, the source of her very being, her caretaker and provider; her protector from danger in the night. He led her slowly, but unrelentingly along paths she only intuitively knew were forbidden. She followed, betrayed by her own body, but deep within herself she cowered with every caress. Her terrifying dreams of fire ceased under his tutelage, and she learned not to cry out in the night. But it seemed she had only replaced one night terror with another.

Soon Justin grew bored with the seduction of his child, and he left the plantation to his overseer, his wife to her nurse, and Louisa to her nanny. Emma Hudson visited occasionally and Louisa stayed at the Hudson place often. The Hudsons had retained a new tutor, and it seemed appropriate for Louisa to take advantage of his skills as well. She began to spend less and less time in her own home, seeking the company, if not the protection, of the Hudson household.

The rare occasions Louisa and Momma came in contact were unpleasant. It was clear Claudia was not herself. Her coloring was grayish, and even her most expensive perfumes failed to cover a sickly sweetish odor that seemed to surround her. She would sometimes provoke ugly scenes with Louisa, accusing her darkly before the servants. Claudia now trembled continuously, and when she confronted Louisa, her quaking was exaggerated. "Do you miss your Papa, child? Little wonder to me—you fast became his favorite girl." Her loathing was barely concealed in her sarcastic accusations. "How odd. You barely resemble a woman, yet. No decent curves or fullness that I can see. But you are seductive in your way, I suppose, depending on one's taste. And Justin surely is a man of varied tastes." She smiled inappropriately at her child. "You are damned, you know, Louisa." Louisa felt guilty and mortified, and began to dread all contact with the woman.

One morning shortly after Justin's departure, Claudia was found on the stair landing below her room. She was very battered from the fall, but conscious when discovered. She accused Louisa of pushing her, and raved maniacally for a short time. Fortunately, no one believed her and Claudia died the same night.

Solemn services were held. They were brief and the mourners' faces were dutifully long, but Louisa suspected few felt any lasting grief. She knew she did not. Her Papa was not present and would not learn of Momma's death for some time. "Will he mourn?" she wondered.

At that point, Justin's properties were managed by the overseer, who answered to Simon Hudson, and Louisa formally entered the Hudson household. Normally, Louisa would have loved this, but there were some changes in the making that disappointed her immensely. First, at thirteen, Marshall, accompanied by Emma Hudson, was sent to travel and study in Europe, something Emma regarded as essential to his development, and Andrew was put aboard one of Simon Hudson's ships to earn his way.

The boys were four years her senior, and Louisa knew she had no right to expect them to spend their lives chaperoning her, but she would have liked them to do just that, and she would miss them. From one lonely house to another, she thought. Now she imagined she understood the term "low-born" as Momma had applied it to Andrew. It meant he didn't have the means to a gentleman's education, like Marshall. Andrew's knowledge of the world would not come from books and museums, as would Marshall's. It would come by his wits, the sweat of his body, and the strain of his muscles.

But Andrew didn't regard his fate as misfortune. He regarded it as an opportunity. He didn't see much future for himself as the son of an indentured white housekeeper. "Just think, Louisa. I'll be sailing all over the world. I've always thought about it, and Mr. Hudson's ships are the fastest in the world. I know I'll have some great adventures." Louisa frowned, viewing his fate much differently, and while she regarded him as much wiser than she, she was struck by

Chapter Seven

JUSTIN'S return to Louisiana was not hurried, nor was his grief overwhelming. He took Louisa into the house again, and into his bed for as long as he stayed. Louisa loved Papa, and her reluctance was overcome by her need to be loved in any way. For now, her feelings of being unclean were put aside. Only loneliness and isolation felt worse.

Soon she began to see herself as mistress of the household. Papa brought her extravagant gifts, silks, and even jewels. "Eventually, I'll take you with me to Europe, Louisa. There are so many things for you to see. And one day soon, you will be something for everyone to feast their eyes on."

Louisa was flattered, feeling and looking like a princess. She worried over the latest European fashions, remembering Momma's preoccupations. When Papa went away again, she remained as "mistress," he said. She imagined herself as such, but Nanny actually wielded the power. Louisa whiled away the daytime hours dreaming and playing—perhaps she was the princess in the fairy tale who was only locked up in the tower waiting for a prince to set her free. In spite of her burdens, she would often lapse into normal girlish playing with dolls. Her collection flourished since the fire, but her dearest doll was the baby rescued from the flames. There were days on end that Louisa would refuse to put the doll down, sometimes rocking her for long periods, holding her tenderly, whispering quiet words. She gave more love to the doll than she could ever remember being invested in her, intuitively knowing what babies needed. And in loving her doll, she began to love herself again. From out of her heart

37

poured needs and tenderness she craved and had long ignored. She even called the doll Louisa.

Papa came and went. He stayed at home for brief periods, taking Louisa out into the world as she lost more of her awkward child's appearance. She was pretty and educated, and only needed time and more exposure to the world to make her exceptional. Justin planned carefully for her. His fortune was secure, but political rumblings made him think of protecting his life-style. A beautiful daughter would no doubt have financial advantages, if need be. He even sacrificed his own wanderings to introduce Louisa to polite society.

But unselfishness has its limits, he thought, as he took his pleasure of her young body.

As Louisa grew more beautiful in her appearance, she was indulged in every matter. Yet she retained a remarkable sweetness and certainly didn't lack for spirit. She often thought she'd been forever corrupted by Marshall and Andrew, because, as she grew older, her taste for excitement increased. She rode her horses wherever she could, disdained chaperoning, and was game for any adventure proposed by companions. She feared no one and nothing, not even her dreams, which to her were no more deadly than reality.

Justin felt his efforts were well rewarded. Louisa was a sensation in the households they visited. Of course, not the least of her attributes was his economic standing, he reflected. Her education needed some rounding out, and that would be taken care of in time. More traveling, more introductions would only enhance her possibilities.

Louisa was eager to go abroad. When she had last seen Marshall, he had just returned from Europe more mature and handsome than she expected. He had been away three years, and she could barely believe her eyes. He was no longer a boy, he was a confident young man. He'd become interested in philosophy, particularly in the slavery issue, and spent considerable time trying to interest Louisa in the ideas he found most compelling, but Louisa grew bored. She tried earnestly, but at twelve years of age, she couldn't be serious with Marshall. She longed to re-create their earlier pastimes, yet somehow she realized those times were gone forever. Louisa coaxed Marshall into re-creating a frog hunt for old times' sake, but she now found she took greater pleasure in long, exhausting daredevil horseback rides throughout the countryside.

Marshall couldn't help but notice that Louisa was on the brink of becoming something more than just pretty and adventurous. She had beauty and intelligence, and a wild kind of gaiety. She had learned to be flirtatious, coaxing and charmingly seductive. Suddenly, he regretted seeing so little of her. Marshall recognized his strong feeling for her was rooted in their childhood, but he suspected his fondness for her was growing into something else. He felt stirrings he'd just begun to comprehend, and Louisa's blossoming suggested desires for her he could not yet face. He would be traveling again soon, and so would she, and they had little hope of much contact, but Marshall knew she held promise and only hoped he would be the one to see her promise fulfilled.

Not much later, they traveled in the same direction, but along separate paths. Marshall stayed for a while in his own country, and Louisa went to Europe with Justin. She loved the sea voyage, wanting desperately to have the freedom men had, to do as Andrew had done. Where is Andrew now? she wondered. Although a seaman's life was not easy, she imagined life at sea was exciting enough to compensate for the hardships. A life in the open air seemed enough for her, with the wind filling the sails, and a work pace busy enough to keep all thoughts occupied, a blessing she would welcome. She stayed above deck as much as possible, or talked with Captain Tomas whenever she could. He was an efficient master of his ship, stern and respected by his men. He had a young daughter her age, he said, "not as pretty, nor as grand, but a sweet girl, too."

Louisa wondered about her, and what it was like to be another man's daughter. "But surely she could come with you on these voyages. I would. I would never go ashore!"

"Sometimes I've had my family with me. But sometimes it's better if they stay in port."

"I would never want to leave the ship. I'd insist on becoming a seaman. I could help with the sails. I'm strong. I can do whatever is needed!"

Captain Tomas laughed.

"I could," Louisa insisted, looking her most determined.

"I wouldn't be surprised!"

But her daydreaming was pointless, she knew. Papa had other plans for her.

Louisa wondered whether she could ever be a proper lady. Louisa knew she was at least becoming a beauty, and her spirit was more alluring than so many of the shy and polite girls she'd met along the way. Had Momma been a proper lady? She doubted it.

"Papa, what was Momma like before she was so strange?"

The question caught Justin off balance as they sat alone in the richly appointed salon painstakingly prepared for select passengers aboard the clipper *Tempest*. "You can't have forgotten her, already?"

"I guess I remember her, but I don't seem to recall more than her being sick all of the time, or when she was preparing for important guests. Is that all mothers do? What are mothers for?"

Justin looked at Louisa. Her life was far from usual, but what did he have for answers to her questions? "Louisa, you have lived differently than most. You are not destined for an ordinary life. Your social position guarantees you'll never have to worry about what mothers do. That's what nannies are for."

What did Papa want for her—a life like Momma's, and eventually a living death? He seemed to want some of the same things for her: beautiful clothes and jewels and the right companions, the right education—a proper finish to his other efforts. Papa was most solicitous of her needs. He did his best to make her feel good, didn't he? Why then, she wondered, did she dream of a life separate from him?

For several months, Justin and Louisa lived in London and were courted by his many friends. Papa was enormously popular, and he often left Louisa to pursue his own interests. He had both business and social obligations to occupy him, and Louisa privately welcomed the relative solitude. A suitable matron was found to oversee her excursions into society. She attended a noted day school, occupied herself with her studies and new friends.

Louisa began to take painting lessons to round out her education. Her painting instructor, M. Ronsard, was pleased with her efforts and soon Louisa was off into her own world of color and imagination. Her talent was extraordinary, and she was encouraged to go her own way. "I am impressed with the life in your portraits, Mlle. Boyd," said M. Ronsard, and he was awed by the intensity of her work as it progressed. "How can pretty Louisa read so much in people at her age," he wondered. "Who is the extraordinary lady in your portrait?"

"She's my mother, monsieur."

"She must be a remarkable woman. Yes, I see a resemblance."

"She was stunning," Louisa mused. Did M. Ronsard see the same things she saw in her painting? Could he see the frozen heart, the madness that lurked behind the beauty and aloofness she tried to convey? "She's dead now. This is how I remember her."

"I'm sorry, Mlle. Boyd. It's a pity."

"No, it's not. It's a blessing for us both," Louisa said quietly without malice.

M. Ronsard wondered at the young woman before him. He glanced at her paintings as they stood propped around the small room set aside for her newfound pastime. Could he know her from the growing collection? She obviously loved the two boys she painted on several canvases. Were they as animated and joyful as she said in paint? And was she the frightened child cowering in the rocker, clutching a very worn doll? Surely not, he hoped. Surely such a child has only a very dark future, and the girl before him promised something more.

At fifteen, there was only a hint of her childishness left. Her body had matured, and with her carriage and apparent worldliness, she was unmistakably a woman. By the time she and Justin left for Paris, Louisa was sufficiently immersed in her art and her studies to no longer be bored. She became more animated and actually started to enjoy herself as she moved into the gaiety of Paris. She was a sensation and was courted earnestly by several young men.

She was happy at last, she thought. Her past receded from memory. Momma became only an unpleasant and even more vague part of her past. Helena, her chaperone, was a good companion, and made an unremarkable, but kindly mother substitute. Papa with his frequent comings and goings became a blur and his interest in her welfare genuine and merely paternal. Louisa felt she might have lived in Paris all of her life.

Only Marshall and Andrew seemed a reality of her past, the only link she wished to preserve. She heard nothing of Andrew, other than through Marshall, whom she saw infrequently. Louisa didn't want to believe it, but Andrew was in deep trouble. He had jumped ship and was considered a fugitive. Louisa ached for him. How incredible it seemed, to think of Andrew as an outlaw! Perhaps, despite her deepest instincts, Andrew was beneath her. Perhaps, just as she'd been cautioned, he was "low-born."

Chapter Eight

AT last Marshall and Louisa were in Paris together, but Marshall found himself only one among a string of Louisa's admirers. He realized his vision of her had been accurate. At sixteen, she was radiant and gay, and very seductive. For the imp he recalled, she seemed surprisingly in her element. He found himself bewitched by her, jealous of her other admirers. He wanted to pursue her earnestly, but his chance never came. She eluded every suitor. Nor was she content to partake of just ordinary fare, often suggesting adventurous and elaborate entertainments for her circle of friends. Her energy seemed inexhaustible, and the pace she kept breathtaking. She seemed always to be in motion, always on the run. Louisa truly believed she could spend the remainder of her life in the French countryside. She loved the elaborate, exquisitely furnished country homes, and quickly succumbed to the self-indulgent style of life. Her favorite pastime was attending dress balls where the music transported her, and the dancing became an opiate, a medium for her fantasies. She discovered her natural inclination for flirting, and any reserve she felt was erased by wine.

She was fond of no man in particular, but it was obvious several young men hoped to single her out. Stefan was probably the most ardent in his pursuit. Justin was pleased with him, since he was financially and politically well connected. "Beautiful, Louisa, you must have been listening more carefully to me than I thought. Stefan is an ideal choice. His father and I have a great deal in common."

Stefan Vinay was the most experienced of her

suitors, the most sought-after himself. He was lean and powerfully built, handsome with intense blue eyes and dark blond hair. Louisa found it increasingly difficult to avoid his advances politely. She had no desire to offend him—after all, his interest in her heightened her enjoyment of life—but it was obvious Stefan was becoming impatient. He was direct with his intentions, and a little menacing, Louisa thought.

Soon, it became more than a game of cat-and-mouse, and the alternatives narrowed. "I'm used to having everything I want, too, Louisa," Stefan cautioned her as he held her while they danced away another night. She had no intention of slowing her pace or narrowing her field of play, assuming her exciting life could continue indefinitely. Stefan saw to it that he was everywhere Louisa went. He tried and fairly well succeeded in monopolizing her attention. He began to wear down her resistance, and over the months, Louisa began to think Stefan was an ideal match. They could have a long courtship and a convenient marriage. She suspected he would soon find himself busy in the world, and would eventually leave her for long periods, as Justin did, and she could pursue her own whims easily. She was romantic, but ultimately practical. Her observation of couples in her circle was that most people married for convenience and advantage, and loved as they chose, aside from any formalized union. Perhaps Stefan would tire of her, soon enough.

Louisa pursued this fantasy, and soon it became popular opinion that the couple would be betrothed. But Stefan did not conform to her ideas. He became increasingly possessive and Louisa grew restless. She found him overbearing, and regarding his apparent jealousy with obvious disdain, she continued to circulate freely.

But despite his public manners, Stefan's nature was not tolerant. He was willful and used to having his whims indulged. He expected Louisa to accept his domination, and was unprepared for and angered by her apparent disregard for his expectations. He began to call her on his disappointments, and was astounded when she failed to take his concerns seriously. She was damned arrogant and elusive, he thought. He became obsessed with halting her habitual flirtations when, to his surprise, Louisa willingly agreed to visit his country estate for several weeks in the fall. Justin even made an appearance, and formally approved Louisa's suitor.

There were several gala parties, yet frequent opportunities for the couple to be alone. Stefan enjoyed their relative seclusion and his monopoly of her attention between social events. Louisa, on the other hand, grew bored and regretted the bargain she seemed to have struck. Nor was she content to recline about the house between evening entertainments, instead seizing every opportunity to ride or take long walks. Stefan eagerly shared these amusements with her, enjoying their privacy. But when there were houseguests, Louisa saw to it that everyone was organized for exhausting excursions, and Stefan found himself even more aggravated by her outgoing nature.

After one particularly hectic week of guests and parties, and with the house still full of revelers, Stefan's temper was short. He wondered if she were deliberately trying to anger him. His mood was especially black early one morning when he insisted on a private afternoon with her.

"I have had enough of sharing you with everyone in the countryside. Today we'll go off by ourselves and let the others amuse themselves as they see fit."

"All right, Stefan. Let's ride down to the pond and sit in the shade for some lunch. After last night and these last weeks, I'm ready for some quiet."

"It's too much to hope for, Louisa," said Stefan sarcastically, but he was not soothed in spite of her pleasant acquiescence. Louisa was weary. She was tired of Stefan, suddenly exhausted by the unrelenting whirl of activities of the past year. And she was faced with a premonition of a life she did not care for. She sensed Stefan wanted to control her, something she deeply resented. She would never again be controlled, not by dreams, not by anything—or anyone. Suddenly, Louisa realized she desperately wanted to go home, yet she couldn't recall anything to go home for. The only pleasant memories of home were connected to Marshall and Andrew, and they were apparently not going home now, if ever.

As she prepared to go out, she thought of another of Stefan's houseguests—How darkly handsome Marshall is. He reminded her of Uncle Simon, but with enough of his mother's gentle warmth to make him irresistible. "Why am I not planning to marry Marshall?" she questioned suddenly, in surprise. "What ever possessed me to consider Stefan. He's such an oppressive bore!" She felt ill-tempered, noticing a pain above her left eye. Too much wine, and the hours I've been keeping, she thought. "Oh, God! A whole day wasted on Stefan," she said aloud, ignoring Helena's presence.

Louisa brushed her shining hair furiously, brooding over her situation. In spite of how she felt that morning, she managed to be beautiful. Yet she wondered if she were on the road to the same kind of life her mother had lived. "How long before I go mad? How long before my skin turns gray?" But for now, all of the out-of-doors activity she insisted on gave her skin a reassuring glow, even if her deepening golden color was unfashionable. When she dressed, her slimness was accentuated by her rich brown riding ensemble, and her pale silk shirtwaist with its cascading ruffles heightened her beauty. She felt cross as she left her room, wondering how she would last the day, not to mention the week remaining of her visit. "If lack of sleep hadn't dulled my brain, I'd never have consented to this outing," she pouted, planning to use her headache as an excuse to come in early. "Oh, won't that improve Stefan's mood!" she scowled.

As they left the house, Louisa said little to Stefan, riding silently beside him, trying to concentrate on the now-familiar scenery. As soon as the horses seemed ready, she quickened her pace, losing herself in the motion and the throbbing of her head. She let the pain consume her, wishing it would burn her up, freeing her from Stefan. Why am I not riding with Marshall? Why am I not planning my life with him? I could

love Marshall, really love him. I'll never love Stefan.
Never! Her thoughts pounded through her pain with
the pulsing of her blood. Stefan is what Justin wants
for me! She kicked her horse furiously. When did
I start wanting what Justin wants?

She didn't think about Justin often. He seemed only
another distant, unpleasant memory from her past.
But now as she concentrated on her disappointment
with Stefan, her heart compared the two men. They
seemed oddly similar in their attitudes toward her—
she was only a possession to both men.

"Let's give these beasts a rest," called Stefan, pulling abreast of her. "Where are you off to at such a
pace?" he demanded as they slowed down. "Let's
head over to the shade of those trees," he motioned.

"I've an awful headache. I hoped it would disappear. Perhaps we ought to make our outing short?"
she said, giving him a soft smile.

He frowned, directing the horses to a small stand
of trees, at the edge of the stream. "Let's see how you
feel after some rest." They dismounted and walked
the horses for some minutes before tethering them,
then Louisa reclined in the warm grass above the water, propping herself on her elbows, turning her face
into the sun.

"It only darkens your skin more," Stefan said
sourly.

Louisa didn't reply, trying to concentrate on the
feel of the warm sun soaking into her body. Make
him go away, magic ball of fire, she incanted privately.

"You're beginning to look like a peasant."

Louisa felt very hot, and she knew it wasn't merely
the heat of the day. She said nothing, and soon Stefan
began to talk about their betrothal and a definite
wedding date.

"Stefan," Louisa interrupted. "Before we marry I
must return to America for a while."

"That would postpone our marriage perhaps a
year!" he said, nearly shouting.

"Why, Stefan," she replied calmly, despite her own
rising anger at him, and at herself, "it's not so urgent
that we marry within the year. We're young yet. Surely

you can understand how I'd want to return to my own country once more before I marry."

"We can sail to America when we're married!" he said sternly, then paused to look hard at Louisa. "But yes, I do understand. You simply do not want to marry me, and I wonder if you ever will. You can't put aside your flirtations. Perhaps you are too young." Louisa stiffened. Stefan was obviously angry. "You American women are immature. You have a beautiful woman's body, Louisa, but you're only a child playing at seduction," he said hotly.

Louisa sat up, rubbing her aching forehead. "Perhaps you're right. Perhaps I am only playing a child's game," she offered, hoping she could take advantage of his train of thought.

But Louisa misread him. Stefan only grew more furious. "You're a bitch, Louisa," he yelled, "and always in season!" He turned on her viciously, slapping her hard across the face, snapping her neck back with an incredible jolt. Louisa's breath was taken away, and before she could regain it, or her balance, he lunged at her, ripping at her clothes. He thrust a hand into the cascading ruffles of her blouse and stripped her bodice to its soft undergarments.

Louisa was totally unprepared for his attack. She reeled from the violent blow he'd struck and from his growing ferocity, believing he would tear her limb from limb, and suddenly, she summoned a strength she hardly knew she possessed. By God, he may kill me, but not so easily! she thought wildly, and began screaming like an animal loosed from the dark depths of Hell.

She lunged at him, gouging his face with her nails, instantly recognizing in her heart the hatred she felt for him. Never again would her body be violated in any way. Although Stefan was a powerful man, he was startled by the furious animal he'd aroused. But all he could think of was inflicting pain on her, of conquering her, torturing her as she'd tortured him. "Bitch," he cursed as he pursued her, ripping her skirt away. She was in tatters, and he flung her to the ground, stripping away her remaining lower garments

Louisa struggled, digging her nails into his flesh, kicking furiously. She sank a vicious bite into his hand as he tried to cover her mouth, yet her struggling aroused him, and he was consumed by his need to punish and humble her. He held her down with an arm across her breasts and arched his body slightly to open his clothing in order to mount her. Louisa took the instant advantage she had, violently driving a knee into his groin. Stefan gagged and fell against Louisa, grasping himself instinctively, yet he managed to seize her flying hair with his other hand as she tried to escape him, wrenching her with him as he rolled in agony.

She imagined he would pull her hair from her head, and in her pain and terror, her own attack became even more furious. As they struggled, she felt the stones jar and tear her flesh, and realizing he would recover soon enough, Louisa searched frantically for a weapon. Grabbing a rock, she forced it heavily into Stefan's already bloodied face, and they looked like what they were: animals battling to the death.

With the blow to his face, Stefan let go of Louisa. She tumbled and fell, getting quickly to her feet to run like a stunned animal, alternately stumbling and recovering. Stefan had hardly regained himself, but he knew he would kill her now, and he staggered after her, catching her viciously. Together they plunged down the stream bank, crashing into shallow water.

Louisa fell on top of Stefan, immediately terrified of nothing else but drowning, when suddenly he let loose his grip on her, and she slipped deeper into the stream. She felt the water only as a further blow, but it revived her, and she bolted from its freezing wetness, putting all of her sagging effort into struggling up the narrow bank, not believing she wasn't pursued.

She ran frantically, falling to her knees sobbing and grasping for breath, rising immediately to run again. She reached the skittering, nervous horses, and in her exhausted wild state had great difficulty getting astride her animal. As she did, Louisa realized she was alone, and curiosity allowed her cautiously to approach the stream in spite of her terror. Looking down, she stared into the agonized eyes of a man she had planned to marry. He appeared frozen, tortured for eternity, impaled on a dagger-sharp tree limb protruding from the gently rushing water. The front of his body was covered with blood.

Louisa cried out, gasping for air. She was exhausted from the life-or-death struggle, both angry and disbelieving. "You poor, goddamned bloody bastard!" she screamed, and her horse bolted beneath her, running into the thicket, throwing her to the ground. What breath she had was knocked from her, and she lay struggling for air.

When she recovered, Louisa was too exhausted to move. Perhaps I'll die here, too, she thought, battered and beyond caring, lying quietly, feeling every inch of aching flesh and muscle, wondering how she had survived the brutal attack. Then she collapsed into unconsciousness.

Some hours later, Louisa awoke cold and shivering in the shade of the stand of trees. Looking for the position of the sun, she realized it was past midday. Her body was very stiff as she forced herself to collect pieces of her discarded clothing. Finally, she walked to the edge of the stream to look briefly at Stefan's body, reassuring herself all she recalled was not just another nightmare. She turned abruptly from the distorted body, wrapping her nakedness in what had been her riding skirt.

She struggled to mount Stefan's still tethered horse and slowly began to ride back to the estate. Louisa knew the pain the horse's motion caused her was real, but surely the scenes that came into her mind must have been dreamed. She was stunned by the events, totally absorbed in her shock and pain, failing to notice the rider approaching her at an ever-increasing pace, until she heard her name being called.

"Louisa! Dear God, Louisa!"

She drew her horse up, and stared blankly into a man's face. Then silent tears streamed down her face. The man lifted her swiftly to his horse and into his arms, pressing her tightly against him.

"Marshall," she choked, unable to control her crying.

Marshall held her soft body against him, trying to console her. "Where is Stefan?" he asked, but Louisa only cried more violently. He realized it would be some time before she was calm, so he turned the horses, riding swiftly toward home. After several minutes, she was quiet, occasionally shuddering against him and gulping in air like a child after a long spell of crying.

Marshall reined in the horses and Louisa turned to him, pulling him to her. "Where have you been all of these months? How did we ever let them separate us?" she cried.

"It won't happen again, I promise you," he said, kissing her forehead gently.

"Yes, promise me," she sighed, still shuddering.

"Now, tell me how I happened to find you in this condition," he said, touching the already discolored places in her face, shoulders, and arms.

"Stefan tried to kill me, to rape me. He went berserk." Louisa began to shake, laughing bitterly, gasping and crying again. "He's dead. God damn him!" she cried with all of her strength, suddenly in control. She sat erect and continued, "We were struggling and fell into the water, and Stefan was impaled on a jagged branch. He's in the stream."

Marshall was stunned. He held Louisa, gently kissing her face and hair, comforting her in a way that seemed very familiar, and for a while they sat in silence. Then Marshall urged the horses forward. "Stefan said some painfully true things to me this morning," Louisa said quietly and put her head down, resting against Marshall for greater comfort. "I'm afraid I've been playing games. I don't belong here." She paused for some minutes, then said urgently, "Marshall, I must go home. I can't stay in Europe. I've had my fill. And you must go with me. No one will dare stop us."

"Yes, perhaps we should go home."

"Now, Marshall, please! Now!"

"Soon, Louisa, I promise. But I'm afraid this ordeal is not over yet!"

They rode on, and when they reached the estate, the other houseguests were occupied throughout the grounds. There was no way for them to enter the yard or approach the family unobserved, so they came to the house with a full audience.

"Mlle. Boyd, what in the world has happened?" shouted Henri, Stefan's older brother, as he rushed to assist Marshall and Louisa. "Summon the doctor!" he called to one of the servants. "Where is Stefan?"

Louisa was mute, lowering her eyes, unable to face the man directly.

"We should go inside before we open this discussion, Henri," said Marshall firmly, gesturing to the cluster of houseguests that had gathered excitedly around them. Marshall helped Louisa dismount and handed her over to Helena, who rushed from the house. Helena was nearly hysterical, obviously expecting the worst. Louisa remembered Helena had overheard her tirade about Stefan when she had assisted her with dressing that morning.

The family hurried into the house. "Louisa, go upstairs. I'll talk with the family."

Louisa gave Marshall no argument. "I ache terribly," she said quietly to Helena. "I'd love a hot soak in the tub and then a soft bed." Marshall and Henri went into the library and closed the doors, but she hadn't ascended the first stairs before she heard their voices grow loud and angry. She wondered if it were possible that anyone could doubt her. Surely her condition would speak for itself. When she reached the first landing, Henri burst out of the study. He shot her a horrified look, shouting for a few of his friends to ride with him, and Marshall quickly followed her up the stairs.

He put an arm around her. "Don't bathe until the doctor looks after you. Also, the police will be sent for. There will be endless questions. Try not to let them upset you. I'm sure it won't be easy." He held her, helping her up the next flight of stairs and into her

room. "Just remember, I'm nearby if you need me."
She hugged him tightly, barely checking her tears.
"Try to rest," he urged as he left her. "I'm going with
Henri to get the body."

Then she was alone, free to remove the remaining
shreds of clothing to examine the bruises and gashes
and swollen places on her body. Her eyes were puffy
and her face swollen and bloodied. She looked like
she'd been in a street brawl, and she felt worse than
she looked. Helena helped her into a soft satin robe
and into an enormous canopied bed.

"Would you like something to eat, Miss Louisa?"

"Please, get me something hot. I'm so very cold."

Helena hurried away, leaving Louisa with her
thoughts as she tried to warm herself in the cold bed.
All that came to her mind's eye was Stefan's anguished face, and she covered her eyes hoping the
vision would be erased. Her efforts were to no avail
and quickly Louisa succumbed to burning, bitter
agony.

Chapter Nine

"IT's hard to believe it happened just as she said. Anyone with eyes knows he wouldn't have had to attack her. I'm certain she's no virgin." Françoise Vinay was adamant, and much more composed than anyone else in the family. As Stefan's mother, she had taken his death with remarkable calm, but Mme. Vinay generally preserved appearances whatever her private griefs. She had loved Stefan as much as she had loved any of her children—with great reserve. They had come as an inconvenience to be nurtured and raised by servants, and they were expected to give support to the family's interests. Status and property were paramount. Stefan's impending marriage to Louisa was regarded as a question of property. Justin and M. Vinay more than saw eye to eye, and would merge many of their enterprises upon the marriage of their children.

"Pay her off, if necessary," Mme. Vinay said, "but she must not make her version public! There must be no scandal. Your sister's future *must* be considered! Annette's reputation must be preserved, at any cost. The Marquis would forbid his son ever to see her again if Mlle. Boyd's account reached his ears."

Henri believed Louisa's story. He knew his brother only too well, and of the battered wenches that were dismissed routinely from their household in Paris. But he agreed with his mother that Louisa's story would be damaging. "I am sure she can be convinced to say they were attacked and robbed by ruffians. It will do her no harm to repeat such a tale."

Françoise Vinay was tiny and ethereal-looking,

having skin like soft white rose petals with the faintest pink blush. Her dark-brown hair was pulled severely from her face, accentuating her large gray eyes. She looked fragile, but there was no hint of it in her manner. She was cold and consummately precise, never yielding to persuasion. "How badly is she hurt? What does Dr. Michaelis say?"

"She's taken quite a beating and is very unnerved, but he expects she'll recover with a few days' rest. There are no broken bones. No deep wounds. She'll look quite grotesque for a few days, and it will be a few weeks before her face heals properly. One eye is quite unattractive."

"Talk to her, Henri, before the authorities do. Send for her father and for yours. I think we may have a problem with her. She is quite proud and headstrong, I think."

Henri remembered his mother's words when he went to talk with Louisa. She was embarrassed by her appearance, her usually beautiful face discolored and distorted. She was calm, almost pensive at first while Marshall sat with her, and the three of them talked quietly over late-afternoon tea.

"I'm very anxious to leave here, Henri. How soon can it be arranged?"

"In a few days, perhaps. Dr. Michaelis wants you to rest for several more days, and you'll want to wait for your father. I've sent him a message and expect him to be here by Friday." Henri could tell Louisa was not happy to learn of Justin's imminent arrival. "Stefan will be buried tomorrow. You will feel well enough to be present?"

Louisa gave him a hostile look. "I've no respects to pay to Stefan, Henri. You heard me say he tried to murder me—and nearly succeeded!" She suddenly seemed very tense, having refused a sleeping powder in spite of the doctor's urging.

Henri sighed. He liked Louisa. She pleased him with her beauty, her innate intelligence, and her spirit. He knew few girls her age who promised as much as she did. What a waste she would have been on Stefan, he mused to himself. He would have abused her without a second thought, and gone on to other conquests, never appreciating her.

Then aloud he began to reason with her. "Yes. Louisa, I heard all you said. And I believe all you say. There is no reason for me to doubt you. I knew Stefan very well. He could be ugly when he couldn't have his way. I'm sure it was mere luck that he didn't hurt you more than he did." Henri paused, watching her carefully, taking time over his tea before he continued. "But I see no reason to do damage to the living. If you fail to appear at the grave, if you tell the truth about what happened, the family will be disgraced. Annette, for one, will suffer needlessly. You know she hopelessly loves Jean. Any scandal would stop their courtship instantly."

"What are you suggesting, Henri?" Marshall interrupted. "Are you asking Louisa to lie about what happened?"

"Simply put, yes. I'm asking her to lie. To—"

"No, I will not lie," Louisa broke in. "Stefan was not the kind of man whose reputation should be protected. And as for Annette . . . she's already turning her eyes elsewhere. I doubt she'll be broken-hearted for long."

Henri rose from the tea table and went to the windows. He took a deep breath, looking out over the carefully manicured gardens, planning what he would say next, finding everything about the day distasteful. "I prefer not to be unpleasant, Louisa. I seek your cooperation with a simple falsehood which will harm no one." He turned to face the couple again. "You fail to see the gravity of the matter. Public disgrace could seriously affect our financial position. Personal scandals of this nature often ruin families, something we are loath to allow to happen." His eyes narrowed, his voice grew very deliberate. "I am sure your father will understand. He will support our request completely."

Louisa froze at the reference to Justin. "Oh, I am sure he would not quarrel with your logic, since it affects money matters—your only real concern."

Henri said nothing.

"No, Henri. I will not lie to the authorities. I have taken a terrible beating, nearly been killed, and I will not lie."

Louisa was calm beyond Henri's expectation. He sat down again. He looked long at Marshall, then at Louisa. "I will ask Dr. Michaelis to see you again."

Louisa stared at him blankly, unable to fathom his reason. "Why?"

Henri looked at her coldly, appraising the usually luscious young woman who normally filled a room with her enthusiasm and charm, and he took a chance, reflecting on what he would have done had he been Stefan. "I am sure he will tell us that you are no virgin, Louisa."

Louisa was silent, disbelieving. She could not bring herself to look at Marshall. Henri had chosen his attack well. She was utterly composed, but she couldn't prevent the color from flooding her face, and she trembled slightly. She stood up and walked slowly to the fireplace and stared into the ornate mirror that rose to the ceiling. She looked at her battered face and felt ugly, ugly beyond her skin, ugly into her core. Tears brimmed her eyes, but did not spill over. She felt disgraced, unclean, and completely vulnerable. She knew Henri could never know her guilty secret. He had only been clever.

Louisa held her breath to keep from crying out.

Henri went on. "Dr. Michaelis will advise us that you have known the ways of the flesh, whether or not my brother enjoyed you, and, whatever the truth of the matter is, the verdict will go against you. Everyone is of the opinion that only virgins can be raped. And you did not lose your virginity today. Of course, it will be made to appear that you seduced Stefan," turning to Marshall in sudden inspiration, "and then your lover interrupted and in a jealous rage killed my brother."

"That's absurd!" Marshall shouted.

"Not so," replied Henri, certain his premise about Louisa was correct. "We have power and influence, and in this country, you have none. It would be a tale easily promoted and readily accepted. I'm sure not a few young men could be persuaded to say they've known Louisa's charms."

Louisa heard and knew instantly that Henri was on sure ground. Her humiliation before Marshall was great. How would he ever understand? He would know when she accepted Henri's bargain that she was no virgin, not the young woman he thought. She couldn't even bring herself to tell him the truth. Louisa heard and watched the men from before the mirror. She did not move. She merely said quietly, "I will think about it, Henri."

Henri Vinay said no more, and rose from his chair quietly. He took a hard, appraising look at Marshall, hoping the young man wouldn't be a fool and discard Louisa over this matter. Finally he shrugged his shoulders. Louisa will fare all right in any event—she's no weakling, he thought as he walked slowly from the room.

To Louisa, Henri's departure seemed to take an eternity, and when he was gone, she put her head in her bruised, scratched hands and cried deeply. Her tears were bitter beyond belief; Marshall did not come to comfort her and she felt abandoned.

In a few minutes, though, she stopped crying. In the sudden stillness of the room Louisa looked into the mirror and was sickened by her temporary disfigurement. She felt contaminated and defiled. I have no one, she thought. I'm alone in this world. And, to her surprise, she was suddenly in control again.

Louisa then turned to Marshall. He appeared to be exhausted, but he looked at her with love and sadness in his eyes. Rising, he came to her and put his arms around her and held her quietly.

"It doesn't matter," he said. "I love you, and it makes no difference."

"I really have no choice but to say what Henri suggests. If I don't you'd be implicated, and we could never prove otherwise." She stopped, wanting to tell Marshall about herself, but found she didn't have words to explain. She felt dirty and ashamed. "I can't tell you about what has happened to me," she whispered, "but it's not what you think. Please give me some time. I'll find a way to make you understand, to make you forgive me."

Marshall smiled at her and held her tightly. "Louisa, it doesn't matter. You're mine now. We belong to each other. Believe me, nothing from the past, nothing else matters."

Chapter Ten

When Marshall left her, Louisa gladly took the sleeping powder Dr. Michaelis had prescribed. She slept soundly through the night, but the day that followed was blurred and painful. Her bruised body ached and her heart was burdened. She followed Stefan's casket solemnly, grieving for him in the tragedy of his short, hateful life; grieving for herself, for the unhappy child that lived inside her, over the knowledge that she had no right to. She prayed with the others, wept with the others, but her prayers and her tears were for herself as much as for Stefan's soul. "Dear God, help me," she begged.

She was a slender shadow in the ponderous black mourning dress and veil. Her tortured face was concealed by the heavily netted bonnet, but Marshall saw her and was touched by her sorrow. He loved her and he remembered the haunted child. He was amazed at the strength that held Louisa together. She might cry, but when her tears were spent, she seemed remarkably whole.

He had thought over her confession to the police officers earlier this morning. She had given them the story that Henri suggested, never faltering when they questioned her. She said she had been too terrified and could not possibly identify anyone. The officers were polite, and the case was evidently closed for them. They were merely completing a perfunctory task.

Marshall also considered the implications of her confession. Over and above her protection of him in the affair was her private admission that she was not a virgin. He would not deny he had wanted to take her for the first time, even have her know him exclusively. What experience has she had? he wondered. Who has made love to her? Then he would remember her promise that it was not as he would think, which only puzzled him. I will trust her because I want to, he said to himself, amused by the simplicity of his solution.

After the funeral, Louisa tried to prepare herself for Justin's arrival the following day. She knew his public behavior would be polite, but she was afraid of how he would react privately. And she feared he would not approve of her deepening bond with Marshall.

Louisa watched from her window as Justin disembarked from the carriage. "Helena, ask Marshall to come here," she said urgently, and Helena rushed after him. Louisa sat quietly waiting, trying to decide how to explain everything to Justin. She had never defied him, and she wondered if she had the strength.

Louisa wore an ice-blue gown. The neckline was high in back and scalloped around her throat, then plunged gently, revealing the fullness of her young figure. The swelling on her face was completely gone, but her skin was still discolored. She looked delicate and exhausted to Marshall; she seemed to be under unbearable strain.

"I cannot face him alone," she told him quietly when he hastened to her. "Please, stay with me regardless of what he says. Please!"

"Of course, I'll stay. Whatever you ask. But what do you have to fear from your father?" he questioned, startled by the desperation in her voice. "He'll accept the truth. What more is there to say?"

"You really don't know Justin, Marshall. Stefan was an approved marriage partner for me. I'm certain our union meant sizable business profits for him and M. Vinay. And I'm merely a piece of valuable property for Justin to shift at will. Now my value is diminished, and even though the scandal is mild, I'm positive Justin will be terribly angry."

Justin interrupted them. "Louisa, dearest Louisa," he cried, taking her into his arms. Louisa was stiff and she shot a desperate look at Marshall. "What a tragedy for you, child! Tell me, what happened? I've only very sketchy information."

Louisa extracted herself politely from Justin's grip. "You look awful," he added, "but, I understand you were not badly hurt. Is that true?"

"I've only aches and pains, cuts and bruises, all of which will heal in time. I'm not sure what you've been told," she said, seating herself across from Justin, motioning for Marshall to sit with her, "but the events are simple. Stefan and I went riding and we disagreed over the date of our marriage. He wanted to marry immediately. I wanted to wait. He turned vicious and tried to rape me, and I have no doubt he would have killed me. But, as luck would have it, he was accidentally killed himself."

It was as if Justin had only heard her say the couple had disagreed over the date of their marriage. He had frowned at that moment of her story, and flashed her a look that caused Louisa to relive the whole hideous scene with Stefan. She had seen hatred just like that on Stefan's face, and she shivered violently, surprised Justin would reveal himself so easily to Marshall. But she wondered if Marshall read what she did in his face.

"Marshall, I would like to speak with Louisa alone," Justin said coldly. He was polite, obviously expecting Marshall to honor his request.

Marshall did not move. "No. I'll stay." And again Justin's face turned malevolent. "What is this, Louisa? Did you betray Stefan? Is Marshall your lover?"

Louisa's hatred for Justin overpowered her. "No, he is not yet my lover, Papa. But he will be, if he'll have me."

Justin quieted himself immediately. "You're over-

wrought, Louisa. I'm sorry. Of course, you're upset."
He paused. "But, tell me why you wished to postpone
the marriage?"

"I knew I couldn't marry him. I hated him. I found
myself doing only what you wanted of me. I wanted to
stop that ugly business." She looked at Marshall and
colored. "I lied about this affair to protect us from a
hopeless mess." She took Marshall's outstretched hand
and held it with all her strength. "But the lying must
stop. Henri trapped me into lying because I'm not a
virgin, and I couldn't say otherwise. I am ashamed
before Marshall because I can't go to him the way I
want to. And I can't even explain my knowledge with
tales of other young men. I've not merely lost my virginity: I've been defiled, defiled by my own father."
And the hatred poured out of her.

Marshall was sickened and angered by what he
heard. He reached to hold Louisa, astounded by her
words, but he was silent.

"Louisa, what madness is this?" was Justin's hot reply. He looked at Marshall. "No one said this tragic
affair had affected her mind!"

But it was Louisa who responded. "Yes, it's affected
my mind!" she screamed. "I will have no more lies!
I'm through with lies. You've burdened me forever,
and I must face the truth of it. And so must you!
You've had your way with me. I've done your bidding.
But now *I am through*. I'll have no more of you, nor
of your plans for me."

"You know," he said calmly to Marshall, "since the
fire years ago, she's had a streak of madness in her.
I'm afraid Stefan's death made her completely mad."

"Yes, the fire left me unsettled, and your merciless
seduction of me from that time on has increased any
inclination I may have for insanity, but I am fully
sane, have no doubt. I only want you to know I am
finished with you forever. I'm going with Marshall.
You've no more power over me!" Her ferocity echoed
in her ears.

"Marshall, are you prepared to take this mad-woman?" Justin sneered. "Let me warn you, insanity is definitely in her blood." He laughed cruelly. "I lived with her mother long enough to testify to that fact." He gave Louisa a hateful glance. "You can have her with my blessing, Marshall. I'm finished with her. She's of no value to me. Precious metal, but tarnished for my purposes." His voice hardened further. "But your blissful plans won't come easily, you know. Your parents, both of them, will oppose a marriage. Emma will object on some high principle," he laughed, "Simon because he wants a political alliance cemented with a proper marriage. He already has his plans in motion, I hear. So, don't count on smooth sailing." He stood up to face them, as if bored by the conversation. "I see little purpose for my journey out here, but I expect the Vinays want to settle some questions of business and I don't want to waste the trip. I'll be returning to Paris tomorrow." A hostile look crossed his face, and he paused to look at the silent young couple. "Welcome to the family, Marshall. You have *my* blessing, but I suspect it will be the only one your union receives." He gave Marshall a knowing smile. "Enjoy her. She's a born whore."

"You filth!" was Marshall's reply as he leapt at Justin, striking him violently. Justin fell dazedly to the floor.

"No, Marshall," Louisa cried as he struck him again. "Please! Please!" she said, touching him desperately. "No more violence." Reluctantly, Marshall stopped his attack, feeling incredible hatred for Justin, an emotion he had never known before.

In a few minutes Justin collected himself and left the room. "My God, Louisa! What he's done is unnatural. What kind of animal is he?" Marshall asked as he held her, wanting desperately to erase her memories, to protect and love her.

"I assure you he is the lowest sort. There is nothing he would not stoop to, no crime he would not commit," she cried, clinging to him with desperate helplessness. "And it terrifies me that I am his child. Perhaps there is no hope for me. Perhaps I can only contaminate you, too!"

Marshall crushed her fiercely against him. He seemed angry, but not at her. "No, Louisa, it's not possible. His evil can't touch us. We start clean and fresh and new, with no past. I promise you, time begins with us, when we begin."

Chapter Eleven

Louisa secluded herself in her room, refusing to see anyone but Marshall. Her father's departure the next morning was attended only by M. Vinay, the two men evidently finding mutual interests in spite of their losses. Louisa stood in her dressing gown, and watched from the window as the men bade each other a jovial farewell. She was appalled at how quickly they could set aside the tragedies of their children. "We were nothing but chattel, Stefan," she whispered against the glass. "Dear God, let me be barren!" she wept.

"Louisa, why are you crying? Didn't you sleep well?" Marshall questioned as he approached her from the doorway, watching her peer out the windows, clutching the draperies, using them to support her weight as she leaned into the glass. At the sound of his voice, she whirled around wildly, startled from her sorrow. Her body was tense and her blue eyes filled with a kind of terror. When she saw him, Louisa relaxed slightly, wiping the tears from her face, trying to compose herself. "Marshall, I didn't hear you."

"Obviously. What do you see?" he said, coming to her, slipping an arm around her. She bristled, which surprised him. "Perhaps Dr. Michaelis can give you something to help you calm yourself? I'll send Helena . . ."

"No. No. I'm all right. I was just watching M. Vinay and Justin. How easily they forget us—Stefan and me —and carry on their business. But we were never on their minds in any other way." She colored. "Except for me. My father thought of me . . . in his own special way. God, Marshall!" She gave a sharp laugh, almost a gasp, and shuddered against him as if she hoped to shake off her memories physically.

Marshall held her tightly, not knowing what else he could do or say. He watched Justin's carriage go through the elaborate front gates. "We can leave this afternoon ourselves," he said. "M. Vinay will lend us a carriage and driver until we leave France. You need do nothing. I'll make all the arrangements." He smiled down at Louisa, very worried about the tension he felt in her body. "Remember, we've promised each other a new beginning. Our life starts now."

"Yes, let's go now—today. This instant is all right with me. Luggage or no!"

Marshall stayed with her and they talked quietly of their happier past and of their hopes for the future. Soon she slept in his arms as they sat in the quiet gray morning, but she seemed tense even in sleep as he lifted her into her bed and covered her with a soft comforter.

"Helena," he called to the woman as she unobtrusively packed their trunks in the morning's stillness. "Go for some sleeping powders. I don't like Miss Louisa's condition."

"Yes, sir. She was up half the night pacing like a caged animal. She's wild for lack of sleep, if nothing else."

"Frankly, Helena, I'm worried about her," Marshall confided with a frown. "I think she might feel better in Paris. How soon can you be ready?"

"After dinner, sir."

"I'll plan on it."

When they were alone, Marshall watched Louisa carefully. She seemed to sleep deeply, but was often disturbed by unsettling dreams. She thrashed and muttered and cried out, waking fitfully. She felt feverish and clung to Marshall when he went to her. "You haven't changed much, Louisa. You used to wake the whole house. Remember?" he whispered, stroking her flushed damp face.

"Oh, yes! I remember! I never thought my dreams could be worse than they were. But, unbelievably, they are!" She pulled him to her tightly. "Marshall, why is my life filled with such horror? I've never hurt anyone. Am I so wicked? Why are my eyes filled with sights that should be only nightmares, not memory!"

"We can do nothing about the past, Louisa. We can only live our future, and try not to let the past haunt us."

"But, Marshall, it does haunt! The past haunts my nights and my days too!" she cried, pushing away from him, leaning into the pillows again. "The voices I hear, the faces I see—my mother, my father, Stefan— they're so filled with loathing. And I feel so small and helpless. They do whatever they want with me. I feel them near me, touching me, hurting me." Louisa closed her eyes, rolled over, and buried her face in the pillows, covering her ears, stiffening her body, sobbing, clenching her fists. She began to moan, the pitch of her voice rising until it became a tortured scream, unheard beyond the room as she burrowed more deeply into the down-filled cushions.

Marshall let her go, sensing into the core of his being the pain that filled her. He touched and stroked her, murmuring her name between her racking sobs. And when her terror abated and she was quiet again, he held her until she fell asleep. "Ah, Louisa," he prayed, his fears only intensified by the long morning. "Let me love you. Leave your dreams behind, and come with me."

Chapter Twelve

Their departure from the Vinay family household was quiet with no formality. Only Henri disturbed himself to bid them good-bye. He offered no apology, but did congratulate Marshall on his behavior. "Glad to see you kept your head, Hudson. You understand my position."

"Perfectly," he replied as he supervised the loading of the carriage.

"Elijah will assist you, until you board ship." Henri turned to follow Marshall's gaze. Louisa was descending the steps, assisted by Helena. She looked frail, enveloped in a blue cape and hood. Her beauty was marred by the gray and green discolorations in her face, and the fading, but unhealed scar curving along her eyebrow.

She barely acknowledged Henri with a sharp glance when he spoke to her. As she boarded the carriage, she turned her head to look out the opposite window, waiting for Helena to settle herself and for Marshall to join them.

She had consented to take a sleeping powder for the trip to Paris, and watched the countryside roll slowly by, mesmerized by the all-too-familiar scenery. When they passed the thicket where Stefan and she had struggled so brutally, she did not turn away, but merely leaned back against the carriage's soft velvet-cushioned interior and stared out silently.

Marshall sat across from her. She had been strangely silent since the episode of violent crying earlier that day. They had dined on the terrace outside her room, with no words exchanged and only the rustling wind in the trees and the calling of the birds to

accompany them. He had watched her gradually withdraw more deeply into herself as they prepared to
leave the house, and he saw her slip even further
away from him as they traveled along the road.

Helena watched both of them anxiously, wondering
what to do if Louisa became ill. She understood Louisa
had broken with her father, and the more she saw,
the more uncertain she felt about Louisa's health. Louisa dozed quietly for most of the five hours the carriage rattled and swayed on the road to Paris, finally
arriving there about dusk.

They went immediately to Marshall's apartments,
startling the housekeeper. "M. Hudson, I did not expect you! You have guests?"

"Good evening, Mme. Braque. Mlle. Boyd and her
companion will be my guests over the next few
weeks. Please, make them comfortable. And a light
supper for us, in an hour."

"Oui, monsieur."

He then turned to Louisa, smiling at her. "Come,
let's go for a walk. Some exercise will do us both good.
We've been confined for days. It's not like you to sit
still for so long."

They began slowly, then quickened their pace. Louisa's eyes shone; ease and laughter crept back into
her voice. When they started out, they moved separately, but in a few minutes they were arm in arm,
enjoying each other's warmth, looking like lovers.

When they returned to Marshall's they dined
quietly and cheerfully, and Marshall began to relax,
hoping Louisa would be all right now that she was in
Paris. "I'm glad we didn't stay any longer. It's wonderful how much happier you are here." He offered her a
liqueur, and she drank it slowly, nestled against him
as they sat on the window seat, overlooking the park
below.

"I know I'll feel even better when we sail for
America. How soon can we leave?"

"I'm certain there's a Vanguard ship leaving Tues-
day of next week. Tomorrow, I'll secure passage for
us."

"How nice to have connections!"

"What accommodations do you want, Louisa?"

Unexpectedly, Louisa sat up sharply, nearly spilling her drink. "Choose whatever you like, Marshall. The decision is yours."

"Not really, Louisa. And what's wrong? Why are you suddenly so upset?"

"I'm tired." She forced a smile, trying to relax again. "I should go upstairs. Do you have any more sleeping medicine?"

"Helena has whatever you need." He rose to go with her up the stairs, puzzling over her abrupt change of attitude. He took her into his arms at her door and she was unresponsive, barely returning his embrace. "What's wrong? Have I done or said something to offend you?"

"Why no, Marshall. I'm just exhausted. I'll be all right by morning."

But Marshall wondered that night if morning would ever come. Louisa took her drug and slept peacefully for several hours. Then, suddenly, the whole house seemed to reverberate with her screams. Marshall, Helena, and Mme. Braque bolted from their beds at the first sound of her voice. By the time Marshall arrived at Louisa's door, Helena was at her bedside attempting to restrain her.

Louisa wept wildly, muttering incomprehensibly. "Oh sir, what is wrong with her?" Helena cried above her mistress's hysteria.

"I don't know." He rushed to take over. "Louisa! My God! What is it?"

"Justin! Justin was here! Didn't you see him? He's come for me. He says he won't leave without me! Marshall, don't let him take me! Please, never again! Please! Marshall!"

"You've been dreaming!"

"No, I wasn't dreaming! I saw him, Marshall! I *saw* him, I swear it!" Her eyes were wild with terror.

"Listen to me! Trust me! No one was here!"

Louisa gasped, clutching her head with her hands, slowly succumbing to Marshall's touch, easing into his arms. "I think you can both go back to bed, now," he said to Helena and Mme. Braque, who were still wide-eyed with fright, as they retreated from the room, Helena in tense silence, Marie Braque muttering a serious request for a benevolent deliverance from ghosts and night terrors.

Marshall helped Louisa into bed again and sat next to her, holding her hands. "I'm so glad you're here," she sighed. "Once again, you're helping me sort out my dreams. But I thought my nightmares would be over."

"Maybe, it's a little soon after . . ."

"After Stefan? Perhaps."

"Give yourself a little time." He put her hands to his mouth and kissed them, then held them against his chest as he bent to kiss her mouth. "We'll soon have dreams to erase the others, Louisa," he added, leaning to touch her lips. He was shocked when she turned rigid at his caress.

"What's wrong?" he asked gently. "I thought you wanted us to be together."

Louisa shook uncontrollably. Her voice was hoarse and barely audible. "Don't touch me, please, Marshall. Please understand. I want you, but not yet, not now. Oh, maybe, not ever." The tears slid down the sides of her eyes.

"Louisa, Louisa, beautiful Louisa," he said in anguish. "What has he done to you?" He touched her face, unable not to do at least that. "I won't hurt you, I promise. I won't touch you until you want me to, not now, not ever."

She held his hands tightly, her tears running fast, wetting her face and hair. "I'm so afraid. Please, don't leave me."

"I'll stay for as long as you need me."

She smiled, calming herself visibly, then took a deep breath, controlling her tears, closing her eyes, seeming to rest. Marshall sat with her, held fiercely in her grip though she seemed to be asleep. He loved her and he pitied her and he longed for her. And now he wondered if he would ever possess her, ever make love to her. He wondered if what he'd heard of the insanity in her background was true enough to harm them. His mother had spoken of it, and so had Justin. Marshall knew little of insanity, having heard only the common tales of miserable wretches chained, raving in asylums. How would he know?

Louisa seemed to sleep peacefully, yet she held fast to Marshall. If he moved, she gripped him more tightly. He suddenly felt weary from the events of the last few days, but he wanted to be with her, comfort her, if he could. He pondered over Justin and his actions against his child. In all his searching, Marshall could not comprehend what sort of lust would overpower a man to allow him to touch a child sexually.

Marshall had eagerly learned about his own needs, finding an abundance of willing young accomplices, and he had hoped Louisa would come to him with as much enthusiasm, long before a formal marriage. But now as he watched her in the night, he felt even marriage might be more than she could accept.

He agreed with Justin's prediction that his parents would object to matrimony, and probably for the reasons Justin had outlined. But soon he'd be twenty-three. On that birthday, he would receive a small fortune as a long-promised gift, and he planned to keep his and Louisa's hopes for a life together secret until he was independent, and could marry with or without approval. But will Louisa be able to marry anyone? he wondered. How awful are your dreams, Louisa?

When she woke again, she saw he was asleep sitting up, holding her as he had been when she drifted off. She smiled softly. I ask a lot from you, too much perhaps, she thought. How can I love you and yet ask you not to touch me? Surely, I'll change. Surely, I'll want you someday. But not now. Please, not now. Please understand.

He had not heard her plea, for she did not speak out loud, but he woke to look into her eyes, "I think I'm all right. You can go back to bed."

"I'll stay as long as you need me," he assured her.

She smiled, deeply touched by his response. "You have the patience to sit by me all night if I ask, don't

Chapter Thirteen

LOUISA slept fitfully throughout the remainder of their stay in Paris, but more quietly than the first night. Marshall arranged passage for the three of them aboard the *Emma H*. At first he insisted Helena and Louisa share accommodations. But Louisa preferred to be alone. "I'll not be watched. It would only make me worse," she stormed.

When their plans were confirmed, Louisa grew cheerful and some of her spirit seemed to return. She laughed and hugged Marshall warmly whenever he returned to the house, but if he approached her as a man would the woman he loved, seeking even the slightest encouragement, a distance could suddenly be measured between them.

When they settled into their cabins aboard ship, Louisa seemed genuinely happy. "I wonder why Andrew jumped ship," she mused, reflecting on her earlier childish thoughts about escaping her life and becoming a sailor.

"Not all sea duty is as good as it is aboard the ships you've traveled on, Louisa. In fact, some of Vanguard's ships ought to be burned without a second thought," Marshall said with conviction. "I'm afraid our fathers earn some of their fortunes in despicable trade, at the expense of others. Perhaps Andrew saw more than he could take. Though I wonder why he made himself a fugitive." He paused to think about Andrew, and the deep friendship they had shared. "Wouldn't you love to see him again? What a threesome we were!"

Louisa smiled at her memories. "I know it could never be the same, but surely we could be as close again." Her voice grew excited as she thought of the possibility of the three of them coming together again. "I'd give anything to go back and relive it all—oh, not all," she sighed, suddenly touched again by her own misery. But generally, she and Marshall laughed and talked and played cards and seemed a very happy couple.

The *Emma H.* sailed and called on several ports in France. They bid Helena good-bye when they finally reached England, delayed on the usual route by poor weather. At first Louisa slept badly, not yet accustomed to the pitch and roll of the ship, nor to the creaking of its timbers. The wind howled in the rigging and Louisa could barely control her agony in the dark as the voices in the wind seemed to cry out to her. "Lou—i—sa, child, you are damned. I war—ned you, but you did not lis—ten," the voice whispered in a gust of air in the passageway.

'Lou—i—sa, my beau—tiful, Lou—i—sa. Let me ho—ld you. Swe—et Louisa. Pa—pa loves you. Come, let me love you."

"Ahh, Lou—i—sa."

Night after night, the wind in the darkness called to her, as she lay frozen with fear until the wind died down and she was overcome with exhaustion. She reassured herself that at least she knew the voices were her imagination, but nevertheless, she was tortured, and though the bruises disappeared and the cuts healed, Louisa's face was marred by lines of tension and fatigue.

"Enjoy her. She's a born whore. Enjoy . . . Enjoy . . . Enjoy . . ." And the laughter echoed in the wind.

Louisa leapt from her bunk and tried to open the porthole. "I must have some air," she cried. Finally, her struggles opened the porthole, bringing a blast of wind and rain to douse her and blow out her only lantern. In her terror, she was caught in total blackness, listening to a raging gust of wind as it touched her body with its wetness and its chill.

"Lou—isa, swe—et little whore." She slammed the porthole closed. "Lis—ten to me . . . You are damned, Lou—i—sa. Damned, Lou—is—a."

Louisa frantically found her way to her cabin door, unlatching it, hastily leaping into the passageway where it was bitterly cold, but at least dimly lit by a lantern. She lunged toward Marshall's cabin, pounding furiously on the door. In an instant it was opened, and she was in his arms, begging, yielding to his comfort.

"I can't bear to be alone anymore. I can't bear listening to the voices," and she uttered their cries for Marshall to hear. "I know they're my imagination, but they terrify me!" She shivered and snuggled against him.

"I've some brandy," he said, turning up the lamp, offering her a glass, pouring some for himself as well. She downed the drink quickly. "Please, let me sleep with you tonight!"

He smiled. "My pleasure."

Louisa flinched, but smiled.

"I want you desperately, Louisa. But I can wait until you're ready," he said, offering her more brandy, watching as she gulped a second glass, obviously debating where she would be most comfortable—with him, or alone in the darkness with her voices.

When he finished his brandy he decided not to prolong their misery. He lowered the lamp and led her quietly to his bunk where, night after night, she slept peacefully and safely against him, knowing at last someone loved her enough to take only what she could freely, lovingly give.

Chapter Fourteen

"ALL hands ahoy. All hands ahoy," shouted the first mate late one afternoon as the *Emma H.* skirted the coast, heading for open sea. The weather was good for a change, and the sudden frantic activity of the crew drove passengers on deck.

"Passengers, go below," ordered the captain. "We can't be stumbling over you. We've got an unidentified schooner in our wake. She's armed and flies no colors. We're running on the wind and will likely elude her, but you best get out of the way! Now, go below!" And he waved them out of sight.

Marshall was with the captain when the schooner was first observed. He knew piracy was not unheard of along this coast, especially lately. And Vanguard ships had suffered more than their share of mishaps. Clippers like the *Emma H.* fared best on the open ocean, but, along the coast, a confrontation with a well-handled schooner could be quite a contest. Marshall remained on deck and his presence was acknowledged by Captain Sebastian. "She's going to give us a bit of a run for our money. Looks as if she's got a sharp crew, and she's heavily armed. If we can get to open water without serious challenge, though, we'll leave her astern quickly enough."

Throughout the remainder of the day, the full crew stayed on deck, and the passengers waited nervously below. Tension built for everyone aboard as the two ships parried with increasing intensity. When night fell, the *Emma H.* had the advantage. The absence of a moon covered them with total blackness and increased their hopes for escape. All light aboard ship was forbidden and the ship's course was altered a few

degrees every hour. The night passed slowly, the
sounds of the sea nearly deafening to those who lay
awake, poised and listening.

"What's going to happen, Marshall?" Louisa asked
anxiously.

"I don't know. Piracy is always a risk, but tonight
the sky is in our favor, and Captain Tomas is the very
best."

"Our trip certainly hasn't been very smooth, and
we've hardly begun," Louisa sighed, only slightly reassured by Marshall's calmness. "I'm wishing we were
still in Paris."

"I'm not. For one, I doubt you'd be in my bed if
we were in Paris."

"One never knows," she laughed, and hugged him
warmly.

It was not the first intimacy she'd shown him in
their bed, for on other nights, they lay together talking, touching. But tonight he turned against her
slowly, kissing her throat, caressing her. She felt stiff,
but seemed willing as he pursued her gently. He
stroked and petted, easing her into his embrace. He
touched her breasts through her gown, then opened
the deep neckline of her negligee, slowly kissing the
length of her torso. Her tension shifted to uncertainty
and then to eagerness at his persistent loving touch,
and Louisa found herself released and unburdened in
his arms. She cried out for joy as warmth surged
through her limbs.

Soon they were naked, exploring and filling each
other with delicious sensations. Marshall coaxed her
slowly but relentlessly until she begged him to penetrate deep inside where her spasms of rapture led him
swiftly to the same ecstatic peak.

Then they lay contentedly with knowledge of each
other, their tension from the previous nights of denial
subdued. They laughed and caressed and planned
their future. And they were oblivious to the dangers
of the night voyage while the *Emma H.* hauled cautiously toward morning.

At daybreak, the unidentified schooner was nowhere to be seen. The ship's course was corrected and

she sped along to the freedom and safety of open water. No one could catch her now.

Louisa now reveled in the voyage. She felt as if her spirit soared alongside the graceful clipper. Suddenly she had no feeling of confinement within the wooden-hulled ship as it flew over the seemingly endless ocean. Louisa was whole again, as free as the wind that filled the sails, no longer a captive of its whistling voices. She was its equal, no longer its prisoner She was filled with strength, at last no one's slave, able to give herself freely with love to Marshall. And when she offered her body, Marshall knew that, for her, it was the ultimate expression of love for him. And they made their plans and dreamed their dreams as only lovers can.

Chapter Fifteen

MARSHALL and Louisa's return to Louisiana was not heralded with great enthusiasm by Simon or Emma Hudson. They were appalled by the story of Louisa's encounter with death, and only grudgingly approved Marshall's accompanying Louisa home, after commenting it would have been better had Justin done so. Their cautious, but unmistakably disapproving response to the couple confirmed Marshall's suspicions that they would vehemently oppose a formal union, and he resolved to conceal his love for Louisa.

"I'm sorry I can't tell everyone how much I love you," he said one afternoon shortly after they had returned. "We'll just have to bide our time, until we're free to do whatever we want."

Louisa willingly accepted Marshall's decision to postpone announcement of their plans. She accepted his love for her as it was given, as something of a miracle. She assumed his presence was providential, as was his love for her, given freely after all the ugly truth was uttered out loud. She would trust whatever he felt was the best for them, unable to question his wisdom, believing only in his merciful love for her, dreaming their love could somehow shield them from the wickedness of others; that it could protect them from grief and tragedy.

Louisa returned to her former home, settling herself uneasily in its still haunting, still vacant rooms. Not expecting to see Justin for several months, she had the place to herself, and closed most of the few previously occupied rooms, discarding or storing furniture and possessions at will. For herself, she chose a room that needed finishing and proceeded to arrange for its

completion, painstakingly decorating it to her taste.
When she was done, her new room was as feminine
and elegant as she was, untarnished by memory, made
holy by the love that filled its space on nights when
Marshall and she joined joyously, promising to share
every moment of their lives.

Then Justin returned to the area earlier than the
couple had anticipated. At first, both feared he would
give them away, but, oddly, he lurked quietly in the
background, infrequently stopping at the plantation.
Louisa and Justin rarely crossed paths, and whenever
he actually set foot in the house, she had either been
away, or arranged to leave immediately. He seemed
to be content with the arrangement and pursued his
own life, and she hers, without comment. But, shortly
before his death, whenever they encountered each
other at a social gathering, he had looked at her
oddly, his physical appearance telling his age, making
him look even older than he was, and, to Louisa's
eye, quite dissipated. She saw him in the company of
people she hardly knew, most frequently it seemed
with a William Easton, an odd, intense man she and
Marshall had met aboard the *Emma H.* Justin's companions were rarely ones she would choose.

The night Justin died, Louisa had seen him at the
Andersons' ball. She had danced for hours with Marshall when Justin arrived—again in William Easton's
company. Justin had stared at Louisa for a very long
time, then approached her while she was surrounded
by mutual friends.

"Let me take you away from our friends, just for a
few minutes, I promise. You can surely spare a dance
with your own papa," and he offered what the world
thought was a loving paternal smile.

Louisa was not above shaming him, but she could
not shame herself before her friends. She politely accepted Justin's request, and, at first, danced with him
with grace and cordiality, smiling pleasantly. "I've
missed you, beautiful child," he soon began in his
most familiar voice. And Louisa stared disbelievingly.
"Tell me you've missed me, too." And he murmured

words she'd thought she'd forgotten, words that were all too easily remembered.

"Please," she whispered, on the verge of tears, "please leave me alone." She moved with him, as if she were in a trance, held fast in his embrace, her blue eyes wide and fixed intently on his.

Marshall watched her anxiously from the side of the room, singularly aware of her misery. He was about to intercede but someone came up to him, requesting assistance, and when he returned his attention to the dancers, Louisa was not in sight. Marshall could barely control his panic. He looked about the room and immediately saw Justin involved in conversation with others. He searched for Louisa within the ballroom and in the torchlit gardens, finally finding her as he heard his name called in the darkness.

"Marshall, I'd like to go home. I'm not feeling well. I think we can leave now without causing a stir, don't you?"

"Of course. I was about to rescue you from Justin, but you disappeared before I could manage it."

"It doesn't matter. I didn't think I could gracefully refuse to dance with him without creating comment, but now I wish I had. Oh, Marshall, I haven't been afraid of him lately, but there's something about the way he looked at me tonight that makes my skin crawl. Did you notice how old he looks? It's as if he's aged ten years."

"I heard my father say, or, that is, warn him to go a little easy on some of his pastimes, referring to his visits to some of the less respectable establishments in town."

Louisa shivered. "Please, let's just go now. I don't want to talk about him anymore."

They left the Andersons' without comment from anyone, for they were not the first to leave and the hour was already late. Louisa was silent on the trip home. "Would you like to stay with us for the night?" Marshall offered as she nestled against him in the open carriage.

"No, I'll be fine, once I get home," she promised. "Besides, I think I'm about to wear out my welcome in your house. I've seen a worried look on your mother's face whenever she's seen us lately."

"She'll just have to worry, won't she?" he said, kissing her eagerly.

When they arrived at Louisa's, the house was quiet and only Clara was up waiting for her. Clara had been with the house for years and considered Louisa her charge now that Nanny was dead. Louisa kissed the ancient woman in greeting. "You can go to bed now, dear Clara," she said gently. "I promise someday to get home early, so you can go to sleep at a decent hour!"

"Good night, Miss Louisa, Mr. Marshall." Clara padded off to bed, feeling her presence was no longer needed. She alone knew of the extent of Marshall and Louisa's relationship, for she was now the only servant sleeping in the house, and she shared their secret with no one, neither questioning nor damning the young woman she remembered from the day of her birth, and from the years of mysterious night terror. And she suspected the man who was her father of the very crimes he had committed, knowing all too well of the appetites of the man for women in his service. Though she had been well beyond his interest, she had tended a number of used, often mistreated women and very young girls from nights with him.

The house lights still burned brightly, for it was Louisa's habit to let them blaze away until she bid Marshall goodnight. As soon as Clara's weary form disappeared into the recesses of the house, Marshall lifted Louisa into his arms and carried her up the stairs to her room. On the nights they shared together, the room was lit only by the glow from the flames in the fireplace and by the love that radiated from them. Their passion had only increased with time, the wait until they would be free to acknowledge their love seeming endless. As Justin had predicted, Simon had been favoring a politically useful marriage for Marshall. Marshall had flatly refused the idea, insisting he had no mind for marriage at the moment. But he was certain his father was wise to his involvement with Louisa and, knowing his father, he suspected Simon was merely biding his time before he confronted them with his suspicions.

The occasions the couple spent together locked in each other's arms seemed too infrequent to them. The moments they stole were intense and sweet beyond earthly measure, their recollection of those hours able to send waves of longing through their limbs. Neither believed it would ever be possible to forget the compelling sounds, the sights, the sensations they shared in both body and soul, and once more the night with Marshall beside her passed too quickly. When he left her, Louisa had fallen asleep immediately, yet it seemed she was only asleep for mere seconds when she felt someone in her bed again. At first, she thought she was dreaming, but the hands caressing her were not unfamiliar, and her body cringed even as she struggled to full consciousness. Suddenly her nightmares touched her, only this was no fantasy. Justin's hands were on her, seeking what they had known of her on many occasions in the past.

Within seconds, Louisa was struggling wildly with a man who, though appearing much older than his age, was still incredibly strong. Louisa used every ounce of her strength as she wrestled with him, panting, crying out, begging him to leave her alone. She was wild with fear and horror, the years of abuse, the feelings of shame and ugliness flashing before her.

Justin was determined to have her again, and he tried to soothe her, even as they struggled. "Louisa, you haven't forgotten how good I could make you feel." But Louisa only screamed at him, "Don't touch me! Don't touch me! Don't touch me!" in an endless hysterical chant. She was now uncontrollable, her strength tapped beyond what anyone would have suspected available to her, and they flung each other around the room until together they fell heavily against the floor, Justin's head thundering into the stone hearth. Louisa's crying went unchecked for some minutes until she realized the man beneath her was not moving, and she moved away from him in revulsion, not knowing whether he was dead or alive.

Later, it would be some time before she could actually recall her next actions, but Simon convinced her of the probable events, and he was surprisingly accurate. She had not for a second hesitated in her motions, swiftly scattering the still burning embers from the fireplace throughout the room, igniting with swift gestures the expensive but quickly flammable draperies and bedding, the canopy, the carpets, the beautifully upholstered furniture, making a torch of a large wooden candlestick. She opened her wardrobes and set her gowns aflame, satisfied the work in the room was done. All of this had taken her only minutes, and she retreated, without looking back, the torch still in her hand.

She passed through other rooms, leaving destruction in her wake, descending the stairs to wind through the house as swiftly as a night breeze. She was at last calm as she heard the fire turn into an impossible conflagration, undisturbed by the shouts that rang from the would-be rescuers as they poured from the slave quarters. Her only thought now was of Clara who occupied a remote room, and Louisa went there as if she'd wanted to make a simple request of the woman. She entered Clara's room to find the tiny woman still sleeping soundly. "Clara, Clara, come with me," she said gently. "The house is on fire again. It's a shame to wake you, but you must come with me." And she calmly helped the terrified old woman through the front doors as men with buckets and armfuls of furniture and other household possessions rushed past them.

"Miss Boyd, thank God, you're safe!" cried the overseer. "Didn't I see your father go into the house tonight?"

Louisa looked back at him without a hint of knowledge in her peaceful face. "Perhaps, you did," was all she said. And in the days that followed, a strange tranquility filled the young woman. None of the excitement, none of the grief touched her. The destruction of the house and of some of the fields by the spreading fire did not seem to distress her in the least. And news of the discovery of Justin's body left her unmoved. Others explained her response as shock. Very few suspected it was relief and satisfaction they read in her face.

Chapter Sixteen

꽃 LOUISA rejoined the Hudson household the morning after the fire and it was only a short time before
Simon approached Marshall and Louisa with his suspicions of their affair and his ultimatum. As soon as
was decent by his standards, as soon as Louisa seemed
cognizant of the events and could confirm what he knew
to be true, Simon brought the couple to his study and
confronted them.

When they were summoned, Marshall suspected
the time had come for his father to admit his suspicions, and to forbid his son's association with Louisa.
He anticipated Simon would threaten and eventually
withhold the property and money he had been promised, in order to secure his cooperation. He even
expected to be coerced into marrying Janna Carson
if he wanted to be financially independent. He had
resolved that, if necessary, he would follow through
with an arranged marriage, but he would not give up
Louisa if she chose to continue their affair. He was unprepared for his father's malicious thoroughness.

"You two have managed to keep a tight rein on
your emotions—at least, in public," he began, when
the couple had seated themselves comfortably across
from him. He sat at his massive rosewood desk in
the cool, darkened room, leaning back in his chair
with obvious assurance, certain of his victory in the
matters he would propose. "Louisa, I know you have
had a difficult time recently, and I know, or I think
I know, what motivated you to do as you did."

She did not reply, but listened while Simon related
essentially what had happened the night of the fire,

confessing he knew and regretted why Justin's body was found in her room. "But that sorrow aside, it appears that you murdered your father, Louisa."

"My God, Father!" Marshall protested. "Your accusation is incredible! How can you even raise the question?" Marshall was stunned, and he felt the blood drain from his limbs and a sudden coldness, knowing that despite his careful anticipation of this meeting, he was unprepared for whatever it was Simon had in mind.

Louisa was mute, as she had been in recent days. And she was numb, not having thought ahead, having lived the last few days from moment to moment, trusting in her love for Marshall to see her through even this phase of her life. Suddenly, the audience with Simon reminded her too closely of the one she and Marshall had had with Henri Vinay in France, some months before, and she suspected the bargaining would be as decisive. She realized for the first time that she had underestimated Simon, having only noticed his charm, having sought his protection in the past, and never suspecting, until now, his sanctuary had its price as well.

"The supposition is not so absurd when you know, and can corroborate, Justin's treatment of Louisa. I'm certain there are others in this parish—on the plantation, even—who know and could be persuaded to reveal what they know."

"For God's sake, Father, why?" demanded Marshall. "Why should you want to destroy us? You may not approve of Louisa, for God knows what absurd reasons—bloodline and all that—I can hear Mother!" He was livid and he felt desperate. "I've even anticipated your demand that I marry Janna Carson. But I'm at a loss as to why you feel the need to raise the cause of Justin's death as an issue. Even so, Louisa only defended herself."

"You forget the codes we live by, Marshall. Justice can be purchased like any other commodity, if you have the means. And I have the means."

"But what of the other codes we say we live by— the codes violated by Justin. Surely someone will speak against what Justin did to Louisa all these years, while everyone closed their eyes!"

"Incest is not murder. In the end, a child is property. And his deeds, though unconscionable, will be overlooked."

Marshall was stunned into silence, and Simon paused to watch the two beautiful young people before him, unable to remember any real fondness for anything but money and power. "I've anticipated your acquiescing that you marry Miss Carson, but I also suspect that nothing, short of a separation at great distance, will keep the two of you apart for long. Yours does not strike me as an easily terminated affair. Am I right?"

Neither replied. They were accused, and Marshall would neither deny his feeling for Louisa, nor simply nod his head in agreement. And Louisa felt incredibly cold and ill. She sensed that the war was lost, and if shock had failed to settle over her the night of the fire, it settled over her now. She sat in the beautifully appointed room and knew she would die even if the trial Simon alluded to never materialized, even if there were no sentence passed on her to be executed for murder. As she heard Simon outline his plan, she knew she would die, because her reason for living would be taken away from her if she were separated from Marshall. And, if by some miracle she did not die, she resolved she would take her own life. She stared at Simon, hearing as if from a distance his plans for her move to California. He seemed to think it would be some marvelous adventure, a future to build dreams on, a new country to go to, as if she were some fortune-seeking pioneer. Suddenly she smiled, then laughed gently, amusedly. Soon though, her laughter became hysterical and her tears wild. She accused Simon incoherently, pouring invective on him as she might have on Justin. When would she cease to be something for others to use in whatever design she could accommodate? Didn't anyone care that Marshall meant everything to her, that she could not live without him?

And then she collapsed. When she woke some hours later, it was to see Marshall sitting beside her on the bed, as he had done in Paris. And because she was calm, and because she did not dare interrupt the sound of his voice, she listened to him tell her what lay ahead for them, in spite of their wants and needs, and, unbelievably, in spite of her faith in their love for each other.

And then Louisa withdrew into herself. It was as if she had at last gone into mourning, or so it seemed to those who felt they must explain her behavior. At first, she listened to Marshall and tried to take in the plans that were in motion. Within three months, they would be bidding each other good-bye for the last time, and while the prospects were very unreal, the truth could not be denied forever. It became clear that Simon's greatest concern was that Marshall's marriage to the Carson girl be untroubled by extramarital affairs, at least, not by one of the intensity that existed in the relationship between Marshall and Louisa. Simon's political schemes, unknown to anyone other than his partners in conspiracy, demanded that Franklin Carson, Janna's father, and Simon have a permanent, unquestionably secure connection, something a marriage between their children would help insure.

At first, Louisa clung to Marshall refusing to believe their fate, and when she heard the facts, really heard them, she retreated from the unbearable. One day, she looked into the mirror and saw her mother's face and followed her for a time down the same narrow tunnel, reaching for the same solace, the same pale, refreshing, mind-distorting liquid. It cheered her, and dulled her pain, even blacked out the horror—for a while. But soon the reflection in the mirror became blurred. Some days she saw Claudia who often gave her a wicked, hateful grin, whose voice taunted her, reminding her that her fate was only what she deserved. Sometimes Louisa saw the little girl she was so many years ago, free one minute, terrified the next. And occasionally, she saw the beautiful woman Marshall was so in love with. And whenever she could, she held him in her embrace, desperate for his touch, blind to everything but the consolation his touch could bring her.

Everyone in the Hudson household worried about Louisa; even Simon grew anxious. His plans would be difficult to carry out with Louisa in her precarious emotional state. Emma could only think of Claudia, worrying that Louisa might have to be confined. But soon the most frightening aspects of Louisa's behavior —her nightmares, her agitation—disappeared. Her swings into deep depression vanished, and what had concerned the doctors as possibly long-term instability was dismissed thankfully as a delayed, but deep grieving response—to the tragic events of the fire and the loss of her father, of course.

For a time, Louisa continued to consume more alcohol than solid food, but her outward behavior leveled off. She resumed her place in society, smiling for the world to take notice of her beauty, accepting, even looking forward to her new life in California. Only Marshall knew, in the now infrequent moments they shared, the agony that still overwhelmed her. She desperately sought his comfort as it was offered. And usually he was incredibly strong. But when he broke down, she found she had no reserves, no solace to give him. At times, he was moody and as needy as she was. Occasionally, he even seemed a stranger to her, and her pain was so unbearable she was certain she would not survive the loss of him.

Then, one day about a month before her departure, something snapped inside of her and she was truly calm. Some time ago, Henri Vinay had recognized the quality within her, and now she saw it, too. It was her strong instinct for survival. No matter how her mind and heart denied she could live without Marshall, her spirit pushed her forward into the new but frightening day. Suddenly it was as if new life filled her and new blood flowed through her veins, and she woke to accept unpleasant reality. Louisa was sure Simon would carry out his threats to destroy them if they did not consent to his plans, and she wondered if there were any room in the universe for love as intense as what she felt for Marshall? She had no sign that it was so, and for the remaining few weeks, and the remaining few hours they could steal with each other, Marshall and Louisa loved each other, knowing for certain the day the world would come to an end.

Chapter Seventeen

THE months at sea, followed by the months on the isolated, almost vacant, California coast had helped heal Louisa. The continuing process had been torturous, and lonely, but not only had she survived her separation from Marshall, she had eventually come to feel confident of her ability to make a happy life for herself and her child. As the new life within her made itself apparent to the eye, and even more apparent to the increasingly self-aware young woman, Louisa's life took on new meaning and new hope. When she came to term, she was only as apprehensive of the process of birth as any novice would be, but even more eager to have her baby safely in her arms, hoping she would not expect too much from the helpless infant, that she would not ask the child to fill her empty heart too fully.

And just when she thought she had accomplished as much as anyone had a right to expect of her, she had been plunged back into terrifyingly familiar and dark waters. Memories stood before her as large as life. Faces she had abandoned, even in her dreams, loomed before her, and more incredibly, a certain face was filled with life, and was attached to a responsive body, which approached her, wanting a great deal from her that was not so easily forgotten.

Now, Louisa sat in what had been her room until last night's fire left it singed and water-soaked. She stared, not really seeing the room where she huddled, rocking slowly in a chair salvaged from earlier fires.

To Aaron, who stood in the doorway watching her for some minutes, she almost seemed to be in a trance.

Once again, he congratulated himself on his luck. She's not proved too difficult. And God knows, she feels good, he thought, closing the door behind him. And so deep were her thoughts, Louisa did not notice. He stood over her before she felt his presence, and was startled when he reached for her.

Aaron was struck by the coldness of her body despite the intense warmth of the day. She felt stiff and brittle as he pulled her against him, and she willed the numbness of mind to leave her, her body quickening to Aaron's desire as she came alive in his arms. How good it was to recognize him, to be utterly free from doubt, for this was no ghost, no desperate fantasy. This man was alive, so alive, taking from her what he wanted, yet intuitively she felt he gave something precious of himself in his embrace.

For now, Louisa would accept Aaron as he came, taking whatever of himself he offered. At this moment, she only wanted to renew her memories of passion, and for whatever unknown time they had, build even a tenuous web of warmth and love. "Love me, Aaron," she whispered. "Make love to me, Aaron. Make me forget *everything, everyone* I've ever known. Can you do that?" she challenged as she lay on top of him, kissing him as deeply as he kissed her.

"What have I got to live up to, señora?" he laughed, helping her undress.

"You have your work cut out for you," she only half teased. Her body was a pleasure for him to touch and see, but no more than he was a pleasure for her. He inhaled her fragrance, and she gratefully breathed in his scent. Louisa wasn't satisfied until he was naked as she, and she could take pleasure in every inch of him touching her. How different Aaron felt in her arms from the man whose face his resembled. Or did she only imagine the difference? No, this man to whom she so eagerly responded was more finely tuned, more taut, more arrogant, more of what she now wanted. What use was there to wait for love when it could so easily be taken from one's grasp? Louisa vowed she would be like the Phoenix, and rise from the ashes. She would make life and love come to her terms. She would take what she could, and give what she could as well.

They made love in the rising temperature of the late morning, never noticing the heat until they were quiet again. They dressed slowly, nearly deciding against rising as they slipped eagerly into each other's arms again.

Then, abruptly, Aaron was totally composed. His voice became harsh and commanding. "Louisa, we have plans to make. We're leaving here, soon. No. No questions, yet," he ordered at her look of obvious surprise. "Isn't that Rachel squalling? Go after her, before Carmen comes for us. When you're finished come looking for me. I'll be in one of the sheds."

"Aaron, I hardly need instructions from you on looking after my child," she said, taken aback by his sudden change of attitude, annoyed by his orders.

"Perhaps not. But you'll have to get used to doing what I say. You and I must get down to other business," he said, pushing his fingers into her blond hair at her temples, holding her head in his hands, kissing her deeply but roughly.

Louisa struggled in his powerful grip, glaring at him when he released her. "Go on," he ordered, his eyes utterly cold. She turned quickly away, looking defiantly at him over her shoulder, the circumstances giving her no choice but to do as he said. She slammed the door in his face, feeling dismissed from the room like a chastised child. Perhaps she'd underestimated his arrogance. Could she live under his terms for very long, she wondered. Dutifully she looked after her child, for the first time resentful of her obligation, quickly handing over Rachel to Carmen when she was done.

"I'm going riding, Carmen. I'll be back at the usual hour."

"*Sí*, señora."

"Have Manuel get Coffee for me," she ordered crossly. So, it's contagious, she thought as she went back to her own room, where she tied her hair tightly at the nape of her neck with a bright yellow scarf that matched her dress. "He can't order me about, I'm not his servant," she fumed. "Perhaps I'll return to my room. He can't force me to occupy his bed. I'll not snap to attention at every command." Louisa hastily discarded her shoes, preferring to ride barefooted, and skirts tucked under her, she lifted herself astride the horse. She took nothing to cover her head, wanting the sun to streak her hair and color her skin.

Louisa made no attempt to find Aaron, and, as was her habit, she took Coffee's reins from Manuel, silently walking the horse to the beach. The heat of the sun was pleasantly dispelled by the crisp breezes from the ocean, and Coffee, seeming to know the trail by heart, slowly approached the surf, to walk at the water's edge on the hard-packed sand. The water lapped at her legs, and soon horse and rider were playing a summer's game, splashing eagerly in the waves, carelessly and joyfully pursuing each foaming crest.

Meanwhile, Aaron expected Louisa to come to him at the shed. After some delay, he went back to the house looking for her. "Carmen, where's the señora?" he inquired impatiently.

"Why, she's riding, as usual, señor."

Aaron glowered. "She's pretty used to doing what she pleases, isn't she?"

It was a question Carmen knew required no reply. She merely stared back at him with a knowing, amused expression.

Aaron left the house angry and quickly saddled his mount. He had thought he'd been very clear with Louisa. This was no game they were engaged in. Other men might play games with women, but for now, theirs was merely a marriage of circumstance; Louisa a bride for his convenience, a pawn in his affairs. What would it take to bend her to his will? "Terror? A sound beating?" he wondered aloud. "This kind of woman won't recant because I raise my hand against her. And, damn it, this affair will proceed more smoothly with her alliance," he muttered as he quickly traveled the small stretch of beach Louisa had just traversed, angrily assessing the situation. "And, God, what a waste it would be to carry out my threats." She'd managed to take him in with her beauty and her sensuality.

She had the look of something almost untouchable,
but touch her and she exceeded his lust-filled imagin-
ings. "Just another whore," vowing not to be taken in
by her elegance and spirit. He looked for her across
the long blinding stretch of sand and water, finally
seeing the flash of her yellow dress intermittently in
the sun's glare. In the distance she appeared like one
of the stalks of wild mustard that blew in a sea of
flowers on the surrounding hillsides. How like those
blossoms she was, appearing beautiful and delicate
against the harsh landscape, but perennially hardy,
lasting in the ever-blowing wind, surviving the beating
relentless sun, blossoming, despite the infrequent caress of life-giving rain.

Seeing a figure in the distance, Louisa nudged Coffee, releasing her to sprint with abandon across the
shore. Aaron couldn't decide if her action was deliberate or not as he sped after her. But he wasn't surprised
by her skill as a horsewoman; he'd expected as much
from what he knew of her. Nor, when he caught up
with her, had he expected to find her calmly waiting
for him, sitting stretched on the black boulders at the
end of the curving smooth-sanded beach. She sat, her
skirts high above her knees, her body turned precisely
to get the best angle of the sun. "It's not the custom,
but I like the sun to color my skin. I come here nearly
every day," she said, coldly casual.

"I told you to come after me when you finished,"
he reminded her as he dismounted. "Do you always
have your skirts up, señora?"

"Only when I choose, señor."

He frowned at her flippant, defiant manner. "Is
your memory so short that you can't recall my careful
warnings?" He paused, hoping his words would have
some effect on her. "As happy as I am to get under
those skirts," he added, quickly stroking the inside of
one of her legs, "I meant what I said."

Louisa drew her legs up, covering herself with her
skirts. "No, I haven't forgotten what you said. But I
won't be ordered about, like some—some witless
housemaid. and I won't be thrown out of your bed to
bow in gratitude as soon as you've had your pleasure."

"You fail to know your place in this situation, woman," he said hotly.

She slipped off the rocks to face him. "My place! Just what is my place?" she stormed. "You've only threatened me, not told me anything. Unless, of course, you expect me blindly to do your bidding." She was furious, standing very close to him, her blue eyes icy with anger. "I'm not some piece of furniture to shift at will, nor some grateful peasant eager to do whatever you command!"

Aaron was suddenly struck by how odd they must look; Louisa flailing as he towered over her. His instinct was to strike her, so vehement was her verbal attack. "Cool off, bitch," he said, easily lifting her into his arms despite her protests. In a few strides, he waded into the water and tossed her unceremoniously into the swelling surf.

Tangled in the weight of her billowing wet skirts, furious and more than a little frightened, Louisa struggled helplessly to gain control in the surging water. Aaron stood in the breakers calmly watching her, obviously satisfied with her situation. She choked repeatedly on the churning salt water, unable to regain her balance.

It seemed an eternity, but Aaron soon waded out to her and dragged her roughly toward the shore, where Louisa gained an unsteady foothold as the waves relentlessly crashed against them. The salt water stung her eyes and she gasped for breath, not fully recovered when Aaron faced her, holding her tightly at arm's length. "You're damned hot-headed, Louisa! I prefer not to use a heavy hand with you, but don't push me too far!"

Louisa was soaked and shivering in the wind. "What?" she cried in disbelief, more angry than fearful. "You've bested me with your superior strength, but I've no reason to ask your pardon! You've been much too high-handed! You came to me in nearly unspeakable circumstances, comforted me, held me, finally made love to me, made me want you—*want you*—not Marshall. And—you snap your fingers and tell me to jump! Do you also leave a few coins for a satisfactory performance?" Louisa's teeth were chattering now, and she shook, whether from cold or from rage it was impossible to tell. "I'm not some whore to have and dismiss, Aaron. Let's understand that! I've freely, even eagerly, come to you. But no more. I won't be debased!"

"You're begging for another salt-water bath, Louisa," he said, not harshly. He drew her cold, unwilling body into his arms and held her firmly but tenderly against him, his body sheltering her from the wind. When she relaxed a little against him, he said, "Perhaps I can afford to tell you more than I have. Then, maybe, we can stop this war between us."

Chapter Eighteen

THEY went behind the towering black rocks that offered protection from the wind off the ocean. Louisa removed her dress, wringing it out, throwing it over the sunbaked rocks to dry. She squeezed as much water as possible from her hair and her clinging petticoat, then sat in the sand spreading the fullness of her underskirt over her legs. She looked nearly drowned as she leaned back on her elbows preparing to listen to what she felt was Aaron's long-overdue explanation.

Aaron had watched her calm herself to listen to what he would reveal. He wished he could tell her everything of the long years that had preceded his arrival here, of the precious things he knew of her, of the tragic things he knew as well. But he felt most of his knowledge would have to wait for another time if it were ever to be revealed.

He moved to sit facing her, close enough to hold her if need be. "Louisa, to begin with, what I have to tell you is not to bring you grief, but to make certain you compehend the danger you are in, to let you know that without question I have no more patience, nor do I intend to tolerate any more outbursts."

Louisa bristled, but said nothing. Aaron watched her closely, taking in the tenseness of her slender body, the wariness of her eyes. He was acutely aware of being torn between wanting to protect the beautiful loving creature he had held so recently in mutual passion, and his desire to control the independent defiant woman whose allegiance and help he could surely use.

"We're certain now that Marshall's death was not accidental," he began. "He was murdered, Louisa. And you must comprehend that tragedy in the deepest part of you. He was murdered to prevent his discovery of the illegal activities from which his father, your guardian, is making a fortune."

"Oh, God, no! You're insane! Uncle Simon would never have Marshall murdered." Her denial was vehement and spontaneous. "How can you believe it?" Louisa stared at him, soon blinded by silent waves of tears. "I don't ever want to hear you say his name again. Never again! Please! I'm begging you." Her face was distorted, her body racked with sobbing. "Is that what you want, to see me crawl and beg? Well, then, I'm begging you!" she screamed, throwing herself at him, clutching him with all of her strength. "Don't tell me these things!" She cried for some time, holding Aaron as if he could save her from her grief. "Don't you know I loved him? Surely, you must! You say you know everything about me."

He let her cling to him, digging her nails into his flesh until she had spent her tears and lay quietly in his arms. "Oh, Aaron, will I never be free?" Then she was silent, finally aware of the sun's warmth as it soothed her aching. "What else do you have to tell me?" she whispered against him, then sat up to look him fully in the face. "I'll listen to whatever you have to say. There is nothing I'm not prepared to hear."

Aaron hesitated, briefly questioning the wisdom of continuing. He looked into tear-swollen eyes, into her stark, fully alert face. She seemed, as she said, ready to hear all he had to say So he went on coldly. "Simon had no part in Marshall's death, I'm sure. But Simon's partners in this affair care for nothing but profit —fabulous profits—and something more precious: power. Marshall was a threat to their undertaking. He was a Southerner by birth only; intellectually he was a supporter of Northern ideas and an advocate of abolition. If he'd discovered the intricacies of the plans here, identified the participants, more than a few heads would have rolled and if not his father's head, at least his father's fortune. You recall, Simon's first love is money?"

She nodded. She was only too well aware of Simon's first love. For all of his charm, Simon's reverence for money above all else could not be concealed. "But aren't you in danger, since you've taken Marshall's place? Who else knows about his death, besides Luther Dobson?"

"No one. And Dobson is safe. Actually, he was instrumental in bringing me here in the first place."

"But Simon's partners must still be threatened by your presence. Or do you already have the evidence that Marshall died for?" She lowered her head and leaned against Aaron for comfort.

"No. But I'm gaining the confidence of Simon's friends here in California; disavowing my—Marshall's —previous political leanings. Money and power have turned many a man's head; Marshall need not be the exception, especially with a wife and child. Ethics are often overcome by practical considerations. His affair with you, 'our' eleventh-hour marriage have occasioned a lot of curious and beneficial gossip. And you've never been a creature of politics. Yet your fortune has always been closely linked to that of the Hudson family, and hence to politics. You and I can circulate in society, where our preference for pleasure and wealth above philosophy will be obvious. Then I will be deemed safe to bring into the intrigue with the full Hudson credentials."

Aaron pressed her against him, hugging her protectively. Then he took her beautiful face gently in his hands, looking deeply into her wide, shining eyes.

"Louisa, I am counting on your love for Marshall, trusting you to share in avenging his death, hoping you'll come with me. I know you have little inclination for political scheming, but together we can untangle a serious, well-financed conspiracy to make California an independent republic, free to feed gold and supplies to the South in a fratricidal war that's more inevitable as each day goes by."

Louisa felt overwhelmed. What Aaron said was incredible, yet his words echoed truth she could not deny, and unwittingly she found herself in the midst of a possibly lethal plot. Would the world ever be safe from greed? she wondered. Would innocent people ever be safe from lust for power and wealth? If not mistaken, she had just heard Aaron tell her of the murder of the man she had, at one time, loved more than life itself. He had also told her of Simon Hudson's corruption, a man she had trusted above her own father, yet a man whose avarice had brought the destruction of his son. And thrust into these thoughts was her memory of Justin, a man who had bartered his soul for lusts of his own. "Why should I trust any man?" she wondered. Of all of the men she had known with any intimacy, only one, Marshall, had shown decency or purity enough to make him worthy of her complete trust. And he was lost to her.

And Aaron? Who was Aaron? Another corrupt man, another predatory animal? Or was he a hope for something more? Despite her doubts, her hesitation was brief. "Yes, I will help you. I'll do whatever I can."

"Good. You can begin by calling me Marshall," he said, brushing traces of sand from her face. "An inadvertent slip of the tongue could endanger us all."

Louisa smiled and sighed. "It's ironic. Now that I've pledged my cooperation, the first thing you ask of me is the one thing I cannot do. Of course, in public your name is Marshall, but between us, you must be Aaron, a separate man with a separate identity. If I can help myself, I'll not live among ghosts." She put her arm around him, kissing him softly. "And when we make love, it will be you I cry out to."

"Cry out to me now, Louisa,' he urged, pushing her down gently ino the sand.

"Aaron," she teased joyfully, wanting him again. "Aaron," pressing her body eagerly against his. She held him tightly, hoping for more from him than he could ever promise. She kissed his mouth and face softly, then pushed him gently away from her to look into his eager eyes. She smiled broadly at him, then laughed, wriggling from his grasp. "It's my turn to throw you out of bed. If we stay here much longer, we'll fry, and in the most indiscreet spots, while I urgently have a hungry baby to tend to."

She threw on her dress, playfully kicking sand on Aaron as he lay watching her. Then she dashed for

Coffee. "I'll race you home," she said gaily. "The one who wins can—" Suddenly she stopped her bargaining, looking at Aaron oddly, feeling her warmth disappear. A sense of *déjà vu* overcame her, remembering all of the similar challenges she'd made to Marshall and Andrew as they raced about their lives. It's an endless haunting, she thought. "Perhaps, ours can only be an unholy alliance, Aaron," she said, leaning from the saddle, reaching out her hand to him.

Oddly enough, Aaron seemed to recognize the source of her hesitation as he stood and took her hand, kissing her open palm. "Not entirely, Louisa, and not forever," he said softly, gazing up into the incredibly beautiful face framed by cascading golden hair.

Chapter Nineteen

By the time they returned to the compound, Louisa was in a turmoil. Aaron's terse explanation of his purposes told her only enough to cause her brain to explode with questions. It was doubtful he would take any more time this afternoon to answer her queries, for when they arrived at the house, he kissed her publicly and affectionately, then left her abruptly.

Carmen gave her a knowing smile when she greeted Louisa at the door, Rachel in her arms. "Señora, did your horse take a fall?" she said in mock concern. "Look at you. You're a sorry sight."

"Salt-water baths are good for the complexion, Carmen, and especially refreshing this time of the year. But right now, let me have Rachel. I rushed back here, for this very event," she said, snuggling her happy infant. "Then, I want a nice hot bath. And please help me with my clothes." Louisa went to Rachel's small room and set her in the heavy carved oak cradle.

"I will get your dressing gown, señora," Carmen said as she hurried down the hall to Aaron's room. "Señora, you will be interested," she said when she returned, "your wardrobe and other things have been moved. Also, the bed. You're all settled in his room."

"My, you've been busy, Carmen. Making all kinds of decisions, it seems," Louisa said pleasantly, yet with faint sarcasm. "Aren't you presuming too much? I know you see all, and probably know all, but leave a few things to me, if you please." Then she patted Carmen and gave her a hug. "But as usual, your intuition is right. Maybe you know my mind better than I." She paused, reflecting on her mixed feelings of the day. "I'd say you merely made a lucky guess this time, my friend."

Louisa discarded her damp sand-covered garments and slipped on a silk dressing gown. Her skin was uncomfortably coated with a residue of salt and sand, and she longed for a bath. Her hair was a mass of knots and tangles, sprinkled liberally with sand. "I look something like a drowned animal. I'm surprised you recognized me, Rachel," she cooed as she picked up the pretty infant who began to suckle eagerly, clearly undisturbed by her mother's dishevelment.

"Please, Carmen. I'll be ready for a bath the moment Rachel's finished." When left alone, Louisa relaxed with her baby who was, as Carmen predicted, faring extremely well. Louisa wondered at the beautiful child who nestled in her arms. "What lies ahead for us, little one? It seems our lives are not our own. It's nothing new for me, but you're starting early to be tossed about. I thought we might be safe here, but I was wrong. Perhaps one is never wholly secure from the world as long as one lives in it. What will become of us?"

Louisa rocked her body silently, a motion as soothing to her as it was to Rachel. In this act of nurturing her daughter, Louisa both gave and received. For Louisa, it was a healing process, remarkable because her wounds were so deep and fetid that it was a wonder any mending could take place at all. But Louisa willed it so. Surely she could right what had been for her a corrupted cycle of loving. Her suffering within the family circle: the broken promises, the perversion of trust and protection, had failed to break her. Perhaps endurance was penance for her participation, she thought, a cruel redemption, but she had endured, a sign from the universe that she could rise from these ashes as well.

Louisa held Rachel tenderly but fiercely, hoping she would again find a man to love her as deeply as she had loved Marshall, and as deeply as she now loved their baby. As she placed the contentedly sleeping baby into her cradle she prayed the hoped-for circle of love would enfold her, and she would feel whole again.

She slipped out of her dressing gown, then sank
gratefully into the foaming hot water Carmen had prepared, relaxing down into the enormous claw-footed
tub until only her face was not submerged, lying
peacefully in the soothing scented water, her mind
drifting pleasantly as she soaked away sand and salt
and pain. She washed her hair and body, rinsing with
cascades of lemon-scented water, then wrapped herself with a huge linen towel, winding it around herself,
leisurely toweling her mass of hair, combing the tangles, sorting the golden threads. She entered her new
room, which adjoined the bath, and sat on the carpet
to dry her hair as the burning heat of the afternoon
sun streaked through the window. Eventually, she
stretched out on her stomach like a cat, her hair
strewn over her back, fanning across the sun-drenched
floor. On the thick soft carpet, Louisa was soon asleep,
luxuriating in the heat, undisturbed by dreams.

When she opened her eyes again, she felt chilled,
for the sun had receded from the window. Drugged
from the nap, she rose slowly to close the draperies
and prepared to dress for the evening. Carmen has
arranged this room perfectly, she mused. All of my
things, even my bed. All so easy. No need to return
to my old room, and no desire to do so. The flesh is
weak, isn't it, Louisa Boyd? From her collection of
perfumes and oils, she chose a favorite lotion and began to smooth it freely on her body, noticing herself
in the mirror. Her breasts were very full, contrasting
with the slimness of her torso. Her flesh was reassuringly taut, the signs of pregnancy completely diminished. She knew all too well the burdens of being
female, yet she rejoiced in her own beauty. For all of
her sorrows, she was glad to be a woman, to be made
as she was, to love as she did. She had long ago accepted her needs as rightful, accepted the responsibility for loving who and when she chose, with no regrets.

Louisa covered herself again with a dressing gown,
and went to the door, opening it slightly. "Carmen,
please help me with my hair," she called, and Carmen
came to brush Louisa's thick mass of satin hair until
it glistened, then arranged soft curls to surround her

face. She prepared to pin the rest against the back of Louisa's head, but Aaron startled them both as he came hurriedly into the room. He stopped short and looked at Louisa, then smiled broadly, pleased with her obvious nakedness beneath the dressing gown.

"Leave us alone, Carmen," he said in greeting.

Carmen looked at Louisa, seeming to question whether to finish pinning her hair but at the same moment letting it fall again.

"I see you're dressed for the evening," he said to her before Carmen could leave the room. He went to Louisa as she sat before her mirror and kissed the top of her head, gently pushing her dressing gown from her shoulders to reach for her breasts. She leaned against him as he stroked their fullness, taking his hands to show him the motion that gave her the deepest pleasure, watching his reflection in the mirror, enjoying the sensations his touch brought her. Soon she rose to face him, approaching him with more passion than he'd yet known from her, suddenly matching the intensity of his needs, burning with the same fire that seared his veins. Aaron felt her wet mouth on his, her fingers pressuring his body, tantalizing his senses beyond his control. Louisa opened her gown and let it fall from her. She took his hands to her mouth, slowly kissing each in turn, releasing them to her eager body, guiding them to the softest part of her, nearly unable to bear the pleasure his touching brought her. Her hands touched him as joyfully, rendering him up to her caresses, and they succumbed to each other, filling themselves to the fullest measure with the sweetness of uniting with tenderness mixed with passion and need.

Chapter Twenty

THEIR closeness lingered as they lay together, their bodies entwining even in rest, and again they made love, each wondering silently if the need to be separate could ever again come between them. They joined with eagerness and growing familiarity, and now even their minds and hearts had a singleness of purpose. For this precious moment, Aaron and Louisa gave themselves to each other completely, with no past, no present, no future existing in a time that was wholly theirs. It seemed as if they were bound together for eternity.

But the spell was eventually broken. "Aaron, I have so many questions," Louisa began when they were still, holding him tightly as she lay against him.

"I'm listening," he said, watching her soft face grow troubled in the dim room.

"Where do you come from, Aaron, and why must we leave here? I've asked you before, and I must know. How do you know so much about me? And who is behind your investigation? Who are the people you suspect? How do they know Simon? My God, Aaron, California seems so far away from the rest of the country, I thought I'd be safe here from the past and the world I left behind."

Louisa shivered against his warm body, and he pulled her more tightly to him. "I can't answer all your questions, as reasonable as they might be. But I'll answer them in time," he promised. "I'm sure you know your father and Simon Hudson were partners for years in various ventures." Louisa nodded. "At Justin's death, you inherited his estate, but Simon is the executor and now the sole director of those mutual enterprises. Both Justin and Simon have long been aware how profitable knowing people in high places can be. If you'll remember, your father courted only those people who could bring him either profit or pleasure. Simon preferred profit."

Louisa sat up, turning her back to Aaron, remembering all too well the temperament of both men. "Who are you, Aaron? How do you know me? And, for that matter, how do you know so much about Simon and my father?"

Aaron sat up to answer her, then reached out to stroke her arms and the straightness of her back, playing with her hair which hung down her back like heavy golden cords. He leaned against her lightly and encircled her with his arms, impressed with her slimness as she leaned into him. "Aaron, many times in my life, I've had vivid nightmares, but waking, I've usually known they were dreams. And though my heart might still be pounding, I could eventually touch something in this world and be certain who and where I was." She paused, twisting slowly in his embrace to face him. "But, Aaron, you tell me things and allude to others that make me wonder. I feel I'm being watched. It's an eerie feeling, and I don't like it."

"Simon and Justin's activities have been watched over the years, Louisa. They were a very clever combination. They trafficked in contraband, as well as conducting perfectly legitimate business—their plans, their profits and losses of interest to many. Simon is, as your father was, a respected citizen. Prominent politicians vie for his support. In government, backs and heads are turned whenever his activities get too blatant, but even Washington has its limits to cuckolding, Louisa. This country will soon be involved in a war, the outcome of which we can't begin to imagine. But it will answer, perhaps for all time, whether the concept of a permanent union of states on this continent will survive. And any activity meant to divide the union, if the movement has any real momentum or backing, cannot forever escape the attention of Washington. Simon's enterprise is grandiose enough to warrant a great deal of interest."

He smiled at her in the ease of their growing intimacy. "I may seem an unlikely arm of the government, but I'm here in an official capacity. There is nothing I'm not authorized to do to prevent California from coming under the control of these mercenaries, these politically ambitious men. They wish to seize power through military action, to establish their own political state, to plunder the countryside for profit. The coming war can only be long and bitter, and in spite of the fact that making California a separate republic is predominantly a Southern preoccupation, men like Simon and his partners ultimately have no loyalties, except to themselves. In the end, these profiteers will sell to the highest bidder.

"Simon's partners are among the most prominent men of this state, as well as including an army of unknowns. California is overrun with adventurers, and has more than its share of ruffians to do the bidding of clever, unprincipled men. We'll be getting well acquainted with some of these people when we get to Monterey. Luther Dobson, by the way, is privy to all clandestine operations here in the south, but he is, in fact, a federal agent. If you should ever need help, go to him."

When he finished relating what information he felt he could give, Aaron took Louisa's face in his sun-darkened hands. He lowered his voice to a softness that Louisa had to strain to hear as he said: "In telling you this, I'm very mindful of other men who've confided in beautiful women in their beds. Yet I'm not worried about treachery. And it's more than simple trust, Louisa," he said with great gentleness. "I have a certain power over you—you're drawn to me for reasons you haven't yet pieced together. And I'll take risks with you because, while you at one time were fond of your guardian, I know you hated your father. I also suspect you are willing to risk everything you own to avenge Marshall."

Louisa looked at Aaron, nearly mesmerized by the things he said, by what he seemed to know without revealing anything. "It's true," she whispered thoughtfully. "You wield a kind of power over me. One part of me trusts you unwittingly; another is afraid. But you don't own me, Aaron. Everything I do, I do willingly." Louisa drew herself away from him slightly. "My first instinct when I look at you is to trust you—love you—as I did Marshall. Then quickly, I see differences only a lover might. Your brow is higher than Marshall's," she said, touching him as she spoke, "and your eyes often cold. You have scars where there were none. Your hands are more powerful and so is your body. You're like a cat, ready to spring and kill."

She paused to stare silently at him, pressing her fingers gently to his lips when it seemed he would interrupt. "You're a very different man from Marshall, and you can have no power over me but what I give you." Louisa halted again, leaning against him, with no gulf between them in the silence. Soon she raised her head to look at him intently. "Aaron, do you think it possible for us to exist with only trust between us, with no secrets?"

He smiled at her gently. "You ask much of me," he said, hugging her protectively. "It's been a long time since I trusted anyone completely—now, I'm always wary." He paused to savor her closeness. "But I'll tell you anything I think it safe for you to know."

With that promise, Louisa pursued him with more questions, but no entreaty would make him say anything further. They dressed for the evening and informed Carmen they would like supper immediately. Louisa fed Rachel, and she and Aaron played with the baby as if it were a normal evening pastime. Aaron felt clumsy as he handled the small helpless infant, but in spite of his awkwardness, he was comfortable in the setting. He enjoyed the feel of the tiny baby in his arms, surprised at his feelings of tenderness and his desire to protect her. Even Louisa's look of happiness while he held her child gave him satisfaction.

He returned the baby to her mother's arms, and watched for a few minutes as the two communicated wordlessly with each other. Then, abruptly, Aaron began his plans. "You must get a wet nurse, someone you can trust. You know we'll be in some danger—you'll have to leave Rachel behind with Carmen."

Louisa's face instantly turned to stone, and she laid the cheerful infant on a gaily patterned quilt beside her. "I've been waiting for you to say I must leave her," she said quietly, stroking Rachel's back. "Loving her, looking after her gives me so much satisfaction, I think I need her more than she needs me." Louisa took a deep breath to force back the tears brimming her eyes. She felt cheated. The circle of deprivation was closing in on her again. A chance to love and be loved was being snatched from her grasp once more. "As long as she's well cared for. Perhaps we won't be absent long," she said, looking to Aaron for reassurance.

"Perhaps," was all he said. He felt he couldn't offer more, knowing in this respect their sense of time was entirely different.

Louisa bundled up Rachel, and held her tightly, as if she dared anyone to take the baby from her. Aaron watched her rock and sing softly to her child, apparently without awareness of his presence. He was not unwelcome, merely unnoticed. He was reassured by Louisa's calm though sad anticipation of the need to leave Rachel behind. He felt she had pulled herself together remarkably in the last twenty-four hours. She seemed to be the strong, resilient girl he remembered, and he felt certain he could trust her to weather the hardships, to withstand the pain—she had surely been bred to it, he recalled.

Soon Louisa put Rachel down in her room, and returned to Aaron, slipping quietly into his arms, urging him to hold her. "I don't think you know how much you're asking of me. You can't know how much Rachel means to me. She's all I love in this world, all I have left of my love for Marshall. She means more to me than I can put into words."

"I'm sure I can't know how painful it is for you, Louisa. I know your life must seem an endless journey from one unhappy place to another. And I can promise you nothing."

She sighed deeply. "I expect no promises. I know

better than to even ask. But I do want the truth from
you. I'll ask again, how you know so much about me?
Have I no secrets? If I do, I'd like to, at least, know
what they are."

He smiled at her, knowing what he could tell her
would now only strengthen their bond. "Your curiosity
has no end. You tantalize me beyond endurance and
then withhold yourself until you get your answers.
Woman—the eternal weapon," he laughed.

"You make me sound like a whore," she said, stiffening. "You ask a lot of me, and I promise to ask a
lot from you as well."

"Louisa, you *know* who I am. You've merely forgotten me, along the way."

She frowned at him. "All at once, I'm extremely
weary of puzzles and games!" she replied impatiently,
real irritation edging her voice.

"I even have something of your own creation to refresh your memory," he said, nearly dragging her
from the house.

To Louisa, Aaron seemed oddly excited, holding
her hand in an iron grip, leading her to one of the
storage sheds where she kept odd pieces of furniture,
trunks of clothing, and a few mementoes. What could
possibly be among those things to make her remember him? she wondered. She held the lantern as he
unbolted the door, noticing several of the crates inside
had recently been opened then carefully reclosed. She
glanced around the shadowed room, trying to remember what each crate contained. Then, her eyes widen-
ing, she set the lantern down. Her hands were shaking.
No, she couldn't trust the turn her mind was taking!
Aaron only smiled at her as she looked at him ques-
tioningly, hastening to one particular crate. "Help
me," she whispered, prying open a resealed crate with
all of her strength. When the contents were revealed,
she paused, feeling apprehensive.

"I want you to remember," Aaron urged.

It was very hot in the stuffy shed, and Louisa felt
nearly suffocated. She reached into the opened crate
and carefully removed, one by one, the canvases she
had painted in London, in Paris, and in New Orleans,

until she found one that had been her favorite long ago. How simple of her, she thought now, not to realize those beautiful children were brothers. Everyone said how much they looked alike, though one was blond, the other dark. It hadn't mattered in the least to her, so she failed to notice the obvious.

Louisa was both thrilled and shocked. She felt plunged back in time, suddenly overwhelmed by the unspoken love between the three wild gypsy children. She moved hastily to Aaron amid the crates and cartons. "Andrew, Andrew," she cried, holding him joyfully. "You promised me you'd come home, but I'd given you up! Oh, I've missed you so, and I've shed more tears than I care to remember without your arms around me." She kissed him repeatedly, hugging him with all of her strength, with laughter and tears mingled in joy. She felt strangely complete, and intensely relieved to find the pieces of the puzzle fitting together, the haze lifting. It was a further reassurance of her sanity.

When Louisa's enthusiasm was, at last, spent, she seemed worn out. Aaron hugged her tenderly and he too felt strangely happy. Yet he held himself back. He would never allow their closeness to override any decisions he had to make, even though the joy of their bond was a lulling pleasure. His memory of their nearly forgotten past was something he tried to bury deep inside himself. He would never again allow anyone to come as close to him as had the needy, innately loving urchin he had loved so many years ago. Their earlier communion was a thing life had hardened him against.

He lived by his wits and his heightened senses, and he could ill afford a blinding love affair, though privately he could not deny his love for her. He would merely be cautious, forever wary. Wasn't that the code he actually owed his life to? Love could be deadly if it made him vulnerable, if it distracted him from the task at hand. He would love her, but not completely, not with the depth that now seemed to flow instinctively. He could afford no such liaison. Their affair might be deeply satisfying, but that fact could only be second to its usefulness.

Surely their affection would only be temporary; surely, it couldn't last. Nothing was permanent, especially love. He needed only to summon the past for undisputed testimony to that fact. So, with careful reasoning, Aaron promised himself certain pleasure with Louisa, pleasure deeper because of their mutual and loving memories, but an armored pleasure, in the name of self-defense. No one could fault him for this choice. Louisa would be the last. There could be no promises for the future.

Chapter Twenty-one

URGENT plans were overlooked for the evening. Louisa could not be distracted from her joy at recognizing the man she would call Aaron. Even Aaron could not suppress the relief he felt in revealing himself to her. Nor could he deny his immense pleasure in the warmth that flowed between them. Their closeness electrified the night, enhanced further by their lovemaking. Louisa slept soundly, clinging almost fiercely to him, and he wondered why a night like this could pass so quickly, how the day could intrude, why their passion could not be the overriding fact of life. But even as he lay there in the comforting night, reality crept up on him, lessening the warmth of their embrace.

Yes, he would harden himself against this renewed inclination to love. He'd learned the lesson before, many years ago. It had been painful, but he had learned. He had forgotten how to love. He had learned to be a man among men when he was merely a boy. He had grown tall and strong and lean and hard. He had hardened his heart as well. Yet his mind had not closed. He knew his heart and his body could be broken in the world, but he found his mind stretched and challenged. Others who traveled with him did not even notice as their minds dulled. Theirs gave way, but Aaron's filled out, as a yearling becomes a seasoned buck.

Aaron lay in their bed, holding Louisa, as the boy Andrew had never even dreamed of doing when he last saw her. Then Louisa was a bedraggled child, and he had loved her, without shame, with no demands of any kind. He barely knew what it was he felt for her, for it was never something to be spoken of. Only in the years of deprivation, in the hours spent satisfying urgent physical yearnings with women less casually taken than others, did he come to recognize what they as children had discovered. He rarely thought of it, for when Andrew last saw Louisa, she held little promise for the woman she was now. And whatever her promise, Andrew never dreamed Louisa would come to him.

Years ago when Louisa and he had said good-bye, Andrew promised only half-heartedly to return. He thought his position was made clear by the very fact of his going. He suspected who his father might be. His resemblance to Marshall was not lost on him. At times, he was bitter that the man did not recognize him, for he wanted a father. But liaisons between servant and employer were never acknowledged in the plantation setting, and he saw no hope for recognition. On that first voyage, Marshall and Andrew occasionally saw each other, but their divergent destinies were clear to both of them. Marshall's life promised pleasure, ease, and elegance; Andrew's hardship, toil, and simplicity, if not squalor. Neither boy had experience or vision enough to see just what lay ahead. They only sensed the years of close companionship were past.

Andrew found sea duty exhausting, but he was vigorous. He learned fast and finally there wasn't a task aboard ship with which he wasn't familiar. In the opinion of even his first master, he would eventually be captain of his own vessel—"what with his connections to the owners."

But skill is not all. Andrew readily mastered whatever task was given to him, tasks often assigned before they might, to test his seemingly inexhaustible capacity. Andrew thrived on challenge, begging for the hours to be filled. For a while, it seemed he would adjust to the rigor of life aboard a ship. Yet Andrew was restless and solitary, daily growing more resentful of shipboard confinement and unquestioned, repetitious obedience.

Eventually he found he had no real opportunity to

advance with the Vanguard line, for it was soon learned that he was not a favorite of the owners. He had merely been shipped out for their convenience. Soon no special duty was afforded him, and there were no special expectations for his future. Word had it that it might even be preferred if Andrew Sutton simply disappeared within the ranks of the other seamen. Andrew was slow to comprehend this, but as the duty he was given grew worse, he began to understand. The first voyages were for Emma Hudson's benefit. Though she knew Andrew's paternity, she would never tolerate his abuse. She had refused to punish his mother, thinking correctly that the young woman had been less at fault than her husband, Simon—a kindness that had been repaid many times in his mother's service to Emma. She had her reasons for keeping Anna Sutton in the household—what surer means of securing a loyal servant, what easier method of seeing Simon keep his promise by winning the confidence of another pair of eyes. But Emma Hudson's kindliness had not secured Andrew permanent good fortune at sea. As she traveled more and as Andrew gradually lost contact with home, he lost her protection.

He spent six years at sea, sailing aboard ships that were among the fastest of their day. With both cargo capacity and speed, the Vanguard ships were built for profit. Simon and Justin were among five Vanguard shipping partners. They had combined with men of similar interests and motives, and conditions aboard their vessels varied from good to grossly inadequate. In the years Andrew spent in their service, he experienced every comfort and nearly every misery known to the lines. At times, he thrived. At others, he was embittered and angry. He saw men break and die before their time, in conditions which were inexcusable. He, at times, found himself weaken when he knew better food, more hands, cleaner quarters would have spared considerable agony.

He grew rapidly, in all respects, becoming a skilled seaman at fifteen, malevolent and dangerous by the time he was nineteen. Early in his career, he returned home on rare occasions, looking forward to seeing

Louisa for reasons he couldn't explain, nor had even considered. They never met, because she, at last, had gone out into the world. Soon he stopped looking for her, and stopped going home. When he thought of her, he realized she had gone as Marshall had, into a world separate from his. And he forgot her.

The bulk of his additional knowledge about women was learned from shipmates. His home experiences had been warm and wholesome, and at first most of what he heard seemed alien. His earliest ship's leave was spent in pleasant circles with seamen who had families. But as he grew older, and became lost in the trade, he began to travel with men whose education, appetites, and dreams never approached his own. But they became his tutors and his disillusionment turned to rancor. He went with them into ports, and sought relief of his normal and intense sexual urges among women he loathed as much as needed. He soon found alcohol as much a solace as the women who opened their palms for him. Still, he was young enough to wonder in his toil if life had more to offer than sweat, and infrequent and indifferent relief of bitter human isolation.

When life at sea eventually became intolerable, Andrew jumped ship in Liverpool to make his way on the docks and in the low, mean streets. The handsome child who left Louisiana at thirteen was gone forever, and a quick, wary animal emerged from its torturous cocoon. He had changed physically as well as emotionally. The blond hair had darkened, and even he was surprised by his own reflection, the likeness of his friend and brother.

Had the two been side by side, it would have been easy to discern which man had labored and sweated, and begun to consume far more alcohol than was wise, which had eaten well and sufficiently. Yet Andrew was a vigorous man, readily employed and eagerly seduced. But there was a shadow cast over his countenance, a hint of self-destruction and self-hate. He drifted amid his sweat and alcohol along the dank waterfronts, and rested in beds which were solitary even when they were shared. He had no plans, no direction, and eventually, he found himself in London.

Chapter Twenty-two

JULIET knew her worth and exacted her price. She was as much an attraction in Joseph Wright's tavern as was the hearty warm ale and nourishing fare. When Andrew first arrived, soaking and grimy from a day's labor, he made little impression on her. She classified him merely as another patron, watching throughout the evening as he filled his spare, well-honed frame with double portions of food and ale, as if he were starving. She smiled to herself. "A few weeks of reg'lar meals and he'll look uncommon handsome." But she dismissed the thought. Who had she ever known with that much promise? Everyone she knew seemed fated to work themselves to death in short order.

Her own good looks would cost her plenty, she thought, though they might make her life pleasant for a time. Yet she realized she would never leave her station in life. She would only bargain as best she could for some measure of comfort, and, as of now, Jake Collins looked like the best prospect for her. "'E's fifteen years older'n me, but 'ardy 'n' prosperous enough," which meant he could support them if money was carefully managed. He was a riverman, gone most of the time, but Juliet accepted that prospect.

Juliet was a product of a hardworking, devoted, but unrealistic mother, and an equally energetic father. Constance Wright looked at her last and only surviving child when she was a toddler and vowed the girl would never break her back in a tavern, or go to one of the crude patrons in order to escape the place, and she took great pains to protect her, working harder than necessary to keep her delicate, raven-

haired child from the thick of tavern life. Joseph
Wright was also won over by his comely child who
had acquired and improved on the best of her parent's features and abilities. He encouraged Constance
and sought to shelter Juliet, but after his wife died
suddenly of a fever when the girl was twelve, Juliet
found herself working in the tavern those same long
hours her mother had, among men quick to know her
prospects and ready to wager for her. Joseph regretted
it, but as he said, "Fate deals the 'and, an' we but play
the cards."

Juliet soon enough learned what was expected of
her in the way of labor, and in the way of charm.
She loved her father, but she was bright enough to
realize sheer toil would shorten his life as it had her
mother's. She was not willing to live out her life that
way. She sized up her future and decided to cast her
lot "on the side o' money." She would trade whatever
she had to escape a certain future of back-breaking
work. She saw her plans in terms of simple survival.

Now she was fifteen and "old enough." Jake Collins
had been a regular patron of the tavern for years,
and when Juliet took stock of her prospects, Jake
seemed the best choice. She approached him, feeling
"a little effort will go a long way wi' 'im." And she
was entirely right. Jake was a rugged, brutal man, but
he could conduct himself intelligently when the circumstances warranted. He had worked for a number
of gentlemen in the past and he'd learned the rudi-
ments of polite behavior. Over the years, Juliet had
seen the best and the worst of this man in his various
stages of drinking His darker side even excited her
as she watched him command respect among his companions.

Actually she knew little of what existence with him
might really offer. But she cast herself with him, stealing into his room at the inn, whenever he was alone,
sealing his affection with glorious charm Jake thought
beyond his reach. Juliet was beautiful and delicate,
almost ethereal, someone more likely to be seen among
gentlewomen than among drunks in a common pub,
and Jake promised her what she wanted. "I can set

ya up proper. Won't 'ave to slave 'ere no more. Yer
father can 'ire a girl." It was completely settled in his
mind.

Yet Juliet prolonged the courtship. She made him
promise to say nothing, and kept a clandestine affair
going. Inns being what they were, with common sleeping rooms, Juliet was not able to come to him whenever he wanted. And Juliet found she liked it that
way. She discovered herself hoping something better
would come along. Joseph Wright suspected her of
singling out Jake, and mourned the fact, all the while
acknowledging she had no better hopes. He imagined
the deal she'd made with Jake and what it was she
offered in "good faith" to firm the bargain. But when
no announcement was made, he worried about the
tack she might be taking, the failure in judgment she
might have made. No one had ever made a serious
bargain with Jake Collins and failed to fulfill the
pledge, without some horrible loss. Jake prized his
reputation, especially in the area of feminine conquest.
Juliet would never survive jilting that man, Joseph
worried.

"Juliet, I 'ave watched you single out Jake Collins.
I wud not trifle wi' 'im. It could mean yer life."

But Juliet only put her father off, embarrassed that
her schemes had been so transparent. "I don't know
what ya can mean. I'm only bein' friendly wi' the
man."

So it was into this situation that Andrew hastened
one stormy evening. What he saw, after filling his
empty stomach and drying the rain-soaked clothes
that hung on his almost emaciated body, was enough
to bring him back to the tavern again and again. What
he had found was enough to begin at last to fill the
cavernous empty places in his soul.

Chapter Twenty-three

As Juliet had guessed, Andrew lost his starved look after a few weeks of regular meals at the pub.

"You don't look so hungry as you used to," she said, one night when she brought him a tray of hot food and warm ale.

"I haven't eaten this well in years. I'm grateful to have stumbled in here!" They had watched each other the first days, speaking only casually. Andrew regarded his attraction for Juliet to be simple need, as well as appreciation for her unusual appearance. She was clean and fair-skinned, flashing a pretty smile from her delicate face, made more so by her pale-blue eyes and her thick shining black hair, and soon she singled him out with special care.

Even Joseph noticed. His daughter seemed especially charming, softening her ways with the handsome stranger. Joseph thought they would have made a remarkably handsome couple in different circumstances, for Juliet's unspoken promise to Jake weighed heavily on his mind.

Juliet learned the stranger was presently working on river barges, and that his name was Aaron Sumner. When he paid for food and lodging, she saw he managed quite well. He dressed simply, and lately he was scrubbed and prosperous-looking. She noticed his few companions held him in high regard, but he had no close friends. He seemed remarkably solitary, seeking no particular comradeship. He often stayed up until the inn closed, watching her as he drank, leaning his chair against the fireplace wall, warming himself in the relentless chill. Juliet had not seen Jake for weeks and he was hardly missed.

Aaron looked better to her than Jake ever had, and after a few days, they began to talk in the late hours of the evenings. In earnest, they discussed their lives, and their hopes, surprising even themselves with the extent of their sharing.

"I'll never stay 'ere forever," she promised. "Think I've found me a good way out wi' a man I know. 'E's not got much, but enough to keep us, I think. Saw my mum drop dead, 'ere. It's not for me. She didn't want it for me. Neither does my pa. Only, he doesn't want me making any bad bargains."

Aaron told her of his life, and she was fascinated by his story, and equally fascinated by the possibilities of attaching herself to him. He was only four years older than she was—a better match for me, she thought, sizing him up carefully. With his experience, his prospects for truly good wages seemed certain to her, and she forgot any plans she had made with Jake Collins. Juliet was as open with Aaron as she knew how to be, and her wants were clear enough to him. She wanted a better, easier life, all understandable to Aaron. And what he wanted from her was not much more than the simplest pleasure and warmth, things that seemed abundant in her nature.

She brought him to her bed, both of them inexperienced in their individual ways. Aaron had wide experience in performance, but much to learn in tenderness. He would not take Juliet as he had the whores who taught him to be more vicious than gentle, and Juliet had more to learn than she knew. But she had eagerness and warmth to offer to their bargain. She told him she had known Jake "a few times, but 'e was rough and I didn't like 'im much. I know I'll like you better," she said truthfully and simply. Aaron was amused, but didn't bother to confess his previous encounters.

Juliet knew Aaron must have known many women from what she had learned about his travels. She accepted his past readily, and sensed what it was he wanted from her. She knew her own beautiful young body well, and was happy to share her private pleasures with him. She showed him the tenderness he ached for, her warmth seeping slowly into his being, and the festering anger and hatred eased out of his bones.

Aaron thought about the joy he was finding in their lovemaking, and regretted that his first experiences had not been like this. Over the years, he'd willingly satisfied his undeniable urges, but so much of what he had known left him empty at best. Juliet satisfied more than his physical demands. At last he could remember what it was he had been deprived of for so long, and, at the same time, he recognized why Juliet's face had been so compelling and familiar to him when he first saw her. He suddenly remembered the intense child he had left in America, and the strong feelings he'd had for her, feelings never before defined, never before consciously acknowledged. But the unspoken words echoed in his memories as he heard himself say, "I love you, I love you," to Juliet, words he uttered for the first time in his life.

Juliet loved Aaron without reserve, from her simple loving nature, and because of what he could promise her. If her love was not unselfish, it was honest and absolutely straightforward, which was more than enough for Aaron. He'd paid plenty before, and he put no credence in love without a price. He believed such a condition rarely existed.

Again, Juliet made plans. She felt an urgency to carry them out, suddenly remembering Jake in his uglier moods. One early morning she packed a few things and left a note written by Aaron for her father.

Papa,
You knew I would be gone someday soon. I am going with Aaron. He promises to look after me. I will have Aaron write again for me, soon. Perhaps Elsa will work in my place.

Your loving daughter,
Juliet

She left the letter under her father's door, and without a backward glance, she and Aaron went out into the damp morning, arm in arm, eager to begin, with no certain plans. In crowded London, it was easy to move a few miles from a former home and never mingle with the same people one had known for years. Juliet was counting on this for an element of safety. As she planned to go with Aaron, she remembered her father's warnings about Jake. But she soon dismissed her fears. She eagerly put her past behind her. At fifteen, Juliet had left her childhood behind. Past was past, she thought, tomorrow a new day. All she saw was a bright future, ignoring the fact that a future is built on a foundation of the past. Juliet had great hope for the future. After all, her dreams were coming true. She was confident.

Finding rooms in London was difficult since housing was always in short supply, but they eventually found two rooms and began a very ordinary life. It was a revelation for Aaron and a relief to Juliet. Aaron seemed to provide for them easily. Her wants were simple enough and Aaron generous. For Aaron, it was a brief time of solace and renewal, and though he began to think his existence dull, he forced himself to relax in the simple atmosphere. On the Thames he developed his reputation as a boat handler and found his opportunities almost limitless. He dreamed of one day owning a craft of his own, but such plans would require more capital than he now had. Yet he was certain he would find a way, and his great energy seemed to grow as he made a new life for himself and Juliet. He even looked like a different man than the one who had darted out of the rain into the London tavern, and both he and Juliet seemed to grow more attractive each day, especially to one another. They were incredibly happy and very young and very hopeful.

Chapter Twenty-four

"ANDREW! Ho! Andrew Sutton!"

He was hailed across the wharf as he tied the final line of Harper's barge. Andrew looked up to see an almost grotesquely enormous man striding toward him. It could only be Mason Jennings. There could be no duplicate of that body, nor that bass voice combined with it.

"I cannot believe my eyes. I never thought to see you here. You caused a ruckus leaving the ship like that!" he roared, laughing. "Thought you'd be home, by now. How is it?" he boomed at Aaron.

"Jennings! What's there to go home for? You never did. I'm fine—don't I look it?"

"I say. Almost didn't recognize you, at first. You looked like hell the last time I saw you!"

"Why not? We were in Hell, wouldn't you say?"

"Can't argue that!"

"What brings you here?"

"Well, something that might interest you. I left the slaver myself, soon after you did. And—and I could use a mug of something. I think we may have some plans to work out." He slapped Aaron on the back heartily, yet with restraint because of his enormous strength. Jennings was nearly six feet five inches tall, a veritable giant. His height was coupled with mammoth girth, muscled in every inch. Had he not been a cheerful man, he would have been terrifying.

Aaron looked forward to an evening with Jennings, one of the few lasting friends he'd made at sea. They sailed together on his last voyage for the Vanguard line—on the *Antonia*, a stinking hole of a ship, whose ghastly mission it was to transport slaves from Africa

to the Indies. Andrew had seen one run aboard
Antonia, which finished his career with Vanguard
ships. Upon leaving he'd destroyed a particularly valuable contraband cargo that left the owners distraught, but with no legitimate recourse, since it was
neither claimed nor legal. He merely disappeared into
the hordes, changed his name, and felt reasonably
protected. For jumping ship, he could be fined and
jailed; for jettisoning an almost priceless cargo, he
could easily be murdered by agents of the investors.
But when he did it, he had done it as an after-
thought, not giving a damn for the possible consequences to himself, a parting gesture of respect for
the owners—all of them, with no special malice toward anyone in particular.

Had he not known Jennings' sentiments to be exactly like his own, their meeting would have been an
anxious one under the circumstances. Aaron quickly
informed him of his new identity and brought him to
Juliet. The contrast between the petite young woman
and his friend was laughable. It was like seeing a
gazelle beside a bull water buffalo. Jennings could
hardly take his eyes from her, several times remarking on Aaron's incredible luck. She fed the two old
friends, glad to see Aaron with a warmly regarded
companion. Only she knew how lonely he must have
been at sea. Sometimes in their lovemaking Aaron
would lose himself, and the bitterness would pour out
of him in cries more of agony than ecstasy. Juliet had
learned much from Aaron and was never afraid of
him, even on those infrequent occasions when he was
rough with her while they made love. She never quite
understood his violence, but she never reproached
him.

Juliet sat by the two as they talked into the night,
eventually falling asleep. Aaron soon carried her gently into the other room and put her into their bed.

"God! Can't believe that beautiful thing you have
there, Andrew. What's she doing with the likes of
you?" said Jennings as Aaron returned to the room.

"Perhaps my luck has changed. And the name's
Aaron," he said, filling their mugs again.

"Yes. Yes. I won't forget," he waved a pledge at Aaron. "Listen, I have a proposition for you. I told you about my ship, but not my cargoes. I took a page from your book, friend. It seemed to me there was a lot of illegal stuff floating on the waters, and those bastards making too much profit on us, not to mention those poor black devils they herd worse than sheep. Anyway, me, and a partner who owns the ship, by the way, are making a tidy profit—pirating, if you'll pardon the expression. I feel I'm collecting some back wages. It's exciting as well. Could use a bitter old man like you aboard. We run a tight ship, but conditions are far better than some of the service you've seen—for a fact. It's dangerous, but we keep her hidden and it'll take 'em a while to get on our wake. In the meanwhile, there's money to be made and we can get out whenever necessary."

Aaron could not say he was surprised, but only said he was presently reluctant to come aboard.

"I can understand it, my friend," said Jennings, sighing heavily and motioning to the bedroom door. "But give it some consideration. I'll be around a few days. I do legitimate cargoes, too. Not so profitable, but safe."

Aaron could not refrain from laughing heartily over Jennings' tale of scuttling one of the Vanguard's particularly disgusting ships, all hands converted to the pirate fleet, the officers set adrift in life rafts. At one time, he could have seen himself readily joining Jennings, but now he had too much to lose in such a venture.

They talked into the early morning as they had in times past. Both men had dreams they would never realize. Jennings possessed an education, surpassing most aboard any ship, including any gentleman captain. But he preferred life at sea above any other. He was often an outcast in other circles due to his enormity, but at sea he was in his element, his size and strength highly regarded. He had broadened Aaron's education with books and conversations that were veritable lectures, to the extent that Aaron could be described as an educated man.

The friends bid each other good-bye, Aaron imagined forever. He joined Juliet, disturbing her slumber to hear her speak amazedly about his friend, but more to fill himself with the joy of loving her, to recall, should he ever forget, his reasons for staying close to London.

Chapter Twenty-five

SHORTLY after dawn, Aaron left Juliet for the docks. He left her reluctantly, his mind filled with bitter memories of his loneliness at sea. Their lovemaking at sunrise had been urgent and full of need, again easing Aaron's pain. Juliet smiled while she lingered in the warmth of their bed. Even though he had gone, the taste of him and his scent clung to her, prolonging her pleasure. She rose and dressed, tidying the previous evening's clutter, remembering Aaron's jovial friend. She was happy to have met him, wondering briefly about the experiences the two men had shared, glad to know there was at least one person Aaron could remember happily from the years he'd spent at sea.

Juliet finished her work and went out to shop before the streets became busy. She filled her basket with soft cheese and fragrant dark bread and a fat sausage. She bought red apples and plump yellow pears, then stopped to choose some yardage for a shirt for Aaron, examining some unusually pretty material for herself. She thought Aaron would like the pale blue flowers against her skin. The fabric was more expensive than she liked, but she thought Aaron would approve her purchase readily. She then searched the now-crowded market stalls for ribbons and thread to match, thoroughly absorbed in her pleasant task, totally unprepared for Jake's rough capture of her arm. Shocked to see him, terrified by the hatred she saw in his eyes, she struggled with him unsuccessfully as he dragged her out of the market through the noisy, unresponsive, unseeing crowd.

Jake had followed her from her door as she did her marketing. He had watched her, his malice ris-

ing as he recalled his disgrace at her sudden departure.
He had boasted of his conquest of the pretty young
girl, filling companions with secondhand knowledge
of her charms. He bragged of their plans and took
bets on the certainty of their open union. When she
had disappeared months ago, he vowed he would see
to it that he would run across her one day, and she
would pay, not only for the wagers he'd lost, but also
for the shame and ridicule he'd borne among his
peers. He had brawled and drunk more heavily than
usual since his disappointment, making himself an
unwelcome patron in even the meaner public places.
His inclination for brutality had magnified, and he
was nearly obsessed by thoughts of hurting Juliet.

He quickly dragged her back to her new home,
flinging her through her doorway to stumble breath-
lessly against a chair. Jake quickly looked around the
tidy, pleasant room, and in the same instant struck Juliet violently across the face, knocking her to the floor.
He picked up a chair and shattered it against the cot,
which collapsed instantly, then swung the dismem-
bered chair like a club, scattering shattered dishes
and paraphernalia from the hutch throughout the
room. Then he turned his attention to Juliet, who
lay stunned in the center of the room. The blow he'd
struck left her dazed but all too conscious of what he
was doing to her body. He raised her limp form with
one hand crushing her upper arm, and slapped her
face several times, causing blood to stream from her
nose and from a gash above her left eye. He beat her
viciously and ripped at her clothes, raising her skirt
to enter her unwilling, helpless body with excrutiating
pain. He crushed her mercilessly, thrusting into her
relentlessly, until he was finished. Blood ran slowly
down her thigh as he pulled himself from her. But
he was not yet through. Her blood excited him anew,
and he shoved her roughly onto her stomach, entering
her where no one had ever known her. Her agony
was unbearable. She thought her own screams would
deafen her, and she wondered why no one heard and
came for her, feeling the warm blood begin to flow
more heavily from her even in her torment. Jake took

his satisfaction from prolonging her torture, and when he was done, she was unconscious. "Cunt," he yelled to her unhearing form, satisfied he'd left her with a lifelong memory of him. He took a small gold ring Aaron had given her from her right hand. "Something to remember you by, bitch."

Juliet lay there, semiconscious and unmoving, that long day, hemorrhaging periodically, seized even in her stupor by unbearable pain from inside her violated body. When darkness and cold covered the little room, Juliet was awake, but still immobile. She desperately wanted to get up. "I must lay the fire," she resolved aloud. "Aaron will be cold when 'e comes in. Why aren't the candles lit?" she wondered in confusion.

When Aaron came to their door, he was alerted by the total darkness of the room. Even in the dimness, he saw instantly that the room had been torn apart. "Juliet," he called when he saw her, afraid he would hear no answer. He stumbled to her, touching her reassuringly warm body, feeling the faint murmur of her pulse. "Juliet, oh, Juliet," he called helplessly.

He went to the fireplace, searching in the blackness with his hands for the matches he knew to be there. He struck one and lit a discarded candle, unwilling to believe the condition of the battered woman lying at his feet. She was soaking in her own blood. Aaron held her gently, not certain she even knew he was there. The horror overcame him with the realization that she would surely die, and tears ran down his face as he lifted her into their bed and covered her. "Juliet! Juliet! Who? Who did this to you?"

She stared at him, as if she did not hear, then slowly whispered, "Jake . . ." Her eyes looked out of her bruised, distorted face, almost reproachfully.

Aaron was covered with her blood, nearly immobilized by his rising grief. He doubted anything could be done to help her, but wanted no opportunity to go unpursued.

"Juliet, I will get a doctor," he said slowly, hoping she'd understand, "so I must leave you now. I love you, Juliet." It tortured him that she didn't seem to know what he said, though she looked back at him. Aaron ran to a neighbor, people they knew well, questioning in his anguish how they had not heard. Immediately, the old man set out for a doctor, and the wife returned with Aaron to Juliet, horrified by what she saw.

"Oh, pray God, laddie," she cried, looking at Juliet. She uncovered her. "And the blood! —'Ad she told you she was having a baby?" she asked him sadly, knowing Juliet had fallen unconscious again. He did not reply, as if he hadn't heard her, but she saw in his eyes that he had not known. "Aaron, poor child, there's nothing to be done." She wept, touching Aaron, whose face looked suddenly sunken. He sat helplessly with her, crushed as if the blows that had been struck had fallen directly on him.

The old woman picked up the broken room, muttering and crying, touched by the stillness and the devastation. She had been fond of these young people whose love for each other had spilled over to the few persons with whom they had even briefly associated. Aaron and Juliet had kept mostly to themselves, but their seclusion had not gained the animosity of anyone. The evident brutality was beyond her comprehension, even in the face of the frequent violence and madness in this world.

Aaron sat by Juliet, nearly blinded with agony for an hour. He heard the old woman speak of an unborn child, and could not cope with any more suffering. They hadn't spoken of the possible consequences of their union, for it had been a union of self-gratification, lived day by day with the future only dimly foreseen. Now he found himself weeping for the sudden loss of their child and their newly promising future. What promises had Juliet made, to be repaid with her precious life, he wondered.

The doctor looked at Juliet, wondering why they had bothered to summon him. "There's nothing to be done, except make her comfortable." He touched Aaron on the shoulder. "Sorry, son."

The old woman hovered about unseen while Aaron

Chapter Twenty-six

AARON sat until sunrise, then collected a few items of clothing and his money. He came across a small gold locket he'd given to Juliet. She had loved the tiny engraved flowers on its face, never expecting to own such a lovely item. Now he tucked it into his pants pocket, then unfolded the bolt of fabric Juliet had purchased the day before. He wrapped her tenderly in the dainty blue-flowered cloth. She had never dreamed it would be her shroud.

Lifting her gently, as if she were sleeping, he carried her into the morning, her shining black hair flying into the wind. A shadow had fallen over Aaron's face as he stared out blankly at the day. He saw nothing, but moved heavily as if carrying an enormous load. It was not the weight of Juliet's small body that burdened him, but what he felt was the loss of his own life.

He moved doggedly toward the Hound's Ear, kicking thunderously at the entrance when he arrived. He heard Joseph Wright grousing as he came to answer, and when he opened the door, Joseph comprehended without asking. His grief was immediate, though he had foretold his own sorrow. Aaron had no comfort to give him, for what comfort could there be? "We were happy," was all he said.

Aaron placed Juliet gently in her old bed, not wanting to look at her again. If he remembered, he wanted only to see the gentle life-filled eyes, the soft unbroken skin, the young eager body giving love and life. Then he sat in the tavern again after these few months and drank ale with Joseph. "Where can I find Collins?" he asked after several minutes of silence.

" 'E'd be down the river. Try Chancey's. 'E's been seen there lately, I 'ear. 'N' if 'e's on the river, 'Ank Cornby shud know where to find 'im." He watched Aaron finish his drink, and he worried about what he saw on the young man's face. It was wrong, he thought, for one so young to have so much bitterness and anger to reckon with. " 'Ave you told the officers about it?"

"No. It's my score to settle. No one else's." He rose to leave, giving Joseph his hand. "I'm sorry. I meant to take better care of her."

Aaron went out of the tavern as he had come nearly a year before, and again the rain ran furiously into the streets. He walked the distance he had already come that morning, this time hurriedly, more for his purpose than for any concern about the downpour. He arrived at Chancey's in time to pass the lodgers stumbling out into daylight. By some invisible instinct, Aaron knew Jake was inside, and he seized one of the lodgers demanding information. There was such menace in Aaron's face that the patron could not refuse to reply. Aaron dropped his small bundle of possessions to one side, preparing to face Jake. He anticipated the battle, his blood stirring, his eagerness for vengeance overwhelming.

Jake was obviously worse for the night that preceded this day, but when he entered the street, he saw Aaron immediately. He had never seen his successor before, but he saw the hapless lodger signal to Aaron, and instantly recognized the look on Aaron's dark face.

Aaron saw Juliet's ring on the smallest finger of Jake's right hand. It glistened in the rain, delicate against the ugly swollen flesh. The sight ignited him, and the two men began to circle each other like animals, the rain showing them no favor as the sky opened up mercilessly. Jake saw passionless control and deadly malice in the man who faced him. He sensed Aaron cared nothing for his own life. He would willingly lose it, and he would give Jake no quarter. Jake smelled his own fear. He had faced death many times but, remarkably, his vision was clear this day, and he knew the battle was lost. Yet this recognition did not prevent him from charging first. Taller and broader than Aaron, Jake leapt at him with considerable force, but his opponent was agile and had the edge of will, spurred by unsurpassable hatred.

Aaron took the blow readily, countering with a vicious attack, memories of Juliet's bloodied, shattered body flooding his heart. Savage screams came from his throat as a crowd gathered even in the rain. Aaron battered Jake's face, gouging his eyes when the two men fell and rolled in the flooding streets. Jake aimed a deadly kick to Aaron's groin, Aaron taking it in the hip as he dodged. He flew at Jake's throat, grasping him with uncontrollable rage. Jake gagged, suffering for his breath. He drew a knife from his boot, sinking the blade deep into Aaron's flesh. Agony seized his body, but his brain was fully absorbed in the act of strangling the life from this murderer, and as Aaron held on, Jake lost his grip of the knife. It slipped from his hands and he blacked out for an instant. Aaron retrieved the weapon, while Jake came to, sputtering momentarily, at the same second leaping at Aaron's disabled shoulder. They rolled in the slippery street until Aaron, blind with a kind of madness, repeatedly and viciously thrust the knife into Jake's groin.

Aaron collapsed exhausted over Jake, heaving for air, slowly overcoming his rage, with no great satisfaction in his deed. He had done what he felt he must, but found his grief no less. He rose awkwardly, then stooped, twisting violently on Juliet's slender ring which was now nearly embedded into Jake's gnarled finger. Then he took up his possessions and staggered into the torrential rain, numb and weak from the loss of blood, moving inexorably toward the river and Mason Jennings.

Chapter Twenty-seven

THE wound from his battle with Jake had left him weak and unstable, yet he trudged unfeelingly, surely toward the docks where he knew he would find his friend. Warm blood oozed steadily into the threads of his clothes, to mingle with the stains from Juliet's life, and as he walked the narrow streets, he looked like a mortally wounded but not yet felled animal. His eyes were cavernous, and shock-filled. He attracted attention, but passersby shrank from him. No one stopped or assisted him, and he sought no aid. Finally, he came to the wharf where yesterday he had agreed to meet Jennings for one last conversation and probably one last entreaty to "quit the land."

He still had time before the hour they had agreed on, and he slumped gratefully against a post on the pier. Resting seemed to stem the flow of blood from his wound, but he knew it needed looking after. "I don't give a damn," he muttered, closing his eyes. He must have lost consciousness then, for some minutes later, he felt as if he'd awakened from a long dream.

The storm had cleared and he heard laughter, coming from a small party of young people heading in his direction. They were no older than he was, but of another class entirely. His presence caused few comments: a broken man in the streets was easy to overlook, it seemed. The party was boarding a fine pleasure yacht, moored perhaps twenty feet from where Aaron lay propped. He watched a pretty young woman ascend the boarding ramp, and he reasoned what he saw was an illusion. Possibly he was delirious, he thought, but he saw Louisa's face, or what could now be Louisa in the years that had passed

beween them. And the young woman saw him, a
look of astonishment passing over her. She hesitated
as she started to board and stared at him, as if she also
recognized him. She seemed pained by his agony, a
look of indecision crossing her brow.

"Don't bother yourself over these derelicts. They
litter the waterfront," interrupted the young man at
her side. And she turned her gaze from Aaron and
walked away. But she stood by the railing closest to
him, watching silently amid the hustle of the other
guests when Jennings came up to him, and she was
gone.

"My God, man! What's happened?" Jennings exclaimed.

Aaron gave no reply, for he had lost consciousness.

Jennings looked him over, knowing well enough
there was a good reason Aaron had deposited himself
at their agreed point of meeting. He picked him up
as if he were merely a few coils of rope and carried
him back to his lodgings, enlisting the aid of one of
the girls he paid handsomely for her careful attention
to his needs during his stay. Between them, they
cleaned and dressed the wound, with no assistance
from Aaron. The pain was enormous and he was very
weak.

"Couldn't be all his blood or 'e'd be dead, Mr.
Jennings," the maid observed, looking at Aaron's
blood-soaked clothes.

"I guessed as much myself, Jenny. And it'll be a
while before he tells us whose blood it is." He sighed
heavily. "I've got some business to tend to, girl. You
watch him carefully."

"Yes, sir, Mr. Jennings."

Aaron slept soundly at first, then a fever settled in
his wound, and he lay fitfully in sweat and pain.
Jenny tended him as best she could, cooling his brow,
feeding him liquid, trying to make him comfortable.

"Aye You've had a bit o' trouble, I think, and you
got some more ahead."

Aaron heard her, but couldn't focus on her.
"Juliet? Juliet?" he called, and then sank again into a
dull haze as a roaring filled his ears.

Jennings went immediately to Aaron's flat, and look-ing around he had no difficulty imagining something foul had happened, and where the quantity of blood on Aaron's clothes had come from. A few houses from Aaron's, he stopped a woman as she left her door. "What happened to the pretty girl?" he asked, motion-ing to Juliet's door.

"Ah, her husband murdered her last night, I 'ear. What's it your biznus?" She stepped back from the giant, all at once regretting she'd spoken to him. "It's none o' my affair, mind ya."

"Where's the husband, lady," he said gruffly, de-manding a response.

"I dunt know. I said it's none of my affair. They're lookin' for 'im though. Killed another man this morn-ing, too. Seems he's gone mad. Seemed like a nice enough sort. It's kinda odd."

"Very," replied Jennings, turning on his heels, not believing for a second that Aaron had raised his hand against Juliet, "but against another man for hurting her, that I know for certain."

Chapter Twenty-eight

AARON barely remembered the next several days as he lay submerged in a fever and hallucinations. The inn where he was staying was owned by Mae, a world-hardened matron whose girls were renowned on the docks for their enthusiasm and their skills. Fortunately for him, they extended their talents beyond what was usually expected of their profession, for one or another of them sat with Aaron around the clock, ministering to his struggle between life and death. Finally, after five long days and nights, Aaron woke with his vision clear and his other senses intact. He felt the burning wound in his shoulder for the first time, the pain somehow reassuring. At least, he could feel it.

He focused on the pretty face of a plump, energetic-looking young woman. He could remember seeing her by his bedside throughout the night, but he was not able to imagine why they would be together, especially with her sitting next to him and not in his bed, though he could not summon the strength to take advantage of her presence, a fact which briefly worried him.

He stared at the small, crudely furnished room with no memory of it, remembering only that he'd seen many like it before. He looked again at the woman who had sat by him most of the night, and she smiled at him, recognizing a look she hadn't seen in his eyes before. "Ye'll be all right now!" she laughed, leaving the room briefly.

Aaron sat back, trying to recall how he had arrived here. And all too quickly, his memory returned. "Juliet," he murmured, aghast at what he recollected. "Why the hell didn't I die," he wondered bitterly.

Then Louisa's face came into his thoughts to torment him further. He suspected he'd only imagined seeing her on the pier, but his memory of her cut into him like another knife. In his mind's eye the innocent faces of both Louisa and Juliet drifted around him, and he mourned the loss of love. He felt now as if he could never love again—in fact, he would deliberately see to it. Love was always wrenched from his grasp and he believed that pain was more unbearable than any other wound he might suffer.

He thought over recent events and concluded again that Mason Jennings offered his only viable escape. He wondered how long it would be before he was fit enough to be of any value to Jennings.

Just then, the man burst through the doorway in his hastily pulled-on pants, obviously overjoyed to have the news that Aaron's condition was looking hopeful. "Didn't know if you'd make it, but you had the most expensive, if not the best night nurses in the city!" he said, smacking the ample behind of Aaron's latest nursemaid.

Then Mason turned serious. "I'm sorry about Juliet," he began, noticing Aaron's expression did not change at the mention of her name. Odd, he thought. Then he added quietly, "You've been accused of her murder, and also Jake Collins'."

Aaron blanched, seeming to retreat into his thoughts. "It's a lie," he said harshly. "But it's just as well. It couldn't matter what they accuse me of, the result is the same." He paused again. "You've got an extra hand, Mason, if you want one. I guess it'll be a while, though, before I'm of any use."

"You can't travel yet, but I've got to get back to my ship, or they'll give me up for lost. Stay here until you're fit. Then go to the Sow's Inn in Dover, and wait for me till I show up. It could be a while, but I'll turn up." He grinned "Ask Max for Angela. She'll set you on your feet again," he roared. Then he sobered. "Keep off the street. You never know. Collins was widely known, and plenty around here are not above collecting the price on your head."

"I'll be cautious."

"You weren't so cautious with all those witnesses to your fight with Collins!"

"I was mad with grief, man. But I won't be so impulsive again." He sank into the pillows, overcome by exhaustion. "I don't last long," he grinned weakly at Jennings.

"Just glad to see you made it, friend. See you in Dover," he added in farewell.

Aaron could do nothing but take Jennings' advice. He slowly regained some of his strength, and he laid low, never appearing publicly. Soon Mae's girls became even more solicitous of Aaron's health, but he put them off, which was as much of a surprise to him as it was to them. But they didn't stop pursuing him for as long as he stayed under the same roof. " 'E's in mournin', let 'im alone," snorted Mae as they discussed his lack of interest. "Some do. But from the looks of 'im, it won't last."

Finally, he knew he was ready to leave London, and he made his arrangements. He left on foot one night, meeting a companion with horses on a deserted road some miles outside the city limits. When he settled into the saddle, he quickly realized how stiff he still was from his illness.

The ride to Dover seemed longer than it should have been, and he knew it might be some time before he would regain his full strength. He worried about the extent of the damage to his shoulder and arm, and it was his only worry now, for he had succeeded in burying the recent past somewhere deep inside of him. It was as if the previous year of his life had never happened, as if he had only yesterday gone ashore from the last Vanguard ship he would ever sail on, as if he had traveled directly from Liverpool to Dover for some predestined meeting with Jennings, as if all the loving he'd enjoyed with Juliet had never touched him.

When he arrived in Dover, Aaron was not much different from the man who landed in Liverpool. A vicious animal was again just below the surface of his personality, waiting to be goaded into action. Over the past year, Juliet had begun to heal his earlier scars, but the recent fever seemed to have reopened those wounds, and now he had fresh scars that might never be repaired. As Aaron descended on Dover, he felt like a hunted, injured animal and no less dangerous than any other cornered, wounded beast.

Chapter Twenty-nine

It was readily apparent why Jennings had suggested the Sow's Inn: the food was plentiful and so were the innkeeper's daughters. He had five, but Aaron turned his back on them. At first, they were reluctant to let him go by without their attentions, but something black in his nature, something fearful that surfaced in his long nights of drinking, a look about him, soon convinced them he was best left alone. It was obvious he was waiting for someone, but he never said who it was. He stayed close to the inn, eventually finding some relief in walking the streets, venturing into the countryside. He built his stamina more slowly than he might have, each night drinking well beyond the point where his physical discomfort became a remote sensation. Yet he found he couldn't drink enough to ease the undefinable pain that also gnawed at him.

Finally, one early morning he realized that no amount of whiskey could drown his grief. He stared at the almost empty bottle he held in his hand, and with a vicious yell threw it violently into the fireplace. The bottle shattered with tremendous force, scattering slivers of glass back into the room. And slowly he began his ascent from questionable survival to certain recovery. When Jennings arrived, Aaron looked more like the man he last saw in Liverpool than the one he'd met in his London flat, but he was sober and alert and gaining strength daily.

From the way his arrival was heralded at the Sow's Inn, it was obvious Mason had spent a good deal of time and a reasonable share of his money in the cozy establishment. "Have you had your fill of Angela," inquired Mason as the girl squirmed eagerly in his grip.

"Even if you haven't, she's mine tonight. Aren't you, lass?"

"Aye!" she laughed. "He's your friend?" She pointed to Aaron in astonishment. "I'd never guess. Not a bit like you, he isn't," she said, rubbing her well-endowed body against him. Mason groaned. "Hold on, Angela, I've got some things to say to my friend." He stroked her body with his huge hands, then shoved her aside good-naturedly to speak privately with Aaron. "You don't say you turned it down?" he asked amazedly. Then without waiting for a reply, he added, "We leave tonight. You look like hell! Do you think you're fit?"

"I'll manage as well as any greenhorn."

"Good enough." He slammed his fist on the table, a wicked gleam filling his eyes. "And now some food for a hungry man. Bring us something to eat, honey," he called to Angela.

He ate ravenously with hardly a word. "Didn't you eat after you left London?" Aaron asked as he watched the trencherman go after an enormous third portion. "You said you ran a tight ship, but you do provision it, don't you, Mason?" he laughed, watching his friend devour the hearty crusts of bread and thick meat-and-vegetable stew.

"We won't find anything like this aboard," he said, leaning back from his plate, reaching for Angela as she whisked past him with a tray full of dishes. "Now for a little food for my soul!" He grabbed Angela roughly, ceremoniously handing over the tray to Aaron. Angela shrieked and laughed for her audience as he tossed her over his shoulder. "Wait for me," he said to Aaron. "I may need help getting back to the ship after a roll over with this one."

Aaron put the tray down and leaned back to wait for his friend. Soon, one of the other girls approached him, ostensibly to take the tray. "Ya sure ya don't want some, too?" she purred. "It'll be a long while 'fore ya git 'nother chance," she said, offering him a good look at her breasts when she bent over to pick up the tray.

Aaron stared at her and took a long drink from his mug, as if deciding whether to take her offer.

"Besides, I 'ave a bet ridin' on ya. Wouldn't want a poor girl to lose a wager?" she coaxed. "I'll make it worth yer effort."

"You were foolish to bet," he said calmly.

She was annoyed. "What's the matter with ya?" Then her eyes narrowed. "Ye're not one a them, are ya? Or, can't ya git it up? Gi' me a chance to help ya," she offered before she saw the murderous look in his eyes.

"Get away from me," he ordered making a great effort to control himself. The girl instantly recognized she was in danger, and hastily retreated from the table. Aaron stood up, not bothering to right his chair as it crashed against the floor. He grabbed his jacket from the peg on the wall, and stepped out of the tavern, badly in need of some fresh air. His mood was black as he walked briskly but without aim. He wanted nothing more than to strike out at something or someone, but not a woman, not with Juliet still fresh in his brain.

He wondered why life had taken him along the paths it had, why nothing but bitterness and alienation seemed to be his compensation. Hatred festered in him and he knew he was perfectly suited to the life he was entering. It would be a sincere pleasure for him to sail with Jennings. He saw it as a sweet sort of vengeance, perhaps a once-in-a-lifetime opportunity to prey on the class and probably the very men who had made his life a living hell. He now welcomed the chance to do damage, to cause grief to men like Simon Hudson.

Aaron returned to the Sow's Inn to be left alone for the now brief wait he had for Jennings. He collected his few belongings and met Mason when he came down the stairs. As they headed toward the water, Mason challenged him. "You created a stir back there," he said, nodding to the inn. "You left them panting and disappointed. Never thought I'd see the day," he laughed.

"Get off my back!" Aaron flashed with unusual heat toward his old friend.

Jennings stopped in his tracks, trying to see Aaron's face in the darkness. "Sure, friend," he said, hugging him roughly with one arm in a gesture of comfort. "I guess it will take more time than you've had before the world rights itself."

"I'm not wanting any favors. All I want is a crack at giving back some grief to the bastards."

"That you'll have plenty of chance to do. Plenty. They're after our butts good, now, but the profits are up. The opium market will make us rich in no time. Might even have to turn respectable and live high somewhere."

"I'm not making any plans."

"Take 'er as she comes, Aaron. Bend in the wind. You're in the hurricane, but she always blows over."

Aaron reflected on what Jennings said as they continued toward the water. In the last few years, his life had progressed like the phases of a hurricane, beginning just as a storm gathers, growing ominous, becoming violent, eventually overwhelming. Then he had entered the calm eye of the hurricane with Juliet holding him fast in her embrace, where a pervasive peace lulled him into hoping and believing the storm had passed, making him forget the eye always passes over, and in its wake is the holocaust.

It was in this final assault, in the furious wind and enormous tides, that Aaron presently found himself. As he rearched for something to lash himself to, against the forces of the universe, he hoped he could remember what Jennings had said: "She always blows over."

Chapter Thirty

MASON had only come into port to retrieve his friend and the two men left Dover quietly that night. They met two of the crew in a large shore boat and rowed out into the channel and traveled along the coast for several miles before they sighted the *Marbella*. She was an undistinguished schooner, a factor which suited her purposes; a working ship with few comforts, but neither the vessel nor the crew actually wanted for anything in the way of equipment or provisions. Jennings ruled her with his enormous iron fist, but he proved a kindlier master than most aboard her could recall. The crew was an odd sort. All were outlaws by virtue of their duty, but they seemed to be a reasonably agreeable band of seamen. Mason tolerated no breach of his authority, weeding out the malcontents, demanding unquestioned loyalty, and offering a fair shake to his followers. He'd seen enough misery himself, and his lust for money in this venture was not so overpowering that he was reduced to running a ship at the low level those he wished to escape.

Though she was a commercial vessel, the *Marbella* was as handsome as any ship of her class, and with the wind filling her sails she skirted the coast as if dancing across the water. In addition to her nefarious duties, she was known to engage in legitimate trade in ports on the Continent, and she was kept in careful order to insure acquisition of legal cargo when it was desired, as well as to make certain her unlawful profits were as high as possible.

It was understood that Aaron would make himself useful however he could, expanding his tasks as his recovery allowed. He didn't quibble over any work

that presented itself, soon losing himself gratefully in
the endless cycle of keeping a ship in working order.
His attention to lesser tasks freed others to do heavier
work, and he spliced countless lines and ropes,
scoured decks, cleaned the brass, charted the course,
anything to keep himself constantly occupied.

He kept to himself as much was as possible in the
tight confines of the ship; he was solitary, but not unfriendly. He was known to be a particular friend of the
captain, but, in this instance, the fact did not go
against him. Physically, he pushed himself hard,
watching the progress of his injury but taxing himself
to the limit with each advance, almost welcoming pain
for its distraction from any useless inclination to regret
his current situation, or worry over his future.

The *Marbella* was a compact ninety feet with a
crew of twenty-four. Mason became distant and gruff
as he assumed command, not tolerating any laxness
on the part of his crew. As a result, the *Marbella* was
unusually secure. The schooner kept a careful eye
along the coast, secluding herself in obscure coves
along the shipping lanes, changing position frequently
to avoid possible confrontation with armed watchmen
whose duty it was to protect coastal shipping.

The *Marbella* was clever and elusive, successfully
catching small and large prey at random, and she was
armed with weapons not usually seen on vessels her
class. She wielded her power with notable accuracy,
occasionally combining her skills with another pirate
vessel to corner her selected victim. Usually her prey
had no alternative but to surrender.

Vanguard's activity in these same waters was heavy
enough to make the line a frequent, if not a favored
victim, and the plundering was sweet. One night *Marbella* parried with the *Emma H.*, a ship which Aaron
longed to take. The *Emma H.* was one of the best-
designed clipper ships and would never have been
compromised on the open sea where her kind ruled
supreme in speed and grace. But along the coast,
where the breezes were lighter and more capricious,
the schooner, with less tonnage and less sail, could
maneuver to advantage. In the open ocean *Marbella*

would not have considered *Emma H.* a possible target, and, as luck would have it, she slipped into the black of night.

By this time, Aaron was chief mate, a post his skills warranted. Jennings welcomed him to the position, trusting him fully, grateful to have a comrade he knew so well as second-in-command.

The kings of commerce railed against the sudden increase in their losses along the coast. A veritable fleet of pirates had sprung up. Or so it seemed to one after another ship limping into port, sometimes with only secret cargo looted, but always the most lucrative ferreted out. The outlaw fleet was small, but seemed to have incredibly accurate information. In fact, the contacts Jennings maintained were a major source of his success.

"Think we must lay low, Aaron. I hear the Crown has a fleet preparing for us. The coffers are full. We ought to quit before we're sunk, or worse, hung for entertainment of the mobs."

"You're sounding like an old man, Mason. The action's just getting interesting and you want to quit! I want to see them bleed a little. We've only made them squirm."

"I like my head resting comfortably on my neck. You don't seem to give a damn for yours. Yours is already in a noose, as I recall."

"If they catch me. And they won't."

"What a braggart!" Mason scoffed.

"What's got into you, man?" Aaron said with some impatience.

Jennings moaned, "Guess I've been aboard this bucket counting my gold too long. I want to spend a little of it before they dangle me from a mizzenmast."

"Let's get into Dover. A few nights with Angela and you'll be good as new."

"And soon limping gratefully back, you think."

"You heard me right."

"Let's go."

This time at the Sow's Inn Aaron unburdened himself in an unfeeling, mechanical way. He chose this form of gratification, never asking for or wanting more than physical release, and the girls greeted him as eagerly as they did his companion.

There were other harbors they moored in, now watching the horizon with greater care, slipping off to the Continent more often than normal to keep their hand in legitimate trade and thereby lessen the pressure on themselves.

Aaron found this duty very much to his liking, his position, the accommodations, the wealth he was accumulating far surpassing his ambitions the day he waited half-dead for Jennings. It was by far a more bearable existence than he had ever known at sea, save for the first months after he left home. And as long as Juliet's memory lay untapped beneath his conscious life, it was the most satisfying experience of his adult life. He knew power and independence. He answered to himself only, worried about nothing, sought only to gratify himself.

He had no deep allegiance to anyone or anything. His life was his own, the only thing of any value to him, and, on the right occasion, it might be offered up if the stakes or the exhilaration were high enough. He was willing to take risks his less-than-cautious friend considered nothing short of insane. The more suicidal, the greater the risk, the more likely Aaron was to press the issue, and Jennings began to have serious misgivings about the future. He retained absolute power as captain, which Aaron never questioned, but Aaron counseled and prodded the ship into ventures that, at times, caused Mason to hold his breath.

One night ashore, Mason rushed unannounced into Aaron's room, interrupting him at a inopportune moment. "The *Consuela*'s captured!" he announced excitedly, seemingly unaware of Aaron's preoccupation. "We'll have to get out of sight. Someone's bound to inform on us to save their necks," he continued without hesitation, ignoring Aaron's obvious disinclination to converse. "I've ordered up provisions to get us a good distance away. We'll catch the tide. Think we're safe for now, but—"

"Mason," Aaron shouted finally, "get the hell out of here! It'll keep."

"Damn it, hurry up!" Jennings grumbled and stomped out of the room, to pace impatiently until Aaron appeared in the hallway in something of a foul humor.

"Don't ever do that again, unless the goddamned house is on fire!" he snarled as he finished dressing.

Mason didn't hear him. All he had on his mind was a safe escape and he worried over Aaron's lack of concern. They immediately left the tavern while Mason outlined his plans. "We've taken far too many risks lately. I've been listening to you too much, been caught up in your enterprising schemes."

"They've worked handsomely, haven't they? You knew the day had to come when one of us would get caught. You're sounding like an old woman. Get hold of yourself," he said roughly.

"Anytime you want, you're free to go," challenged Mason.

"My work unsatisfactory, Captain?"

"Not as long as you know who's captain!"

"Aye, aye, sir," Aaron laughed.

"Then go get Hastings and Jensen. We'll head for Calais as soon as we get everyone aboard."

"Mason." Aaron stopped abruptly in his tracks to make sure he had the man's full attention. "Have you thought of going home?"

"Home? My God! —Home's any brothel." He hesitated. "What do you mean, the States?" he asked incredulously. "Why? You're not going to tell me you're homesick."

Aaron laughed humorlessly. "It just occurs to me, it'd be a fresh start. This part of the ocean is getting too crowded, especially if our name comes up."

Jennings pondered a few minutes, taken immediately by the logic and simplicity of Aaron's idea. "Won't a few people be surprised to see us?"

"No one's even missed us, you fool!" he laughed. "I left behind quite a stableful."

Aaron roared. "Don't expect them to be pining for you."

"They'll be glad enough to see me." Then he was serious again. "Never thought I'd go back."

Chapter Thirty-one

SOME months later, Jennings would revise his appraisal of the wisdom of ever taking Aaron under his wing. They crossed the Atlantic, established the *Marbella* legitimately along the Southern and Gulf coasts, and enjoyed a prosperous existence. But Aaron missed the precipitous danger of their former profession and acquired another ship for use in more lawless ventures. Soon their base of operation centered around the Louisiana coast and into the mouth of the Mississippi. Aaron began to reacquaint himself with the area he at one time called home. Having severed all ties with home years ago, he rarely considered seeing his mother; more often he thought fleetingly of Louisa or Marshall.

He spent his free time along the waterfronts and sought his pleasures in the highest-priced houses. At *La Petite Maison,* Madame Lilly welcomed him warmly whenever he entered and Aaron reflected on the things money could buy as he lay back in one of her comfortable beds in a dimly lit, but lavishly garish room. Aaron watched Katherine in mirrors over the bed and on the walls. The red-velvet and silk-draped room glowed pink in the soft light, and no detail was overlooked. There were even vases of enormous red roses to fill the air with their heady fragrance. Aaron had paid for a night without sleep, but he was ready to welcome a few hours rest. He lay back watching Katherine satisfy herself again, envying her insatiable needs and her seeming ability to go on forever. To his surprise they were interrupted by a soft, but persistent rapping on the door. Katherine disturbed herself to answer, and Lilly intruded apologetically. "My pet, I am so sorry to disturb your rest," she smiled, patting Aaron's face, speaking soothingly with genuine affection. "Another patron has insisted he speak with you. He is a very frequent and welcome guest. But, of late, he's seemed very unsettled and I'd prefer not to offend him, you understand, my love." She motioned to the glassed slit in the wall, where for a suitably high fee, certain customers took their pleasure by watching others take theirs.

"Who is it?"

"Oh, I couldn't reveal his name, you know. But I'd not interrupt your pleasure for just anyone, you can be assured."

"I take it he's not asking for any favors." Aaron grinned at her.

"Oh, no!" she laughed.

"All right, send him in." Aaron reclined in the bed, as if receiving visitors there was customary.

Katherine sought to arouse Aaron while they waited. "Perhaps his eyes are failing and he wants a closer look," she giggled, urging him with her tongue.

"Perhaps," he said, declining the temptation she offered, and he covered the both of them with the coverlet.

He had no idea nor even speculated who the intruder might be, but he was totally unprepared to see Justin Boyd walk through the door. Aaron recognized him after all these years in spite of what age and dissipation had done to him, for Justin's particular hauteur outlived even the ravages of time. "You recognize me, don't you," Justin began with unquestioned authority in his tone.

"If I do?" Aaron shrugged noncommittally.

"I want to know who you are for certain," Justin demanded.

"My name would mean nothing to you."

"But your face does."

"What can my face mean to you?" Aaron asked calmly.

"You resemble someone of great interest to me, and the resemblance could mean a great deal to both of us."

"I'm not wanting for anything," Aaron replied easily.

"Few of us ever have enough, true?"

"Perhaps."

Justin seated himself in a chair which he pulled to the bedside. He looked at Katherine coolly, and then at Aaron with a hard, calculating expression. Aaron noticed the man shook almost imperceptibly, and close up, he was frail-looking. His eyes had a glassy appearance, their color faded from the intensely blue piercing gaze Aaron recalled from childhood, when the eyes betrayed the man as cold, if not cruel. Now the man appeared as cold-blooded, perhaps, but more distracted, more distant. "You won't deny you know who I am."

"I know you," replied Aaron.

"Then, you could only be Andrew Sutton." Justin smiled, seeming very satisfied.

Aaron hesitated, drinking deeply from a glass of champagne Katherine offered him. "Some years ago, that was my name . . . what could it matter to you? Surely, the reward for my jumping ship is of no consequence, and you've long since recovered your other losses?"

"You do remember Louisa?"

Aaron's eyes narrowed. "Very well," he answered quietly.

"She's grown into a remarkably beautiful woman," Justin said, extending his glass to Katherine for a refill. "She and Marshall are very fond of one another, it seems." He paused to drink again, a hard look covering his face. "Their union has been kept secret, as secret as such a pastime can be," he smiled, lingering over his thoughts.

"So, they've climbed out of the swamps into each other's beds—what has that got to do with me?" His voice was edged with growing boredom.

"I want your signature . . ."

"What can that possibly do for you?"

"Your signature and your appearance at Marshall's bank at the appropriate moment." Aaron's blank look annoyed Justin, but he went on. "Marshall will soon reach his twenty-third birthday. At that time, he will receive a sizable gift from Simon—a fortune, in fact."

"For God's sake, Justin, you broke?" He roared with laughter, annoyed by the peculiar plan the man advanced and by his nervous behavior. Justin suddenly seemed barely able to control a hostility that seethed beneath a thin veneer of respectability.

"I'm not at all insolvent," he stiffened. "Marshall and Louisa have not exposed their affair because a marriage would never be agreed on by the family. But Marshall will seek no one's consent once he is independent."

"You're saying you don't approve of Marshall for a son-in-law?"

"Oh, no, it's not that I don't approve of Marshall. I just want Louisa back." He stared into the distance as if he saw something that transfixed him.

Katherine rolled her eyes at Aaron when he frowned in her direction.

"What are you saying, Justin? I don't get your drift. What is it you want?" Aaron demanded.

"Why, I love Louisa and I want her again. I've missed her. If Marshall cannot support her tastes, she will have to come to me."

"My God, Justin. You sound as if she were your lover!" Aaron exclaimed.

"She was. Before Marshall took her away from me."

"Christ!" Aaron cried in disbelief.

Justin continued, oblivious to Aaron's response. "It's very simple. If you impersonate Marshall, take his fortune, Louisa will have no other recourse." He smiled with an odd innocence, as if believing his own logic.

"You son-of-a-bitch." Aaron growled, his body stiff with fury. "Get out!"

Justin appeared to be genuinely shocked at Aaron's response. "Why I thought you'd understand," he said, gesturing to the room and to Katherine.

"I understand. Now get out!" He rose from the bed, moving angrily toward the man.

Justin sighed, and retreated with obvious reluctance.

Aaron was stunned. "The man's crazy," he shouted at Katherine when they were alone.

"Oh, you'd be surprised," Katherine said almost casually, beginning to pet him again. "Plenty of girls have known their fathers."

For a few minutes Aaron only stared at Katherine. Justin's visit had ruined the night for him. All his mind could see was Louisa, the face of the young woman he thought he'd seen last in London, or the tragic child who clung so desperately to him years ago. No wonder she was crazy, he thought. She only seemed sane when Justin was away from home. Why was everyone so blind?

"More wine, or would you like something else?"

"My heart isn't in it."

"I don't want your heart, *chéri.*"

He smiled at her, relaxing again. But even in his pleasure, thoughts of Louisa filled him, and he was obsessed with the idea of seeing her once more.

Chapter Thirty-two

AARON didn't seem able to stop thinking of Louisa. He had been "home" a long time, and now the need to reopen the past was overpowering. He found his activities bringing him in closer and closer contact with the Boyd and Hudson properties and investments. Along the Gulf Coast, hardly a cargo of any value was transported without Justin and Simon having an interest in it. Anything he pirated affected them somehow. And nights ashore found Aaron disguising his appearance, moving closer to home, little by little getting information he wanted. He actually saw Marshall one evening. He was shocked by the face of his friend and brother. Few would have told them apart had they been groomed and dressed alike.

And when he saw Louisa, he knew he had seen her that morning in London. She did not see him this time, and he watched her longingly from the shadows of a small street crowd while she danced with Marshall in the garden at a gala waterfront party. Aaron brooded over her beauty and her joyfulness as she danced and flirted so close but so far from him. She seemed to be something from out of a dream, certainly only a dream for him. For surely she would shrink from his touch, as she would from Justin, he thought. Who would not want her? he wondered. To anyone with even half an eye, the couple who danced together radiated love for each other, yet, as much as he desired Louisa, Aaron was both glad for his friends and greatly surprised by his own charity.

He was somehow satisfied at seeing Louisa and Marshall again, and by knowing they had so much pleasure with one another. He no longer felt any need to go home again, and what regrets he had about his friends, and especially Louisa, seemed to be settled. He thought he was done with her at last.

But he hadn't given up his game before he was observed by Jason Russell. The resemblance between Aaron and Marshall was not lost on the man who, over the years, had spent a good portion of his time noting the comings and goings, the griefs and the joys, the profits and losses of both the Boyd and Hudson families. Russell was well known to both Justin and Simon, and they were even better known to him. He knew them as well as they knew each other, and perhaps better than each man knew himself. At first, he had been employed by Northern competitors to spy on the men for business reasons. But with the nation's future in balance, his information became a serious political interest. Russell's loyalties were strongly for the Union, though his sentiments were unknown to his Southern friends. When approached for information about Southern intrigue, he rather naturally extended his efforts to furthering the Union cause, providing any enlightenment he could.

Russell moved comfortably in the Hudson household since he and his wife Kathleen were special favorites of Emma Hudson. Russell was a quiet man, and he saw and heard more than most. He knew an incredible amount about the affairs, business and otherwise, of the Boyd and Hudson households. He was certainly the first to recognize the bond between Marshall and Louisa, the first to suspect the extent of their relationship. And he knew whose face he had seen in the shadows from time to time recently.

He followed Aaron, and made discreet inquiries until he learned his present occupation, and then he meticulously pieced Aaron's past together. He saw to it that Aaron's future whereabouts would be known to him, not knowing until after the fire, when Louisa's plans for California were made, just where Marshall's look-alike might fit in. He learned about Aaron's bitter and violent life and suspected his motives and his hatreds. He also suspected who it was that drew Aaron close to home, and caused him to take the risks he did.

He knew Aaron had the temperament if not the loyalty to participate in the yet amorphous plan to stop

Southern influence in the West. All that needed to be done, as Russell saw it, was to coerce Aaron to cooperate. "Jennings!" Russell concluded, as he pondered over the problem. "Jennings, of course. The man saved his life and their friendship goes a long way back. You'll have to arrest them both and hostage Jennings."

"What do you mean?" inquired Major Arnett, lighting a cigar while he and Russell discussed the means of securing Aaron's assistance.

"The only chance to secure Sumner's cooperation is by endangering his friend. Oh, he'll agree to help us with the right amount of financial persuasion, and because we can promise to hang him for piracy and those other warrants on him in England, but he'd slip away from us the minute our backs were turned, unless he had a personal stake, such as an obligation to Jennings. We can promise to hang Jennings, unless Sumner agrees to and successfully impersonates Marshall Hudson."

"And what do you intend to do with Marshall Hudson?" countered the major.

"We'll keep him under wraps for as long as necessary."

The major rose to leave. "You've my okay. Just let me know when you want us to arrest this Sumner."

"I want him now. We ought to begin right away. The man may take some convincing, as well as training. Hudson and Sumner may be brothers, but one was born in the house, the other in the stable."

"We'll bring them in immediately. You'll hear from me soon. Sumner and I have at least a few mutual acquaintances, and I imagine it will be only a little while before I can lay a snug trap for him."

Chapter Thirty-three

ON the whole, Aaron and Jennings were more occupied with legitimate trade than they were in piracy, but on occasion the temptation was sufficiently great, the risk just dangerous enough, especially for Aaron, to lure them into criminal activity. Sometimes even a lark would send them into action, such as when Lilly's rum supply got precariously low. "We'll get you some—cheap," offered Mason in an expansive mood which found the *Marbella* stalking the *Caspian Sea Witch* one night soon after. "Anything to keep the whores happy," muttered Aaron in the darkness. He was growing bored with his existence. It didn't lack for vigor, nor did he want for anything material, but, except for certain rare occasions, monotony was pervasive, and, with it, an unquenchable emptiness. In his boredom, he filled himself with hard labor, alcohol, and companions of the meanest sort. For him, life had no particular goal, no measurable worth, no perceptible reason. Only danger seemed to gratify him, and it came only fleetingly.

That night the *Marbella* stalked the *Witch* with ease. The night was made for stealthy maneuvers, the moon gone dark, the water churning to the will of the wind. There was no light aboard and the crew was dressed in gray, silent, almost unmoving, except in response to the *Marbella*'s demands as she crept patiently after her prey. The pursuit seemed remarkably easy, everything in the *Marbella*'s favor as both vessels skimmed along the coast toward a treacherous stretch of road before safe entry into the channel leading inland. Jennings hung safely back, waiting for the right moment. When it came, the *Marbella* flew swiftly and precisely, striking and cornering her equally fast victim where she was vulnerable. Light flashed suddenly on the *Marbella,* unmistakable challenge given, the shots startling the seemingly complacent *Witch.* Her choices were few in the narrow bed between the shoals, and total effort was required to save her. She could either stop dead in the water or slither out of reach in precious little space. There was no other way to avoid the arms of sand stretching from the depths, eager to impede if not cripple.

Orders were cursed from both ships, the *Marbella*'s opponent taking the one tack she had with breathtaking effort, Jennings' countermaneuver meant to drive her back again. Suddenly Aaron's blood stirred as it hadn't for an interminable time. He began to think the chase might be worth his while, the *Witch* as wily as any craft he'd seen in a long time. She backed off, but, as Jennings pursued, she abruptly changed her tack putting the *Marbella* instantly in danger of being hammered and probably run aground. "Starboard tack . . . ease off!"

The *Marbella* parried, seizing the moment, surprising her victim with her dexterity. "It's going to take more than wit on this one," cried Jennings, unmistakable excitement in his voice. At the same time, he was sorry the prize would be no more than cases of rum. "Draw your weapons!" he bellowed.

Soon acrid smoke filled the darkness. The first explosions brought quick counterresponse from out of the darkness. But the wind shifted suddenly, and the play of weapons was dropped in frantic attempt to keep both ships from off the sand bars. The *Witch* miscalculated and broached, slamming onto the shoals, stopping with fierce suddenness. Chaos prevailed and the *Marbella*'s crew, adept at this work, quickly controlled the scene, taking her share of the cargo and a surprisingly good bonus from the captain's sea chest. "Not a bad way to spend the evening," commented Jennings as he stashed the bundle of crisp notes for safekeeping. "She'll have a devil of a time extracting herself," he motioned as they retreated. "Looks like a storm's coming up. She'll be lost in a good blow. Too bad, she had a lot of spirit."

But his words could have been for his own ship, for

she soon found herself being overtaken by a larger brig, armed and signaling him to halt for boarding. "Looks to be a federal," commented Jennings, deciding to try to make a run for it. "We've got a good chance." But Aaron was instinctively uneasy. There was no one to observe their encounter with the *Witch* and, therefore, no reason for *Marbella* to be halted in the open water. But he had little chance to speculate as fire rained from her pursuer's guns. "I'd say they're serious!" Mason shouted. "Haul her in!" he commanded, and the race was on. Mason figured he'd make his way to one of the slender inlets on the coast, to slip to safety in the dark, out of reach of the larger ship. But the federal followed relentlessly, closing the distance with unmistakable determination. The ships did an undulating seductive dance along the water with the tempo to the music altered from time to time, but always the little *Marbella*'s steps were picked up by her partner, until she found herself edging into an untenable position, the beach looming dangerously before her in the black of night. She tried again to slip from the arms of her pursuer, but as she stared at guns that peppered the water much too closely now, she signaled defeat to her aggressor, reluctantly accepting her fate.

"God damn!" was Mason's only response as he stared down the barrel of cannon that would have easily blasted *Marbella* and her crew to oblivion. "To be caught on an errand of mercy!"

"For some reason, we were set up, Jennings," was Aaron's instant appraisal. "And I'm not sticking around to learn what they've in mind," he said eying the shore.

"Are you crazy?" was all he heard as he discarded most of his clothing and dove over the side into the cold but invigorating water. But it was as if his every move had been observed, for he was instantly seized in the water by swimmers who overpowered him and bound his wrists, not without a furious struggle. He was dragged into a dinghy, soon to be accompanied by Jennings and the crew and dragged aboard the federal ship.

"I should have known never to trust a woman I had to pay for—but why? What for?" grumbled Jennings.

It was an answer that took several days to get.

Aaron proved a truculent prisoner, all of his anger and hatred seeming to surface in total disregard for his safety. Yet he found he was treated benignly and even his most outrageous behavior and insults were ignored. It was as if it had been ordained that no blows would fall on him. Finally he pushed too hard and the butt of the sergeant's rifle was aimed and driven precisely into Aaron's still tender shoulder. Amid his agony, Aaron heard the warning as it boomed out at him. "Shut your mouth, or I'll personally open that wound for you again." It was obvious the arrest was more than the capture of coastal pirates, but he could not fathom the reasons.

"Take the prisoner Aaron Sumner to Major Arnett," and Aaron was singled out, and carefully transported to headquarters.

"Justin," scowled Aaron. "Justin." But he didn't quite believe his encounter with the man would have provoked such a careful plot to arrest him. Or is the man more deranged than I thought, and this simple revenge for turning him down? he wondered.

At New Orleans Federal Army headquarters, Aaron was placed in a remarkably comfortable, but heavily guarded locked room. He was kept uninformed, and even his simplest inquiry was not responded to by stone-faced guards, a fact which infuriated, then bored him.

"Let them play their goddamned games," he finally muttered, but the oddness of the situation, and the growing suspense nearly drove him wild as he waited with no word, day after day.

Then, finally, he was roused from sleep one night and escorted through town to the cellar of a home he recognized even in the dark. The man who soon faced him was also well known to him. Jason Russell confronted Aaron in a small cell which was simply furnished, damp and dimly lit. At first, the men stared at each other, unspeaking.

"It's been a long time, Andrew."

Aaron made no response, unable to guess what the

man had in mind. He was curious, but also bored, even by the prospect that Russell knew his full history.

"I spotted you when you came into the area, though you evidently did not want to be recognized. Lucky for us, you kept hidden."

"Lucky for you? How could my showing up here be important to you? Surely a man who jumps ship is of little interest to anyone?"

"But a man with your face is of great interest to us."

"Who the hell is 'us'?"

"The Federal Government."

"My face is of interest to the United States of America?" Aaron chuckled. "That's an amazing fact, if I ever heard one. You've obviously a lot of explaining to do."

"Before you take what I say in too light a vein," he said, seating himself across a small table from Aaron, "let me tell you what I know about you and what choices you have."

Aaron shrugged his shoulders, alert and no longer bored.

"You're a wanted man on several counts—for jumping ship—a minor offense; for piracy, for two murders—those being capital offenses."

Aaron scowled. "The most serious of those crimes being committed in a foreign country. I'm an American citizen returned home."

"It could easily be arranged to send you and your friends back to England. We're very anxious to respect British law since we hope to discourage our foreign friends from supporting the South if she secedes from the Union. And in your case, I'll guarantee you see British soil again, if you choose not to help us."

Aaron started to interrupt, but Russell halted him with a raised hand. "If you cooperate, there will be substantial monetary reward, and you'll be exonerated for your crimes of record by diplomatic agreement. In addition, you'll be settling some very old scores with Simon Hudson and men like him." He halted, waiting for Aaron to respond.

"Go on. What do you want from me?"

At least, I've piqued his curiosity, Russell thought. "What we want," he continued aloud, "is for you to impersonate Marshall Hudson. Just when you will begin the charade is uncertain at this time, as is precisely what your stance will be. But those are details that will be worked out as we go along. What you have to do now is learn as much about Marshall Hudson as is possible: we have substantial information regarding his whereabouts over the years, his tastes and inclinations. You'll have some fine points of etiquette, handwriting, speech habits—many other things to absorb."

"And what am I to do with this information and training?"

"You will involve yourself in the midst of a political intrigue and obtain information to be passed on to me. Simon Hudson and two other partners intend to take over political and economic power in California, eventually to establish a separate Pacific States Republic. They have a great deal invested in property and commerce there, and they expect war between North and South to increase their wealth greatly. Southern ports will surely be closed in a war, and the South will need other sources of income and supplies. She also needs places to market her cotton and other goods in order to survive separation from the Union. If Simon and his friends can succeed in uniting a political force in California and other Western territories in favor of the South, the South will be in a very favorable position for success. She can then easily establish foreign trade and obtain recognition for the new government. The West's supply of gold, silver, and other minerals, its ability to supply grain and cattle are enormous. A transcontinental rail line is already being planned to make the Southern states a formidable power. These and other things Simon has foreseen." He paused, waiting for some response from Aaron. Getting none, he went on. "As I said, it appears the plan is to make California a separate republic. We're not sure yet just what the plans are, and that's where you fit in. You're a natural—or, that is, Marshall is a natural to get the information we need. He could represent Simon's interests in California and get all the inside information we need to make arrests and put down the movement. California is populated with a good many Southern immigrants. Southern sentiment is strong and the populace only too ready for action."

Aaron was slowly digesting it all, liking especially the opportunity to interfere with Simon and his friends, perhaps to bring them to ruin. "The intrigue interests me, but don't you think intimates of Simon and Marshall would recognize me?"

"I have a very keen eye, and you're a dead ringer. Otherwise, there's the matter of a few rough edges to smooth down, but with your cooperation, you soon should pass even close inspection."

Both men were silent for several minutes. Aaron took a deep breath and leaned the wooden chair back on two legs. He stared hard at Russell's face, contemplating his alternatives, and his desire to crush Simon Hudson. He couldn't believe he might actually have the power to see Simon and Justin and their partners ruined. It seemed too good to be true in spite of the risks, which only made the plot more savory to Aaron.

"You'll hang if you turn us down," Russell interjected matter-of-factly.

Aaron grinned. "You drive a hard bargain." He sat up straight. "But there's one thing in addition to the other offers you made that you must agree to."

"What is it?"

"In addition, you must agree to protect and exonerate Jennings and my crew, all or none of us." His eyes glinted with unquestionable firmness.

Russell smiled at Aaron's final bargain. "It will be arranged, they will be held until your work is complete. Then, like you, they will be free to go as they please."

"Then I give you my word to help you."

"One other thing," he paused, wondering if Aaron would be able to conceal his interest in his next remark. "There is a woman involved. You remember, Louisa Boyd?"

Aaron was visibly startled. "Yes, I remember her," he said, suddenly tense, which surprised him. He thought he was finished with longing for her.

"What has she to do with this?"

"She will be going to California shortly, and will be living in San Diego, in the southern part of the state near the Mexican border, where Simon has interests. Simon is her guardian since Justin's recent death."

"Justin's dead? When? How?"

"A few weeks ago. In a fire at the old house which was never really finished. It burned down again."

"God! Fire seems to follow her around," he muttered. "Not that Justin didn't deserve to die that way," he added with conviction.

"What do you mean?"

"Nothing," he countered.

"There's something you know?" pursued Russell.

"Why? What would I know?"

"Well, her departure is something I didn't anticipate. To my eyes, Marshall is obviously very much in love with her, and she with him. I expected them to marry, perhaps soon. But his engagement to the Carson girl, Janna Carson, has already been announced, in spite of the fact that Marshall and Louisa have been lovers for some time. Their affair began in Europe and its intensity hasn't seemed to diminish at home."

"What do you know of Louisa?" Aaron was very intent.

"All there is to know," he answered simply.

"All?"

"Why do you ask?"

"Do you know, then, that Justin interfered with her sexually over the years? Did your spies see that, too?" he inquired hotly.

"No, we didn't see." Russell was stunned. "How do you come by that?"

"The bastard told me himself. He also asked me to impersonate Marshall, to help him get Louisa back for him to use again."

Russell was silent, his eyes suddenly cold, staring hard into Aaron's, but he was obviously sifting through the information he had stored in his head. "Perhaps, then, the fire was no accident." He hesitated again. "Louisa was living at the house alone, so Justin's death there was surprising. If he was so frank with you, he may have approached her openly." His face was grim. "It all fits. No doubt, Simon has blackmailed the couple to separate them. The cause of Justin's death must have been subject to question, and to protect Louisa from a murder charge, Marshall must have agreed to marry Miss Carson, and Louisa has been ostracized. Marshall's marriage, by the way, will enhance Simon's fortune. It will be a merger of heirs." He sat silently for several minutes more. "All very interesting. But I don't think it will affect us much, other than you will probably meet Louisa in California. She's now using her guardian's name, by the way."

"I'll make a point of seeing her. I don't think I could pass up the chance to confront her with my impersonation."

Russell smiled broadly at Aaron, then stood to leave. "That's sufficient reason, I suppose. But you'll want to be careful not to put your disguise under too close scrutiny."

"I'll be careful, but this escapade is not without its risks," he countered.

"And its danger only heightens your appetite, I know. It's the code you live by. Good luck, Andrew Sutton. Good luck to us all."

Chapter Thirty-four

KATHLEEN Russell was small and slender with dark hair, now liberally streaked with gray. She was a woman Aaron had known as a child and now she was his tutor. She taught him about the finer points of life that had never been of concern to him. She taught him which fork to use, what wine to choose. She taught him how to dance, even to enjoy it. "When you have a beautiful young woman in your arms, this will come more naturally," she said, and she was right.

She painstakingly helped him refine his speech and soften his tone. "We're remarkably lucky your voices are almost identical. We've been so lucky. Even your handwriting is similar to Marshall's."

And so it went, very easily. Russell saw to it that Aaron had a considerable new wardrobe, all fit for a gentleman like Marshall, all perfectly tailored, and he was groomed to look precisely like his brother.

"Jason, whatever happened to that wonderful young man to make him so bitter?" Kathleen Russell asked her husband when Aaron went out late one night to ride, his lessons well learned, his body craving exercise.

"What do you mean, you probably know as much about him as I do."

"Perhaps more. There's a melancholy in his nature. . . ."

"Now, Kathleen, don't be sentimental. I'm sure it's hard on you. You knew him as a child and now he's training for a rather perilous mission. But if a war comes, there will be a good many of us in danger."

"I suppose—but there's a bitterness in Aaron that endangers him over and above his mission."

"His bitterness only increases his chances for suc-

176

cess and for survival. He relishes the idea of destroying this conspiracy and bringing Simon down. I'll admit I've rarely seen such hatred in a man and not seen it destroy him. Let's hope Aaron can make use of hate, and not let it use him." He sighed thoughtfully. "I rather like Aaron, myself."

"You don't think he murdered those people in London, do you?" Kathleen pursued.

"He's never said. But his friend tells it that Aaron was accused wrongly of the girl's murder. That he killed the man to avenge her."

"Well, then, that's better," she said, satisfied she was right about Aaron. And she began to pray earnestly for his success in this mission and for an end to his sadness. To her regret, Kathleen Russell had no children and she wondered about Anna Sutton, Aaron's mother, whom as a friend of Emma Hudson, Kathleen knew quite well. Some years ago, Kathleen had learned of Anna's distress at losing all contact with her son, and, according to Emma, when the news that he had jumped ship reached her Anna never again mentioned Andrew's name. Kathleen wondered what it would do to her to lose a son that way, and she wished she could tell the woman her son was safe for now, at least.

And Aaron felt safe. He was confident of his disguise. His appearance mirrored his brother's, and thanks to Kathleen Russell, he surely would pass most tests. He even had occasions to observe Marshall at close hand. On one occasion, the Russells thoughtfully arranged a small summer evening dinner on their terrace, inviting the Carsons, the Hudsons, and Louisa who was living under their roof since Justin's death. Through opened French windows in a darkened room above them, Aaron had watched the affair. As often as he could take his eyes from Louisa, he observed Marshall who was carefully occupied by either Mr. or Mrs. Russell, or by his fiancée, Janna Carson. Neither young woman seemed terribly tense in the presence of the other, possibly because their fates were seemingly so certain and, perhaps, because the liquor flowed so freely.

During the evening, Aaron noted Louisa's lingering but moody observation of Marshall, sensing her longing for him. He watched intently as she remained distant in her exchanges with him, almost aloof. And he wondered at the copious quantities of champagne she drank. Aaron was nearly blinded by her. To him, she sparkled and shone, seeming gay and self-assured, and exquisite. He found himself stirred by her, cursing the barriers that now separated them. Why did she seem always to be out of his reach? Before he could not approach her because of his position as an outlaw, and because of her involvement with Marshall, and now that she could not have Marshall and was free, he still could not go to her.

Again, Louisa obsessed him, and often when he went riding late at night, he would enter the Hudson property. He had learned from Russell which room in the house was hers, and he'd seen her many times on the balcony. He drew Russell out on the subject of Louisa, learning about her distant, almost distracted manner, her consumption of alcohol, her increasingly fragile, ethereal appearance. He grew concerned when he heard of her erratic shifts of mood. He heard she careened from inappropriate, seemingly unshakable calm to periods of great agitation with spells of depression, returning to haunted dreams and apprehension-filled days.

Aaron found himself plotting and planning an encounter with her, wondering if she, of all people, would recognize him. And yet he knew that was not the only reason he wished to confront her. He knew he was willing to risk anything to hold her in his arms.

His chance came unexpectedly, as, he realized, many of the other events of this charade would. A furious downpour trapped the Hudsons and Marshall and Louisa for the night at Russells'. The roads were awash and impassable from the storm, and the condition of the guests made them unwilling to depart, even if the weather had permitted.

The evening had been a lavish celebration of Jason and Simon's mutual acquisition of certain land titles. It marked the first of perhaps many new ventures the men were considering. At dinner each course was accompanied with the appropriate wine or liqueur, and by the end of the evening, everyone was languishing in a state of drowsy contentment. But Louisa had, as she now frequently did, indulged even more heavily than the others in the beverages, consuming little solid food, and she was very inebriated and moodier than usual.

Emma Hudson looked at the beautiful young woman, sad to see her slipping in the same direction her mother had, many years ago. At the same time, she was relieved to know that Marshall had chosen to sever himself from her, and even more relieved that Louisa was leaving within the next several weeks to settle far from temptation's reach—she hoped. Emma conveniently failed to connect the increase in Louisa's consumption of alcohol with the arrangements the two young people had suddenly made. Oversight had now become a way of life for her. She chose to believe Justin's death and the fire were responsible for Louisa's unstable behavior.

Louisa retired early, escorted to her room on the third floor by Mrs. Russell. In deciding sleeping arrangements, Jason thoughtfully made Marshall's access to Louisa nearly impossible, but Aaron's quite easy. If Kathleen knew her husband's understanding of Aaron's need to put his new identity to the extreme test, she gave no hint as she assisted Louisa up the stairs, the young woman unsteady, weaving slightly, seeming quite giddy.

Kathleen Russell had also watched Louisa follow in Claudia Boyd's footsteps, but unlike Emma, she knew the reasons Louisa sought solace the way she did—all of her reasons—and she connected none of them to heredity, but to her need to escape all too painful reality. She, too, had watched Louisa regress from a forward-looking, happy young woman to the withdrawn child everyone remembered from years ago. Kathleen connected the haunting dreams she'd learned Louisa had these days, not so much to the effects of alcohol, but to the effects of fires from the distant and recent past, to the love that was either perverted or inaccessible. She knew Emma condemned Louisa, though Emma never said so out loud, yet Kathleen wondered if anyone would condemn Louisa to live solely in reality if they knew what her real world was like.

Louisa's room was available to Aaron by an interior connecting room which was not visible from the street or from the landing. The only access to the outside from this private room was a skylight from the roof. This concealed place had provided Aaron comfortable, but private quarters, once his cooperation was certain. Earlier, Louisa's room also provided Aaron the opportunity to watch events in the garden below, and, if necessary, to descend the servants' stairway in order to gain access to other parts of the house.

When the decision was made for the party to stay over, Aaron had gone to his room, dressing in perfect imitation of Marshall, then waited impatiently for Louisa to settle down. In spite of her hazy condition, she was quite restless, and called for a bath to be prepared against the oppressive heat. Asking the maid not to disturb her again, she sank into the soothing water, her hair pinned carelessly against her head. The tensions of the past weeks, the ghosts who followed her no matter how hard she tried to drown them and herself, the pain of the immediate future were telling in Louisa's limbs, and she sighed deeply as she tried to relax. She closed her eyes, drifting silently among her fantasies, her tears washing her face, spilling into the already overflowing water. "Marshall, Marshall," she murmured in the warm, stifling night.

"What is it, Louisa," the voice answered, and she sat up from her bath, sincerely frightened by what she heard. She peered into the shadows, and shivered when she saw him as he moved into the dim light.

"Oh, I didn't hear you come in!" she cried, her heart pounding.

Aaron had watched her silently from the shadow-filled room, stirred by her beautiful body. "I'm not surprised," he said, going to the door to bolt it.

"I didn't expect to see you tonight."

"Where there's a will . . ."

"There's a way," she said, completing the phrase,

laughing. "Oh, but where's our way to stop the future they've planned for us?" she sighed, slipping again into the soothing water. She closed her eyes tightly. "You'd think I'd have drunk enough by now to be oblivious to the bargains we've struck, but it doesn't seem to make me care any less." She sat up again. "Marshall, how can I live without you, how can we do what we've promised?"

Louisa began to cry tears of torment. "I want to die! I can't take any more!" Her tears flowed as torrentially as the rain outside the house.

Quickly Aaron took her towel from the bed and went to her. Taking her hand to help her rise, he folded the soft fabric around her slim body, lifted her from the tub, and carried her to the turned-down bed. He held her, trying to shelter her in an almost instinctively familiar way, calling her name as he had many times in the past. He unpinned her hair and toweled her gently, stopping to caress her breasts with his fingers, to admire the soft satin feel of her skin. He groaned softly as his desire for her intensified, forcing himself to control the wild urge he felt to take her without further delay, yet smiling in his agony, knowing how different their lives had been, how accustomed she must be to sweet slow seduction. As he kissed and caressed her, she knew his need for her, and reached out to touch him, to caress him, to help him undress.

Aaron knew he could not expose his chest because his scarred shoulder would instantly give him away, so when she began to undo the buttons of his shirt, he took her hands in his and kissed them, returning them to his body to stroke him nearly beyond endurance. He found he could not control himself when he slipped into her surging warmth, but she was ready to receive him and their voices joined their bodies to sound their joy.

Immediately Aaron wanted to pursue her again, to taste her warmth, consume her, fill himself until he could take no more, but he was reluctant, fearing the intensity of his hunger for her might alert her, even in her nearly irrational state, and expose him. S' seemed desperately in need of his comfort, telling him how grateful she was that he had found a way to come to her. The sweetness and depth of her response both excited and depressed him, for she had called another man's name in her ecstasy, and he knew it would never be different. He feared he could never reveal himself to her, even if, as he hoped, they came together in the intrigue that lay before him.

He became silent and withdrew into his thoughts as they lay together quietly, and Louisa responded, holding him as if she were afraid their final separation would begin the moment he left her embrace. She pressed more closely against him at each shifting of his body, and she stroked and kissed him while they nestled closely.

She laughed softly at him. "You were so eager you didn't even get your shirt off," and she began to unfasten the remaining buttons when she touched a heavy gold chain which was concealed underneath. "What's this?" she asked, curiously lifting the unusually thick chain from inside his shirt. Aaron held his breath, furious with himself for the loneliness and sentiment which caused him to wear these mementoes of Juliet. Louisa fingered the delicate locket and slender ring, lifting the chain over Aaron's head. "A gift for me, Marshall? Or, a souvenir from Janna Carson?" she said with open jealousy in her voice.

"A gift for you, Louisa," he said, taking the chain from her hands, placing it around her neck. He raised the locket and ring to his lips, and then arranged them between her breasts, moving his mouth to her body, at once shifting her attention to the sensations he stirred within her.

He had endangered himself by careless sentiment, and it raised his anger and lured him to risk more with her. Louisa's mood was now edged with petulance and she responded to his ferocity with a fierce- of her own, arousing feelings which were new xciting to her. "We may never love each other ut you will never forget me," she promised.

never forget you, Louisa. Never." And he pressured her until she begged for satis-

faction from his body, but instead he took pleasure of
her with his tongue as her own pleasure transcended
what she believed possible. But he was not finished,
and he explored sensations with her she had never
known, leading her slowly, gently, persuasively, easing her reluctance when she hesitated. "I won't hurt
you. We'll stop whenever you want," he promised,
and she surrendered to him willingly.

Aaron caressed her thighs and buttocks, slowly,
gently penetrating her with his fingers, anointing her
with the excess of her own sweet fluid that seemed to
flow without cessation, entering her only when she was
ready to accept him. Then he took her hand in his
and led her fingers with his inside of her to the softness and vibrations they felt intensify until they both
lost control and escaped together into ecstasy.

When they were overwhelmed and still again, Louisa was very silent, drawing Aaron's arms around her
for comfort. He settled against her, savoring her
sweetness, longing for her even in his exhaustion,
knowing it would be months if not a lifetime before he
held her again. "Why did you take me that way, Marshall?" she whispered.

"I want to know every part of your beautiful body,
every sensation of touching you. We'll soon have only
memories to live on," which was as true for him as it
was for Marshall, wondering over Marshall's decision,
whatever the cost, to separate himself from Louisa.
He pushed the mass of her hair from the back of her
neck and began to kiss her again, sending delicious
shivers along her back and into her limbs. Soon she
was writhing and crying out whenever his lips touched
her. Suddenly she turned to face him, fiercely seeking
his mouth and his body with her own. Aaron matched
her intensity and they fed one another until there was
nothing left to feast on, and at last no more hunger.

And they cried together in their joy and in their
separate sorrow: she, for what she was about to lose
forever; he, for what he never had.

Then they slept peacefully for several hours, entwined in each other's arms and in their dreams. In
the early morning, Aaron woke and prepared to leave

Chapter Thirty-five

SILENTLY he unbolted the door, returning to Louisa's bedside to watch her for several minutes more. As quickly as he could leave her, he descended the servants' stairs, and through the same network went to Russell's door, rapping softly but persistently. Russell soon answered, and led him quietly to a study adjacent to the sleeping area.

"Sleep well?" Russell inquired, closing the study door.

"Well enough, thank you," Aaron replied politely.

"As of this morning, what do you think your chances are for recognition?" Russell continued bluntly.

To that Aaron smiled. "I've passed a very severe test, even if the lady was heavily under the influence."

"And success is sweet?"

"Very," Aaron replied with a contented note.

"As soon as our guests leave today, we'll go over the plans to get you to the Coast. We're sending you overland to San Diego. You should get acquainted with the Western Territory firsthand. Sergeant Heller, whom you've already met, will be your guide."

"Isn't he the one who offered to open up my shoulder? We ought to get along real well," he shrugged.

"You weren't the most cooperative prisoner we've had. And while your loyalties are reasonably sure, it won't hurt to provide you with an escort with a temperament similar to yours."

Aaron resented that his word was questioned, but he accepted the reality of his situation, and spent the remaining weeks preparing diligently for crossing the country. He studied maps and government documents

185

and the latest military briefings. Intermittently, he thought seriously of Louisa, even worried about her. Their encounter had not diminished his desire for her, but he tried to put his thoughts of her aside, immersing himself totally in the project at hand. She left for California shortly before he did, and he wondered briefly how she would fare, and what condition he would find her in when they met again. He admitted to himself that he would not be able to keep away from her. He knew, however, if she were in any way approachable, she would soon discover his charade. He readily recognized the luck of their first meeting, and wanted to approach her openly, hoping she was as well as he heard she now was. Perhaps she would join with him—perhaps she felt as much rancor for Simon as he did, perhaps she would forget Marshall —perhaps she would come to him—and even then, he cursed her, and himself, for the way she possessed him.

When he found her in San Diego, so pathetic and broken by her loss of Marshall, he was bitter and uncertain. His assignment would be difficult at best, his adversaries cunning and clever. And he saw no way to avoid involving himself with Louisa. It was common knowledge at home and among Simon's friends in California that Marshall had broken his engagement with Janna Carson because of her, and there was no way to postpone their meeting. At first, when he saw her, he doubted he could get close to her. It was obvious she had again retreated from reality, and he feared for her sanity. But as he watched her over the weeks and especially over the last days, he was encouraged by what lay beneath Louisa's turbulent exterior. Beneath the threat of storm and disorder lay a reserve of strength in which he believed he could even trust his life. It was risk he would take, because Louisa had always been strong, all the years he had known her.

And, no doubt, she would survive even him. Regret would stalk him, but he knew he would use her however he needed; yet, the most difficult part of his growing alliance with Louisa was the caution he imposed on himself, the agony of discarding a second chance to love freely. His painful memory of Juliet, his need to protect himself from decisions made from a position of loyalty to a woman he knew he could love without reason or even an element of caution, made him retreat from her. And now as she lay in his arms, she stirred, sensing his wakefulness and discomfort, waking momentarily, to snuggle more closely against him. Then she slept again, with Aaron still awake and increasingly miserable.

With Louisa entwined with him, the scent and feel of her soft body filling him with longing, he remembered another young woman whose softness he'd lost himself in. Juliet was a wound never completely healed, much deeper than the still tender scars that disfigured his shoulder. Her memory was usually buried with the physical discomfort he'd grown used to, surfacing only when something unusual called the pain to his attention.

As he had risked himself in his vengeance of Juliet, because he saw no other course, he found himself committed to this assignment in California through an obligation to himself and a surprising sense of loyalty to, and love for, his cruelly murdered friend and brother.

He remembered his own shock, peering into Marshall's silent face and seeing his own, grieving at never having had the opportunity to really know the man, remembering only the boy who was so close to and so like himself. In a sense, Aaron felt he was avenging his own death, for in many respects, he felt himself murdered when he was sent to sea, sent by some of the very same men whose plotting was instrumental in Marshall's death. Again he must do what he must, even if it meant another part of his life was sacrificed.

His bitterness overwhelmed him, making him inaccessible. All that surfaced were needs readily satisfied, especially in Louisa's arms. He would keep her by him for as long as possible, probably only for as long as she could live with his isolation, and now he turned to her in the darkness, pulling her from sleep, arousing her with caresses. He touched her full breasts with his fingertips, her nipples erect at his touch. Her legs pulled him to her, and she moved against him slowly, rhythmically. He took her breasts to his mouth and drank deeply of their sweetness, touching her with gentleness he'd thought he'd forgotten. Her pleasure grew as he kissed her deeply, reaching into her hair, urging her slowly. Louisa cried out at his motions, feeling herself fly to his caresses. She sought him hungrily, and her calling only made him pursue her more eagerly. He suppressed his great desire to soothe her aching with his body, and watched her as she responded with ecstasy to his hands.

He held her when she was quiet, filling his senses with the softness of her skin, the sweet aroma of her body, the warmth of her mouth, unwilling to let her go, overpowered by his desire to fill her body with his own. He touched her again, raising the intensity of her desire until they joined with mutual soaring joy.

When they slept, they slept without dreams. When they woke, they were grateful for the new day and to see each other again. And Aaron watched as Louisa fell into his satin-lined steel trap. Coldly, he appraised the success of their union, believing his plans were well on their way to a successful outcome. Louisa was his to manipulate in his schemes. If there were anything left for them at the conclusion of his work, he would pursue it with great eagerness. But, as of now, he thought his heart was closed.

Chapter Thirty-six

Їђђ Тнеір preparations for the trip to Monterey were begun immediately. The barkentine *Isabella* was expected in two weeks and messages were dispatched, advising the conspirators that Marshall and Louisa Hudson were coming to take their places among them.

Louisa prepared for their journey with both sadness and joy. She relinquished Rachel to a young woman whose baby had died days earlier, hoping the two would find great comfort in each other. And she knew Carmen would fill in for her very happily and very adequately.

Within the next few days Louisa sorted and packed her trunks with clothes she had almost forgotten she owned. "Perhaps these are out of fashion," she worried to Aaron. "I'll have to have new things made."

"It will be part of the charade. I'll enjoy pampering you, getting whatever you like to make you feel beautiful."

She looked over her small but impressive collection of jewels. She'd had no occasion to wear them in recent months. "I believe I may actually enjoy some of this affair," she said, holding up piece after piece of jewelry. "I haven't danced for months, not since I left Louisiana. Do you know how to dance, Aaron?"

"I've been very carefully prepared for my assignment, señora. They've made a silk purse from a sow's ear, this time."

She laughed. "I never thought you coarse. Momma said 'low-born.' But I never saw it. I loved you so. God only knows what 'low-born' means. My mother had no right to use the word," she reflected, then turned to face Aaron lightheartedly. "Now, show me how to dance, if you can."

He stared at her.

"I mean it," she coaxed. "We don't want to look awkward when the time comes." She went to him and took his hands, trying to pull him with her. "If I didn't know better, I'd say you were shy—I'll even provide some music," and she began to hum softly, dancing in his arms.

He was seduced by her, in spite of his vows, and it worried him. He danced with her, amused by her gaiety, taking advantage of a sudden invitation to make love to her.

"Does this go with every dance, señora? I'm new to all of this."

"Only if your name is on my dance card, señor."

"Well?"

"Let's see. There are three names: Marshall, Andrew, Aaron. Who are you, by the way?"

"Take your pick."

"Andrew—I've never made love to Andrew."

"Which Andrew do you want? The boy who left you, or the man who forgot you?" His voice was edged with bitterness.

"I'm wrong. I've made love to Andrew—that sweet night I learned who you are. Which was he, the boy or the man?"

"The man would have loathed you, abused you. It's best you leave Andrew alone. And the child is gone."

"Oh no, Aaron. The child is never gone, especially not now." Louisa kissed him, aware of his loss of interest. She stroked and soothed him, aroused and loved him in his need, giving and responding with the depth and sweetness he had been afraid he'd never know.

Afterward she watched him, wondering about his thoughts as she lay against his back, encircling him with her arms. He had seemed to take deep satisfaction from their lovemaking, but now he brooded silently, almost unaware of her. She couldn't know his thoughts, but he worried over the immense pleasure he felt loving her. Their union was much more than a purely physical response. She touched him to his core and he knew his only concern must be with the success of his assignment. Then, slowly, the usefulness of his easy and deeply felt attraction for Louisa struck him as he realized their closeness would only make their association more authentic, the charade more convincing. I'll be careful, he swore to himself, turning to her to immerse himself again in the joy of holding her in his embrace.

Chapter Thirty-seven

"WE leave at noon tomorrow, Louisa," Aaron announced one morning. "The *Isabella* is in the harbor." He paused to look at her. "Are you ready?"

"Yes," she sighed, "I'm ready," and continued to arrange clothes to be stored in her absence.

"You might want to know I've written Simon. I've informed him we're married and I've told him about Rachel. I've also reminded him we're both going to Monterey." He showed her the letter that would go overland, and watched as Louisa seemed to withdraw into herself. She shivered as if suddenly chilled.

"Whoever tutored you, taught you well," she said quietly. "I'd have sworn this is written in Marshall's hand." She paused. "Surely you know Simon forbade our marriage?"

Aaron sat down in front of her, taking her hand in his. "At first he did. But when Marshall learned you were pregnant, Simon saw his opposition was useless, and he accepted Marshall's going to California."

"How did he ever learn I was pregnant? I was well out to sea before I was able to admit it to myself."

"One of the crewmen from the *Winged Horse* left the ship at Cape Frio and returned to New Orleans with a message informing Simon."

"Ah, yes . . . Captain Tomas."

"The message was accepted and read by Marshall before Simon even saw it. And when Emma found out, you should've heard the row. She never quite approved of you, but, truthfully, she liked Marshall's alliance with the Carson girl even less. And when Emma learned of your bargain with Simon, and Marshall's agreement to marry Janna Carson, Emma brought the house down. No one had ever seen her in such a fury. I would have loved being there!" He laughed to think of Emma Hudson in a rage. "She was angry with Marshall who willingly admitted his affair with you, even when she tried to protect him by saying you were notorious."

"Was I notorious?" Louisa bristled.

"You still are!" he laughed at her sudden sense of propriety. But he sobered quickly and tried to placate her. "Marshall was adamant in his decision to go after you. No threats from Simon moved him. And in Emma's disgust with Simon, she sided with her son. I guess all those years of gentle forbearance with his infidelity finally came to an end when she saw her son involved in what she regarded as a disgrace. And in a clearer moment, Simon reconciled himself to the fact that he couldn't stop Marshall. In fact, it inspired him to think of using Marshall in his California intrigue. After Marshall's departure, he wrote to Peter Melville in Monterey telling of Marshall's pending arrival. He explained that he expected Marshall to be useful—all of this without Marshall's knowledge. Obviously, someone doubted Simon's judgment in the matter, but we'll change their minds," he said, pulling her against him, trying to capture her in his arms, hoping to arouse her.

Louisa frowned, almost pouting as he concluded. Aaron had stirred many ugly, unhappy memories for her. "Your sources are very accurate, which should reassure me, I suppose." She was silent for some minutes, taking in Aaron's words. "Poor Marshall. Coming to rescue me," she said sadly. "It was so like him." She looked away from Aaron's gaze, staring quietly into the afternoon.

He watched her for a while, then spoke quietly, letting her go. "I must take care of some final details, Louisa. Don't wait for me this evening. I won't return until very late." He kissed her mouth softly, knowing he interrupted her lonely thoughts. "Someday, I hope there will be no more sadness in your eyes."

"It will be a long time coming, I'm afraid." Then

she kissed him. "Please wake me when you come in."

When he left her, Louisa sat amid the trunks and baggage. She had one final trunk to organize. She opened her jewel case and looked at the glittering stones. "I've quite a collection for a castaway," she thought aloud, holding up her favorite necklace, a gift from Marshall. It was a large tear-shaped pearl, clustered with diamonds in a platinum setting. "The shape is very symbolic of our life together, isn't it, Marshall? But I have no more tears, even for you. I am empty."

Louisa would never have believed it possible to be finished with Marshall. He had meant everything to her, solace, salvation, love, and sensual gratification. Their life together had been a mixture of deepest pain and profound pleasure. They had drifted in and out of each other's lives, weaving threads of love and fulfillment. He seemed always to come to her when she needed him, and she gratefully acknowledged the blessing it had been to be loved by him.

Now Louisa sat staring at her precious gift from Marshall. The diamonds in the necklace sparkled in the lamplight, and the pearl had a luster all its own. She held the necklace against her throat and admired its beauty against her skin. "I would almost rather die than lose this necklace," she whispered, staring into the mirror, blinded by the flashing of the jewels in the glass. She felt foolish to have said it, but the sentiment was undeniable. This gift from Marshall was the only possession she had that truly meant anything to her. Everything else could be easily sacrificed, if need be.

She slipped the precious necklace into its velvet pouch, which she slipped into a secret compartment in the trunk that only she was aware of. Then she packed the other jewels in the mahogany case, and into the trunk. Soon I'll be traveling again, she thought, and as far as the world is concerned, I'll be with Marshall—surely, no one will suspect. I wonder if even Emma could tell. She worried over the dangerous charade, praying the ghosts from her past would rest peacefully in their graves, and her sanity would go unchallenged in the night.

Louisa ate a light supper of bread and wine, fruit and cheese with Carmen and Soledad, the young woman who so readily nursed Rachel. Why did my mother who had nothing but destruction to give, not lose her child? she asked herself. Why has this simple, loving woman lost hers? Where is the order in the universe?

When she finished her meal, Louisa took her cloak, and despite a disapproving frown from Carmen, she went out for a last walk on the beach. The moon was enormous, suspended as if by magic over the dark mountains to the east, filling the night with unearthly luminescence. The tide was very low, and Louisa walked barefooted in the unusually quiet surf. The ocean murmured rather than roared and Louisa basked in its stillness. She let the sensations of sound and light wash over her, filling her with an extraordinary peace. Taking leave of this land and of her child was unreal, the separation would take time to settle into her being.

Louisa strolled the water's edge, as aimless in her wandering as the curling of the water against the sand. The mild night air caressed and soothed her and she walked the length of the beckoning shore, past the boulders where she had not long ago confronted Aaron, until she reached the caves. Normally, the wave-carved hollows were at least partially submerged, but tonight the receding tide exposed them. She discarded her unneeded cape on the sand and crept through the gaping mouth of one tunneled-out boulder to stand her full height, then inch her way, in total darkness, the few feet to its exit. There, the surf surged gently, threatening to rise the few inches to flood the hollow. Louisa sat in the damp tunnel as if watching from some secret tower, and looked out over the water. She leaned against the cave's wall and settled in silence to stare without conscious thought into the shimmering silver sea.

She thought perhaps she could spend the pleasant night in the cave, but prepared to return to the compound when a longboat edged around the cove. She retreated into the cave's darkness and watched as two men beached the craft and began to unload small crates into a natural bunker, well above the waterline. They worked quickly and silently, pausing occasionally to scan the beach. Louisa froze as one of the men raised his hand to halt the work of the other, and they hurriedly covered their cache and shoved the now empty boat into the surf, one man proceeding with silent oars across the water, the other returning to the beach toward Louisa.

Her heart pounded wildly. She stood holding her breath, innocent of what she had witnessed, yet certain her observation had endangered her greatly. She shrank into the recesses of the slim cave, hoping it offered protection, for the depth of the tunnel would never save her. The cave was perhaps ten feet in length and at most six feet wide, so she was trapped in only a few feet of shadows. It would be suicide to step out onto the moonlit sand, she thought, suddenly knowing the terror of a stalked animal. She glanced into the water, instantly deciding what she must do. What brings him so accurately in my direction? she wondered in her panic. Then she remembered the cloak she'd thrown aside and the diamond-encrusted button reflecting in the rays of moonlight.

Watching the man stride quickly toward her position, Louisa disrobed within seconds and slipped over the other edge of the cave and into the warm water. She splashed silently into deeper water, swimming a few feet, hoping to be sheltered by the shadows of the prominent glistening rocks protruding at this end of the small bay. She looked back, and saw the figure filling the open mouth of the cave. He held her cloak and an armful of her discarded clothes.

"What?" She started in the gentle swells, hearing her name called.

"Louisa! Damn it! Come out of the water!"

Louisa laughed in spite of herself.

"Damn it, I know you're there. Your clothes are still warm."

Now Louisa laughed heartily. She rose and waved

at him, laughing harder. "You nearly scared me to death!" she yelled. "Come for a swim, Aar—Marshall, the water's wonderfully warm." She laughed uproariously, splashing back into the water, drifting at will.

"Come on, get out of the water! I've no time for games."

"Damned if I'm getting out yet. I'm very wet already and enjoying this unexpected moonlight swim. Come and get me, Marshall."

He retreated into the hollow to appear a few minutes later, naked, striding vigorously into the surf. He dove after her as she swam further into the shallow pool. He caught her quickly and she wound herself around him eagerly as they stood in elbow-deep water. He was no longer angry with her as he stroked her satin body.

"What are you doing here, Louisa?"

"What am I doing here? Why, I was out for a walk."

"You're quite a distance from home."

"I'm healthy and able to walk! What are *you* doing here, and how did you know it was me?"

"Your clothes have your fragrance," he replied, beginning to touch her in an urgently familiar way.

"Mmm, but that doesn't tell me what *you* are doing here."

He was exasperated at being interrupted. "We're storing munitions here and there, in preparation for possible armed conflict."

"In this light?"

"Ordinarily, we wouldn't have risked it, but we're pressed for time. We're leaving tomorrow, remember?"

"I haven't forgotten." She leaned against him, holding him fast, suddenly more in need of comfort than caressing. "You really gave me an awful fright, you know."

"Sorry," he said, lifting her, kissing her throat, licking her breasts as she rode him. She held him, moving her body fiercely against him. "Aaron, Aaron," she soon called. "Now, Aaron." And they clung together in mutual elation.

They held each other joyfully for several minutes more, then separated to swim side by side in the crystal bay, soothed and rejuvenated. Then he touched her and brought her with him onto the sand. He wound her cloak around them and drew her close to him to share their warmth.

"You owe me one, Louisa," he said as he savored the feel of her body against him.

"What do you mean?"

He opened her cloak, spreading it on the sand. "You slipped out of my arms here on the beach one afternoon, and, before we leave, I think you ought to settle your debts."

"Gladly!" she replied touching him, making his body yearn for hers again.

"Why can't I get enough of you, Louisa?"

"I don't want you ever to have your fill. I want you always to be a little hungry."

"But must I always be starving?" he laughed.

"Good," she said, her mouth wet on him, tasting the slight saltiness of his skin.

"Ah, Louisa," he groaned while she stroked and teased. "You think you have me in the palm of your hand."

"I do now, don't I?" she laughed.

"Not for long," he laughed, and grabbed her roughly. He rolled over onto her, trapping her beneath him, pinning her hands over her head with one of his. He kissed her, taking her breath away. Then with his free hand, he slowly teased her flesh until she cried out, begging him to finish, arching her body uncontrollably toward him, her breath forced out of her involuntarily in little gasps. The duration of her joy surpassed what she'd known before, and soon he came into her and filled her with his own rejoicing.

Afterward, they were quiet for some time as they rested pleasurably together. "In a way that was nearly a kind of torture, Aaron," she said. "I felt as if you might never let me go!"

"I never want to let you go, Louisa," he answered, lying against her. Then he raised himself and took her chin in his hand, hurting her in his intensity. "But I cannot love you and you must not love me. Not

now. Do you understand? We can make each other
no promises."

"I understand only too well, Aaron," she said quietly to his fierceness. "Have you forgotten what you
say you know of me? I'm an authority on broken
promises. That you promise nothing is in its way reassuring." She took the hand that held her face, making
him release her, then said gently, "But you cannot forbid me to love you. Do *you* understand?" she asked,
kissing his hand as she held it.

"Yes," he said, smiling as he relaxed against her.
When they were dressed, they embraced again, each
filled with what they believed was a new understanding of the other, then walked the distance to the house
in comforting silence.

Chapter Thirty-eight

❧ BEFORE they reached the steps of the house, Louisa touched Aaron's arm to stop him. "Wait, Aaron. Before we go away, there is one thing I must do."

"What is that, Louisa?"

"I have one farewell to make before we leave."

"Yes?"

"Please, take me to his grave," she whispered, looking at him, drawing him into her moonlit eyes.

"Why, Louisa?" his question as soft as her plea.

She hesitated. "Oh, Aaron, I don't know why. I only know I can't leave here until I go to him." Her voice was quiet, but urgent, pleading. "I've asked so little of you in all of this. Please, just trust me. I must do this one last thing before we go."

"All right. If it will ease your mind. He's buried a little east of here, on property owned by Dobson. We can ride there now, if you like."

They remained at the house only long enough to get horses and for Louisa to dress for riding. She hastily pinned up her hair and tied a dark bandanna around her head. This time she dressed more appropriately, wearing a riding skirt and boots. She met Aaron at the door, the amethysts of the rosary hung around her neck glistening in the moonlight. "Slip that inside your shirtwaist," he motioned, "we don't want to attract attention if we're noticed on the road."

She obeyed and they rode out swiftly, traveling easily in the light. They wound their way through the thick, low-growing shrubs, following the river along its north bank. They traveled for an hour, then headed due north. There was no one on the Dobson property, but Aaron led her directly to an immense and ancient oak tree, stopping his horse abruptly. He dismounted and assisted her. "You are standing beside his grave, now. There is nothing to see, the ground was carefully prepared so that it would go unnoticed."

Louisa gave him the horse's reins, then lifted the rosary over her head and knelt quietly. Aaron walked the horses a short distance away and tethered them, then stood and watched her pray in the silent night, wondering what comfort she found in this act, a question even she could not answer. He did not begrudge her her prayers, or the gesture of farewell, though it was inconvenient on this last night of preparation. He simply failed to comprehend her faith, in view of all her grief, and if it was not faith, then the empty gesture. "How could anyone, most of all Louisa, trust in God?" he wondered.

Louisa stood, then went to Aaron and put her arms around him. "Thank you," she said, hugging him gratefully. Then she mounted her horse and turned south again without another word or a glance back.

As they passed by the Dobson house, there was a light shining and Aaron halted, Louisa quickly doing the same. "As long as we're here, I want to talk with him," he said, leading the horses toward the house.

Luther Dobson opened his door. "Who is it?"

"Hudson."

"I didn't expect to see you, but come inside. Who's with you?" He squinted in the darkness. "Oh, Mrs. Hudson."

"We've been paying our respects to the oak tree," Aaron motioned.

"I see—of course. Come inside, Mrs. Hudson, Excuse the clutter. I'm rarely here. Usually live in town." The house was adobe, built soundly, but it obviously hadn't been lived in regularly for a good while. The inside looked more like a storehouse than a dwelling. "Just brought out more supplies. Jackson has a good shipment this time and there's to be more the end of the week. If it keeps up, they'll be able to supply a formidable army.'" He motioned to the stacks of ammunition, rifles, and other provisions. "I hope Washington has accurate information regarding the scale of this operation or we're wasting our time."

"The information I have seems to coincide with whatever I've been able to verify on my own," Aaron responded. "There must be nearly thirty thousand sympathizers and with sufficient leadership and arms, this part of the country will easily fall into the South's camp. The only real uncertainty is how much time we have. Who is our contact in Easton's household?"

"Samuel Davis, free Negro servant in Easton's employ. Damnedest situation. Easton's the biggest slave advocate around. I guess Davis plays it his way for his own amusement, hiring out for high wages and hoping eventually to put the final screws to Easton." He shifted his weight and looked sideways at Louisa.

"Easton? Easton?" she mused. "Not William Easton?"

"Yes."

"Of Richmond?"

"Yes."

"My God, I know him!" she stared.

"Yes, you do! And a lot more I haven't had time to tell you."

"What's his role in all this, Aar—Marshall?"

"William Easton is to be the President of the Pacific States Republic."

"I knew him for a short while," commented Louisa, unable to hide her astonishment. "He's clever and dangerous, and a bit demented in my estimation."

"Precisely." Aaron turned to Dobson. "We'll see you tomorrow?" he asked. "Has the courier come in?"

"Yes, he's waiting for you. I was surprised to see you tonight."

"Something unexpected came up," he said, smiling broadly at Louisa. "I'll take the señora on, and then get the pouch."

"Good night, Mrs. Hudson, I'm glad to see you so well."

"Good night, Luther. Thank you."

Dobson watched them ride into the night, and hoped their masquerade would go unchallenged.

Chapter Thirty-nine

WILLIAM Easton looked over the peninsula as it stretched south from his windows. The grand house of stone, redwood, and leaded glass looked as natural in the heavily wooded setting as anything man could make. He would regret the necessity of leaving this place when his schemes were realized, but the quest for power overrode any feeling he had for Crane's Nest. Hudson's arrival signals their full commitment to the Republic, he thought, satisfied with the prospects he saw for himself. Soon, he expected to realize ambitions most men never dared to dream. He had dreamed from unlikely places and origins, single-mindedly certain of his destiny, though its actual form was unclear until recently, when he met Simon Hudson, Franklin Carson, and Peter Melville.

He had been born to zealous, Bible-beating parents. His father was an overworked merchant; his mother an ambitious woman whose aspirations surpassed her husband's abilities and her own strength. William was the last of four children, by far the brightest, by far the most overwhelmed by his mother's illnesses and dissatisfactions, and by his father's torturous retreat into alcohol. As the years wore on, James Easton increasingly hated life and himself, despising his ability to take his own sermonizing to heart; committed to seeing that his children would "enter the Kingdom of God" even if they passed through those gates with multiple bruises, testimony to their submission. William sought his mother's protection early on, but Marta offered comfort after the fact, never questioning James's authority to oversee his children's access to God.

William could now look back on the beatings philosophically. "One could say they fostered my destiny." He believed he would soon realize a kingdom of sorts, but "better yet, a kingdom on this earth where I wield the power, control the destinies, bow the heads." It was a simple self-deception, common among inflated puppets who come to prominence, believing their success is of their own making.

The only area where William seemed to gain his father's approbation was in his studies. He was a quick and gifted student, soon surpassing his teachers. James Easton's fortune was small, but he was able to send his son on to school, eventually to the university. His ambition was for William to be ordained, a mission never realized before he died, nor after, when William acknowledged he had no intention of pursuing "God's work." His mother was not disappointed and she encouraged him to pursue his interest in law.

She was less enchanted by his attraction for Anna Clarkson, and, while she was alive, Marta was unalterably opposed even to William's platonic pursuit of the young woman. Anna Clarkson . . . reflected William. He could only wonder how different his life would have been if their relationship had come to anything. A son's attraction for Anna Clarkson might have been approved by most mothers, except she was lame, and sometimes quite disabled. William met her through a fellow law student, a cousin of Anna's. She came from a prominent family and would never have seriously encouraged William as a suitor had she not been incapacitated. She was pretty and bright and charming, but in reality, a pariah by virtue of her infirmity. In his youth, William saw her as a star in a constellation he would not have aimed for. He knew he would never have caught her eye if she were not an outcast. Nor would she have appealed to him, had she been whole, for he sensed he did not deserve anything that was not in some way deformed, which was the way he saw himself. He was small of stature, and very slight, almost too thin. Now, he would be described as intense, but when he was younger, his intensity made him odd. He was not one immediately to command the respect of those around him, although those with whom he mingled came to respect his intelligence, if not concur with his philosophical viewpoint. He was not very strong physically, nor athletic, but he respected strength, or at least its manifestations. He made himself a proficient marksman to compensate for his self-acknowledged deficiencies and he often carried a gun, usually concealed, because it gave him a sense of power and worth.

It could not be denied that William was brilliant and shrewd, but when younger he was far too rabid. He favored the law, not out of a sense of justice, but for its more lucrative considerations, and perhaps even for its opportunity to inflict abuse on those at its mercy. Today, he might appear austere but elegant, for he had acquired manners to suit the nature of his ambitions. Flattery, patient civility, polite attentiveness were added to his politically keen sense of the moment. As a student, he was a fanatic, hate-filled and angry. Remarkably, Anna softened him with her innate gentleness, which flowed over everyone. "I can thank her for that," he reminisced, "otherwise I would have destroyed myself before long." But even with her help, William was unpopular in his profession, unable to keep clients, and when Marta Easton died, William's inclination to proceed with the law disappeared. He had hoped to marry Anna, but her family forbade it, as much because of his lack of social standing as for his personality, or for considerations of her health.

William was eloquent though caustic, and a loquacious nature fostered by courtroom battles predisposed him to politics and to his next occupation. By the time the law profession soured on him, he had found a supporter in Amos Freeland, a journalist and zealot who welcomed William to his camp. When Anna died of pneumonia after a long incapacitating illness, William sank into his newfound career. Under Freeland's tutelage, William developed a gift for adroit, remarkably popular editorials which brought him unfamiliar notoriety. He began to circulate among people whose fortunes he could enhance by virtue of espousing their opinions and gaining public approval for them.

To his astonishment, he became a favorite of the rich, courted and cajoled. He was grateful, solicitous, and useful. He was rewarded monetarily, and even attained a satisfying amount of local prestige. The horizon opened for William, and he sailed off into it, expanding his interests, indulging his whims. Eventually, he came under the patronage of Justin Boyd, who rounded out his education in all matters, grooming him for whatever service suited Justin's varying disposition.

Louisa was not aware of William's lengthy relationship with her father. She was aware the men were acquainted, but not of the nature or the extent of their association, or that he was informed about her in intimate detail. William now looked forward to seeing Louisa again, "perhaps of knowing, at first hand of her reputed charms."

Chapter Forty

Louisa had no way of knowing what reception awaited them in Monterey as she stood watching the last of their luggage being taken aboard the barkentine *Isabella*. Emotionally, she had left her home and her child as if she were returning very soon, perhaps the next day. She stood at the bow of the ship watching the final preparations for sailing, waiting for Aaron to join her for the weighing of the anchor.

When the *Isabella* headed gracefully around the lighthouse point, Aaron stood behind her with his arms holding her fast against him, his mouth warm against her ear. Louisa watched the town and its cluster of dwellings recede into the landscape, feeling quite detached. The sea breeze was crisp on her face and she let her hair fly freely into the wind while they watched the barkentine tack north past the small compound above the beach. "Now, it begins, Louisa," Aaron whispered to her, kissing her throat gently as she nestled for a moment in his warmth.

But soon his attention riveted to the ship, and she caught his excitement as he made himself at home among the other seamen responding to orders from the captain. He seemed exhilarated to be at sea, and she smiled at the pleasure he seemed to have aloft. He was agile and catlike, which only slightly reassured her as she watched him high above her in the sails.

"Don't you miss this life?" she asked when he came down. "I watched you and you seem to belong aboard a ship, there are so many things I've not asked you, Aar—Marshall."

"There's a lot you have to learn about me, Louisa. First of all, I'll break your neck if you call me anything but Marshall, here on out!" he whispered harshly, sounding as if he meant it.

She looked at him sharply, and he softened toward her. "I love being at sea," he continued. "It's a vigorous, challenging life, but unless you have command, it can be a murderous existence, and most of what I saw was solitary and brutal. Yet, only chance brings me here. Right now, I'd be sailing my own ship, if I didn't have an obligation I can't avoid."

"How did you ever get involved? The last I heard, you were in Europe."

"It's too long a story to tell. I've other things to say first. Let's go below."

They went to their cabin which was small but, like everything else aboard the *Isabella,* well tended, even comfortable. "If I'd seen nothing but duty like this, I'd never have left the Vanguard line, Louisa," Aaron remarked as he settled into a chair.

"Your past has been bitter, too, hasn't it?" she said, touching him softly as she seated herself on the bunk next to him.

He looked at her, unwilling to trust what she offered. "Past is past, for now, Louisa. We need to concentrate on the present. You said you knew William Easton."

"Yes," she replied, trying to focus her thoughts on the odd little man Aaron wanted to discuss. "Marshall and I first met him aboard the *Emma H.* and I saw him, from time to time, in my father's company when I was last in New Orleans. He's very strange, but he's refined and commands attention. I suppose he'll cut a good figure as the president of a republic."

"We'll be staying with him in Monterey . . . he's written he's looking forward to seeing you again, and to congratulate us on our marriage. I understand he knew you and Marshall very well."

"Well enough to recognize you, if anyone does!"

"What would you say my chances are for escaping recognition?"

She looked carefully at Aaron. "Extremely good in physical appearance. William had no occasion to know whether or not Marshall had scars of any kind." She paused, smiling slyly. "You're aware of his tastes?"

"I've heard. You should be prepared to woo him a a little if need be."

"So should you!" she laughed.

"I'll do my best to avoid it," he grinned. "But remember, he was well aware of your affair *sans* legal sanction, and in the course of this venture, I expect you to use your head—and your body—if the need arises."

"I can assure you, the need won't arise," Louisa snapped, glowering. "You were asking about whether William would recognize you," she changed the subject. "Physically, no, but you're more arrogant, less refined, a lot tougher than Marshall. A shade of difference, perhaps, but not, I think, to William's eye. Perhaps, it could be explained away with the hardships of marriage, and so on," she teased, "but, I doubt it."

"I can be charming when I put my mind to it."

"With considerable effort, might be more accurate," she parried.

He looked at her, glad to have her with him, confident she would do whatever was required. "We'll soon be at Easton's and as the son and daughter-in-law of his most prominent backer, William will be entertaining us like royalty. It will be good to see you in your finery—and, I imagine, in your element." He paused to take a long look at her. "I've a gift for you, Louisa. It was to have been your bridal gift from Marshall. I've saved it to give to you at the beginning of our official relationship as Marshall and Louisa Hudson, in Marshall's place." He reached under the pillows of their bunk, and pulled out a slender but wide green velvet case. He hesitated, "Let it be a gift from me as well, Louisa. It's something I'd give you if I could." He placed the case in her hands, then leaned over to kiss her.

She returned his kiss, lingering over his touch. "Of course, it can be a gift from you both," she said, opening the box, which was heavy for its size. "Oh, it's incredible!" she gasped, taking the necklace from its case. The jewels shown brilliantly with a fire of their own, the heavy V-shaped collar of emeralds gradually descending to a point from which hung a large lustrous stone. "I've never seen anything so beautiful!"

"Let's see how it looks on you," said Aaron, reaching for the throat of her dress, helping her with the buttons and then with the golden clasp of the necklace. She revealed herself as might the bodice of an evening gown, with the collar covering her throat, the larger stone nestling perfectly between her breasts.

"A jewel among jewels, Louisa," he said caressing her breasts. "I don't know if you'll be safe wearing that in public," he said as he unbuttoned the rest of her bodice.

"I'm definitely not safe with you!" she laughed, starting to unclasp the heavy collar.

"No, leave it on."

"That's an odd request," she teased, disrobing without haste, turning around slowly. "Is this the way it should be worn to advantage?" she asked. "I'd be a sensation at Easton's, don't you think?"

"They'd dethrone Easton and make you empress of the new republic with no regrets." And they laughed as they lay together.

Then she was quite serious, touching his face, outlining his features with fingers he kissed whenever she touched his lips. "Thank you for this beautiful gift, Marshall," she whispered, looking deeply into Aaron's eyes.

"Thank you, Louisa, for the gift you give me," he whispered in return, taking her with the tenderness and love he felt but wouldn't admit. He made love to her gently, much as Marshall had on the first voyage they made together. And though she would have denied it, Louisa's heart was now lost somewhere in the space between the two men she called Marshall.

Chapter Forty-one

AARON lay in their bunk aboard the *Isabella*. Normally, if he did not have the watch, nothing would have kept him awake in the early hours before sunrise. Unless it's a matter of pleasure, he reminded himself, listening to Louisa's rhythmic breathing as she lay close to him. But he had already filled himself to the brim and had slept deeply for several hours. He lay next to her thinking over the usual scenes of an early-morning watch, recalling the sense of wonder that filled him each time he witnessed the breaking of day on the open sea. If he could pause for these moments, the stillness, the promise, the sensation that was like no other, overwhelmed him.

But now he was below deck and wide awake, feeling unusually irritable, restless, and resentful. "A clever trap this has turned out to be," he grumbled under his breath. Politics was of no interest to him. And though he abhorred the institution of slavery and found the philosophy which tolerated it incomprehensible, he never expected to endanger himself in any cause that might abolish the system. He truly cared nothing for the argument over the preservation of the Union, having long ago divested himself of any such loyalty. His first and only responsibility was to himself.

Oddly enough, it turned out to be a circular devotion. He first sought to save himself from hanging, then he found himself seeking vengeance for his brutalization, and, finally, he became committed to revenging Marshall's death. In the process he would render service of the highest order to his native country and assist in the downfall of a detestable system of human bondage. But, certainly, without this simple duty to himself, he would never have found himself enmeshed in such a complex web. He would have slipped away unseen, and gone his way without a second thought. What am I doing here? he wondered silently. I should be at sea again myself—with no time for loyalties to intrude, and even less time to brood over the woman warming my bed, he thought. There's a lot to be said for a good whore—no obligation after the price has been settled.

Over the three weeks at sea, Aaron's hunger for Louisa had been tempered by his growing concern for his mission, and by the fact of her eager presence. He was only too aware that her accessibility, her needy response to him took the edge off his desire for her. But let her appear indifferent or distracted and his craving for her surfaced very quickly.

As he stared out at the new day from the warmth of his shared bed, he remembered countless early-hour watches when he would return to his solitary bunk. Never before had he rolled over in his bed aboard ship and looked into shining blue eyes, nor been drawn into a warm embrace in the chill of morning.

"Good morning," Louisa said softly, at his urging lifting her body to lie on top of him, teasing his face and chest as strands of her soft hair brushed lightly against his skin. She kissed him eagerly, and moved her body against him, sure of his responses, sure of her power over him, greatly enjoying the pleasure she gave. Aaron wondered again what possessed Marshall to abandon Louisa. Surely, he thought, no sum of money, no political advantage, no loyalty could be worth the trade. Yet he found himself irrationally accepting the idea that he might lose her in his responsibility to what had become his cause, and as they seduced each other in the comfort of the growing light of day, Aaron silently cursed everything but the instinct that brought them together.

They spent the final day aboard the *Isabella* leisurely preparing to arrive in Monterey, neither eager for nor regretful of the commencement of the charade. Aaron was sure their relationship would appear authentic, and he trusted he could conduct himself appropriately—his rough edges worn smooth with proper tutoring and through Louisa's more recent nurturing.

He hadn't told Louisa of some unexpected news he'd received just before their departure from San Diego. He had thought the strain of leaving Rachel was enough for Louisa to cope with for the present. He had not relished the news and had wanted time to weigh the possible implications, and any alternatives open to them. Actually, he questioned whether he needed to worry or not. Emma Hudson was a woman with a keen intelligence and distinct love and regard for the well-being of her son.

Mother and son had been separated for a long time, and, in recent years, their comings and goings were separate even when they were under the same roof. Aaron remembered the woman's watchful maternal eye and wondered whether Emma would detect the nuances in his protrayal of her son. Am I skillful enough to deceive her? he wondered. She was to arrive in a few weeks, depending on the speed of her journey around the Cape, and there was no way to avoid meeting her that he could foresee, at this time. She had decided to come to see her grandchild whom she knew would have been born by now, and whom she expected to be in Monterey since the child's parents were due there. Aaron hoped the masquerade would be sufficiently underway, the others successfully convinced of his identity and new political persuasion, and that Emma could be kept at arm's length long enough to give him all the time he needed. Perhaps she could be convinced she was needed in San Diego and, if necessary, dispatched there with Louisa.

Aaron worried about what Louisa's reaction to Emma would be. The women had parted on friendly terms, but Emma had at that time been unaware of the depth of Marshall and Louisa's involvement. Their fondness for each other was inescapable to anyone but the most blind, yet mothers are often unobservant, especially where a son's love affair is concerned. Surely, she knew, but overlooked the obvious, thought Aaron. Yet Emma had consented to Marshall's engagement to Janna Carson, never openly questioning the sudden public end to Louisa and Marshall's romance. And, by her reaction to the news of Louisa's pregnancy and her willingness to defend her son in the matter, she had been oblivious, at least, to what went on in private between the two lovers.

Janna Carson had not been Emma's choice of a mate for her son. She found Janna shallow and cold and selfish, but since Simon was so in favor of the match and Marshall not opposed, Emma had accepted the prospective union as a means of discouraging Marshall from further inclination toward Louisa. It had been remarkably easy—too easy, she would reflect later when the news of Louisa's pregnancy came to her.

The means of separating the lovers had angered Emma most of all. Emma would not have chosen Louisa for her son because of what she knew of the family history—the dissipation, the inclination to excess, the questionable sanity of both Louisa and her mother. But Simon's conscienceless coercion of the young couple to end their affair and promote his selfish plans was beyond her comprehension, and beyond her tolerance. Whatever her misgivings about Louisa's heritage, they did not warrant the wrenching apart of two people who had risked a great deal to love each other. Emma realized too late that her son and the girl she had sheltered on many an occasion had loved each other secretly to avoid the disapproval of the family, and to insure a means to make their open union a reality by waiting until Marshall became financially independent and able to support them whatever the family reaction. Finally, threatening Louisa with prosecution on a murder charge in Justin's death, in circumstances which could never be proved but which would disgrace the couple, regardless of the outcome, would forever damn Simon in Emma's view. At last, Emma faced the reality that Simon would do whatever was necessary to get what he wanted.

At first Emma could not comprehend what would make Simon believe he could threaten Louisa with the murder of her father, but she learned to her horror what both her son and her husband knew. She was sick and furious and outraged, and only half placated when Simon swore that he had only recently learned of Justin's abuse of Louisa. He swore he would never have tolerated it, but now Emma had severe doubts about her husband's morality, a rift that now would never be mended. She only hoped her coming to California, her expression of regret, her request for pardon for disregarding Marshall and Louisa's right to choose whomever they might as a partner in love would allow her access to her grandchild.

Emma was, for once, feeling her age, and somehow the grandchild loomed as a beacon for the future, a link to immortality in the chain of generations. Her distress over Marshall and Louisa's affair, the grief she felt over Simon's growing lust for power and money, the sorrow she felt for a child she might have protected, and her other disappointments long past remembering, had suddenly aged Emma. She saw the war that seemed more possible with every passing day, and her husband's involvement in the South's prospects for success, to be more ominous than exciting. Whatever premonition she had of the future was clouded by her growing distrust of Simon, and by the disgust she felt over what she was learning of his affairs.

At first Simon's takeover of the family business was an arrangement which pleased her as she watched her fortune and status grow under Simon's clever management. From time to time, something would give her great distress, yet each event could be explained away and, with enough time, forgotten. Now these grievances boiled up from the past to compound the current rift; Emma's discontent further encouraging her to travel west. She needed time away from Simon. These were things that Aaron knew from contact with the Russells, and he feared what Emma's reaction would be when she connected Simon to Marshall's death. Perhaps, he reflected, the punishment for the sins of omission was as severe as for sins of commission. He knew Emma would never escape an overwhelming guilt in the death of her son, and he wished he could save her from it.

Chapter Forty-two

THE bay at Monterey was beautiful and refreshing to see. The town spread gently, spaciously at the edge of the water against the backdrop of hills covered with dense trees and greenery. Aaron and Louisa left the *Isabella* late one afternoon, rested from their sea journey, restored by the days and nights of private, dreamlike solace they took in each other. No promises were exchanged, few words of endearment spoken. Yet Aaron and Louisa heard each other's silent voices and their bodies responded with what promises they could make. Both would later remember their time together aboard the *Isabella* with longing and sadness.

The couple was met at the port by William Easton's carriage and carried to Crane's Nest on some truly spectacular roads that lifted above the whitewashed, red-tile-roofed town. As they entered the heavily wooded hills, the air became crisp and cold, and Louisa snuggled into her cloak while the carriage ascended slowly to William's secluded home. She watched Aaron's face intently, reassured by the confidence she saw there and by the knowing smile he gave her. They said nothing to each other as they rode along, immersed in their private thoughts and last-minute anxieties.

When they arrived, William greeted them warmly in the dusk. "Marshall, Louisa, so good to see you. So good to have you accept my hospitality at Crane's Nest! Louisa, it's been such a long time since I last saw you, and that's my loss. You're more beautiful than I remembered."

"Thank you, William. I'm happy to be here. What

a magnificent location you have. Won't you be sad to leave it?"

"Why, yes, I will," he hesitated, uncertain of what she knew. "Come inside. The best is yet to come," he promised. They climbed the gray stone steps and passed through massive, dark, carved wooden doors into a brightly skylit foyer. Before them ascended an enormous white marble staircase, at the foot of which extended spacious, treasure-filled rooms. Louisa began to comprehend the extent of William's schemes as she took in the priceless furniture and objects that adorned the place. She could barely hide her astonishment at the riches she saw. She had seen plenty of estates filled with rich possessions, but nothing to rival this. She wondered where the man had acquired his taste, not to mention his possessions. She never suspected the source of his good fortune was Justin and men like him.

Aaron was prepared for Crane's Nest, if not for William Easton. He knew well of the backing the plot to take over California had. But now he came face to face with the cold hard reality of the importance of his mission, of the importance of stopping Simon and his partners. Apparently nothing would stop them from trying to gain power; money was obviously no object; ordinary loyalties meant nothing, even common decency was not respected. Any means of success was fair in their minds, the end was paramount—even a son's life could be offered up to their dreams. If he hadn't understood it before, he comprehended it now: only exceeding cleverness, superior strength, relentless pursuit would make him and his mission successful. And nothing would interfere with him. Any lack of commitment he had vanished in the instant it took him to grasp the stakes of the game he was now engaged in. Any concerns he had about his sentiment for Louisa were diminished. He realized his life was on the line as he stared into a richly mirrored wall and watched William show Louisa a particularly favorite painting which hung in the room. Aaron's blood raced through his veins, and he felt prepared, even excited, to be involved in so severe a test of his wits.

"And next week," he heard William promise the two of them, "this room will be filled with some old friends, as well as new, anxious to meet the younger Hudsons, the children of our benefactors." He looked at Aaron. "It's a shame, but I doubt your mother will have reached Monterey by then, but no matter, her later arrival will merely give us another occasion to entertain, something I love to do, and there are so few real events to warrant it here."

Louisa carefully concealed her surprise at William's remark. She looked at Aaron to receive no hint from him. What else hadn't he told her? She realized the facts she had were few, and she would be better off saying as little as possible. By doing so, she would risk less and probably learn more.

"Won't she be disappointed to learn you left her grandchild behind?" continued William to Louisa. "I suspect her journey was more for the purpose of seeing her granddaughter than for 'reasons of state'!"

At that, Louisa could barely control herself. But miraculously, she only offered him a polite smile as he escorted them up the winding staircase to their rooms, which overlooked an untouched wilderness. The view from their windows gave them the feeling that they were perched high among the tree tops, secluded and totally alone. The wing they were in extended into the woods farther than any other portion of the house. In the light of day, nothing but trees, and later, deep blue ocean and sky filled the horizon. No sound but that of the forest reached them. It could be a very private place.

When they were alone, Louisa immediately brought up Emma's arrival. "Why didn't you tell me? What if she discovers who you are? Oh, what if she learns Marshall and I are not actually married? She'll try to take Rachel from me!" Her eyes were wide with fright, her body very rigid.

"Louisa, you're being irrational," he said, going to her, taking her in his arms. He slipped inside her cloak, drawing her very close to him as a means of comforting her, and as a means of distracting her, as well. "I have good reason to think she'll not recognize me. Don't you think I've been successful with Easton?"

"Why, yes, so far," Louisa said, still not able to dismiss her sudden fright. Aaron was well aware he had not been able to placate her totally. He let Louisa out of his embrace and watched her as she paced in front of the windows looking out over the now-darkened woods.

"I didn't tell you because I needed time to sort out my own worries and thinking. And I've concluded we're in no way endangered." He went to a piece of luggage and took out Emma's letter, handing it to her. "I'm sure you'll agree that she only wants to make amends, to see her son's child, probably to escape Simon for a while . . . I think she may even be finished with him, as finished as a woman of her class can be with her husband. I doubt you have anything to fear from her, even if she learns who I am, and that there was no marriage." He looked hard at Louisa. "What do you know of Emma Hudson to think she would take your child from you?"

Louisa hung her head. "Nothing. Of course, nothing." Tears brimmed her eyes and spilled over onto her face. "You're right. I am being irrational, but my life has already been filled with too many irrational events." Aaron went to her again, letting her nestle and cry against him. "Also, I've just realized that I won't see Rachel for a *very* long time, something I hadn't really faced before now." Aaron held her while she cried, knowing she had to face this issue sometime, and now, at the start, would be as good a time as any.

They prepared and dressed for dinner with Easton. Louisa suddenly looked very tired and pale in the candlelight, in spite of the restful voyage she'd had. Both men were stirred by her distant and ethereal quality. William always dressed for dinner, even when he dined alone, and every meal was an occasion. Had she not been so upset, Louisa would have enjoyed this first meal in the elegant house. No expense, no formality was spared, and in any part of the country, one would have had a difficult search to find a better table. Easton was living like an emperor already, and even in her personal discomfort, Louisa wondered what need of William's made him pursue a political position. He apparently wanted nothing. What could being a puppet monarch give him that he didn't already have?

Louisa graced the table with her beauty. She wore a pale pink silk gown which clung delicately to her slender body. Everything about her shimmered in the light: her skin, her hair, her eyes, the fabric of her dress, the diamonds at her throat. She looked carefree, and no one would have guessed her heart felt like a stone. The conversation was lively and polite, while they dined on delicacies, many of which had been imported from as far away as the Sandwich Islands, and, of course, Europe. The wines were carefully chosen for crab legs and filet of beef, delicate vegetables and perfect sauces. Aaron and William ate heartily, Louisa sparingly. Papayas and mangoes, pineapple and pears adorned the fruit tray with cheeses from France and Germany. Louisa had last seen such extravagance in France, and she shuddered imperceptibly.

They dined leisurely into the night, and chatted about their shared experiences aboard the *Emma H.* Louisa carried the conversation easily, amused by Aaron's look when Easton mentioned their voyage together.

When they retired, Louisa paced the room nervously while Aaron undressed for bed. "This isn't your wedding night, Louisa," he said as he watched her catlike movements. She threw open the terrace windows and stepped out into the night in her thin gown, but returned rather hastily as the chill air enveloped her. She closed the windows and hurriedly removed her clothes to slip into Aaron's waiting arms.

"Mmmm," she shivered against him. "What was that look I saw on your face at dinner?"

"What look?"

"When we were discussing our trip aboard the *Emma H.*"

Aaron laughed heartily. He grabbed Louisa roughly and rolled around with her in the bed while she laughed with him. "What is the matter with you?" she demanded as he wrestled with her good-naturedly.

"Perhaps you ought to tell me all of your experiences with Easton, so I won't be unprepared," he smiled. "According to my memory, at the time you were aboard, *Emma H.* was pursued by an unidentified vessel for a day and a night. Do you have any recollection of that event?"

"I certainly do. Why? How could you know?"

"I was on the ship chasing her. Had I only known you were aboard, I never would have let you escape!" he said, pursuing her even now.

But she wouldn't be distracted. "You mean, you were a pirate—among the ones causing so much grief to Simon and my father's ships?"

"The very ones."

"Oh? What could you have done if you had captured us, and found Marshall and me aboard?"

Aaron stared at her, suddenly remembering his frame of mind at the time they were discussing. "Probably nothing, other than lift the most precious cargo and any jewels from the passengers—but, in your case, I might have made an exception and taken a captive, one I would have never ransomed," he said, fondling and kissing her breasts.

"You wouldn't?"

"It wasn't our usual style, but you'd have been difficult to let go unmolested!"

"I really don't know very much about you, do I?"

"You know about all you *need* to know," he said, covering her mouth with his, kissing her deeply, wanting to stop their conversation. His tongue caressed her mouth, then slowly sought her breasts, drifting down her belly into her groin. Louisa was delighting in his touch, and, as he returned his mouth to hers, she held him eagerly in her embrace. They stroked and petted each other, pushing and tantalizing, prolonging their reach for satisfaction until the sensations were nearly unbearable.

"Kiss me, Marshall," she whispered. "Why don't you ever kiss me?" She seemed to be a long distance away as she spoke, her eyes closed, her body tilting urgently toward him. Then she opened her eyes with an odd, almost questioning look, and said, "Kiss me, Aaron," and he needed no further urging as he lowered his mouth to her, and with his tongue filled her with a kind of pleasure she had known only once before. Louisa was wild with joy which magnified his own, and when they came together, at last, their union was deeply felt and intensely satisfying.

"I would have stolen you from Marshall," Aaron promised her, caressing her beautiful slender body that gave him so much pleasure. "And I would never have given you up. Never!"

Louisa smiled at Aaron, and at the intensity of his pledge. She looked into his shining dark eyes, marveling at their blackness, feeling herself pulled helplessly into their depths. She drew his mouth to hers, succumbing again to the wonder she felt in his embrace, seeking his warmth and consolation, and she knew, at last, that she was in love with him.

Chapter Forty-three

WHEN Louisa woke the next morning, she found herself alone. At first she luxuriated in the warm bed watching the early light filter though sheer draperies, glancing leisurely around the room to reacquaint herself with her new surroundings. She felt as if she were in a palace whose furniture adorned rather than filled the rooms, every piece excellently made of the finest woods, carefully preserved, and rubbed with the best oils.

A Swiss clock, which was as much a work of art as it was a timepiece, told her it was still very early, in spite of the bright sunlight filling the room. Louisa turned over, wishing more than soft covers enveloped her lithe body in their satin folds. For a few minutes she considered drifting off to sleep again, then decided she would do what she presumed Aaron had done—go exploring on the grounds.

She rose from the warmth, reaching for a silk robe laid out for her on the chair beside the bed. The fabric was wonderfully pleasing against her skin, and its pattern of large colorful flowers set sharply in a black background made her seem more fragile, even more beguiling than usual. Where's Aaron, she thought again as she gazed at her alluring self in the mirror, suspecting he would find the garment winsome. The gown did not belong to her and she wondered who had left it for her.

As she moved about the room, Louisa discovered her trunks had been unpacked and each item carefully arranged for her convenience. Her gowns hung in matching wardrobes, all meticulously pressed and waiting for her to don them. Then she thought of the gala dinner William had mentioned last night, and began sorting through her dresses, wondering what she would wear to impress Easton's important guests for whom she and Aaron would be on display. When she remembered the emerald collar Aaron had recently given her, she immediately decided what she would wear.

Louisa pulled the shimmering gown from the closet and tossed it on the bed while she searched the bureaus for her jewels. Finding them, she removed the emerald necklace, wondering at its beauty and its expense; realizing again her fortune was directly tied to the Hudson wealth. Simon was executor of her father's estate, and she presumed that if the Hudson fortune floundered, so would hers. Louisa was certain if the impending war did not go in the South's favor, if Simon's schemes failed, she would somehow suffer the consequences. She eyed the sparkling jewels in her hand, as well as those lying in their mahogany case, trying to reassure herself that whatever the outcome of Simon's dreams, she would not be penniless for a long while.

Louisa sighed, putting the elaborate collar away in its velvet box. As she tucked it away, she uncovered an odd gold chain Marshall had given her one night shortly before they separated. She frowned at this necklace and its pendant which had always distressed her. The chain itself was beautiful old gold, heavy and thick, but incongruously attached to it was a delicate locket and tiny ring. The discrepancy between chain and ornaments annoyed Louisa, and she had never worn them, except on the night they were given to her. But now she stroked the heavy loops of gold in her fingers, suddenly lifting the unusually long chain over her head, staring at herself in the ornate mirror wondering not only about the necklace, but about the night Marshall gave it to her. Even at this distance and expanse of time, she could feel the sensations of that evening—the strange fear mixed with desire; the longing she had felt, and, afterward, Marshall's odd unresponsiveness to her shy requests for him to touch her that way again. "Aaron," she murmured without recognition, staring into the glass, not hearing her own voice.

Suddenly Louisa remembered another necklace Marshall had given her, this one more precious than any other, and of its secret hiding place in her trunks. Their luggage had been carefully emptied and stored, and she made a mental note to retrieve the necklace from its niche without delay.

Louisa dressed in a soft challis gown and rang the bellpull for some assistance with her hair. While she waited for a response, she opened the windows and stepped onto a broad terrace extending from the room over a patio below. The air was crisp and cold as she looked over the pristine estate. Nothing seemed disturbed by the presence of this magnificent house. It was as if she were alone at the top of the world, and she stood peacefully until she felt someone's presence.

Louisa had not heard a sound except the shimmer of wind as it occasionally passed through the branches arching above her, and she was startled to turn and find a breathtakingly beautiful, though diminutive Oriental woman a few feet from her. The woman waited silently, eyes downcast, with no perceptible motion, even from breathing. Unexpectedly seeing the young woman, Louisa cried out softly in surprise, and the girl bowed submissively.

"I have come to answer your call, madam."

"Oh, yes," Louisa said, composing herself. "I need help with my hair—and, perhaps, something to eat before I go out."

"Yes, madam," replied the woman. "My name is Loo Kim. I will assist you any way I can," and she bowed again.

"Thank you." Louisa hastened inside and seated herself before the dressing table, watching the girl skillfully and quickly pin her hair. "How long have you been in Mr. Easton's service?"

"For as long as he has settled here."

"How long is that?"

"Perhaps a year."

That would be about right according to Louisa's calculations. She last saw William Easton in New Orleans shortly after her father's death. He had offered her his condolences, and said he wished he could assist her in some way. "How little he knew," Louisa said aloud, absorbed in her thoughts.

"Excuse me, madam? I did not understand."

"Nothing. I was lost in my thoughts."

The maid silently disappeared, almost before Louisa noticed her departure. At first Louisa paced the room, then seated herself on a richly brocaded divan, stroking the fabric absentmindedly. She felt restless and uncomfortable, and from the surprises sprung on her the day before, she realized she knew far too little of what was actually going on. She felt herself merely an ornament, and decided the time had come for her to pin Aaron down about details and to find out what was expected of her. "Just how am I going to force anything from him?" she laughed, interrupted in her musings by Loo Kim, who carried a remarkably heavy silver tray laden with ornate serving dishes.

A delicious feast was soon artfully arranged before her while she sat at an elaborately carved table. Louisa looked out into the treetops and basked in warm sunlight which settled into her body like a salve as she ate the simple but elegant meal, the setting complete with a bowl of fragrant exotic flowers to fill her senses. If nothing else, thought Louisa, dining here will certainly be a pleasure. For her enjoyment there were enormous, perfectly ripe red strawberries resting in a bed of geranium leaves, partially covered with heavy sweet cream; large golden croissants, sweet butter, and hot aromatic tea. And since she had not eaten much the evening before, the food revived and soothed her.

When she finished, Louisa took her great cloak, engulfing herself in its folds, and left the room. She stepped onto the second-floor landing to be drenched by sunlight which poured from the partially glassed-in roof above. There were no sounds to assail her ears, and it seemed as if she were totally alone in the house. She strolled the circular corridor slowly, moving from one ornate door to another, speculating on the rooms behind each one, admiring the rich tables, the works of art adorning the walls, and the lush plants that care-

fully decorated every part of the house. Descending
the staircase, Louisa went directly outside, wandering
aimlessly at first, wondering where Aaron had gone.
The air was very crisp, and so thick were the trees,
hardly any sunlight reached through to offer her
warmth.

She was glad she had worn her heavy cloak as she
hurried into the forest, hearing nothing but the rustling of her skirts in the underbrush and the quiet
sounds of the woods. After months in southern California, Louisa was refreshed by the rich abundant
pines, the ferns and oaks waving their arms in the
constant undulating drafts and wisps of air. She
quickened her pace, soon growing warm, lowering the
hood of her cape when she climbed to the top of a
gentle hill. From there she could see a few buildings
clustered together a short distance away, and she wondered if Aaron might be there.

Finding a broad and clear path that allowed the sun
to drench her in its soft warmth, Louisa almost ran
toward the buildings, discovering they housed horses
and other livestock; a variety of workshops she assumed were used to keep the estate running smoothly,
and a large, well-stocked greenhouse. She heard a
horse whinny and stamp its feet, but otherwise the area
was quiet. She found the silent, abandoned atmosphere
eerie, but the greenhouse intrigued her, with its strange
blooms she could see through moisture-clouded windows. None of the doors to any of the buildings was
locked, so her entry to the garden enclosure was un-
impeded. The sultriness of the air struck her immediately, and she discarded her heavy cape just inside the
door, draping it over a large wooden chair set before
a well-used, utilitarian desk, piled high with ledgers
and botanical charts.

The shed was filled, floor to ceiling, wall to wall,
with trays and tables thick with plants whose foliage
was lush and overwhelming, spreading even into the
aisles. Louisa walked curiously among the raised
planter boxes, the rich smell of the potting soil pleasing
to her senses. From time to time, she was impressed
with some fragrance wafting from a beautiful or, oc-

casionally, odd bloom. She became engrossed in inspecting this luxuriant vegetation, and didn't notice the intruder until he put his hands on her. Trying to whirl from his grasp, she felt her heart take flight, and her screams were shrill in the thick, still air.

Aaron laughed at her wide-eyed terror.

"My God, Aaron!" she gasped, her face flushed, and her breathing labored. "You've gotten in the habit of scaring me nearly witless," she snapped, then relaxed slightly. "Please don't do it again—how did you know I was here? And why didn't you wake me, and tell me where you'd be?" she continued, her excitement still high, not giving him a chance to reply.

He pulled her tightly into his arms. "You, lady, seem to have the habit of leaving your cloak around to give you away." He kissed her warmly in greeting, feeling her still trembling body, noticing her breath was short and her body restless against him. "I saw you let yourself in here. Did you find anything interesting?" he asked, casually reaching for a strand of blooms, breaking it from the plant, twisting the flowers becomingly into her carefully dressed hair. Louisa was calm now, responding to Aaron's gentle manner, noticing the fragrance from the blossoms on his hands as he caressed her face, raising her mouth to his again. She moved more closely into his embrace, the scent of the flowers, the warmth of the air having its influence on them as they gradually lost all sense of where they were.

Suddenly Louisa wrenched blushing from Aaron's eager hands, the look on her face causing Aaron to turn quickly, his tension lifting when he saw the man Louisa reacted to. "Sorry," he chuckled. "I got distracted—forgot you'd be following." Aaron turned back to Louisa. "This is Samuel Davis, Louisa. You know, of course, who this is, Samuel."

"It's a pleasure, Mrs. Hudson," responded Samuel, his voice rich and melodious, with a softness that belied his height and his confident bearing. Louisa stared momentarily at the handsome black man. He seemed young, but something in his presence told her he was years older than she or Aaron.

"Hello, Samuel," she said, having regained most of her composure.

"Perhaps you recall," Aaron said, putting his arm possessively around her, "Samuel is our contact here at Crane's Nest."

"Oh, yes—and I also recall I know little else of this affair—a fact that should be remedied. Soon!" she said resolutely.

"The less you know, the better."

"Is that so?" she countered, her annoyance obvious. "I can be trusted with your precious secrets," she snapped.

"It's not a matter of trust," Aaron replied, his voice edged with the beginnings of impatience. "It's simply the less you know, the less danger you'll be in. Murder is not beyond them, if you'll remember," he reminded her sternly.

Louisa blanched at his warning, then raised her head defiantly, her eyes narrowing. "I'd rather be informed," she said coldly. "I can't behave very intelligently, procure information of any use if—or am I only to be an ornament?"

"That role would suit you well," Aaron replied lightly, turning immediately to Samuel. "We'll establish a routine for riding, and insist on your aid, perhaps, your personal attention to errands, whatever suits us— the prerogative of the class," he said sarcastically.

Samuel addressed both of them. "Easton rarely surfaces before ten o'clock. I imagine you'll have no difficulty choosing your pleasures at least till then. I'm about from sunup, sometimes before—at night, you can find me in the servants' quarters, behind the summer kitchen." He turned his eyes on Louisa. "My duties are varied—whatever suits Easton—bodyguard, manservant, groom, gardener," raising an arm to gesture to the greenery surrounding them. "Not my exclusive responsibility, fortunately. You should see this place at night. Sometimes it's lit, but just enough to compete with your worst nightmares."

That Louisa doubted, but said nothing as the threesome left the hot, sultry enclosure, all relieved to be in the bright, crisp air once again. Aaron wrapped her cloak gently around her.

"Good day, Mrs. Hudson," Samuel said, nodding in her direction. "If I can ever assist you, it will be my pleasure." Then, nodding to Aaron, he left them quickly, disappearing with great strides into the thickly wooded grounds.

Louisa stepped back from Aaron slightly. "Now, tell me what you can. I can't go on like some nitwit—something I'm not and will never pretend to be."

"You're here mainly to warm my bed, Mrs. Hudson," he said lightly, closing the distance between them, reaching into her cloak, his hands drifting familiarly over the soft curves of her body.

Quickly Louisa withdrew from him. "Is that right? Well, you just snuggle up to something else for a while —perhaps one of William's alabaster statues will warm up for you—if not, then maybe your tongue will loosen—that is, if your teeth aren't chattering too wildly." Her retort was teasing, but not completely meant to amuse.

"A wife must honor her vows, madam," he said, approaching her again.

She caught his hands and held him off. "What vows —I was delirious, as I recall."

"Nonetheless, the union is legal," he smiled.

"But not with you!"

"A mere technicality, Mrs. Hudson," he said, scooping her forcefully into his arms again. "And I'll hold you to your promises."

"Damn you," she said softly, meeting his hungry mouth eagerly, despite her threats of only moments before.

Chapter Forty-four

By the time they reached the house, there were a number of servants unobtrusively engaged in the myriad tasks required to maintain the splendor of the place. They seemed all to be Orientals, but Loo Kim was not in evidence. A stately manservant, seeming to Louisa like he should know all the secrets of life, inquired of their needs. Aaron asked about Easton, to be told he would not rise for hours. Then they were ushered politely into Easton's impressive library.

The room was cool, and, despite its size, it had a close, intimate feeling. There were several large windows, but that side of the house, like the others, was so shrouded in trees, the only real light came from ornate lamps positioned strategically around the room. The walls were perhaps twenty feet high, covered with books and collections of porcelain or bronze miniatures. Aaron seemed ill at ease, but Louisa began poring over the shelves, handling volumes as they caught her eye. "If my existence as an ornament gets too dull," she smiled at Aaron, "I can at least amuse myself reading. I wonder if anyone's even looked at some of these books." Many were richly bound in leather, the pages edged in gold; some were obviously rare, beautifully illuminated manuscripts.

While waiting for a breakfast tray for Aaron, Louisa lifted an obviously unread volume of Nathaniel Hawthorne's short stories from a shelf. She seated herself comfortably close to Aaron and began to read expressively. He listened to her soft, pleasing voice, watching her intently as she gradually relaxed into the enormous leather couch, but not paying as close attention to her words, as to the sound of her voice, very aware of its

233

natural seductiveness. Soon they were interrupted by a servant with an amply filled tray, and when they were left alone, Louisa continued to read, intermittently stopping to sip from a cup of strong fragrant tea or to steal something from Aaron's plate.

"If you're hungry, I'm sure they'll let you have a tray of your own," he said, condescendingly offering her a bite from his fork.

"No, I'm fine," she said, reaching for a croissant he'd just buttered, continuing to read between nibbles.

"You seem to have settled in comfortably," he said, interrupting her storytelling again.

"Have I? Well, it is a magnificent setting, but so eerie," she said, closing the book, putting it on the table in front of them. "At times the place seems deserted; then, just as suddenly, crawling with people who appear from nowhere—and the oddest apparition is Easton himself. Did you see the way he looked at me last night?"

"I saw," Aaron remarked casually, shoving the silver tray aside, leaning again into the enveloping cushions of the soft couch. "You can't tell me you aren't used to being stared at—you're very aware just how remarkably beautiful you are. You attract attention, if not outright leers, from even ordinarily polite men."

"How nice to hear you say so," she mocked, stroking Aaron's arm, moving her fingers to the front of his shirt, touching the buttons one by one, at last stroking his chest in a slow circular motion.

"Elegant speeches aren't in my nature, Louisa. I'm not here to seduce you—that's already been accomplished." His voice was full of comfortable self-satisfaction, as was his countenance.

"And she jumps whenever he calls her name," she snapped her fingers in his face. "The little hussy!" Louisa huffed in matronly disdain, beginning slowly to undo the buttons of his shirt. "Tell me, Aaron, how shall we spend the morning waiting for Easton to emerge into daylight?" Louisa teased, her tone revealing she had at least one idea of how to while away the remaining hours. "I can't think of a thing to do, can you?"

Aaron's eyes flashed as she moved quickly into his arms, and he met her kisses with a passion that amazed him. Surely, he thought, she would one day cease to arouse him with such intensity, even as she now moved with him, each hungry for the other. In other circumstances, he would have made love to her then and there, so careless did she seem, so wanton was she in her caressing of his body. But he willfully controlled himself, lifting her into his arms, rising to cross the room, the door opening before he could touch it.

The motion startled them both, as did the man who was ushered into their presence. Neither had seen Franklin Carson for nearly a year, the time it had been since they were last in New Orleans. And he found them engaged in what he imagined to be their natural and favorite inclination—pursuing each other romantically. A stern, yet indulgent look greeted them. His journey had obviously been long and arduous, and he longed to rest comfortably. He was in no mood for anything but polite confrontations.

"Well," he said to the obviously startled and embarrassed couple, "I can't say that I'm surprised to find you embraced in this fashion—considering what has come to pass. But isn't it a little early in the day?" he questioned, entering the room casually.

Louisa blushed furiously as Aaron lowered her gently to the floor where she met the open, knowing stare of the father of the woman Marshall had disgraced in polite New Orleans society. Aaron interrupted Carson's frank gaze by extending his hand to the man, and he was greeted with a warm handshake.

"Your father and mother send their love," he said to both of them. "The storm seems to have settled—in your house, at least. Can't say the same for mine—oh, Janna has recovered well enough—ice water being what it is—but Mrs. Carson will, doubtless, never recover. I'm quite happy to find myself in California—alone."

Louisa watched as faint lines of tension were erased

from Aaron's face and he moved into his role as Marshall with confidence. "I'm relieved to find you bear no hard feelings, sir."

"Your decision shows you have good sense," Carson remarked absently, sinking gratefully into a less than comfortable, but artistically perfect chair. Franklin Carson was ordinarily an energetic, vigorous man, but the long trip he had just experienced was telling on him. He seemed hunched with weariness, his usually distinguished white head and carefully trimmed beard now only making him seem old. He was some ten years older than Simon Hudson, a fact that was never before in evidence, but the Isthmus passage which disabled or killed multitudes of travelers hoping to reach California more quickly than by the Cape or overland routes had proved an unfortunate itinerary.

"We didn't know we were to have the pleasure of seeing you here," remarked Aaron, ushering Louisa to the couch again, but, in fact, he was expecting Carson's appearance at any time.

"Doubt you were thinking of anything but getting yourself out here. Yet, Simon seems to think you've a mind to involve yourself in our enterprise. But I wonder if you've the inclination to immerse yourself in the project," he said with a thoughtful look in Louisa's direction.

"There's time enough for both," Aaron said coolly.

Louisa gave Aaron a look of sweet acquiescence, which belied her feelings of embarrassment and fury. Yet she could not deny it was a response entirely in keeping with her adoring, and, now that she thought of it, almost simple-minded relationship with Marshall. My God, she thought to herself, I've forgotten what soft clay I was.

"You seem quite tired, sir. Did you have a difficult trip?"

"The Panama jungle is merciless, and I wasn't lucky enough to escape the rigors of it. It would've taken me less time, with fever and all, to have come around the Horn! I just hope to get my full strength back—and soon. I need to rest even now. How long will I have to wait for Easton to appear?"

"Another few hours."

"Mmm—so you were going to occupy yourselves pleasantly for the time—this is, before I arrived," he chuckled then frowned slightly. "William will soon have to give up his self-indulgent ways if he's to be head of state. . . ." he remarked as if taking notes for the future. "How's the food around here? I've been promised a light repast."

"You'll find everything—the accommodations, the food—surpassing anything available at home," answered Louisa respectfully, finding the man's demeanor more accepting than insulting. Reflecting on the past, Louisa recalled that Franklin Carson was a realist, more practical than ruthless, perhaps more crude socially, but more humane in many respects than Simon Hudson, and, certainly, more so than her father ever dreamed of being. Where Simon offered flamboyance and ambitious thinking to the triumvirate's scheming, Carson gave cautious balance and thoughtful, calculated consideration to the workability of plans which were forthcoming from Simon's and Melville's, as well as Easton's fertile brains. He provided the sorely needed temperance amid the occasionally capricious dreamers, and his worth was acknowledged by his fellows.

"California may espouse a free-state position, but it makes full use of these Chinese devils," he remarked in passing, devouring the plates of filling, delicious food, which were set graciously before him in the dining room by Easton's Oriental servants.

Aaron and Louisa sat with him, listening to tales of his recent, unpleasant travels by boat across the steaming jungles of the Central American country. But the time passed quickly enough, and soon they were joined by the master of the house, whose needs were ministered to by the breathtaking Loo Kim. Louisa watched in fascination as she devotedly hovered over William, and she amusedly watched Aaron and Franklin Carson, both of whom saw her for the first time. The two men devoured the graceful young woman with their eyes, and Louisa acknowledged the jealousy that surged in her blood in the face of Aaron's obvious enchantment. He failed to even give her the opportunity to cast him a reproachful look, so engrossed was he in the attractive and submissive servant.

Carson repeated his tales for Easton's benefit, and when William was finished with his light meal, Loo Kim escorted Carson to his quarters to rest until he would be summoned for tea later in the afternoon. Then William turned his attention to the handsome couple who remained in his presence, and with whom he preferred to occupy himself in the first place. Over the next week, travelers would be arriving periodically, disturbing the careful routine he had established, and he reluctantly anticipated its permanent disruption. But this was the future he'd been waiting for: his future was now his present, and he was beginning to find its arrival was tinged with aspects of self-doubt and terror, as much as with a sense of fulfillment for dreams long harbored.

Aaron and Louisa spoke politely of what they had discovered in their brief explorations on the estate, and arranged for Samuel Davis's assistance whenever his aid was required. "He is at your beck and call," William announced in Samuel's presence. "Consider him to be in your employ," he said graciously. "Also, Loo Kim will see to whatever needs you might have, Louisa. She is most solicitous, and I cannot imagine that she would disappoint you."

"I'm sure she'll be a great help to me," Louisa replied, hoping Aaron's smirk was not as obvious to their host as it was to her, wishing he was sitting close enough for her to give him an unobserved but effective kick in the shins for the prospects that she suspected had crossed his mind. "If you gentlemen will excuse me now," she added, smiling sweetly at Aaron, "I'd like a short rest myself. I find the long journey we've just made leaves me more fatigued than I expected.

Both men rose as she did. "If an hour is sufficient time for you to catch your breath, I would like to show the two of you some of the more spectacular sights on the property."

Louisa seemed to revive before their eyes. "Actually, I find the idea of an excursion very refreshing. I'll rest when we return."

"Excellent," William smiled broadly, his usually inanimate face lighting up enthusiastically. "I suggest a cape to protect you from the wind. The horses will be waiting whenever you're ready."

Aaron and Louisa retreated to their room, where he caught her fiercely as soon as the door was closed behind them. "No time but to say I expect you to live up to your earlier promises," he said, drawing her even closer to him.

"What promises?" she inquired, trying to wriggle from his grasp. "I made no promises."

"The hell you didn't!" He caressed her full breasts, then pulled her more tightly to him, moving urgently against her compliant body as she laughed and squirmed against him.

"I'm sure if you make your needs known to our so very gracious host, he'll be excessively polite, and grant you whatever time you think you'll need to satisfy your every demand."

"And perhaps he'd provide me with a more willing servant—he seems to have an abundant supply, and they all seem *very* agreeable," he said, releasing her, bowing in exaggeration. "For instance, I think Loo Kim might be easier to handle than you."

"I *knew* I read that look on your face!" she said, her voice hardening, her teasing manner disappearing in a jealous huff that amused Aaron and shocked and infuriated Louisa. She turned her back on him abruptly, seeking her cloak which had been carefully replaced in the wardrobe. When she faced him again, Louisa found she hadn't yet shrugged off her sudden, deeply possessive feelings, or her longing for Aaron's exclusive interest in her. She recalled those same feelings from Marshall's association with Janna Carson, but, then she reasoned, she'd had the right of possession. Now, Louisa realized she had no rights, not even those formalized in their legal union, but she could not deny how she felt, nor the strength of her emotion. And when he approached her again as they were leaving the room, caressing, teasing, tormenting, Louisa briefly yielded to him with a fierceness neither could believe, and both were resentful of the events that kept them from each other's arms.

Chapter Forty-five

THE countryside William showed them was exhilarating, the contrasts of forest, meadow, streams, soaring cliffs, and sheltered beaches easing the disappointments of the day. Louisa even joyfully planned excursions of her own into these wondrous regions, soon expecting to have more time to herself than she would really like. With Franklin Carson's arrival, she focused on the politics of their journey to Monterey, and she could foresee many solitary hours. She glanced frequently at Aaron, who, as often as not, met her stares filled with anticipation for the evening before them. His eyes wandered over her, lingering at her breasts which, with her cape thrown back in the temperate air, her soft challis gown pleasingly accentuated. She watched his open gaze drift to her hips and down her belly to her thighs, and she knew, well enough, his thoughts were of the promising warmth sheltered there.

Easton rambled endlessly on, providing them, in spite of himself, with interesting information about the flora and fauna, knowledge which Louisa never suspected he would have, until she recalled the impressive greenhouse she had browsed in early that morning. When they returned to the house, another feast awaited them, and this time even Louisa's appetite did justice to the lavish fare. Franklin Carson joined them, emerging earlier than expected, hands full of documents and letters to which he insisted William give his immediate attention.

Louisa and Aaron lingered at the table briefly, then relaxed in silence on the terrace underneath the balcony which extended from their own room. When it became apparent Easton and Carson would be occupied for some length of time, Louisa and Aaron's lack of conversation turned to smiles, and to giggles on Louisa's part. "I blame it on the wine," she said, meeting Aaron's unmistakable look of lust with gales of helpless laughter. "And to the fact that I *am* exhausted."

"And a little rest might revive you?" he grinned, standing to escort her.

"I've no doubt about it," she replied knowingly. "Would you care to assist me up the stairs?" The assignation made, they moved quietly into the house and slowly climbed the long graceful staircase, arm in arm, seemingly alone, little by little drawing ever more closely together.

"Who else that I already know will be coming here?" she whispered, sheltered by his arm held around her tightly.

His reply was hushed. "Probably Peter Melville is the only other person you know. He's the third member of the financial and political hierarchy—Carson and Simon being the other two. Easton is a puppet monarch, to be tolerated only as long as his presence is useful. Melville is the most ruthless of the three." He stopped when they reached their door, and when it was closed securely behind them, Aaron released Louisa from his comforting grasp and walked thoughtfully by himself to the balcony windows. He drew the sheer draperies aside, his legs spread, arms raised, reaching out, leaning his body against the wooden frame. He was silent for some minutes. Louisa remained near the doorway where he had left her side. She was mildly surprised by his change of mood as she watched his pensive, almost sad figure bending before the bright glassed door. His lean powerful body, now accented in the sunlight, made her extremely aware of her own eager body. She had expected to find this man ready for an energetic, not very restful afternoon, but instead, when he turned to face her, she saw only weariness and tension. A responsive apprehension filled her as they moved wordlessly toward each other, meeting at the center of the room, not touching, both wondering

what lay within the other's mind, their earlier careless
mood dispelled.

"I feel I must warn you about the distinguished
Peter Melville. *Never* trust him for an instant; *never*
turn your back to him." His look was tender, protective; his voice hard, threatening. He stared at her flaw-
less skin, her intensely blue eyes surrounded by thick
dark lashes, at the sensuous, promising mouth, reminding himself the woman before him was a mixture
of strength and vulnerability.

Louisa did not interrupt him, watching as his eyes
drifted over her face, then thoughtfully, rather than
erotically, gazed at her body. He brought his hands to
her waist, casually encasing her slimness in the expanse of his grip, tightening his hold briefly, then releasing her. "Melville is responsible for Marshall's
murder—at least, for the order. He's the man we'll
have to reckon with." His words were cold, precise,
and after they were uttered, he was silent and the
abrupt stillness in the room rushed over them in
waves.

Aaron gave Louisa no opportunity to react, his
shifting moods holding her full attention. He now
stared mutely at the flowers in her dress, in no way
responsive to the shock she registered at his words.
His gaze was fixed intently, almost quizzically. Then,
as if he'd suddenly remembered something—someone
—important, something he'd almost forgotten, he
reached to touch the fabric of her gown. Slowly he
began to trace an oddly familiar trail of small ice-blue
bouquets from the high throat of the dress, down her
breast, then along the placket of buttons, his fingers
stopping just below her waist. His gentle touch made
Louisa's pulse quicken and made her dress feel unbearably warm.

The dress had no collar, its modest design softened
by crisp ribbons of narrow lace edging her throat, the
round neckline descending only far enough to expose
the slight natural depression at the base of her throat.
She saw something glint in Aaron's dark eyes as he
moved his hand into the lace, carefully grasping the
nearly hidden loops of a golden chain lying concealed

beneath her dress. He looked at Louisa strangely, then suddenly let go of the chain, raising his hands to her hair, unpinning the careful curls and braided twists, scattering the fragrant garland of flowers he'd arranged there earlier. Louisa began to help, moving as if directed by his command, but none was given, though she listened, hearing nothing but his breathing, which, at times, almost seemed to stop. She was caught up in the longing she saw in his eyes, and by the grimace of agony she saw pass over his face. He was tensely absorbed in taking in the fragile beauty of the woman he caressed, yet he seemed not to see her. "What is it, Aaron?" she whispered, but he did not answer, for, in fact, he did not hear her.

When her hair was loose, and he had his fill of its softness, he undid the strand of buttons on the front of her dress only far enough to make his access to the necklace easy. He removed the heavy chain from the recesses of her bodice. Its ornaments were warm from the heat of her body as he held them in his hand. "Somehow, these don't seem to belong to you —perhaps, on another chain . . ." He lifted the necklace over her head, catching it tightly in one of his hands, pushing the other into the thick mass of her hair, forcefully drawing her against him, bringing his hungry mouth to hers, lowering them into the bed. He let the chain fall beside them, turning his full attention to his growing passion to consume her, and to his own need to be consumed.

His breathing was ragged, his desire for her as great as it had ever been, and Louisa responded in kind. They undressed each other, touching, searching joyfully along paths of pleasure, losing all touch with reality. Soon their cries were primitive and unrestrained, like the fire that raged inside them, with little tenderness in their embracing. Their joining was wild and fevered, easing what soared between them for the moment only, and for both, a disturbing hunger persisted. Neither would release the other, each coming into the atmosphere of full consciousness only for as long as was necessary before diving again into the warm, reassuring sea, hastening to submerge from all but the other's reach. They devoured each other with kisses, their fervor slowly turning gentle, soothing, giving. But all too soon, Louisa watched that same dark sadness cross Aaron's wonderful face, and his voice again filled more with the sound of agony than with ecstasy, frightening her, bringing up her own pain. "Aaron, Aaron," she called urgently, trying to reach him. "Tell me!"

But he did not even hear her. Desperately, she tried to soothe him, but he was too distant, and Louisa was overcome with loneliness. She cried out to him, kissed and petted him, her mouth soft, wet, exciting on his body. Slowly, she turned over in his embrace, inviting him, and he thrust eagerly into her consoling vibrating warmth, moving steadily, fiercely, her own motions driving him more deeply into her. And, suddenly, against her cries of pleasure, in the midst of their heat and rhythm, Aaron was at last released to her, with her name on his lips, and in his heart, as well.

Then he lay against her, their bodies still joined, both reluctant to be separate again. Aaron felt as if they had united with his love spoken out loud, and when she turned to face him, she held him fast in her arms. "So you have ghosts, too," she said quietly.

He watched her, loving the soft, giving look of her. "A few," he replied gently, "but they rarely come out of the dark."

"Mine have been instructed to stay there, too," she insisted emphatically. Then she shuddered and quickly nestled into him as if she were frightened.

"Good luck," he sighed, kissing her deeply, and they both relaxed, their thoughts drifting separately, aimlessly, in the afternoon. Then he slapped her soundly on the backside, changing the mood intentionally. "You'd better dress, unless you want Easton to do more than leer. It's teatime, beautiful—but wear something a little more fetching." He motioned to her blue-flowered gown, now crumpled on the floor. "I don't care for that dress at all."

"You could have fooled me!" she winced, reaching

to rub his already visible red handprint on her skin. She got up, collecting their garments strewn about the bed and the floor. When she again turned her attention to Aaron, she found him examining the gold necklace he'd taken from her throat, and she reached out for it. "I've never really cared for it," she said pensively, turning the locket and ring over in her fingers, "but Marshall gave it to me—probably on the night I conceived Rachel," and she glanced away, her words falling on him unobserved.

Aaron merely smiled and propped himself up against the pillows, crossing his arms behind his head, and watched leisurely while Louisa arranged her hair and covered her wonderful body with a flattering, even seductive dress. Filling the role to perfect order, he thought. She was clever, he mused, intuitively so, and he wondered, almost absently, if she suspected him as the father of her child, or if she were only beginning to fit the pieces together. He had realized the possibility, even preferred to believe it was he who had filled her body with new life, finding it in no way changed his course. He believed the chance would only work to his advantage, should she ever take that night from out of her memories.

Chapter Forty-six

⟡ OVER the next week, the activity at Crane's Nest increased dramatically. Callers arrived from midmorning until late in the afternoon. Easton's time became less and less his own as the days passed. At first the intrusion on his privacy seemed to affect his usually polite temperament. But as the week wore on William's courtly manners reappeared, and he seemed at ease again. A few guests arrived and took up residence within the estate; others found quarters in Monterey. And finally, on the morning of the gala dinner William had planned for Aaron and Louisa's formal introduction to the emerging political society, Peter Ulysses Melville and his wife arrived.

The event was not observed by either Aaron or Louisa, for they were occupied, as far as everyone else was concerned, in a pleasant outing with Samuel as guide. In fact, during the days they mingled very little with the few other houseguests, except at dinner which served to advance Marshall's changed political position, the evenings often turning into heated diatribes against pro-Union thought. No dissenting opinions were offered at these times—though the opposition's tactics and philosophy were debated between the serious planners on other occasions.

On these evenings, Louisa was a glittering decoration amidst the men. In this era of California's rapid expansion and exploitation, not only were the numbers of women very limited, but a woman of her elegance and beauty was truly exceptional. There were hundreds of men for every woman in the state, and even the eyes of men of wealth and significance betrayed them. She felt relatively secure, her status as the wife of a soon-to-be-prominent aristocrat allowing her the freedom to amuse herself as a temptress—a role she hadn't played before any large audience for sometime. Louisa soon realized she could tease and torment all she pleased, and retreat whenever it suited her—games to play when she got bored—and, oh, what boring times she anticipated in the company of the men who sat and plotted at Easton's table.

Aaron was occupied with his political role, only occasionally looking to her, but careful for those present to note his adoration, his devotion, his obsession. It was she who had brought him here, his responsibility to her that enlightened his philosophical leanings, the fruit of their union which made him reconsider the future of his world—and of his fortune. And the others envied him and coveted Louisa, their respect for his capture of such a prize raising him in their esteem. The rumors of their affair, its duration, its ocean- and continent-spanning episodes titillated most, as did the looks and gestures of the couple. The show was made, and the audience was responsive.

While Louisa mingled with these men, she could not help but overhear and eventually listen to their more serious discussions. And gradually the years of inattention to intellectual matters, especially to politics, began to come to an end. Her natural curiosity, her early training with good tutors—the same who helped shape Marshall's and, for a time, Andrew's minds—began to rise to the surface. She flirted safely before her admirers, *and* she listened and learned, finding her brain engaged again, though she was unable to publicly question the ideas she heard. These were not evenings to exchange ideas, or broaden thinking. It was a time of monologue.

Her hours alone with Aaron were scarce enough, for even on their excursions with only Samuel in attendance, strategic information was passed between the men, with little opportunity for discussion of concepts she now wanted to pursue for the sake of expanding her own range of knowledge. And when she found herself alone with Aaron, he had had his fill of politics, and she, too, had little inclination to rehash the endless words, happy to engage in other pleasures in their private moments together.

Her flirtations with those other men were not regarded seriously by Aaron, not seen by him as any sort of threat. She was, after all, meeting the obligations of her role. But he was not yet immune to her. He was confident her responses to him sprang from her deepest feelings, that for her no affair could ever be truly casual, but he wondered why she gave herself to him so openly, so freely. She must somewhere still be confusing him with Marshall—as she did on that night long ago. That had to be an answer. What else could explain her passion? She was a prize—he had only to look up in Easton's salon, and be reminded just how precious a jewel she was. Even those men of wealth and prominence in the company found her alluring, and few, if any, of them would disdain possession of her. Her loyalties to Marshall's memory explained most of her cooperation, he thought, though she was a creature of the flesh, something he knew better than any man alive. These were the explanations that seemed logical to him in those moments that required logic, and he remained uneasy in the wake of his own passion.

The afternoon before Easton's carefully arranged festivities, Louisa indulged herself in leisurely preparation for the evening. Bathing seemed to be an art form in this house with its enormous sunken tubs made of lustrous enameled tiles, in rooms where the air was thick with steam and heavy with the aroma of eucalyptus. Today she was attended by Loo Kim, and Louisa wondered how William did without her, for Louisa seemed to be taking more and more of the girl's time.

Often, without much trouble, Louisa lured Aaron into the water with her, where, time and inclination allowing, they seemed to do most of their conversing. But this afternoon, Louisa was alone with Loo Kim hovering about. After a splendid soak and a soothing massage from the young servant, whose abilities seemed unending, Louisa wanted to know more of the girl and began to question her, knowing with reasonable assurance that Loo Kim would not dare refuse to answer.

Louisa sat, wound comfortably in a towel while the maid dried and prepared her hair, watching Loo Kim's activity from the mirror. "I'm very impressed with you," she began. "Mr. Easton is very lucky to have you in the house."

Loo Kim responded with a slight bow, her hands busy with the dark golden tangles of Louisa's mane. "Please tell me how you came to be employed here—perhaps I could steal you from him?" she smiled.

Loo Kim smiled gently, never ceasing her work. "I do not think so, madam. Oh, but, of course, you may inquire," she added hesitantly. "Mr. Easton bought my contract from Su Ling, and I am bound to him for a very long time."

"What do you mean, he bought your contract?"

Loo Kim's voice was always quietly restrained, but now her voice was hushed to the point of being nearly inaudible. Yet, she was careful to see that Louisa heard and understood every word, and it was as if these two were the real conspirators in the house. "In my country there is great poverty and hunger. It is not unusual, almost customary, for female children of promise to be sold for a sum of money—it is necessary, you must understand. Some of us are even lucky enough to come here to California as I did. We sell out labor for a time, and then, sometimes—if one is lucky—we are free to go home."

"Is that what you want to do, Loo Kim? Go home to China?"

"Oh, yes, and see my family."

"The family that sold you?" Louisa found it hard to believe.

"They had no choice. I am sorry if I am unable to make you understand my words. I have tried very hard to learn your language."

"Oh, you've learned very well, Loo Kim."

"It is a great honor and hope to be with Mr. Easton, madam. I am treated very well. I would not have so much hope if I had stayed with Su Ling."

"Why not?"

"I would have been just another girl, perhaps."

"I doubt you'd have been just another girl." Louisa laughed softly. "If so, my white sisters would find some way to see that your sisters were not imported, or, at least, not brought into their households."

"Oh, most of us do not work as house servants!"

"Oh? —Oh!" Louisa colored at her own simplicity. "I see," she said quietly, an old anger smoldering as she reflected on Loo Kim's status.

Loo Kim heard the anger and worried that it was meant for her. "I am sorry to offend you, madam."

"You do not in the least way offend me, Loo Kim," Louisa answered kindly. "I understand only too well what your position is," her voice now cold.

But Loo Kim was confused by Louisa's altering emotions, and she hastened to make her understand. "If I had stayed in Su Ling's house, I was bound to seven years' contract. I am bound that many years to Mr. Easton. But in the cribs, I would be allowed one day off each month, but for every day I do not work, ten days is added to a contract, and there would be little hope. But, here, it does not seem to matter, I can work every day, and I have not been sick. It would not be so easy to stay well in the cribs."

"I can just imagine!" was Louisa's startled response.

"Most of the girls die before their contracts are up—but, even so, it would not be any better at home —perhaps they would not even live so long. I am very lucky I am in this house."

"I guess you are, at that," replied Louisa, beginning to comprehend the girl's devotion to William, as odd as Louisa thought he was. "How old are you, Loo Kim?" she wondered suddenly.

"You would say fifteen."

"I would say—nothing," finding it hard to believe. Louisa looked at Loo Kim gently, trying not to frighten her, knowing her emotions were confusing the girl. She would have guessed they were the same age, but Loo Kim had a timelessly beautiful face, seeming both childish and worldly—which surely she must be, thought Louisa. Then she looked at her

own beautiful face in the mirror. She stared long
and deeply, concluding that although she had long
ago relinquished her childhood, she too had some
of the same look about her, and she felt a bond to the
girl which Loo Kim never suspected.

Louisa was left alone for a few minutes while the
maid sought a tea tray. While she was gone, Aaron
came into their room, and when he reached to draw
her fragrant soft body against him for a brief moment,
he was greeted with a stiffness he knew he didn't deserve.

"Hey, what's this reception?"

Louisa was in a definite huff. "Oh, I've just been
talking with Loo Kim," she announced distractedly.

"Then I suggest you not talk to her anymore," he
said, whisking the towel from her body, instantly
leaving her naked for his perusal. But in her frame
of mind, it was the last thing he should have done.

"Give that to me!" she snapped, grasping furiously for the towel, which he threw at her.

"I hope your temper improves a little by this evening, honey," he said sarcastically, sitting heavily
in a large, cushioned chair, beginning to remove his
boots. "This is *the* night we've been waiting for all
these weeks, and in some respects, all these months.
Need I speak to Easton? Should I tell him his servant
is upsetting you?" he asked harshly.

"Don't you dare!" she flashed.

"Well, then, what in hell is the matter with you?
—It doesn't matter," he waved at her wearily, "just
behave yourself tonight, is all I ask." And he flung
his boots and gloves into a corner, and they looked
at each other sullenly for a few minutes, until Louisa
smiled, rushing to him, kneeling between his legs,
stretching herself against him comfortably. He closed
his legs and his arms around her, this time finding his
reception more to his liking. "You feel like satin,"
he sighed, stroking her, "wonderful, soft satin," kissing her mouth, pulling her even closer. "Care for another bath?"

"It would spoil my hair, if I know you!"

"You're right. Just don't bother dressing—unless

you don't mind taking off your clothes again." He smiled, easily raising them both from the chair, beginning to remove his own clothing.

Aaron had disrobed when Loo Kim returned, and, to Louisa's shock, he made no effort to conceal his nakedness, even though her entry was announced before she came into the room. Aaron seemed not to notice, and neither did the servant, but Louisa blushed for both of them, very relieved when Aaron disappeared into the bath. She soon dismissed the girl, thinking wickedly Aaron might not bother with even that formality when he came back with only one thing on his mind.

She ate and drank from the tray that had just arrived, then wound her untangled, but not yet arranged hair into another towel, piling it into a turban on her head. She entered the steamy bathroom and sat on the floor above Aaron. "Why didn't you tell me about Loo Kim? *You* knew she was more than just a simple servant."

"Anyone could guess that by looking at her. There aren't many 'simple servants' that look like she does— even at home—if you'll recall," he said, submerging into the superheated water for an instant.

"Well, Easton has a better eye for women than I'd heard."

"There's nothing wrong with his eyes, that's for sure. Nor with mine," he said, rising from the tub, toweling quickly, seeking what promised to be more than an afternoon of idle conversation.

Chapter Forty-seven

THE guests began to gather early, daylight extending late into the evening. Aaron had entered the party some time before Louisa came down, and when she stood preparing to descend the now seemingly precipitous staircase, in yards of billowing skirts, she could hear the usually quiet house resonant with deep, forceful voices. She listened briefly, hearing echoes, thinking they might have come from the past when, as a child, she would perch above her father's entertainments, those occasions also having a purpose, always a means to an end. She remembered Momma—the glittering ornament—and Louisa felt herself pale. "I follow in your footsteps," she murmured. "But not forever," she vowed, beginning her descent.

Servants at the ballroom doors bowed, and she entered quietly into the collection of men, who momentarily seemed intent on their conversations. The room was crowded, the lamps not yet raised, dusk only beginning to settle, and for a moment, Louisa stood motionless and unnoticed, framed in the now closed doorway. Slowly, eyes began to turn to her, and she appeared as another of Easton's priceless paintings, a portrait—classic, perfect woman—the dimness of the room only illuminating her beauty. One by one, conversations dropped off, and soon Easton was at her side, with Aaron close behind. Her effect on the gathering was just as she had planned, her success evident even in Aaron's eyes. The emerald collar alone captured everyone's attention with its alluring plunge into her cleavage. The men in her presence were neither immune to her—nor to the value of the jewels at her throat.

As she watched the gathering admire her, Louisa
noted she would have her share of amusement this
evening, suspecting her audience was already anxiously considering the skill of her dressmaker. She had
never before worn the gown, though it had been made
for her when she was in Paris, and she had declined
for the very reasons she now wore it. Though the dress
was carefully made and very secure on her body, the
absence of straps to support its incredibly shallow bodice would render almost anyone to speculate on and
watch for her fate through the night. The shimmering
ivory satin fabric caught the essence of the now raised
lamplight, and as Louisa moved for introductions into
the small clusters of elegant but darkly clad men, the
contrast of light and dark at once softened the décol-
letage, and made her even more compelling. For her
audience she appeared both daring and vulnerable.

Her host was delighted with her, feeling as if she
were somehow an extension of his own splendid
surroundings, and thereby a credit to himself. He
thoroughly enjoyed circulating among his guests to introduce her, even if his remarks did have to include
the handsome husband at her side. She met senators
and bankers, ranchers and businessmen, mining czars
and professional men, and slowly conversations resumed, but the tone was more subdued, and the assem-
bly proceeded to take its cue from her. Soon most of
the others had arrived. A few men escorted their wives
or other women, and what easily could have been another political gathering took on the aspects of a pleasant social function.

Franklin Carson made a point to spend a few moments with Louisa, candidly admiring her appearance.
"At least my eyes didn't fail me on the crossing!" he
sighed. "It would have been a pity to miss such a
sight," he beamed at her. "My regard for Marshall's
intellect increases measurably every day," he sighed
with his eyes fixed on the enormous solitary emerald
nestled pleasantly between her curving breasts. Louisa
sipped champagne and giggled at him almost conspira-
torially as he took her arm and whispered, "As Janna's
father, it may seem traitorous, but from what I've seen,

Marshall would have been a sap to marry her and
abandon you. In fact, I can't imagine whatever possessed him to think of it." And he left her side to seek
another drink, one which, even this early in the evening, he could scarcely use. Louisa suspected if he
often drank so heavily, in addition to his continuing
malaise from recent travels, his usefulness to the operation at hand would be severely limited.

She watched the other guests arrive, most interested
in the women, finding each had an enthusiastic reception in the woman-hungry group of men. None, however, was quite as spectacular as she. The one who
came the closest to her radiance, even in her own estimation, was Marguerite Augusta Hill, the wife of
Colonel Philip Hill, assistant to the United States'
Commandant of the Pacific, a man whose knowledge
was precious to the planners, and whose honor was
respected among his peers, his true nature not yet fully
revealed.

Marguerite and Louisa were both undeniably beautiful women, yet a very pleasing contrast for the eye.
Marguerite's skin was fairer than Louisa's, creamy
white beneath a rosy glow, fragile but exuding health.
Her smoky dark brown hair with short wisps of curls
framing her face balanced a heavy twisted knot of luxurious hair laced with pearls and pinned at the back of
her head. Thick black lashes and delicately curved
brows enhanced her pale, wide aquamarine eyes,
which, as Louisa noted, seemed to have a quizzical
look, a look that suggested the need for a response
—and the room was filled with answers to any questions she might have, Louisa smirked to herself when
she paused to assess her only real rival of the night.

Marguerite was dressed simply but effectively in a
silk gown the same color as her eyes, the design without affectation, covering her promising and sensuous
body without concealment of any curve. A long rope
of baroque pearls did nothing to hide the deep V of
the dress's neckline nor obscure her shapely full
breasts, and, in its way, the design of the gown was as
bold as Louisa's. Marguerite's movements were fluid
and politely suggestive. She was neither plump nor

slender, with a conflicting aura of maternal woman's knowledge and virginal innocence, and Louisa was certain she escaped the contemplation of few, if any, of the men in the room—including Aaron. And Marguerite was frankly curious about her only apparent competition, seeking Louisa out, her soft, husky voice requiring the listener to strain slightly to hear her words.

"We've been so anxious to meet you and your husband," she said warmly, gesturing in Aaron's direction. When Louisa's eyes followed, she saw Aaron watching the woman with a pleasant, thoughtful look on his face. He smiled broadly at the two when he found their eyes on him. Marguerite gave him a cheerful nod, then turned her attention back to Louisa. "Peter expects you to come to live in San Francisco with the rest of us."

"We've settled in San Diego, but, perhaps, not for long," Louisa replied, then glanced around the room. "I've not seen Peter for a number of years, and I'm looking forward to seeing him again. What delays him tonight—have you any idea?"

"Oh, he never arrives promptly. I don't think I've ever been to a party where he was not the last to arrive. It's very annoying if you're the hostess, but his eventual presence always seems to make up for his tardiness—at least it always has for me." And Louisa wondered if there was anything to the flicker she saw in Marguerite's eyes.

Her recollection of Peter Melville was not good. She'd seen him frequently in her father's house over the years, but she'd never had any opportunity for any real contact with the man. She really knew him by reputation only. Like his partners, he was enormously wealthy and influential. At one time he had considered high political office, soon finding his taste was more for manipulation than performance as a public figure. He preferred the rewards of power over its outward manifestations. She knew also, from Aaron's remarks, that he was dangerous, not to be taken lightly. For a moment, Louisa felt afraid, more for Aaron than for herself, because her losses to the man's authority were already more than she could comprehend.

Louisa's musings were brief, as suddenly Marguerite and Louisa's attention was distracted by the addition of music to the sounds in the room. Over the rumble of conversation and laughter came chords of music from a piano. The notes lifted Louisa's spirits from the edges of her memories, and from the tight grip of grief threatening to take her in hand. When she looked in the direction of the music, she found a screen that held a rich medieval tapestry moved aside, and behind it sat a piano whose keys were played as if the musician were merely a working part of the instrument. He played beautifully, effortlessly, and the music captured Louisa's heart. She looked to Easton as if he were a magician, her look of astonishment and appreciation gratifying him. In her excitement, Louisa moved quickly toward him in a spontaneous gesture of gratitude. "Oh, where did he come from? And why haven't you paraded him for my pleasure before this?" she demanded, teasingly but sincerely.

"I would have, if I'd been able, you can be sure. But even I cannot have *everything* I want," he replied pleasantly. "Yet, a little pressure applied in the right circumstances usually works. People rarely say no to Peter Melville."

"He's that influential? I *am* impressed."

"The pianist is not always up to performing. It seems he came out here along with the others to make his fortune in the gold fields, and along with many, found it was more work than he cared for. Can you imagine, Louisa, some assumed fortunes in gold were lying about for the taking."

"There are a lot of things I find hard to believe." Louisa smiled at him innocently, putting her arm on his, strolling with him to stand by the piano.

"Our musician now practices his art in San Francisco, often for Peter's enjoyment, and, sometimes, in lesser places of music." He made other remarks but she barely heard, being taken so suddenly and completely with the strains of melodies she had not heard for far too long. But when Easton left her side to greet

latecomers, she could not disregard Aaron's hands as
they came around her waist, pulling her briefly against
him. Aaron was impossible to ignore for long that evening, his clothes cut perfectly for his tall magnificent
body. Even in this group of carefully groomed, stylish
men, he was outstanding, the rich deep black fabric of
his frock coat and trousers sharply contrasting the
shock of a pure white, fashionably ruffled shirt. He
looked born to this style of dress. No one, save Marshall himself, could look more comfortable, Louisa
mused as she gazed happily at this darkly handsome
man who devoured her with undeniable hunger in his
wonderful eyes. When the light was as it was this instant, the pupils of Aaron's eyes were enormous, their
color more black than brown, and the intensity of his
look electrified her and made her pulse seem to stop.
His gaze seemed to penetrate to her very soul, to pull
her away from herself and into his domain. Under
his magnetic stare, she felt she would do whatever he
might command. Yet she composed herself and spoke
to him lightheartedly, as if he had no effect on her.
"Isn't this a wonderful surprise? Can you believe
you're hearing such music here in this wilderness?"

"You're the best surprise of the night!" he whispered. "What keeps you decent?"

She tossed her head back and laughed at him.
"Something you and nearly everyone else in this house
wants to know!" she said, sipping enthusiastically from
another glass of champagne. "I'm beginning to get
giddy. How long do you suppose it will be before dinner?"

Aaron frowned slightly. "We're waiting on Melville.
He runs the operation, on this front at least, and he
doesn't bother to wait on others. He lets everyone else
wait on him. But the senators are here, so 'His Emi-
nence' won't be long now," he said under his breath.
"Tonight Easton's table will be graced with men from
both sides of the aisle, but most have strong sympathies
for our grand scheme. The only real exception is Ellis
Crawford, and he is, first of all, a politician, and per-
suadable—perhaps. 'We' are treading around him
carefully. He's in camp tonight for wooing. By the way,

Chapter Forty-eight

In appearance Peter and Arabella Melville were the cream of Southern gentility. Those standing superficially on the sidelines would admire them, wish for the same existence, and be grateful society had such models. "A fine Christian man," it was said, "an exemplary citizen," much honored and much respected. And Arabella Melville was probably all of the things her husband was not, according to Louisa's scant information: fine and honorable, but dreadfully, purposefully ignorant of her husband's real motives and inclinations. Both were of stoutest Southern conviction, but politics were not even a peripheral interest of Mrs. Melville. Her duties lay in the management of the home, in total subjugation to her husband, having relinquished her rights in deference to him. Truth became whatever "Mr. Melville" said it was, if there was even an occasion to ask. And if his interest lay in other beds, it was easier not to see, than to question his authority, or his right.

Mr. and Mrs. Melville quickly greeted most of the congregation familiarly, and hastened to become better acquainted with the young Hudson couple. Soon the guests were summoned to dinner, Peter Melville seated between Louisa and Aaron. He did not hesitate to take full advantage of his view of her, nor, despite the distraction, did he fail to draw out Marshall Hudson on the subjects of politics and ethics, and the probable future of the world if the government in Washington should pursue the economics of federal supremacy over its sovereign states.

As expected, no detail, no expense was spared at Easton's table. William Easton outdid himself, and his hospitality was greatly appreciated. They dined in the room with mirrored walls, and it seemed to Louisa the greenhouse must have been emptied and its plants moved to the house for this occasion. The tables were set with gold service, strewn with flowers, and lit with gracefully tapered candles set in golden candelabra. The scene was resplendent, its opulence, and the luxury of the plants, magnified in effect by the shining mirrors. The meal was long, and many of the guests, though gratified by its sumptuous presentation, were more than ready to adjourn to deeper after-dinner conversations and lighter pastimes, keeping the few women present well occupied in dancing to the rare musical accompaniment.

Louisa scarcely had a moment to herself, which was also the fate of the other women. When she charmingly begged for a rest, she was not rescued by Aaron as she had hoped. She wanted to ask him about some of the men with whom she danced, or, in some instances, inquire more about the men who had stepped heavily on her feet in clumsy imitation of dancing. Through it all, though, she was dazzling, and if Aaron's acceptance was to be scored on her behavior, not a vote would have gone against him.

Instinctively, Louisa seemed to know who the more important men in the collection were. She met the five senators and the others, all of her senses keen to what each man wanted to find in her, treading carefully, surefootedly, being demure, or clever, or intelligent, or bewitching, whatever the customer wanted. "Have I missed my calling?" she remarked snidely to Aaron in a brief moment of privacy, one she arranged for them to have in the evening that went on and on. He only smiled and quickly escorted her into the surprisingly mild night. Other guests had also escaped the crush, and were conferring on the pleasant, lantern-lit terrace. Aaron took her hand and they walked into the moonlit grounds for a few moments of seclusion. "I don't think you have a prayer of a chance to convert Crawford to 'the cause,' " she began in a hushed voice. "He's a man of the people—and aspires for nothing more than their approbation. He definitely doesn't

want a place among the likes of William Easton." She
paused to evaluate the men she'd so recently met. "I
think Taylor is your best bet: he has schemes of his
own, and belongs among the vain and powerful. He
even looks like he belongs at court with the rest of
them. Isn't he from Mississippi?"

"You've been busier than I'd suspected. It seems to
me, though, you'd have no time to consider anything
but keeping your dress up to accepted levels of mod-
esty."

"*Stop it* and listen to me—answer my questions for
once!" she demanded, pushing away his probing
hands.

He accepted her rebuff, knowing he could not now
afford to consider her charms seriously. "You've as-
sessed the situation remarkably well, Louisa. Tonight
the herd is being thinned, and I imagine Crawford is
out. And if I read Melville correctly, I'm sure we're
in. My performance is very good—don't you think?
I'd have gotten on without you, in the long run," he
teased, "but you're blinding them to any flaws I might
have. Even Melville would vouch for me based on
your assets—and your potential. Don't be surprised if
he asks for a few of your sweet favors."

"Mmmm. He'll just have to go away empty-
handed," she said without hesitation. "But perhaps
Mrs. Hill will oblige him."

"He's interested in a new conquest, and for him,
Mrs. Hill is old, very familiar territory."

"I thought so," she purred with feline satisfaction.

They had walked far enough into the still woods to
be quite alone. Aaron stopped, and turned to Louisa,
taking her in his arms, gently seizing a fleeting moment which came quietly on them. The tension of the
evening, the teasing, the flirtations evaporated for an
instant, and they embraced as the loving couple they
pretended to be. There was a strange absence of the
soaring passion that so often swept them away, and
only an odd, piercing warmth flowed gently between
the two. Aaron's mouth was warm, the taste of him
good and fulfilling, and he savored her in every sense.
The touching was brief, yet the feeling haunted them

both, even in the din where they returned to resume
their acting. Whenever they caught the other's eye, the
looks they exchanged were soft and loving, and, just
before the evening drew to a close, Aaron claimed his
wife, holding her surely in his arms to dance before
the company. There were other couples on the floor,
but all spectators' eyes were on the powerful, lithe,
and unquestionably male animal who held his delicate, worshipping prey easily, but firmly, in his hands.
And a few saw that what they did, in their polite acceptable motions, was make love to each other, the
two actors on the stage forgetting they were only playing a game, or that their bond was only a loosely woven
web. The music seemed to be only for their ears, and
the late hour, the wine, the success of the charade
climaxed in their movements. They had no sense of
time or place or others, and, for the seemingly few
bars of music, they were totally alone, of one body
and one spirit.

Chapter Forty-nine

"MARSHALL, Louisa could be of great assistance to me, if you don't mind," William Easton suggested brusquely after an annoying interruption during a meeting he and Aaron were having with Melville and Carson.

"Oh? What can she do for you?"

"I'm expecting a man to arrive here shortly to assume duties as my secretary and aide, but in the meantime, I cannot keep up with supervising the affairs of this house and with my growing correspondence," he said impatiently. "I must concentrate on more important matters. The man has been delayed, I suspect through no fault of his own. Your father is sending him with his recommendations. In fact, I imagine he and your mother are traveling together."

"I'm sure Louisa will welcome the diversion. She'll do whatever she can to lighten your burden." Aaron was certain Louisa would relish the opportunity. With Peter Melville's arrival the signal had been given at Crane's Nest. He, Franklin Carson, and Simon's proxy in the form of his son Marshall, were aligned, and under the guise of pleasure and relaxation, formal plans began to take final shape. Carson and Melville conferred at all hours of the day and night, with Marshall included in the discussions with increasing frequency. But Easton was kept busy more with domestic considerations than with affairs of state, a condition he remedied by approaching Louisa through Aaron.

And she was delighted, hoping the tasks would at least prove to be distracting if not informative. "I gladly accept!" she said enthusiastically when Aaron brought up Easton's offer. "Just think—a chance to be something more than an ornament—something to do besides *just* warm your bed."

"If you perform as well for Easton as you do for me, you may have a permanent appointment with the new regime. Would you like that? Now I've been taken into the fold—I'm sure I can arrange it. Your title could be Mistress of State!"

"Very amusing. And what will you be? Court Jester?" she laughed at him and at her own joke.

"Let's see if I can make you laugh now," he said, grabbing her, throwing her onto the bed playfully, tickling and teasing her until she was helpless and begging for him to stop. And when he did she lay exhaustedly against him, snuggling happily.

"We haven't had much time to ourselves these last few days—or nights," she mused, kissing him lightly. "By the time the night ends we collapse with fatigue and nerves—I think I'll complain to William. He ought to be treating his guests with more courtesy, don't you think, Marshall, love?"

"Well, now you're in charge of seeing to the comfort of his guests—but you needn't extend yourself too generously," he cautioned, pretending to take a generous bite of one of her breasts.

"Why, I thought you wanted me to give my favors wherever they might do the most good? You never know when a kindness might pay off, isn't that how it goes in politics?"

"You're catching on, Louisa. Perhaps a little too quickly. Remember you don't want to be too generous —the rule is, a few promises, but you try to keep from having to pay off—keeps the treasury flush."

"Let's see if I can remember that." She closed her eyes tightly, pretending to memorize this code of ethics. "Promises only; no payoffs."

"Got it!" he laughed at her. "Hey, where do you think you're going?" he demanded harshly, catching the hem of her skirt as she leapt from the bed.

"Why, I'm putting your words of wisdom into practice. Promises only—for *all* customers. Fair's fair!"

"Doesn't apply to your mentor, honey," he said, leaping on her, finding she wasn't in the mood for much of a struggle, so it was a race to see who could cast aside their clothes more quickly.

"Not fair!" she insisted, still tangled in petticoats while he waited for her smugly on the bed. But when she'd lost the contest, Louisa took her sweet time, he noted, teasing him with gradual exposure of her sleek beautiful body. And when she was fully naked in the streaming rays of early-afternoon sun, her skin glistening lightly, her perfume heavy in the air, she stood motionless, waiting, contemplating. And Aaron waited for her.

Finally she pulled the pins from her hair, letting it tumble wildly as she shook her head, the flying curls shining like spun gold in the sunlight. And still she stood before him, realizing, as she looked at him, that she loved every part of him—the taste, the scent, the look, the feel, the sounds of his voice when he made love to her. She had no recollection of ever being quite so overwhelmed; there was no memory of quite this kind of feeling. She'd loved before—oh, yes! But this yearning for Aaron went beyond what she'd known— these feelings for Aaron were fierce, consuming passions which made her confront emotions she would have said were alien to her. But gnawing at the edge of her passion was an unnamed fear, which, for now, she tossed aside as easily as she did her gown, succumbing to more enticing sensations. She found it a joy merely to fill her eyes with the sight of his lean, hard male body. And when she went to him and touched him, she could not imagine the act gave him any more pleasure than it did her. "Now that I'm in command," she whispered, "I order a siesta every afternoon according to the custom of this country. Surely, it's only our *duty* to establish traditions for the coming empire, and I think some of the old ways were not so foolish," she sighed, soon sailing with his caresses into what seemed to be all too few moments of bliss.

Later, Louisa approached Easton and began her new duties, relying heavily on Loo Kim since most of the servants spoke little or no English. And since Loo Kim already performed the function of head housekeeper, all Louisa needed to do in that regard was make final decisions as the mistress of a grand household would. What she found most interesting, and what heightened her interest in the political affair she and Aaron were engaged in, was to aid Easton, and soon Melville and Carson, with correspondence to various men throughout the country who were in league with their schemes. There were perhaps forty men with whom they regularly corresponded, and whom Louisa came to recognize from their names alone when they called at the estate. Louisa found herself caught up in the activity and the plotting, and, had she not been so painfully aware of Aaron's and her purpose in the mansion and among the conspirators, she could have easily lost herself in the excitement, for soon the plans were laid before them, piece by piece, each fragment painstakingly thought out. And when she sometimes sat alone with William Easton before the lamps were lit in the waning afternoon sun, drinking tea, reflecting silently over the day, she was sure she could sense the dreams that filtered through the pensive man's brain. When their conversation ceased and he stared into the distance, she knew he saw the same splendor he had seen on the fringes of the court in Paris, and probably other capitals of Europe. But there he had only been in the galleries. Here he believed he would reign, if not rule. She saw his visions in the way he gazed at the possessions of the house he now occupied. She'd learned most of the treasures did not belong to him but were merely the trappings, and, if necessary, the collateral of the new state whose birth was imminent, waiting only for the correct moment, the inevitable tide of natural consequences.

The business of state moved slowly but steadily, and the tension of the days was always between Louisa and Aaron at night. They had few private moments, and some days they did not see each other, except for meals, until their door closed behind them at night. And often before a word was exchanged, before a lamp was lit, Louisa knew by the way he seized her how the events of the day had gone for Aaron. It became a source of amusement. "I think I like it best when you've had a unproductive time with Peter and Franklin," she purred, one night after he'd made love to her, and she was feeling particularly contented.

"Mmmm. That so," he replied, in less of a mood to converse than she. He had to force himself to listen to her whisper of the things she had done and learned. At those moments he told her what, if anything, he wanted her to know, worrying silently that she was much more involved in the project than he would like, thinking also he continued to be much more attracted to her than he believed wise, beginning to realize a romantic alliance with Marguerite Hill was inevitable.

Aaron was drawn and openly welcomed into the conspiracy, but he sensed and then learned from his own sources that what was revealed to him, as well as to Easton, was not the complete picture. Aaron suspected the whole of the operation was known to one man, and that man was Peter Melville. Franklin Carson thought he knew the total, but Aaron was certain Melville had more in his portfolio than was revealed even to Carson. Perhaps Simon Hudson was privy to it all, but that was doubtful. Aaron was sure Peter Melville's schemes outdid them all. His life-style was opulent, even by Hudson standards, and Aaron knew Melville's tastes were bred in greed that far surpassed his partners' lusts.

As Aaron lay in the darkness next to Louisa, thinking himself drained of passion for the night, he considered his probable liaison with the colonel's wife. He smiled broadly, his expression hidden in darkness, telling himself it would be good—and the best way possible—to remember Louisa was not the only woman who could arouse and satisfy him. She was, after all, only a woman, and he was positive Marguerite had abilities of which he only needed to take advantage.

Yet, even as he considered the probable delights of future conquests, the beguiling woman next to him

Chapter Fifty

PETER Melville studied the men who came to his attention, and soon the field captains were selected, the maps unfurled. Each man's devotion to the success of Southern dreams, power, and rights was placed above the value of their individual lives. The holy oaths were given, the duties assigned, and the plans set in motion. Like Melville, the select men were prominent, unsuspected, taciturn; their infrequent conversations held in parlors where no one could overhear, or in grand houses like Easton's, where the ears of any uninvited listener were unschooled to any but specific English commands. Each man was then charged with choosing a trustworthy agent who would be expected to search out a group of men, each unknown to the other, but ready whenever called to come forward without knowledge of their mission— a lethal, conscienceless, adventure-seeking lot—men whose natures were strikingly similar to the man who not long before had sailed the coasts of Britain and the Gulf states of his native country. And the lures for this new company of soldiers were the same that had stirred Aaron's blood—money and excitement—but without the loyalties, or the dreams of vengeance, or the emotion of hate—at least, not yet.

Unknown to the secret army, when summoned they would be expected to lay siege to and capture key military positions and arsenals within the state, and, if Franklin Carson did his job, the soldiers would be equipped as well as "the enemy." Then the territory could be declared to be in the Southern camp, or become a separate state as the moment and the triumvirate dictated.

While the army was cautiously being recruited in the countryside, editors of some of the more popular newspapers began assisting the conspirators, usually as a result of sincere personal conviction, with no connection to the conspiracy. The papers announced the news from home, the editorials raging in favor of Southern opinion, and slowly the California populace grew to be aware of the nation's impetus toward disunity, if not actual war. The onslaught was slow, the momentum gradual, but, from the conspirators' point of view, prophetic.

It was hoped Colonel Hill would turn out to be a significant figure in the final act. It was expected he could be persuaded to cooperate, for his assistance would be crucial to the plans. In his position at the headquarters of Western military operations, he could assign soldiers sympathetic to the South to key locations where, when attacked, their resistance to the invading army might be strongly affected by their ambivalent loyalties. The true nature of Colonel Hill's personality was unclear for the present. His personal honor seemed strong enough to make his oath to the government in Washington a matter of fact, but his assignment to the San Francisco command had been secured by Edwin Taylor, a congressman whose sympathies were openly, unabashedly Southern. And for the time being, the inner circle at Crane's Nest was very optimistic about the future of Hill's allegiance. His vices were scrutinized, and his potential for corruption developed whenever possible. Slowly his gambling debts in private games with socially prominent San Franciscans began to mount. These obligations among gentlemen were of no great concern to anyone —for the present. The sums were merely recorded as the action progressed.

All throughout the planning, Aaron listened and watched as if his life depended on it. He moved casually, easily, within the circle, his innate capacity for intrigue giving him an advantage where a better educated but less intuitive man would have failed. His handsome, well-groomed appearance, his seemingly natural aristocratic bearing afforded him entrée to society, and there was no suspicion of his charade. Only Louisa read his tensions and she did all she could to soothe them. If there was any hesitation, it was on Peter Melville's part, and it pertained only to Marshall's previous philosophical inclinations. He actually never considered the possibility of Aaron's impersonation of Marshall. He merely acknowledged Marshall's lucky escape from injury aboard the *Golden Lady*. When Louisa paled visibly at his comments, he apologized for unnecessarily bringing up uncomfortable memories, never knowing how close to a nerve his remarks had struck.

Aaron schemed on several levels, just as he suspected Peter Melville did. He regarded Colonel Hill as a likely traitor, but expected to hedge his bets with Marguerite Hill. He knew little of the woman, except what his eyes could plainly see. The rumors about her were many; the facts few. But as he began to observe her, he suspected the truth would tend to confirm rumor. He knew for certain Peter and she were occasionally lovers, and the more Aaron saw of Marguerite, the more her general boredom with life became obvious.

Her preoccupation was self-indulgence, and she had endless opportunity to see her whims and fantasies, as they pertained to men, were realized. She had no family in California, and no children, with no hopes for any. In fact, Marguerite made it plain, when she queried politely about Louisa's new baby, that she really preferred to remain childless, and would not give it another thought, "except Colonel Hill would die with regret if we did not someday produce an heir." Her inclinations were strictly toward self-gratification, her pleasures taken without her husband's knowledge, and without the inconvenience or discomfort of conscience. She professed love for the colonel, and believed whole-heartedly that her affection rested solely with him. It was simply a matter of her preferences diverging from accepted standards. She would have openly indulged herself with other men, but she did accept the reality that her husband would never understand. Her behavior was not flagrant—she "carried on," as she so aptly described it, in secrecy, but only for the sake of the security of her social position and her very comfortable life, not for any principle, or regret. Her tastes were very democratic, and only fear of exposure prevented her from too often crossing class and color lines—and the sometimes transient fear of producing a child of strikingly dissimilar features. She was the kind of woman Aaron knew best. And he knew he could play any game she cared to name, and at any stakes she cared to set, for it was a contest of equals.

When Aaron contemplated Louisa and Marguerite, he alternately smiled and shook his head, or frowned. And when he reflected on his pending liaison with Mrs. Hill, he occasionally considered the probable duration of Louisa's fidelity to him. At first he immediately dismissed the notion that Louisa would betray him in another man's bed. He did so, more out of high regard for his own prowess than from confidence as a man of her equal. And gradually his doubts ate their way to the front of his mind.

A few times the questions surfaced in their bed, where—for now—there was no need to fear Louisa had any inclination to move on. She was hungry and he gratified her as no one ever had. He knew it, because she told him so.

And yet—and yet she had come to him very easily, something for which he did not condemn her. But she could just as easily turn away from him, couldn't she? When this game they played was over, when the excitement was up, the high of living on the edge of discovery gone—what then? He would again be the low-caste pirate, though his crimes would have been erased from official record, if promises were kept. And Louisa would still be a woman of wealth and education. Wouldn't she then be wanting a man of her own class and temperament; a man who could be a suitable father to her probably high-born child? Wouldn't she prefer a man with wealth and social position, comfortable in refined society, not merely an actor playing a role in which he preferred not to be cast? Aaron's was only an act on a stage where he would never be comfortable. If he had a choice, he would instantly cease his performance and resume a life similar, if not identical, to the one from which he was so abruptly torn. While sometimes he enjoyed the ease and comforts of this new life, he often grew restless for his independence and the freedom to choose his own kind of pleasures. He identified with Marguerite's boredom with the life she led. He felt it would be good for him to get better acquainted with a woman who wanted nothing more than to be entertained, a woman who cared nothing for the permanence of a relationship, and who had no hold whatever on his emotions.

But before he was finished with his thoughts he heard Louisa's voice calling softly across his schemes. She wound her arms around him, pulling herself against his back while he lay on his side, his face turned away from her. "Marshall," she whispered coquettishly in the dawn, her hands gently stroking his chest, moving swiftly down his firm, lean belly to caress and excite him. "Wake up and make love to me," she urged, aware of her success in arousing him, and quickly he turned on her, only too happy to fulfill her request. He found her refreshed and vigorous after sleep, and for the moment he could not recall any desire to be anywhere but tangled helplessly in her talons, willing prey to her kind of torture. He knew it would be a very long time, if ever, before he would be free of her.

Chapter Fifty-one

THE day that had begun so early was a day filled with surprises and pleasure. Recent days and nights had been hectic, but this one would be leisurely and private. When they rose, they discovered the beautiful clear mornings they'd enjoyed since their arrival were over, that those days came infrequently and they had been lucky to enjoy so much sun. This morning the trees outside their windows were thick with mist, which might have promised a day shrouded in fog, but Easton, in warning the days had been especially beautiful in honor of Louisa's arrival, had also promised the fog would burn off by noon, this time of year. "Oh, I hope so!" cried Louisa.

"What's that?" inquired Aaron since her remarks were not prefaced by any other statement.

"I hope William is right about the weather," she replied, turning from the French doors. "He promises the sun will appear in spite of what hangs outside our windows right now. Wouldn't you know, the day we at last have to ourselves, the sun would disappear!" she said unhappily.

"We'll just slip off into the fog and no one will ever know we've gone," he suggested cheerfully. "We can do whatever we had in mind just as well in the dark as in the light," he added, grinning.

"Is that right?" Louisa asked, pretending uncertainty.

They'd arranged an excursion into the countryside on their own. The Melvilles were being entertained by local friends for the day, and both Easton and Carson were looking forward to a restful break in the last weeks' frantic pace. "Samuel and Loo Kim will have arranged everything by now. Let's not keep them waiting."

"Ready," she laughed, snuggling into her cape. "It would have to be pouring rain to keep me here!"

As ordered, their horses and an elaborate picnic lunch were waiting for them downstairs. Samuel waved them off into the mist, and soon they rode along some of the same trails Easton had showed them, then entered areas that seemed never to have been violated by man, finally, about noon, reaching a high meadow at the edge of a thick stand of trees.

Just as they had been promised, the sky had become clear and the air wonderfully warm, and their cloaks had been discarded long before. During the last hour they had traveled along the banks of a narrow stream which now converged into a sunlit pond, its green crystal depth inviting in the heat of the sun. They felt as if they were alone in the world, perhaps the only ones in the universe. The horses slowed their pace, seeming to have reached a familiar resting place. Aaron and Louisa were in wordless agreement, and soon dismounted, strolling arm in arm along the granite edges of the pond, then sitting down, perched above the inviting water. When Louisa began to braid her hair on one side of her head, Aaron put his hands into the remainder and gently braided the soft warm strands, tying the pigtails with ribbons from her petticoat. He couldn't help but smile when the pigtails were hanging heavily against her back, recalling the child whose hair he'd pulled playfully long ago, the child whose beautiful young face he could see even now. "Oh, God, I love you," he said silently, kissing her mouth, touching her warm fragrant body with urgent caresses. She seemed bound to every good memory he could summon, in the echo of every joy he could recall.

Soon they were lying in the sweet, soft meadow grass, among the sun-loving wild flowers, overcome with the joyousness of being one again. Aaron felt his body reverberate with unspoken love, his seed thundering into her, and Louisa heard, and her soul echoed the same silent words. Afterward he held her with

a fierceness she knew only too well. She had clung to
Marshall that way many times when their hours together were numbered. And though Aaron still had
said nothing to her, nor made promises he couldn't
keep, Louisa knew he loved her. Yet she was afraid—
afraid to trust her instincts, afraid of his silence.
Does he love me? she questioned. Or did she only
imagine it because her need for him to do so was so
deep, and she was so in want of love? And even in
the warmth of his embrace, Louisa felt cold and
lonely.

Then she relinquished her fears and held him fast,
taking what she knew was given, even if it was offered
in silence, giving herself freely. "I love you," she said
against him softly, and she felt his body shudder almost imperceptibly. "I cannot help myself. I love you,
Aaron—and I know you love me." And in response
he held her even more tightly, kissing her, calling her
name as if, even while he held her, she were a memory from a dream.

When he released her, they lay happily side by side,
petting and stroking, and teasing each other with
blades of grass, wrestling and enjoying the beautiful
day. He tied her pigtails in knots, as he'd done years
before, and chased her into the ice-cold pond as she
screamed, to capture her struggling and breathless
from laughter and cold. They swam and played as
freely and happily as children, drying themselves
stretched out on the sun-baked rocks, talking of nothing and everything, embracing finally with gentleness
and love.

The afternoon was idyllic, the scenery breathtaking,
the escape from Crane's Nest satisfying, their pleasure
profound. They dressed and ate their lunch in the
cooling shade of willow trees, and when they were silent, the meadow grew restive and they watched a
small parade of wildlife. A family of deer wandered
within a few feet of them, alert and interested in their
presence, staring mutely with their sad pensive eyes.
The smaller creatures were more brazen, approaching
them openly for samples of their picnic.

"It makes me think of home—when we were children. Do you remember, Aaron?"

"I remember the little girl who couldn't kill a frog. But she had a fondness for lighting fires. . . ."

"Something I've outgrown."

"I hope so."

"What do you mean, Aaron, you hope so?" she frowned at him.

"Nothing, really. Yet fire seems to haunt you, doesn't it?"

"I've given up ghosts, or don't you remember?"

"Even in your bed?" his voice now mildly sarcastic.

"*Especially* in my bed!" Louisa was puzzled by his questions and attitude. She felt as if he were reprimanding her, and she turned away from him to look out over the beautiful meadow, hoping the mood would change. Several minutes passed, and Louisa relaxed again, and when Aaron moved next to her, she nestled comfortably in his arms.

"We'd best get on our way, if we want to get back before dark," he cautioned.

"I'd just as soon not ever go back."

Aaron smiled at her. "And what would you rather do? Live in the forest like an Indian?"

"Perhaps."

"You'd never make it. A few days, maybe a week, and you'd be begging for the comforts of Crane's Nest. Louisa among the wild creatures," he laughed, "the game would be very short."

Louisa was annoyed by his low estimate of her stamina, and by the sarcasm edging his voice. "You're probably right," she stiffened against him, "but I'm faring very well in the *games* we're playing at Easton's. I'm no weakling, Aaron, you needn't sneer at me. What's wrong?" She sat up and looked directly into his mocking face, watching his deep black eyes stare into hers. In reply, Aaron grabbed her and held her tightly and close, but far enough away from him to watch doubt and tension spread across her beautiful face. He seemed to want to speak to her, but instead he kissed her almost violently. She wanted to struggle against his fierceness, but his desire for her overtook them both.

"I thought we had to be on our way if we wanted to get home . . ." she suggested lamely amid his kisses, torn between her emotion to resist his insulting attitude and her need to submit to her undeniable passion for him.

But he only continued to caress her, his approach now kind, his gestures loving. Then unexpectedly he slowed his pursuit, interrupting those delicious feelings he encouraged. He lay with her, continuing to touch yet backing off from his passion, seeming ill at ease, undecided. "Tomorrow I'm leaving Crane's Nest for a few days," he began, putting his hand quickly but gently over her mouth when she started to protest, kissing her again as soon as he lifted his hand from her lips. "I'm running an errand for Melville. Making sure 'our' interests are seen to in negotiations with Indians they suspect will be happy to distract the federal troops from 'our' other activities."

"Why can't I go with you?"

"It'll be a rugged trip into rough country."

"That's the reason for your earlier remarks? To convince yourself I couldn't make the trip, and you could leave me behind without a whimper?" Her eyes flashed at him, but her lips trembled at the prospect of remaining alone at Easton's. "Aaron, I'm *not* going to stay here without you!"

"You've no choice. The trip isn't one a lady the likes of you would be welcome on. It's strictly business; for men only."

She squirmed under him, unable to free herself, then sighed resignedly. "Why didn't you give me more warning? I could've used more time to consider your absence."

"I wasn't informed myself until late last night, and, as I recall, you weren't in the mood to discuss much when we were finally alone," he smiled.

She smiled back at him softly, touching his handsome face, running her fingers into his thick black hair, drawing his mouth to hers. "I'm going to miss you so," she whispered. "How long will you be gone?"

"A couple of weeks—four at the most."

"That's considerably more than 'a few days,'" she protested.

"You won't even know I'm gone."

"I won't? You underestimate yourself," she teased. "But perhaps I should take you at your word, and since you say I won't miss you—and you, therefore, won't miss me—you can get *off* me and we'll be on our way home!"

"Not so fast. You misunderstood. I've no plans to go home. Not quite yet, Louisa." And eagerly but leisurely, they finished what they had begun.

Chapter Fifty-two

He woke suddenly in their bed, listening alertly in the deep black of the night, hearing what sounded like an animal whimpering and then crying out softly. He lay quietly, then turned to her, lifting her into his arms. "Louisa, Louisa. Don't cry. It's all right, you're dreaming. Wake up now."

But still she cried, even as she came from sleep. "Marshall, please don't leave me. Don't leave me."

"Shhh," he said softly, cuddling her against him. "It was a dream," he said just as he had years ago. "I'm here beside you. You're safe now, love."

She breathed in deeply, shuddering against him. "I dreamed you were leaving me, Marshall, and we would never see each other again," she said, not fully awake.

Aaron held her tightly. "Louisa, it's me, *Aaron*. We're in Monterey, remember?" he said quietly, stroking her, trying to soothe away her sadness.

Suddenly she was very still, seeming to think over his words carefully. Then she relaxed slowly in his embrace. "Yes, I remember," she murmured.

He kissed her in the darkness. "I'm the one leaving you today. But I won't be gone long. How could I stay away from you?" He kissed her again, filling himself as fully as possible with the sensations of being close to her. There was no light in the room, no moon to illuminate their joy. "They say, if one is blind, other senses are sharpened. If I were blind, Louisa, I'd want my sense of touch to be more acute," he sighed as he caressed her satin-smooth body, moving his hands gently into her hair, petting and arousing her, making her forget her dreams and her terror. "You're so wonderful," he gasped as he entered her, holding her eager body tightly to him, restraining her motion until he could regain some composure.

"I love you, Aaron. And I love the way you make me feel," she said joyfully, trying to ignore the fierce hold he had on her.

"You'd better be still, or this will be a very short joust," he laughed, struggling with her and with himself.

"Mmmm," she said, kissing him aggressively, lying none too quietly in his arms. "Let me go!" she demanded, and it wasn't long before his pleasure filled them both. "I'm going to miss you! Oh, am I going to miss you!" she giggled.

"It's good to be appreciated," he grinned, "but I won't ask what it is about me you'll miss most! —You're making it damned hard to leave here, you know," he added almost harshly.

"If it were light, you could see me smile," she whispered, kissing him. "I've no desire to have you go cheerfully." And it wasn't long before they came together again.

Not much later Louisa felt Aaron's hands on her, shaking her gently. "Wake up, Louisa. I'm leaving now."

She opened her eyes to dim lamplight, and saw that Aaron was fully dressed and ready for traveling. It was not yet light, but he and his companions were all set to depart. He looked especially wonderful to her, his dark skin, the blackness of his hair and eyes contrasting with the fawn-colored leather coat and leggings he wore. She stared at him sleepily, thinking his look seemed loving, and Aaron brought her gently into his arms and held her. "Try not to get too embroiled in the goings-on here while I'm gone. You're safer if you keep out of it. I'm the agent, you're here to amuse. Don't risk yourself. Remember that baby of yours needs her mother to come home to her one day." To Louisa's ears, his words sounded incredibly gentle, and he kissed her with as much caring and feeling as she could recall.

"I love you, Aaron. I'll miss you so! Whatever am I going to do at this place without you?"

"You'll find something," he said, giving her one last loving touch, then leaving her to stare after him.

A few minutes later, Louisa rose from the bed, quickly covered herself with a heavy, concealing robe, and ran down the stairs after him, dashing through the front doors. The men and horses stood in the torchlit darkness, momentarily startled as she burst outdoors. She stopped short. "I wanted to see you leave," she said apologetically.

Aaron grinned at her childish, charmingly tousled appearance. "You were almost too late," he said, gesturing to the others who mounted their horses in response. She threw her arms around him. "Good-bye, beautiful," he whispered, catching her fiercely.

"Good-bye, Marshall, my love," was her nearly inaudible reply. And she stood several minutes watching them quickly disappear into the now faint light. She stared after them for what seemed a long while, then re-entered the house to wander distractedly about the downstairs rooms, not wanting to go back to her empty bed where she dared not dwell on the weeks ahead without Aaron to confide in. Nor did she want to consider the time she would have to long for him and not have him lying next to her, ready to offer consolation.

But eventually Louisa climbed the long stairway to their room, and lay on their now cold bed, finding it difficult to get warm again. This was that time of day she struggled with most, but the thoughts that surfaced would not have been easy at any time. And they were especially troubling now. "I'm certain he loves me," she concluded, and for the time being she was resolute and secure.

The day progressed very slowly, Louisa rising again, taking breakfast downstairs alone, long before anyone else in the house except servants stirred. She ate an unusually hearty meal, then requested the lamps in the study be lit, where she began to sort through and complete correspondence which had accumulated from the one-day holiday the company had taken.

Louisa thought she could begin to see the pace slackening now that the conspiracy was in motion, but still there seemed plenty to do. The Melvilles would be going back to San Francisco, probably before Aaron returned to Easton's. Then the house would be nearly empty, except for Easton and Franklin Carson. "At least I won't be alone in the house with Easton," she reassured herself. Easton had always been polite and gracious to her, yet she never lost a sense of uneasiness in his presence. She had looked up on many an occasion to find him watching her with a look that made her want to shudder. As Aaron had pointed out, she was a woman used to lengthy consideration by men, but the look she sometimes found on Easton's face suggested he knew more than he should.

Just before the other members of the household appeared, a very weary messenger arrived with a thick packet of letters. They were from the *Carolina,* a Vanguard clipper that had put into Los Angeles harbor only two days ago. The letters preceded the ship by overland messenger, and in the mail was an envelope addressed to Marshall in a familiar hand. Louisa regarded the letter for some minutes, then sat before the now blazing fire she had requested, wondering how she could possibly feel cold when she sat so close to the flames.

She tried to warm herself, staring at the envelope, dreading the now imminent confrontation with Marshall's mother. Louisa anticipated her relationship with Emma would be a difficult one at best. No one but Marshall had stood to defend her when she was so troubled, not even Emma, the one person she might have expected to give her some support. As she gazed at the still unopened letter, Louisa felt bitter, and a sick kind of fear, and she wished she were not alone, that Aaron had not just left her side. He could reason with and reassure her, she thought, feeling a sort of panic creep over herself. She closed her eyes tightly and tried to compose herself, knowing Aaron would demand, if not expect her to control her fears.

Over these weeks at Crane's Nest, Louisa had thought often about Rachel, finding her separation from her child nearly unbearable. She had at times cried inconsolably, knowing she exasperated and tried

Aaron's patience. Yet he had been remarkably, end-lessly patient and understanding, which surprised and gratified her, and eventually his attitude had helped her to accept the unacceptable. She came to believe leaving Rachel behind was what was best for her child, knowing in her heart it would have been impossible for her to refuse Aaron's request for help in avenging Marshall's death, certain she had left Rachel with persons who would give their lives for her, if necessary—at least, Carmen would.

But now with Emma's letter in hand, Louisa's certainty about her actions were shaken, and again she went through her reasoning, concluding again that what she had done was right, feeling she could face the letter and eventually the woman with confidence. At last she took Easton's jade-encrusted letter opener and cut the envelope, and began to read.

Dearest Marshall and Louisa,
This has been a very long and difficult passage, made more so by my eagerness to see my precious grandchild, Rachel. I long to hold her in my arms and see just who she resembles. I wonder who chose the name Rachel? It seems perfect for a small, innocent baby. I have a trunk full of beautiful things for her. I was afraid you might not be able to find what you need in your part of the country. Of course, it's only my excuse to begin spoiling her.

I so regret the misery and unpleasantness that finds you on this coast and away from your natural home. But for now it cannot be helped. Perhaps we will soon all be able to live under the same roof again, but I am doubtful. Perhaps we will not even be living under the same flag for very long. But Louisa and Rachel and I will leave those matters to you men, and enjoy ourselves with more feminine concerns.

The captain advises me it may be several more weeks before we reach Monterey, due to the prevailing winds. I hope your passage along this route were less fearsome than the trip I have just experienced. I would never have believed such dreadful storms as we encountered coming around Cape Horn. If I have to travel that way to return home, I may choose to remain permanently in California. Yet I understand traveling across the Isthmus of Panama has risks of its own.

The only compensation of this journey has been a very nice fellow traveler who will also be stopping with us in Monterey. He is Alexander Fielder, the man whom Simon recommends to William as his aide and secretary. I am sure he will perform most admirably. He is a few years older than you are, Marshall, and has studied in many of the same places as you have. All in all, he is very compatible. Alex would have joined your party sooner, but he was delayed at home with a very ill wife and new baby, who are now, I am delighted to report, well on their way to recovery. In fact, they will probably join him in a few months.

I cannot tell you how anxious I am to arrive at Monterey. We all have been separated far too long, and due to the most unpleasant of circumstances, which we will have to make up to each other.

> Your loving mother,
> Emma

The reading was not as difficult as Louisa had anticipated. Marshall's mother was probably as regretful and conciliatory as Aaron believed. It was simply difficult for Louisa to trust anyone after all she had been through, especially someone who had failed to come to her assistance at a time when it was reasonable to expect support. Louisa wondered how much Emma's desire to reconcile herself to the couple would affect her ability to recognize the man who only used her son's name. She wondered just how keen Emma's sense would be; after all, a grown man changes in many ways, not only from the child with whom a mother could be expected to be familiar, but often from the person he was months before. It was possible that

Chapter Fifty-three

✍ THE Melvilles departed as planned in spite of Emma's approaching arrival. They promised to return, if only to greet her, should she choose to stay on and not go to San Diego to be with the grandchild she had come so far to see.

Louisa kept busy even in the now quite empty house. Easton was reluctant to resume making household decisions, and gratefully left those things to Louisa. The time she had to spare was spent outdoors on her own, or sometimes in the company of Samuel Davis, for lengthier excursions. Occasionally she would stop to sketch, finding it had been much too long since she had engaged her artist's eye. At first she was impatient with her efforts, eventually forgiving her first attempts and looking forward to the times she could pursue her talent.

She drew gnarled trees in fields of wild flowers; chipmunk, squirrel, and wood-rat families; deer and many winged creatures who inadvertently posed for her. She rode with Samuel to favorite fishing coves and sketched men unloading their catches; sat above the ocean and even captured the curious sad-eyed sea lion on her paper. She ordered paints and canvas and waited their arrival like a child anticipating Christmas. And while waiting she made portraits of the people around her, and from her fond memories. She found her drawings of Marshall and Aaron identical only to "strangers," and her single portrait of Rachel too painful to look at, the likeness too perfect. She would save it for the child's grandmother.

One afternoon she came in from a very satisfying period of sketching to meet Easton in a particularly jubilant mood. "Your husband's mother arrived while you were out," he proclaimed before she could put her drawings down.

Louisa pretended to be pleased. "Did you give her the bad news—about Rachel still being in San Diego and Marshall being on an errand?"

"No. I leave both unpleasant tasks to you. I only saw to their accommodations, I'm afraid."

"Oh, I wish you'd helped me out a little more," she sighed pleasantly.

"They'll all be down for tea in a few minutes."

"Then I'll rush upstairs. I'd prefer to greet Marshall's mother in a fresher state. Would you ring for Loo Kim, please," she asked, flying up the stairs.

In a few minutes Loo Kim was there to assist her, and soon Louisa felt she was ready to greet Emma Hudson. She chose a suitably demure gown, one Aaron would object to as being too modest. It would suit her mother-in-law's taste, she thought. The peacock-blue dress and her skin, which was especially tan from the last several afternoons in the sun, made her own blue eyes seem unusually pale. Loo Kim brushed her windswept hair away from her face, tying it simply at the nape of her neck, allowing the mass of curls to flow softly down her back. She fixed some delicate plumeria blooms at the knot, helping Louisa to appear more delicate than she felt. A good impression for Emma, thought Louisa.

She was the first of Easton's guests to arrive downstairs for tea, and she'd wished she'd sent Loo Kim to notify her when the others were already waiting. Easton admired her openly, staring longer than Louisa felt necessary. "I think you will please your mother-in-law very much."

"You forget, she already knows me quite well," she said nervously.

"I don't forget at all," he replied as the doors opened to admit Emma Hudson, Alex Fielder, and someone Louisa and Aaron never expected to see—Anna Sutton, Andrew Sutton's mother. Louisa felt flushed, and in her astonishment, all the polite remarks she'd considered for her first encounter with Marshall's mother vanished from her tongue. Everyone noticed how ill at ease she was, and Emma bridged the uncomfortable moment and quite naturally went to her, to embrace her gently.

"I'm so glad to see you again, Louisa. You look wonderfully well."

"So do you, Aunt Emma. I was afraid from your letter that you might not have fared well on the trip," replied Louisa, feeling very self-conscious, her usual confidence all but evaporated.

"It seems I did better than I'd thought. But I'm not anxious to make the return trip very soon, I can assure you."

Louisa greeted Aaron's mother quickly, who stayed with them only to share a cup of tea, then disappeared upstairs to oversee the unpacking. Alex Fielder then came to Louisa's attention, and, as Emma had announced in her letter, he seemed a very amiable sort. As soon as the introductions were complete Emma asked of her grandchild.

"I know you'll be terribly disappointed, but we left her in San Diego."

"Oh, no!" cried Emma, her surprise and disappointment evident. "Whatever for?"

"Marshall felt it would be too much of a journey for so young a child, and yet, he felt it was our duty to be here at this moment," she said lamely, laying the blame for the decision squarely on the woman's son. "She was left with my housekeeper who will lay down her life for her if she's asked."

Emma was not pleased with the news, but said nothing further to indicate her unhappiness. "I guess I'll just have to pack up again and get aboard another ship bound for San Diego," she smiled. "While it's good to see you, and I'm most anxious to see my son again, I did come to see that child. Where is Marshall, by the way?"

Louisa smiled gently at the woman, and sighed. "I know I'm going to disappoint you again, but what can I do? Marshall is away for a few weeks. I'm hoping," she looked to Easton for support, "he'll be here again in three weeks, perhaps sooner."

"I'm sure we'll see him by then," added Easton encouragingly.

"Well, then, I guess it won't be a waste of time for Anna to unpack," Emma sighed. "How disappointing the news is this afternoon! Just think, to come all this way and find I've traveled too far." But she managed a cheerful smile for Louisa, who returned it, thinking sadly that Emma didn't dream the extent of her actual disappointment. How much more tragic it would be, Louisa thought, for her to learn the truth, and how impossible it would be to simply shrug off that unhappiness if she were to learn of the death of her wonderful son.

Chapter Fifty-four

FIVE hard days of travel on horseback found Aaron eating his mocking words to Louisa. It was he who was longing for the comforts of Crane's Nest. By far he preferred the feel of an ocean-going deck to the back of a horse. His traveling companions were somber enough, and the long hours crossing steep ravines, or on paths hundreds of feet above endless twisted canyons, gave him time enough to contemplate the events of the past few weeks. He journeyed with two of the countryside's veterans, Calvin Lewis and Emil Joseph, the excursion posing no discomfort for either of these men.

Lewis was a gnarled, often dreary man whose life had been spent along the seemingly endless frontiers of territories claimed by the United States. Like many of his fellow frontiersmen, he could not tolerate inhabited areas for any length of time. Whenever he ventured into such places, he would quite literally soak up what the civilized world had to offer, then when he dried out sufficiently from his expedition, he would pack his horse and mule, and head as far from society as possible, to trap, or mine, or hunt as it suited him, swearing he would never venture into civilization again. He was thoroughly acquainted with the country, and a more proficient guide could not be found. And as far as Aaron was concerned, the fact the man was nearly mute by choice made him an ideal companion on the trail.

Aaron's second companion was less taciturn. Emil Joseph was essentially Peter Melville's agent in the conspiracy. In some respects Joseph did not fit the strictly imposed criteria for an agent in this enterprise, for his loyalties were not tied to the South.

But he was an adept, multiskilled man whose talents were for hire and who, once he joined an enterprise, would pursue his duties as if the cause were his. No one in polite society would have connected Melville and Joseph, for their contacts were always surreptitious. Nor were they in any way social equals.

Joseph was perhaps twenty years older than Aaron. His life had been very like the one Calvin Lewis had led, but Joseph favored more contact with people and lived among others whenever possible. In his travels he'd had two informal marriages with Indian women, and had lived peaceably near or in their camps most of his life. He knew their ways and of their general abuse by white men. He neither despised nor particularly admired the Indians, seeing them only as fellow travelers in this short life, who were due no less and no more of life's bounty or misery, as the case may be. By most people's standards, Emil Joseph was at least an amoral man, yet, in his thinking about Indians, he was considerably more charitable than many upstanding citizens.

Aaron felt a kind of kinship with Emil, for in many ways their lives had been parallel. Joseph had even lost his first wife to the woman's Indian lover, in much the same way as Aaron had lost Juliet. If circumstances had been different, the two men might have been as close as Aaron and Mason Jennings had been. But on this journey and in this circumstance, they saw each other in a much different light. Aaron went with his companions as a representative of the elite, and Joseph came along as his minister to implement the conspirators' plans.

The three men traveled into California's interior to meet Juan Delgado, a man whose fervent hope it was to fulfill those same plans. In California, like elsewhere in the country, the Indian had been pushed out wherever the white man thought he wanted to settle. If the Indian's natural habits were somewhat nomadic, the increasing white population, which forever infringed on Indian settlements, made it impossible for them to locate their communities permanently. And each new environment they were pushed into was, as a rule, more inhospitable than the last. They were driven and harassed with little mercy from any quarter, their labor was sought by ranchers, but, usually, only on a seasonal basis, and where other workers were not available. Indian women and children were commonly abducted, abused, and sold; their lands, their stock and crops, their means of survival destroyed whenever circumstances permitted.

Those who were not beaten down beyond hope were ripe with hatred, but ordinarily they had no means to seek vengeance. Now, for a few, the time was right, and the means for revenge at hand. Juan Delgado was a man well known to Joseph, and his was the first name to come to mind when Melville discussed his interest in arming suitable groups of Indians. His plan was to distract federal army troops from larger military centers into the frontier regions by staging Indian uprisings at convenient moments. Then the conspirators' other plans would be set in motion.

Delgado was a perfect choice to lead his people, his desires exactly fitting the needs of the conspiracy. He was a man widely respected by his brothers, and one dangerously angry about his people's condition. He had watched and waited for the three men who came into his territory with an eagerness only such a man could know, approaching their camp shortly after the moon had risen. He was young in years, but old in appearance, of medium stature, with extremely black hair pulled severely from his face and tied with rawhide strips. His face was wide and dark, as were his eyes. He seemed to be heavyset, his musculature suggesting a powerful, strongly built man, but, in the light of the campfire, it was evident that there was far too little flesh on his bones, and, from his general ragged appearance, it was plain that the well-honed body was likely a result of persistent hunger rather than self-discipline. He supported himself and his family by working on ranches in the valley, staying as long as the jobs lasted. When they ended, he pulled up camp with his fellow herdsmen and looked for another position, welcome where he had been before, if there was work. But work grew scarce. A constant and plentiful supply of white men was now available to crowd the Indian laboror out, and under the specter of being herded into the confines of reservations which meant certain death, Juan Delgado and his people retreated farther into the country, where they barely eked out an existence. They became shadows in the landscape that had once been theirs, imprisoned where they had once been free, intimate with and responsive to the murmurs and seasons of nature.

"We're offering guns and horses, food and other provisions—all that you'll need. What we want from you is some assurance we've come to the right man. Proof you can use those weapons to our advantage." While Aaron listened, Emil Joseph did the negotiating. Lewis was excluded from the conversations, and stood an informal lookout, seeming not the least bit curious or interested in the business of the other two men he had guided to this spot in the wilderness.

Juan Delgado made demands for specific quantities or certain special arrangements, his general manner passive but nonetheless earnest; his questions, his commitment convincing; his general loathing for the white man unmistakable. He had seen his father and other members of his clan murdered when he was young; his mother and his older sisters brutally and repeatedly raped and carried off. And over the years his fears and horror gave way to smoldering hatred, but, for the sake of survival, the embers were never stoked adequately. Now, in the changing winds blowing throughout the country, the sparks began to fly. Juan knew nothing of the nation's growing impetus toward war, but he heard the offer Joseph made, and saw what before had only been visions of a foolish, starving man become a very real possibility for redress. And miraculously, it would be revenge sanctioned and supplied by brothers of the very men he hoped to cut down. He believed it was a sign from his gods the time to dream had ceased; the time to act had come.

He promised Aaron and Emil they came to the right man, and he would give proof within two weeks.

They arranged to meet with him again in a fortnight, and the three white men traveled farther south to meet with another prospective soldier of fortune, returning to Delgado's territory at the appointed time. And from the gathering of a hundred men who appeared in their camp late the night they expected to see one man, Aaron and Emil concluded Delgado was resourceful enough to meet their needs. He assured them there were more men like these he'd summoned, men with malice enough to mete out disaster very proficiently to troops who cared to challenge them, provided the Indian army was prepared as agreed. And while Lewis looked on nervously from a distance, oaths were exchanged between Emil Joseph and Juan Delgado, neither man doubting the course of their lives would forever be changed.

Chapter Fifty-five

THE return to the coast seemed less arduous than the trip to the interior only because the territory was now familiar. Aaron's companions grew more solitary, Lewis separating from the trio about midway in their journey home. Joseph continued to Crane's Nest planning to consult with Franklin Carson before going on to San Francisco to report to Melville. Aaron envied Emil his usually independent life. He truly seemed to be a man who was totally free to come and go as he pleased, with no personal attachments to bind him to any one spot for longer than suited his appetite. And from the man's report, whenever he got homesick for a more domestic life, there was opportunity enough to indulge himself in one for as long as it proved agreeable. Though women were not plentiful hereabouts, perhaps Joseph was a better breed of muskrat than was usually available, and the female of the species merely waited for his call, Aaron reasoned drily over coffee at their last campfire before reaching Crane's Nest. Well, whatever the luck, Joseph's had to be a better situation than his, at least for the present.

As he had many times on the trail, Aaron dreamed of Louisa that night, now anxious to hold her again. His thoughts of her hadn't exactly troubled him on the trip, but his memory of her seemed always to lie just below the skin, and there were times when he would have been glad to find her actually in his presence.

He wondered if it would be best to conceal his plans to romance the colonel's wife, or whether he would be wiser to tell Louisa of his intentions in advance. Either way, he suspected, neither the prospect nor the result would please Louisa. He wondered just how she would handle it, whether she would be philosophical or a green-eyed spitting cat. For now he would love to have even the wildcat with him in his bedroll; at this moment it would have been his pleasure to try to tame her.

When it was light the men were on the trail, soon crossing Easton's property, quickening the pace until the house loomed pleasantly before them. Aaron left the horses for Joseph to look after, and stole into the mansion. He was acknowledged by a servant who opened the door for him, but no one else appeared to be up. "So even Louisa's succumbed to Easton's way of life," he chuckled to himself, remembering her usual morning restlessness. "Time to get her reaccustomed to waking early, even if she doesn't get out of bed." Rapidly he climbed the stairs, carefully turning the handle of their door, pushing it open without a sound. He stepped inside the room and removed his hat, holding it in his hand, looking to the bed for the form of the shapely woman he was ready for.

The room was bright, although heavier velvet draperies had been pulled across sheerer ones to minimize the daylight. He saw Louisa tangled in her satin comforter, her cascading hair strewn over the pillows, swept away from her face as she lay peacefully on her back. She seemed to be deeply asleep as Aaron dropped his hat and cast his gloves aside. Standing over her, she stirred and as she opened her eyes, he lowered himself to her, capturing her though she withdrew instinctually. At once she realized who held her so powerfully, and she shuddered in relief. "One of these times, you're going to scare me to death, I'm sure of it!" she panted. "Did you intend to have me die in your arms?"

"Not quite," he said, trying to kiss her.

"You look like a wild man!" she said, struggling. "I'm not sure I'd call you a welcome sight—maybe after a bath and a shave—a bath, at least."

"Now is that any way to greet your husband?" he teased, handling her roughly.

"Are you sure you're one and the same?"

"Let's find out!" he said, pulling the covers away from her naked body with a flourish. "You were waiting for me!"

"It may seem that way," she said, fleeing from the bed when he released her to undress, "but I can wait until you bathe." She pulled a dressing gown hurriedly over her inviting body and lit a lamp.

"I see what you mean," he said, catching a good look at himself in a mirror that hung a few feet behind Louisa. He looked just as she said, like a wild man, his black hair almost bushy, several week's dark growth of beard covering his face, his black eyes flashing, the dark olive skin deeply tanned by the sun. "Mountain men don't appeal to you?" he laughed, relaxing into the warm soft bed, still heavy with her scent.

"I won't know until I get a better look, and a little soap and water will solve that problem nicely," she said ringing for Loo Kim, who appeared within moments. "Prepare a bath for my husband," ordered Louisa casually. "Then bring us a tray," she said, dismissing the girl with a smile. Aaron lay fully clothed in the bed and she went to him now, seating herself at his side. "I'm so glad you're back," she whispered softly, kissing him in spite of her preference for his more usual appearance. He quickly put his arms around her, grasping her hungrily, turning over onto her, finding her yielding and eager. "I wondered if you'd come back."

"You doubted it?" he asked, undoing the sash of her gown, seeking the soft curves of her body with his mouth, stopping his pursuit only when they were interrupted by Loo Kim's noisy re-entry into the room.

"Your bath is ready," she announced, bowing, seeming not to see, retreating from their presence.

Aaron lifted Louisa with him, not willing to let her go, insisting she join him in the tub. While he undressed, Louisa braided and pinned her hair against her head. When she finished, her gown clinging lightly about her slim young body, she looked fresh and incredibly innocent to Aaron. She saw his look and read his mind, then slipped into the water before he reached her, forcing him into the water beside her. After some initial struggling, he succumbed to her insistent, soap-filled caresses, laughing at her teasing, playful demands.

"I suppose you're going to insist I have a shave and a haircut before I get what's rightfully due me," he said sarcastically.

"No, I'm not. I think you'd do well to leave the beard—for a while," she said thoughtfully.

"Why?" He was obviously surprised. "You like mountain men, after all?"

"Not much," she said, climbing the narrow steps of the sunken, tiled tub, beginning to towel herself. Then she sat at the water's edge. "Your mother arrived while you were gone."

"Oh?" he replied distractedly. "You think the beard will help conceal my identity? I didn't think my physical appearance was a problem."

"The beard will only help you. But I mean *your* mother is here."

Aaron stared at Louisa, then the flash of recognition crossed his face. "I hadn't expected *her,*" he said quietly, stirring the hot water absently. "God, it's been a *long* time," he sighed.

Louisa reached to touch his now wet beard, then put her fingers on his lips, drawing his mouth to hers, leaning to kiss him. "It's been a *very* long time for me, too," she whispered with every intention of bringing him from the water. And he gladly joined her, letting her gently towel his wet body dry, her hands working their magic. "Welcome home," she said as he lowered her into their bed again. "I missed you." But no more than he did her, or so it seemed from the way he made love to her that morning. "I love you, Aaron,"

Chapter Fifty-six

AARON trimmed his beard carefully to suit the style of a perfectly groomed gentleman, and when he finished, Louisa nodded her approval, kissing him enthusiastically. "Now you could pass for a respectable man of good breeding and means," she teased.

"That so?" he replied, dressing as perfectly as he was groomed. "Do you think 'my mother' will recognize me?"

"Which one?"

"Does it matter?" he asked gruffly, obviously annoyed by the circumstances. "Shouldn't you be downstairs by now helping Easton with his correspondence, or something?"

"I believe you've got a slight case of stage fright, Aaron."

He frowned at her. "Does it show?"

"Don't worry," she said, putting her arms around him tightly stealing another kiss. "You'll do fine. Only I could tell the difference, and *only* when you have your clothes *off,*" she teased. "And you needn't shoo me away this morning, Easton's aide arrived with your mother. He's assumed his duties very adequately. At least he can do without me this morning. After all, I'm busy looking after my *long* absent, *dearly* missed, loving husband—like the proper wife I am," she smiled, falsely demure and adoring, and with a curtsey for emphasis.

"I don't think I could stand too much of that. I'd think something was wrong if you didn't snap at me occasionally." Then he offered her his arm and they went downstairs to greet Emma privately before the others were summoned for breakfast.

Emma Hudson seemed stunned by her handsome son. She was awed by the look of love she saw in Louisa's eyes, and soon there were tears she could not conceal in her own eyes. "Oh, wouldn't it have been tragic, if you two had been separated as planned!" she said finally, beaming at the beautiful young couple standing radiantly before her. "Thank God, you're together, in spite of your foolish parents, Marshall!"

Aaron put his arms around Marshall's mother, warmly embracing the woman for whom he still had a deep affection. She seemed tired, perhaps older than she had when he last saw her in New Orleans. "I'm glad you've come to be with us, Mother. Sorry I wasn't here when you arrived."

"Your absence wasn't my biggest disappointment, son. As it turns out, you had the poor judgment to leave your baby in San Diego. Whatever possessed you? How very unfair to demand that Louisa do so! That's not something a woman does lightly. . . ." Then she stopped her brief lecture. "Grandmothers are the worst sort of meddlers," she added kindly to Aaron's sudden look of bewilderment.

Louisa could barely keep from laughing at his discomfort, and she put her arms around him. "She's on my side," she said comfortingly. "Your mother thinks the baby would have borne the trip easily, just as I said. I told her *you* insisted we leave her."

"Did you?" he inquired. "Perhaps, Louisa," he offered coolly, "you and Mother *should* go to San Diego. There's certainly no reason for Mother to remain here, and probably no reason for you to stay. I could join you soon, I'm sure." To Aaron, Louisa looked as if she might faint. Her color, which had been high, drained from her face. "I would miss you," he said, putting his arm around her slim waist, "but perhaps it would be best," he added with conviction, and, to Emma's ears, he sounded convincingly unselfish.

Louisa was speechless. But Emma was not. "Of course, she can come with me. But I'm not putting up with any delays. I'm leaving here as soon as possible. I only waited long enough to see you, Marshall, and

I'm going to see my Rachel, with or without her mother in tow. Now, let's have some breakfast," she said airily. "You can decide what's best, later."

Breakfast was an unusually cheerful event, both Easton and Carson remarking on Aaron's stylish new appearance, and the vote among the men was for him to retain the beard, with both Emma and Louisa stating they were undecided. Emma announced she would leave whenever a ship's passage to San Diego could be secured, Marshall promising to see to the arrangements after breakfast.

From Louisa's icy stares, Aaron found that the prospects of Louisa going with Emma were not open for discussion before the company at the breakfast table, and as soon as they were alone, Louisa struggled with her mixed emotions, tearfully incoherent at first. "I can't leave you just yet."

"You don't have to go. I just thought you'd want to see your child," he pressured.

She shot him a helpless look. "You want me to go, don't you?" she questioned with both surprise and dread in her voice.

"Yes. And no," not feeling he needed to conceal his own mixed feelings. She could go or stay. Either way would suit him, he thought. It would be convenient not to feel any necessity to explain his actions as the charade progressed, but then, her presence was undeniably to his liking and, for the time being, it suited him just fine to share his bed with her. "You don't have to go. Stay with me for now. There's always another ship heading south, whenever you want to go." She frowned at him, obviously not very pleased by his casual indifference to her decision, so he made the choice for her, seating himself beside her on the bed, beginning to make love to her. "Stay," he said. "I want you with me." And when he had finished, and she was bound to earth again, there was no further question about what she would do.

Aaron then left the house to make Emma and Anna's arrangements for travel, and Louisa found Emma in the library where they spoke cheerfully with one another. Over the days they had waited for Marshall to return to Crane's Nest, Emma and Louisa had grown hesitantly close. At first it had been very difficult for Louisa, but Emma was genuinely warm and painfully regretful of the events and the oversights that had allowed her son and Louisa to be separated in the first place. Louisa did not speak as freely as Emma did, but gradually she began to relax with the woman again, slowly feeling as she had long years ago, when she, Marshall, and Andrew had had the run of the Hudson house and the run of the countryside, sure of Emma Hudson's approval and loving concern for their welfare.

"Let me show you what I'm making for Rachel. Oh, it will be a little bit before she can wear it, I imagine," Emma said, holding up a delicately crocheted infant's sacque for Louisa's approval.

"It's lovely, Aunt Emma. And you'll be surprised, it won't be long before it will fit her perfectly." She sat next to the older woman. "You seem to know how hard it was for me to leave Rachel behind," she began quietly. "I think you know how much I love her. Perhaps you even know how much she means to me. But I'm *not* going home with you. I can't leave him just yet —I've only just found him again." She paused and took a deep breath before she could continue. Louisa couldn't look Emma in the eye, and she sat silently for a few minutes, hoping and praying the woman would understand. "Aunt Emma, I have loved your son for as long as I can remember. There was a time when I loved him more than life itself. I'd have gratefully given my life for his. I would have killed to save him. When I thought I would never see him again, I was certain I would not survive. But miraculously I did, with his child growing inside me to give me courage when I had none of my own. And I know our baby is well cared for—you'll see for yourself. I hope you can understand why I can't leave here, yet."

"I understand. And I believe what you say about your love for Marshall. It was obvious all along. If only—if only I'd . . ."

"Aunt Emma," Louisa interrupted gently, "I've said 'if only' often enough for both our lifetimes." She took the woman's hands in hers. "Now, you must promise me you'll tell Rachel I love her—tell her so every day. Carmen's supposed to do that, but it won't hurt for her to hear it in double measure," Louisa said warmly.

"I suppose not," she smiled at the beautiful girl-woman before her, and sighed. "I'll make sure she hears her mother's name often." She watched Louisa silently for a moment, then began more animated conversation. "When Marshall gets back, I want to show him the things I've brought for her before they're packed away finally. Also, he must greet Anna. *And* I'd like a long chat with him before either he or I leave this place. For years he's been in such a hurry to get someplace or another, I've rarely had a chance to have a good talk with him—especially after the two of you came home together—oh, if I'd only had the eyes to see the obvious!" she sighed again.

" 'If only,' " Louisa interrupted, teasingly reminding her of her earlier admonition.

The two women now sat comfortably with each other, Emma resuming her crocheting, Louisa browsing absently through one volume or another in Easton's collection. "Tell me, Louisa, what do you think of Marshall's becoming embroiled in the politics Simon and his partners are conjuring?"

"He seems quite interested and excited by it all. . . ."

"That's not what I asked you, my dear."

"No. It wasn't." Louisa paused thoughtfully. "You know, Aunt Emma, I'm about the least political creature ever designed. It's enough for me that Marshall is happily occupied in their schemes. My only concern is for his safety. I care nothing for the promises of being a member of the 'new aristocracy' William speaks of so enthusiastically." She stood and paced very slowly along the book-covered walls, circling the room silently. "Oh, I was caught up in the excitement of details before Alex arrived, but it merely spared me from dreadful boredom in this beautiful but lonely place. I fear it's all very dangerous business, though. And if the plans fail, if there are spies somewhere in their midst to give them away . . . treason is a hanging offense. And lynching is a sport in California; the mobs have been known to cry loudly for blood," Louisa shuddered, then continued.

"From all I've heard, the plotting is careful, as well as daring, but truthfully, I'd prefer Marshall were out of it. He's much too precious to me. I care nothing for prominence. I'd just as soon live well out of the intrigue."

"Even though your life has always been lived among the scions of politics and society? What else do you know?"

"Perhaps my desire to retreat is because of my all-too-clear memory of life at that level," Louisa replied politely but harshly. "My memories of the elite of society are extremely bitter. I know very little of what it's like to live simply, but if I could choose, I would at least try—but as yet it is *not* within my power to choose. I am Marshall's wife, and I will do his bidding."

Emma stared thoughtfully at her beautiful, now very determined daughter-in-law. "As much as I love my son, Louisa, from experience, I caution you to question even the man you love. Never do anyone's bidding blindly. Know what it is you stand to lose, and be certain you are willing to sacrifice whatever it is you have chosen to risk."

Louisa sat down and listened to Marshall's mother. Her voice was quiet, her words almost wistful. "My error was to see only what I wanted to see, to hear only what was pleasing to my ear, to acknowledge only the pleasant, and ignore the painful. I can no longer afford such luxury—it seems Simon and his fellows would risk more than you or I care to offer to the bargain."

Louisa did not reply. She only stared helplessly at her hands which were now folded tightly in her lap. Emma's confessional words rang in her ears. Were they overlaid with double meaning, Louisa wondered, or were her nerves only on edge? Emma was very calm, more calm than she would be if she suspected Marshall to be an impostor, Louisa assured herself.

"I understand how you must feel, Aunt Emma," she said calmly. "I understand your regrets. I know how

much you disapproved of me in the past, and I'm
grateful for your acceptance now. But I have no reason not to trust Marshall's judgment. In fact, if I can't
trust him, I can trust no one. He saved my life by
loving me. I'll do whatever I can for him; I'll do whatever is asked of me for his sake." And Louisa prayed
Emma did not know what she did for Marshall's sake
was at the request of a man who only resembled him.
She hoped it would be a long while before Emma
learned what it was she had sacrificed by ignorance.

Chapter Fifty-seven

THEIR conversation was interrupted by a dutiful servant bringing tea, and soon Alex joined them, presenting Emma with a letter from Simon. Her face reflected annoyance as she perused the envelope, and then placed the unopened letter into her basket of yarn.

Alex had a more welcome parcel for Louisa. Some of the paints and yards of artist's canvas she'd ordered had arrived, and her response was joyful and animated, greatly contrasting Emma's subdued, dismissive response to the mail. Louisa quickly opened the packages, fingered the brushes carefully, and inspected the canvas. "Samuel can make a palette and easel in no time," she announced, wanting to rush off to find him and make her request. She knew he would welcome the chance to please her. She'd done several pencil sketches of him which had pleased him enormously, and, except for one with which she refused to part, she'd given them to him, a simple gesture that somehow stepped briefly over the confining boundaries of position and race. Samuel and she laughed at her mistakes, and wondered how it was she had seen, not to mention captured his expressions, when most would have said he was a mountain of unflinching stoicism, a man whose opinions, as well as his emotions, were unfathomable—that is, of course, *if* he were capable of any but simple brutish concepts.

"I promise not to be too greedy with these," Louisa offered to Alex. "I said I'd share, and I shall." Alex Fielder was an artist, too, one more advanced than she, and with a keener eye for landscape. They'd made a few excursions together, and he'd proved a pleasant companion as well as an able teacher. "Now we'll see who has the best eye for color," Louisa challenged, "that is, if William will indulge me and allow you a few hours away from your multitude of duties."

"He does like to keep me busy."

To bolster his own sense of importance, Louisa thought to herself, a slight pout appearing on her pretty face.

"For your sake, though, I'm sure he'll be lenient with me."

"And I'll make sure he knows how badly I need an outing with you to escort me," she added. Alex then handed her another piece of mail. It was a letter from Carmen, written for her, as usual, by Luther Dobson. Louisa recognized his handwriting, and whenever she saw it her heart lurched with a mixture of joy and alarm. Momentarily she regretted her decision to remain with Aaron, but knew even in this fleeting instant of remorse that she could not leave him. She hastily opened the letter and greedily read every word, hearing Carmen's voice as she did so. Luther carefully preserved Carmen's dialect on paper, much to Louisa's joy and comfort. It made the distance between the correspondents less, and Carmen's words of reassurance about Rachel's good health and perfection touched Louisa as if she were actually there to observe their truthfulness.

"Here you are, Grandmother," Louisa said gently, offering Carmen's letter to Emma, "words of comfort from home. And while you read it, I'll go upstairs and get something I've been saving for you." Louisa excused herself to search in her room among a stack of drawings for the sketch she'd made of Rachel, the one she'd saved for Emma, because the likeness had been too perfect, too difficult for the young mother who was more painfully torn between love for her baby and her growing love for Aaron than she cared to admit.

Emma was delighted with the sketch, and pleased by the loving letter from Rachel's guardian. "I still find it shocking that Marshall insisted you leave the baby behind. It seems so unlike him. As I recall, when he was a youngster, he would mourn over the separation of pups from the bitch. I can't imagine him deserting his own child—you don't think he was jealous of the attention you gave her, do you?"

"Oh, no, Aunt Emma. Not your son. It never occurred to me he might be envious. He was with me when she was born, and has always been touchingly loving, even at his most awkward moments." She smiled to think of Aaron and Rachel; how he had cried with her at the exhilarating moment of birth, how occasionally he had held them both in his arms protectively while she nursed the infant in their bed; how wonderful the contrast was between the tiny bundle of life and the secretly sensitive man who held her with awe in his powerful hands. And it was with some awe that Louisa realized how easily she had accepted Aaron as a substitute for Rachel's natural father in that same bed; how she had so readily taken him into her heart, as well. "I can't explain it, but it wasn't jealousy that urged him to leave her at home."

"Men can be funny that way, sometimes. And in spite of what you say, it annoys me terribly that she was left behind."

Louisa was disturbed by the woman's growing irritation on the subject, and decided not to defend herself or Aaron's actions any further. She finished her tea and politely excused herself from the room. "I've got a fitting in town for a new dress. Samuel is probably waiting for me now. Would you care to come along?"

"No, thank you, dear. I'll wait for Marshall and we'll have that long-overdue chat I've promised myself. And I probably ought to write Simon," she sighed. "I've not done so since I arrived. Go along without me. You'll be home in time for dinner?"

"I'll be back in plenty of time, I'm only going for a fitting. I don't plan to do any other errands—unless there's something you want?"

"No. Nothing. I'll be making a list for Anna before we go on our way. She can search for whatever I need some other time." Emma reached for Louisa's extended hand, and kissed her on the cheek in a gesture of farewell.

Wearing only a light cape in the late-morning sun, Louisa was glad to be out of the house. Samuel drove the open buggy quickly, but surely, down the hills and into town. "Isn't that Marshall's horse?" she inquired as they passed Swenson's dry goods store.

"Sure is."

"Then let's stop. I'd like to speak with him a moment." Samuel turned the buggy, and Louisa entered the tidy but bursting store, greeted pleasantly by Mr. Swenson. "I saw my husband's horse outside and thought he might be here," she said, surprised to find no one but a few other women looking among the shelves and barrels.

"Yes. He was here, Mrs. Hudson. Just left a few minutes ago with Mrs. Hill, helping her with some awkward bundles."

"I see. Thank you, Mr. Swenson." Louisa was disappointed, hoping to warn Aaron of Emma's wish to have a long talk with him. "If you should see him when he returns, please tell him I'm at the dressmaker's."

"I surely will, Mrs. Hudson," he smiled cheerfully. "Did you get your paints?"

"Oh, yes. Thank you. I didn't expect them so soon. In fact, I'm going to use them today, if time doesn't get away from me." Louisa hoped the session at the seamstress's would go quickly. She was in no mood to stand still for too long, feeling eager to get out and find a place to paint or perhaps ride, feeling a bit jittery without knowing why. She'd be glad when Emma was safely on her way south. It was Emma who was making her uneasy, she thought, whether from Louisa's past associations or from any sense that Marshall's mother was uncomfortable with her "son," she couldn't say. All she knew was, she'd breathe more freely when she and Aaron were alone again.

The fitting went badly. The dress didn't fit as it should have. The bodice was too tight, the waistline more snug than was comfortable. Mrs. Stevens was embarrassed, and at a loss to explain to this most coveted of clients how the errors had been made. And Louisa found herself uncharacteristically cross over

such a simple matter. Normally she'd have been good-
natured about so minor a problem, for the alterations
were easy to make. But instead she found herself reflecting like a common scold on the ineptitude of
people on this coast. Then, noting how nervous Mrs.
Stevens was, Louisa realized she was frowning. "I'm
sorry, I know the dress can be easily adjusted, as you
say. I've been very pleased with your work in the past.
I've no cause to be so cross. Perhaps I'm overreacting.
I'll simply have to be less indulgent." Louisa pulled her
own dress on again, noticing for the first time how snug
it felt. She took a long look at herself in the dressmaker's full-length mirror. Her breasts strained heavily
against the dress's fabric and her belt seemed tighter
than usual. "I think it less your fault than mine," she
said pensively to Mrs. Stevens. "When shall I come
back? Saturday morning, at the same hour, perhaps?"

"Yes, that would be fine," Mrs. Stevens replied,
very relieved at Louisa's willing admission that her
work was not at fault. She knew many women who
would have never acknowledged such a possibility.
Then Louisa browsed over some yardage and laces
just received, selecting several yards of linen and lace
for new petticoats, and a bolt of brown-and-blue plaid
wool for a beautiful cape of simple design, both Mrs.
Stevens and Louisa expecting the result to be dramatic
against Louisa's coloring and figure.

When she entered the buggy again, Samuel noticed
Louisa was not pleased, but said nothing, and they
turned to the main street, seeing Aaron's horse
tethered in the same place as before. Louisa thought
little of it, but it didn't cheer her either, and they rode
to the estate in uncharacteristic silence, Louisa's perfunctory thank you when they arrived at Crane's Nest
the only words uttered on the journey. The front door,
of course, was opened for her, but she was grateful no
one interrupted her on her way upstairs. She had arrived just before the customary main meal of the day,
finding she was neither hungry nor in any mood for the
company of those who would be dining with her. Yet
she didn't feel she wanted to make excuses and have
her absence from the table fussed over. The least of all

evils would be to appear, eat a little, and fake con-
geniality, so she rang for Loo Kim after deciding on a
quick bath to refresh and perhaps lift her spirits. But
when she was ready to join the others for dinner, she
found her attempts to improve her mood had been in
vain. She would have to be charming through sheer
will, and to the faintly nagging worry she harbored
about Marshall's mother, she added the suspicion she
was pregnant. The signs she had ignored the first time
from simple ignorance were not easy to dismiss now
she knew what they were. In her bath she'd confirmed
the increased fullness of her breasts, her thickened
waist, the sudden hardness of her already firm belly.
They were implications she wished she could ignore
and, perhaps, she could have for a while longer than
she did, but Mrs. Stevens would not allow it, it seemed.
In a few days she would know for sure. In the meanwhile Louisa would lie in limbo, uncertain how the
truth, whatever it would be, would make her feel.

Chapter Fifty-eight

THEY were seated and the meal started when Aaron arrived. He was in a very jovial mood, kissing Louisa gently on the cheek before seating himself next to her. He then apologized briefly for his tardiness. "I've arranged for you to sail next week on the *Isabella,* Mother. She's a pleasant vessel, though small, but I think you'll be comfortable. Yet, you could wait a few weeks for better accommodations, if you wish."

"Oh, Marshall, she's a lovely little ship. We've sailed on her. Don't you remember? The accommodations are very adequate," Louisa said, turning to Emma, hoping Aaron's disclaimer would not discourage Emma's quick departure from Monterey.

"I'm sure she'll suit me just fine. As you know, I'm in a hurry," Emma smiled.

Louisa relaxed a little, turning again to Aaron. "You must see the things your mother has for the baby before she packs them away, Marshall."

"And you must promise me a little of your time, son. Louisa's going out this afternoon, and I intend to monopolize your attention. Do you think you could spare me an hour or so?"

"Of course, Mother," Aaron replied with natural ease.

"By the way, Marshall, you haven't met Alex Fielder," interrupted Easton. "He arrived with your mother, and has assumed responsibilities as my secretary, freeing Louisa to do as she pleases. And it seems he's an able artist, as well. He'll be escorting Louisa this afternoon. I can't refuse her request for his attention. They've convinced me the correspondence will keep, but the paints will not."

Aaron and Alex Fielder exchanged greetings, Aaron taking notice of the man for the first time. Though seated, it was apparent Alex was about the same height as Aaron, perhaps a little shorter. He was slender and well built, of medium complexion, with dark blond hair and light topaz-colored eyes which gave him a magnetic sort of appearance, and Aaron suspected Louisa enjoyed the man's looks as much as she did their common interest. Aaron and Alex spoke congenially of their mutual experiences in Europe, and of some of the same haunts they had known on holidays, remarking it was odd they'd not run into each other since they'd seemingly been in some of the same places at the same times. And both Aaron and Louisa breathed easier when the meal was concluded pleasantly.

Louisa hastened to their room to ready herself for a few hours of painting. "You don't mind?" she asked of Aaron. "There's nothing I can do to save you from the interview with Emma. And I've the feeling it's not going to be an easy one. She's really been harping on our leaving Rachel behind, telling me how softhearted Marshall was as a child when the pups were separated from their mother. Remember? Well, we all thought it a trifle sad, as I recall, but Emma seems to want to make something of it. I think she's uneasy, but I can't imagine why. How I wish she'd not come!" Louisa fretted.

Aaron frowned. "I'll just have to get through it as best I can. I won't allow her to pin me down. Marshall had a way of being evasive with Emma when it suited him. She didn't know all our mischief. We managed to conceal whatever we wanted."

Louisa smiled. "I guess we did at that. Little did we know what we were training for! Good luck, my love." She kissed him sweetly, then gathered up her artist's materials. "Come after us, why don't you? As soon as you can get away. We won't be able to do much painting, we've got too late a start, and the light won't last long. Promise you'll try?"

"I promise," he said, taking a long kiss from her warm mouth, touching her full breasts with eager hands. "You've added a little roundness while I was away. *Very* nice," he whispered, then kissed her, pulling her close, moving his body suggestively against hers.

"We'll discuss it later," she said abruptly, slipping with some effort from out of his arms. "Alex is waiting."

When he was alone, Aaron sized himself up in the mirror, convinced there was nothing about his physical appearance to make Emma Hudson suspicious. With the addition of the beard, there was even less chance she'd identify him. Though it had been a good many years since he and Marshall had been inseparable companions, Aaron had carefully recalled all he could of the nuances of Marshall's interaction with his mother. Unlike Louisa's childhood contact with Marshall, Aaron's had been daily. They had lived like brothers though there had never been acknowledgment of the fact, and while it was always clear to others who the young master of the house was, the boys were unconcerned with social rank and each seemed to be the other's shadow.

Aaron stared sharply at himself in the glass. In a few minutes he would speak to Marshall's mother as if she were his own, and greet Anna Sutton, his own mother, with fond but casual regard. Forced to contemplate feelings he had readily buried long ago, he felt suddenly strange and sad. Shame and sorrow came over him, and then very quickly that pain was replaced by the deep, self-sustaining bitterness that fueled him in this enterprise. It was his apprenticeship at Simon's direction that had forced him from home, and from the simple woman who had originally nurtured and loved him. Circumstances beyond his power had driven him away, eventually making the chance of his ever being welcomed home improbable. Surely Anna would not wish to acknowledge an outlaw for a son. Her own sins had weighed heavily on her soul, something he as a young child had sensed and learned gradually. Aaron never intended to burden her further with his own offenses. Today, after all these years, he would face his mother and then turn his back on her again, as if he had no memories to cherish.

When he went to Emma's door, it was Anna who answered his knock. She seemed startled by him, then cheerful warmth replaced her surprise. "Oh, you look just wonderful! I'd heard you added a beard, but not how much you look like your father did many years ago," she said, opening the door wide for him to enter. She stood and looked at him a few moments, listening to his polite inquiries and comments. They laughed at the furor the Hudson household had been in the last time she'd seen him. "Things settled down a little after you left for California, but your mama was *very* hard on your father," she laughed quietly, and from the sudden flicker in her eyes, it was as if it were a private joke. "I was very glad I was not the source of her fury, although the whole house was under its influence. Your mama is something to behold when she is angry!" Anna shook her head and smiled. "At least from your looks, marriage agrees with you." Then she lowered her voice, "I'm glad you two finally got your way. It's the way it should have been all along." She paused to look at him more closely, seeming quite pleased with what she saw. "Your mama is on the terrace waiting for you," she said, leading the way. "She's longing for a good chat."

Anna left them alone; closing the terrace doors. Aaron kissed Emma's hand and then her forehead, a gesture typical of Marshall in years past. Then he sat close to her on the redwood couch while she alternately crocheted and scrutinized her son. They spoke at first of things at home, of his favorite horse, the books yet to be shipped to his residence in California, wherever that might finally be, of Janna Carson, of a university friend who had called on the Hudsons shortly after his departure. Russell had kept him well informed, well prepared for this inquisitive lady.

"I'm afraid I've been a little hard on Louisa about Rachel. I know my last remarks nearly caught a flare of her temper. Still I can't get over your actions. It seems so unlike you, and more than that, Louisa needs her baby, perhaps more than most mothers.

You can't wrench mother and child from one another like that. Surely you haven't forgotten how fragile Louisa's health can be?"

"Of course, I haven't forgotten! Don't forget how many years I've loved her, Mother. Much longer than you know. Even as children, Andrew and I held Louisa in our arms hoping to ease her terror. At first I tried to comfort her; much later I made love to her," he said frankly. "I love her more than even she knows, and I know better than anyone what her strengths and her weaknesses are." He spoke quietly but passionately, his words, his aggressive but polite stance very like Marshall when he was determined and unwavering in his beliefs. Yet Aaron was acutely aware how much the words he spoke mirrored his own feelings. He had been unable to tell Louisa how he loved her, but he told Emma, and she heard and believed him. "We left our child behind with servants just like you did occasionally. We've not abandoned her."

Then the tone of his voice became irritable. "And why, if you're concerned for Louisa's health, do you rub salt in her wounds? She doesn't need to be reminded of Rachel." He stood up then and paced the terrace slowly, hoping to put Emma on the defensive, to wring a few apologies from her, to distract her from any but her own guilty feelings about Louisa and Marshall.

"Haven't you yet forgiven her for always seeming to disrupt our lives? Have you forgiven her for loving me? For the crimes committed against her? Do you forgive *me* for loving Justin and Claudia's child? Is she too unclean for 'the cream of Southern manhood,' too corrupt to mingle her blood with the Hudson line of thoroughbreds?" His anger was unmistakable now, and Emma's face registered shock, just as Aaron wanted.

"Marshall, you're being cruel and unfair! I've told you how badly I feel. I've come in conciliation, you *know* that's so!"

"I also remember how you cautioned me not to come here, not to go after Louisa when she was unwed and carrying my child. I remember the modest, but nonetheless pointed accusations you made."

"You must forgive me! I was half mad with shock over all of the incredible events!"

"You say you were 'half mad,' and yet you wonder about Louisa's sanity. Among those whose sanity is not in question, we speak very loosely. It seems to me, Mother, if Louisa ever does lose her mind, she's had more than sufficient excuse. Let's not shove her too hard with self-righteousness." He pulled a small pine cone from a tree whose branches dipped onto the balcony, then threw the cone forcefully into the woods, allowing his anger to ease slightly. "I'm sorry we didn't bring the baby with us. It was mainly due to my selfish wish to have Louisa all to myself. I'd appreciate it, though, Mother, if nothing more on the subject was said," he concluded, certain Emma would say no more.

"I'm sorry," she said, tears brimming her eyes, and Aaron went and knelt by her, and hugged and kissed her gently, quite satisfied by how the interview had progressed in his favor. "I'll have Anna get us some more tea," he offered. "You were going to show me the things you're taking to San Diego. Louisa will be very disappointed if I don't see them."

Emma was relieved to have the conversation so easily turned. Her emotions were in a turmoil. She felt she had been unduly accusing with Louisa, and she felt appropriately but harshly chastised. Yet something nagged at her. Something was not as it should be. She sensed it even in her present despair, even in the guilt Marshall had so adroitly touched and wrenched from her.

Chapter Fifty-nine

Louisa and Alex returned to their favorite location for sketching. Some time before, they'd discovered a perfect clearing, edged with an outcropping of boulders, open on one end to the horizon, surrounded on its other edges by the forest and its creatures who ventured out, seemingly for the artists' pleasure. However, this afternoon was providing neither good light nor subjects of any interest, and Louisa was very unhappy about the way the outing, as well as the day, was going. "William won't be pleased when we come back without some splashes of color on canvas," she said, picking up her more familiar pen and paper. "Nothing seems to have gone right today."

"Don't let your husband hear you say that!"

"I guess not!" Louisa laughed. "It wasn't a very flattering comment his first day back! I know he wouldn't appreciate it." And they laughed heartily. "When do you expect your wife to join you? I know she was ill from childbirth, and that's why your own arrival was delayed."

"I don't expect her for several months. She needs to get her strength back. I left her when she was safely out of danger, but she wasn't well."

"It's going to be lonely for you."

"Very."

"I know better than most what it will be like," Louisa sighed. "You've no doubt heard about Marshall and me? Did anyone in New Orleans not hear the gossip?" Alex nodded. "The loneliness was almost unbearable. I expected never to see him again—you at least have the comfort of knowing your family will come as soon as possible. I came here thinking I had to forget the person I loved most in the world."

"What would you have done if he hadn't come? As I heard the story, it was only by chance Marshall learned of your circumstances."

Louisa shook her head. "It was odd, Alex, but nature seemed to be on my side for once, or, more probably, on Rachel's side. Miraculously, as the birth got closer, I focused more and more on the future, and less on the past. I actually seemed to get stronger, even confident. I wouldn't have been able to get through it otherwise."

"Perhaps, you underestimate your strength of character, Louisa."

"Perhaps. But let's not waste the afternoon talking." She closed the subject. "Let me sketch you, and you can send the results, if they're good, to your wife. It would cheer her up, I'm sure. I seem to have more skill at portraits than landscapes, as you already know! Just turn to face me a little more. No, that's too much. Now lift your chin about an inch. Perfect." Soon Louisa lost herself in her subject, in the shapes and lines of his face, in the shading of his hair, in the look of his startling, pale eyes.

Alex sat silent and still, an ideal, knowledgeable subject sensing she preferred not to have her work interrupted by conversation. He watched her carefully as if he were also observing a subject for drawing. He doubted he could do justice to her on paper or canvas, feeling there was something too elusive about Louisa, too mercurial to capture adequately with brush or pen. She didn't seem to be as accessible as her great beauty and natural allure implied.

Alex wondered about the man who had managed, by her own admission, to capture Louisa's emotions so completely. As a couple, Marshall and Louisa were strikingly handsome, an artist's image of perfection with Marshall's darkness and apparent strength vividly contrasting Louisa's splendid fairness. Alex found himself wondering if such a combination, so amazing to the eye, was not in some way too bold. Often, it seemed, opposites never managed to find a lasting

common ground. Only luck seemed to determine the
destiny of that kind of union. But perhaps these two
were more like primary colors on the artist's palette,
free to combine into infinite shades on the spectrum,
free to blend and compliment, or to contrast effectively
and dramatically. It would intrigue him to watch the
pair. So far, he had enjoyed Louisa's company immensely, especially their mutual interest in art, and he
wondered if he could cultivate a friendship with her
husband, or whether the sensual beauty of the woman
would somehow prevent the men from developing
more than a very superficial relationship. If she were
his wife, he knew it would be difficult for him to be
comfortable with her attachment to another man,
whatever the grounds. And he wondered if any man
could feel secure in Louisa's presence.

"Finished," she said. "No, just one minute." She
looked thoughtfully at Alex and at the sketch. "Yes,
I'm done," she said finally, and Alex moved very close
to her. "It's not bad, but I think I could've done a
little more justice to your eyes. You'll have to let me
try again."

"My pleasure. Mary will be very pleased," he said,
reaching for the drawing, wondering if his very innocent young wife would sense the longing he saw there
in his eyes, the yearning Louisa had evidently read
and transferred to the pen-and-ink drawing. He felt
transparent, but perhaps Louisa didn't see what he
did. If she did, she made no overt sign.

"Send it with the courier, and she'll have it in a
very short time." When she glanced up, Louisa looked
over Alex's shoulder to see a man seated on his horse
watching them. She covered her eyes and squinted,
then stood and raised her arms to wave at him. "It's
Marshall," and though he was still a good distance
away, she hurriedly gave her materials to Alex and
began to run in Aaron's direction.

Aaron had come into the clearing just as she'd finished the portrait. He watched with surprise as Alex
moved familiarly close to Louisa, and it seemed to
him they sat cozily for quite a while. Perhaps this was
the man Aaron had feared. Alex Fielder was certainly

a man very like the one Aaron had conjured as a potential adversary, and as Louisa started in his direction, Aaron remained stock still. Just an hour before, he had confessed his love for Louisa aloud for the first time, and now he felt the specter of a more suitable lover for this woman breathing down his neck. He had come after her full of satisfaction, and very full of his feelings of love for her. Now, as they faced one another, he found bitter reality rearing its head, hissing its venom. Yet when he began to approach her again, and met her with her arms reaching out to him, her love for him not the least concealed in her face and posture, he forgot his fears and gathered her into his arms eagerly, easily lifting her with him onto the horse.

They held each other tightly, and kissed passionately, Louisa quite breathless from scurrying toward him across the meadow. "Well? Tell me how it went. I can see from your face, it must have gone well."

"It went perfectly!" he said emphatically.

"Ahhh! What luck," she sighed.

"Luck? Hell! Skill!"

"Pardon me!" she laughed, hugging him. "You'll have to tell me about it later."

"I'll tell you a lot of things later." And she knew just what he meant, his hands seeking more than she preferred with an audience, even though the observer was a good distance away.

"Aaron, you're in polite company, just now. You don't want to give yourself away—Marshall would be more circumspect," she cautioned, loving her ability to torment him just a little.

"Yes, good old well-mannered Marshall. How did he manage it?"

"Only in public."

"I see. And what about the little public display a few minutes ago?"

"What public display?" she asked, truly dumbfounded.

Aaron motioned toward Alex. Louisa's eyes widened. "You're jealous!" she said, hugging him, laughing wildly. He could get nothing more than helpless

Chapter Sixty

A few nights later, Louisa lay still in spite of the intense pain. She'd been unable to sleep, at first feeling vaguely uncomfortable, then increasingly weak. Her body grew tense and restless, and soon she was swimming in perspiration, suddenly frightened of whatever it was that was fast coming over her. When the pain came, it was vicious, taking her almost by surprise. Never before had it come so suddenly, almost without warning, and she wondered, when she pulled her legs up instinctively to shield herself from the force that struck her, why she had not called out. Or did she only assume she had not cried, because Aaron was still sleeping soundly beside her, his face serene and loving, just as she remembered from the moment she slipped from his embrace to confront her odd discomfort.

At first she could tend to nothing but the pain. Later, when a reprieve was given, she rose from the bed to find she was shaking and unsteady. Despite her weakness, she felt the need to pace the floor, and throughout the night she alternately lay in torment, sometimes in stillness, or walked about the room impatiently, like a caged animal. Aaron woke several times, but she assured him he could do nothing more than he did, so he held her whenever she turned to him. He insisted she drink a small glass of whiskey, and she protested, but he won out in the next bout of pain.

The night passed slowly, and only at sunrise was Louisa finally able to rest, sleeping as much from exhaustion as from relief. Hours later, she woke to find

Aaron dressed and sitting beside her in a chair pulled next to the bed. "That was a rough night!" he said, standing to ring for Loo Kim. "She'll bring you something to eat, and look after you. Think you've recovered? Or do you want some laudanum?"

"I hope that was the worst of it. I don't think I want any laudanum, but I'd have been grateful for one of Carmen's potions last night. I don't remember ever being so ill before," she sighed wearily. "What time is it?"

"It's past eleven and you've kept me from my appointments, as well as kept me awake most of the night." He smiled at Louisa, sitting next to her on the bed.

"Sorry. I hope I haven't interfered with the important affairs of state," she mocked, kissing his mouth when he came close to her.

He stroked her hair, pushing a few disorderly strands away from her face. "You ought to give up hard liquor so early in the morning," he remarked, lifting the whiskey bottle from the bedside table to pour her another small drink. "This will help you sleep," he said, offering her the amber liquid.

"Last night I was afraid you might make me drink the whole bottle."

"Believe me, the thought crossed my mind."

She smiled at him weakly. "I'm going to spend the day in bed."

"So you can keep me awake all night again?"

"Perhaps," she countered, pulling him close, caressing him.

"Don't tease—I've been away much too long to tempt unless you're up to it, he said, again smoothing her hair away from her pale face, kissing the pulse beating rhythmically at her throat, moving his mouth familiarly along the swelling curves of her breasts as they pushed invitingly at the low neckline of her sheer nightgown. But he stopped himself there, taking a deep breath, arising reluctantly from her embrace. "I'll be back late this afternoon. Get some rest."

"If you're going to town, tell Mrs. Stevens I won't

be in for my fitting? Or send a message for me, please."

"Any other errands, madam? Anything to oblige you."

"Go!" she ordered, smiling back at his cheerful teasing. How wonderful to have him with her again, she thought, as she fell into hazy, uneasy dreams.

When he left the room, Aaron's face betrayed nothing of his thoughts. He'd spent the early part of the morning with Marshall's mother, relating Louisa's indisposition, briefly discussing his change of politics, and his expectations for the regime Simon and his partners envisioned. Emma seemed keenly alert, listening earnestly, saying little, apparently happy to have more time alone with her son than she expected and pleased to find there was no residue of anger from their confrontation a few days before. She would leave day after tomorrow and seemed only to want to draw a little closer to her son again, to heal permanently any remaining scars.

Later, Aaron sat by Louisa for perhaps an hour, watching her sleep, wondering about the intensity of her pain, brooding silently over the woman and what he knew of her various agonies. He wondered if what he felt for her was actually love. If so, how could he do, or even contemplate, the things he did? Yet he could not recall ever feeling any emotion stronger than what he persistently, though distressingly, felt for Louisa, and he acknowledged what he felt for her was in no way diminished by the moments he'd spent with Marguerite in the past couple of days.

The morning he returned to Crane's Nest, he'd begun to court her. And just as he'd suspected, there was little need for a formal or prolonged courtship. She was of like mind and readily gave her favors. They met on his now daily trips to town, and it seemed Marguerite had missed him in his absence from Monterey nearly as much as Louisa had.

Aaron was reassured to know his passion for Louisa had not affected his ability to be eager for and aroused by the touch of another woman. The assault of Mar-

guerite's heavy sensuous perfume, the heat of her inviting body easily worked their magic on him. When
he found himself in her embrace, enjoying the new-
ness of her touch, he savored the difference between
the women and the excitement of a change from
what with Louisa was profoundly, completely satisfying. Marguerite was a selfish and demanding lover,
her ecstasy coming in violent aggressive lovemaking.
Her preference for rough treatment surprised him, because she had a soft, almost childish look about her,
but Aaron more than gladly obliged her whims. He
discovered his reserves of anger were quite sufficient
to play her brutal games, and his experience with her
never failed to please him in the end. Best of all, beneath the surface of passion there were no bonds of
affection for him to struggle with, no feelings he had
to deny, and never any fear that he could not walk
away from her unscathed. He pretended all the necessary emotion to lure Marguerite to his needs should he
want information from her, but beyond the fleeting
release he found in her arms, he took no satisfaction,
nor did he lose anything of himself he could not regain.

By the time Aaron returned to Crane's Nest, it was
early evening, and Louisa was up, looking pale yet
radiant, seeming to enjoy a glass of wine with the others before supper. Her hair was swept high, away from
her face with cascades of curls left to trail down her
back. She wore a new white linen dress with narrow
grass-green stripes widely spaced in the fabric. The
neckline was invitingly low, tempting all four men to
speculate on the glorious sensations awaiting the man
who unfastened her bodice.

Louisa had spent most of the day sleeping. When
she woke, she discovered the bleeding had all but
stopped, and she wondered what it meant. Last month
she'd bled, but very little, now that she thought about
it. And this time, the pain had been incredible, the
bleeding heavy, yet, within hours, the flow had diminished to an insignificant amount. Maybe there's a doctor in town, she thought absently, and the signs she

suspected were unmistakable, persisted. She said nothing of her doubts to anyone, and when Aaron joined her in their bed that night, Louisa welcomed him without restraint. He sought her as he always had, without hesitation, barely noticing her condition, aware only, when he took her into his arms, that her cries were not from pain but for the joy of his touching her.

Chapter Sixty-one

꘎꘎ THE next morning Louisa woke to find Aaron turned on his side watching her while she slept. "You got in the habit of sleeping in while I was gone. You're getting spoiled!" he said as he began undoing a long strand of satin-covered buttons to free her from a filmy negligee. "These things are a damned nuisance," he remarked, struggling with the small, tightly fastened satin pearls.

"They're for security. Protection from unwanted intruders."

"She wears yards of transparent gauze over her wonderful body, and openly lures me into her bed. Then she hopes twenty buttons will save her virtue!" He caressed her breasts through the sheer fabric, opening the neckline when Louisa had finished with the buttons, his mouth fast seeking her rose-colored nipples, his fingers familiar and gentle on her soft skin. She sighed under him, soon losing her way in the morning, her eyes closed as she yielded herself. Soon she was writhing in his arms, caressing and wanting him, bringing him swift release when at last he entered her.

"Which one of us needs protection?" he wondered softly, his mouth against her ear as he lay holding her close.

"I'll defend you," she promised, stroking him with gentle, soothing hands. "You're safe with me," she laughed.

They lay quietly, talking and teasing, and momentarily Aaron was able to forget his need to be separate from Louisa. In those fleeting minutes it was as if they were more than lovers, much more than conspirators

whose allegiance to one another would cease when all
the schemes were uncovered and the plans overturned.
But Louisa spoiled the illusion, whispering "I love you
so," fiercely yanking him back to reality. In disbelief
Aaron found himself beginning to utter those same
words to her, and he hurriedly retreated from her
reach, alienating himself; safe, once again.

Later he promised to join her downstairs, planning
after breakfast to spend one last morning at Crane's
Nest with Emma. Louisa bathed and dressed leisurely,
having a good deal of time to herself before everyone
would gather for a formal morning meal. Yet when
she entered the dining room, she was surprised to discover neither Aaron nor Emma present.

"I expected Aunt Emma to be down by now, William? In fact, *I* expected to be the tardy one."

Easton smiled at Louisa's fresh appearance. The
pale blue dress she wore made her skin as translucent
as the fragile china adorning his table. She thought
Easton stared at her longer than necessary before re-
plying to her remarks. "Anna says Emma will be confined to her room for the day, just as you were
yesterday. Perhaps what incapacitated you is contagious," he offered with no apparent concern. "She says
her travels have at last caught up with her."

"And no doubt the anticipation of another sea voyage is not improving her health," added Franklin Carson who still suffered from his recent journey, though
he anticipated eating a hearty breakfast this morning.

"Perhaps I should see her before I sit down,"
Louisa suggested, turning to leave the room.

"I think you might wait until you've had something
to eat. Mrs. Sutton is looking after her, and Marshall
has been up to see her already."

"Oh? Where is he now, do you know?" she
asked, moving to the table.

"He said you and he were going to ride this morning, and I presume he went to make those arrangements. He left the room only a few minutes ago. Sit
down, Louisa," he ordered kindly. "Enjoy your breakfast. You look much too pale to be skipping a meal.

He'll be after you in a few minutes, I'm sure. And Emma is not as gravely ill as the look on your face suggests."

Louisa smiled at Easton, surprised he had noticed her state of concern. She'd come to think the man was too involved with himself to pay much attention to the condition of others, which was unfair of her, perhaps. She sat at the table reluctantly. Lately her appetite was not good, and this morning, with the news of Emma's indisposition, she felt even less inclined to eat. Her uneasiness about Marshall's mother was heightened by the woman's sudden illness. Something intangible, something at the back of her neck, told her Emma's illness was not the contagious kind. She worried the woman's ailment might be more dangerous than some simple communicable infection.

Louisa ate very lightly, not waiting for Aaron, then excused herself from the table. "Please tell Marshall I'll not be riding with him this morning," and she disappeared up the stairs, soon rapping lightly at Emma's door. Anna admitted Louisa to the room.

"She's dozing just now," volunteered Anna. "If you would sit by her, please, I could take care of some things needing attention downstairs?"

"Of course, Anna."

"I think she would like your company if she wakes." Anna gathered a pile of clothing and prepared to leave the room. Then almost as a second thought, she went again to Louisa. In the enormous room, Emma's bed was quite a distance away, but Anna lowered her voice so there was no chance of being overheard. "I think Mrs. Hudson is worried about her son for some reason she has not confided in me. She is not physically ill, that I can tell, but she is very depressed today, so unlike her usual self." Anna Sutton sighed, pausing to look at Louisa kindly. "I'm really quite worried about her. These last few months have not been happy—what with the family being so upset." She stared silently at Louisa, seeming to consider whether to proceed, watching for some hint in the young woman's intent face.

"Miss Louisa, I have known you for a very long time—forever, as a matter of fact. I speak frankly with you, because we go a long way back. I think we have few secrets the other does not know."

Louisa thought she would faint for fear of what Anna might say next. Her breathing became shallow in anticipation, but Louisa merely looked back at Andrew Sutton's mother, and nodded, encouraging her to continue. "Do you remember Andrew, Louisa?"

She could barely reply. "Why, of course, I do!" she said when she found her voice.

"I've not seen him, nor spoken his name aloud in years, but there has not been a day that I have not thought of him. So I know what it is to worry about a son." Louisa felt huge tears welling in her eyes, grateful the room was extremely dim for the comfort of the patient who still slept soundly in her bed. "I know you are joyfully married to Marshall, and that you have loved him for years. I'm very glad everything worked out as it did. I, for one, never quite understood why you separated in the first place, but it was not mine to decide," she sighed. "Also I bring up Andrew's name because I wanted you to know, when he first came home, I suspected he came more to see you than he did me," she smiled. "He was always so disappointed when you were not at home. I used to laugh at him—privately, of course—for even a young man's pride is strong. He told me once, in an odd moment of secret-sharing, he wished he were Marshall—oh, I think, not for Marshall's easy life, or his wealth, but because of you." This time Louisa's tears were not to be contained, and they ran down her face silently without a chance of stopping them. "I just wish he had kept in touch, even in his trouble. I would have forgiven him anything."

Louisa was overcome, taking the woman into her arms. "I'm so sorry, Anna. I wish I could do something," she cried, much less composed than Andrew's mother.

"It's all right, child. I suppose there's nothing to

be done," she said, settling her emotions, once again resuming her steady, reliable stance. "Now if you will sit with her for a while?" she motioned to Emma.

When Anna left her, Louisa seated herself as comfortably as possible. She stared blankly into the room which was faintly lit by light creeping around the edges of closed draperies. At this moment she was sure she felt at least as weak as Emma did. She'd been quite apprehensive when Anna began to speak of Andrew, and the woman's sorrow, as well as her words, had touched Louisa deeply. She wanted to believe Andrew had loved her when he was young, just as she wanted to believe, and did believe, he loved her now. Silence, Louisa was reassured, was just his nature.

While she sat in the dark, she tried to relax a little and reason out her uneasy feelings concerning Emma. Certainly, anyone is entitled not to be well once in a while. Surely, Emma is tired after the strain of her trip, and the disappointment of not seeing Rachel, and by Aaron's pointed scolding. Preparing for the trip to San Diego took its toll, and as Anna had said, so had all the last unpleasant months. There was nothing out of the ordinary to make Louisa uneasy. Wasn't Aaron confident? Yet there was a feeling she had in the pit of her stomach, a sixth sense told Louisa the woman was suspicious. "But so far, thank God, whatever her doubts, she's remained silent," sighed Louisa.

"Louisa, child. What are you doing here?"

"Oh, Aunt Emma, did I disturb your rest?"

"Not at all. I've got to wake up sometime. I thought a little extra sleep might do me good. But now that you're here, come and sit next to me on the bed. And light the lamp—or, better yet, draw the draperies, please."

Louisa did as Emma requested, first opening the draperies, then sitting very close to her on the bed, reassured to note Emma looked very well. "Louisa, I think you look more pale than I do. Perhaps you should have stayed in bed, too."

"I was worried about you."

"You mustn't worry about me. I'm as strong as an ox. And just about as dogged when I've my mind made up." She paused to look at the young woman next to her. In all honesty, she doubted she had ever seen a woman more beautiful than Louisa. No wonder her son set his eyes and his heart on her. "What a fool I was," she said aloud. Louisa looked startled, but said nothing. "I've been thinking over what you said the other day. It's wonderful to have so much love for a man—as much love as you have for my son. I never for a minute doubted your love for him. I doubted the wisdom of your marriage, and I was very wrong."

Emma Hudson stopped talking, ostensibly to arrange the pillows at her back and to straighten the covers for greater comfort, but she really wanted a few more moments to order her thoughts. Soon she seemed to settle comfortably, smiling gently at Louisa. "Something else troubles me deeply, and I'm struggling to understand. But I cannot provide any more of the answers without some help. *You* must give me the answers."

Emma reached for Louisa's hands and held them tightly, then smiled kindly at Louisa. Suddenly her face hardened slightly and she sat upright, her body filled with tension. Her voice was controlled and soft. "What I want to know—what I *must* know, Louisa—where is my son? I'm sure I know who the man posing as my son is—and doing an excellent job of it. But not good enough for me. He'd fool Simon, I'm sure, as he's obviously fooled everyone else. But he cannot fool me, Louisa. *Not me!*" Emma was incredibly calm, yet it was obvious she was determined and unshakable in her suspicions.

Louisa was stony silent and absolutely motionless. She too was calm, though speechless. How could she find the words, she wondered, and what would the consequences be if she spoke the truth? God knew she had loved Marshall, but now she loved Aaron, and she could not bear to risk losing him. In this fleeting moment, she even wondered if it were possible that she loved Aaron more than she had Marshall.

"Louisa, don't stare mutely at me," Emma said gently. "Answer me. I've thoroughly gone over the possibilities. And I swear, I'm prepared to hear whatever you say. *But I want the truth.* And I want it now, *this minute,*" she said firmly.

Louisa gently pulled her hands from Emma's. She stood and walked to the windows in silence, then turned to the bed to sit down again. For a few minutes the women stared wordlessly at each other. Emma felt apprehensive, and, in spite of her resolve, a heaviness took possession of both her body and spirit. She'd been truthful with Louisa. She had carefully, rationally, logically thought over her son's disappearance, but while she waited for what she hoped would be truth from Louisa's lips, she felt old and haggard beyond words.

Louisa looked at the petite, elegant older woman, who was as much a mother to her as anyone in her life had been. She'd always thought of Emma as a woman of great spirit and pride; somehow always thought of her as youthful. Now she saw the gray streaking her jet black hair; now she saw the lines at her eyes, and the relaxing of the flesh in her face and body. Emma was no longer the young woman who readily dropped her guard and played tag with three spirited children. She was someone else now, and Louisa wondered if she had the strength to hear what had to be said if she were to know the truth she demanded.

Louisa took a deep breath and reluctantly began to speak. "There is only one person on the the face of the earth who *might* have loved Marshall more than I did, Aunt Emma. And not even in the darkest moments could you ever doubt how much I loved him. I would not be here—I would not have left our child —if I had not loved him so much." Louisa stood up again, suddenly feeling very distraught and trapped.

She turned her back on Emma Hudson, then whirled on her emotionally. "My God, how can I tell you this, without it killing you—and me, too?" she cried.

Louisa sucked in her breath and tried to control herself as the tears began to flow. She sat down once more and took Emma's hands in hers, whether to comfort the other woman or to have someone to hold onto, she did not know. "Aunt Emma," she said, nearly unable to force the words out even in a whisper, "Marshall was murdered! Murdered by men who scheme to make themselves rich and powerful, by men we both know only too well!"

The color had drained from Emma's face and she closed her eyes, as if the truth had accomplished what Louisa had feared. But soon both women were overwhelmed by their tears, neither able to offer the other much consolation, yet they held each other fiercely as if their touching might somehow help them.

Chapter Sixty-two

BEFORE the women could find words again, they were interrupted by knocking at the door, and Louisa pulled herself away from Emma's grieving arms, trying desperately to wipe away her own tears and make herself presentable.

"Who's there?" she called through the door.

"It's Marshall. May I come in?" he inquired, not waiting for a response as he opened the door and let himself into the room. His fears were confirmed the instant he saw Louisa's face. "What's going on?" he whispered harshly.

"She knows!" she replied, also in a whisper. Aaron frowned deeply, glancing at Emma who lay with her back turned to them. "And I've just told her about Marshall's death."

Cold tension filled Aaron's face, but oddly he did not feel the apprehension he might have. Though Emma's sensibilities had been overtaxed in recent months, he knew when the woman's tears were spent, she could be relied on to be level-headed and, probably in this circumstance, vengeful. "What gave me away?" he asked casually.

"Instinct, I guess. We both feared it. I think she's been suspicious all along. But I'm certain she's said nothing to anyone." Louisa reached for Aaron's hand and walked with him to the bedside. Emma had covered herself with her robe and sat on the edge of the bed. She was ashen and her eyes were very swollen from crying, but she seemed remarkably composed.

"Sit down, both of you," she said, gesturing to chairs next to the bed. "You have a great deal yet to tell me. I must know it all, Andrew. *All,* not one word less."

She took a deep breath, suppressing the tears threatening to spring from her eyes, reaching to hold one of each of their hands as they seated themselves before her. "My God, Andrew, I never dreamed you'd grow to be so perfect a likeness of my son. Your resemblance is breathtaking."

"That's just what I said when I collected my senses, Aunt Emma. You're a good deal more calm than I was at first," Louisa reassured her.

Emma Hudson took another deep breath. "Perhaps I should have some tea before I hear it all. I suddenly feel weaker than I have in years."

She rang for a servant, staring helplessly at Aaron in silence until her request was taken. Then she listened in horror to Aaron's suspicions about Peter Melville, to the story of Marshall's murder, to a very brief outline of the plans of the conspiracy, agreeing to go to San Diego as planned, to wait for Louisa to join her, to be patient, and to help them however possible.

"And to think, just the other day, Louisa, I cautioned you to be careful, to be certain what you risked was worth the sacrifice!" Now her tears would not be contained. Both Aaron and Louisa reached in one motion to touch her, hoping to lend her comfort, knowing in some primitive way they too were her children. When she was finished crying for the moment, she stared at them. Her look was kind yet hard, the look of someone who at last has confronted reality, and is not pleased. "And what of the other part of your charade? Are you the lovers you pretend to be? Or is that an act, too?"

The couple was silent. Louisa lowered her eyes from Emma's strong questioning gaze, but Aaron looked at her head-on. "That portion of the charade is no act. We share the same bed as husband and wife. What I told you the other day is true."

"Good," Emma sighed, and Louisa looked up in surprise. "If you'd said anything different, I would have doubted the truth of everything else you've said." She reached for Louisa's very cold hands. "I wonder if God will ever forgive me?" she said. "I wonder if you can forgive me, Louisa."

"Yes. I have forgiven you. Long ago. Now you must forgive yourself."

Emma nodded her head, and leaned to kiss Louisa's cheek. "Let me rest for a few hours. We'll have our dinner together here in this room. Make some excuse to Easton. I'd just as soon not see him ever again, at least not until the morning when I say my farewells."

"I'll arrange it," Aaron promised. "Keep this to yourself, Emma. Reveal nothing to anyone, not even to my mother."

"Poor Anna. To have her son within reach . . . she's never uttered your name since you jumped ship abroad, but I know she's never for an instant forgotten you. Andrew, you too have a lot to forgive me for. It's very easy to make Simon the guilty one, but he hasn't sinned alone, it seems."

"We'll save our conversation for later, Aunt Emma," he said, taking Louisa's hand again, ushering her from the room and into their own. Louisa threw herself on the bed, lying face down, covering her head with her arms, silent and feeling exhausted. When she raised her eyes she saw Aaron at the windows, staring silently into the noonday sun. "It was wishful thinking to believe she wouldn't know. You trust her, don't you, Aaron?"

"Almost as much as I trust you, Louisa. Her pain must be as great as yours," he said solemnly.

"Don't be so foolish as to believe that," she said quietly, rising to stand beside him when he turned to face her. "No one, not even his mother, loved him like I did."

"But her love has never changed, and, if I am to believe you, *you* love *me* now."

"I love you, Aaron, but I will always love Marshall. Love doesn't disappear when the grave is closed. Surely you realize that."

"I know very well," he replied, turning back to the windows. "But I'll never get used to a ghost standing over my bed."

Louisa stood behind him, slipping her arms around his waist, leaning against his back. "I have never made love to you thinking you were anyone but who you are. You've never been Marshall in my arms. I swear it."

Aaron stood very still, beginning to be aware of the pleasure of Louisa's body against his, and for now he didn't bother to confront her with the truth, instead turning to her to hold her tightly, hoping that in her loving embrace he would be relieved of the anxieties of the painful morning.

Chapter Sixty-three

AFTER bidding good-bye to Emma at the Monterey waterfront, Aaron and Louisa returned to Crane's Nest, riding into the hills as they had that first evening. But this time they did not ride in silence, nor did they feel the same apprehension as on the night of their arrival. The black man who drove the team of bays this morning was their confidant; the rich and varied landscape now seemed comfortingly familiar, and the errand they'd just completed lifted a burden from them, even if it did not lift their spirits. Emma Hudson politely said her farewells to William Easton, Franklin Carson, and Alex Fielder as if she knew nothing more of the intrigue this morning than she did when she first arrived. She seemed only the pleasant, gracious wife of Simon Hudson, very removed in her interest in their politics. No one but Aaron and Louisa knew the extent of her knowledge, and even her farewells to them had been full of restraint, with no questions or last-minute doubts. Her questions had been answered the night before, forthrightly and sometimes coldbloodedly by Aaron, and she trusted the truthfulness of the man she intuitively had known was not her son. She alone continued to believe Marshall's ideals would have been unwavering, even in the circumstances, but she acknowledged she had no proof, only a mother's confidence.

On that last night with Emma, Louisa had learned much about Aaron, realizing then how much she had accepted on faith while desperately trying to deal with the difficult present. But Emma had no night terrors to shut doors on, and she pointedly asked for answers to questions to bring herself up to date on the child she had too readily forgotten when he went out of her home and off to sea. Aaron told them about his life, touching truthfully but briefly on the external facts, but revealing little of what actually made up the man, leaving Louisa to speculate on the shading of his words, adding meaning to this history when she recalled other very familiar, less articulate, sounds of his voice.

With Emma on her way to San Diego, Aaron again became deeply embroiled in plots and plans hatched over conference tables and, now, even at late-night suppers with select and knowledgeable guests. He was watchful, alert to all possible outlets for information, and careful to keep Marguerite happy. He was discreet, but he found the lady was less inclined to secrecy. When the Hills dined at Crane's Nest Marguerite was bold and something less than diffident. She sought Aaron's attention openly, and only Colonel Hill appeared to be oblivious. Louisa found herself wide-eyed, and Easton watched with great and open interest.

Marguerite flirted with no apparent regard for propriety, though in public Aaron was guarded. "What do you suggest I do, Louisa?" he shouted at her late one night when she railed at him, her jealousy obvious in face of Marguerite's flagrant behavior. "Potentially, she can provide us with invaluable information. She lies in more beds than her own, and I suspect she could pry information from a sphinx if she set her . . . mind to it."

"Is she prying anything from your lips, Aaron?" Louisa flashed, pulling her dress over her head in preparation for bed, but she received no reply as she struggled with buttons that became tangled in her hair. When she extracted herself, she stood staring at him silently, watching him undress with his back to her. She folded her dress in her arms, watching as his muscles rippled under the smooth dark skin of his back and arms, longing for him, eager to touch and caress his lithe body. But when Marguerite's face came to mind, Louisa bristled and pursued her inquiry. "What 'state secrets' has Mrs. Hill shared with you?"

Aaron was tired from several long days and nights, and his temper was strained. At Louisa's question, he froze for an instant, the tension of his body apparent. Then he whirled on her with uncharacteristic venom, surprising them both, and betraying his weariness. "What is it you want to know?" he demanded, his voice brimming with suppressed violence, his shining eyes coal-black in the dim light. For several minutes they stood motionless, and he stared at her waiting for a reply. When it was obvious she had none, he turned away from her and they did not speak to each other again, finishing their preparations for bed as if the other was not present. Yet each was very aware of the other, and alternately angry and sorry for the way the day was coming to a close, but neither was willing to make the first move to alter the climate in the room. Louisa took an unusually long time with her hair, unpinning the coils, brushing the gold threads to an unsurpassed luster, while Aaron watched from the bed, turning away from her when she at last extinguished the lamp.

Though they were both exhausted, they lay sleepless in the darkness. Finally Aaron reached to touch her. At first she pulled away, but instantly she felt the uselessness of her gesture, knowing she had no real wish to deny herself the pleasure of his embrace. Within moments their angry exchange over the colonel's wife was forgotten. But in the remaining weeks of their stay at Crane's Nest Marguerite's name often came between them, and, at times, it was debatable whether ghosts or the living wielded a stronger influence in determining the outcome of the affairs at hand.

They were often entertained at the Hills' and in

other splendid homes in Monterey. The atmosphere was intimate and friendly, though Colonel Hill and his wife were not yet formally drawn into the conspirators' circle. His allegiance to the federal government was "a matter of honor," he declared. But, he vowed, if war came, he would resign his commission to support the Southern cause. Therefore Colonel Hill was only courted, not yet invited into camp. However, it was hoped he might still be useful.

For most, the colonel's loyalty was above reproach, but open-eyed observers suspected Marguerite's fidelity to her husband, and those who watched closely wondered about Marshall Hudson, as well. Their exchanges were more friendly than necessary, thought Louisa, and whenever they danced together they seemed to enjoy each other's embrace a little too much, or so it appeared to her.

Other doubts began to cloud Louisa's emotions. Was Aaron less interested in her own attentions lately, or was her imagination running away from her? When he did make love to her he was never careless, never thoughtless, always full of passion, his hunger for her undiminished, but he seemed to have less and less time for her. Of course, Peter Melville had returned to the estate, and the days were long and exhausting. Aaron did not explain the details to her, yet Louisa knew there was discord and some sort of difficulty from the number of couriers who rode onto the property, lingering only long enough to eat and sometimes sleep, then to carry messages bound for destinations unknown to her.

Eventually Louisa could not contain her suspicions. She found she could not deny the look she saw in Marguerite's eyes whenever Aaron was in her company. To Louisa it was the unmistakable look of a woman who enjoyed more of the man than his embrace on the dance floor. But for now Louisa did not confront Aaron. She simply withdrew a little from him, and nursed her pain. She attended to the odd intermittent physical discomfort she had begun to live with, and she accepted the reality of her pregnancy with regret and apprehension.

Louisa bled irregularly, and though the amount was insignificant, it was abnormal. She might have overlooked this aspect of her pregnancy, for she knew it was not unheard of, but the infrequent but intense stabs of pain could not be ignored, even by a woman who, in times past, had often chosen to retreat to other levels of reality. Her discomfort was more acute because she faced it alone, and because it was mingled with other, less identifiable pain.

In indecision and growing doubt about Aaron's affection, Louisa drew gradually and hesitantly close to Alex Fielder. Aaron was forever tied up with his political colleagues, but Alex found time to schedule occasional outings with her. She had finally prevailed upon Samuel to build palettes and easels; paints and canvas arrived as ordered, and seemingly there was nothing to prevent their self-indulgent excursions into the countryside. From Easton's study, Aaron often caught glimpses of them when they drove down the path in William's carriage. Sometimes he would see them off on horseback, their charcoal or pastels and paper carefully tucked into saddlebags. Aaron thought Louisa seemed more cheerful, even radiant, after these outings with Fielder, and he was correct, for she was cheered by the open air and scenery, and by the companionship of a warm, literate, and compassionate man who sensed she was lonely and silently suspected her husband, just as she did.

Louisa was attracted to Alex for reasons she didn't care to explore with herself too deeply. He had a gentleness about him reminiscent of Marshall, and in contrast to Aaron. She knew Alex admired her, and suspected she might easily trespass on his loneliness with his willful cooperation, but Louisa knew he would not demand anything from her. He would be satisfied with the pleasure of shared friendship.

But Aaron soon began to wonder whether Louisa and Alex were not drawn together by more than artistic talent. Aaron had seen Alex look at Louisa with open admiration. Who didn't, he reminded himself, when he chose to be rational. But Alex was the sort of man he feared as a competitor for Louisa's lasting affection. He was all the things Aaron was not: a man of education, breeding, wealth, and social position. In addition he was physically the kind of man who might compete with him in satisfying Louisa's other undeniable, perhaps unquenchable, needs. He'd watched them dance together occasionally, seeming to fit together like interlocking pieces of a puzzle, their common fairness making them seem like shafts of wheat undulating together in a prairie wind. These two were much less of a contrast than he and Louisa were. In many respects Alex and Louisa seemed like kindred spirits, far less strident, more melodious than he and Louisa would ever be.

They were like two smooth stones from the wave-swept beach, pleasing to the senses, matched in so many respects, and he began telling himself, for reasons of his own, that Louisa would betray him, confirming his doubts at every turn. So when, as he descended the stairs one morning, he saw Louisa embrace Alex with considerable strength and passion, he felt the muscles of his body tighten, but he was not unprepared. What he did *not* see, what he did *not* hear was the man's tears, nor did he know that Louisa only reached out instinctively to Alex to comfort him in his grief. And, unfortunately, for some reason in the now chaotic pace of the household, Aaron never heard the news about the death of Alex's infant son, nor did he learn the news struck nearly as intense a blow to Louisa. It was as if the message which arrived that morning had been for her. It was news that promptly summoned all of her carefully suppressed feelings— those guilty feelings she had put in their shallow grave to make her temporary abandonment of Rachel something she could live with.

Momentarily frozen in his descent of the stairs, Aaron watched Louisa hold another man fiercely in her arms, watched her give comfort, saw her press her

Chapter Sixty-four

Louisa hoped the shearing pain that edged along her ribs and seemed to constrict her lungs was not visible, especially to the woman who sat glowing and confident before her. Aaron and Colonel Hill conversed energetically by the windows and it appeared they and other guests had no hint of her misery. The afternoon kept everyone else comfortably occupied and amused. The wines and liquor, the delicacies from Easton's kitchen were in plentiful supply, and the house and garden patios were thronging with amused and cheerful guests.

Louisa tried to ignore her unhappiness, tried desperately to be entertained by Marguerite's conversation. Why did the woman single her out, Louisa wondered. She would have preferred to be ignored, or at least politely overlooked. But it was not the way it was, just as there was no longer any way for Louisa to ignore Aaron and Marguerite's affair. Even Easton knew, she was certain, otherwise he would never have been so bold as to touch her the way he had.

He had discovered her reading in his study late one night, trying to find sleep between pages of a book when it would not come naturally in her half-empty bed. Aaron and Melville had dined with Colonel Hill that night and had not yet returned to Crane's Nest. Aaron was often, though explainably, late to return, and his absences from the estate were now more frequent. The times that disturbed her were the times he came in alone, though in the course of meeting his new responsibilities, she simply lost track of his agenda. She told herself she had no reason to suspect him, but she knew it was a lie. Hadn't he told her he expected her to use her body if it were to their advantage in this intrigue? She had no doubt about his stance as it applied to her, and no reason to think he would be more circumspect about his own behavior.

Easton had brought her a glass of sherry, then joined her on the leather couch, seeming relaxed and intently concerned about her comfort. They'd talked for perhaps half an hour, Louisa sharing with him her first effusive letter from Emma. They'd laughed at grandmothers in general and he spoke kindly and with apparent understanding of her loneliness for her child. They had remained in Monterey far longer than she had expected, she said. "Perhaps I should go home," she sighed wistfully. "If I were to leave tonight, Marshall's so occupied with his affairs it would be days before he'd even notice my absence."

"You're mistaken, Louisa," William had offered, taking her hand in his, quickly moving closer to her, reaching into the deep V of her robe, touching her breast through her night dress, his hand swiftly descending down her belly. She shuddered and recoiled, hoping surprise rather than her revulsion came through as she shrank from his touch. She wanted to scream at him, but maintained a presence of mind well beyond what she would have thought possible had anyone suggested Easton would approach her in such a fashion.

"I can't believe you'd forget yourself so!" she blurted with incredible calm, wanting to lash out at him with all of her strength, not knowing where she found the nerve to stare at him, sweetly portraying bewilderment when all she felt was fury and loathing. But she lost little time in retreating from the study, flying up the stairs, locking her door behind her, ripping her robe and gown from her body, feeling unclean.

Aaron's knocking at their door came quickly thereafter, and the mood he found her in was not one he expected, not one he relished. Wildly pacing the floor in the nude, she was not yet calm from her encounter with Easton, and related her tale in a harsh whisper. Aaron smiled wickedly at her lack of clothing, but his grin disappeared soon enough.

"I'm leaving here. You've no further need of me. I've carried out my bargain. I'm only in your way," she tossed out her challenge, finally opening the subject she had delayed as long as possible. "Then you'll be free to make love to Marguerite with my blessing."

Aaron frowned at her as he removed his clothes, standing barefooted now, in only his trousers, with his shirt open. She'd flung herself in the bed with her last accusation, pulling the covers protectively over her body, staring back at him with obvious fury. "I've not asked for your 'blessing,' " he tossed back at her, feeling tired and drained, not wishing to bring up this topic for discussion at this hour of the mornng.

"Well, thank you, for at least not lying to me," she hissed. "At least you don't come into my bed protesting your innocence."

His dark eyes narrowed. He had expected the subject to come up sometime, he'd only hoped it would come at a time when he was less exhausted. "Louisa-the-pure-in-heart. What about you? What of your affair with Alex Fielder? And you can claim no better motive than pleasure!"

Louisa's mouth dropped open, finding no possible reply for his accusation, her head beginning to spin. But he took no notice, his intention now only to injure, to inflict pain, and he knew his approach would be precisely on target. He threw back the covers of the bed, exposing her beautiful naked body, nearly unable to restrain himself from a sudden impulse to cease this form of attack and begin another, one far more gratifying than the one he forced himself to pursue.

"Tell me, Louisa. What promises have I broken? What words have I said to you to make you believe I would be faithful to you? In fact, didn't I assure you I could make no promises? I warned you not to fall in love with me. And I don't have to remind you, do I, this is not a children's game of hide and seek. People die in war, Louisa, and for us, this *is* the war, our own little battleground. Maybe no blood has been let on these priceless carpets, nor men's guts splattered on the elegant furnishings, or on the richly brocaded walls, but the time is coming. Maybe not here, in this house, but soon—somewhere." His voice was hushed but vicious, his eyes flashing, black and ominous. "And I'll fuck whoever I think will give me the answers I need —and I'll do it *before your very eyes,* if she asks!"

Louisa looked back at Aaron's ferocity in horror, knowing what he said was true, trusting he was capable of doing what he threatened, and though she suspected he had suggested it to make his point, she shuddered, the images in her mind all too clear.

And suddenly Louisa remembered this man who stood before her was not the man he pretended to be, not the gentle man of good breeding and wealth, not the protective lover whose name he used. Suddenly she realized she too had found his performance as Marshall Hudson believable. She too had acclaimed him another man when, in fact, he was not. Aaron Sumner, né Andrew Sutton was "low-born," as someone long ago had so aptly pointed out. Just recently he had told her briefly of his coarse and violent life, admitting he only revealed the simplest facts. Now she could imagine he had shared only the best of his experiences, though his revelations had been adequately shocking, and Louisa realized she knew very little of the man who stood angrily before her.

Aaron watched Louisa carefully, silent for several minutes, certain his words had stunned her. Some of his tension eased, and he sat down on the bed next to her. She said nothing, lying against the pillows staring at him, her luminous, expressive eyes full of pain. Her immobility concerned Aaron, for rarely, if ever, had Louisa not spoken her mind to him. But he ventured on, and though he was a little uncertain of her response, or lack of it, he pursued his course.

Aaron quickly removed the rest of his clothing, his eyes filled with the woman he preferred and longed for above any he had known, and at least his physical attraction for her was evident to both of them. He moved next to her in the bed, taking a reluctant hand, opening her clenched fist, forcing her to hold her fingers around him, increasing their pressure slightly, then taking her hand from him again, rolling onto her, holding her hands at bay, and with the weight and motion of his body forcing her thighs open, nudging himself just inside her moist sensitive body. She struggled vigorously with him, but cried out almost pleasurably at his entry. Without volition her body fiercely acknowledged his, and when he stopped short, her look was at least one of surprise, if not disappointment. "You think yours is the only body that can make mine sweat and ache and deliver satisfaction?" he began sarcastically, his voice low, constricted. "You are wonderful—God knows, how good you feel!" he cried with feeling, moving quickly, his rough words reproduced in the movements of his body. "But let me assure you, Louisa," his voice uneven amid his thrusts, "yours is not the only . . . pleasurable cunt . . . here . . . or anywhere else."

As he spoke, Louisa at first lay tense and still beneath his familiar weight, but when his words registered on her, she became convulsive. She spit in his face, and struggled wildly, screaming furiously, incoherently at first, trying in her rage to shred his face with her nails. Aaron was amazed at her sudden strength, wondering momentarily if he'd not gone too far. Hell hath no fury . . . , he reminded himself as he defended the most vulnerable part of his body, finally besting her. Louisa was outraged beyond comprehension. He had forced her onto her stomach, and was lying heavily on top of her, pinning her helplessly on the bed. "You going to behave when I let go?" he taunted her harshly.

"You *consummate* bastard!" she hissed into the bedding.

"Make up your mind—I could probably sleep soundly all night—just like this," he said, stroking her soft, shapely body.

"Yes! Yes!" she replied exhaustedly under his crushing weight.

He let her go and she turned on her side, curling her legs against her body, lying helplessly at first, her breathing hard, arhythmic. She closed her eyes, alternately feeling both stone cold with shock and burning with rage. Her body was rigid with anger, and she forced herself to relax, lying still for some time. When she opened her eyes in the faintly lit room, she found nothing had changed. She turned to find Aaron was still beside her, lying, she noted, a good distance from her in the bed. And then she began to laugh, softly at first, then uproariously, which did a good deal to upset Aaron's sense of accomplishment.

Then as abruptly as she'd begun to laugh, she stopped, quickly rolling next to him, gripping his upper arms, digging her nails into his flesh, looking him savagely in the eye. "Aaron, my sweet," she hissed between clenched teeth, "mine may not be the only 'cunt,' as you aptly pointed out, but mine is the only one you really want. You may spill yourself all over creation, but here is where you want to be!" She suddenly let go of him, shoving herself away, sitting up, leaning back onto her hands, enjoying his hard but questioning look. She offered him a good view of her silhouette in the lamplight, turning her luscious breasts for his full perusal. "I may not know every detail about your past, *but I know you.* I've made love to you, and held you, and you've *made love* to me—you've poured yourself out to me—in every respect—whether you know it or not. You may not love me, Aaron, but if you don't, there's no one on earth you love. And you'll never be done with wanting me! There's only one 'cunt' for you, Aaron, and it's *mine!*"

With tears streaming down her face, Louisa jumped from the bed, dashing for the wardrobe, seeking her most protective nightrobe, but Aaron was beside her wrenching the garment from her hands, throwing it wildly across the room. She struggled with him, crying helplessly now, her own bold words shocking her, making her feel like something from out of the gutter—a place she felt Aaron had helped her into. He carried her, kicking and protesting, crying and screaming invectives at him, and threw her and himself on the bed. He lay with her, his arms crushing her against him until her sobbing ceased, and for some minutes she shuddered and gasped for air. When she was still, he began to kiss her gently, but she lay tense and unresponsive. He rolled onto his back and drew her on top of him, and, for what seemed like a very long time, he rubbed her back, pulling her against him until she seemed to relax into him, and he held her quietly. Then he released her, and lay next to her, watching her. She seemed lonely, her eyes wide with sadness, but when he began to kiss her again, she returned his kisses and caresses, at first tentatively, then with passion. He touched her in the gentlest of ways, slowly moving his hands and mouth on her compelling body, touching her at last where he longed to be. "You *must* stay. I won't let you go," he said as he slipped into her body. "Promise me, Louisa."

"I promise," she whispered, moving with him eagerly. He was tender, and she responded to him as if his hateful stinging words had not shattered the night, both of them knowing what she'd said was true: he wanted her—only her—and he would never stop wanting her. And for the time being, nothing was really changed between them.

Chapter Sixty-five

WAS it any easier, Louisa asked herself, now that she knew for certain? Hoping Aaron loved her, believing he only toyed with Marguerite for other purposes, had, at best, a very hollow satisfaction. The next time she saw Marguerite, Louisa's face became very flushed, prompting Marguerite to ask if she were feeling ill. What was worse, the woman didn't leave Louisa's side, and Louisa began to down considerable amounts of wine, listing between barely contained tears and giddy escape into drunkenness.

"You must come with me to San Francisco," she heard Marguerite purr in her low sensual voice. "I'm leaving early next month. I'll take you to the best dressmaker on this coast. When we come back, we'll really turn their heads—something which seems to be increasingly difficult," she sighed, gesturing to the men who retired to another room, closing the doors on the two women.

"That sounds like a splendid idea!" Louisa laughed. "It would be nice to have a really good dressmaker rather than whoever is available." Then Louisa pouted, impatiently holding out her wineglass to a servant for a refill of the deep crimson liquid. She drained the glass very quickly. "A very good idea," she said again to Marguerite, and giggled uproariously, silently thinking her private thoughts. How perfect, she mused. *His* wife and *his* mistress traveling together— what tales we could exchange! Or is it his mistress and his mistress—all the same to him. God damn him! She frowned soberly. He only uses me, too—just as he pledged, promising nothing else. She closed her eyes

and leaned back into the cushions of the couch, feeling
herself whirl, not unpleasantly, under the effects of too
much wine. She was tempted to drink away her pain,
to swim far below its surface, but she'd tried that
before, she remembered, and it didn't work. "To the
realities of life here in this marvelous house," she said
flippantly to Marguerite when she again opened her
eyes, raising her glass gaily.

Marguerite imitated her, and took a sip more of
wine. "Do you feel all right, Louisa?" she said, laughing lightly at Louisa's false but convincing gaiety.

"As a matter of fact, no. Please excuse me," she
said, standing quickly, hastily leaving the room and a
bemused Marguerite. Louisa hastened up the stairs,
feeling the blood pound in her head, stumbling blindly
as her tears ran down her cheeks. Louisa shut the door
to her room forcefully, then leaned against it, sobbing
until she could no longer stand, all of her strength
drained away. She collapsed at the foot of the door,
trying slowly to recover her patrician façade.

When she was calm she turned to ice, turning
abruptly, knowing she was not alone in the room. She
turned her head and the terror in her eyes dissolved to
more tears before the gentle Loo Kim. Louisa covered
her face and cried out her grief incoherently, while
Loo Kim came slowly to her, stooping with effort,
reaching to comfort her. Louisa was unsure what, if
anything, the servant knew, but neither woman was
immune to tragedy, nor were they hardened enough
to let the gulf of class prevent tenderness and sympathy to flow between them.

When Louisa was quiet again, she looked up at Loo
Kim, really seeing her for the first time. Her eyes widened and she sucked in her breath. "What's happened
to you?" she asked, startled by the girl's swollen eye
and the splash of blue bruises on her jaw and cheek-
bone.

"It is nothing, madam," she replied, standing with
difficulty yet reaching to assist Louisa from the floor.

"What do you mean, nothing? And it's not just your
face," she said in horror. "Let me see your arms and

legs," noticing more bruises and swelling on her hands.

Loo Kim stood motionless, frozen in her awkward and painful attempt to aid Louisa.

"He's beaten you, hasn't he?" she whispered.

"You are mistaken, madam."

"No, I'm not!" Louisa glared at her. "Don't lie to me! He's beaten you, hasn't he?"

Loo Kim cast down her eyes. Louisa threw back her head and screamed, "God damn this house and all the people in it!" She leaned against the door. "I made him angry and he turned on you! I wondered why you didn't come to me this morning, why there was someone in your place hovering over him at breakfast. The filthy bastard! I hope he rots in Hell with the rest of them!" She covered her eyes with cold fingers, feeling them burning from her tears, her body sagging heavily. "What do we do now, Loo Kim?" she whispered, feeling defeated, lost, and very lonely. "You're a captive and so am I." She reached out her hand to the girl, who helped Louisa to the bed and brought her cool scented cloths to apply to her face and eyes. Soon Louisa's face was soothed and she decided to return to the library to play out the evening's performance.

While Loo Kim carefully rearranged her hair, Louisa studied herself in the mirror. She smiled a benign, empty smile to the face she saw there, then glared at the beauty reflected back at her. This time, as last, pregnancy only made her glow. She was pale but radiant, her body not yet showing any distortion, her curves only enhanced, made more appealing. "No one, especially you, Aaron, will ever know," she said aloud.

By the time she returned downstairs, the men had joined Marguerite, again, and though she wanted to spit in Easton's face, Louisa was polite but diffident, expecting him to assume she was still uncomfortable in the face of their awkward confrontation. She sought out her handsome husband, slipping her arm through his, holding him for reassurance, smiling into his wonderful eyes that seemed to smile lovingly back at her, glowing brilliantly for him and for his comrades. And when they were alone, she made love to Aaron, seducing and draining him of every ounce of his passion for her, while concealing her torment, her fury over her position, her loathing for being used by him, all the while watching him, knowing he was self-satisfied and complacent, his victories and his conquests sure, his losses less than certain, if not unknown.

Chapter Sixty-six

In the morning, Aaron seemed very reluctant to get up from their bed. He lay for a long while on his back staring at the canopy over them. When Louisa woke, she had a slight headache. "From the amount you consumed last night, you deserve worse," he grinned, turning on his side to look at her.

"Why aren't you up by now?" she asked, noticing the time on the clock behind him on the dresser.

"We're taking a holiday. And I'm thinking of spending it right here," Aaron said as he began to play gently with her nipples, which fast responded to his touch. "Is it my imagination, or do you grow more beautiful with every passing day?"

"Which is it, Aaron, are you going to be charming or sarcastic today?" she queried with obvious annoyance.

"Don't be so rough on me, Louisa," he teased.

"My head hurts," she replied coldly.

"A little distraction to help your head," he said, moving his fingers into her hair, kissing her mouth, very easily shifting her focus of attention. "Oh God, you give me so much pleasure," he cried, and she went after him hungrily, listening to him murmur about the way she made him feel, exciting her, making her forget her displeasure of the night before, wondering if she had any strength of character as she responded to him wildly.

Long afterward, they still held each other, neither seeming the least inclined to get up and face the day. "We'll miss breakfast," Louisa said finally with no real conviction.

"Who cares?"

"The rumors will fly," she teased.

"*Fact,* not rumor."

"Don't you care anything about our reputations?"

"Our reputations will only be improved by a day in bed."

"We could say we had a fever."

"We could," he said, grabbing her for the sheer pleasure of feeling her struggle against him and his rough play. When she had stopped her helpless laughter, smiling up at his own smiling face, she threw her arms around him and held him warmly in her arms. "Oh, Aaron, when will we be able to leave here?"

"Soon." He held her, savoring her gentle embrace.

She pulled away from him doubtfully. "What do you mean *soon?*"

"Soon.'"

"That's not going to do! When? I want to know the exact hour!"

"You know, Louisa," he said, suddenly quite pensive, "if I weren't obligated to do what I am, I'd be tempted to join these bastards in their enterprise." Louisa stared at him in disbelief. "They've got a plan for one of the islands lying off the southern part of the coast that very much appeals to the sailor—and the pirate—in me. They're planning to set up a fortress to control shipping along the coast, and possibly to launch military action. I'm to be in charge of seeing the base is set up. We'll be sailing south soon."

"I'm ready to go now. I've been away too long. I have very little stomach for this whole affair. It's much dirtier business than I thought."

"You thought Marshall's murder was a good beginning?" he inquired harshly, annoyed with her unrealistic attitude. "You knew from the beginning you weren't going on a picnic, Louisa. Didn't you hear anything I said to you?"

She pulled away from him. "Perhaps not."

"And speaking of stomach," he said, stroking her belly, his fingers pushing gently against a slight but definite roundness in her firm flesh. "Are you pregnant?" He moved his fingers to explore the fullness of her breasts, then caressed her cheek, waiting for a reply.

Only a few minutes ago she might have easily told him the truth, but the force and sarcasm of his last words still stung her, and though her flesh began again to succumb to him, she looked back at him and said effortlessly, "No, Aaron, I'm *not* pregnant.'"

He moved his hands over her body again, lingering at the slight roundness of her belly. "Not for lack of effort," he smiled.

"I have to get lucky, sometime," she said back to him. "The cards have to go in my favor once in a while." She looked at him coldly. "I don't want your baby, Aaron. Not in these circumstances. Not in this sewer."

"And where did you conceive your last?" he frowned. "The beds may have been clean, but as I recall, the stench, and the rats scurrying about were not too different from the ones who cluster under this roof."

"How would you know?"

"How do I know? You heard what I told Emma. I was under the same roof as you were on a number of occasions. I watched and longed for you in the shadows, while you lusted after my brother, Louisa."

"You make me sound like a slut, when you know it wasn't like that at all," she bristled, trying to pull herself from his very tight grip.

Aaron scowled, releasing her. "You could do worse than . . . we've taken to quarreling a lot lately —you sure you're not pregnant?"

"Very sure," she lied.

He stared at her, his look lingering and hard, sweeping slowly over the length of her still slim body. His voice was cold, even bitter as he said, "It would be a shame to disfigure you with my child. I enjoy you too much just the way you are. But be sure no one else leaves his mark on you, Louisa."

"You've nothing to lose any sleep over!" she snapped, rising from the bed. "No one else will leave his mark on me. Just be careful where you leave your calling card!"

"Marguerite plays far too many games of chance to point the finger at me."

"Perhaps there's safety in numbers," she laughed derisively. "Maybe I should sit at her feet and take instruction," she flashed, her voice teasing and seductive.

"Do, and the mark I'll leave on you will be black and blue."

"Aaron? Why, I think you want to be the only rooster in the yard!"

"The only one in your nest anyway," he replied, pulling her into bed again. "Goddamnit, Louisa, shut up for a while. Whenever we speak to each other lately we end up brawling. God knows, I didn't intend for the morning to start this way," he added, offering as close to an apology as she knew she'd get from him.

She smiled wickedly at him, rolling onto her back. "What you meant to say was, 'Lie back, close your mouth, wait patiently,'" pretending to follow those instructions.

"Precisely," he said, forcing his mouth on hers roughly. "And if I haven't already, I'm going to leave my mark on you this morning!" and he went after her, and she after him, as if they were both determined to have him do so.

Chapter Sixty-seven

THE tension between Aaron and Louisa seemed to lessen. Louisa tried desperately to accept Aaron's alliance with Marguerite philosophically, trusting the tenderness of his embrace spoke more truth than any other act. In spite of small voices that cautioned her, Louisa gave herself to Aaron wanting to believe what she felt for him held sufficient promise. He made it easy for her, seeming to make extra time for her, seeming to see less of Marguerite than he had.

For her part, Louisa now went out infrequently with Alex. She spent a good deal of her time cloistered in her room, or on one of the patios, drawing scenes from her memories, recounting her pleasures and her pain, hiding from herself none of the joys and few of the nightmares. Often, at night, she and Aaron shuffled through this growing portfolio of sketches. He laughed and, sometimes, cried with her as she turned the pages of her life. The pain in her heart and the occasional pain inside her womb drove her to reflect on her agonies. She concentrated on that aspect of her life, hoping to be done with it, to empty her spirit, to open herself fully to peace and, hopefully, love. And whenever Aaron was beside her, his body connected with hers, Louisa trusted his heart was hers as well.

She expected to go south in a month and the prospects gave her more joy than she could contain. But she was brought up short late one afternoon as she was leaving the dressmaker's and met Marguerite, who was on her way to consult Mrs. Stevens.

"Ah, Louisa, you must come with me to San Francisco next month," she offered again. "Your sweet Marshall will approve, I'm sure. It will be a great diversion for you. Peter will fete us grandly. What do you say?"

Louisa barely heard her, staring in disbelief at the woman's eye-catching necklace. She felt weak, gripping the white fence railing surrounding Mrs. Stevens' little yard. Marguerite hurriedly got out of her carriage and came toward her. "Louisa, are you all right? Where's Samuel?" she asked, looking about for the black man. "You've turned quite pale."

"What a lovely necklace, Marguerite," Louisa said quietly, ignoring the woman's concern for her health. Her mind whirled and raced, knowing even as she considered the possibility of a duplicate necklace, there could be no other like it. Marshall had purchased the pearl with her in mind, and he had designed the swirl of diamonds that surrounded it. Louisa had long ago memorized every detail of this most precious of her possessions. For her, it was the symbol of their loving union.

Marguerite cocked her head a little, and looked slyly at Louisa, touching the large tear-shaped pearl hanging so decorously at her throat. "From an admirer. You know me, Louisa," she smiled brilliantly. "I'd find life too dull without a few flirtations."

"Perhaps that's what's wrong with mine, it's devoid of proper excitement," Louisa said drily with amazing calm.

"Well, then, come to San Francisco with me. We'll do more than shop, if you like," she smiled. "Are you sure you're steady on your feet now?"

"Very. My head is suddenly clearer than it's been in some time."

"Good. Then we'll expect you at seven tomorrow." Marguerite patted Louisa's arm, and smiled innocently, immediately entering Mrs. Stevens' little shop.

Louisa had told Samuel she would meet him at the inn, and she bolted there, breathless when she arrived. He immediately helped her into the carriage, noting her agitation and high color. "Take me to the shipping agent," she demanded first thing, to his surprise. She ignored his look and made her demand a second time. Louisa tried to book immediate passage to San Diego, but found it would be weeks before she could make suitable arrangements. When she got into the carriage again, she sat silently for some minutes, then called on Samuel to assist her.

"You said when I first met you that I should feel free to ask you for help if ever I needed it."

He nodded. "I did; and I meant it."

"Can you arrange for someone to escort me to San Diego?"

"When?"

"As soon as possible. Tomorrow."

"I doubt I could make arrangements that quickly. Mr. Hudson hasn't spoken to me."

She stiffened. *"He's* not making the arrangements. *I* am. I've not consulted him," she bristled.

"I see."

"No, you don't see. This is not his affair, not his decision to make. Will you help me, or not?" There was a wildness in her eyes he'd never seen before.

"Yes, Mrs. Hudson, I will help you, if you are determined, and you appear to be just that."

"Thank you, Samuel! Let's go back to the vipers' nest, now!" she ordered. "Wait! Where are my trunks stored?"

"In the shed behind the greenhouse."

"Take me there first." In response, Samuel hurried the horses home. Louisa shivered under her heavy cloak. Samuel lit a lantern and showed her into the shed, leading her to the trunks which were stacked neatly to one side. "I want to open the one on the bottom of the pile. Also, I'll want that one, and the one on top, brought up to my room immediately."

Samuel shifted the trunks, opening the one she requested. Quickly she removed the drawer and maneuvered the hidden panel, reaching for the welvet pouch she'd hidden there when she packed the luggage in San Diego. She sucked in her breath when she found it, but knew instantly it was empty of what should be there. Louisa opened the pouch with icy fingers. In the necklace's place she found a square leather envelope with a seal on the flap. Inside was a letter written on heavy bond, signed and sealed with the same insignia. "God damn you," she whispered, slipping the envelope and its letter into the pocket of her cloak. "I'll walk back to the house," she said. "Please bring up the trunks I mentioned."

She didn't hear Samuel's reply, nor did she see the path she walked on. Storming through the doors of the house, she was grateful she encountered no one. Once in her room, she rang for Loo Kim, and ordered her brusquely about when she arrived. "My trunks will be arriving in a few minutes," she began. "Pack everything in that wardrobe," she pointed to one of the tall chests, "and all the things in these bureaus. The rest will wait till I've a definite departure time." Louisa went to the desk, and pulled out pen and ink, and began writing. "Get me some tea before you begin." The girl skirted away, letting Samuel in with one of the trunks. "You won't forget what you promised?" Louisa asked him.

"Of course not," he replied as he rested the trunk on the floor in the center of the room.

"I'm counting on you."

With his promise, Louisa turned away abruptly and began to draft a hasty letter to Emma, advising her to expect her within days, telling her she was making arrangements now, and would let her know the details when she had made her final plans. "Your son is very well indeed," she concluded tersely, and signed her name. "The bastard!" she muttered, sealing the envelope.

When Samuel returned with the second trunk, she gave him the letter and made him swear he would put it in the hands of a trusted messenger, insisting the note should arrive as soon as possible. Loo Kim returned with a tray, and quickly began to do as Louisa had requested. While she drank her tea, Louisa tried to calm the murderous feelings that welled within her but found she had little success. She closed her eyes, again feeling a slight cramping in her ab-

Chapter Sixty-eight

Louisa tried to relax, to let the fury and tension recede from her a little. She felt tricked and betrayed and stupid. She'd thought she and Aaron had reached an understanding, trusted again that he loved her, knew she loved him without a doubt. Louisa had even believed she could tolerate his affair with Marguerite, though the extent of his involvement was repugnant to her. But quickly her charity had been shattered. Where had she learned, where was it recorded in her diaries, where was it promised that loving and trusting was worthwhile, sensible, or sane behavior?

Louisa watched Loo Kim carefully carry out her instructions, packing her beautiful gowns away. The things being packed now could be sent to her whenever a ship was due to go to San Diego. She would travel with only the necessities, and, of course, her jewels. Surely, for the right price, Samuel Davis would find someone willing to escort her. She would not stay under any circumstances. Yet, in spite of her feelings about Aaron, she did not want to endanger the successful outcome of his mission. "I've invested too much—time away from Rachel, and, God, revenge for Marshall's life means something!" She glanced around the large, beautifully furnished room and fleetingly thought how appropriate cleansing by fire would be for this house as well. She closed her eyes in the early evening and envisioned the act accomplished, feeling enormous satisfaction, a sensation from her past.

"Enough daydreaming. What's going on?" Aaron asked pleasantly, obviously puzzled, turning up the

371

lamp on the table next to her. "It'll be a month before we leave. Aren't you getting ready a little early?"

Louisa had not heard him enter the room, and at his voice her eyes flew open, her look alerting him instantly he was about to deal with a venomous animal. In one motion Louisa flew out of the chair toward Loo Kim. "Leave us alone. I'll call you when I want you," she ordered crossly, waiting for the girl to leave, staring at Aaron with unmistakable loathing.

"God damn you, Aaron! How dare you? How could you? What right do you have to give my possessions away?" She flew at him with insane disregard for his strength and capacity for violence. She knew he'd killed at least one man, and she'd sometimes sensed the volcano beneath his exterior, but reason escaped her in her anger.

Aaron caught her easily, holding her at bay. "Hold on!" he commanded, resisting her as she struck hopelessly at him, and she struggled all the harder, kicking at him, her tears falling fast, her words becoming choked in her rage. Quickly he twisted one of her arms behind her back, pulling her against him fiercely. He increased the pressure of his arm around her, lashing her against him until she could no longer breathe. When he sensed she was subdued he lessened his grip minutely. "Jesus, you're a hellcat!"

The instant she found the strength and breath, she tried to pull away from him, and he only tightened his grip once again. "Give up yet?" he demanded, crushing her a little harder, and she was soon quiet, panting, defeated but not conquered. She couldn't speak, and she gulped in air and began to cough convulsively. Suddenly he turned her loose and she collapsed as he shoved her away from him.

While she regained her breath, he removed his coat, all the while watching her, flinging it over one of the yawning wardrobe doors. "Where the hell do you think you're going?" he demanded.

"Home," she whispered when he strode to her, grabbing her wrists, dragging her to her feet, insisting she answer him.

"What makes you think so?"

"I can't stay. You've spit on me for the last time," she cried. "How could you? How could you give *my* necklace to her? Oh God, you're such a bastard," she screamed, sobbing wildly, trying to cover her face with hands Aaron still held tightly at the wrists. Then he let go of her hands, grabbing her tightly against him with one hand, the other shoved roughly into her flowing hair, slowly pulling her head back until she looked up at him awkwardly, her crying all but ceased. Her face was very wet from tears, and he watched her intently, waiting for her breath to return, feeling the tension of her body increase the longer he held her, his own tension quickly shifting downward with the pressure of his body against hers.

"You will not leave here!" he ordered with a certain indisputable finality in his voice, his deep brown eyes flashing. His voice was hoarse, and, though a whisper, it reverberated in the stillness of the room. "Louisa, I promised you, I'd do whatever was necessary in this charade. Exchanging one of your baubles for information was included in the possibilities," he reminded her heatedly.

Louisa had not been afraid of him since he had identified himself to her that night long ago in San Diego. But now fear crept along her spine. Even so, she was nearly mesmerized, his eyes boring into her, penetrating her deeply as his body often had, and swiftly he began to approach her in a more familiar way, with urgency and compulsion, trying to overcome her, to seduce her to his various needs. She was acutely aware of the hardness and pressure of his body as his mouth closed over hers with eagerness and violence, as if by force he could take her will and bend it to his own. Louisa struggled against him, yet feared she would lose—he would eventually win out—her body would give assent to this power he had over her. Her body would not deny her want of him though she raged against him. "I *will* leave you," she swore weakly. "I cannot stay."

His mood was violent and he pursued her in that fashion, ripping as well as undoing her soft garments, holding her forcefully in his grasp. Then he stopped his harshness. His fingers, which had just bruised and punished her, held her gently, softly stroking her nakedness. "I love you, Louisa, in spite of my silence, in spite of the ugly things I've said. Please," he begged in a moment of tenderness, "you must not leave me—I need you."

Louisa's mind tumbled after his words, shocked by what he said. The unexpectedness of his approach was reflected in her eyes, which widened and became black, dangerous pools. He felt her trembling in his now gentle embrace. How long she had waited and longed to hear him say he loved her! And now his words fell on her like blows. Louisa's face became flushed, and her body raged with heat. "You would say so—anything—to keep me here!" she spat at him like a cat cornered, and for the moment unsurpassed hatred escaped from her into the scant space between them. "You use and lie and betray—whatever means suit your end—and you expect me to bend to your confession of love like a simple fool!"

She laughed at herself sarcastically. "Oh, I understand how you might think so," she whispered venomously against him as he returned his hands to the luxurious softness of her hair, crushing her more tightly against him. Even as she railed, he felt his desire for her, and he was committed to keeping her by him. "You've had your way so easily with me from the beginning!" Only fury kept her tears in check as she pushed strenuously against him in what she knew was a futile effort to escape as she read his body and his desire to consume her and impose his will on her. "You'll no doubt have your way with me now," she seethed as she struggled, feeling his wet mouth on her throat, his kisses soon descending to the swelling of her breasts, "but whatever you do, however I respond, I will not stay one minute longer than I am forced to!" she raged.

It was then Aaron knew he'd lost. Short of keeping her a virtual prisoner, he suspected there was nothing he could do to detain her. There could be no hope of soothing this fury. And the worst of it was, he feared that if she fled she would be lost to him forever, and he sought to bind her to him, hoping to repeat the now countless occasions they had been profoundly intimate. He felt desperate and incredibly needy, and Louisa sensed his urgency, trying all the harder to withdraw from his rough, nearly violent caresses. "Get away from me! Get away!" she hissed, but his mouth and hands persisted against her furiously.

She continued to try to wrench herself away as he moved her, seemingly without resistance, lowering her onto the bed. He caught her hands, which reached frantically to push his mouth away from her breasts, and pinned her arms to the side of her face, looking into her angry eyes—eyes he knew implored him not to take her this way—closing his own, seeking to erase what he saw. He seized her mouth with his, kissing her forcefully, and she fought for her very breath.

Then he relaxed slightly, drawn into his love for her, wanting to feel again the pleasure of her fullest response to him. And slowly Louisa began to fight with herself as much as she did with Aaron. She hated herself, and battled with her own body and mind, for she had come to give herself to him completely—"stupidly," she raged. Whenever he was present, his very nearness aroused her. Even now her anger failed to lend her protection, and soon the heat of rage turned to something more compelling, her struggles becoming movements of surrender and pursuit. She yielded to him and to herself—as if there would never be another time for them.

She shivered and cried out to him, his touch like fire, searing and spreading desire throughout her body. "Louisa, my God, Louisa, believe me, I love you!" he pleaded, kissing her deeply, soon descending from her mouth to softer, more eager places. He wooed her in ways he knew she could not resist and when he at last came into her, filling himself with that incredible joy, her reply was so intense, he dared to hope he had some chance of keeping her with him.

But when the chains of ecstasy were loosened, Louisa cried bitterly in his embrace. He tried to comfort her, to reassure her, but she would have no part of his offerings. "I could *never* trust you," she said finally, soon yielding to exhaustion, falling into a deep but troubled sleep. Aaron covered her body with his own, drawing her to him, pressing himself against her as heavily as he dared, at last following her to sleep for a few short hours, lying awake the rest of the night.

She did not stir when, just before dawn, he rose from their bed for perhaps the last time. He looked at Louisa, his heart filled with bitter longing, certain she would do just as she said, and his darkest, deepest fears about their mutual venture would be realized. He hadn't feared the possible loss of his life in this enterprise as much as he'd dreaded the moment when Louisa would turn her back on him, when he would be alone again. He wondered now where his life would lead when he was safely out of this damned plot. Where would he go when, after all these years, he was a free man again? Now he could only think that there would be nowhere to go—Louisa was all he really desired from this life, something he'd come to grips with not very long ago in this very bed. And surely he would never again have her except by force. "God damn you, Louisa," he swore under his breath. And even in his grief he began to retreat to the protective corner of anger and hatred.

Chapter Sixty-nine

ON the surface there was no change in their relationship once the couple stood outside the bedroom doors. Aaron announced Louisa's plans to go to San Diego, discovering, he said, his plans to head south were probably premature. Louisa could not bear to be separated from Rachel any longer. Easton was consulted and several possible escorts to San Diego were suggested. Then Samuel set out to make the arrangements.

In public the couple acted out their roles, Marshall seeming more attentive than usual. "It's obvious he's going to miss you," purred Marguerite the following night at her dinner party. "I was hoping you would be traveling with me, not heading south!"

"Marshall must remain here, but I simply can't stay away from Rachel any longer."

"We'll look after Marshall for you. We'll see he doesn't get too lonely."

Louisa nearly gagged on her own polite response, seeking the cold night air as soon as possible. Franklin Carson followed her into the damp, offering her his coat. "Thank you," she said, wearily accepting his kindness. "It's stifling in there."

"We'll miss you, Louisa."

She smiled at him and patted his arm. Louisa had grown oddly attached to Franklin Carson. He had not regained his health as he should have, and he seemed weighted down both by his insidious tropical illness and by the plans to which he had committed himself. Louisa suspected he had serious doubts about the enterprise. She wondered if he would remain involved if he believed he had any alternative now that he'd come so far.

"As much as I've come to despise travel on this side of the country, I almost wish I was going with you— especially since you've the good sense to choose *not* to go by sea."

"You must plan to visit me soon. Perhaps when Marshall comes home you could pull yourself away from here for a while."

"It's a thought," he said, turning in response to the opening of the door behind them.

"There you are," said Aaron pleasantly. "Careful, Carson, in this dampness you'll catch your death with your coat off. I'll get your wrap, Louisa," and he disappeared into the house again.

On the lantern-lit porch, Carson couldn't avoid noticing the flash of hostility that momentarily crossed Louisa's face. "I hope I detect nothing wrong between you. That's not why you're going, is it, Louisa?" He paused to watch her. Her eyes flickered an apparently stiff retort, then washed serene. "Don't worry about Mrs. Hill. In the long run, she can't hold a candle to you. He won't stray for long."

Abruptly Louisa turned her back on Franklin Carson, not wanting to discuss the subject even briefly. Everyone with any brains, and two good eyes knows! she raged to herself, saved from the silence by Aaron's return to the porch.

Franklin claimed his coat again. "I should go back inside," he suggested, leaving Aaron and Louisa to themselves.

Aaron placed the short satin cape lovingly around Louisa's bare shoulders, carefully tying the fastening ribbons across her breasts before she could begin to do so. "I'd like to go home now," she whispered.

"The night's just getting started," he protested.

She glared at him. "For you I'm sure it is. But I've no inclination to remain. I'll make my excuses. Someone from the colonel's staff will see me home safely."

"I'll see you home," he said firmly.

"Whatever you prefer," she said, moving past him.

Aaron reached for her. "Louisa," he said, pulling her against him, feeling her trembling, wondering if it was the night air that affected her. He kissed her, though she resisted him with a stiffness in her body. "Don't go. Don't leave me."

He held her tightly. "Marguerite has promised to see you're not unhappy in my absence," she said coldly. "She's a very charitable woman. You'll not go begging—what an enormous pleasure this assignment must be for you," she sneered. "Even if the purse isn't high, the other benefits haven't been ungenerous. There seems always to be someone in line eagerly to meet any need you have."

"You won't face the truth, will you. Louisa?" He held her roughly now, snarling at her in a hoarse whisper. "When you don't like what you see, you merely ignore the facts and retreat to your fantasies."

"My dreams seem no uglier than broad daylight—over the years not much has changed, has it?" She made a futile effort to extract herself from his grip. "I said, I want to go back to Crane's Nest," she added calmly when she stopped resisting his tight hold on her, coolly staring back at his intense gaze.

Aaron glared at her a few minutes more, both tantalized and infuriated by her. In the lantern-illuminated dark she was alluring, and even what he regarded as her irrational stance did not make her any less appealing. She could be stark raving mad, he suspected, and he would still be aroused by her. "Where do you spring from, woman? Heaven, or Hell?" And to this whispered question she only gazed at him enigmatically, unresponsive. almost overpowering him with her beauty.

"I'll see you home now, Mrs. Hudson," he said quietly, when he could.

"Thank you, Marshall," she said sweetly, turning from him forcefully the instant he released her.

With Aaron at her side, Louisa found Marguerite and bade their hostess an early goodnight. "You know, at times lately, I've noticed you haven't looked well, Louisa. I hope it's nothing."

"I've been very weary lately, Marguerite. I must be homesick. I doubt it could be anything else."

"Well, you won't need to worry when you're gone. We'll look after Marshall. We'll see he isn't too miserable without you."

Louisa smiled and returned Marguerite's affectionate hug in kind, reserving her murderous thoughts for herself only.

Aaron gave them a hair-raising ride home, Louisa wondering if he hoped to get a rise from her as he drove the horses much too fast even though the road was very familiar and the night bright. But she remained passive, despite her concern and her rising anger at his lack of caution. She tried to focus on the graceful sometimes eerie trees rushing into and receding from view with incredible speed. There was a time she would have loved such a ride, even reveled in the experience, perhaps demanded the speed to erase an unpleasant evening from memory. But such a time was long past.

Louisa felt very tired, heavy in body and spirit. If she didn't have Rachel to go to, she wondered what she would do at this moment. The new life in her womb gave her no solace, no hope as the other child had. There was little promise, and no joy. How odd it was. This time the man who had joined her body to make a new life was by her side, and the love she felt for him had been as overwhelming as her love for Marshall, perhaps deeper. For although she had gone to Aaron in great need, she had gone to him a woman, not a lonely, desperate child. Yet their union was, in its way, ending as dreadfully as the one with Marshall had, and she saw no hope for it.

When they arrived at Easton's estate, Louisa was relieved to have arrived at all. "Your years at sea didn't diminish your skill with horses, thank God," she snapped as Aaron assisted her from the buggy.

"There was a time you'd have been disappointed in less of a ride."

"Let's say I've finally come to my senses."

"Promise?" he said, lifting her easily into his arms, carrying her despite her protests.

"Put me down, please." she said, making an effort to be polite before the servants who assisted them with the horses and into the house.

"You said you were weary. I'll spare you the climb upstairs. I'm the gallant sort, or hadn't you noticed? Never one to turn down the needs of a lady—I'm a gentleman of good breeding, remember?"

She laughed in spite of herself. "I think gentleman is an exaggeration, but 'breeding' certainly applies!"

Aaron laughed with her, but the moment was short. When they entered their suite, it wasn't only the night air from the open terrace door that made the room seem chilly. Louisa hastily undressed with her back to him, covering her body with as concealing a nightgown as she could find. The deep rose satin gown edged with delicate ivory lace did not do what she hoped, but clung invitingly to her curves, plunging deeply into her very round, firm breasts. She'd not worn the nightdress before, and Aaron's pleasure over the way she looked was obvious. She pretended not to notice, meticulously preparing her hair for bed, praying against all she knew was likely that he would fall asleep before she finished.

Louisa dimmed the lamp on the dressing table, but did not go to bed, instead sitting on one of the lounges at the far end of the room, leaning against its soft cushions. She tried to relax, thinking she might sleep. But she thought bitterly of the man who also lay awake, and she could not sleep. Soon her rancor turned against herself. Louisa, you are such a fool, she thought painfully. Then a voice inside her, one she at first did not recognize, laughed crazily and sneered, You're as much a bitch as Marguerite. You loathe him and long for him the same instant. It was as if she could feel his eyes and his hands on her in the darkness, and she wanted to wound him one minute; console him the next. You deserve him, Louisa, you're two of a kind.

Louisa sat up instantly and shivered, pressing her

hands against her ears, but her reply to the voice came immediately. *You're right! You're right,* she screamed silently inside her head.

Louisa stood and paced in front of the terrace windows, unaware of Aaron, unaware of anything but a sudden numbness in her heart, a blessed anesthetic suddenly flowing in her veins. For several long minutes she stood motionless before the windows, staring at the moon.

As he watched her, Aaron was stirred beyond his ability to endure, and he went to her. She seemed nearly in a trance, seeming to have forgotten her wild struggles of the night before, seeming to have no memory of the caustic retorts she'd flung at him throughout the day, allowing herself to be eased into his embrace and carried to their bed. She let him extend his passion, seeming to respond just as he wanted.

But when Aaron touched her she was not with him. She was somewhere beyond his usually sure grasp, and though she was touchable and cunningly lured him, he soon discovered her coolly detached. Louisa was deliciously sweet and yielding in his arms, and she played him until he was not sure whether she offered more pain than pleasure, and when the explosion came between them, for all his effort, it was felt only by Aaron, and she left him wanting and needy and oddly lonely. She lay with him but was not there, and she went to sleep leaving him physically gratified but profoundly solitary, even with his arms full of her.

He pressed against her tightly as if he hoped to take something more from her, something of herself she had refused to give, something he had been accustomed to having in the past.

Later in the night he awakened her, and let her know his need for her, and again she gave him her body easily and willingly, meeting the rough urgent desperation in him with passion to match his own, but he sensed it was all for show, having been there many times before, having in the past paid the fees for the best in the house.

"You're whoring for me!" he said, grabbing her fiercely moments after she had turned away from him. He forced her onto her back, pinning her with his body, holding her hands in his across her breasts, staring with obvious anger into her passive, unresponsive face. She looked fragile, otherworldly, untouchable in the silver shades of moonlight, and she watched his eyes, the tension in his face, and felt his body brimming with violence.

"Haven't I satisfied you? I did my best," she purred. Then a malicious smile curved at her mouth. "But the fee is not adjustable. Not now. Next time, perhaps—but only in advance."

At her words he involuntarily thrust his body against hers, crushing her, his grip on her hands extremely painful. For an instant he knew he could have killed her, but she did not wince, nor did she move to resist him. He spread her arms, pinning her hands in his at her shoulders. He stared at her, and an incredible weakness swept over him. He put his cheek against hers, his mouth against her ear, his face in the fragrant silk of her hair. "Don't whore for me, Louisa," he whispered, pulling her against him, rolling with her onto his side, wrapping himself around her tightly.

"You can have me no other way," she replied without emotion. "As long as I'm here I'll be your whore. But you can have nothing more of me than my body. After all, that's all you ever wanted. You told me so from the beginning, only I didn't listen." She was very restrained, very distant, speaking quietly with complete control. "But I've heard you at last," she sighed. "I agreed to help you, Aaron, and I'll faithfully play out the last act of this charade. I've lived up to my word. And so have you." Louisa yawned suddenly, as if bored with the late-hour conversation. "As you say, you've broken no promises."

It made him ill to hear her ice-cold voice, her frozen words. "Bitch," he cursed in disgust, releasing her; turning away. And with no apparent effort,

Louisa was soon asleep again, while he lay awake the rest of the night. In the few remaining days before she left Crane's Nest, even though he lay in torment, certain Hell could offer no greater agony, Aaron did not touch her. And the worst of it was, Louisa didn't seem to care.

Chapter Seventy

A few days later Louisa met Ben Patrick and Jack Herbert. They were coarse, rugged men, but they had the experience to see her to San Diego. They had worked occasionally for Easton, and any anxiety Louisa had gave way to her desire to be out of Aaron's presence and home again—if she could call San Diego home. As she made her final preparations to leave Crane's Nest, Louisa felt more like a nomad than a woman with some definite place to go. It seemed to her she was forever packing her belongings, forever going elsewhere, never resting in one place for very long, never really secure when she laid her head on her pillow at night. Someday that feeling would disappear, she insisted. Someday she would be safe and comfortable. Perhaps when she settled in again with Rachel. Surely no one would come after her now. Who could possibly want anything further from her? She had nothing left to give.

The last few days and nights at Crane's Nest were like a dream. Most of the time Louisa felt detached, only a voyeur. Numbly she watched the affairs and the people of the house. Those around her couldn't fail to notice her silences, her slowness to respond, but they excused her distraction, knowing she would miss her husband. She almost seemed drugged, though she slept fitfully most nights, usually alone in her bed until the very early hours of the morning.

She told herself the anticipation of her journey home was responsible for her sleeplessness, but there were too many moments she would lie waiting, wondering when Aaron would return, and in what condition. On the last night of her stay in Easton's magnificent house she barely slept, the minutes ticking away soundlessly in the murmurs of the night wind.

Shortly after Louisa heard the clock announce 4 A.M. she heard her door open. With her back to him, she listened as Aaron slowly undressed, discarding his garments recklessly. He walked unsteadily around the bed and stood before the windows, his slim body etched against the glass in the moon-bright night. Louisa stiffened against the familiar rush of feeling, the warmth that washed over her. When he turned toward her, she closed her eyes, seeming soundly and peacefully asleep.

He watched her for what seemed an eternity, then went to the empty side of the bed where her back faced him, and sat heavily, remaining motionless for several minutes. Louisa's nostrils were assailed with the odor of liquor, which, with his very slow movements in the night, told her his consumption had been excessive. Then another scent came to her and left her feeling sick and somehow violated. It was the heavy musk fragrance Marguerite always wore, and Louisa struggled desperately to keep from retching. It was only outrage that prevented her from crying aloud and letting Aaron see the tears which poured out of her eyes. Louisa did not want his attention as she lay inhaling the scent of another woman, who only recently had lain with the man to whom she had given herself so completely, and to whom, truthfully, she could gladly give herself forever—if only circumstances were different. And although she could say logically that Aaron did not deserve her love, or the depth of her feeling, the wounds and the pain were not diminished. In those moments before Aaron lay with his back against hers, and those few minutes with his wakeful body touching hers, Louisa thought her lungs, if not her heart, would burst. And when she heard his heavy breathing and she knew he was lost to sleep, her agony slipped from her in tormented, overwhelming tears, and only Aaron's drunkenness spared her from discovery.

From the dullness of her body and the numbness of her spirit the next morning, Louisa would have

sworn she had not slept at all. But in fact she had
drifted off to sleep once her tears were spent. She
woke to an empty bed, and to burning eyes, which
Loo Kim soothed with cool, mildly scented cloths
pressed against her eyelids. Louisa bathed and
dressed for travel, eating a light breakfast in her room,
sitting as she had the first morning of her arrival at
Crane's Nest, alone and wondering where Aaron was
at this moment.

He joined her before she was finished, looking none
the worse for wear, and she marveled at his capacity
for self-abuse. He seemed untouched by the late hours
he'd been keeping lately, or by his heavy consumption
of alcohol. He looked wonderful—dark and lithe and
powerful. Part of her couldn't believe she would separate herself from this man; another part could barely
wait the hour more it would be before she would bid
him good-bye, hopefully for the last time.

Silently he worried about her. She didn't seem well,
but she seemed strong enough to travel, and there was
no persuading her to wait for a ship, if she didn't wait
for him to travel with her. So determined was she to
be out of his presence, he guessed she would walk
south if there were no other way to go. For several
days, they had barely said anything to each other in
private. There seemed nothing left to say. Actually
he only came to her now because he felt failure to do
so would cause comment.

"It won't be long now. The captive bird will be set
free within moments." He looked at her light eyes
with their dark shadows under them, at her very pale
skin, at her slenderness, and wanted to forbid her to
leave; then he laughed at himself. He had no such
power over her. "For the sake of the charade, see if
you can muster a show of regret when we part this
morning," he said, taking her face gently but resolutely in his hands, bending to kiss her tenderly at
first, then savagely. She struggled uselessly. "You were
right about one thing, Louisa. I'll never be finished
with you. You can expect to see me again." It was a
threat, his dark eyes looking into her fury without the
slightest concern.

"You'll never have me again, except by force."

"That can be arranged," he said casually, watching her eyes widen. Then she lowered her gaze, seeming to ignore him, and he walked away from her.

Soon Samuel came for her trunk and handbags, and it was time to go. Aaron offered her his arm a last time and they descended the staircase. Easton, Franklin Carson, and Alex met them at the door, bidding farewell and wishing her a safe journey. She was gracious and cheerful. Embracing Franklin Carson warmly, she said, "I expect to see you soon."

"Maybe," he replied. "Maybe."

She also hugged Alex without regard for the curiosity of onlookers. In this instance she truly didn't give a damn. "I'll miss our outings," she said warmly. "I hope Mary arrives safely and soon," she said, kissing him on the cheek.

With her good-byes said, Louisa descended the front steps of the house with William and Marshall. "Personally, I'm very sorry to see you go, Louisa, but I understand how you would wish to be with your child." Finally he extended his hand to her. "We will meet again soon." He smiled at the young couple. "Now, I'm sure you'd like to say your farewells in private." He climbed the steps again, leaving them alone but within his observation.

"We've said all there is to say, haven't we, Louisa?" Aaron's face was seen only by her, and his words were for her ears alone. And where there was sadness, she read only hostility; where there was warmth, she felt his bitterness. "Give my love to 'my' baby, and to 'my' mother," he said, kissing her with gentleness, holding her beautiful face in his hands. Then quickly he opened her cloak and pulled her against him, his kiss turned passionate, his hands drawing her forcefully to his hard male body. "Only you will know how much, and in what ways I'll miss you," and she heard arrogance and insult in his voice, not the anguish he carefully controlled in his harsh whisper.

Tears of fury and humiliation spilled onto her face, but Easton and the others who looked on from the windows of the great house, and the men who waited for her, saw only a husband and wife whose separation would be difficult. For Marshall's sake, Louisa did nothing to dispel the illusion, taking Aaron's hand for assistance into the carriage, instead of slapping away what she believed was a hateful smirk. But when she stepped inside and seated herself in the carriage, withdrawing to privacy, she returned his final lingering kiss with a warmth she forgave herself under the circumstances.

"*Hasta luego,*" he said, slamming the door abruptly, waving the carriage on, and when the coach turned and she should have had a last glimpse of him, she only saw his back as he entered the house, and she knew it was finished. She might see him again as he had threatened rather than promised, but she had no hope the future for them held any suggestion of happiness.

Chapter Seventy-one

EXHAUSTED, Louisa closed her eyes and tried to get accustomed to the motion of the carriage. She'd had little sleep the last few nights, and, as she tried to relax, recent scenes filled her mind, as did memories of other retreats from grand estates. Now would begin the process of forgetting Aaron. "The process of forgetting," she sighed. It was a skill she'd refined to an art.

As soon as she settled down, Louisa felt cramping in her abdomen. Over recent days the pain worried her increasingly, but nagging discomfort was set aside, and she dozed exhaustedly, adjusting to the rocking, occasionally jolting motion of the ride. Sometime after noon the carriage pulled to a stop, and Louisa and the men hired to see her safely on the road ate a light lunch.

"We'll be stopping for the night in about four hours. That'll bring us to a place you can put up." It was Ben Patrick who informed her of their itinerary. He was a stocky man of medium height, slightly taller than Louisa. In general, his appearance was loathsome to her. Even though he appeared to be freshly washed and shaved, he had an unkempt, ragged look. In spite of his appearance, his reputation for hard work, knowledge of the road they would travel, and skill as a driver and general hired hand, had recommended him for the journey. It outweighed his infamy for periodic disappearances, because he always turned up, usually none the worse for wear, ready to engage wholeheartedly again in his more usual pursuits. His absences rarely interfered with any but his own life. They seemed merely to be a part of his basically unsociable nature. Sometimes he returned to his nor-

mal haunts with pockets full and with tales of his ex-
ploits along San Francisco's Barbary Coast. These
outbursts of confession followed particularly jubilant
bouts of gambling, carousing, and other pleasures
whose adventure seemed to need repeating. Usually,
however, his return was noted, but not discussed.

Louisa's exhaustion was pronounced. She felt
drugged and very lethargic, blaming these sensations
on the monotony of the long ride, looking forward
to a good night's sleep in a bed some distance from
Crane's Nest and that much closer to home. But she
was not removed enough from awareness of the
things around her to ignore the stares of the men who
accompanied her.

Ben Patrick regarded her more casually then did
Jack Herbert, his younger companion who watched
her with undisguised interest. He was dark-skinned
and dark-clad, appearing slim and wiry, his wide
hat covering thick blond, almost white hair and
shielding pale blue eyes. He had a dark blond mustache, which cut across his narrow face handsomely.
His general appearance was much neater than Patrick's, but there was no mistaking he was as coarse
as his mentor.

In the past, Ben Patrick had been a loner, but for
the last year Jack Herbert and he were rarely seen
separately. Herbert was new to the state and had attached himself to Ben almost immediately. It was an
unlikely father-son relationship, yet the older man
shepherded the younger, though his instructions de-
graded rather than uplifted him.

Louisa tried to dismiss her uneasiness, and was relieved to be on the road again after a short stop.
Even though she slept, she didn't feel rested, and
she was very ready to stop for the night. They pulled
up to an umpretentious but comfortable-looking house,
and Louisa was given a small but tidy room for the
night; Ben and Jack accommodated themselves outside, not far from the house.

Louisa enjoyed a simple evening meal with an ordinary family, an experience almost entirely foreign
to her. The house was cozy though sparely furnished,

and the people who occupied it seemed much the same: polite and modest, but apparently happy. It was an existence for which Louisa would have gladly traded the sum of her inheritance. The family was small, the two children reserved, the young girl, perhaps eight years old, extremely curious about Louisa. She stared at as elegant a woman as she had ever seen, from time to time lowering her eyes in embarrassment. Louisa smiled warmly at the child and willingly answered her shy questions.

But she did not linger with the family after dinner, retreating to her room, seeking the soft bed early and gratefully. She slept several hours, waking late in the night, listening to the night sounds, feeling peaceful in the quiet house. The night was mild and her window was open. For a while she propped herself up in the dark, and looked out the window. She saw the carriage waiting next to the barn, and nearby two seated figures, presumably Ben and Jack. Louisa saw the glow of their cigarettes in the gray night, and from time to time she could hear a faint rumble of the men's voices. There seemed to be some topic about which they could not agree, but eventually their conversation stopped and they bedded down for the night.

Still Louisa lay sleepless. A dull, despondent ache in her abdomen had been with her all evening, and now it gave way to extreme tenderness deep inside. She felt a dampness against her thighs and feared the bleeding had started again. Louisa was suddenly cold with fear. What would the outcome be, she wondered. When she rose to look after herself, she nearly fainted from a knifing pain in her womb, then sunk onto the bed again, sorry for an instant she had left Crane's Nest so hastily. But the cramps subsided and she slept again.

She woke the next morning to a gentle rapping at her door, and greeted Mrs. Adams cheerfully. The woman carried a hearty breakfast tray, and Louisa ate ravenously of the simple food. She was served eggs and freshly baked bread, even bacon and a mug of truly delicious coffee topped with heavy cream—

less elegant fare then she'd recently grown used to, but definitely more satisfying.

"I hope all the places I stay on my journey measure up to your lovely home," Louisa said with genuine respect.

"Why, thank you, Mrs. Hudson. I only wish every one of our guests was as nice as you," she cried, clearing away Louisa's tray. "They said to tell you they'll be ready to go soon," she added, gesturing to the window.

Louisa followed Mrs. Adams' hand to see Ben and Jack harnessing the team of horses. She frowned. "Tell them I'll be ready shortly."

Louisa dressed with care. The morning was crisp, and she felt very chilled, and, in spite of a good night's sleep, listless. Why should I feel wonderful? she asked herself frankly as she tied her hat over her curls. There's little cause for rejoicing, she noted. Not when I find I both love and hate in the same breath.

She took a final look at herself in the mirror. In spite of the depression hanging over her, and the heaviness in her womb, she looked beautiful even to her critical self. She sighed, hoping her uneasiness about her guides on this journey was only a factor of her weariness. Surely she was only distraught because of her unhappy affair with Aaron; surely the company in Monterey would not send her away in the hands of truly dangerous men. Surely they only looked menacing.

Chapter Seventy-two

LOUISA read most of the morning, taking her pick of several volumes Easton had insisted she take in her traveling bag. In that manner, she tried not to dwell on thoughts of Aaron, tried to think of how the house in San Diego would look to her after all these months of absence; tried to imagine how wonderful her baby would feel in her arms. She deplored the months of separation, feeling the bitterness of her experience with Aaron to her core. It was right for her to assist him; wrong to have left her child behind.

Tears of regret slid down her face; all at once turning into tears of severe pain. Louisa held onto the dangling support straps fiercely as the carriage swayed on the rough road, and drew her legs up, sweat suddenly drenching her body, her mouth very dry as she gasped tormentedly for breath. But just when she thought she could endure the pain no longer, it subsided, and if she thought she'd felt exhausted before, she found new meaning in the word.

Louisa trembled from weakness. She was very frightened, and she was unable to decide what she should do. Should she stop the carriage? Should she go back to the Adams place? Should she return to Monterey? No answer was forthcoming, and she leaned against the carriage's velvet-cushioned interior, and tried to rest.

When the men stopped to eat the lunch Mrs. Adams had packed, Louisa asked for a piece of fruit, a small portion of cheese, and some water, refusing to leave the coach.

"You feeling all right, Mrs. Hudson?" Ben Patrick inquired. "You look a little peaked."

"I'm fine," she answered coldly.

Ben and Jack ate hastily, glancing in her direction as they talked. They spoke heatedly, but were not overheard, and Louisa felt increasingly uneasy. She prayed this journey would not turn out to be one she would regret, but her thoughts didn't remain with Ben and Jack for long, as she abandoned the largest share of her small lunch to attend to what she now recognized as the beginnings of a siege of intense pain.

The carriage started up again before the full force of agony broke, but again its duration was not more than a few minutes, and she was left numbly weary. This time she abandoned her concerns and fell asleep in the rocking motion, holding onto the support straps with one hand, stretching out as much as possible on the carriage seat. When she woke her outstretched arm was asleep, and she spent several minutes restoring normal feeling to it. When she felt her limb revive Louisa noticed it was late in the afternoon. She hadn't been informed of the day's plans, but from the lengthening shadows, she suspected they would be stopping for the night very soon.

But the carriage traveled on into the dark. She grew apprehensive, losing track of time, having no sense of the direction they were traveling. Finally she rapped soundly against the front of the coach, and shortly, after an obvious turn off the main road, the steadily rocking motion ceased.

Jack Herbert came to the door. "Guess this is as good a place as any," he said, opening the door for her.

"What do you mean?" Louisa inquired more calmly than she felt.

"Just what I said," was his curt reply, stepping into the coach, reaching roughly for her arm.

Louisa wrenched her arm from him, and he grabbed her roughly. "There's been a change of plans, Mrs.

Hudson," he said, dragging her with him as she tried vainly to resist.

He was not much bigger than she was, but he had incredible strength, and there was no possibility of struggling from his grasp.

"Careful with her," Ben growled at his comrade. "She'll not get us what we want if you mangle her."

"What is it you want," Louisa demanded as soon as she recovered in Jack's tight grip.

"Let her go!" Ben demanded with authority. "Rest yourself," he offered, pointing to the trunk of a fallen tree. He spoke quietly to her, slowly, softly, as one might address an overwrought animal. "We've been considering your assets."

"My assets?"

"Yes. Don't see a lady the likes of you very often. Not just pretty like you are, but smellin' o'gold."

Louisa's eyes widened in surprise, but she said nothing as she tried desperately to focus on the man's words, almost but not quite able to overlook the now familiar cramping in her womb.

"You see, we been watchin' the comings and goings at that fancy house where you come from, and we couldn't help but notice a few things. First, nobody but the richest sort ever seems to set foot in the house for more than a few minutes, and you been there quite a spell. And treated like the high an' mighty while you was there."

Louisa was undeniably intent on Ben Patrick's words, and he smiled at her obvious interest. "I ain't sure just what's going on, but I smell gold, and lots of it. Know for a fact a Mr. Peter Melville's got a heavy interest in the mines out here, and in Nevada, too. And Mr. Easton, queer sort he is, has his share of money, from the looks of it."

"I believe you're mistaken. I've not heard either of them speak of investments in mining."

Ben smiled. "Well, let's just say you must've been around for other conversation." His implication was as unmistakable, as was his lengthy gaze. His remarks drew a deep chuckle from his companion.

Louisa gave Jack a scalding look which momentarily stopped his laughter. "Don't think you're too good for me, lady," he threatened, reaching into her cloak with both hands to clutch her breasts roughly. "I can make it nice or nasty, whatever you wish," he suggested coarsely as she shrank from him in revulsion.

"Get off her!" Ben commanded. "We'll get what we want from her—but ya gotta decide what ya want. Do ya want a few shots at her, or do you want your pockets full o' gold?"

Jack had every intention of satisfying himself right then and there, but Ben physically interfered. "Damn it, man! Let her be!" he shouted, grabbing the younger man roughly. "This isn't what we figured on!" and the younger man let go reluctantly, and Louisa found herself unbelievably moving toward Ben, knowing her safety was not the least sure.

"Let's get camp set up," Ben barked in the next breath. For a few short moments, Jack stared at his friend, then did as Ben ordered without comment. Soon a campfire was blazing, Louisa sitting motionless, close by. Jack looked after the horses, while Ben offered Louisa leftovers from the ample noonday meal. Louisa was nearly too afraid to eat, but reasoned she'd better eat while she could, suspecting the next meals might be harder to come by.

As soon as she finished, she stood up. "Where'd you think you're going?" Ben inquired sharply.

"I need a few minutes to myself."

"You'll not get 'em," he said, rising to his feet.

Louisa's astonishment was seen clearly in her face. "I'll be goin' with you."

"But . . ."

Before she could protest further, he grabbed her arm brusquely, and dragged her with him into the brush, stopping some distance from the campfire. "Well, get to it."

Louisa stood and stared at him.

"Get on with it, woman!"

"Mr. Patrick! I'm unused to an audience," she said with consternation.

"I ain't leavin'," he said impatiently.

Louisa stared a moment longer. "You will at least turn your back!"

"Give me that bag," he demanded, snatching the carpetbag she clutched. "Got yourself a weapon hidden there?"

"No. Only a few things I'll be needing." Unable to withhold the bag from him, she watched as he searched the contents.

"Only this and that? And some cloth?" His voice was amused.

"Just that."

"You travel light for such a fancy lady," he sneered.

"If you'll give me my bag, and turn your back, please." He complied, stepping away a short distance, allowing her only very little privacy.

Despite the pain she'd experienced, Louisa was relieved to confirm her bleeding throughout the day had not been excessive. She hoped, if necessary, this very condition would spare her from what it was clear Jack Herbert, at least, had in mind. She prayed her condition would repulse him enough to protect her. Why, she asked herself, when she first saw these two unsavory men hadn't she at least thought to carry a gun?

"You may turn around, now," she said, moving toward Ben.

"I thank you, ma'am," he replied sarcastically, taking her arm again, escorting her back to camp, roughly ordering her to sit close by him before the fire. "I think someone is a-goin' to want to pay a high price for your safe return," he said as she sat obediently and uncomfortably where he'd insisted.

"I can't think who it would be," Louisa retorted with sarcasm.

"How about that fancy-looking husband of yours?

Now, he looked like he was surely goin' to miss you!"
Jack smiled as if he had tales to tell, and Louisa
quickly righted herself, glaring back at him hotly.

"There's lots o' rumors about that fancy place you
been visitin'," Ben continued, "and maybe you could
tell us a few things we'd like to know."

"I doubt there's much I could tell you. My husband
and I were merely houseguests. Those people you saw
are friends from home. My husband's family is in the
shipping business. That's the extent of my knowledge
of his affairs!"

The men stared at her, both questioning whether to
believe her or not. "While you were out walking with
the lady, I found some interesting things in her baggage," Jack said with obvious satisfaction. He pulled
her jewel case from behind the rock he was sitting on.
"And from the looks of what's here, there'll be a nice
purse for her safe return—for her return, anyway," he
corrected himself.

Ben grabbed the case and greedily sorted through
the jewels, giving a low whistle at several items, shouting when he clutched the emerald collar. "God Al-
mighty! Would you look at that!" And he was silenced
as he watched the stones glitter in the firelight.

"Now I'd've guessed she was some fancy prize,
but she must be somethin' to warrant that!" Jack
offered, eying her forthrightly.

"I'll say!"

"Bet some queens don't have so much."

"Could be," Ben speculated, taking a longer, harder
look at Louisa. He smiled greedily. "Seems we've come
into a piece of good luck."

"At least into a piece!" Jack roared.

"Look, Jack! Cool off! We gotta think this through
a little more. There's more to this than we thought."

"Yes, sir, you've said just exactly what I'm thinking!"

Ben grabbed the younger man's arm. "Shut up and
listen to me. And listen good. If you touch her I'll kill
you. We've got a chance to grab something big, and

Chapter Seventy-three

SOME minutes later Louisa found her wrists and ankles bound together. For the sake of speedier travel, Ben decided to abandon the carriage, and Louisa sat crouched on the ground while the carriage was moved to a less obvious place some distance away. While the team horses were freed to forage for themselves, Ben and Jack's saddle horses were left tethered near the campsite. Louisa's single truck had been thoroughly searched. This time nothing of interest to the men was discovered. She was permitted to retain only the clothes on her back, her carpetbag, and the wool cape Mrs. Stevens had designed and made.

While Jack hid the carriage, Ben prepared for the three of them to move a little farther from the main road for the night. The moon was bright and they could travel easily. "You'll have to ride with Jack. My horse has all it can do to carry me. I trust you'll behave yourself," he snickered.

Louisa made no reply, not in the least relishing a moment's contact with Jack Herbert, praying earnestly for her safety, but not at all hopeful as the prospects of the night loomed before her. Ben untied her feet before he helped her roughly onto Jack's horse, but her hands were kept bound, and she sat rigidly in front of her captor. "Relax a little, honey," he suggested. "It'll feel good in a while." His free hand roughly explored the contours of her body. "My God!" he exhaled in a whisper, not without admiration. She could feel the tension of his body, and his nearly involuntary motion against her as he pulled her to him forcefully.

She struggled vigorously, repeatedly pushing away

his probing hands, shrinking from his eager mouth on her neck, nearly toppling the both of them from the horse. "Leave me alone!" she begged. Real terror began to clutch at her; she felt like an animal trussed for sacrifice.

Ben halted sharply on the road, turning around in his saddle. He pulled his revolver, and cocked it, aiming casually. "I'll put one of you down to walk if there's any more of it." he growled. "And by God, it doesn't matter to me who."

"I'll gladly walk!" Louisa offered, almost begging.

"No. It'll slow us down. Move ahead of me, Jack. You lead the way," he motioned with the gun. "Keep your eyes on the path, and, for now, your hands to yourself."

Louisa was relieved, but feared it was only a reprieve; very conscious of the hardness of Jack's body, she sensed the animal hunger in him, knowing he had to make every effort to concentrate on anything other than her.

They traveled at least an hour, coming to a thick stand of willowy trees, near some apparently cultivated fields, but not within eye range of habitation. "This'll do us for the night," Ben announced, dismounting, coming immediately to take Louisa from Jack's grip, giving his reins to Jack. "Bed 'em down. I'll see to the lady."

Louisa relaxed slightly, knowing if she had any hope it was in Ben's hands, as unlikely a protector as he might seem. Ben untied her hands and spread a blanket for her on the ground. He pointed impatiently and she lay down, and he folded the blanket around her. Then he proceeded to settle himself for the night. He pulled a bottle of liquor from his possessions and tucked it under his arm, relieving himself a few feet from her without a second thought. Louisa turned away, and he laughed. "Haven't been around real men much, have you, pretty lady," and she shrank into the blanket in horror.

Then she thought hopefully she heard him settle in his position for the night as the whiskey bottle cork popped and Ben gasped for air after a long draft.

Jack joined him, bringing his own bottle. "Did ya offer the lady a swig, Ben?"

"Guess I forgot my manners," he chuckled. "Seems she don't want our company—got her back turned to us already, and the evenin's young," he snorted.

"Some prefer it that way. Maybe she's one," he offered congenially.

Louisa closed her eyes tight, not moving, though she was swept with a wild stabbing of pain, exhaling the breath she held as slowly as possible when she could no longer bear the pressure in her lungs. Sweat came from every pore as she listened, not believing what she heard, or what was felt within her body.

"Now, friend," Jack continued amiably, "how are we going to manage the night?" He drank heavily and fast from his bottle of whiskey. "You can't tell me her grand husband won't want her back if we take a little for ourselves, and besides, who's to tell him before he gets the package back?"

Ben gave a low, growling laugh. "No one." He grinned in the darkness, eying Louisa slowly, savoring another long drink. "Who goes first?" he asked after a lengthy silence.

"Me!" replied Jack as if it was his indisputable right, as if he meant to kill to insure it. "My idea; my right," swilling another deep draft of alcohol.

"No! No!" Louisa screamed, rolling to face them, at the same time struggling to rise, backing away, not succeeding in her attempts at either motion. "Please! Please!" she begged. "I'm going to have a baby. It's not as it should be. I'm bleeding, and I know if you touch me, I'll lose it." She hoped to repulse, if not obtain sympathy. Her terror was unmistakable as she attempted to reason tearfully with her adversaries.

At first the men were dumbfounded. Then Jack uttered a mirthless guttural laugh. "What a cunning bitch!" he said, approaching her viciously, pulling the blanket from her, beginning to struggle with her, to rip at her petticoats and bloomers. "And the more you scream, the more I'll like it!" he grunted at her, finally freeing her of her protective clothing, grabbing her hands, wrenching them behind her tightly, in the same motion penetrating her tense body with his maleness. She involuntarily gave him what he said he preferred, her screams frantic, full of terror and pain, the invasion of her body violent and terrible. She writhed helplessly under his brutal assault in the worst agony of her life, while her attacker carefully prolonged his pleasure. "Sweet Jesus," he exclaimed finally in satisfaction, slumping heavily against her when he fiinished.

At first, watching Jack rape Louisa excited Ben. But when he sobered, it was too late. "God! Get off her!" he cursed. "What'd I let you talk me into? She wasn't lying! Look at the blood! You're covered with it!"

Jack pulled himself away from her, seeing the dark stain on the whiteness of her petticoats and on himself as well, bloodying his hands as he rearranged his clothing.

"Shit! She's no good to us dead! Why the fuck did I listen to you? You could've had every whore in Frisco for as long as you liked for what we'd've got outta her old man!"

Louisa retched violently, her body shaking uncontrollably, now oblivious to the men who stood over her. She felt there was nothing more they could do to increase the pain she was suffering, and she gave herself up to it. From the beginning she feared she would miscarry, but this suspicion was no comfort now as she felt the new life within begin to leave her, and Louisa wondered, very briefly, if it might be better for everyone if she went with it.

Chapter Seventy-four

BEN and Jack stood quietly, still unmoved by Louisa's seizures of pain. She lay panting, her body and face contorted, trying to gain some control as spasms racked her body. Suddenly Ben advanced on her, as if he might take his turn at her, and Louisa's terror was magnified. His face was dark and furious, but he only wrenched away the blanket he'd given her earlier, and with great effort Louisa turned away from him.

"What now?" Jack grumbled, and Ben struck at him with a meaty fist.

"Sonofabitch!" he howled. The blow caught Jack slightly off guard, but he soon reacted, with equal violence. For the moment Louisa was forgotten, the tension and anger of the men suddenly focused elsewhere, but her terror was not abated, and between agonized contractions, Louisa crawled through the brush, not knowing where she went, collapsing helplessly whenever she was overcome with pain or weakness as she bled profusely. She had no clear thought, yet some primitive instinct drove her away from the brawling men.

By the time the air was cleared between the men, Louisa was not in sight, and they argued whether to search for her or not.

"If she can scurry away, she's all right," Jack reasoned, touching his broken nose very tentatively.

"Even so, she'll be too much to deal with," Ben insisted.

"She probably ain't havin' a baby—just bleeding, like they all do."

Quickly Ben agreed, and they began to search, both

liberally using whiskey to facilitate their endeavor, cursing the darkness when shadows turned out to be shadows.

"Goddamn! This is useless!" Ben shouted finally. "Ya can search the rest o' the night—the rest o' your life—but I'm takin' them stones and getting what I can for 'em."

With that announcement, Jack was quick to join his partner, their interest in Louisa waning, now confined to the price her small but impressive collection of jewels would bring. "She'll never make it alone. If nothing else, the coyotes'll hunt her down," Jack assured his friend.

Louisa heard the men search on foot for her, and she concealed herself as best she could, her terror rising with every night sound, but she'd eluded them out of some luck she would never have believed possible. Now she heard the horses approaching her, certain she would be found or at least trampled to death. She dragged herself with effort, and, against all instinct, threw herself into the thickest part of a cluster of low-growing shrubs, not trusting she could be safe anywhere in the bright night. She cowered, head bowed as the hooves of the men's flying horses kicked sand and debris on her in their retreat, the sounds of the animals thundering at her, the feeling of impending attack from a crazed enemy pushing her mind to the brink of snapping.

After the men abandoned her, Louisa lay in her thorny nest for nearly an hour. She was unaware of the slashes on her face and hands; unaware of the gashes in the thick wool of her cape made by the brambles into which she'd plunged herself. She tried to endure her pain silently, as if silence would assist her, but soon the night echoed with her pain. Some of the time she neither heard her own voice, nor felt the pain. She was detached, as if watching some other weary, trapped animal struggling for its life within its man-made death cage. For a time she floundered, certain—even grateful—she'd lost the struggle. Then she was granted a stay of execution, the contractions subsiding, exhaustion giving way to semiconsciousness.

The reprieve was short, but during it she gained strength from some unknown source. When she opened her eyes, she felt herself to be in possession of her senses, a fact which became clear within moments when pain again grasped violently at her womb. She shut her eyes tightly, then peered into the starlit night through the net of brambles when pain released her. Her contractions were very close and intense, and her vision grew distorted, the limbs of shrubs turning into spidery webs of thorns; clawed hands reaching in the dark to inflict awful and familiar abuse.

Again Louisa struggled along the ground, crawling she knew not where, but away. Always away. Perhaps she could escape this time. Perhaps she could find a warm safe shelter—somewhere. Never before in this life—but, surely, somewhere there was a truly safe place. Not just momentary sanctuary, but enduring, permanent peace. Some place where there was light. Some place that was never dark. Never lonely. Nor painful. Nor unprotected. "Please, God!"

"Hail Mary full of grace . . ."

Louisa collapsed, sweat and tears mingling with the dust of the roadbed. She cried out pitifully, screaming and heaving for air.

"Please!"

Begging. Crawling.

" . . . the Lord is with thee . . ."

Reaching for whatever lay in her path to pull her along; any means to free herself from pain and terror.

"Blessed art thou among women, and blessed is the fruit of thy womb, Jesus . . ."

Where was there shelter? Where was there safety? There seemed to be none for her—anywhere—ever.

"Holy Mary, Mother of God . . ." she pleaded.

Was there nothing but misery in this night's darkness as well?

Louisa crawled until her strength gave out, and she was engulfed in a sea of slender stalked plants, or were they the lances of the enemy, and their leaves the pennants of an army that had surrounded her? What did the voices chant in the distance? Or was it

Chapter Seventy-five

"JUST received some interesting pieces last night. All from the same party. The necklace has to beat all." The man stood respectfully in front of the enormous gleaming desk. He pulled a dark, square-shaped, green velvet case from a coarsely wrapped package, placing the case before the other man. The case was soiled rather than worn, and the prospective buyer surveyed the stains and matted velvet with obvious distaste.

"I thought it best to bring it in its original box," the pawnbroker added apologetically. He was a pale, tall man with a considerable paunch to contrast with his otherwise slim build. He appeared not to be very strong, but this appearance was deceptive, for he had considerable strength. He both used and required strength to deal with some tougher customers in his business on the fringes of San Francisco's Barbary Coast.

As if certain he would be contaminated, Peter Melville did not pick up the velvet container. He only lifted the lid carefully. At first his eyes widened, then narrowed, his face turning very hard. "How did you acquire this, Kilby?" he demanded quietly, but obviously expecting a complete answer.

Benton Kilby had dealt with this man before, and from his own experience and from the man's reputation, he knew a brief but precise answer would be the only one accepted. As a rule, Kilby protected his sources, but not in this instance. "A couple of men brought me some good stuff last night. Didn't think you'd be interested in the rest, but, as you can see, this piece is exceptional," he said, gesturing nervously to the glittering green stones. "That's how I came to think of you first, sir."

Melville nodded. "What of the other jewelry?"

"Still have most of it—though it's good enough to change hands quick."

"I want to see all you have of this collection," he said firmly.

"Yes, sir."

"Leave the collar with me—to consider. I'll sign for it, if you have a receipt."

"That's not necessary," Kilby said, pleased to have gained this man's interest. He knew he was right in coming.

"Can you get in touch with the men who sold this to you?"

"Yes. I've not paid them yet. Wasn't sure I'd get what I wanted, according to what the sellers said they'd accept. They're not desperate to sell—as yet. If you're in no hurry, Mr. Melville, we can wait them out."

"I'm in no particular hurry," he said, standing up to conclude the interview, "but I want to see the other jewels as soon as you can arrange to bring them. I know someone who will be very interested in seeing both this necklace, and whatever else you have."

When he finished speaking, a servant appeared to show the pawnbroker out, giving Kilby no time to question Melville's remarks.

Kilby returned to his shop immediately, quickly gathering the pieces of Louisa's jewelry he still possessed. All of it was beautiful, yet, he'd thought, none but the emeralds were exceptional enough to capture Melville's attention. He shrugged his shoulders. Perhaps he was wrong. Yet Melville seemed to be interested in more than the jewelry, and Kilby wondered what intrigue the two trail-worn men, who'd appeared at his shop late last night, were involved in.

Kilby expected Melville to be interested in buying the necklace, if anyone in the area was, but it never occurred to him the man's interest would go beyond that.

He polished and wrapped each shining piece of

jewelry in velvet, and placed the small collection in another pouch. He closed his shop again, hurrying back to Melville's impressive stone house a few miles across the frantic, often corrupt, constantly expanding metropolis. The city, if it rightfully could be called that, was only now really beginning to take on the appearance of something other than a coarse frontier town. The influx of men to this gateway to the gold and other mining fields had given San Francisco the general appearance of a very temporary city of drifters, its residents coming and going rapidly, not encouraging the construction of permanent or sturdy buildings.

But here and there, durable or noteworthy structures were found, and Peter Melville resided in one of the more impressive homes dotting the landscape. Outside his gates the road might turn to a quagmire of mud and filth when rain inundated the coast, but behind the lacy grille of his wrought-iron fence, the grounds were green and immaculate, and in a few years the young trees on the property would be imposing and graceful. This dwelling, sitting pretentiously on a rise of land at the edge of the city, would for a long while capture the attention of onlookers.

When he arrived again, Kilby was advised to wait. A yellow-skinned servant showed him to a small dark library on the north side of the house, where it seemed he waited a very long while. Kilby grew restless. He fidgeted, not liking to be kept waiting but aware it would do him no service to be impatient or discourteous to his host.

After about an hour, another servant came for him, ushering him into the room where he'd been interviewed by Melville earlier the same day. Another man whom Kilby did not recognize was present, but from his looks, it was obvious he was Melville's social equal. With nothing more than a gesture of acknowledgment, Melville asked to see what he'd brought.

"This gentleman and I," Melville began by way of introduction, "would like to see what else you have.

All that you'll show us is from the same source, am I correct?"

"Yes, sir," Kilby replied, opening the pouch and carefully, almost nervously withdrawing its contents, unwrapping and laying the first item before the two men. The newcomer, standing to one side of Melville's chair, made Benton Kilby very uneasy. Though he had the unmistakable appearance of a man of wealth and breeding, there was something very disturbing about the coldness in his eyes and face. There was a tension in the man's body that warned Kilby to be accurate and cautious in his dealings with him.

Before the first glittering jewels rested on Melville's desk for more than an instant, the stranger lifted the drop diamond earrings for his closer inspection, his face turning darker and even more menacing.

He spoke before Kilby could unwrap another small bundle for scrutiny. "What did the men who sold these look like?" the man demanded, his eyes seeming to pierce Kilby with their intensity.

Kilby's mouth was dry as he gave a very general description of Ben Patrick and Jack Herbert.

"How did they come by the jewels? Where is the woman these belong to?" Aaron demanded, moving to Kilby, reaching for the man's lapels, the strength in his hands apparent, the fury in him contained with obvious effort.

"I've no idea—that is, I've no idea where the woman is—exactly. The men said they'd brought a 'high-class bitch' into town, and she wanted to raise a little money. I gathered she's a whore. They said they worked for her." Beads of sweat stood out on his face, and he licked his lips with a nervous motion of his tongue.

Aaron looked as if he'd explode. "These jewels belong to my wife whom I sent off in the company of the men you've identified. Her destination was San Diego, not San Francisco. She's no whore!"

Kilby winced at the force of the man's words, at his barely controlled need to lash out. "I—I—don't say she is! That's just what I understood. They must've lied."

"Relax a little, Marshall," Melville cautioned, rising to separate the men, if necessary. "Kilby, you said you'd not paid the men for the jewels," he said when Aaron released the pawnbroker. "How can you get in touch with them?"

"I've paid for all but the collar—we couldn't agree on a price—they're to come to my shop next week."

"I can't wait a week!" Aaron said angrily, turning to Melville, hardly able, in his concern for Louisa, to preserve his role as Marshall. He tried to smooth the edges of his desire to react violently, tried to show control where there was little ability to be even rational. He presumed the worst, or ransom would have been demanded in Monterey for Louisa's safe return, and Aaron's need to know for certain was nearly overpowering.

Peter Melville spoke calmly to Aaron. "I understand," he said, thinking he comprehended the man's intolerable and agonizing situation. Then he turned to Kilby again. "Have you any notion where these men might be?"

"None at all—not with their pockets as full as they were when they left my place. Without the windfall, they'd've spent time goin' from one dive to another. But with some sprucin' up, and some new clothes they could partake anywhere—as you well know."

"Yes, they could be anywhere," Melville sighed. "Kilby, if you have any thoughts between now and next week; if these men turn up before the appointed hour, let me know immediately." Then he gestured to the pouch of gems on his desk. "I'll take these for safekeeping. A little insurance from you, shall we say?" he said, ringing for a servant.

Kilby nodded compliance. "You'll hear from me directly," Melville added, and the man was ushered immediately from the room.

Melville gestured for Aaron to be seated, then went to a crystal-laden sideboard where he poured two generous drinks, handing one to the younger man.

"My mind is spinning," Aaron groaned truthfully.

Melville smiled grimly. "Let's not assume the worst. It's possible she's even in the city. White slavery *is* a common practice. I imagine those two didn't fail to notice her beauty—she'd fetch an excellent sum."

Aaron put his drink down and leaned his elbows on the desk, pressing the heels of his hands against his eyes, trying to think clearly. At first, all he could see was Louisa's lovely face, and remember the misery he'd so often seen in her eyes long years ago. He was certain her mind, if not her body, would never survive an encounter such as the one Melville suggested. She would never survive the assaults of countless men lined up for her favors. Perhaps, he thought, all he needed to do now was inquire after a beautiful mad-woman in the streets, and he could not conceal his grief, even from himself.

Chapter Seventy-six

MELVILLE summoned Emil Joseph and before Aaron left the house a plan was set in motion. Aaron did not intend to let another moment go by before beginning his search for Ben and Jack, their faces looming like gargoyles in his mind's eye. If it was the last thing he did, he would find them. If necessary, he would abandon his assignment. His former shipmate and partner, Mason Jennings, as well as his crew could hang, but, he swore, he would find Louisa's abductors.

While waiting for Joseph, Peter Melville studied Aaron, wondering at the younger man's metamorphosis. Clearly Marshall Hudson had a capacity for violence he'd not suspected. "Perhaps we all do," he muttered to himself. In spite of an obvious dalliance with the winning Mrs. Hill, it was evident Louisa had penetrated Marshall's soul deeply enough to turn an ordinarily gentle man into one of venom; one probably capable of murder, if Melville read the man accurately. He filed this insight away for future reference.

Almost immediately after Louisa departed Crane's Nest, Aaron had traveled from Monterey to San Francisco with Marguerite. She'd planned to come, having twice invited Louisa to accompany her. "The Colonel," as she was fond of calling him, stayed at his post in Monterey, and she needed an escort for traveling. Marshall and Franklin Carson were at the same time summoned by Peter Melville. "How wonderful," she purred. "You're a far more desirable companion than Louisa!"

The situation also suited Aaron's purposes to perfection. He would be able to immerse himself in the plot which became more and more to his liking as plans for a fortress at Santa Catalina Island took shape. And, he hoped, it would afford him ample opportunity to immerse himself in forgetfulness with Marguerite. What better way to erase the memory of one woman than by indulging himself with another. And he set about that portion of his assignment with lusty determination.

And while he exhausted himself, insisting the pleasure of it was sufficient, he wondered how long and what else it would take to rid himself of visions and sensations that, as yet, hadn't diminished. "Damn you, Louisa!" he cursed in the emptiness and loneliness of his bed in San Francisco. It wasn't enough just to go through the motions, but at the moment pride would have seen him go to his death insisting one woman was as good as another.

Yet with the news Melville gave him after summoning him abruptly from lunch with Marguerite, Aaron wondered if his assumption about women was accurate. The words he heard struck him nearly blind with rage and sorrow. When he saw and touched Louisa's emeralds for himself, his emotions exploded, and he seemed to go mad inside himself. For some indefinite time that afternoon, he felt himself adrift. None of the possibilities looming before him were tolerable, and at the edge of his consciousness was a nagging memory of another young woman who had loved him, and whom he had loved, as well.

As he dressed in rough, common apparel to scour San Francisco's muddy streets, Aaron armed himself with both a gun and knife. No one in his right mind would venture into the dens into which he would be going without weapons, nor face the men he hoped to find without some source of protection. He had rehearsed this act only a few years ago, he recalled, yet it almost seemed centuries had passed since he had walked in a torrential London rain to avenge Juliet. Now his memory of her ate at his heart. She had only been a child, secretly carrying one of her own, and she had died brutally, because of her love for him. His loving her had in no way shielded her, and Aaron feared the same for Louisa. He now strongly suspected that she too carried his child—*still* carried his child, he hoped against hope.

Finally, in addition to the weapons he secured against his body, Aaron slipped a heavy gold chain over his head. Minutes before, while sifting through the jewel pouch Benton Kilby left behind, Aaron came across his mementoes. They lay incongruously among Louisa's brilliant stones, and he'd removed the simple chain and its pendants from the rest of the glittering collection. He pressed the still cold metal against his chest, against his heart. This time, he swore, he would not part with them. They would have to be taken from his corpse.

Peter Melville had summoned two other men, and, with Aaron and Emil Joseph, they spread out to cover the city's more notorious places of business and pleasure. If it had been within his ability, Franklin Carson would have joined the party, for word of Louisa's probable abduction grieved him deeply. But, with Melville, he would wait in the stone house until midnight when everyone would reassemble to share information.

It was not by chance that the roughest section of San Francisco claimed the name Barbary Coast, for every vice imaginable, every sort of low humanity could be discovered within the district. And there was little honor among the thieves who congregated there. They plundered and murdered among their own kind nearly as often as they did their eager customers.

Aaron and Joseph started their hunting among the more "respectable" houses, an experience they both might have enjoyed in different circumstances. At several places, they were authorized to give Melville's name as a means of introduction and, perhaps, to insure that more truthful information was obtained. No one confessed knowing or hearing of anyone of Louisa's description nor had anyone seen Ben Patrick or Jack Herbert.

At the "Patrician Hotel for Young Women" Aaron met an old friend he was in no position to recognize. He wondered if coarsely garbed and bearded as he was tonight, he was sufficiently disguised to remain

Marshall Hudson for her. Lilly, now Elena, gave no
indication she had ever set eyes on him before he
entered her establishment in San Francisco that evening, and after the first tense moments passed unre-
markably, Aaron reminded himself, almost cheerfully,
it wasn't only members of his sex who could forget a
face.

But Elena didn't hesitate to recognize his prominent
name from New Orleans, nor did she deny being well
acquainted with Peter Melville. She promised to put
her sources to work within the community to locate
both Louisa and the men Aaron searched for.

It was very late at night when the two men arrived
at Elena's hotel, and while they relaxed briefly over
strong, well-aged Scotch, Aaron noted trade was brisk,
though the prices were high. He recognized some of
her customers from more polite gatherings. This establishment, like Lilly's in New Orleans, was splen-
didly garish, her girls all pleasing to the eye in one
way or another. He even thought he recalled one or
two now very experienced women.

It seemed like a long time ago when he had fre-
quented Lilly's place, and others like it. Now, oddly,
he thought, he didn't yearn much for the freedom of
his earlier life. As he sat quietly detached from the
hustle in Elena's parlor, tired and on the brink of
bereavement, he wished he'd been more forthright
with Louisa. He wished he'd withheld less of himself
in their affair, for concealing his true feelings, conflicting though they were, had not insured Louisa's safety,
nor, he suspected, would it protect him in any way.
Had he only told her how much he loved her, had
she known it was only fear keeping him from revealing the extremes of his passion for her. How could
knowledge have done her any greater harm than ignorance?

For an instant it seemed to him grief would sweep
him away; and he steeled himself against it. He must
find those men; he must find Louisa. He must tell her
those things he should have said months ago. If he
had only been less arrogant about his right to do whatever he felt necessary to accomplish his goals, if he'd

simply told Louisa the truth about how he happened
to give Marguerite the necklace—perhaps, then, Louisa would have understood—if not forgiven him—perhaps, then, she would never have left him and would
now be safe.

Aaron felt his eyes haze over, and the weight of his
sorrow. He took a deep breath, and slammed his glass
down on Elena's stiffly starched linen-covered table.
"Shit on hindsight!" he said under his breath, rising
from the table to go again into the streets, Emil's diverted attention swiftly brought back to his obviously
distressed companion. "We've rested long enough,"
Aaron said less vehemently than his more private remark.

It was best not to think at all, he concluded. It was
best to do what he had done before—search with purpose, without questioning or regret, listening only to
his instincts, doing what he had to without mercy or
second thought. He would find Herbert and Patrick if it
took his last effort to do so; he would find Louisa, if it
killed him.

Chapter Seventy-seven

AT midnight they met again at Melville's. No one had anything significant to share, and they went back to the streets, agreeing to meet again at noon the following day.

Aaron and Joseph split up, determination etched in Aaron's face. He didn't stop until dawn, sagging against the worn, unpainted siding of one of the more typical saloons of the district. He'd decided the chances of finding men of Jack and Ben's character in the high-priced brothels were nil. Maybe they'd spend one night extravagantly, but after that they'd seek lower levels of enjoyment.

Wearily he entered a dingy saloon, at this hour purporting to be a café. He ordered breakfast, though he wasn't especially hungry, and attempted to sort out his gloomy thoughts over perhaps the strongest coffee ever poured. He had descended finally into the meaner part of the district, but probably it was the section of the city he could be most at home in, he thought sardonically. These were the people he knew best: the prostitutes, smugglers, gamblers, thieves, murderers, and aimless drifters, few with any creed above survival, few with any hope for life above the lowest level.

When the grimy cook, cigar stub clenched fiercely in his jaws, shoved Aaron's sizable breakfast at him, he was the only patron in the place. "Business isn't too lively," he offered.

"You're a little late in the day."

Aaron smiled ruefully. "I'm looking for a woman."

"Like I said, you're a little late. Come back this evenin'. They're catchin' their beauty rest," he gestured with a nod upstairs, a tooth-filled grin dissolving into a phlegmy cough, which did a good deal to further dissuade Aaron from attacking the grease-filled plate sitting before him.

He shoved it aside. "She'd be new. Slim. Pale hair. Light blue eyes. Not too tall. Soft, beautiful."

The cook gave Aaron another wide grin, and a very doubting expression, waving the well-savored remains of his cigar at him. "Now what do ya suppose a dame like that would be doin' here?"

Aaron didn't answer. "Maybe you've seen her companions," he said, and described every detail he could remember about Ben and Jack.

"Could be half dozen of the men I see every night."

Aaron frowned. "Keep your eyes open," shoving some gold coins at the man. "There'll be more if you report anything worth hearing. The name's . . Hudson. You can leave word for me at the stone house on Drydock Hill."

The cook eyed the money, which amply covered the indigestible fare Aaron had merely surveyed. "What'd you say your name was?"

"Hudson," Aaron answered from the doorway. "Marshall Hudson."

It was a series of questions and descriptions he gave the rest of the day, returning to the stone house in mid-afternoon, collapsing for a few hours of sleep, and the first edible meal he'd had in more than a day. On his way out again, Aaron glanced at himself in an ornate mirror in Melville's foyer and saw a face he'd almost forgotten, noting he was already beginning to take on the appearance of the kind of men he was rubbing elbows with along the Barbary Coast. The looks of a gentleman wear off fast enough, Aaron thought to himself, seeing hard lines of tension in his face, and the already soiled patches on his warm, coarsely woven pea jacket. "In a few days, I won't be admitted to this house through the front door."

And that was as it should be, he reasoned. He was only a gentleman for the charade. The habits he'd acquired, the mode of dress, the style of life were only part of the masquerade. If—*when* he found Louisa,

the act would resume—but only for as long as it took
to be done with this affair. "Water seeks its own level,"
he cautioned himself before the glass. Louisa would
forever be above his reach, regardless of his restless
dreams. By his side she would suffer, and, Aaron
sighed, he already knew enough of her sorrows.

Aaron turned away from the mirror, and left the
house hurriedly. Light was fading and the crisp evening
air was damp. Soon it would be pouring. "Wonderful
night," he said aloud. "At least the dives'll be full."

Hours later, he found Emil scouring the same establishment he'd stumbled into. "Anything?"

"Not a trace," Joseph growled over obviously cut,
disagreeably sour whiskey. He poured Aaron a glass.
"I've seen my share of these places," he offered, "but
the way they spring up's an amazing thing. Haven't
been on this street for a while. Haven't missed much."

Aaron winced at the first swallow of liquor.

"Not like the stuff at Melville's!" Emil laughed.
"This sure must be an eye-opener, son."

Aaron nodded. At least he continued to deceive
someone, he sneered to himself.

"Not too many places in the country depraved as
this one. Watch yourself. You're a sore thumb. Fact is,
you'd best tag with me the rest of the way. One body's
enough to be searchin' for."

The assessment stung Aaron, although he was well
aware the possibilities were slim Louisa was still alive
—for, if she were, she'd likely be wishing she were
dead. "No. We'll continue separately. We'll cover more
ground."

"Naw. Melville'd personally slit my throat if you
didn't come back." The decision for him was final, and
he leaned a little more heavily against the bar. "Ya
know the little game they play here? Convince some
fool they've got him a virgin all primed and eager to
get it over—just on account of him. And for the same
price he can do her sister. Well, the two ladies see to it
he's properly sauced, then help him out for a little air.
They take him for a few spins around the block, and
in again the back way. They help him off with his
britches, and the 'virgin' for the hour invites him in.

While he's on his way to paradise, the 'sister' brains him for all she's worth, and someone drags him off, dumps him in the alley, and if he's lucky he wakes to see another day."

"Probably none the wiser," added Aaron, having heard of the game before.

Joseph laughed. "There's not a virgin over thirteen years old within a thousand miles of here! You'd think everyone'd know that!" He took a hasty swig of his drink, turning slightly more serious. "Been into Virgil's yet?" Aaron shook his head. "Not my favorite place. Not bad-lookin' gals though—considerin'. He's a mean sonofabitch, and he keeps a tight rein on 'em. They don't last long, even at the prices he pays. That's what attracts 'em. Laces the booze he insists they drink with cantharides and keeps 'em dancin' even if they burst. Some show! Maybe we'll have some luck there—our men haven't been here," he added with a sweeping gesture.

He'd been leaning over the noisy bar, and now he straightened, hunching and rolling his shoulders to ease his fatigue. "Don't give up—we'll find 'em yet. They've got to be around. They'll not skip with their tickets to fortune stashed with Kilby," he reasoned. "It's just a matter of us gettin' lucky." And he put his thick arm around the younger man's back, and ushered him into the rain-soaked night.

Chapter Seventy-eight

There was an especially brutal and foul air at Virgil's, its reputation for depravity well deserved. Six scantily clad women, in various stages of inebriation and discomfort, did their best to keep up with the discordant music pounding from a much-scarred upright piano next to the crude raised dance floor. All the dancers wore long black stockings held up with scarlet garters, their sheer blouses clearly displaying all for the prospective customers. Their black skirts just reached the tops of their stockings, and none were allowed undergarments.

An equal number of "girls" circulated among the patrons of the very packed saloon and gambling house, selling drinks which they shared with their customers in full strength, though it was an unusual practice. They also hustled their other wares to whatever willing customer was available for snaring, and the takers were plentiful. The traffic between upstairs and down, from main to back rooms was constant.

"If they haven't been here, they've been done in," was Emil Joseph's wry assessment. He and Aaron circulated and spoke with each of the girls, prying their already loose tongues with coins.

"Maybe I seen 'em," a husky damsel who called herself Mabel told Aaron. "Especially the one with the sliver of a mustache," she added to the clink of his gold coins in her palm, shoving her other hand between his thighs, urging him roughly. "Vicious bastard, too," she added, smiling.

When Aaron pushed her hand from him, the whore's smile faded. She attempted to push the wisps of her dirty blond hair back into the bun at the nape of her neck, staring at him cautiously. "What is it you want 'sides information?" she inquired suspiciously.

Just then Emil joined them. "The barkeep says he's seen 'em!" he said jubilantly. "They've been in every night since they arrived; spendin' freely, drinkin' heavy, and whoring plenty." He paused. "No sign or word of a woman," he added quietly.

Aaron shoved Mabel aside. She growled an obscenity, but quickly went on her way to more willing prospects while Emil and Aaron seated themselves near Virgil's main entrance, several tables back against the wall. They bought a bottle of uncut, but poor quality whiskey—"the best in the house"—and proceeded to wait.

Beyond the din of the place, Aaron heard the rain pour down, the storm filling every dive on the street with more than the usual assortment of revelers. As the night wore on, Virgil's increasingly crowded patrons grew steadily more drunk and disagreeable. Through it all Aaron and Joseph sat silently watchful, surveying every new arrival, every fistfight and quarrel, every public exhibition. After a while the bottle they shared even seemed reasonably acceptable refreshment.

Emil Joseph sat patiently and considered his companion. He remembered Mr. Marshall Hudson from the weeks he'd spent on the trail with him. Emil recalled how displeased he'd been when Melville said a gentleman would be accompanying him into the interior. But he'd been pleasantly surprised to discover the man was in no way a hindrance, finding him an expert horseman, even if it did take him a few days on the trail to regain some comfort in the saddle. Joseph had also been amazed at how easily the man adjusted to the other rigors of the trail, and it wasn't long before Mr. Hudson seemed as at home in the countryside as his two guides. Emil had a great deal of respect for the young man, and it had only increased these last few days and nights as they combed the saloons and bawdy houses together. He expected the man could hold his own in the confrontation they hoped to have, although he had no specific knowledge to make him certain. But the man's preparations, his conduct throughout the search suggested Mr. Hudson could take care of himself. It was as if he'd had more than a gentleman's education.

While Emil regarded him, Aaron scanned the customers, his anticipation high, his desire to act against the two men he'd entrusted with Louisa's safe journey rising with every passing minute. He watched the night tick away on a battered German clock above the otherwise unadorned entryway, and wondered why someone hadn't long ago put the whimsical parading figures out of their misery. At predictably regular intervals, two gaily painted lovers would appear and clasp each other fervently to a trite melody not often heard above the roar of Virgil's place. Then the wooden couple would disengage and disappear. Whenever they appeared, Aaron watched the pair hypnotically as he drank, momentarily feeling the heavy numbing effects of alcohol and grief.

He felt as wooden as the clock's carved figures. Certainly his experience with women was in many respects not exceptionally different from the comical male doll who paraded mechanically each quarter hour. This minute, Aaron's encounters seemed as brief, as unsatisfying, as empty, even when he'd felt love. And he found himself contemplating putting a final end to the misery of the hapless wooden lovers who strutted unnoticed in the foul-smelling saloon.

He leaned back on two legs of his chair considering such action, suddenly inching upright when he saw Jack Herbert step surely through the doorway. Jack quickly scanned the mob in Virgil's, but took no notice of Aaron. Ben followed his friend out of the rain in the same ignorant condition. Without raising his eyes from Aaron's face, Emil knew instantly the men they waited for had arrived. In the younger man's countenance he read unmistakable hatred and unflinching purpose. He suspected only extreme self-control prevented Aaron from swiftly murdering the new arrivals.

Because of the crush inside the hall, Ben and Jack stood near the doorway relaxed and unprepared. As if by signal, Aaron and Joseph acted in concert, rising

from their chairs, moving in one motion. By prear-
rangement they'd chosen who to grab, Aaron deciding
Jack was more his equal in age and strength and Ben
and Emil a suitable match.

Before either Ben or Jack had time to sense the
presence of their adversaries, Aaron and Joseph seized
the men from behind, their weapons drawn. Strangling Jack with one powerful arm locked around his
neck, Aaron felt a special thrill as he thrust his knife
against Jack's lean belly. One powerful unrestrained
thrust and the man's life would begin to flow from
him, and it was nearly impossible for Aaron to refrain
from the motion, so sure was he that any information
these men provided would be long past helping Louisa.

At first, the life-and-death movement in the barroom
went unnoticed, but soon a wide circle opened around
the four men and the roaring of the place ceased. Ben
and Jack were frozen, their breathing restricted in the
death grips of the strong arms of their captors, their
awareness of the damage the blades would surely do
momentarily eliminating any other response.

In the suddenness of the attack, Ben was the first to
guess the reason for the confrontation, the first to
know it would be a fight to the death, if, in fact, they
were given an opportunity to defend themselves.

In the surprising stillness Aaron's voice was unfamiliar, but Jack instinctively knew his attacker. "Where is
she?" Aaron bellowed, pressing his knife point to penetrate the surface of Jack's skin.

Jack shrank against Aaron, away from the blade,
feeling a trickle of his own warm blood begin to spread
slowly. He struggled helplessly in Aaron's grip, Ben
faring no better in Emil's hands, though the rage
emitted from Aaron's every pore was lacking in his
attack.

In Emil's grasp, Ben struggled for breath, eyes bulging, and tried to speak, his voice rasping incoherently.
Emil loosened his grip slightly and it was all the man
needed, arching and twisting, successfully wrenching
the knife-wielding arm away, doubling both himself
and his attacker, crashing head over heels into the

saloon, onlookers trampling each other to avoid the two. Ben and Emil struggled desperately, the knife lost, slithering along the floor out of reach.

The brawl seemed to be a sudden invitation, and soon it seemed the whole of Virgil's erupted in long pent-up violence. Rapidly Aaron lost his control of Jack, and the two were shoved outside, losing their balance as they tumbled into the mud-wet street. They grappled furiously, the most vicious aspects of each man's nature rising instantly to the surface in the no-holds-barred fight. The rain pelted them, making their grasp of each other more difficult with every passing minute. Jack received the advantage in their expulsion into the street, immediately pressing the full weight of his bent leg into Aaron's stomach, battering Aaron's head and face as fast as his arms could swing. Aaron's only advantage came in Jack's still short breath, and he managed a decisive, still powerful fist squarely into Jack's throat, knocking out the man's wind and toppling him backward into a pond in the muddied street.

Aaron threw himself onto Jack, pushing him deep into the puddle. They struggled and thrashed like two mud-and-water-soaked primeval creatures. Expecting the move to find him free of his pursuer, Jack planted a violent kick in Aaron's groin. Aaron roared in agony, but his grip was only momentarily, and insufficiently loosened, and his pain magnified his rage. He managed to shove his opponent beneath him again, feeling Jack struggle under the surface of the water. His own head safely above the water, Aaron gasped for air, nearly blind with fury and discomfort. Had he not wanted something more from the man than his life, Aaron would have easily drowned Jack without mercy. But he wanted more. He wanted to know about Louisa, and he raised the man by his hair from the shallow but deadly water, pressing his bent knee squarely, heavily into the man's gut.

Jack labored for breath, unrecognizably covered with slippery brown ooze, his eyes bulging. Aaron waited a few seconds, until he was sure the man had recovered enough to blurt out what he wanted to hear.

"Where is she?" he demanded again, pressing his body down slightly to remind Jack who was in control.

Jack shook his head weakly. "Don't know," he gasped. "God's truth, I swear!"

Aaron wrenched the man's hair all the harder. "Where'd you leave her?"

With difficulty, Jack coughed and rasped. "Just west o' the Salinas River—east o' Los Burros."

Aaron tightened his grip again. "Why isn't she with you?"

At first, Jack was mute. Fear could be seen in the man's mud-smeared face, which was now streaked clean in patches by the fast-pouring rain. He begged shamelessly for mercy in Aaron's grip. "She . . . she was dying—havin' a baby too soon."

"And you left her alone, not sure whether she survived or not?" he bellowed, not giving Jack the opportunity to reply, his horror and grief finally turning to insanity, his hands clutching Jack's throat in a moment that seemed to be suspended in space and time, the seconds seeming eternal, the night and the strength of his hatred seeming to lift him from his own earthly body as he thought he watched Jack's soul leave his body, and the physical shell sink into the river of a street when he released it.

Aaron's effort nearly spent, he raised himself hypnotically from the scene with effort, now only vaguely aware of the continuing general melee around him. Something reminded him his business was yet unfinished, and he staggered painfully into Virgil's again. He looked around the battling throng for Emil, finding him losing his fight with Ben. Without hesitation, but feeling as if he were weighted and hardly moving, Aaron disarmed a fallen patron and, amid the roar of the place, put the .45 to Ben's ear and pulled the trigger.

The effect was ghastly, but Emil was saved. With effort Aaron shoved Ben's mutilated body from Emil, and lifted his disabled partner as best he could. Incredible pain shot through Aaron's groin as he did so, but the two men managed to stagger from Virgil's, jostled in their exit by still, and incomprehensibly, brawling customers.

Along the way, in the cold but unnoticed downpour, the two battered men stopped briefly in their trek across the city, Aaron suddenly aware he continued to grasp the execution gun. He stared at the weapon momentarily. This time his acts of vengeance registered in him with satisfaction, and he was unrepentant. He knew he would not hesitate to commit the same crimes again. This he was sure of even before he knew the full horror of Louisa's experience.

Chapter Seventy-nine

LOUISA had wanted, even prayed, not to survive. But she had. That she had lived through the long, long night seemed a miracle—no, a curse.

The worst of her agony was spent in the shadow-filled night, and in the early morning she finally closed her eyes and slept deeply, well beyond the reach of dreams. She slept perhaps two hours, waking stiff and cold in the crisp air. When she noticed the sky above her, the dark gray clouds threatened rain, and turning her head, she could find no promise of anything brighter on the horizon. Her mouth and throat were parched, and she thought she would welcome a downpour. It would, at least, be refreshing, perhaps even cleansing.

Louisa was very weak, nearly unable to move. I'll rest a while longer, she thought, turning her eyes to her immediate surroundings, realizing the army she'd both feared and beckoned to assist her in the terrifying night were only long rows of corn stalks. And the pennants the soldiers waved were only flapping leaves. She heard something shuffling in the undergrowth beside her head, and twisted slightly to see a tiny silver mouse standing inches from her, regarding her with his enormous black jeweled eyes. He was no bigger than a large walnut, watching her curiously, his small nose twitching furiously to inspect this intruder in his domain.

Louisa couldn't help but smile at the inquisitive creature. I'd move out of your way, she thought wearily, but I haven't the strength. When she did move slightly he scurried away, and her attention was suddenly focused on herself again. She felt a rush of blood between her thighs, and she wondered what would become of her, how long she could lie here unnoticed, whether she would be found alive or dead. "Does it matter?" she asked aloud and bitterly.

She lay a few feet within the rows of corn, in a blood-soaked nest. Pulling herself with an effort to a cleaner patch of ground, she was too exhausted to go more than a few feet, and collapsed, finally sleeping again, but less soundly. She heard low voices, and suddenly dark threatening figures filled her head. Soon she felt something touch her body, someone touch her face, and shake her shoulders gently. Louisa's eyes flew open, and she cried without volition trying to wrench herself weakly from whatever touched her.

They saw the terror in her face and eyes, even before she saw them, and they muttered among themselves quietly. "Señora, señora," said the woman whose hands tried to rouse her. When at last she was able to focus on the woman's broad dark face, and see the gentleness of her round black eyes, when she could hear the softness of the voice, Louisa's heartbeat began gradually to slow to a normal rate.

Louisa's first thought was of Carmen, but she knew instantly she was mistaken. "What do you want?" was all she could think to say, frightened, but oddly relieved to be no longer alone. The woman's face did much to soothe her.

Then Louisa heard a gruff male voice behind her. "Hurry! She's bad luck. Gotta do it now, before it's all ruined."

Louisa had no idea what the angry man meant, but she felt herself recoil, certain he regarded her with malice.

"No, we wait for the Father!" the woman insisted.

"No!" and the man's face loomed suddenly before her. Louisa saw both resolution and revulsion in his eyes as he leaned over her, and, seemingly without effort, lifted her from the ground. He carried her quickly without another word, but not roughly, and laid her about fifty feet from the cornfield. Immediately the Indian woman silently stooped next to her, covering her with a heavy but ragged blanket, and then turned her attention to the men.

Louisa lay propped at a slight angle and watched as six men and as many children set fire to the stand of corn where she had spent the night aborting Aaron's child. The strangers' hurried act and the heavy smoke made Louisa shiver, and, even under the heavy blanket, she began to tremble. Quickly she felt the darker woman's hand on her forehead. "Soon as it's done, we take you with us. Father Hidalgo comes soon."

"What are they doing?" Louisa inquired, still shivering.

"Sucking bugs have come. Because of you. You're unclean. We burn the field to save the rest. Or many will starve again. A bleeding woman cannot go into the fields. Or with the stock. It is forbidden."

Louisa was startled. "I didn't know," she whispered defensively. "I didn't even know I was in a cornfield," she sighed, remembering the distorted shapes of the field "I lost my baby in there last night," she confided to the woman. "I was very early."

The other woman frowned. "Tell nobody," she cautioned, and though she spoke quietly and without malice, Louisa was frightened. These people *were* Indians, and though they dressed much like other poor people in the countryside, and spoke of having summoned a Catholic priest, Louisa's pulse began to race again. The woman called her "unclean" and said she was to blame for the ruin of part of their crop. From the looks of these ragged people, they could ill afford to lose even this small plot of land.

Louisa began to sweat. What dark superstition made them believe she was responsible? What cruel practices did they have to punish one who brought such a fate on their meager existence? The woman who sat by her even warned her there was danger.

Louisa's head felt light. She was weak from loss of blood, as well as from hunger and fatigue. The wind shifted and blew smoke from the fire directly on her, making her feel even more weak and uncomfortable. Fire, smoke, pain, feelings of contamination were forever weaving through her life. She coughed convulsively in the engulfing draft of smoke, suddenly unable to breathe, feeling blood gush from inside her empty womb, and the tears that originally sprang from the irritating denseness of the air turned to tears of hopelessness.

She fainted then and when she woke again she was lying in a straw bed on the dirt floor of a small whitewashed house. Underneath a heavy multicolored blanket, Louisa lay nearly naked, with only a well-worn but clean peasant's blouse barely covering the upper half of her body.

The only furnisings in the one-room shelter were two poorly made, unpainted chairs, and a small trunk which probably served as a table as well as a bureau. There was no window, and only a blanket to cover the doorway. A crucifix hung at the foot of her straw bed. It was crudely carved, but somehow touching. Louisa thought the agonized Christ must have been rendered by someone who knew the meaning of pain, for he certainly managed to convey it. She suspected she would have many hours to reflect on the rough wood figure before her, but for now at least, she was warm and comfortable, as comfortable as her hosts could make her.

Suddenly she had no more time to contemplate her situation, for the blanket serving for a door was pulled aside and the woman who helped her earlier entered the house carrying a steaming cooking pot. She gave Louisa a shy but friendly smile, rested the pot on the floor, and reached for a clay bowl on a shelf above Louisa's head. The woman stooped and ladled a good portion of a thick stew into the bowl. The aroma was unfamiliar to Louisa, but not unpleasant, as was the actual flavor of the concoction. Propping herself up weakly on her elbows, Louisa ate it eagerly as it was spoon-fed to her in silence.

"My name is Rosa," the woman confided.

Louisa smiled. "Thank you for your help, Rosa. Is this your house?" she asked, relaxing down into the straw again when she was no longer hungry.

"No, it's empty for a long time. You must not live

with others when you bleed. I bring you clean straw.
I do what I can. The Father came. He come back in a
while. I told him you was sick. I told *him* the truth."
She smiled at the pale young woman. "Sleep now, and I
cook up something good to make you strong."

Louisa had no strength to do other than what Rosa
recommended, and several hours later Rosa woke her
and brought her clean straw. "Father Hidalgo
here again, señora," she reported quietly when Louisa
was settled once more in the simple bed.

At first all Louisa could do in the priest's presence
was cry. He prayed for her, and when she seemed
calm, he asked her questions. He seemed to Louisa as
gray as his habit, and not nearly as sturdy as its fabric,
but he had a quiet steady approach which helped her.
"Who are you, señora, and how did you get here?
There must be someone I can send for?"

"You must send for no one!" she said emphatically.
"You must promise me!"

"I can not promise," he replied, a bit startled by
Louisa's sudden vehemence.

"I'm sorry, Father," Louisa sighed. "Please forgive
my rudeness." She gave him her name and told him
of her abduction and miraculous escape. "Please don't
send for anyone until I'm well. Please understand I
need some time to recover, to be by myself. I can't
leave here for a while anyway. It would do no good to
send for someone."

"There's a doctor. You won't object to him?"

"No. You may send for him."

"I'll look in on you again, señora," he promised as
he left.

The doctor did not come for several days, obviously unhappy about entering the Indian camp. Louisa wondered why he'd bothered to come at all. She'd
hemorrhaged badly once more before he came, and
Rosa's foul-smelling and sensation-numbing potions
were as adequate as any she suspected he would ever
brew. "You the wife of someone important?" he asked
gruffly when he discovered there was nothing for him
to do.

"Why do you ask?"

"Wouldn't have come out here if the priest hadn't insisted. He didn't say who you are, but I don't usually come all this way for just anyone."

"I'm no one important, Doctor. Sorry you came all this way for nothing," she said harshly. "You obviously misunderstood the Father."

Late the following week Louisa was on her feet. She was weak but gaining, beginning to wonder what she should do next. She was dressed like the few other women in the camp, in garments Louisa previously wouldn't have even considered worthy of the description rags. And against the caution of her "nursemaid" Rosa, Louisa sponged herself with water brought to her from the river, even washing her hair with a very diluted solution of strong yellow soap, drying the heavy mass of it in the sun, making one long braid to hang down her back when it was dry. But even though she dressed just as her newfound caretakers did, and even though she learned a few of their ways as her strength and curiosity permitted, gathering roots and skinning small game, it was obvious the slender, fair-faced, fair-haired child-woman was not one of them.

While she waited in their camp, Louisa lived from moment to moment, thinking of nothing but what she saw before her eyes, on the task of living alongside, if not actually among, a people who were in most ways very foreign to her. She neither thought of the past nor the future while her body healed its bleeding wounds.

Then one afternoon she cuddled another woman's infant while the child's mother ground corn in preparation for the evening meal. Louisa held the baby naturally, without a second thought, and the infant nestled instinctively, seeking Louisa's breast through her thin dress, growing steadily annoyed when his clutching hands and mouth found only softness, but no satisfaction. Soon the infant was screaming in fury, not to be soothed by anything Louisa had to offer, and it was then Louisa knew the time had come for her to go. Now she was only a burden to her new friends—as she had been all along, she thought. She could not impose on their open-hearted kindness any longer. She was well enough to leave them.

Again there was unpleasant reality to face, even if she preferred not to face it. Her own baby had fared well enough all this time without her, according to all the news she'd had, and though she feared her child would be better off without her, Louisa felt her obligation keenly.

But before she could even go home, she had no choice but to send word to Aaron. All she had were the rags she wore, and even these did not actually belong to her. She had no means to go home, except by him. She had purposefully postponed this moment, perhaps longer than necessary, she acknowledged. She dreaded the hour she would meet him face to face, and that moment when she would be forced to confront her wildly conflicting emotions.

Chapter Eighty

THE boy José went for the priest very early the next morning, with a request that he come to camp bringing something for Señora Hudson to write on. She also sent word she must leave for home as soon as possible. Father Hidalgo did not return with the young messenger, but he sent a ledger and a stub of pencil to her in José's safekeeping.

When Louisa saw José returning to the camp alone, she at first was alarmed. "Where is Father?" she asked the boy anxiously.

"He says he cannot come today. I'm to bring back your letter to him," he said proudly.

Louisa hugged José tightly, taking the ledger from his outstretched hand. She quickly seated herself in the shade of her tiny house. She wrote three letters: the first to Father Hidalgo explaining herself and her situation a little more precisely; the second to Emma, briefly explaining her delay, knowing the woman would be half-crazy with worry by now; and the last, and the briefest to Aaron. She informed him of her whereabouts—in case he had noticed and was concerned about her disappearance. In formally polite sentences, she asked him to come for her, and it was clear she expected him to honor her request for help.

The next day Father Hidalgo prepared to send Louisa's mail, tucking her letters along with others into a leather pouch to be picked up later in the week. His attention was diverted by the scurrying of squawking hens in the yard outside his door and he looked up to see a very determined-looking man ride up, halt, and dismount from his horse in one motion. The stranger tethered his animal hastily, and approached the priest's living quarters in an obvious hurry.

The man's face was partially hidden by the hat he wore to shade his already dark skin. From his dusty appearance it was obvious he had been on the road for several days. When he saw the priest, the young man removed his hat, in what the Father thought seemed an unlikely gesture of respect, in view of the coldness of the man's eyes, the nearly brittle tension in his body.

"Father!" the man said, seeming starttled by the priest's sudden and silent appearance in the doorway.

"Father Hidalgo," he informed him.

Aaron nodded, not inclined to even simple polite conversation. "I'm looking for a woman. Perhaps you've heard of her, maybe even seen her. She'd have arrived here about four weeks ago."

The priest looked surprised. "And you are . . . ?"

"Her husband—Marshall Hudson. My wife's name is Louisa—she's fair, about this tall," he raised his hand to his chin, "blue eyes."

Father Hidalgo turned his head and looked at the small collection of letters he had just prepared, now lying on his desk. He smiled at Aaron. "I have a letter for you. I was just this moment preparing to send it to Monterey."

Aaron's face suddenly reflected a mixture of misery and joy, the first flash of life the priest had seen in the man's eyes. "Where is she?" he demanded in a voice that sounded more fearful than harsh.

"Not far from here. She's asking you to come to her," the priest said, reaching for his mail pouch.

"How long have you known she was here?" Aaron demanded.

"Nearly as long as she's been in the area," Father Hidalgo responded quietly.

"Why wasn't I sent for?" Aaron seemed not to believe he had not been notified.

"She begged me not to. Why? Perhaps, you know the answer better than I." It was a small challenge.

But Aaron did not take it. Instead he tore open Louisa's crisply cold letter as soon as it was handed to him. "Yes, I know the answer to that one," he muttered. He stood silently for a few minutes. "Tell me. How is she?"

The priest sat down on his unadorned, uncomfortable desk chair and motioned for Aaron to sit in the only other seat in the small, spare room, a hard bench against the wall.

"In the physical sense, she seems well enough, when you know she nearly bled to death not once, but twice. In fact, my son, it is only one of God's small miracles that she is alive." When her husband did not seem startled by the revelation, he suspected the man knew at least something of what had happened to her. "What do you know about what has happened?"

"I know she was abducted and abandoned to die."

"I assure you that is not *all* of it." Aaron scowled, a wave of hatred rushing over him when he thought of the men to whom he'd entrusted Louisa, despising himself, as well, for his lack of foresight. "She was brutally attacked and left to die. She has lost your child—one doesn't know whether she will ever conceive again," he added to the man he thought was her husband, and rightfully concerned about such matters. "You must *not* blame her for what has happened."

Father Hidalgo didn't know how to interpret the look on Aaron's face. Again his expression seemed blank and uncaring, exceedingly cold, if not cruel, and the priest worried about the young woman who recently had begged to recover anonymously and in private.

"How do I find her?"

"I will go with you."

"It's not necessary for you to trouble yourself, Father."

"I assure you, it's no trouble," he said firmly.

They traveled more slowly than Aaron wished in order to accommodate the elderly priest, who tried to draw Aaron out a little, to inform him about the countryside, and of the people who had sheltered Louisa and whom she had eventually come to trust. But the priest soon began to feel he prattled to himself, finally giving up his efforts, and they rode more than half the two-hour trip to the camp in total silence.

When they arrived, Aaron created a great deal of interest among the Indians. Except for his fine features, and his somewhat taller body, he could have been one of them. He was nearly as dark-skinned, and his hair was as black and his eyes as brown as any of those who collected silently around the priest and his companion. Everyone who was not working at some nearby ranch had returned from their own cultivated fields for the noonday meal and there was quite a gathering. When Rosa looked up to see them, she knew at once the reason for their presence, and she approached Aaron and the priest directly to answer their questions before they were uttered.

"She's down by the corn," Rosa said, pointing in the direction of a path that led from the small cluster of thatched and adobe huts. "She's not far. She's not real strong."

Aaron started out immediately on foot, firmly insisting he would go alone. "I insist," he said flatly to Father Hidalgo, and he turned and strode hurriedly in the direction Rosa pointed. The path wound gently, finally bringing him to a slight rise of land from which he could see a woman in the distance. He knew from the figure's impression on his senses, it had to be Louisa.

For a moment as he stood watching her, he asked himself how she could affect him the way she did? Why didn't he forget her? Why was he obsessed by this woman? "For God's sake, she's only *one* woman!" he cursed aloud. She was made like countless others, he reminded himself . . . not very unique . . . but not very like anyone he'd ever known. There were other beautiful women, but she seemed to please him especially. Others were sensuous, others had aroused and gratified him . . . yet not quite the way Louisa had. She seemed to possess some elusive power he couldn't even name. Whatever it was, it made her irresistible, and he wanted to despise her for it. She made him feel weak. She had a frightening kind of power over him, and he did not conceive of himself as a man who was weak or easily frightened.

How was it possible this slender beautiful creature who, if he chose, he could kill with one blow—how could she exert control over him to the extent she did? She was like a demon in his soul, a fever in his blood; and he wondered if there were enough hours in an ordinary man's lifetime to make him forget her.

As he stood there, Louisa did not see him, for her back was still turned as she continued to walk. When she stopped, she was reassured by the distance she had come from the campground, knowing her strength was at last returning. In the few weeks she had been among these simple people, in spite of their superstitions about her being unclean, she had felt more protected, more an object of sincere concern than she could recall in a very long time. She was grateful for their caring shelter, aware that she owed her life to them, especially to Rosa, knowing she could never repay their kindness. They gave of themselves when they had, by most men's standards, nothing to give.

Louisa walked to the edge of the small cornfield, taking refuge nearby in the shade of a sparse stand of trees that spread their thin arms along the edge of a shallow stream. She seated herself on a large rock, and leaned against one slim sapling, closing her eyes for a few minutes in the midday heat. When she opened her eyes, she could see the figure of a man approaching her. Something in her stirred, a pulsing that made her tense and breathless. She knew who he was even before she could see him distinctly, the movement of his body familiar to her, imprinted on her, probably forever.

Louisa tried to collect herself, forcing tranquility from some reserve she was amazed to find she had. And by the time he stood before her, she was able to greet him coolly, yet wanting to fling herself into his arms, to feel the insistent pressure of his body, the wonderful comfort of him, to cry wildly of her loss and pain.

Instead, Louisa withheld herself, offering him her

hands when he reached out for her, her body rigid, giving no consent, no sign of longing in her impassive, even unfriendly face.

Responding to her remoteness, Aaron was just as distant. If she had even smiled at him, he might have abandoned his resolve to keep away from her. She looked pale, though not frail, and he was grateful, seeing no apparent strain in her beautiful face. She's made of steel, he thought, nothing will ever bring her down. But he remembered Father Hidalgo's words, his promise that it was only "one of God's miracles" that Louisa was alive. "I'm sorry," he said quietly, his voice sounding casual to Louisa's ears. "If I could change what has happened, I would."

He paused to look at her, hoping for something more than the incredibly aloof response she gave him. "The men who hurt you are dead." She only nodded at him, afraid to speak for fear she would give herself away. "Why didn't you send for me immediately? You didn't have to stay with these miserably poor people. You should've had a doctor. You almost died, you know."

Louisa pulled her hands from him as if he'd insulted her. "No one could have done more for me than they did!" she said hotly. "And for no reason other than simple kindness. They expected nothing from me in return." He felt her luminous eyes dig into him.

"I'm not here to exchange bitter words, Louisa," he said calmly. "I'm very grateful to them for looking after you," he said, his voice seeming to take on the cold edge of authority Louisa remembered from their earliest association. And she responded as she had then, with defiance, retreating from his sympathetic words, hearing only their crisp tone.

"What *have* you come for?"

"I've come to see you safely to San Francisco, then home."

"Safely? I don't recall I'm particularly safe with you," she replied caustically.

Her words pierced him, stabbing into his gut. It was true, as he had reminded himself often, she was not safe with him, and probably she never would be. But he wanted to grab her, hold her, beg her to overlook that truth. He wanted to plead with her to forget his silences, the pain, even the insults he'd flung at her when he did speak. He wanted to tell her he loved her, but he saw in her flashing eyes, in her tense body, what he thought was the uselessness of speaking those words.

"In any event," he heard himself say firmly, "I've come to see you home. They're waiting for you in San Diego."

His reminder startled her, and left a look of sadness in her eyes. "It will be good to get home, at last," she sighed quietly, moving away from him hastily, leaving him to stare after her as she abruptly began the walk back to the small shelters in the Indian camp.

Chapter Eighty-one

WITH a few long strides, Aaron caught up with Louisa on the path back to the campground. When he reached her she seemed terribly pale beneath her sun-tanned skin, and within moments he carried her in his arms. "The sun is too hot," she said before she collapsed, her legs no longer able to support her.

Her weakness frightened Aaron, and he hurried back to the campground feeling helpless and distraught. Rosa rushed to them the moment they were visible, and led Aaron to Louisa's hut. He placed her gently on her straw bed, and Rosa quickly sponged Louisa's face and throat with cool water. Louisa revived, but remained resting in her bed of straw, not feeling strong enough to stand, or even sit. She looked silently and hard at Aaron, seeing sternness in the lines of his face, but in reality it was worry and sadness that marked him.

Rosa was more astute, and as soon as it was apparent Louisa was all right, she slipped quietly from the tiny house. "You're not as strong as you thought," Aaron remarked, kneeling close to her on the dirt floor.

"It's an especially hot day. I'm sure that's all," Louisa said more weakly than she intended. "I'm ready to go, but I need clothes. Perhaps Father Hidalgo can help you get me something more suitable than this," she said, indicating the faded dress she wore. It was too large for her, hanging on her slim frame, the thin fabric concealing little of the outlines of her curves, even with a ragged petticoat to offer its concealment. And Aaron was not above feasting his eyes on her, the bodice of the dress wet from her recent sponging. Louisa's always inviting breasts were now very prominent, her nipples poking at the fabric with infuriating firmness. She gave Aaron a scalding look, but it did nothing to relieve the swelling ache in his groin, something they were both acutely aware of. Less visible but just as pronounced was Louisa's surge of response, but she managed to conceal her feelings with ease.

"For all I know, my trunk is still in the carriage. But I don't have any idea where it would be. Perhaps it's been discovered. The priest might know," she offered.

"The priest knows more about what's happened than I do, Louisa." He hesitated. "But you can tell me all about it when you're stronger. I don't want to upset you."

"How kind," she sneered softly. "It's a subject that will wait, thank you." Her hostility was unmistakable, and she refused to apologize for words she, on second thought, felt were too sharp.

"You insisted on going. I begged you to stay," Aaron said hotly.

"Please. Not now. Please just make arrangements to get me home, however you suggest this time. I was a fool to travel with those men—but you sent me with them!"

"I sent you? Jesus, Louisa, I—" Aaron took a deep breath. "I see no point in discussing it now," he said coldly.

"I agree." Her eyes brimmed with tears she hated herself for. "You can go back with Father Hidalgo tonight and return whenever you can."

"Not on your life. I'm not leaving here without you. Whatever you need can be sent to us. And I'll determine when you're ready to travel, not you. Perhaps I'll have to leave you to arrange for a wagon or buggy, but otherwise you can count on my presence until I hand deliver you to Emma Hudson." There was no room for doubt that he meant just that. "This time I *will* make you a prisoner, if necessary."

"It won't be necessary. I've paid for my foolhardiness. My crimes have been punished severely."

"I know, and I'm sorry," he said gently, reaching to touch her, but she pulled away from him, tears spilling from her eyes. She covered her face and rolled as far away from him as possible, wanting him to pursue her and give her comfort, yet wanting to be alone.

Aaron looked stricken, but she didn't see. He reached out to her, them withdrew his hand before he touched her. He was bewildered, wanting to console her, but feeling she had every right to despise and shrink from him. "I'll go speak to your priest, and see what he suggests," he concluded slowly, leaving Louisa to her angry, broken-hearted tears.

"I don't know if she's well enough to travel," he confided to the priest. "But she's determined to go. I'll need a good buggy or wagon." He and Father Hidalgo sat in the shade and discussed the alternatives. The carriage Ben and Jack had abandoned had been discovered, but the trunk with Louisa's clothes and few belongings had not been with it. The carriage was at Ellison's ranch where Aaron could claim it and obtain a team of horses. Father Hidalgo gave him directions and Aaron expected to complete those arrangements the next day.

Father Hidalgo read Aaron's worry, and it was a great relief for him to see it. Until then, the priest had worried deeply about what he had interpreted as the man's cold nature. He feared for the safety of the frail young woman who had sent for this, perhaps, cruel husband. Yet he knew he was powerless to intervene in their final arrangements. He had no authority, nor was there any law to protect this woman from her husband. "Thank you for your help," Aaron said warmly then they finished their conversation, and the priest left the camp in much better spirits than when he'd arrived.

Aaron looked after his horse, then looked in on Louisa. He pulled aside the blanket door, and when his eyes grew accustomed to the dark interior, he quickly saw she was asleep. While he had talked with Father Hidalgo, Rosa had doubled the size of the straw bed. Aaron smiled, anticipating Louisa's less than friendly reaction if he should accept this as an open invitation to join her. Everyone assumed he had more rights than he did, and it amused him perversely to know he would be expected to share this shelter with her tonight.

Aaron found the thick-walled, tree-shaded little room surprisingly cool. Yes, it would please him to spend the night next to her, but more so if she would yield her body to him, if he could know her as he had in the past. Would there ever be another time when he could hold her in his arms and vent his passion? It didn't seem very likely.

As if she had read his thoughts, Louisa turned to face him drowsily. When she opened her eyes, she looked relaxed, and even gave him a faint smile. "What have you arranged?" she asked, sitting up and stretching, beginning to pick straw from her golden hair, still plaited in one thick braid.

He sat down beside her. "You seem to have had a good rest, but are you sure you're ready to travel?" He looked at her, trying to make some sort of responsible judgment.

"Believe me, I wouldn't have sent for you if I hadn't thought so!"

"That's clear enough! Tell me, Louisa, are we going to wage war from now on? Or can we call a truce?"

"I'm agreeable to a truce," she said simply. Aaron reached to pull a few pieces of straw she'd missed from her hair, and she recoiled. "Only there will be no resumption of what you believed to be your former rights under our 'truce.' "

"What about the increased size of your bed?"

"I'm not responsible for Rosa's assumptions."

"I take it you expect me to bed down with the horses."

"No, I don't expect that. I merely want you to leave me alone—you know what I mean."

"I know well enough. I won't touch you. I've no plans to force myself on you." He said it calmly, and she relaxed visibly, tension seeming to drain from her body.

"I'm surprised my word is good enough for you!" He didn't seem able to resist being sarcastic.

"Isn't it?" she bristled.

"Yes. Of course," he snapped, regretting his thoughtless retort. He reached for her hands, insisting she give them into his. "A full truce, señora, is granted with all your rights protected," he promised, then smiled gently, releasing her from his grip. "Tell me, Louisa, what happened? Why didn't you tell me you were pregnant? Why did you lie to me? If I'd known, I'd never have let you go.

"That's as good a reason as any," she said quietly. "But it's not the only reason. You know the reasons as well as I do. It would serve no purpose to go through it all. Not now." She took a deep breath. "And as for what happened, I don't think you could ever understand how horrible it was. Perhaps you have to be a woman to know what it means to be raped. Perhaps not. I couldn't, if I sat here the rest of my life, tell you in words how horrible it was. I can only swear to you I don't ever want another man to touch me. Never. I have had enough of men to last me several lifetimes." Louisa was very calm. She spoke as if giving solemn testimony before a court, and at the moment she uttered her preference for a lifetime of abstinence, she truly meant it.

There was enough resolve in her voice and in her face to make Aaron certain it would take an act of God to persuade her from her oath. And if a mere mortal were capable of changing her mind, it would, he thought, certainly take more of a man than he was, for, it seemed to Aaron, she equated him with the men in her life who had abused her.

Yet, after she'd said what was on her mind the climate in the little room was more comfortable, if only temporarily. And slowly, as if in a confessional, Louisa reached out to Aaron with words, telling him what she could remember, which, regrettably, was just about everything. She was restless and distraught as she related her story, sometimes self-consciously trying to wrap her loose gown around her body as if to conceal her shame, to protect herself from a too clear memory of the violation of her body. She undid her braided hair absently, seeming to use its long flowing strands to shield herself a little. Yet she knew there was no point in hiding, finding that as she began to face her pain, she began also to slowly purge herself of its agony.

She told him of the long, tortured, specter-filled night, of her terror in the smoke- and accusation-filled morning. But she did not voice her grief over her prematurely empty womb, for she knew to speak of it at all would force her to look Aaron in the eye and say aloud she'd loved him, and that it mattered that she'd lost his baby. Neither could she face the fact she might love him even now.

Whenever Louisa cried, Aaron held her fast in his arms, not with longing, but in disbelief and sorrow. He clutched her fiercely to his body, yet she never saw his tears as they slid silently out of his eyes, falling unnoticed as he put his face against the thick fragrant mass of her now unbraided hair. And though they were in some ways very intimate, they failed to shatter the silence which really separated them, building yet another bridge between them that might never be crossed.

Chapter Eighty-two

FINALLY Louisa had nothing more to say, and retreated from Aaron's arms self-consciously. She wiped away the last traces of her tears with her fingers, and smiled hesitantly at him. "I'm exhausted again," she said meekly.

"Then rest. It's still very hot. You should stay in till evening when it's cooler anyway." Aaron gave her a cup of water from a clay jug on the floor next to her straw bed. Then she lay down, and he sat against the wall, watching her from time to time as she drifted off to sleep.

He'd underestimated her, remembering his speculation she'd never last any time at all in the wilderness away from the comforts she was used to. She'd survived a lot, more than he'd have laid bets on this time, and the elements were the least of what she'd overcome.

Aaron was weary too. He'd been on the trail for more than a week, leaving San Francisco in haste even before he'd recovered from the sleepless days and nights he'd searched for Ben and Jack. Emil Joseph had traveled with him out of San Francisco to the approximate area in which Jack had confessed to abandoning Louisa. Then they'd gone searching for her in separate directions, planning, between the two of them, to circle and canvass the entire area. Finding Louisa alive was beyond Aaron's expectations. He'd been afraid to hope, and hadn't begun to prepare for her reaction to him until he'd read the letter the priest handed him this morning. These last few hours of confrontation and worry had taken their toll on his emotions, and he felt numb, beginning again to deny his love for her, feeling only the torture of their association for himself, and for her as well. If there were ever star-crossed lovers, he and Louisa were a pair, he thought. Shouldn't defy the universe, he said to himself as he fell asleep propped against the wall across from the woman he wanted to lie next to more than he wanted anything else in the world.

They were both still sleeping when Rosa entered the room. She carried a tallow candle in one hand, setting it on the low table. She also carried a pot of steaming food, and a basket with two small loaves of bread, and perhaps two handfuls of pine nuts. She considered the figures resting separately, wondering if they also had customs about bleeding women, though she knew Louisa was no longer "unclean" by Indian standards. She was afraid to wake the man, and didn't want to disturb Louisa, feeling the young woman wasn't as strong as she pretended. Rosa left the candle and the food and quietly disappeared into the evening.

Aaron heard her slip out of the room, opening his eyes slowly, feeling stiff from the unrestful position he'd chosen. He inhaled the unfamiliar aroma of the food Rosa had brought them, feeling suddenly famished. He glanced at Louisa before he stood up, noting she seemed to sleep soundly, but when he reached above her for eating utensils she turned over and opened her eyes. Aaron smiled at her sleepy stare, and at first she smiled broadly, her eyes full of warmth, hands pushing her tousled hair away from her face. Then it was apparent she remembered where she was and her wide, welcoming smile disappeared.

Aaron ignored her change of heart. "Hungry?" She only nodded, starting to rise. "Me, too. There seems to be plenty—even for two starving people. What is it? Do you know?"

Louisa surveyed the pot. "Wild herbs and roots, potatoes, onions, some sort of fresh game—squirrel, probably—sometimes it's best not to ask. Rosa will soon bring us some mint tea. I'm practically drowned in it—it's a restorative, she says!"

"You've done fairly well—from all that I hear."

"I remember your saying I'd never survive in the

country. I surprised us both." Her smile returned briefly as he filled a bowl with the hot stew, and they both ate greedily.

"If only the elite of Monterey could see us now," he grinned between mouthfuls.

Louisa laughed. "Can you imagine William Easton stooping to this cuisine! I think he'd rather starve."

"He's a fool, but I suspect you're right. This fare suits me as well as anything from his table."

"Frankly, I wouldn't mind a good Southern breakfast sometime soon," Louisa sighed.

"Getting soft so soon?"

"And a good bed, and a *hot* bath, and . . ." She seemed to drift off.

"You'll have all those things in a few days, I promise. The carriage is at a ranch nearby. I think we can leave day after tomorrow. I have to meet with a friend, but we should be on the road by the end of the week." Aaron paused a few minutes before continuing. "Louisa, the charade must begin again."

She stiffened and sat more erect. "Yes, I know," she said quietly.

"That'll mean sharing my bed, permitting me certain public familiarities—we're married, remember. With all that's happened we'll be even more the subject of gossip."

"I should think my experience might excuse me from the public eye. That's what I intend."

Aaron frowned. "I suppose you have that choice. I won't insist you do otherwise."

"And a separate bed."

"If you wish."

"I wish."

Aaron's frown deepened, and he tossed the last crust of his bread into the empty cooking pot with obvious disgust. "Kindly don't be too difficult, Louisa. I've still a lot to do to get everything Washington wants."

"I don't expect to interfere with any of it."

"You have already."

"I beg your pardon," she said coldly.

"Remember, we have a truce, Louisa. All I'm ask-

ing is reasonable cooperation. I'll be very busy when
we get back, and I'll not spend much time in your
bed—you forget I have other interests—besides, hus-
bands and wives often share the same joyless bed."

"We're not husband and wife."

"You get my point, nevertheless. It may not be possible to sleep separately in Melville's house. I'm just
warning you in advance."

"You're in San Francisco?"

"I left Monterey right after you did."

"With Marguerite?"

"That's right."

Louisa gave him a hateful look. "The colonel?"

"He remained behind to see to his duties."

"And you, no doubt, found ample duty of your
own."

"Ample." They stared at each other. "You understand what I said? I expect you to live up to the charade at least marginally. I promise not to impose on
you, except when necessary. And not in bed—unless,
of course . . ." he smiled.

"There will be no 'unless,' I can assure you," Louisa
hastened to inform him.

Aaron's smile faded. "A truce, remember?"

Rose appeared then, and Louisa dutifully drank the
steaming fragrant tea. "It's almost a ritual," Louisa
whispered to Aaron when Rosa left. "She credits it
with stopping the severest of my bleeding. I must've
drunk gallons by now! But it's very pleasant, don't
you think?"

Louisa was smiling again, and Aaron basked in the
friendliness of her smile as long as he could. "Come
on, let's take a walk in the cool night air," he said,
picking up her blanket from the straw, wrapping it
around her shoulders. "We won't go far."

Louisa was very agreeable, taking his arm when he
offered it, and they walked a little way from the camp
and sat silently listening to night sounds of frogs and
crickets, the occasional howling of coyotes, and the
rustling of the breezes in the tall grasses nearby.
Aaron sat behind Louisa and she leaned against him

comfortably and watched the stars. "Do you remember any of them?" he asked.

"Of course, I do!"

"It was a *long* time ago."

"I've an excellent memory. I'm not as simple as I look," she snapped.

Aaron laughed. "Simple you're not!" he said with feeling, and Louisa couldn't help but laugh at the way he said it. He put his arms around her and hugged her gently. "Truce?"

"Truce," she promised easily.

Chapter Eighty-three

WHEN they returned to the camp, they said nothing, made no further bargains, and slept the long night next to each other. Since they didn't need privacy according to their agreement, Aaron took down the blanket door and used it to cover the straw mattress for further comfort, and they lay down using Louisa's blanket for the both of them. At first they were restless lying together in the darkness, but soon enough Louisa fell asleep, and Aaron followed her not much later. Twice she woke, sitting up with a start, and Aaron was aroused by her alarm. He soothed her quickly merely by telling her who he was, and she lay down again without much hesitation. "The nights aren't always easy," she whispered after the second interruption of their sleep.

"I know," he said, wanting to pull her against him, to make the night more bearable, at least for him. But with effort he kept his hands to himself. Not much later, he was pulled from a very heavy sleep by her weeping. She tossed feverishly, and muttered words he could not distinguish, yet she did not wake. This time he touched her, and moved against her, calling her name, trying to reassure her. She seemed to relinquish her nightmares, but didn't wake. And he held her close with no further sleep for himself in the few short hours until morning.

In the first light Aaron sat up and began to watch her, noticing for the first time the faint pink lines etched erratically in her usually perfect skin—the only visible scars from her experience, he thought, remembering she'd said she'd plunged herself into thorn bushes trying to escape Ben and Jack that night.

He noticed a smudge of dirt on her chin, and considered the rags she wore. It reminded him that in spite of the last two wakeful hours pressed against her, and his normal response to her closeness, she was only human after all, not some bewitching mythical goddess. But the fact remained, his senses were not convinced.

She had taught him the real meaning of sensuality and desire, and those lessons were not easily, if ever, forgotten. In the faint morning light, with a gossamer mist sifting over the valley, covering them silently as it drifted into the open room, Louisa seemed more delicate and beautiful than he remembered. He longed to touch her, to lift her against him, to feel her eager and responsive in his arms. He reached out to her, then hesitated, his hand stopping in midair. "I love you," he said, the sound of his voice drowned in an early greeting from the songbirds that filled the oak trees surrounding the primitive whitewashed house.

Louisa stirred, moving closer to him as he dipped his hand in the luxury of her satin curls. How often he had stroked the wonderful softness of her hair, how often he had nestled with her, the both of them draped in shimmering cascades of fragrant silk. Suddenly he clenched his fist, crushing those golden strands in his grip. It was a mistake, he cursed silently, a mistake to spend the night here next to you. God, what a fool I am! He knew for certain it would be one of those cold days in Hell before she would give herself to him again. She'd been very clear about it. He felt nearly ill with longing, his body all too willing, but he would never again force her into his embrace. And when he thought of the brutality she'd recently known, his desire was slackened by anger and pity and sorrow, and, for the time being at least, the spell she cast over him was broken.

She'd exacted his promise, and he would not touch her, unless—unless. He smirked to himself, thinking of the days ahead, lying in the same bed with her. He would see to it she had what she wanted—a separate bed, so he might get some sleep. Yet, he thought, just knowing she was under the same roof would probably be enough to give him many sleepless hours. He would have to make certain he exhausted himself with Marguerite. And remembering the woman's capacities, he was reassured that with proper effort on his part, he should have no trouble sleeping, even with Louisa next to him. He'd done it before, but, he recalled, not without effort and concentration.

Louisa woke to see him sitting next to her with a bewildered look on his face. It surprised her, and she smiled, raising herself on one elbow. "Didn't you sleep well?"

"All things considered. I slept very well."

"Sorry. I often have difficult nights."

"A very good argument for separate bedrooms."

"Why, yes, it is."

"I'll do my best to get you one," he promised, but not for the reason she assumed. "After I have something to eat, I'm going after the carriage. Then I'll get you some clothes, along with provisions for travel. With luck this will be the last night you spend here."

Aaron spent the rest of the morning collecting the carriage, finding Emil Joseph on the same road. Ellison's ranch was in Joseph's portion of the territory they'd divided up for searching and the trail he followed brought him to the same destination that morning as Aaron. Aaron returned to the Indians' camp, sending the other man on with the carriage to provision it for their travels. When Aaron returned, Louisa seemed happy to see him, and after a light meal at noontime, he lifted her onto his horse and they went to buy her a more suitable traveling wardrobe.

She rode in front on him, savoring the feel of his body, even in the sweat-producing heat. It seemed to her they'd slept very close to each other the night before. She had no specific recollection of her nightmares—they were all too common once again—but she did think she recalled being held in Aaron's arms, her memory seemingly full of the sensations he usually evoked in her body. Her vow that she never wanted another man was, in its way, not a lie. In fact, she wanted no other man. She wanted Aaron. But not under the terms he offered. She would not share him, whatever the reason, noble cause or not. She suddenly stiffened in his arms at the thought of Marguerite and the woman's oh-so-coy, so-solicitous ways. Louisa could just imagine how beguiling she could be, and how cheerfully Aaron—this admitted pirate—would succumb!

"What's the matter?" inquired Aaron, when she suddenly sat erect and as far away from him as possible in the saddle, for no reason he could fathom.

"Nothing at all!"

He didn't bother to reply, not exactly sorry to have the disturbing pressure of her soft body against him decreased, especially since he knew there was no hope of relieving the hardness she aroused in him.

When they arrived in the dusty town, their appearance drew more than a few stares. Louisa was an unusual sight, ragged and barefooted, and, in spite of it, disarmingly beautiful. Speculation as to what she might do with her charming body drew a fair number of catcalls and whistles before the two newcomers could enter the general store. It was obvious the storekeeper's wife had second thoughts about serving these customers, but the clatter of Aaron's gold coins on her counter dispelled any doubts she had. The selection of women's garments was decidedly poor, and more for the thick frame of the storekeeper's wife than Louisa's little figure. Louisa was nearly in tears as she considered traveling to San Francisco in what she now wore on her back.

It was a silly thing to be upset over, but at this point in time she was not beyond being unreasonable. "I can't wear any of these things!" she said tearfully, tossing aside everything but a small stack of bloomers and two inferior muslin chemises. She found a pair of shoes, and two pairs of stockings. The only garters available were more suitable for display on the legs of a dancer in one of the saloons they'd passed, but she tossed them impatiently into the small pile she was managing to assemble. "If they stare at me in this costume, I wonder what kind of reception I'd get in San Francisco if I arrived in just my underwear?"

"You'd get some reception, believe me. We wouldn't get within fifty miles of the city before you'd be stolen again."

"Well, what am I going to do?" she asked seriously, collecting a hairbrush, several bars of "decent" soap, and a quaint bonnet, thinking for once she'd had enough sun on her face.

The scarlet garters gave Aaron an idea. "Are you sure you can't manage with something here?" he asked impatiently.

"I'd rather not."

"Well, I've two other ideas," he said, paying for the things Louisa had reluctantly selected, waiting without further comment until her purchases were bundled in coarse brown paper and tied with string. Then he took her arm, and ushered her to the noisiest saloon on the main street.

"I'm *not* going in there," Louisa huffed when he pushed open one side of the swinging doors for her to enter.

"Yes, you are," he insisted, taking her arm roughly. Her sudden presence in the barroom produced absolute silence within seconds, then robust cheers when her sorry condition was properly surveyed. Louisa blushed furiously, and gave Aaron the most scathing and furious look he'd ever seen on her face, but she practically stood on his boots trying to get closer to him and his imagined protection. When he went to the bar, Louisa walked next to him as close as she could manage.

"I want to speak to whoever is in charge of the girls upstairs," Aaron announced. Louisa could barely believe her ears.

"What for?" she demanded in obvious disbelief.

"First door up the stairs," replied the bartender giving Louisa a cheerfully wicked leer before Aaron could reply. Louisa put her arm through Aaron's and followed him up the stairs without another word. "She'll be a nice add'tion," was the man's parting comment, and Louisa sucked in her breath.

Estelle Handy was the name of the establishment's madam, and she was dressed perfectly for the part.

She was well past her prime, but comfortable in her domain. She was asleep when Louisa and Aaron knocked persistently at her door. She bellowed at them, but they would not be dissuaded, and finally she greeted them with puffy eyes, quickly rouged cheeks, and none too carefully arranged hair. She wore a white satin, feather-trimmed dressing gown. It could have been made for a lady of high fashion, but it clung unflatteringly and comically to Estelle's sagging and bulging flesh.

"I'd like to buy some clothes from your girls, if you have what I want," Aaron began.

Estelle looked at him in surprise, as if she weren't fully awake, and as if she'd not understood him correctly. She looked at Louisa with the same curious expression. "You planning to set up competition?"

Aaron smiled broadly. "No. The lady needs some traveling clothes, and could find nothing to her liking at Parson's store."

"I have to special order with the dressmaker, or from Parson's." She went to Louisa and gathered her oversized dress tightly at the waist and across Louisa's breasts and hips. "Ya sure you're not going to set up business?" she asked of Aaron again.

"Positive!" Louisa answered for him.

"Well, haven't got anything that'll fit exactly, but Fancy'll have some things that'll be close enough." She reached for a key ring hanging over her dressing table. "Have a seat. I'll be right back."

"Leave it to you to think of such a clever solution!" Louisa was not exactly pleased.

"Do you have a better idea, Princess?"

"I'm afraid not," she sighed.

Actually the dresses Estelle brought back fit her reasonably well—a little tight through the bodice and a bit loose at the waist, but otherwise just fine, and not badly tailored. Louisa approved of all three dresses Estelle brought to her, and Aaron paid, rather handsomely, for them.

"I'm afraid you were robbed," Louisa said, clutching her carefully folded dresses on the way back to camp, "but I thank you." She was anticipating a bath with the scented soap she'd bought at Parson's, and the luxury of nice clothes on her body again; already thinking about more comfortable surroundings in San Francisco, more familiar food, and a softer bed. She leaned easily and absently into Aaron's willing arms, falling asleep against his chest in the very warm afternoon. Aaron's horse walked slowly bearing his passengers, Louisa's sleepy head filled with very pleasant dreams, and Aaron very wakeful with the very same notions crowding out any other thoughts.

Chapter Eighty-four

SAN Francisco was not quite what Louisa expected, but Peter Melville's stone house overlooking the city was just what she'd imagined. Surprisingly, she wasn't as tired as she thought she'd be after a two-week journey, but she feigned fatigue to be left alone as much as possible. After Aaron saw her settled, she rarely encountered him. At first she had a separate room in Melville's house, but when the house filled up with guests, Louisa found herself in Aaron's bed again, often sleeping with his heavy arm thrown over her body, finding it easier to sleep that way than to wake him. And safer too. Initially, Louisa was determined to forbid his touching her, but her struggles to wake and convince him she had meant what she said had only aroused him almost beyond either of their abilities to resist. Now she lay tangled with him quietly when, and if, he joined her in the bed, protesting his closeness only in the light of day and safely out of his reach.

Upon his return, Aaron was quickly occupied with plans to travel south, and, more interesting to him, with plans for Santa Catalina Island's occupation by the pro-Southern conspirators. With Carson and Melville and two very seaworthy ship's captains, now in the San Francisco port and obviously at the disposal of these Southern sympathizers, Aaron discussed a variety of possibilities for the island. They might set up a formidable smuggling operation, handling both men and supplies for the South's army; or perhaps, totally disrupt shipping on the western coast. With Indian uprisings where and when they chose to supply the necessary arms and provisions, California would be cut off from the rest of the nation and subject to persuasive ideas with which her populace was already becoming familiar, and to which a good number of her citizens were increasingly very sympathetic.

Marguerite had been the first to rush alarmedly to Louisa's bedside as soon as she'd arrived. She came with armloads of clothes and her dressmaker in tow. "Oh, my dear, Louisa, Marshall has told me everything!" she cried, seemingly with genuine grief. "I'm so sorry you've had such a dreadful time." She pressed Louisa's hand to her cheek. "But now Miss Wilson will cheer you up," she said, indicating the thin, very plain seamstress she often raved about, insisting Louisa get out of bed that instant for the taking of her measurements at least. It was easy and yet hard to hate Marguerite, Louisa thought. At times she was very pleasant, even kind, but woefully empty-headed and amoral. Is that it? Louisa questioned when Marguerite had left. "I *still* hate her," Louisa raged aloud, sinking back into bed, pulling the covers over her head.

As soon as she'd arrived, Louisa had a marvelous, nearly scalding bath, feeling her skin begin to soften again in the oil-rich water and from the luxurious creams Arabella Melville had generously given her.

Now with Marguerite finally gone, Louisa hid beneath the covers, alone with her murderous thoughts for the woman. But she heard her door, and when she peeked out from under the comforter, she saw a very handsome man standing by her bed. "Oh, you shaved off your beard!" she cried, and sat up without thinking, the comforter slipping to her bare waist.

"And scraped a few layers of dust off the rest of me."

"Why, Aaron, don't tell me you're getting soft?"

"I haven't been in that comfortable condition for weeks," he replied, his eyes fastened hungrily on her breasts. Louisa frowned at him, suddenly aware of her naked body, hastily pulling the comforter up under her chin, leaning back on the pillows. "You needn't worry. I gave you my sacred word of honor!"

"I'm not so sure you're very honorable."

He shrugged his shoulders. "I suppose in some circles it's open for debate."

But he remained true to his word, in spite of the obstacles in his way. For one, Marguerite made it plain she was occupied for the time with a new lover. "He's very attentive, but he won't be with us much longer. I *do* miss you," she purred. "But he's a very important friend of the colonel's. You *do* understand."

He understood her houseguest was very welcome, and that he was being punished. Marguerite had been miffed with him for leaving the city in such a hurry even if it was to go after his wife. Aaron only smiled at Marguerite when she said she didn't know just when she could see him, then told her flatly he didn't expect to be kept waiting very long. She gave him a very pleased look when he released her after mauling her savagely, raising her skirts, taking her quickly and violently amid only very faint protests on Melville's thick parlor carpet the same afternoon he'd arrived with Louisa.

Another obstacle was his continued craving for Louisa. Their infrequent contact, now that they did not share the same bed and she rarely appeared outside her room, did little to relieve him. When they began to sleep together again, he'd even considered raping her at one of his lowest moments, and it was then he'd left the house in the middle of the night and headed straight for Elena's hotel.

It was a place where he was recognized as a good friend of Peter Melville. It was how he was acknowledged by Elena herself, his reputation enhanced by the news of the way he had handled his wife's abductors. The first night he patronized her establishment, it amused Elena immensely to introduce him to a woman she swore she only introduced to very special clients. "Rita comes and goes as she pleases, and she's always welcome. You may settle your preferences with her," and her smile erupted into a wild mirthful laugh.

Aaron was ushered into a dimly lit, lushly blue-carpeted room designed to look like a ship's stateroom. The furniture was rich dark oak and carefully preserved, the enormous bunk mattress covered with white satin, strewn with an abundance of white satin pillows. Aaron propped himself in the bunk and waited, startled yet pleased with the woman Elena ushered into his presence. He roared with laughter when the door was closed behind Marguerite, who stood wrapped in a red silk dressing gown, just like all Elena's other whores.

Marguerite clapped her hands for joy. "Elena promised me, when she could keep from laughing that wonderfully wicked way she does, she promised I'd just be thrilled with tonight's customer."

The games they played that night and on many other nights were paid for in hundred-dollar gold pieces, the fee seeming to add something to the pleasure of the experience for her. And these often prearranged nights they spent together made the time Aaron remained in San Francisco a little more bearable. Marguerite craved violence and abuse, never happy when Aaron chose to be gentle, begging him to make her terror a little worse each time, her pain a little more intense. She was merely lucky the man she goaded on these occasions was not as sadistic as it seemed she would have liked. There were times Aaron thought Marguerite actually wished to be murdered. But at least he went to Louisa's bed exhausted, if not satisfied.

Chapter Eighty-five

CAPTAIN Will Hansen had his eye on Louisa from the first moment he met her. From a respectful distance he surveyed Louisa's youth and great beauty, and the grand looks of Marshall Hudson, speculating theirs was a delightful combination, something to envy. "No fool, that one," the captain speculated aloud. "There's a gentleman who'll never spend much time at sea, even if he does own most of the ships afloat. Couldn't be leavin' that one for long."

He was struck dumb when the couple settled aboard the *Crystal Mae* in separate cabins. And further puzzled when it became obvious Marshall Hudson never visited with his wife in private for more than a few minutes. Could it be this woman who seemed so ripe and appealing, whose every curve invited wishful thinking about the levels of passion to be coaxed from her sensuous body, could it be her spirit was cold and forbidding? Now that would be a hell of a spot, the captain thought. To get yourself all worked up and find it hardly worth your while.

He found further speculation worthless, but he kept his eye on both of them, He found the gentleman very knowledgeable, though he'd never been formally a member of a ship's crew. But that came from growing up with ships, as Marshall Hudson had, and he soon could see why Melville had chosen the man to oversee the plans for Santa Catalina. Mr. Hudson seemed to have a native ability, a natural craftiness, a sense about the complexities of such a project. With Marshall Hudson, Captain Hansen further confirmed his thinking the rich were at heart only a well-dressed bunch of pirates.

Travel south was swift in spite of choppy seas and changing wind that made keeping the course steady a difficult task. They reached Catalina Island in three days from San Francisco, pulling into Isthmus Harbor on the southwest side of the island. Fog still hung over the top of the island when they anchored offshore. There was little evidence of habitation on the island though the ocean-battered remains of a crude landing wharf could be seen at the shoreline. A longboat was soon lowered from the *Crystal Mae* and before it reached the beach with Aaron and Captain Hansen aboard, two men on horseback appeared, obviously waiting for the men to arrive.

Louisa stood at the ship's railing and watched the crew beach the boat. Aaron stepped gingerly into the rough surf, and he and the captain greeted the two other men with hearty handshakes. Aaron rode off with one of the men while the other returned to the *Crystal Mae* with Captain Hansen, and soon her work boats were busy hauling supplies ashore.

Wanting some fresh air, Louisa stayed topside, but out of the way. She'd spent little time above decks on the swift journey, hoping to keep out of Aaron's reach in the close quarters of the ship. While they were in San Francisco, her moods seemed to shift erratically. At times she wanted to reconcile with Aaron, especially during the days and nights when she saw very little of him. When they slept in separate beds they rarely saw one another, sometimes not even at meals.

Louisa rose late in the morning and if she had a companion for breakfast it was usually the benign Arabella Melville. She often skipped lunch. Dinner and early-evening conversation was always cluttered with other guests, Louisa able to give as little or as much attention to her husband as she liked. She maintained the appearance of devotion, but found Aaron's hands on her in Melville's parlor now produced uncharacteristic blushing, which obviously amused Aaron, for he seemed to seek her out and put his arms around her whenever there was the slightest excuse.

Sometimes when he touched her, it took restraint on her part not to gasp at the rush of feeling in her body. But when they again began to share the same bed, she was usually hostile, his touch making her angry and defensive, though once she almost approached him even while she sensed he was doing his utmost to control his passions. And once she had thought he had reached his limit of saintly behavior. For an instant she thought his mood was so black, he might rend her limb from limb, if not make love to her. In the mood she was in that night, he would have had to rape her, and he seemed to know it. She could feel the incredible tension in him as she lay stiffly next to him, and that night she would have fought him with every ounce of her strength. Since her experience with Jack Herbert, there were times she could not have faced any man willingly. She doubted even Marshall could have approached her without her turning against him. Sometimes her memories of Jack, mingled with her memories of Justin, were overwhelming, and anyone's hand on her, in love or otherwise, would have been more than she could bear. There were moments she thought she would kill to be left alone.

After that especially unpleasant night when Aaron had left their bed hastily, she was often alone most of the night. She didn't know for sure where he spent his time but she suspected he didn't lead a monk's existence. On occasion she was certain he'd been with Marguerite, for a trace of the woman's favorite heady perfume seemed to cling to his body, which did nothing to improve Louisa's mood.

In private Louisa and Aaron usually stood off from each other like two stray cats eye to eye on the same fence, one waiting for the other to make a move. Sometimes when she caught his eye, she read the kind of longing she wanted to respond to. She was sure she saw the hunger for love she herself knew so well. But Louisa accused herself harshly. Fool, she charged silently. She'd not go begging. Never again. He'd made a fool of her before, and she'd never crawl to him. She swore he would have to come to her—on her terms or not at all.

But when Louisa lay in her solitary bed with her body urgently wanting Aaron's, her words only seemed ridiculously brave. She would scream and pound her fists on her pillows, replacing her physical hunger with anger. "You're Justin Boyd's daughter for certain! You're low and immoral. You'd take *anyone* into your bed—a born whore, just as the man said." Louisa no longer needed other voices to accuse her; she was now very adept at self-indictment.

Yet as the *Crystal Mae* sped down the California Coast, with the wind howling at Louisa as it often had, she managed to stay sane. Pensively, she watched Aaron watch her. He stared after her in the passageways, on the deck, at the mess, his eyes disturbingly full of desire, and desire was rekindled in her—with unmerciful ease. Even now she stood at the ship's rail waiting for Aaron's return from the island, wanting to see him, knowing in a few more days when, at last, the ship left her in San Diego, she might never see him again. And it seemed like a death sentence.

But when he returned to the ship for the very purpose of seeking her out, to invite her to go ashore and ride with him for a tour of the island, she agreed in what he described to himself as her "rich man's whore" attitude.

When the boat was close to shore, Aaron lifted Louisa against him, high above the turbulent surf, bundling her skirts around her. He enjoyed holding her in his arms, feeling her cling to him, her arms tight around his neck, her face close to his. As he watched the swirling sandy water, trying to keep her layers of skirts out of the water, he felt her eyes on his, and he yearned for her as if all the unpleasantness between them had never existed.

Earlier Aaron had had the pleasure of surveying this very interesting island. It seemed perfectly suited to the plans now in motion. What the islands in the Caribbean would probably do for enterprising ship owners on the Atlantic side of the continent, Santa Catalina and perhaps other islands along this

coast could do for California's conspirators. There
were natural advantages to Santa Catalina Island
that made it an ideal headquarters for privateers.
There were several good harbors. It was a perfect
place to station ships whose goal would be to interfere in normal coastal shipping, or to launch military
action against the coast or at sea. The island could
support a permanent settlement, having ample supplies of wood and water, good soil for self-sustaining
crops, an abundance of good pasture land, and a
plentiful supply of fish. If armed properly, it could
be a perfect settlement for pirates. The prospects very
much appealed to Aaron, but it occurred to him he was
getting almost too fond of this part of the operation
for his own good. With Louisa now riding by his
side, obviously enjoying the rugged beauty of the
island, he could even imagine keeping her captive,
spending long hours persuading her to love him again.
It was a very appealing daydream.

They rode a long while, at last reaching the other
side of the island. Louisa was very impressed with all
she saw. It was a lovely, if lonely, setting. What a
shame, she thought, for this place to figure in the
empire-building schemes of men like Simon Hudson
and Peter Melville. It would be a wonderful place
to seclude oneself away from the world, something
which part of Louisa longed to do. She thought she
would very much like to take Rachel and retreat,
perhaps to this very island. Somewhere. Anywhere.
But soon Catalina would be no haven. Soon it would
be swarming with men, many with less than honorable
motives. A suitable nest for Aaron, she thought in a
moment of bitterness.

She was frowning deeply over her thoughts now,
though not many moments before she had watched
Aaron as he led them on a narrow trail, her eyes full
of his powerful body, her senses overcome with longing, wanting desperately to hold him in her most
intimate embrace. If at that instant he had turned
and confronted her, she would have been powerless
to resist him. How could her emotions swing so violently within the space of minutes, she wondered,

catching Aaron's eye, a scowl deeply etched in her face.

Aaron halted their horses and dismounted, reaching to assist her. "I thought the scenery might improve your temper, Mrs. Hudson. Obviously, I was wrong." He spoke sarcastically, and she ignored his glance as best she could.

"My spirits will improve *only* when we set foot in San Diego."

"Only one more day to wait. Tomorrow, señora, I set you free."

Yes. Free. Free of memory and desire for him. Free to forget all. "Please let me be free at last," she intoned privately while they looked down the steep rugged slope at a sandy beach on the eastern side of the island. Seeing the lazy, deserted shore made Louisa suddenly remember their early encounters in the sand, and the promises she'd hoped eventually to hear from his lips. She knew even then she probably asked too much of him, if not the world.

Aaron's thoughts wandered in the same direction, and he grabbed her suddenly, moving his hungry body fiercely against hers. To her horror, Louisa's instantaneous response was just as violent, but not the least defensive. She didn't want to struggle against him, and protested his approach not at all, her arms reaching around him, clutching him with all of her strength.

His kisses, the pressure of his body inflamed her, and there was no possibility of turning back. Soon they were lying on fog-wet grass, her clothes seeming to fall away from her eager body, his warm mouth quickly on her breasts, tugging at her nipples, pulling low animal cries from deep inside her throat. Under her skirts his hands were fast but, for all his passion, amazingly gentle. She met his probing fingers with cries of obvious pleasure, totally blind to normal vision when he entered her; lost when his hardness touched her, seeming to be in agony, meeting his thrusts with sharp cries, but locking her legs around him so that he could not have escaped even if it had occurred to him to leave her.

Louisa's softness seemed to liquefy under him, the

pressure of her body on him extreme as he drove himself deeply into her warmth, wanting to attach himself to her, never to be unfastened. Aaron postponed his own moments of rapture, coaxing Louisa's body to new heights of response, repeatedly and lengthily feeling her body and spirit soar against his, finally taking blessed relief in the momentarily subdued depths of her body.

Afterward Louisa was weak and trembling in his arms, at first unable and unwilling to move away from him, yet unable, when he helped her dress and onto her feet, to look him in the eye, tears streaming down her face, not hearing anything he said, not the least aware of his tone or the meaning of his words. Suddenly she did not want him near her, and he stepped back, at first dismayed, then angered at the constantly mercurial side of her nature.

By the time they boarded the *Crystal Mae,* they were once again adversaries, Louisa retreating to her cabin in shame and regret over her extremely passionate response to a man she knew would leave her behind indifferently the very next day; Aaron boiling, his face as dark as the black storm clouds that were fast filling the southern horizon, but soon too preoccupied with getting the ship safely out to sea to brood over Louisa.

Chapter Eighty-six

THE sudden and violent storm blew them away from the coast. Twice they passed uncomfortably close to another large ship in the same waters. Louisa stayed below, appearing only for meals. For three days they were reduced to the simplest fare of cheeses, beef jerky, stale biscuits and honey, fresh oranges and apples, and strong black coffee. Once, when she sat in the mess, Aaron came and sat directly across from her. She endured his stares in silence, successfully managing her plate of food and hot drink in spite of the unpredictable pitching and rolling of the ship. He studied her with his dark eyes, waiting for her to speak, but she had nothing to say.

They spent three nights off the coast trying to outrun the fury of the storm, at times taking terrifyingly enormous waves over the bow, in dire fear of being swamped. Louisa wondered if she would ever get to San Diego, if there was not some evil force trying to keep her from returning to her home, and to her child. Why did it seem the simplest pleasures were so hard for her to come by? Why did it seem a simple existence was always just out of reach? She was not many miles from shore, so very close to embracing her child again; but in the storm, in the danger of the open ocean, she might have been on the other side of the world.

Before Louisa could sleep on those nights, she would endure other torment. She felt longings she could easily satisfy, if she chose. But Louisa's pride overrode her desire, the voices raised in her heart and head doing shrill battle, until her body gave up in exhaustion and she slept, but without peace. Now, unbelievably, it seemed the next morning would bring her home to San Diego, and she tried to trust Captain Hansen's cheerful announcement. The night was favorable; the winds perfect. She would be in her house tomorrow! "Please, dear God!" she whispered.

Louisa's spirits were buoyed. She smiled at almost everyone during the evening meal; her only harsh glances were for her husband, the captain noted. The young husband didn't seem to notice, though his eyes were fixed on her intently.

When she retired, Aaron stared after her, exceptionally silent as the lamps were lit and the captain smoked his after-dinner pipe. There was no drawing him out in conversation, and, with only a courtesy nod in Hansen's direction, Aaron went topside and paced the deck for over an hour, taking the helm after a long discussion with the first mate, finding momentary pleasure in the task. The clear sky pleased the sailor in him, but the unfaltering course toward San Diego countered any joy he felt at the wheel. After another hour, Aaron went below, and after only a few brief words with Captain Hansen, he went straight for Louisa's cabin.

Her door was not bolted as it usually was, and he slipped inside the room undetected. Her lamp was low but not yet extinguished. Aaron watched her, smiling at the softness of her face, the innocent, almost beatific look about her. She lay on her stomach, one arm reaching above her head with fingers tangled in the flowing mass of her satin curls tossed away from her face. She slept on the far side of the bunk, her other arm seeming to reach toward him, her hand outstretched, palm open as if inviting him to join her.

Why did he torture himself this way, he asked himself. What drove him to feast his eyes on her when there was no hope of touching her again the way he wanted? But after tomorrow he might never see her again, and at least for these few minutes he could stare at her without interruption, without her hostile eyes demanding he look away. This was the reason he stood in the near-dark and watched her, or so he told himself.

Then before he realized what he was doing, he had disrobed except for his soft cotton sailor's shirt, and was gently pulling back the quilts that covered Louisa's nakedness, slowly easing his body next to hers. Still sleeping, though less soundly, she moved toward him, sighing as she felt him and his warmth.

Oh God, how he ached for her while he caressed and renewed his memories of her sweet body. He moaned in pain-tinged but joyful appreciation of the softness of her skin; her aroma; the firmness of her flesh. Her eyes were closed, but she was awake, and she pressed her body into his, her voice beginning to sing its own wordless song, seeming to want just as much from him as he desired from her. He called her name and she touched him knowingly. When his mouth sought hers, she yielded passionately, opening her legs to seek and embrace him with at least as much ardor as he possessed. She welcomed his wonderfully hard body with joyfully fierce cries, seeking the same joy he did, taking wild abandoned pleasure from his body, joining him in splendid and transcendent ecstasy.

When his heartbeat had slowed, Aaron gazed at Louisa to find she was already asleep in his arms. He did not want to leave her even briefly, but quietly got out of her bed and left the cabin. He would approach her about the future in the clear, more rational morning, if the light of day did not color the shades of night too differently.

Chapter Eighty-seven

SHE woke just as the cabin door closed behind him. Louisa sat up in astonishment and swiftly rising fury, outraged and furious to think Aaron would make love to her the way he just had, and leave without a word as quickly as he could get his pants on! But it was just like the damned pirate he was, she raged to herself. He was obviously an expert at dead-of-night operations on open water. Louisa flew out of her bunk and bolted the door, pounding her fists, but no one was there to hear her. Then she threw herself into the bunk again, covering her head with pillows, screaming out her anger over Aaron's behavior, and, more especially, her own. Finally she'd had enough of him. "At last!" she screamed bitterly, and cried herself to sleep.

In the morning there was no one to bring her cool, scented cloths to soothe her eyes, no one to arrange her hair to perfection. Yet she managed to be alluring by her own hand, even though she scowled at the results. Aaron was not at the mess when she arrived, and she ate little, returning quickly to her cabin, hoping to avoid him.

She packed the last of her bags, and slipped into her heavy charcoal-gray coat, fastening the pearl buttons securely, tying her lynx hat over her curls. She took the matching fur muff and left the cabin for the last time, expecting to see the rest of the journey in the crisp November air from the windy deck of the *Crystal Mae*.

As she stood at the railing watching the barely familiar land very slowly come closer, Louisa stared at the landscape intently, hoping to see the Hudson compound at any moment. But she didn't concentrate so

deeply that she didn't feel Aaron approach her. At
first he said nothing, reaching for a stray blond curl
that whipped behind her head in the wind, tucking it
gently beneath her fur hat. Louisa turned her ice-cold
eyes on him and looked into his, believing she found
his face full of smug satisfaction. Aaron stroked her
cheek softly, then held her head in his hands, reaching
for her mouth with his lips, expecting her to kiss him
with the same warmth and tenderness that made him
not notice the very cold morning. But he found her
lips and body stiff and unyielding. "What's this reception?" he asked as if he were due better.

"The only kind you're entitled to."

Aaron frowned. "And last night?"

"Is not open for discussion," she said firmly, and
turned away to look out over the ship's railing again,
apparently absorbed in the rust-, brown-, and green-
splashed tops of seashore cliffs.

"Louisa Boyd Hudson, you're the damnedest
woman on the face of the earth. What is it you want
from me?" He was both puzzled and furious, having
reached the end of his rope with her.

She turned flashing, spark-filled eyes on him. "I
want precisely nothing more of you. I *want* you to
leave me in San Diego, and get out of my sight, and
my life, once and for all. If there is some minor thing I
can do to assist your escapade *from a distance,* you
may call on me, but otherwise, keep away. *Just keep
away from me!*"

Aaron stared at her. "I'm of the opinion only daily
beatings will make you easy to deal with. But, it occurs
to me, if I were to pitch you into the ocean right now,
you might behave sensibly for a few more hours. It's
something that's worked well in the past."

Louisa stepped back instinctively, and Aaron
reached for her, grabbing her roughly. He shook her
as one might shake an unruly child, drawing her very
close when he finished. "I tell you it's a very tempting
thought. But one of us has to keep his head." She felt
the tremendous strength of his arms and the anger in
his body, even before she heard the same emotion in
his voice. "I'll keep away from you, Louisa, if that's

what you want. But you and I both know it's not what you want. And all I'd have to do is lift your skirts to prove you've no more strength of character than I do. You howl at me for taking Marguerite. You refuse to listen to reason. You look down your nose at *me,* at *my* past, at *my* origins, but you, pretty, well-bred Louisa, have better instincts than any whore who ever spread her legs for money!"

Louisa had turned exceptionally pale, but he seemed not to notice. "You told me once, I'd never be finished with wanting you. Well, I've much the same news for you. You, my fine gentlewoman, with your perfect skin, and perfectly educated tastes and manners, you'll never be happy till you take me back into your bed. But, believe me, when that day comes—and it will, my hot-blooded gypsy bitch—it will be on my terms, I promise."

Louisa held her breath and choked back outraged tears as best she could, but the biting wind spilled them down her cheeks. "That day will *never* come, I swear it," she hissed when she recovered her voice.

He gave her a bitter cold smile, then released her from his grip and walked away.

Louisa stood helpless with furious tears running freely. She tried desperately to calm herself, finding herself unable to think clearly, concentrating on one object then another to find and keep her composure, until the *Crystal Mae* was finally anchored in the bay. Louisa didn't see Aaron again until the shore boat was lowered over the side, and Captain Hansen came for her to go ashore. Then Aaron, still dressed as a common seaman as he had been throughout the voyage, suddenly stood next to her as if nothing had happened between them, and when they landed, Luther Dobson greeted them enthusiastically. "At long last, Mrs. Hudson!"

"At long last," she cried just as emphatically, offering him her hand.

"There's a great deal of news." he whispered to Aaron. "How long will you be in port?"

"Only long enough to see Mrs. Hudson settled." Luther Dobson couldn't help but notice the way

Aaron's eyes wandered over Louisa as if he were admiring her beauty for the first time. "Not long at all."

"Just be sure to see me before you pull up anchor." Aaron nodded. "Take the wagon, Mr. Hudson. I see no need for you to wait for your carriage," he added more loudly.

It was an offer Louisa hoped he'd make. "We'll send someone for the trunks," Aaron said, helping Louisa onto the wagon seat, quickly sitting next to her, turning the horses almost before he was settled. The trip was made in silence, the horses driven with haste, and at the compound Louisa was on the ground flying into Carmen's arms even before the wagon came to rest.

Louisa was home at last.

But it wasn't quite the homecoming she had hoped for.

Carmen was just as ebullient as she'd expected, and Emma just as welcoming. But in the excitement and confusion of greetings, Rachel cried tormentedly in Louisa's arms, seeking Carmen frantically with her hands and eyes. Reluctantly and sadly, Louisa returned the screaming baby she'd longed for in the worst of her hours to Carmen. Obviously, Rachel thought Carmen was her mother.

Defeat not jealousy surged in Louisa's heart as she watched Carmen soothe Rachel's distressed cries. It seemed to Louisa that Rachel cast her especially reproachful looks as she responded to the older woman's voice and hugs. Louisa tried not to feel crushed, yet, after all that had happened since she'd left San Diego, none of the motherly words of reassurance from Emma and Carmen helped her. Rachel's natural responses only rekindled Louisa's fear that she somehow ruined everything she touched.

Aaron knew better than to interfere, watching Louisa's transparent emotions. Her desperate torment seemed to echo inside him, and he knew she cursed the day she'd left her home.

Emma had immediately greeted Aaron warmly, but he watched Emma's eyes cloud over briefly when she first saw him. He wondered if she would ever get used to the idea that a man who was her son's double was not in fact her son.

When they at last went inside the house and sat in the parlor, Louisa tried again to hold Rachel, this time with great success, and the tears that flowed this time were hers. She laughed and cried and hugged the bouncing, vigorous baby, not able to believe Rachel was really her very own. The child's black newborn hair had given way to bountiful and very blond curls, and there was a rosy glow about the very fair child to reassure her mother. Those brown, brown eyes were Aaron's without a doubt, she thought. What did she mean? Louisa was horrified by her mistake. Rachel was *not* Aaron's child! How could she make such an error, even at this emotional moment! She gave Aaron a slashing glance, and he wondered what thought of him had entered her mind to produce such a hateful look.

Rachel was taken by the deep pleasing sound of Aaron's voice, often glancing in his direction, staring intently at his smiling face, giving him more than a few of her happiest smiles. "Señora, you must let baby get to know her papa a little," Carmen said cheerfully, reaching for Rachel to hand her to Aaron.

Louisa forced herself to keep from offering a hot denial of Aaron's responsibility for Rachel's paternity, keeping the charade going even in this circle. Before she could refuse Carmen, Rachel was in Aaron's arms, flashing as much charm on him as her mother flashed sparks. Rachel seemed quite at ease with Aaron, and it was too much for Louisa, who quickly left the room, causing everyone to look after her. Obviously she wouldn't be missed for a quick inspection of the house, she raged, poking into every closed room, finding her old room now arranged for Rachel's convenience, and what had been Aaron's and her room waiting with a turned-down bed. "Carmen, you're more than a little wicked," Louisa said aloud in disgust, hearing the door close behind her.

"She's just assuming that all is well," Aaron said, pulling her against him. "Shall I lift your skirts and prove the point I made earlier, señora?" he said, grabbing Louisa forcefully, kissing her without giving her a chance to respond. She struggled as best she could in his grip, but it was fast and sure, and she had nowhere to go but closer to him as he crushed her against his hard body.

"You're safe for now, Mrs. Hudson," he said when he released her from his kiss, still holding her securely in his arms. "I don't have time to bed you properly, or even improperly. But I promise you, it won't be long before you're missing me. God knows I'll miss you."

"You conceited bastard! Let me go!"

"Reluctantly, Mrs. Hudson. Reluctantly!" and she found his mouth on hers again, one hand moving familiarly down her back, the other fast caressing her breasts. Her will was beginning to slip away, and she found that she had to force herself to struggle. Yet finding it was a very great effort to resist him made her anger more real, though it was fury directed more at herself than at him. When he released her she slapped his face with all of her strength, which was only sufficient to make him smile. *"Hasta luego,* Mrs. Hudson," he said, and left her in tears, standing in the middle of their room, her last memory of him with an amused and too knowing smile on his lips, his eyes full of mocking laughter.

Chapter Eighty-eight

AARON found it difficult to concentrate that evening. The meal had been long and heavy, the wines plentiful. The German host was a fine example of what dining at his table too often could do to one's physique. He was a short man with a barrel shape, and a booming authoritative voice. He had a painful, sometimes debilitating affliction in his spine, and always carried a heavily carved solid silver cane to assist him, if need be. He swore by the Los Angeles sunshine—"saved me from being a damned invalid," he reminded his guests from time to time, as if he were in awe of this part of his good fortune.

If he were in awe of his luck in the matter of his health, it was one of the few things in life that truly impressed him. He seemed to take all else in stride, as if it were his due. He was, in fact, a German peasant who had arrived in America like the multitude of his fellow countrymen—very poor and very eager, and willing to do whatever was necessary. He had long ago forgotten his origins, long ago amassed a fortune. He'd even come to California long before it was fashionable, and was quick to make more money when California exploded in the world's imagination. He invested in banking, mining, freight hauling, whole shiploads of mining and other supplies, lumbering ventures, farming, cattle and other stock. If an enterprise made money in California, Herman Brockheim seemed to have a share of it.

Very early in his adventures in California, he saw his future in the territory, then held by Mexico. He had a sixth sense about it, he said later when his prospects turned to pure and assayable gold. He'd been shrewd enough to marry into a prominent Mexican family, securing a sizable *rancho* as a dowry, as well as a sizable maiden for a wife. And he considered himself lucky. The offspring he and Carlotta produced pleased his father-in-law immensely, and at this man's death the bulk of the estate fell under his German son-in-law's administration. The peasant was now a king.

And Brockheim readily saw merit in the conspirators' plans. Peter Melville appeared to take him into his full confidence, though Melville never trusted anyone to that extent. Brockheim was like his newfound comrades, a man with allegiance to himself alone, his citizenship and oaths of loyalty subject to the opportunities of circumstance. He had been a German national, then a citizen of Mexico, and was now an American citizen in very good standing, but he had no prejudice toward permanent affiliation with one country or another. He was in a way a man without a country.

It was for this reason, and others, that Melville, Carson, Aaron, and Easton were enjoying Herman Brockheim's hospitality. The private discussions after dinner were lively, the proposals expansive. The German gave them his full support, and further influenced Senator Edwin Taylor to lend an ear to the flourishing schemes.

Even Aaron's mind caught fire. The men with whom he seemed to plot were frighteningly close to being next of kin. In other circumstances he could have gladly done business with them. They had imagination and daring and fearlessness about the future. They regarded the risks of their schemes—the loss of fortunes and position—as worthy of the gamble. At the root they were ruthless and corrupt, risking far more than their own property and lives. This fact, made so apparent by the murder of Aaron's actual kin, Marshall, kept Aaron at his distance at moments when the game he played became too real, the charade overwhelmingly self-deceptive.

The schemes were advancing with steady and thoughtful precision. Plans for privateering on this coast as well as the other were reinforced by decisions to order construction of appropriately designed ships. They would go to British and French shipbuilders. Northern shipyards would not be available during the now inevitable war. South Carolina had just withdrawn from the Union, and the coming inauguration of the despised Abraham Lincoln would see more states follow her, it was certain.

The conspirators foresaw the problems of foreign shipbuilders selling ships to the enemies of the United States. They would find supporters in other foreign countries, and register the newly built ships in the investors' names under foreign flags. Later the conspirators would purchase the ships from those private persons. It would definitely be a war of economic advantage to the rich, especially those with a provident eye on the future.

New to the plotting, Senator Edwin Taylor was a man with a rich imagination and questionable loyalties. He was foremost an opportunist, a man of sometimes wild vision. He sprang from the South, and settled in the West when, like Brockheim, he foresaw the possibilities the region held. He vigorously promoted legislation advantageous to the West, and saw many bills through the rigors of passage in the U.S. Senate. He was also a darling of foreign courts whenever he traveled, even as a private citizen.

Senator Taylor firmly believed all of the West would follow California's lead if she declared neutrality in the coming conflict. Neutrality in the war could be the first step in the move toward a fully independent West. Taylor would use his eloquence where necessary, his plain-spoken phrases when it better suited the audience. He would sway large numbers of people to his convictions.

It was not beyond the realm of the possible, he said, to think the commander of military forces in the Western territory might declare California and the rest of the region neutral. Once the West was securely in the conspirators' camp, the government in Washington would be powerless to reclaim it. The business of war would guarantee their success. Why, he asked, should the West, with its abundant resources and dynamic citizenry, be bound to North or South?

He would, at first, speak in favor of neutrality, but the senator ultimately preferred the idea of California rising as an independent republic. He had schemes of his own. Mention of his dreams caused a responsive gleam in Peter Melville's eyes, opening the doors for Aaron's long-held speculation that no one really knew the extent of Melville's own plans. Senator Taylor saw the eventual boundaries of the new republic to be the Pacific Ocean, the Rocky and Sierra Madre mountain ranges. He did not dream on an ordinary scale.

But he did not recommend abandoning the South—"my homeland," he called it—to fate. He still had too many business interests in the South, despite his residence in the West, and contrary to Congress's gentleman's code of ethics. Perhaps if the tide ran in that direction, the Pacific states might openly declare allegiance to Southern ambitions. Eventually the West and the South might join to become one mighty and separate nation. Even now there were militant pro-Southern citizens residing in California. Several, especially in Southern California, had openly declared themselves to be in the South's camp. Some were armed and already practicing military maneuvers among themselves. These militants could easily be added to the existing army, bolstering the numbers of soldiers who hailed from the South.

A railroad connecting the South with the West through sympathetic territory was not an impossible dream. The debate for a transcontinental railroad had long been echoing in Congress, one of the biggest obstacles being the route across the interior—northern or southern—and the war might decide that issue too. Among those at Brockheim's, linking the South with the riches of the West was deemed a necessity for the South—if the war should last more than a few weeks.

Many optimistic Southerners boasted the North would crumble immediately in the face of brave Southern soldiers. But the men who now convened in the hills east of the port of Los Angeles were more farsighted than the braggarts who thumped their chests over the superiority of their region's manhood. They saw early skirmishes turning into protracted battles; battles turning into campaigns; thin wisps of smoke from a few muskets becoming clouds of suffocating cannon fumes. There would be red stains on a few bandages at first, but later the streams would be full of the stench and color of blood. If necessary, these men at Brockheim's could see to it.

Taylor even revealed he had spoken of his sketchy dreams in the French court, and his ideas had drawn considerable interest. As yet, Europe officially supported the government in Washington, but Southern ideas were not rejected out of hand; there was still room to bargain. In order to survive the long haul of war or separation from the Union, the South would have to establish firm trade ties with and diplomatic recognition in Europe and the Orient. California could provide that link as an independent republic. Certainly the South's ports would be closed in war, and since she relied heavily on Northern and European mills to convert her valuable cotton crop to cash, as well as demanded the importation of many goods to make life livable, she would need an open source of ocean trade. The friendly Pacific Ocean loomed as the means of trade she needed. The conspirators counted their blessings.

Very highly placed French officials took a special interest, however, in Senator Taylor's discussions of the eventual boundaries of an independent Western republic, and in his points regarding abandoned gold and silver mines in Sonora, Mexico. The French had their own designs on Mexico. Taylor impressed his friends at court with his knowledge of the region, and even managed to spur the court's interests in it.

Now the senator pointed out to his listeners in the California hacienda, just as he had to the foreign secretary, that *all* the millions in gold extracted from California did not *even begin* to equal the amounts mined in Sonoran mines in past centuries. These mines had been abandoned primarily because of the fierce Indians of the area. But with proper use of military forces, Sonora's mines could be reopened. The region

Chapter Eighty-nine

On December 20, 1860, South Carolina seceded from the Union. The word passed quickly, and when the news arrived in California by telegraph, Peter Melville was one of the first to receive it. At Brockheim's, the news was celebrated temperately, champagne glasses raised among the silent thoughts of those who gathered at Casa del Sur. The conversation then turned very earnest. By Christmas Eve, the Melvilles, who had planned to stay in Southern California until after the New Year's fiesta wound down, left with Franklin Carson for San Francisco. William Easton remained behind to enjoy the German's hospitality, and Aaron rode to San Diego to enjoy Christmas with Marshall's wife and family, and to see Luther Dobson again.

Aaron was accompanied on the trail by Easton's servant, Samuel Davis, and the two men arrived at the Hudson compound very early Christmas morning. Aaron entered the house, quietly greeting a startled Carmen with a satchel full of packages.

"Señor! I did not expect you! Señora, your wife, did not tell me," she said, looking up from an array of less than traditional holiday dishes in various stages of preparation, instantly considering whether there could be enough food for another guest. Satisfied she could feed an invading army, Carmen turned again to Aaron to concentrate on his reply.

"The señora is fond of surprises."

"Oh, *si,* señor," Carmen agreed.

"I've some things to put under the Christmas tree," he waved the satchel at her.

"There is no tree, señor, but a special place in the

parlor." Carmen gestured in that direction, then led the way, stopping only to put a heavy kettle down on the crowded worktable.

The house was decorated with greenery tied simply with red and green silk ribbons scattered throughout the branches, and here and there were a few ornaments Aaron seemed to remember from years past. The only elaborate decoration was a fine China crèche on the mantel. He distinctly recalled these figures. He had been with Marshall in the Boyd household when the valuable pieces had been unpacked after one of Justin Boyd's many trips abroad. Louisa had been enthralled by the fragile, exquisitely rendered figures, and it didn't surprise Aaron to see they were among the things she chose to bring to California. It was a woman with a deep longing for permanence who collected these mementoes from her shattered past—a woman he could long for but never make a life with.

Seeing the crèche again, so far away from their original home, so carefully preserved and transported, made something suddenly very clear to Aaron. These shining figures reminded him that women like Louisa Boyd Hudson were like priceless ornaments designed and finished to decorate other men's fine homes. He could admire them, perhaps even hold them in his arms for a few short hours, but they, like the figures in the crèche, would eventually shatter into uncountable pieces if he tried to take them from their rightful places. He could look. He could touch. But he could never possess.

Aaron seemed unusually thoughtful to Carmen as he placed his packages with the others. "Oh, señor! *La cocina!* The señora is still sleeping," she said, flying from the room.

Aaron smiled after her. He emptied the satchel, then closed it, taking the last two bundles, heading for Louisa's room. He opened her door and went in.

"What time is it, Carmen?" Louisa asked, still lying on her stomach with the covers thrown almost completely over her head.

"It's still very early, señora."

The response brought Louisa to a sitting position instantly, her face showing how startled she was.

"Good morning, Mrs. Hudson," Aaron said cheerfully, sitting next to her quickly, before she could react.

Louisa blinked at him, then leaned into her pillows slowly. "Good morning, Aaron," she said quietly, pulling the covers under her chin protectively. She looked sleepy. "You didn't warn us you were coming."

"I thought you liked surprises."

"And you're an expert at surprises, aren't you?"

He smiled and leaned to kiss her gently on the cheek. Louisa shrank from him. "Just a friendly holiday kiss, señora. The man would be expected to call on his beloved wife and family on this day, especially when he's so close to home."

"Close? Where have you been?"

"For the last week—in Los Angeles. You asked me to leave you alone, remember? Just honoring your requests, señora." He gave her a slight bow from the waist, though still sitting next to her on the bed. "But perhaps you've had a change of heart?"

"Don't get your hopes up," Louisa said firmly. "Why *did* you come?"

"For appearances. To feast my eyes on you. And to give Luther Dobson enough information to keep him happy indefinitely. The fire is hot, Louisa. South Carolina seceded from the Union a few days ago."

"Oh? I hadn't heard."

"You will."

Her attitude softened a little. "Well, it's just what you've been waiting for. Now what?"

"I keep dancing till I get further orders, or till some overt act to overthrow the government is made."

"How long will you be with us?"

"I won't trouble you long. I'll enjoy the Hudson hospitality today, but my real business is with Dobson. Then I'm on my way north again." He told her briefly of some of the schemes.

"Actually it's very intriguing, isn't it?" she offered, turning on her side as she listened to him. "I knew Senator Taylor was a schemer!"

"He and Melville come closest of all to each other's thinking. Although Melville said little to reveal exactly what his thoughts are, he seemed very impressed with Taylor's ideas—as if he'd heard an outline of the senator's plans before."

Louisa stared thoughtfully at Aaron. "It's a strange situation for you to be in, isn't it—opposed, not aligned with, these men?"

Aaron's face grew pensive then turned cold, but his eyes burned into her. "There are many things I want but can't have in this affair," he said, and they were silent for a few minutes, Louisa absolutely frozen in Aaron's gaze. Then he relaxed, seeming to have lost his train of thought when one of the packages he'd brought to her room slipped from the bed.

Aaron bent to pick it up from the floor. "Merry Christmas, Mrs. Hudson," he said, handing the pale, tissue-wrapped gift to her. "Something to match your eyes."

Louisa smiled at him gently. "Thank you. I'll wait to open it with the others."

"If you wish."

Louisa hesitated. "You know I've never been able to do that," she said, immediately untying the elaborate blue satin bow. "Obviously someone else tied this for you," she laughed.

"Obviously," he smiled. Louisa unwrapped the package and unfolded a blue silk nightdress. Its design was very simple, without sleeves, with a gathered neckline. The hem, neckline, and armholes were edged with white eyelet lace, threaded with narrow pink satin ribbons.

"It's very pretty. Thank you," she said, folding it again.

"I hoped to see it on."

Louisa laughed. "I'm sure you did!" she said casually. "What else do you have there?" She reached for the other small package.

"Something for Rachel."

"Ah, Aaron, how thoughtful." There was surprise in her voice. "Let me see. Rachel won't know what to do with a wrapped package. I'll have to unwrap it for her."

He handed the present to Louisa, and she discovered a small linen doll, exquisitely finished with silk-embroidered curls, and a pretty embroidered face. She was dressed complete with lace-trimmed pantaloons, and a gay pink frock. "Oh, she'll love it. It's just the right size for her little hands. How did you ever think of it?" She looked at him curiously.

"Arabella Melville."

"Thank you, Arabella." Louisa sat up in the bed, closed her eyes, and stretched. "Carmen should be bringing Rachel any minute. You should hear her," she said triumphantly, "she calls me 'Mama' and has accepted me as if I'd never left her," she sighed.

"That should've been easy," he said, pulling Louisa against him. She stiffened and tried to push him away at first, then slowly relaxed, and let him kiss her.

"What do you think you're doing?" she asked softly with her arms around him tightly.

"Getting a Christmas-morning hug is all."

"As long as you understand that's the extent of it!" Then she sighed sadly. "I wish you hadn't come," she whispered as if she meant it. "I never dreamed you'd come. I've no gifts for you."

Aaron groaned in a familiar way. "We could say our gifts were exchanged in private," he offered with a hopeful grin.

"Mmmm. We could, but we won't," she said firmly, squirming out of his grasp.

At that moment there was a knock at the bedroom door. "Come in, Carmen," Louisa called cheerfully. "So good to see my girl," she cried, reaching out for Rachel with a sly smile to Aaron. "Just at the right moment, too," she giggled.

"What do you think of your daughter, Marshall? Who do you think she looks like?" she asked as Carmen left the room.

Aaron studied the gleeful child. "She has my eyes, or Marshall's, that is. Your nose." He studied Louisa for a few minutes. "Actually she looks like Andrew

Sutton. You've seen the photographs, haven't you?"
He seemed serious.

Louisa looked stunned, then frowned deeply. "I
fail to see the humor in your suggestion," she said,
clutching Rachel tightly all of a sudden.

Rachel let out a squeal. "Sorry, baby, Mama didn't
mean to hold you so tightly," Louisa apologized.
"Here, see what your papa brought you," she said
glumly, offering the pretty doll to Rachel. Rachel's
eyes lit up as she squeezed the doll in her hands. She
made a variety of obviously pleased, untranslatable
comments, which made both Aaron and Louisa laugh,
then put the doll in her mouth for further inspection.
"A pretty baby for my pretty baby."

Then Louisa offered Rachel to Aaron. "Will you
hold her while I get a dressing gown on?"

Rachel went to Aaron without hesitation, with
charming smiles for his seemingly natural banter as he
sat with her on the bed, Louisa covertly watching the
two as she tied the sash of a blue-gray dressing gown
over her pink challis nightdress. She was frowning
again, but neither Aaron nor Rachel noticed. Why,
she wondered, had Aaron compared her child to Andrew Sutton? To tease her? To pique her anger? To
insult her? Louisa had also made the disturbing com-
parison, and for some unexplainable reason she had
not been able to dismiss the thought. Now, suddenly,
what should have been only a fleeting, annoying observation became an obsession, an unavoidable and
very real thorn in her side.

Chapter Ninety

EVERYONE had gone to bed. The house was quiet, and she was tired from the long and pleasant day. She lay in bed for over an hour, but did not sleep. She seemed to be waiting for something. Someone. Louisa was uncomfortably conscious of her mood, and she frowned in the dark. "I am *not* waiting for him," she said aloud, as if to reassure herself.

Don't lie to yourself, came the immediate reply inside her head.

Louisa kicked off the covers and sat up, drawing her legs against her body, clasping her arms around her knees. For several long minutes, she sat and stared out the bedroom window, listening, watching—waiting. "I *am* waiting for you," she whispered finally, sitting in the soft nightgown Aaron had given her early that morning. She knew she wore it hoping he would come back tonight and see her in it just as he had wished.

The whole day had been wonderful, almost unreal in its pleasure. Aaron's presence had made it more of a celebration than Louisa had expected. She had prepared for the holiday by unpacking the few Christmas ornaments she'd brought from New Orleans, and with help from Emma and Carmen and Anna, boughs from a large pine tree had been hung above the mantel and decorated. Louisa arranged her precious créche beneath the greenery, but none of the decorations had cheered her in the least. She'd wrapped presents, yet only the anticipation of Rachel's first

Christmas gave her any feeling of excitement, and
even that expectation did not arouse her emotions as
she thought it should.

Emma had seemed cheerful throughout the preparations. She smiled a lot. But her eyes were vacant. She spoke of Christmas holidays they'd spent in
Louisiana, and for a while both women daydreamed
aloud of happier moments. Then the reality of Marshall's absence from their midst slammed the door
on their happy memories. Yet instead of Aaron's presence depressing Marshall's mother, he seemed to make
Emma's eyes shine. It was obvious Emma Hudson admired Aaron, and her fondness for him was real
enough to convince anyone she doted on her "son."
Perhaps that was why Louisa had so easily warmed
to him today. Emma had only set an example for
her.

The day had gone so smoothly, and she had been
happy. Her husband played his part perfectly, and
"his baby" even joined the charade with special
enthusiasm. Rachel hung on Aaron's every word,
following him with her eyes, reaching out for him
with her eager small hands more often than Louisa
could believe. And Aaron took to Rachel as if he'd
bounced countless babies in his arms. Rachel straddled
Aaron's hip throughout the day, more than she did
her mother's. Rachel was Aaron's captive. Just as I
am, Louisa said silently in her now dark room.

Her restlessness was overpowering, and she rose
from the bed, pacing the room without purpose, deciding a glass of sherry would help her sleep. She
wrapped a wool dressing gown around her shivering
body, slipping her feet into soft lambswool-lined slippers, and in the dark made her way through the house,
easily finding the sherry decanter on the sideboard
in the dining room.

Louisa helped herself to a glass of wine, and sat
for a few minutes in the parlor. Then she took her
glass and the decanter outside to rock slowly on the
wooden porch swing where she and Rachel custom-

arily spent many hours of the day. While Rachel slept or watched the world around her, Louisa propped pillows around the baby, and painted at her easel or sketched in her lap. The month they'd been reunited had passed very quickly for mother and child.

But in other respects the month had been an endless one. The last time she saw Aaron, Louisa swore he would never have her again. She was certain she could forget him, and she found she could forbid his memory in the day. But she could not control the sensuous warmth that flowed over her in sleep. Her dreams forced her to remember him and the ecstasy of his touch. She would wake sweating in the cool winter night air, tingling and sick with longing, aching for the hardness of his body and the weight of him bearing down on her.

In other dreams it was as if she were wide awake to feel him brushing her nipples lightly with his gentle fingertips, and his mouth taking possession of hers. She too vividly remembered the contrasting textures of his body against hers—the firm, lean muscles, the crinkly soft hair, and his smooth, warm skin.

Sometimes she was brought from slumber to feel again his penetration of her and the sensations his touch would bring. And she was frightened that only his memory obsessed her. Never once did she dream of Marshall. How could Aaron with his duplicity, his willful, unfeeling use of her, how could he possess her so completely? Was it true what those voices had said long ago? Was it true she was damned? Damned, never to be loved; never to be whole? Louisa had been whole when Marshall loved her, but her love had only destroyed him. Was she as contaminating as she'd feared?

Louisa had thought she could live beyond her past. Now she knew she was mistaken. Only her kind would seek out and possess her—a sort of man like Aaron—or Stefan—or Justin—manipulative, selfish, cruel. They would seek and find her, because she was a corrupt as they. Louisa said she despised these men she named in the darkness, but the intensity of her hatred for them was only a fraction of what she now felt for herself.

Louisa stood up, and paced the porch. Her wine-glass was empty, and she filled it again, deciding without a moment's consideration to walk on the beach. "It will help me sleep," she reasoned. Though the night was deep, Louisa knew the path well enough, leaving her slippers on the rocky soil ledge when she descended into the soft cool sand. The ocean's waves were violent, and she sat well out of their reach as they pounded the shore relentlessly. Louisa watched the dim outline of the water hypnotically, clutching the crystal decanter and her half-empty glass of sherry. The surf roared in her ears, and her heart seemed to pound in reply. She wondered how long she would have to wait before she would forget Aaron. "How long? How long? How long?" she demanded of the night. "Never. Never. Never," was the answer, and she jumped to her feet, throwing the decanter with all of her strength, shattering the crystal against the water's low lapping edges. "No!" she screamed. "No! NO! You are wrong!" she cried, flinging her wineglass after the decanter, and herself into the sand.

But there was no comfort in doing so, and when she finished crying, she rolled onto her back and stared at the sky. The stars reached down, and seemed to whisper to her, confirming the ocean's assessment of her plight. They assured her she would never forget Aaron. Angrily Louisa turned onto her side to face the violent waves again. She took a deep breath, stretched out, resting her head on her arm, and stared into the night until she fell asleep.

How long she slept she didn't know, waking when she felt herself lifted from the sand, recognizing her captor instantly, even in the darkness. "How did you find me?" she asked drowsily, offering no resistance to his strong warm arms.

"Just say I'm very clever," he laughed.

"Why are you here? I thought you'd be on your way by now."

"Tell me you want me to go and leave you alone."

Louisa stared at Aaron in the dim night, then rested her mouth against his ear. "I want you," she whispered.

When he realized she had said what she intended, he pulled her more closely against him and carried her without another word to bed. "I expected more of a struggle," he teased as he lay caressing her compliant body.

"Is that what you hoped for?" He laughed at her. "If I wake Carmen screaming for help, you won't be in any condition to make love to me."

"But I'm your husband."

"You think that would matter to my self-appointed guardian angel?"

"Carmen likes me well enough."

"We'll see." But Aaron clasped his hand over her mouth firmly before any sound could escape.

"If we wake them at all, let's wake them with other sounds," he whispered, lifting his hand to cover Louisa's mouth with his. They were a joy to one another, seeming to forget the tumultuous recent past, seeming to create new memories, with Louisa soon free of her new silk gown. "You've yet to see it in the light. It's really very pretty," she said as he tossed her nightdress aside.

"I was more interested in helping you off with it than seeing how becoming it is."

"Is that so? I'd have never believed such a thing of you, Aaron," she teased as she undid the buttons of his shirt, tugging at his clothes, playfully trying to increase the speed with which he disrobed. "You're so slow!" she giggled as he discarded the last of his garments.

"And you're so anxious all of a sudden."

"If you only knew how I've tossed and turned in this bed!"

"Show me how much you suffered," he said as he grabbed her, finding Louisa as passionate as he'd known her, yet seeming to offer more. They were as loving with their caresses as they were hungry, giving to each other from the depths of their racing hearts. But they were silent about their feelings, promising nothing to each other in the darkness. Nor did they dream of their future when they closed their eyes to sleep when it was light.

Chapter Ninety-one

IN the morning, no one came to disturb them. On the surface it appeared they had reconciled. But in fact, they had no understanding, no pact, no hope. They had only what they found during the moments they were locked in each other's arms, and soon Louisa's memories became treacherous and painful.

At first she was merely numb without Aaron. To those who saw him leave the Hudson compound late that morning, Louisa and her husband parted with affection. He'd gently kissed her hair and forehead, then lingered at her mouth, and, to all who watched, love seemed to flow between them. Once again when he left her he whispered, *"Hasta luego, señora,"* and his words echoed at her in the night. At first, she heard them as words of longing, but they fast became a chant to make her burn with humiliation. Soon the words said she would be his whenever he came for her, whenever it suited him. He was the one who said she was no better than a paid woman. Had he also called her, "a born whore"? Or was that someone else?

Louisa's feelings blurred. She ached and she raged. And she was very silent. Her nights were filled with ghosts again, but this time she knew whose face haunted her, and when she called him "Aaron," he always answered her. In her dreams, she never hesitated to go to him, and, even in her dreams, she knew it would be the same if she were awake.

Emma watched Louisa. At first she hoped it would only be a few days until Louisa's spirits improved. She worried privately until she could bear the silence no longer. In the past she had kept her concerns about

501

Louisa to herself, and she had ample reason to regret it. Emma swore she would never make the mistake again.

"Louisa, we have a great deal to talk about," she said firmly one morning. "Carmen can look after Rachel until we're finished with our chat," and she whisked the baby out of the room, returning with her arms folded determinedly at her waist.

It had been years since Louisa had seen the "no nonsense now" expression on Emma's face. The three children who from time to time upset the orderly Hudson household had seen it regularly, and when they did, promptly buckled under whatever edict was issued. Though the look on Emma's face made her almost instinctively sit up and take notice, Louisa was no longer a child to be intimidated.

"I suspect we've at least a few months of waiting before this escapade is finished. And I don't look forward to watching you pace and brood all that time. Not long ago I stood aside while you nearly went mad. And believe me, all of us who watched you were not far behind you with worry and grief. But I don't think, with all that's happened since, that I could sit silently by again." She was stern, yet kind, very like the woman Louisa remembered from her childhood. "Louisa, this time you must share your sorrows. This time you must confide in someone. If not for yourself, for Rachel. In the past, keeping everything to yourself has helped no one, least of all you." She smiled gently at Louisa who stared back at her pensively. "Talk to me, Louisa. Tell me what troubles you. This time I have not shut my eyes to things I would rather not see."

What Louisa felt and did not feel was reflected in her mirror. Her face was drawn; her color poor. She knew she desperately needed to accept Emma's offer to listen to her troubles. But Louisa's habit was to hide herself, to go alone someplace where she thought no one could see her, to conceal her shame, or guilt, or misery. She had done this as a child when she retreated to her nightmares, taking comfort reluctantly and only to save herself from unbearable pain. When she had reached out to Justin, her horror had only been magnified. When she reached out to Marshall, she had been saved—for a while. And in Aaron's arms she'd found both more than she dreamed, and more than she'd bargained for.

But as yet Louisa had not lost the instinct to reach out. She still had hope. She wanted to believe she could truly trust someone again.

Now Louisa leaned against the settee in the parlor, finding its cushions hard and unyielding. She raised her fingers to her eyes and pressed the lids gently, taking a deep breath. "Aunt Emma, I'm all right. I'm only tired. I just need more time to settle in."

"Nonsense, child. You've settled with Rachel well enough, that's very plain to see. It's not Rachel who troubles you; it's Andrew. You might have avoided your feelings for a while longer, if he'd stayed away. But something happened between you two when he was here." Louisa didn't have a reply. "Louisa, there's no need to deny anything. Your face reveals so much. Even Carmen's reviewing her list of potions and concoctions, wondering what remedy will put you on your feet again. I've heard some of her ingredients, and, if I were you, I'd try my suggested cure first!"

Louisa smiled. She could just imagine Carmen brewing something to put the color back in her cheeks. She felt tense, and tried to relax a little, visibly letting go of some of the strain in her face and body. "I'm grateful for your concern, Aunt Emma," she sighed, "but can you tell my why I have women to mother me now—you, Carmen, even the Indian woman Rosa? Tell me why didn't I have a mother when I needed one most?"

"Your mother was . . . she was . . ."

"Insane?"

"At times. She was not well. We must not judge her."

"Must not judge her?" Louisa was aghast. "*Emma*, she *knew* about my father! She *knew* and did nothing to protect me. In fact, there were times I'm sure she was jealous of me. My God!" Louisa choked on her tears. Her body stiffened, repulsed by her awful memories.

"Oh, Louisa, Claudia *was* insane! God will punish her if He sees fit." To that, Louisa laughed, but her tears spilled, and she sobbed uncontrollably. Emma put her arms around Louisa and rocked with her slowly, anguished by the younger woman's sorrow. "Why didn't you come to me? Why didn't you tell me? *I* could have stopped him. I would have taken you home. He would not have dared cross me."

Louisa pulled away from Emma gently. "What could I have told you to make you understand? I couldn't put in words what he did to me. I didn't know the words. How could I tell you? How my flesh shrank at first, then didn't? How do I explain that? Even now! He called me a 'born whore,' Emma," she whispered. "He used my body and confused my mind. I both hated and loved him. I was so ashamed; so unsure. I knew the way he touched me wasn't right, but he was my father. It's wrong, you know, to hate one's father. 'Honor thy father,' the priest said. Everyone respected him, then, and I thought he ruled the world. *Everyone,* even the governor, foreign ambassadors, all the important people, or so it seemed to me, came to my father's house. I must be insane, I thought—like Claudia sometimes was. And I saw in your grown-up faces that you thought so, too. Only the boys, in their childish mercy, really accepted me."

"Louisa, no one knew what made you behave so strangely. We were afraid for you, and a little afraid of you, too."

"Afraid of me?" she laughed, thinking of herself as she was then: a slender, wispy, haunted child.

"You were like a wild creature. No one seemed able to approach you, at times, except the boys."

Louisa took a deep breath and checked her tears. "The boys," she murmured. "The boys grew up and so did I. And now, Emma, I'm whore to another man I find I hate one minute, and love the next. My head is no clearer about Aaron than it was about Justin so many years ago. Aaron uses me for his own purposes, and I respond like no decent woman would dream of doing. Do I shock you?" Louisa glared hard at Marshall's mother, looking for recrimination in Emma's face or posture, something to confirm her own feelings of degradation. But she found nothing in Emma's face to make her stop—no horror, nor any righteous indignation. Could it be she saw understanding, she wondered in her momentary silence?

How was that possible? No one could sympathize with what she felt, least of all someone as refined and correct as Emma Hudson. But Louisa went on. "It's as if I have no volition. Aaron touches me, even looks at me in a certain way, and I'm powerless. I can refuse to think of him during the day, but at night—at night, I dream. *Then* there's little question about what I'd do if he wants me. Even though I know I'm just another whore to him, all he needs to do is summon me, and I'm bowing at his feet like some grateful slave." She took a deep breath. "It's just as it was when I was a child: all the shame doesn't matter when he takes me in his arms. At those moments, I know for certain I love Aaron like I've loved no one else in my life, and I know he loves me, too."

Louisa brushed away a few more of her tears distractedly and looking into Emma's eyes directly, facing her confessor without averting her eyes. "But when he's left me, and I'm alone, I'm not so sure. He's made no promises, and I have no reason to trust him. He told me he loved me *once*—only to convince me to do what he wanted. But, Emma, the way he makes love to me. Surely no one can pretend that kind of emotion." She laughed with her tears still streaking her face. "You see how my mind reels from one side of the argument to the other! And you wonder why I'm pale!"

Emma gave Louisa another handkerchief, which she gladly accepted, and continued. "For me, love seems to be a trick, just some carnival trick, and I'm the perfect fool. I reach out, only to be taken in by the man's sleight of hand. When the carnival leaves town, I'm left with my hands and my pockets empty, to be forgotten until the next circus passes my way."

"Louisa, Louisa," Emma shook her gently by the shoulders, hoping to stop her growing depression. "Have you forgotten how much Marshall loved you? You can't say he played tricks on you. If ever a man loved a woman, he loved you. Surely, you remember."

This time Louisa lowered her eyes, nodded her head, and sighed, letting her breath out slowly. "Yes, but that seems to have been a trick, too. Not Marshall's, but a trick just the same. Where is he, if his love wasn't a trick, as well?"

Emma had no answer for Louisa's question, and the women stared silently at each other for several long minutes. "I've no simple words to change your impression. But I know you're mistaken about Andrew, Louisa. He may be a clever liar to fool these conspiring men, but he did not lie to me about you. You'll *never* convince me he did." Louisa's face revealed she did not know what Emma alluded to. "That afternoon he and I had our little chat in Monterey, Andrew told me he loved you."

Louisa shrugged her shoulders. "He was only playing Marshall's part."

"*No,* Louisa! *Andrew* was telling me how much *he loved you!* The words came from Andrew's heart in a way only a man who truly loves a woman can speak. I heard much the same emotion from my son before he came to California, and there was no mistaking what Marshall meant. And, if you'll remember, I confronted Andrew that afternoon at Easton's in your presence. Perhaps you did not understand him, but I certainly did. There is no doubt in my mind but that he loves you. He was emphatic. He swore what he'd told me in private was true, and I could see in his eyes he meant exactly what he'd said."

Emma took Louisa's hands and held them. Louisa lowered her eyes, and Emma waited for her to look up again. When she did, Emma stared deeply into her lonely, almost wild eyes. "Louisa," she whispered, "Andrew has always loved you, just as Marshall did, and there is no doubt in my mind that he loves you now. *Nothing* could change the kind of love he has for you. I came to realize sending you away would never have changed how Marshall felt about you. It would only have kept the two of you physically separated. Listen to me, Louisa. I know Andrew loves you at least as much as Marshall did," Emma concluded firmly. Then she sighed as if she were disheartened. "Yet it's not a matter of believing me, child, but of trusting him."

Louisa was not as calm as her now dry eyes suggested. "Emma, when I don't know my own feelings, how will I ever be able to trust him?"

"Give yourself more time, Louisa. You only need a little more time." They were words she uttered on many other occasions, for in the months that followed Louisa and Emma talked on this subject often. With slightly different words each time, the women said much the same things over and over to each other in their conversations, and it was a long while before Louisa could admit she loved Aaron as much as she did, and an even longer time before she began to hope, if not believe, Aaron really loved her, too.

Chapter Ninety-two

IT was obvious, even to William Easton, he was being shoved aside. Peter Melville had revised the conspirators' original plans, and no one contested his decisions. But it was not an easy defeat for Easton to accept. In fact it was not one he could tolerate. He had set his sights on becoming president of the Pacific Republic. He had been involved with planning the West's future almost from the beginning, and he could not imagine the schemes accomplished without visualizing himself in a ceremonial position. The honor could not rightfully be bestowed on anyone else, even though the moves of the game were always to have been flexible. The end, as Easton saw it, was always to have been the same: he would reign.

Now Easton realized would never ascend to the heights he had come to expect when he first mingled with these men of power and influence. In his place, Senator Edwin Taylor was being groomed. Taylor's ability to rally the mobs had given him the advantage over Easton. He had the notoriety and the presence to swerve thinking in favor of an independent West, and had already influenced a strong minority in favor of Western neutrality. Even among those who favored support of one side or the other, Taylor managed to sow seeds of doubt.

William Easton privately acknowledged Taylor would be more widely applauded and supported by the general population than he would ever be, and quietly retreated to Crane's Nest. With his future undecided, he tried to settle unobtrusively again in Monterey, soothing his tensions and his sudden, blinding, sound-amplifying headaches with the almost magical powders Loo Kim supplied. As soon as his head seemed clear, Easton would set about making plans of his own for the days to come.

Peter Melville also returned to Crane's Nest. Surreptitiously the estate once again became the conspirators' headquarters. On drafting paper, plans for Santa Catalina Island were developed in detail. Supplies were secretly stored on the island and in other locations on the Southern California coast. Fortification and development of the island was not yet begun in earnest for fear of attracting too much attention so early in the game, but "mining" activities were gradually increasing. Was it true there was a rich lode just discovered on the island? The rumor surfaced from time to time, especially along the Southern California coast.

Marguerite Hill followed Melville to Monterey in February only a few days in advance of Aaron, who arrived at Melville's summons. When he disembarked from the ship, he looked like one of the crew, having thrown himself into the Catalina project with abandon. No one could fault him for enthusiasm. Since the first of the year he'd spent a fair share of his time at Casa del Sur at Melville's request. He kept Herman Brockheim informed of the plot's progress, and his visits to the hacienda soon became a pleasure. Hospitality his host never dreamed was being offered to him was extended to Aaron.

Esperanza Brockheim was her father's youngest child and only daughter. She was willful, and a student of nothing but her own whims, having outgrown her tutor, if not outsmarted him. She was very marriageable, but flatly refused the suitors who proposed. Her father's patience was wearing thin in this matter, and she knew her days were numbered. When Aaron reflected on Esperanza's choices, it was apparent to him she had decided to make the most of what freedom she had, for as long as she had it.

Esperanza was a surprise to all who saw her within the family circle, resembling her rather homely parents only in that she had her mother's Castilian coloring—jet-black hair and milk-white skin. Her sparkling brown eyes, her energetic body belonged to her alone. Esperanza's figure was fuller, her hips broader than Louisa's, a fact which made her more fashionable, if not more appealing than Aaron's slender wife. Yet her smooth, lithe flesh was very pleasing to his touch, very compliant to his needs when, by surprise, she first stole into his apartment within the hacienda, and treated him to her not very virginal charms.

She's learned more than conjugation of French verbs from her teacher, Aaron smiled to himself in the semidarkness of his room. And he carefully helped round out her education, finding her a very apt pupil, hardly an ingenue, though sweetly curious and willing. She was definitely less temperamental than Louisa Boyd Hudson, he thought, and, gratefully, she seemed not to have the least interest in making lasting demands of him. She asked a few inquisitive questions about his wife, about whom she'd heard a few flattering details, much to Aaron's amusement.

"If she is as beautiful as even you say, she has lovers, too. Tell me how to find a husband as tolerant as you, señor, because I hope to have many lovers, also." Esperanza sighed finally, and Aaron found himself frowning. In Esperanza's conclusions, Aaron again discovered unwillingly, he was opposed to Louisa being as generous with her favors as he was with his own. The thought of Alex Fielder, or a man like him, still haunted Aaron, though increasingly Aaron tried not to think about Louisa. When he did, he reminded himself he was only in California to play a dangerous game. The stakes were keeping his neck, and the neck of his former partner Mason Jennings out of the hangman's noose. If, at times, Aaron despaired of his role in the political affairs in which he found himself, when his loyalty to Marshall's memory was obscured he needed only to remember his friend Jennings. He certainly owed him something, the least of which was his all-out effort to save the man's life. And at these moments it was clear to Aaron his prize in this affair would not be Louisa. She had been only a source of extreme pleasure: a bonus, just as he'd originally thought of her. But she was also a complication, if she had not endangered him.

Aaron lay on his back with his arms folded behind his head, waiting for Esperanza to dress and leave his room, knowing it was best to forget Louisa; knowing it was smarter by far to take his pleasure with women, like the German's daughter, whenever they came his way. What did Louisa have that Esperanza lacked? "Nothing," was the very obvious answer, and Aaron managed to drive down all retorts that sprang to mind, reaching out to Esperanza again, forgetting all else when she slipped into his arms, murmuring his name as if she loved him.

Chapter Ninety-three

MONTEREY was much darker this time of year than when Aaron had been there with Louisa. The most apparent reason was the forbidding slashing rain which swept continuously over the coast during the last week. Little seemed to have changed at the estate, in spite of the new focus of attention on Senator Taylor. He was definitely the man of the hour, much more prominent than Easton had ever been; obviously catered to like a head of state, his travels throughout the West in order to obtain support for neutrality were followed with intense interest.

During the week of isolating rain, a document was drafted and within days its subject matter was discussed from one end of the state to the other. In the public eye it became the manifesto for those who favored the state's neutral position in the pending armed conflict between North and South. Senator Edwin Taylor's supporters were accused of being responsible for the doctrine, but it was never acknowledged by the senator, nor by any of his associates. Yet it sounded very much like, and was, in fact, his handiwork:

Whereas the ability of the United States government to protect California on account of its geographical location is in doubt, and due to the needful preoccupation of its military forces with the coming conflict, the citizens of this state declare their neutrality in the issues which divide the nation, retaining their rights to conduct their affairs, both personal and business, as they see fit, according to their best interests. We, the sovereign citizens of the State of California and the Western territory will neither promote nor discourage the outcome of the issues which now divide the United States of America.

At first the document was rumor only, but its rumored existence quickly captured the attention of Washington. In Marguerite's bed Aaron speculated over what would happen if the people of the state rallied to the idea of neutrality. The possibilities seemed to rivet public attention, and opinions were varied. Everyone had a different notion about the number of citizens who actively supported a neutral West. The strongest support for neutrality was in Southern California, where voices were also most strident in favor of secession. These aims were fanned by secret contributions from the conspirators' treasury, and a great deal of vocal encouragement from drifters who collected on the edges of crowds at public gatherings.

Aaron and Marguerite laughed about the prospects of a separate nation on this side of the continent, but in a moment of lucid observation, Mrs. Hill named Peter Melville as a likely source of agitation. "Wouldn't he just love the opportunity to found a new country. It would be just like him: King Peter the First. You could be prime minister, Marshall. What great fun we could have at court!" she purred thoughtfully.

"And your husband, what side would he take?"

Marguerite sighed dramatically. "He would be a bit of a bother. He's very loyal, you know. His honor and all. Even now, he's on the verge of resigning his commission. Mr. Jefferson Davis need only summon him to the cause of Southern justice."

"And you? Where is your allegiance?"

"You already know the answer to that question, love," she smiled, rolling onto Aaron, touching his handsome face with gentle fingers. "My first loyalty is to my husband," and she burst out laughing, giggling helplessly for several minutes.

Aaron found her mirth off balance, though he laughed with her. What a mockery her marriage was; what a deceitful bitch she was, Aaron snarled to himself even as he fondled her. She was so beautiful, yet so treacherous, and he laughed the harder, realizing he was sympathizing with the woman's husband even though he had no respect for the colonel, and only moments after doing his part to further degrade the man's reputation. But a cuckolded husband was to be pitied, regardless of the circumstances, Aaron thought. A wife could only too easily make a fool of her husband.

Quickly, however, his mind turned back to getting information from Marguerite. In spite of her behavior, she appeared to be her husband's confidante. How the man avoided knowing of his young wife's affairs was beyond Aaron's comprehension.

"Where do you think the troops they've massed are headed?" he asked her casually.

Marguerite stretched out beside Aaron, and propped herself on an elbow, stroking the length of Aaron's torso with long slender fingers, leisurely returning to his chest to twist the black hair there playfully. She stared into Aaron's face a few moments more before answering. "The general's quite upset over a letter that's been circulating. No one's actually seen any document, but it's made everyone nervous. They're gathering men wherever they think there might be unrest. The colonel's expecting to go to San Francisco any day."

"And you?"

"Why, I'll stay here, of course," Marguerite replied softly, staring deeply into the enormous pupils of Aaron's eyes, feeling herself drawn into those black pools. "Where I'll be safe from any real danger."

"Good," he whispered, pulling her against him. She gave him just what he wanted of her body and of the

information she had. As yet the powers-that-be had
no idea what the source of the unrest was. At the
moment, a properly mounted campaign on the part of
the conspirators had a very good chance of being
successful, and when the skies cleared, Aaron sailed
south again. His visits to the Brockheim household
were a diplomatic assignment and at the top of Melville's list of Aaron's responsibilities. Melville wanted
to be certain he kept the support of the powerful and
influential German.

Aaron's duties were secretly sweetened in the cool
shades of night by his host's agreeable daughter, and
when the old German asked him to escort "my Esperanza to her brother in San Diego," Aaron only smiled
pleasantly.

"It will be my pleasure, sir. I was intending to visit
my own family soon," he added. The short sea journey was more circumspect than the eager señorita
liked. She had rebelled against the idea of visiting her
brother, which no one seemed to comprehend, since
only weeks before she had begged to see him. But
that was prior to Aaron's return to Casa del Sur. Yet
no one connected Aaron's arrival with Esperanza's
sudden reluctance to travel, and her odd behavior
only made her father's resolve more firm. No amount
of tears changed his decision, and her bags were
packed and she was escorted reluctantly to San Diego
for a long visit.

Esperanza cried distressfully because Aaron would
be returning almost immediately to the hacienda in
Los Angeles, and her childish petulance and dramatic
tearfulness made their brief voyage uncomfortable,
at best. Aaron's relief at depositing her at her brother's house two days later was enormous.

It was a pleasure to then turn his attention to Luther Dobson, seeking out the man in his cluttered
office, finding him listening skeptically and officiously
to the story of a recently arrived ship's captain whose
claimed cargo was in dispute. The duty Dobson levied
was excessive, the captain declared vigorously, but
Aaron's arrival terminated the argument, with Luther

waving the fuming man hastily from the dishevelment which was his office.

"Well?"

"It's my bet it'll be a quiet revolution. All the paper is in Monterey just waiting to be confiscated: maps, and letters, enough evidence to hang scores of men up and down the coast."

Dobson gave Aaron a half-smile and shrugged his shoulders. Leaning wearily against his chair, he stared at Aaron, who seemed to sit with catlike anticipation of orders to spring for the very evidence he offered. "The order is still do nothing. Take no action."

Aaron's impatience with the imposed caution was mirrored in every fiber of his body. "What action will there be to take when the whole state rises up in favor of neutrality one day very soon? By then it'll be a damned hard, if not impossible, sentiment to stop."

Dobson shrugged his shoulders. "They're not doing anything as yet as one state after another secedes, so you can't expect too much on this coast. Just have to hope the pro-Union effort here succeeds." His voice was more wishful than certain. "Keep doing what you've been doing. Russell's mighty pleased."

"Great!" Aaron muttered disgustedly, then stood abruptly. "I'll be at the compound—at least overnight," he added as he left, but Aaron's horse seemed more eager to travel in that direction than he did. Yet he didn't halt the animal until he stood outside Louisa's front door.

Almost immediately, Carmen cheerfully gestured him toward the beach. "She is riding."

Aaron turned quickly in that direction, suddenly discovering he was more anxious to see Louisa than he cared to admit. He raced after her trail in the recently disturbed sand, thinking of the few months they'd been separated. He believed his longing for Louisa had diminished. At times he'd even thought he might be free of her, yet during the time since he'd last seen her, Aaron had not anticipated holding anyone with quite the same emotion he now felt. What special power did Louisa have to make him follow her, even when he questioned the wisdom of his acts? She was only *one* woman, he reminded himself once more, yet again he felt himself drawn to her by some unexplainable and powerful force he knew he might never understand.

Chapter Ninety-four

THE wind blew in Louisa's face, tossing the hood of her cloak from her head. Though it was late in the season and the sky was a sharp, clear blue, the mountains to the east were still capped with snow and the air was distinctly bitter. Louisa was glad she'd worn her warmer boots and clothing, but she was definitely looking forward to another warm spring, and the hot summer sun.

The tide was at its low point for the day as she rode Coffee along the edges of the shore, totally unaware of Aaron's approach. In the whipping wind, Louisa did not hear Aaron until he was beside her, dragging her from her saddle and into his arms. She met his fierce kisses with passion and sweetness to stir his blood, and he knew instantly why he'd come after her.

Yet in a few moments she was scolding him. "We've had no word from you, Aaron!" she frowned.

"Were you worried?" he asked, holding her tightly, turning the horses back in the direction of the house. Independent as his mistress, Coffee persisted in trailing riderless behind them.

"Of course not. You're quite capable of taking care of yourself. And, I seem to remember, there's always someone to look after whatever demands you have. How *is* Mrs. Hill, by the way?"

Aaron sighed impatiently, and gave Louisa a vexed look. "Just fine, señora. She sends you her best wishes."

"How thoughtful."

"Why do you pursue it, Louisa? You know I won't lie to you."

"I must be insane," she said coldly. "It's in my blood."

"I know! I've worried about you on more than one occasion!"

"You've actually worried about me? How flattering!"

"But I'm not worried now. You appear irritatingly healthy. And scrappy as ever."

"I'm just fine, thank you," she snapped, and it seemed there was nothing more to say. Aaron was suddenly silent, regretting he'd come after her, but within minutes Louisa relaxed against him and some of his anger slipped away. "I missed you, Aaron," she sighed without apology, kissing his cheek and trying to nestle more closely against him.

"Is that right?"

"Where have you been?"

"Racing up and down the coast waiting for some definite move to be made."

"Then what will you do?"

"God knows! I've been ordered to lie low, which, sure as hell, makes me wonder why I was ever sent on this damnable mission. There's already enough evidence in Melville's files to hang more than a few men for treason."

"And what brings you here? Tell me you came just to see me," she teased, kissing him again.

"I would, but you'd no doubt learn I escorted Brockheim's daughter to San Diego. She's about as high-strung as you are, and her father wanted some peace and quiet."

"And you?"

This time Aaron laughed at her frank jealousy. "She's a *homely, pale peasant*. Satisfied?"

"Should I be?"

"Louisa," Aaron said with a warning note in his voice, "I've a night here with you, maybe two. I hope to spend it just as you do," he said, moving a hand under her cloak, beginning to caress her breasts. She twisted her hips, turning a little more to face him in the saddle, kissing his mouth with the warmth he longed for.

"But we're not far from home," she whispered, when he suggested they lie in the sand.

"What shall I say to Emma when I sail past her with you in my arms? I could nod her a greeting as I kick the bedroom door shut," he suggested, lowering Louisa to the sand.

Louisa giggled. "It would be awkward, but I think she'd understand," she said as Aaron joined her, leading them to a sheltered spot away from the water against the cliffs.

"You two are getting on better than I expected."

"We get along remarkably," she said, wrapping her arms around him tightly as they lovingly began to renew their knowledge of why they could not forget each other, all thoughts dissolving into wonderful sensations, all sound but their own soft cries erased by the wind.

For Aaron something happened when he made love to Louisa that never happened in anyone else's arms. He was at a loss to explain what made this blending of his body with hers so profoundly good. At times it was something of a frightening mystery, but for now it was only a joy to relish, a feeling beyond all others, and the reasons did not matter. Louisa's kiss held him, soothed and inflamed him, and the deep passion he mysteriously felt for no one but Louisa poured out of him.

"You bewitch me," he said, kissing her gently and repeatedly when they lay quietly side by side, both just beginning to regain their awareness of the world around them.

Louisa smiled, taking the kisses from his lips as if they were sips of nectar and she were dying of thirst. When they were separated, she often felt as if she were withering in the heat of the sun, but while she lay in his embrace, she had a sense of blooming, a sense of peace and perfection, of great contentment, hope, and joy. "If only these feelings could last forever," she thought now in the churning wind, gradually feeling the cold as their warmth slipped away from them.

Soon they reluctantly rode back to the house and greeted Emma Hudson, who had been waiting. "You're looking very fit, son," she said, pouring tea for the three of them as the radiant couple seated themselves before her. "How long will you be with us?"

"Not long. I'm only here to bring Herman Brockheim's daughter to San Diego. You've not met him, but he's embroiled in the plot now, too. One of my duties is to keep him happy."

"Oh?" Emma seemed surprised. "There could only be one man in California with that name, surely. Short, stout; a sometimes crippled man? His daughter was, let me see, Esperanza, correct?"

"Correct." Aaron felt suddenly uneasy.

"Didn't she marry recently? I traveled with the family from Mexico, up the California coast on my way north. She was to have married soon after arriving home, I believe."

"She refused at the last minute."

"Again?" Emma laughed, rolling her eyes.

"I'm surprised such a homely girl would have so many suitors," offered Louisa, her eyes narrowing fiercely on Aaron.

"Whatever gave you that idea, Louisa?" asked Emma. "Esperanza Brockheim is far from ugly."

"Marshall described her just that way for me," she said coolly, but with her eyes blazing.

Emma stopped stirring her tea, and added a little cream to the hot liquid. "I suppose it's a matter of opinion. Now, tell me, Andrew, what messages do you schemers have from Simon?" she added hastily.

Louisa did not linger to hear the reply, nor did she bother to excuse herself. Her face burning with color, and her thoughts in angry disorder, she went directly to her room and turned the lock, slowly changing her clothes for dinner, glad Aaron did not follow her. Her head seemed to reel with confusion and disappointment. What possible pleasure could he take in making a fool of her, she wondered. Especially since it was so easy for him to do so.

Louisa only left her room when Carmen rang the brass bell for dinner. At the table she was polite, but decidedly icy, so Emma carried the burden of conversation. Louisa refused even to look at Aaron, escaping from the dining room with a fretful Rachel as quickly as possible, gratefully rocking and playing with her baby on the floor of the nursery playroom, almost able to forget the unpleasant turn of events.

For nearly an hour mother and child lay opposite each other on an eyelet-edged comforter, Louisa tantalizing and amusing Rachel with various soft toys. But when Aaron entered the room, Louisa's smiles faded to a frown, and when he sat next to her, reaching his arms out for the baby, Rachel grinned with a special light in her very brown eyes.

Louisa felt her body stiffen with displeasure. "She certainly could be your baby from the way she responds to you," Louisa grumbled, tossing a cloth-stuffed toy at him with obvious scorn.

"She could. But it wouldn't please you in the least, would it?"

"Not in the *least!*"

"She's a lot more agreeable than her mother. Perhaps she's acquired her father's sunnier nature," he said, baiting her pleasantly.

"Perhaps," Louisa said quietly, and leaned to give Rachel a kiss. "Good night, lovey," she sighed, then stood. "Soledad will take her when you two have finished your tête-à-tête," she added curtly, motioning to the woman who sat unobtrusively in a corner of the room. Then Louisa hastily retreated, turning the key in her door and also in the door to the bath. She disrobed for bed, and was half-naked when she heard

Aaron try the door. He rattled the handle several times.

"Let me in, Louisa," he demanded firmly.

"No!" she replied with equal force, quickly removing the rest of her clothes and slipping into a heavy robe, securely tying the sash around her waist.

His voice was louder this time. "I came for the night, remember?"

"But you'll not be spending it in my bed!"

There were a few seconds of total silence, then the house shook as Louisa's door buckled on its hinges. Louisa retreated to the far side of the room, furious and suddenly afraid of Aaron's violent reaction.

"Stop it! Stop it, damn you!" she screamed, but the hinges of the door gave way under his assault. Aaron entered the room, and grabbed Louisa from the corner, lifting her into his arms, then dumping her forcefully onto the bed.

"I came to spend the night in *this* bed next to *you!*" His voice was low but furious, and his eyes flashed with a cruelty Louisa had never seen in them before.

"I thought you came to deliver the German's *homely* daughter! Poor ugly child! You're so deceitful, Aaron! I suspect you haven't a truthful bone in your body."

Aaron glanced at Louisa for a moment then leaned the door against its opening, and turned back to her once more, his intentions obvious.

"No!"

"Yes!"

He moved toward her, quickly extinguishing the lamps. In the next instant he lay fully clothed next to her on the bed. For a few minutes Aaron did not touch Louisa, and as he undressed, he listened to her nervous breathing. He waited, expecting her fright as well as her anger to diminish, but she lay stiff and unbelieving, afraid to move, suddenly recalling the first night she'd spent with him. Then, she'd been afraid he'd rape her, and now the same apprehension filled her. The months they'd spent together had strangely come full circle. So much had happened between them, and yet not much had changed. They had been lovers, but it seemed they always remained adversaries.

When Aaron's hands slipped under the soft folds of her dressing gown, his mouth suddenly on her breasts, his fingers quickly penetrating the warmth inside her legs, Louisa tried desperately to withdraw from his touch. "Get away from me!" she demanded without much hope, trying to push him away. But she found herself crushed in his arms, his mouth hungry and violent on hers. When she finally wrenched away from his kiss she was hysterical. "Don't you understand?" she cried, her voice shrill and full of tears. "I can't live with your lies. I don't want you to touch me. Don't you understand? I *hate* you, Aaron! *I hate you!*"

"Give in, Louisa," Aaron commanded as he struggled with her. "Take your pleasure, and don't ask for more." He held her surely, his fingers searching again for the softness her tense tight body now concealed, and when he bent to kiss her, she bit his lip with lashing anger.

"Don't touch me!" she screamed when he recoiled in shock and pain.

"Bitch!" he yelled, and slapped her face, grabbing her shoulders, dragging her to a sitting position. "You like the taste of blood?" he demanded, and again kissed her violently, his blood running into her mouth.

Louisa pulled away and ran from him, but he caught her easily, tearing off her robe, flinging her roughly back onto the bed. She sobbed wildly, trying to retreat against the wall as far from him as possible. "Are you going to rape me, too?" she cried, the honest terror in her voice stopping him midmotion. In spite of his great fury, her question, and the sound of her voice, ripped into his flesh like a knife.

He had raised his hand to slap her a second time, and now he stood motionless, slowly lowering his arm to his side. For endless minutes, Louisa watched Aaron's silent shadowy figure in the terrifying darkness, all the while pressing her body more forcefully against the wall, unable to move or make a sound, watching as Aaron sat down on the edge of the bed with his back to her, as if she weren't there. Frozen in her exaggerated posture, Louisa watched Aaron dress with what seemed weighted slowness, and when he left her, he left the room and the house without another word, and without once looking back. Then Louisa collapsed into the unconsoling bed, and for a long while stared after him, shocked to hear herself weeping, not in fear, nor even with relief, but as if she were grieving.

Chapter Ninety-five

As if someone had heard Luther Dobson's entreaty, California's support of the Union cause heightened. Secret and not-so-secret organizations in favor of the South brought out at least equal support for Northern ideology. A Pacific States Republic banner was raised in Central California. Overnight word spread throughout the state, and soon American flags were flying in protest. A furious war of words was launched in the California press and in her pulpits, but still the question of loyalty was unresolved.

When Fort Sumter was fired on on April 9, 1861, the state's mood grew especially tense, and a new military general suddenly appeared from Washington to take over the command of the West's military forces. General Johnston resigned his San Francisco command and left California to join the Confederate Army. His replacement was definitely a matter of loyalty, but Colonel Hill remained in his position, affirming his own loyalty to the Union. His roots had so obviously taken in the West, his sincerity was not questioned further, and he expected to rely on his charming wife to dissuade the new general from any lingering doubt. From San Francisco, Colonel Hill wrote to Marguerite in Monterey. He summoned her, and she turned her back on Crane's Nest for good.

Not long after, others at the estate had similar inclinations, but there was no overt sign. Since his last encounter with Louisa, Aaron's temper was restive and at times decidedly black. He forced her from his thoughts, blaming his do-nothing orders from Russell for his irritable moods, and threw himself into the details of the Santa Catalina project. To those at the

Monterey estate, he appeared to have become something of a zealot. Franklin Carson could only shake his head at the resolve and tension he observed in Marshall Hudson, but, he reflected, everyone's nerves, not just William Easton's, seemed to be at the breaking point.

In early May, William Easton accompanied Arabella Melville on a short trip to the stone house in San Francisco. There were a few details she wanted to oversee in the temporary closing of her house, a number of possessions she wanted with her in Monterey. While they were in San Francisco, Easton paid his respects to Marguerite. She was cordial, all the while wondering what brought the man to her door, and a little perplexed when he left without giving her any significant message. When he appeared a second time, she grew even more curious.

"William, it's not like you to make such informal visits."

"I'm merely renewing our friendship while Arabella collects her treasures," Easton answered politely.

"Well, it's always a pleasure to entertain you, William, but you seem to have something more than refreshment on your mind." She poured the man more tea, and herself a glass of sherry, relaxing into soft cushions, stretching her long legs casually over the length of the couch. "Is there something in particular I can do for you? I know I have something you want," she said softly. "You've not come merely for tea."

Easton's eyes narrowed momentarily. There was a note in her voice she'd never before used with him and he found the invitation nearly irresistible. But he thought better of it. She was too beguiling to be trusted. Better to state his business, then follow up other suggestions at another time. "I would appreciate an introduction to General Johnston's replacement, Marguerite. I know you are, by now, well acquainted with him."

"Such a simple request, William? Of course, I can arrange for you to meet General Hoffmann. You needn't have been so sly in your request. But why does Peter have you approach me in so roundabout a fashion? You need only have asked. You, of course, can come to dinner tomorrow evening? Would Arabella care to come?"

"Tomorrow will be perfect." Easton's face lit up cheerfully. "But I prefer to come alone."

"Alone it is, William; but I'll see to it you won't be lonely. It's going to be a lively occasion. I'm anticipating some of our favorite wines and foods will be harder to come by in the near future, so our party tomorrow will be extravagant. I'm thinking of it as rather like the last event of the season."

"Aren't you being rather pessimistic about the future, Marguerite?"

"Aren't you?" she asked coyly, and he only stared at her coldly, abruptly standing to leave.

"Thank you very much for the tea, and for your kind invitation."

"My pleasure, I'm sure." She waved at Easton with her glass, ringing for a servant to escort him to the door, rising to watch him leave her house in Melville's fine landau carriage. She wondered what his purposes were, suspecting she would never learn of his mission from his lips. He's come representing himself, this time, she conjectured, and her curiosity was piqued beyond endurance.

Marguerite's thoughts turned to Aaron, and the skillful ways he'd kept her interested in him. Lately she was uncertain just what his motives had been in seeking her out. She sighed in the increasing grayness of the afternoon light, and leaned into the cushions of the cut velvet couch once again. Everyone at Crane's Nest had secrets, she remembered. Some they seemed to share with one another; others they kept to themselves. It had merely been her pleasure to mingle with a few of the men there, not yet learning many secrets, but "there's still time," she suggested aloud, and sure, at least for the moment, that Aaron's reasons for approaching her had been simply a matter of desire, she closed her eyes to dwell on what, for her, were very pleasant memories.

The next evening's party was just as festive as Marguerite had hoped. Her table was laden with food and her guests were exceedingly well satisfied. French champagne flowed more freely than water in the fountain at the house's entryway, and anyone coming onto the gathering would have believed the guests were celebrating some momentous occasion. Forty well-heeled partygoers lifted their voices in general merriment and the occasion lasted well into the morning.

Just as she'd promised, Marguerite introduced Easton to General Hoffmann, watching whenever she could to see what interaction occurred between the two men. But not until late in the evening did she have anything on which to speculate.

About midnight, as most guests collected along the edges of the patio to listen to her accomplished fiddlers, William Easton approached General Hoffmann for more than idle conversation. The general was an impressive man. His appearance spoke well of his selection for command. His bearing, his apparent dignity seemed to demand respect, and respectfully was just how Easton approached him. Yet William Easton did not in the least lack for dignity himself. Tonight he was especially polished, informed, and precise. He had information the general wanted and he spoke to get the man's attention.

Tonight William Easton was playing a role vastly different from the one he preferred, but nevertheless he performed with poise and distinction. He was no ordinary informant, but one of studied loyalty to his country, a man of conscience, even if his devotion was a bit delayed. At first the men spoke of General Johnston and the unfortunate circumstances that divided the nation. Easton's remarks enabled him to draw General Hoffmann a little distance from the crowd, and slowly the man's full attention was focused on William.

Very shortly, the general took Easton's arm and escorted him to a more private room within the house, where he shut the door quietly behind them. "What you've told me thus far has indeed captured my attention, Mr. Easton," General Hoffmann began, seating himself comfortably in Colonel Hill's dark leather chair. "You say your client is prepared to provide us with documents to back up your accusations, as well as a list of names, all of which are verifiable by signed correspondence?"

"Correct."

"In exchange for safe passage out of the country, and five thousand dollars in gold for the informant?"

Easton nodded confirmation.

"At least sixty documented names, you say?"

"At least."

"Most impressive. Hardly an offer I could turn down. What are your client's estimates of the force of men available to this conspiracy?"

"I believe they compare favorably with your own estimates, General. At most forty-five thousand men."

General Hoffmann stroked his silver mustache thoughtfully, and stared at Easton silently for several minutes. Easton sat still, staring back at his inquisitor with unwavering eyes. His demeanor was one of poise and detachment: the barrister offering a bargain to the court. And it was obvious his was an offer impossible to resist.

"If your client's evidence is worthwhile, Mr. Easton, I am prepared to agree to your terms."

"I will be in touch with you very shortly, sir," William said, extending his hand to the general, then departed the room leaving General Hoffmann sitting in the dim golden light of the brown-leather-filled study. For several long minutes, he sat swirling brandy in a delicate crystal snifter, considering the slight but self-assured man who had approached him with precisely the kind of evidence that brought him to this assignment only weeks before. If he managed to obtain the information he'd been sent to uncover, his efforts would not be forgotten. Lincoln's favor would assuredly be his, and he could name his position in the conflict at hand. History would not forget him.

His slight smile was one of obvious self-pleasure, and Marguerite did not fail to notice it when she quietly opened the double doors to the study. "General Hoffmann," she chided sweetly. "You're one of my favored guests this evening, and you mustn't seclude yourself. Why you'll damage my reputation as a hostess by doing so!" She reached for his arm, and he stood at her direction.

"No one could tarnish your reputation as a hostess, Mrs. Hill."

"Thank you," she smiled graciously. "But weren't you speaking with William Easton?" she said, looking around the study.

"In fact, I was."

"Where did he disappear, would you know?" The general shrugged. "It's not like him to take his leave without comment," she added as if she were puzzled.

"Perhaps he had a great deal on his mind."

Marguerite gazed sharply at Hoffmann. "Perhaps you're right, General. It would be just like him," she added softly, ushering him into the midst of the party-goers. "But for now, General, I *order* you to think of nothing but me and my reputation." And as if to keep her happy, General Hoffmann danced with her into the morning.

Chapter Ninety-six

IN the predawn very shortly after the revelers at the Hill house left for their own homes, William Easton and Arabella Melville were comfortably ensconced in their staterooms sailing for Monterey. Easton was quite satisfied with his encounter with General Hoffmann. He would have his way. The last scene might not be the one Easton had originally expected, but he would have the satisfaction of seeing the last act played according to his direction. He might not have what he dreamed would be his place in a new society, but he would see the other schemers brought to their knees; humbled just as they had humiliated him by placing Senator Taylor above him in their designs. Their crimes, he noted with an odd sense of pleasure, were matters of treason.

Fantasies of hanging men drifted through Easton's head, even in daylight. His head had ached with greater intensity in the last few days, and he was driven to increase the dosage of the powders he took to relieve the pain. At times his hands and limbs shook and at night he did not sleep normally, but lapsed into unconsciousness. His nightmare visions were distorted yet remembered as pleasurable. Melville's swollen and grotesque face encircled by a hangman's noose obsessed him. But the sweetest satisfaction was Easton's notion of Marshall Hudson's death. It was not the physical taking of Marshall's life that pleased Easton as much as what he willed the outcome would be. There would be a young and beautiful widow to console: one who had declined an advance made to her in the past, declined sweetly, as Easton recalled the incident. Probably only the time had not been right. Now,

Easton was certain his time with Louisa was coming. He combined his memories of her with the enticing stories he'd heard, seemingly a long time ago, from her own father, and his eager anticipation invigorated him.

William Easton appeared to have been restored by his trip to San Francisco. Franklin Carson noticed the man's agitation had decreased, and his acceptance of a diminished role in Melville's designs appeared complete. "So Easton is a realist, after all," muttered Carson to himself. By Carson's thinking, the point itself was becoming increasingly moot. On the very day Easton and Mrs. Melville returned to Monterey, California's legislature passed a resolution pledging the state's loyalty to the Constitution and the Union, in spite of the fact that many of those assembled to vote had strong Southern leanings. But, pass it did, and Melville's next decisions followed suit.

Aaron arrived in Monterey two days after Easton, and in two more days he was dispatched to collect a cargo of pirated munitions to be taken directly to Santa Catalina. With Easton's knowledge, definite but unobtrusive packing was being done for the principals at Crane's Nest. The Melvilles and Carson were soon to be on their way for another visit to Herman Brockheim's household. Senator Taylor was not in residence, but messengers kept him informed of all that went on.

There was no mention made of Easton's future. He was very obviously being overlooked. He'd not been evicted from the grand estate, but no plans for him were mentioned. So, unobserved, he decided his own future, and, he hoped, the future of several others.

"Loo Kim," Easton said sternly, "I have an errand of the greatest urgency for you. If you perform as I expect, I will forgive a year of servitude from your contract."

Loo Kim could scarcely believe her ears, and she could not believe the simplicity of the task required of her. He merely planned to send her unescorted to San Francisco with a letter she could not read. She was instructed to hand the letter to a General Hoffmann at the city's garrison headquarters and wait for his reply. Then she was to return immediately to Crane's Nest.

Loo Kim made her way to San Francisco with remarkable ease considering her astonishing beauty, but she had a purpose well worth her while, and nothing, especially uncouth jostling, could distract her.

When Easton's unusual but able messenger sat silently before General Hoffmann, he alternately eyed Easton's correspondence and his agent. Loo Kim also watched the man she had been sent to see, awed by his presence, certain she sat before a person of considerable power. But she did not blanch when he gruffly demanded more information from her, and it was soon apparent she had nothing more to offer.

"I come only to deliver my master's letters, and to await your replies," she said over and over again. Finally, she was ushered to another cold, starkly furnished room where it seemed she waited an interminable amount of time, and when a young sergeant called for her, it was quite dark outside.

"My reply is ready," General Hoffmann said when the door to his office was closed behind her. He handed her a large leather pouch. "Give this to Mr. Easton. Tell him I agree to his terms."

These were the exact words Loo Kim repeated to Easton when she returned to Crane's Nest. Easton accepted the pouch from her hands with no indication of his vast excitement, and although she expected no thank you from the man, she expected some acknowledgement of her conduct in the affair.

But no words were forthcoming, and Loo Kim bowed, leaving the strangely silent man sitting and staring at what she had traveled some distance to obtain. Easton's heart pounded, and when he was left alone, a broad smile of self-satisfaction settled on his face. At first he did not open the pouch, but leaned back thoughtfully into his chair. In exchange for a short listing of unverified names, and the promise of details about an upcoming raid on one of the army's

arsenals and of correspondence to verify the names
he gave, as well as others, General Hoffmann had advanced Easton's client one thousand dollars in gold.
The unverified list alone was extremely tantalizing,
just as William had expected.

It seemed hardly necessary to confirm what he knew,
but Easton counted the payment to the last coin.
There was no stopping him now.

As he had agreed, he wrote Hoffmann what he knew
of the details of plans to pirate munitions. He knew
who would be receiving the crates and barrels, but, he
cautioned, he did not know who among the general's
men had conspired with those he named to deplete
the army of these supplies. Gladly, he gave the name
and a thorough description of the man to be seized
first in this operation—the one who could answer any
unanswered questions. His letter was dispatched as
soon as he finished it, with no one the wiser. And he
waited for the outcome of his actions.

But the nights that followed were longer than Easton
anticipated. Franklin Carson and the Melvilles went
south as planned. Samuel Davis went with them.
Fielder was with Taylor at the capitol, and Easton remained to haunt the estate, diminished in size from his
already small stature by his medications that took away
his appetite, as well as his pain.

The Oriental servants became apparitions in the
corridors; the plants cast eerie shadows on the walls
sometimes reaching out to him as he passed. The paintings stared back at him; the ornaments whose positions
had never varied from month to month appeared in
new locations. At times the furniture seemed to rock
and reel at him. But the worst was the hideous whispering from behind the walls. Yet all the odd events
he'd noticed helped him decide what he had to do. In
fact, he was grateful for these extraordinary signs.
They gave him much-needed counsel when the hours
of the day seemed far too long.

Loo Kim had faithfully done what he'd told her, and
she was now waiting for him aboard a small but comfortable ship. In less than an hour they would begin a

sea journey. He would stop for Louisa Boyd Hudson
in San Diego, for by then she would have received sad
news of her husband. By then she would badly need a
man by her side to comfort and revive her.

At length Easton imagined how wonderful it would
be to assuage the young widow's grief. He could see
Louisa beside him, and together they would pursue his
revised, more realistic plans. The fame, the fortune,
the empire Easton had foreseen with the likes of Simon
Hudson and Peter Melville more reasonably lay in
Mexico's yet to be reopened silver mines, the very
ones Senator Taylor had so glowingly described. All
that had been necessary, Easton acknowledged to himself now, was for him to see this reality of his destiny
clearly. And in spite of the thick smoke that drifted
in his direction as he went to meet Loo Kim, Easton
was certain of his destiny. Burning Crane's Nest and all
of the evidence he'd promised General Hoffmann
gave Easton enormous satisfaction. None of the priceless treasures belonged to him, though on numerous
occasions his imagination had claimed title to most of
what filled the house.

Easton now sat a short distance from the conflagration, watching the interior flames spread rapidly, the
window coverings evaporating to reveal orange bonfires
behind glassed windows. He imagined the rich, not-to-
be-duplicated furnishings, paintings, books, and art
objects turning to ashes. How quickly the trappings
of wealth could be reduced to insignificance! But, he
also considered, how easily these refinements of life
could be replaced if one had the means. Easton
clutched a satchel containing General Hoffmann's advance payment and suddenly urged his horse toward
the bay.

He had lingered at the fire until he was positive nothing of value remained, viewing his destructive act as
his revenge against his enemies. He was proud of having tricked a clever general into financing his new
Mexican venture and smiled with satisfaction over his
insane act. He would have all that he wanted now.

As he approached the waterfront, William Easton

thought of Louisa Boyd Hudson again, and smiled to think of her. She was someone who knew, just as he did, how to purge herself of her enemies. She would understand his actions this afternoon. She would know and applaud the means he had chosen to cleanse his spirit for her.

Chapter Ninety-seven

The weather favored them and they arrived in San Francisco two days early. They lay off the coast one night, then landed, confining almost all crew aboard ship for the additional night. But Aaron went ashore, a privilege of his position, for a change. Many times in the past, he had been penalized just as the crew of the *Crystal Mae* now were, but, happily, tonight there had been little grumbling from the men. Captain Hansen was not injudicious, and his crew had relative ease compared to Aaron's memories. It simply would not be wise to let the men loose on the town the night before they would load a considerable quantity of stolen arms and munitions. These days it would be too easy for rumors to fly in this city. There was far too much temptation here, and the city was more ripe than usual.

Dressed as a seaman, Aaron drifted aimlessly along the waterfront, and eventually into the saloon district, remembering his last excursions there. He wanted a woman tonight, and though he was in no mood for self-denial, the girls who willingly offered themselves for a price from the doors of innumerable canteens had little allure, and he kept walking. Eventually he passed Elena's, where he'd been a frequent customer of the much-touted Rita, but Elena had her standards to maintain. He would not be permitted upstairs dressed as he was now. She fancied her merchandise above the common customer.

Not much later he passed Melville's stone house, noting it was lighted, but for no one but the servants these days. He wondered what brought him as far as he'd come in his meanderings. He'd been very restless lately, and tonight it seemed especially good to get off the confining ship and walk. Why was he now thinking a ship confined him? What had this damned assignment done to him, he wondered. All he could think of lately was returning to his former existence. What alternative did he have? After all, before Russell snatched him off the coast, he was living the life of his choosing, was he not? In any event the only life he was likely to know.

In his wanderings, he came to Marguerite's darkened house, stopping before it. There was faint light in her bedroom—the one place in the house with which Aaron was well acquainted! She'd soothe him for the night at least, he thought. The question was, where was Colonel Hill? And if he was absent, was she alone? Aaron smiled to himself, knowing the lady's appetites. Was she discreet enough to not question his sudden appearance or his manner of dress? His temper was such that he really didn't care whether his actions created a stir. Daily the whole California affair was going more sour. Risk was not alien to his nature, nor to this assignment, after all.

He might have gone to the front door, but the idea of scaling the Hills' fence, and breaking into the house, in addition to the pleasure of contemplating the probable rewards, were enough to make his decision easy. Within seconds he was over the locked ironwork fence, and, in a few minutes, easily climbing the carved porch pillars to a second-floor balcony. The window was another matter. It was locked securely. The French doors were also secured against intrusion, but a thick carpet running the length of a hallway to the very edge of the doors would silence any broken glass.

Aaron pressed the small pane of glass nearest the handle with the heel of his boot until it shattered almost silently, smoothing the edge of the window frame so he could reach his hand safely through to the door's handle. Perhaps he had another calling ahead of him, if, in fact, he found life at sea too confining. He smiled as he let himself into the house with relative ease. The hallway was dark, but once he maneuvered to the stairs, it would not be difficult to find his way to Marguerite's room. He'd found it in the dark many times before. Indeed, he could find her room on the third floor with his eyes closed, if necessary.

But was the lady alone and unoccupied tonight? He listened outside her door for several minutes, not hearing a sound, reluctant to try the door.

Then suddenly the light in Marguerite's room went out, and he heard what sounded like someone getting into bed. Aaron waited several long minutes, hearing no other sound. He smiled to himself. If the lady were not alone, there would not be so much silence.

He waited a few more minutes, then entered the room noiselessly, watching the small dark figure beneath a satin down comforter. He listened to her sigh and turn over, and before another moment passed the flash and fire of a pistol, the first bullet passing within inches of his face. Instinctively, he fell to the floor.

"Marguerite!" he shouted. There was another shot, this time well out of his range. She was firing blindly, and he lunged at her, struggling with her silently, at last covering her mouth with his hand, choking the breath from her, until she heard his voice and at last relaxed in his grip.

"For God's sake, woman!"

"For God's sake, nothing!" she retorted, kneeing him gently but pointedly. "Get under the bed, without another word!" she ordered. And he scrambled for the hiding place just as her door flew open. Three servants, two with lamps, and all in a very excited state burst into the room.

"Madam!" a middle-aged man cried when he saw her calmly sitting in the middle of her bed, her small revolver dangling casually from the index finger of her upraised right hand.

"I believe my imagination got the best of me, Harrison. There's entirely too much tension in the city these days. I thought I heard someone. It was nothing. Go away now."

"Shouldn't I send for the colonel?"

"No. Of course not. This silliness isn't worth disturbing him at his post. Do as I say and go," she said, with annoyance this time.

Astonishment was clearly written in all of their faces, each furtively surveying the room with their eyes, following Marguerite's orders reluctantly, but obediently. All the while she sat smiling with odd amusement in her dark eyes, her hair and gown disheveled, as if she'd been in some sort of struggle. The servants' expressions showed they questioned her, but there was nothing for them to do but finally retreat as she'd demanded.

Marguerite waited, enjoying every moment she kept Aaron stretched unseen beneath her bed. "You may come out now," she giggled. "Whatever possessed you to do that? You could have got us both into a peck of trouble!"

"Let's say it never occurred to me you'd have it in mind to defend your virtue," he said without a hint of anger, swiftly loosening the straps of her sleeveless gown, burying his face in the softness of her breasts.

"You are a very reckless man," she murmured, "more so than I would have ever dreamed. Is that what makes you so desirable, sir?" And they exchanged few other words until he left in the early, still dark morning.

"You have my permission to come this way again, anytime you choose," she said when he was dressed and ready to leave. "I'll not fire so quickly next time."

"I'd just as soon take my chances at Elena's, and pay your exorbitant fees," he laughed.

"What brings you to my door in such an unorthodox style? You're all getting a bit queer lately, it seems to me. Must be all this war business."

"What do you mean?"

"Easton called on me not long ago."

"So?"

"So? Well, he wanted an introduction to General Hoffmann, which of course, was a simple matter. But instead of asking outright, he slithered around me until I could bear it no longer and had to ask what it was he wanted of me." She giggled. "I thought for a moment he wanted what you always come for." She paused and her voice suddenly took on a very serious tone. "What *do* you come for, Marshall?"

Aaron didn't answer immediately, but sat on the bed again, taking her face in his hands. "You've always known just what I wanted. At least, I've never gone away wanting more than you gave." He kissed her mouth, hoping she'd not question him further. "But next time, I'll try a more formal approach." He covered her with her satin comforter. "Let me make my exit with less excitement than I made my entrance. I know the way." And he left her smiling at him in the darkness.

Aaron went out the way he came in. The morning air seemed excessively damp, and all of a sudden especially heavy. He turned up the collar of his pea coat, and walked swiftly toward the *Crystal Mae.* So, he thought, William Easton had wanted and obtained an introduction to General Hoffmann. What for? If Peter Melville had wanted to establish contact with the general he certainly would not have sent Easton as an intermediary, Aaron reasoned as he hurried along the fog-wet streets.

Tonight Aaron's instinctive wariness was unusually keen as something ill-defined began to gnaw at the back of his neck. He knew for certain the raised collar of his coat would not ease the feeling, and he began to move and feel like a stalked animal once again. Instincts he'd almost forgotten were still available from the recesses of his more haunted past, and he called on them once again for reasons he was not yet sure of.

Chapter Ninety-eight

AARON did not stand watches. He was not officially a member of the ship's crew. His name was not listed in the ship's log, even as a passenger. But often out of habit, he would stay above decks the span of a watch, if there was no other matter to claim his attention. Usually, when he did, he did his share of work, and today he handily spliced line. To any who noted his occupation, it appeared he was thoroughly absorbed in his task. His hands did their work mechanically, in mindless repetition, but his mind was not idle. He sat in the damp, dull morning and mulled over Marguerite's remarks about Easton, conjecturing the man's purposes, and the information he could pass, if he chose. Aaron weighed the possibilities. He had never regarded Easton seriously. Perhaps he had been wrong not to. But it was an error Aaron felt sure other members of the conspiracy had made, as well; a fact which could make Easton all the more dangerous now.

Aaron reviewed his information about Easton. He knew the documented details of the man's life, and had observed him firsthand. William Easton was not an ordinary man by anyone's standards. He was a man overly impressed with his own worth; inclined to pettiness; autocratic. He appeared refined, cold, efficient. He was ambitious; otherwise, he would never have joined the men with whom he plotted.

Then suddenly without discussion, without his consent, Easton had been replaced in the schemes. Everyone involved had believed Easton accepted these changes without a murmur. But this Aaron doubted. Easton may have reconciled himself to the new situation, but, Aaron suspected, chances were Easton would be vindictive. There was certainly nothing in the man's demeanor to suggest he was particularly generous. He would never accept his dethroning philosophically. More than likely, he would plot the destruction of his enemies. The question was only when and where.

In the morning the *Crystal Mae* weighed anchor and moved to a new mooring. Late that night, they were approached by a nearly invisible boat, followed almost immediately by another when the first cargo was unloaded. A methodical, rhythmic string of boats approached the *Crystal Mae,* one after the other, distributing their crates and barrels with precision in the silent, black night.

No one should have been the wiser. To the uninformed observer there was nothing of note going on aboard Hansen's vessel. She was only doing what she claimed: waiting for cargo and passengers yet to arrive from Carson City. But there were no uninformed observers. All those who watched had extraordinary information. They knew what they watched, when to pounce, and who in particular they wished to snare. The only information they lacked was who was responsible for pirating the damning government cargo. There was no clue in the dark night, and every attempt to follow the small boats that sailed to the *Crystal Mae*'s berth failed.

When General Hoffmann threw out his net, he was sure he had what he wanted. He demanded enough evidence to hang his captives, or at least the principals, and when he gave the signal, dark-clad soldiers, as inconspicuous as the ghosts who wordlessly paraded the ship's decks clamored from out of nowhere on the pier. Their prey was totally unprepared for seizure. Almost no one aboard had anticipated interruption; there had not even been a guard posted. It was as if the crew merely engaged in a business transaction, and not an act of war.

But there was no mistaking Gereral Hoffmann's intent, and his soldiers understood their orders were extremely serious. They were to subdue all those aboard the *Crystal Mae,* and one man in particular. It was Marshall Hudson, as well as the illegal cargo, that the general wanted. Marshall Hudson had been carefully identified as the key to unraveling the rest. Above all he was to be captured. Three of the general's hand-picked soldiers dragged the marked man before their commander, and Hoffmann breathed more freely than he had since he'd given the exceptionally beautiful Chinese agent payment for Easton's client. With Hudson's capture, Hoffmann had every reason to believe the other men on Easton's list were authentic.

General Hoffmann stared at Marshall Hudson, noting the man's apparent arrogance despite the fact he'd taken quite a beating from his captors. From out of the bloodied face burned deceitful and disrespectful eyes. If he were a sample of the types who favored the South in this state, Hoffmann concluded, martial law should be declared until the crisis was well in hand. California was on the brink of being turned upside down.

It seemed odd to him that the conflict that gripped the nation so many hundreds of rugged miles away could have so seriously disrupted this state's far-flung population. But, General Hoffmann reflected, causes were not solely a matter of geography: above all, causes afflicted men's hearts. He watched his soldiers struggle fiercely with the man he sought most for questioning, and, probably, execution if the information he'd been given proved correct, reminded that greed often determined men's politics above more noble emotions. In the end, Marshall Hudson's reasons for treason would be of no consequence; it merely would be interesting to know what motivated the man.

Hoffmann suspected, as he glared into the arrogant young man's eyes, commitment to principles did not chart this man's course. Marshall Hudson had the look of pride and insolence that damned him even before his case was heard. And, in Hoffmann's view, this very air of superiority, this sense of right above law, would be what would eventually make the North victorious in the conflict Marshall Hudson's Southern comrades would soon call "Lincoln's War."

Chapter Ninety-nine

LOUISA had welcomed the warm spring weather as she would have welcomed a healing salve upon an open sore. Whenever she relinquished Rachel to any of a number of other eager hands, Louisa and Coffee were inseparable. The mare had trimmed down from months of near idleness, now expecting Louisa to take her out at certain times during the day, neighing impatiently if her schedule was overturned.

Whenever possible, Louisa and her horse flew together across the sand, sometimes venturing into overgrown canyons, or along the river. A few times they had ventured as far as Luther Dobson's property, stopping for a while at Marshall's unmarked grave beneath the oak tree. Louisa had brought Emma there once, and not long afterward she thought she saw a certain drawn look fade from the older woman's face. There was something very soothing about the setting chosen for his grave, a comforting timeless feeling beneath the aging arms of that giant tree. Beneath those heavy dark green limbs, Louisa was certain death held more promise than the grave, and she sensed Emma felt so, too.

Not many weeks after Louisa and Emma's outing, Louisa returned to the compound with both horse and rider exhausted, surprised to see a strange carriage secured in front of the house. She couldn't begin to speculate who would be visiting, but the expression on Emma's face when she greeted her told her, even before the woman spoke, it was someone she would never expect to see.

"William Easton and little Loo Kim are here,"

Emma said, as if she also found it difficult to believe.

"Oh? What does he want?"

"He hasn't said. But he's made it *very* clear he wants to speak to you—alone."

Louisa patted Coffee and stroked her nose, handing the horse's reins to Manuel. "It could be about anything, knowing him," she whispered sternly, beginning to climb the steps into the house.

Emma reached for her arm. "He looks odd," she cautioned.

Louisa's mouth twisted a little into a tight wry smile. "More so than usual?"

Emma nodded.

"Well, I guess I'd better find out what he has on his mind." Louisa laid her gloves, the one concession she made to a proper riding outfit but only to save her hands from abuse, in the drawer in the hallway, taking a few minutes before the mirror to arrange her hair, then pushed open the door to greet Easton and Loo Kim.

"Hello, William," she said, extending her hand, appalled by his paleness and by the lack of strength she felt in his arms as she shook his hand when he rose to greet her. "Loo Kim, you are as lovely as ever," she said to the girl who stood a few feet behind her master, and the servant girl bowed as demurely as ever. "Has Emma offered you some tea, or perhaps lunch?" she asked, glancing at the clock on the table beside her when she sat down opposite her guests.

"Yes, it's been offered, but I have declined. My appetite, with traveling, has not been good."

Louisa nodded, trying not to stare too obviously as she slowly sized up Easton's appearance. "Tell my why you've come this way," Louisa ventured, hoping to have the interview over as quickly as possible, upset by the man's nearly cadaverous look.

"Surely you've had word by now?"

Louisa shrugged her shoulders. "I've no word of anything worth mentioning, William. San Diego seems to be a very out-of-the-way place. I'm not informed in the least."

He frowned. "I had not intended to bring you the news."

"What news?" Louisa demanded almost impatiently, feeling a sudden wave of tension grip her.

Easton chewed his lip for a moment. Something was wrong. He was suddenly anguished. This would not be the meeting he'd planned with her. But he had come this far, and he was compelled to continue. "Your husband has been seized; condemned as a traitor and sentenced to hang. I did not learn the date set for his execution, but it is possible the event has already taken place."

As he spoke, Louisa's eyes widened and she paled under her suntanned skin. Suddenly she realized she was holding her breath, and she sucked in air, releasing it with effort. She felt as if Easton had struck her head with some heavy object; there was a tremendous pressure on her ears, and a ringing in her head. Her eyes blurred with tears, which for some reason did not run down her cheeks, and it seemed an eternity before she could really focus on her guests again.

"I've heard nothing at all about this," she whispered finally. "Why wasn't I informed sooner? When was he arrested?"

"It's been weeks now. Perhaps no one else knows."

"Why not?" she asked in total surprise.

"The house in Monterey burned. Perhaps they've not discovered where everyone has gone."

"The house burned? How? Where has everyone gone?"

"I expect Peter and Franklin remain at Brockheim's."

"You mean you don't know?"

"Not for certain."

Louisa felt at least as confused as Easton seemed to be. "How is it you know about Marshall?" she asked. "Where is he precisely?"

"I don't know his circumstances exactly, but he was taken prisoner in San Francisco the night he loaded a shipment of stolen government munitions aboard Captain Hansen's ship. It seems the authorities were informed of the maneuver. General Hoffmann also has a very complete list of names of those involved in the conspiracy."

"He does?" Louisa frowned. "How did he come by such information?"

"I can't tell you, my dear."

"So the plot is up, then, William? Is that what you came to tell me?"

"Why, no! I imagined you'd be advised by now. I came to console you in your sorrow. I came to invite you to come with me."

Louisa had no reply. She was too stunned. She raised her eyes to Loo Kim, who seemed not to have moved the whole time she and William talked. Louisa was struck again by the passive beauty of the young woman, surprised she was still at Easton's side in the changed circumstances. "Come with you, William?" Louisa asked, unable to conceal the incredulous note in her voice.

"I'm on my way to Mexico, to investigate and re-open some of her vastly rich silver mines. A man of vision and ambition should be able to see to it easily. The fortune that waits for us, Louisa, is unsurpassed in this century. The mines will produce wealth to ex-ceed anything we've seen in California. There are no real obstacles to opening the mines again. I have the means to accomplish it."

"The means?"

"The capital and the intelligence."

"I see," Louisa said cautiously, "but, as you can see, I am in no position to go with you, William. Your news has taken me totally by surprise. What is more, I have no intention of leaving here, nor of ever travel-ing under your protection."

Easton felt the insult of her words. "You might be implicated in the political schemes," he suggested, choosing to ignore she had declined his offer.

"Did you implicate me?"

"No, of course not!"

Louisa's eyes narrowed on him fiercely. "You're the informer, then."

Easton licked his lips nervously. "You misunder-stand me, madam," he said sharply.

"I have never misunderstood you!"

"Nor I, you, Louisa," he said, calm once more, changing the tone of his voice suddenly to one that made Louisa's flesh crawl, making her remember Easton had been a friend of her father.

Louisa saw Easton read the flash of recognition that passed over her face. Perhaps, she thought, he was not as dull as he appeared. What accounted for his wasted appearance, Louisa wondered all of a sudden, but she had no time to consider the possibilities as she listened in horror and disbelief while Easton spoke of Justin Boyd. "Before he died, Justin told me of your needs, Louisa. He promised me you were most seductive. Is it any wonder I've not wanted to leave without you? All of your life you've been under a man's protection, and I've come to offer mine to you now."

Louisa was astounded, and rose to her feet. "Get out!" she demanded. When Easton did not move, Louisa lowered her voice slightly. The sound of her voice had a hollow, tormented quality that Easton could not fail to respond to. "I said, get out. Get out, or I will have your blood on my hands, as well!" she whispered ominously, and he did not doubt her for a second.

Easton stood quickly, gesturing for Loo Kim to go before him and open the door.

"Loo Kim, you needn't leave with him!" Louisa called after her.

"She is under contract!" Easton interrupted indignantly.

"I doubt you're in any position to contest any breach of contract," Louisa said sternly. "Loo Kim?"

"No, I will go with him, madam," Loo Kim said softly. "I will take care of him," she offered, standing erect, looking poised and strangely determined, for once looking Louisa directly in the eye. "I will see to him. I have promised."

Louisa could scarcely believe Loo Kim would follow after Easton as she watched them leave the compound. In Louisa's estimation, William Easton wasn't entitled to the devotion of a dog. Then suddenly it

Chapter One Hundred

When Emma heard the carriage start up, she came from another part of the house to find Louisa wiping tears from her eyes. "Louisa?" she said.

"It's not over yet," Louisa assured Emma, and quickly related the scant information Easton had given her.

"Surely Easton was the informer."

"I'm certain of it. But why didn't Luther Dobson come to me about Aaron? He surely knows I—you don't suppose he's not heard himself?"

"My God, do you think they'd hang him? After all, he can prove he's been sent here to investigate, not participate in the conspiracy—which William didn't know, of course."

Louisa turned pale. "Wouldn't you think this new general we've heard of would know about Aaron's activities?" Both women were silent, staring at each other helplessly. "If not, he has no means to prove who he is because I have his papers, Emma." Louisa then began to pace the room. "I'll take them to Luther now, and he can send them to the proper authorities. Have Manuel saddle Coffee again," she called to Emma as she dashed to her room.

The trunks Loo Kim had packed in Monterey to be carried by ship had arrived safely in San Diego long before Louisa had. When they arrived in San Diego,

553

Carmen had unpacked Louisa's possessions carefully, but Aaron's papers, which Louisa had discovered in the secret compartment where she had hoped to find her precious necklace, were still hidden there, unless Louisa's memory played tricks on her. While in Monterey, the last thing she had done, before locking the trunks, was tuck Aaron's leather-covered identity papers into that special hiding place.

Now Louisa collected the keys to her trunks, and ran to the storage shed, unlatching the bolt from the heavy door. The heat inside the shed was intense but she hardly noticed, hastily searching for her baggage within the dim interior. When she found the trunk she wanted, she opened it immediately, her fingers finding the leather envelope as soon as she probed the compartment. Louisa's heart was beating furiously, and now she breathed a little easier. Why? Why hadn't Luther come to her with information about Aaron? And why, come to think of it, why was she so upset now? Aaron had been an animal the last time she saw him. Why should she be in such a state over him?

Louisa was frowning, whether over her thoughts of Aaron, or at herself for her great and obvious concern for him, she couldn't say. "He doesn't deserve to hang for treason," she said aloud finally, and continued her haste, leaving the shed door gaping open, mounting Coffee quickly as Manuel held the animal still. "I'll be home again in a few hours," and she hurried Coffee to the harbor.

Louisa had not been into town for some time. In fact in the last few weeks she'd not even considered mingling with the few townspeople she knew, for there had been a severe outbreak of fever in the county. Louisa thought it best not to see anyone outside the compound, and no one within had contracted the fever. Louisa feared most for Rachel, knowing the greatest number of deaths had been babies and small children, though a few adults had died as well.

A watery-eyed sailor sat propped in the shade

against the door of Luther's office. "Excuse me," Louisa said, impatiently reaching over him for the door's handle.

"Ain't here."

"Oh?"

"Ain't been here for days. Since he went out to his place east. Didn't feel well, and he left. Guess he got sick out there."

"Didn't anyone bother to find out?"

"Everybody's sick," and he coughed violently as if to prove his statement. "Not even unloading much. And nobody gives a damn neither, that's how sick they are."

Louisa wasted no further time conversing with the man, doubling back to the river and heading east, afraid of what she'd find once she reached her destination. She felt a tight knot growing in her stomach. Something was wrong, she was certain, otherwise Luther would have informed her of Aaron's capture. Her thoughts raced on just as Coffee did. Perhaps Easton had informed, but Aaron had eluded the trap which had no doubt been set for him. Of course, that must be it! And here she was very upset for nothing!

Louisa slowed Coffee's pace a little. "Nearly breaking your legs for no reason," she said, patting Coffee's neck. Aaron was, after all, a very elusive man, she recalled. How well she knew it. It occurred to her he was probably sitting somewhere quite cozy right now, not the least bit endangered. Yet she continued to travel east, and her pace was not really leisurely.

When Louisa first saw Dobson's adobe house, there was no sign of life, but she tied Coffee securely in front of the house and knocked on the door. There was no answer. She went several yards behind the house to the lean-to, seeing Luther's wagon beside it, and his horse tethered on the far side, in the shade.

Louisa went back to the house quickly, and pounded on the door this time, letting herself in when there was no answer, nearly retching in the close rank air that assaulted her. She squinted her eyes in the darkness, and found Luther alive, but barely so.

"Luther, Luther," she called at him sympathetically. He opened his eyes, appearing to focus on her briefly, then shut them almost immediately. Louisa pulled back dust-thick curtains from one of the two windows in the room, and strained to push open the window on its hinges. In the greater light, Louisa searched for matches and lit the lamp on Luther's small table, to be even more appalled by the condition of the man who lay very ill before her.

Louisa ran outside again and with great effort primed the pump, filling a bucket with water. She ripped up one of her petticoats and tried to soothe the man's fever and wipe away some of the foul debris from his body. She helped him drink, and tried to make him comfortable. Luther babbled at her incoherently, from time to time calling her Dorothy, pleading with her not to leave him.

Her heart sank as she listened and tried to help him, worried that there was nothing she could do, and, if so, nothing she could do for Aaron. In the stinking house, Louisa began again to fear the worst, rapidly succumbing to depression.

Luther lapsed unconscious or slept again, Louisa wasn't sure. While she tried to decide what to do, she rifled through some of his papers, hoping to get some clue about Aaron's situation, but all she found were papers of little significance, and nothing pertaining to the conspiracy. "Of course, he wouldn't leave anything important lying about!" she said crossly. "Luther! Luther!" she called to him when he opened his eyes again. "What about Aaron?" she demanded, then shook her head furiously. "What about Marshall Hudson? Tell me, Luther!"

"Dorothy. You're here," he smiled at her weakly, closing his eyes very quickly again.

"Oh, damn! Luther!" she cried to the unconscious man, putting her head in her hands for a few minutes, resting her elbows on the table. "Now what?" she asked angrily, desperately fearing there was no hope for either Luther or Aaron. Then she stood and partially closed the window she'd opened, and gently covered Luther with another blanket. "I'll send someone to look after you," she promised to the sleeping, unmoving form, and left the property even more quickly than she'd come.

Chapter One Hundred One

Louisa had no idea what to do next. Who could she turn to? Aaron had said Luther Dobson would help her if she ever needed someone. Now Luther was in need himself.

As soon as she returned home Louisa dispatched Anna Sutton and Manuel to Luther's aid. They would remain with him as long as necessary, and Manuel would come for her as soon as Luther's head seemed clear of fever.

But what if he didn't recover? Louisa felt totally helpless. Her thoughts ran on endlessly about Aaron. All day she was swept with familiar, loving sensations, to be very quickly brought back to what she regarded as brutal reality. She felt the violence Aaron had used against her keenly at times, and the sting of his occasionally vicious, low words gave Louisa a clear idea of his opinion of her.

Late in the day, Louisa sat down to rest, without thought reaching for something to ease her thirst, pouring a glass of bourbon. She tried to sort her thoughts out, pouring another drink when the first was gone and no solution to her problems became apparent.

Emma Hudson was no help to her as the two women dawdled over a very late meal that would have been served at midday in ordinary circumstances. Emma said nothing of Louisa's choice of beverage, but Louisa was not oblivious to Emma's anxious glances. "Don't worry," she wanted to say, but didn't. "That's all over now," she reassured the woman silently.

Finally, Louisa pushed her plate away as if in disgust, and she rang for Carmen, who appeared instantly.

"Carmen, where is Alfredo?"

Carmen raised her eyebrows. "Alfredo, señora?" Louisa nodded. "I am not certain." She waited for another question from Louisa. "My sister, his *madre*, should know," she offered finally.

"Find out immediately, and let me know. Also who is the very slender hand we have working here—the man about my size?"

Carmen wrinkled her brow. "Michael Brown?"

Louisa shrugged. "I'm sure I don't know. But get me some of his clothes—pants, shirts, a hat, and a heavy jacket. Give him money to replace whatever you take. Then send the foreman to me."

"*Si*, señora."

"What are you thinking, Louisa," Emma demanded as Carmen left the room.

"I'm thinking there must be something I can do."

"But what?"

"I don't know," she said, rising from the table. "One minute I can barely sit still wanting to do something. Then I remember the last time I saw Aaron, and I'm not as eager to know his fate. . . ." Louisa's voice trailed off. "Perhaps, it would be best if it has ended as Easton said." Louisa closed her eyes, hoping to stop the tears that glistened on her lashes, and Emma knew her last remarks were very much a lie.

Then the dining-room door swung open and Carmen entered the room with a bundle of men's clothes, just as Louisa requested. "I have sent someone to my sister for news of Alfredo. 'Señor Billy waits to see you, also. And so does *la niña*," she said, motioning toward the sound of a fussy baby.

"Emma?" Louisa said, and the woman hastened to her granddaughter, with Louisa following her from the room to greet Señor Billy, the man who oversaw the work within the compound. Louisa quickly led him outside again, and went directly toward the barn. "I need the very best horse we have, the one with the greatest endurance—actually, I'll probably need two of that description."

"We've excellent stock, probably some of the best horseflesh in the county—it's a prejudice of mine."

"Good! And a packhorse, as well. I want you to provision the packhorse for a least a week of heavy travel—nothing fancy, but adequate. Understand?"

"Of course."

"Have them ready by daybreak."

He nodded, and began to carry out Louisa's requests the moment she turned away from him to race back to the house where she grabbed the clothes Carmen had just collected for her. She looked for Carmen in the kitchen and found her mulling over the half-eaten remains of lunch. "Señora, you must eat better."

"I will, Carmen, but, for now, get a needle and some heavy dark thread, and come with me."

Carmen eyed the men's clothes a moment, then followed her mistress who flew down the hallway. By the time she reached her door, Louisa had most of the buttons on the front of her dress undone, and once inside her room, was undressed very quickly. First she tried on the shirts, and Carmen noted how much to decrease the sleeves to make them manageable, then the pants. Their length was basically all right, but there were several inches to spare in the waistband. "Let everything else in the house go, Carmen. These must be ready for me at daybreak."

"*Si* señora."

As Carmen finished with dressmaker's pins, Louisa opened her wardrobe and chose one conventional change of clothes and folded it carefully. "Bundle these and take them to Señor Billy." Carmen nodded. "I'm going to rest now. If Manuel comes back, come and get me instantly. Otherwise, let me sleep. I won't have dinner. Just leave a tray of something in the parlor. I'll eat when I wake up."

When Carmen left her, Louisa at first lay on her bed very wakeful but eventually she slept heavily for several hours. When she woke Louisa found Emma still up and sitting in the parlor. The women said little to each other while Louisa ate from the tray Carmen had left for her. When she finished, she poured herself another drink and stared thoughtfully at the needlework Emma pursued wordlessly.

Now that she was rested, Louisa was both compelled and hesitant about her plans, and she wondered if it could ever be different where Aaron was concerned.

Her hastily made plans seemed to be falling into place perfectly, and she felt almost as if she had no control over them. When she woke, Carmen informed Louisa that her nephew, Alfredo, was working for Eduardo Diaz, one of the few people Louisa knew and liked in the small community. He would help her however he could, she was certain, and word had already been sent for Alfredo to come to the compound. He would likely arrive by midnight. By morning, escorted by Carmen's fierce-looking nephew, Louisa hoped to ride north to San Francisco.

The papers she would carry with her would free Aaron, and with his mission finished, she would be done with him forever. In this respect Louisa's outlook was hopeful. Why then, did she feel so uncertain?

Louisa poured herself another small glass of bourbon, then began to sort through the clothes Carmen had altered so very efficiently. She chose a shirt, and a pair of pants, and the jacket, and set them aside, calling Carmen to take the rest to Señor Billy. "Have him pack these with my other things," she said impatiently.

Carmen only nodded, but cast a worried glance at Louisa before she left the room. Louisa noted the servant's look of concern while she finished the last of her drink, and smiled to soften her command. "Good night, Carmen," she added with a faint, but warm smile. She also bid goodnight to Emma. "I'll see you in the morning," she said as she left the room on her way to look in on Rachel once more.

It was late and Rachel was already asleep for the night. She'd not seen her mother the usual number of hours today, and Louisa missed her. She found it difficult to believe she would be leaving Rachel by choice once again. "I must," Louisa whispered in the dark, stroking the child's satin-soft cheek. "I love you, little one. I won't be gone long, this time," she said, kissing Rachel's slightly damp forehead, gently pushing soft blond curls away from her little face. "Whose

Chapter One Hundred Two

 Louisa dozed in her bed, fully dressed until Carmen came to get her. "Alfredo is here, señora," she said. Quickly Louisa made her arrangements with Carmen's nephew, specifically wanting him to accompany her on the trail. He was an enormous, fierce-looking man, half-Mexican and half-Sandwich Islander, the latter accounting for his enormity. His size and apparent, but deceptive, ferocity were sufficient reasons for making him desirable as a companion, but he also knew the route they would travel as well as he knew the trails in San Diego County. A man from the Hudson compound would be selected by Señor Billy to accommodate Eduardo Diaz in Alfredo's absence, and Louisa sighed as she shut her door for the last time that night. Her plans were made and final.

Yet she was nagged by a feeling that refused to go away: Why should I do this? It's none of my business, after all. I've not been kept informed. My position in all of this affair was made clear from the beginning. I was only an ornament for pleasure and not much else. Aaron knew where his papers were. If he needed them, he'd have sent for them. But did he know, she wondered. The last time he'd seen them, she'd tossed them in his face when she confronted him about the necklace he'd given Marguerite.

Louisa burned again with fury as she thought about her necklace. Aaron had never offered her an explanation nor an apology for his actions, and it was his arrogance that made her most furious. Aaron had always presumed too much in their relationship, she thought. "You are an arrogant bastard," she muttered aloud. Perhaps it had been his downfall.

Louisa poured herself another drink, suddenly seeing Emma's face in her mind's eye as she did so. Tonight Lousa had seen the faint lines of worry on the woman's face turn to deeper ones. She'd seen Emma watch as she poured herself small but frequent glasses of bourbon, consuming them like the veteran she was. "Thank you for sparing me the lecture I deserve," Louisa now sighed in the dark.

She sat without lighting a lamp, staring into the so familiar room, remembering the first night she came into it with Aaron, and how fearful she'd been, and how very soon she entered it by choice. Lately, though, it had been very haunted and lonely.

As it often was, the room tonight was lit only by moonlight, every object having an unearthly soothing brilliance, now exaggerated in Louisa's eyes by the effects of alcohol. Louisa was at that stage where the world looks slightly better than it really is, the place she tried to stay when he drank. Louisa stared at the weighted crystal decanter sitting within easy reach, knowing she could sustain the plateau where she now languished for hours, perhaps days, maybe weeks—at least, she could try. But eventually she would have to descend, "crawl," she said aloud, the truth only slightly jarring the beautiful night.

A breeze stirred and drifted over her, momentarily cooling the ever-present fever she had spent so much time denying, and now tried to drown in bourbon. But the sudden breeze only reminded her how Aaron sometimes playfully tried to cool her heat and how his efforts to do so had failed as well.

In spite of herself, Louisa smiled at the sometimes silly things they had done together, forgetting, again, her vows to put her memories of him away forever. She even smiled in the darkness, and remembered how she laughed at him while he insisted he could cool her fever by blowing gently along the curves and hollows of her body when, after making love, her heat would linger. She would thrash about the bed trying to get comfortable, kicking off the covers, opening a terrace door. Aaron would capture and hold her down, and talk about her hot blood, blowing his cool breath across her skin at her throat, dipping his tongue between her breasts, then licking each nipple slowly, descending to her belly. When he finished, her temperature was much higher, but he always managed to distract her from it.

When she dared to think about him, Louisa's thoughts and especially her emotions were a patchwork of confusion. She recalled her pleasure very clearly, and far too many times it seemed as if he were only inches from her, not long miles. The feelings never seemed to diminish, nor did the ache. If anything, it deepened. When she countered those memories with unpleasant ones, Louisa only covered her feeling of love for Aaron with a thin dressing, not unlike the way she in the past had tried to drown pain with alcohol, and the effects were much the same: only temporary.

"God, Aaron! You make me crazy!" she screamed in the empty night. "You make me *crazy!*" Tears ran down her face, and she put her head on folded arms and cried. There had been no answer in the lonely room, only another drafty gust from the night wind.

Louisa sat up again, and stared at the bourbon decanter glistening before her. "You may make me crazy, Aaron," she whispered gently as though he were next to her and she could caress him with her words, "but I promise I'll help you, if I can. Only—only, I wish I didn't love you."

She reached again for the liquor-filled bottle, starting to pour another drink. Then before she poured a drop of the golden liquid, Louisa abruptly stoppered the container. "You make me crazy, too," she cried, heaving the decanter powerfully through a lace-edged window a few feet away. She stared after her handiwork, smiling contentedly. "I should break every bottle in the house," she concluded, greeting Emma and Carmen with a simple and satisfied expression when they burst into the room moments after the crash of glass woke them both.

They stared even harder at her when she calmly turned to them and said, "Goodnight," then turned

Chapter One Hundred Three

DAYBREAK seemed to come exceptionally early the next day. Manuel came as expected to say Luther Dobson was no better. *"La señora* say he is *malo."*

Louisa had expected nothing more in the way of news from Anna, but she had hoped for decent weather, her spirits this morning depressed by a constant drizzle. In addition, her head pounded unmercifully, the fact she had brought this form of pain on herself doing nothing to improve her condition.

But within half an hour after sunup, Louisa and Alfredo were ready to travel. Louisa was disguised by Michael Brown's clothing, her face concealed very successfully by his wide-brimmed hat, her hair pinned severely against her head. Her sex was further concealed under the loose oilskin drape she wore as protection against the wet morning.

As they left the compound, Louisa felt as weighted down by her strange clothing as she did by the task she had taken on, and though her mind was set on San Francisco, she was still burdened by fear and misgivings.

What if she was too late?

No. She had to put that thought aside.

Louisa reasoned her journey would be hard, at best, whatever Aaron's fate. She prayed for Aaron's safety, but she had no other expectations. It seemed obvious she and Aaron had no future together, nothing good to offer each other, spewing hatred, anger, and distrust at one another, and when she dwelled on that part of their experience, she could forget the loving.

Now the harshest of memories fueled her and

made her strong, able to face the difficult road stretching nearly the length of California from San Diego
to San Francisco. She traveled without illusions and
beyond the pain of her relationship with Aaron. In
one corner of her heart, she accepted the knowledge
that she loved him, but, as it was between them, as
he had last left her, there could be no accommodation.
Louisa knew very well there were some things in life
one could not have, ever, no matter how desperate
one's desires.

It was plain Aaron would never come to her on
her terms. He was far too arrogant, too independent,
too selfish, perhaps even too cruel. She would not
spend her life crawling after him, eating whatever
morsels he offered from his hands. She could not,
would not, sustain herself on blind devotion. At least,
Louisa consoled herself, when they separated this
time, they would part definitely and finally, and she
could begin to live again without him. Again she
entertained the hope she would be free, at last.

On the road the first day, it drizzled continuously.
They traveled slowly, stopping only when light gave
out. The night was wet, uncomfortable, and endlessly
long, but the sky was clear the next morning when
they set out again. They moved much faster on the
second day, continuing until both they and the horses
were well fatigued and it was too dark to travel.

Over the next days their movement north became
a hypnotic, unalterable course. By the fourth day they
traveled well into the night because the sky was clear
and bright. They encountered no one in their journey
to cause them concern, moving with determination,
not stopping in populated places except to buy a
newspaper, hoping for word of some sort. But there
was none.

Louisa's weariness and worry began to show on
her face. She was grateful she had lately spent so many
hours riding Coffee, for she was certain she would
never have tolerated the journey otherwise. The first
days seemed especially trying and she would have
sworn during many of the long hours on the trail that
her mind was completely empty, her total concentra-

tion aimed at staying upright in the saddle. But often her mind focused on Aaron's handsome face, seeing the soul-touching smile he often flashed at her, the same smile that had encouraged her to love him with the intensity she did.

She reminded herself that his smile was one of the reasons he had his way so easily with women, but when she fell asleep, the very instant she lay down on even the hardest of ground, his presence filled her dreams.

When she was awake, she dreamed of finding him alive, ruling William Easton a fool, if nothing else. She occasionally envisioned Aaron sitting comfortably and coolly, not the least in need of her assistance, and the thought of it provoked her anger. Yet part of her hoped it was the case, and that her efforts were unnecessary. Aaron would then have an amusing anecdote among his memories of her, and the thought made her cheeks burn with rage as she pressed her horse to increase his seemingly plodding speed to begin the day.

"One more day, señora," Alfredo promised, and she gave him an exhausted smile. One more day. This was the sixth day, was it not? If Aaron had the cheek to laugh at her attempts to rescue him, she'd spit in his face, she swore. It would be just like him to laugh, she fumed, remembering how his eyes could mock her.

Louisa's charity was wearing thin with exhaustion, and that night she had nightmares of his leaving prison with Marguerite on his arm. "Thank you, my dear," the woman said as she and Aaron drifted out of her vision. And Louisa woke screaming incoherently and sweating, feeling feverish, certain she could slit Marguerite's throat gleefully.

Louisa's sudden outburst startled Alfredo from a sound sleep, and he staggered blindly to her defense, only to confront the empty night. "Sorry, Alfredo," Louisa apologized lamely, and he soon fell asleep again.

Louisa did not have the same luck. She lay awake the few hours until morning, feeling restless and uneasy, grateful that the next night would find them in San Francisco.

When they arrived it was dark, the city's nightly revelry well underway. At first Louisa's only thought was to find a room for the night, but she thought better of the plan, stopping their progress in the city to get her bearings, and think.

When she was last in San Francisco, she had gone out very little at night, or in the day for that matter, and the city was very alien to her. But she remembered that Melville's house had been a prominent landmark, and with some effort they made their way to his gates. It was not the destination she had in mind, she noted when she saw the impressive house and grounds, but from Melville's stone house she hoped she could make her way to Miss Janet Wilson's, praying the woman would recognize her after all these months. There she might change her clothes to the more conventional ones she had carefully remembered to pack. And if the woman were as kind as Louisa recalled, she might brew Louisa a very strong cup of coffee to give her courage. She must see General Hoffmann *tonight*. Tomorrow might be too late.

Chapter One Hundred Four

FROM Melville's house, Louisa proceeded to the seamstress's shop without hesitation even in the dark, wondering if Marguerite was still consulting the woman, or whether someone of greater talent had come to the area. Louisa knocked on Miss Wilson's door, knowing the woman lived alone and would be startled by a late-night visitor. In this raucous city, a knock on the door in the middle of the night was not especially welcome.

There was no answer and Louisa knocked more loudly, feeling more and more frantic. Then Alfredo began knocking too, and soon a lamp was lit inside the house and not much later Miss Wilson's figure could be seen behind the curtains.

"Who is it?" she asked in a calm and businesslike voice.

Louisa sighed with relief. "It's Louisa Hudson, Miss Wilson. Perhaps you remember me. I was referred by Mrs. Hill, if you'll recall."

The woman pulled aside the curtain over the door's glass window, and stared without recognition at the dark figures who stood outside. Suddenly Louisa realized the woman would never recognize her, and tore away her broad-brimmed hat, unpinning her hair swiftly. Slowly the door opened to her.

"Please forgive this unconventional appearance, and the hour, but I have a favor to ask you," Louisa said, stepping into the woman's house.

"Yes?" she said, standing aside for her visitors, closing the door and lighting another lamp in the sitting room that doubled as a waiting room for customers. Miss Wilson surveyed her guests, obviously uneasy in Alfredo's presence, tightening the large shawl she held around her nightgown. "What can I do for you?"

Louisa smiled at the woman wearily. "I need a place to freshen up and change my clothes"—she held out a bundle of clean clothing for Miss Wilson to notice—"and, if you would be so kind, a very strong cup of coffee. I know this is an imposition and must appear insane, but I've good reasons. I'll explain as soon as I can."

"Of course, Mrs. Hudson, come with me. The gentleman can wait here," she said as if she were speaking to one of her customers.

Louisa followed the seamstress into the workroom where she had been many times for fittings after their introduction by Marguerite. "Have you any recent newspaper—perhaps the *Alta California?*" she said, beginning to peel away her travel clothes when the workroom drapes were pulled behind them.

"One or two."

"May I see them?"

"Certainly. I'll get them as soon as I get you some water for bathing, and as soon as I get the coffee started. Something to eat?" she offered kindly.

"Please!" When the woman left her to fill the china pitcher with water for washing away some of her trail dirt, Louisa raised her eyes heavenward in gratitude. Her mind was clouded with fatigue, and she only felt half-alive, yet she'd remembered the one person in this city who might help. Louisa's suspicions had been correct. Miss Wilson catered to Marguerite Hill, for it was her business to do so, but Louisa had guessed it was an indifferent association at best. With Marguerite, Miss Wilson was coldly efficient, and her execution of Marguerite's wishes prompt and artful, but unenthusiastic. Yet, Louisa remembered, Miss Wilson's response to her had been almost warm, quickly filling her empty closet with beautiful gowns, the designs and selection of materials envied and commented on jealously by Mrs. Hill. "I'm not at all sorry you're going home soon, Louisa," Marguerite had said, reviewing Miss Wilson's work. "It seems my dressmaker, the best on this coast, prefers to sew for you. Let's hope someone better comes along, and I can have the pleasure of giving my business to another seamstress. In the meantime, I'll be a little more demanding."

So it wasn't only jealousy over Aaron's affair with the woman that made Louisa dislike, even hate, Marguerite. Other people found Mrs. Hill less than charming. The fact was somewhat consoling.

As she bathed and dressed, Louisa wondered what reaction Marguerite Hill had had to Aaron's arrest. Probably little—it wasn't as if the colonel's wife was loyal to her lovers, after all. Even if Aaron was especially good, he was only one of many, or so Marguerite had confessed.

The newspapers the seamstress brought to Louisa were devoid of any news Louisa was interested in. They rabidly supported the Union cause, and if the papers were any indication of the mood of the city, the fever was high.

Louisa felt feverish herself, but she ignored it, dashing into the night as soon as she was dressed again, and as soon as she and Alfredo had a delicious odd-hour breakfast. One would have thought the two of them were starving from the joyful way they consumed Miss Wilson's food. She joined them at the table, not asking for more information than Louisa gave, but directing them to the fort with a curious expression when she was asked for those directions. "You'll be back?"

"Yes, thank you," Louisa said when they left the seamstress's small shop, patting the pocket of her coat to reassure herself the envelope she'd come this long distance to deliver was safely tucked away, and a few minutes later, her heart began to pound in anticipation as she and Alfredo entered the San Francisco Presidio where, despite the lateness of the hour, she was escorted to General Hoffmann's quarters.

Chapter One Hundred Five

AARON knew something had gone very wrong. He had been imprisoned far longer than necessary. Word should have come from Russell long ago, his identity established, and he should have been released. He'd given Hoffmann and his aides all the information he had, but instead of satisfying them, his cooperation only seemed to make his captors insanely furious. He detailed his work on the Union's behalf at length, but there was little appreciation for his efforts. Each day he was identified in muster as "the prisoner, Marshall Hudson," a situation that grew to be more and more discouraging.

In the several weeks he languished at General Hoffmann's whim, Aaron had been interrogated endlessly. The same stupid questions were put to him until he no longer had an ounce of patience, and the exchanges, which at first had been reasonably polite, became hostile and aggressive. His hosts insulted him, and eventually the prodding raised devils in Aaron's nature, and he responded in kind. Rations were reduced, and he was held in solitary in a nearly airless, damp cell.

The general's rationale escaped Aaron. He'd been cooperative, yet it didn't satisfy the man, and he suspected the general of having reasons of his own for not wanting Aaron's information to prove correct. He suspected it would not suit General Hoffmann's schemes if he turned out to be someone other than Marshall Hudson.

Late one night someone had even entered his cell and roused him with a beating, but the outcome of the attack had been a draw, for though he'd been battered into semiconsciousness, the last thing he remembered of the night was two guards entering his cell to remove his equally disabled attacker. The general's mistake in that case, Aaron reflected later, had been to have him approached before the inadequate rations of food and water had taken their toll. The general had not realized the man he dealt with had known even worse conditions. As a seaman he had been expected to do hard labor, and survive with no better fare than he now received, and it would be a while longer before Hoffmann's prison would turn him into the kind of creature who could not fight back.

Soon enough, however, Aaron began to dream of food and fresh water. He'd grown used to comfort, and the discomfort of hunger was something he hoped he'd never again experience. For a while after his late-night visitor was carried from his cell, Aaron was almost ignored. His rations were thrust at him at regular intervals, but otherwise his days and nights had no interruptions. He grew increasingly miserable with lack of exercise and fresh air, and only a blanket for a bed. In the brightest hours of the day his cell was dimly lit. He only hoped the vermin he saw in that light were not doubled in the dark.

In the darkness, his thoughts were filled with Louisa. In the light of day, with conscious effort, he shoved his memories of her aside. But whenever he slept, amid his dreams of ample food and cool, refreshing water, Louisa haunted him. Then the sensations and gratification of loving her woke him as his body betrayed his conscious repudiation of her. He tried to erase her from those night dreams, to fix his eyes on someone else—anyone else—but he failed.

With these dreams, Aaron's confinement began to get the best of him. He had no clear indication about what General Hoffmann wanted from him that he had not already provided. He already seemed to know the names of the men Aaron identified as members of the conspiracy. He already seemed to know many of the details Aaron gave of the conspirators' latest plans. He had seemed especially interested in the details about Santa Catalina Island, though less concerned about the future plans for restive Indians. Oddly, it seemed what he wanted most was to have Aaron confess to being Marshall Hudson.

Finally, Aaron was advised, if no word came by the end of the week, his capture would be announced to the public, and with the temper of the city what it now was, he should hope he remained in military hands for a swift and efficient death. The mobs, he was cautioned, would not treat him so humanely.

And as the week wore on he thought more and more of Louisa Boyd Hudson, now having more hours to dwell on her than he'd ever wanted. When he'd been summoned to his brief trial in Hoffmann's office, the evidence against him was overwhelming. The officer who spoke for him had nothing but the sworn statement he'd given when he was captured that first night, and he was condemned with little more than the suggestion that if what he'd sworn was true, there had been ample time for evidence to arrive in his favor. No one in Washington had ever heard of him, and they showed him the correspondence announcing that fact. "We have no knowledge," the response to General Hoffmann's queries began.

But as he waited in his cell, Aaron found he was a condemned man in more ways than one. He was condemned to die, to relinquish mortal life, but, he reasoned, the gallows would at least free him of his obsession with Louisa. In these last few days she'd begun to torment him as nothing else in his confinement had been able to do. "Something to be grateful for, after all!" he sneered. Perhaps the chaplain was right—"sweet release" would be his at last.

He began to feel a reprieve from the hangman's

noose would only condemn him to burn, for there was a fire in his blood that would rage for as long as he lived. Perhaps it would smolder unnoticed for a time, but unless the embers were finally quenched, they would flare up at some unsummoned memory, and the heat of his passion would once again sear and scar him.

Finally, he asked what he could do to save himself from her—if that reprieve should come, for almost every condemned man harbors the fantasy of pardon and Aaron was no exception. Surely there was a way to overcome Louisa and the power she wielded, he reasoned. If he could elude the hangman, surely he could outsmart her.

What was her power, her undeniable fascination, her ability to make him weak, to make him vulnerable? How, without his consent, did she have the power to torment him?

The answer came out of nowhere; out of the four corners of his rank cell; out from under the layers of stonework piled carefully around his heart. "You love her," said a remarkably clear voice, "and you will never have any peace until you face it."

Aaron had been alone in the cell for weeks, and he shuddered at the response he was sure he'd heard. He was certain he'd not spoken his curious questions aloud, and though it was nearly pitch black that night, he peered cautiously, even suspiciously about the tiny enclosure. Then he laughed, and his laughter soon became raucous.

He went to the barred door and clenched the ironwork with angry hands. "Come and get me, you bastards! I'm ready," he shouted. "You win! I'm Marshall Hudson!" and he laughed uproariously.

Even dousing with a bucket of ice-cold water failed to quiet his booming laughter. Then for no apparent reason, he was silent, finally leaning with his back against the wall, slowly sliding into a sitting position where he waited the rest of the night, certain he had his answers, believing the gallows would be an easier fate than facing the truth. Humbling himself before

Chapter One Hundred Six

LOUISA felt as if her eyes were full of sand, and, in spite of her anxiety, she knew if she closed them for more than the second it took to blink, she would fall asleep on her feet. She waited with a young sergeant on the porch outside General Hoffmann's quarters. The sergeant's eyes were frankly curious about Louisa, and his interest was not purely military.

Her demand to see General Hoffmann at 2 A.M. was at first met with humor. But when she told the night officer she had information about the prisoner Marshall Hudson, there was no further hesitation. The major had cast her an odd look, and eyed her companion with serious interest for a few minutes, then ordered Alfredo to wait while he escorted Louisa to see the commandant.

While she waited the sergeant offered her a porch chair. "No thank you," Louisa said wearily, afraid she would fall asleep instantly if she sat down, and the two of them stood eying each other in silence until the major appeared again.

"General Hoffmann will see you, madam," he said, and showed her into a modestly comfortable parlor. Almost immediately, the general joined them, and Louisa stood calmly before him, feeling her pulse quicken as he surveyed her.

"You have information about a prisoner," he began, not offering her the comfort of a chair.

"Yes."

"How did you learn he was being held?"

"A Mr. William Easton gave me the information."

General Hoffmann frowned. "And what is your interest in the matter, madam?"

Louisa lowered her eyes, then raised them immediately, to stare directly into the general's. "I don't happen to believe innocent men should be executed for crimes they did not commit."

"You have proof the man is a federal agent."

"Yes. And unless I'm mistaken, he has provided you with a great deal of valuable information."

"The information he has given me is useless," Hoffmann said gruffly.

Louisa's shock was evident. "How can it be?"

"It's not a matter subject to discussion just now, madam. What do you have for proof?"

"First, General, tell me about the prisoner. Where is he? And how is he?"

"He will hang this morning if you fail to produce anything of interest," he said coldly.

Louisa felt her knees give out, and the sergeant reached to steady her. "Perhaps you'll have a chair now," he suggested kindly.

Louisa sat down. She touched her forehead wearily with her hand and took a deep breath to give her strength. Then, from a deep pocket inside her long coat, she withdrew the leather envelope she'd come all this way to deliver.

The major took it from her immediately and handed it to General Hoffmann, who examined the small square of leather with obvious interest. He ran a finger over the familiar seal stamped into the envelope, looking up at Louisa for a few moments, then removed the identity papers, reading them carefully, examining their official seal. "This will have to be authenticated," he said finally.

Louisa nodded. "I'd like to see him tonight."

"It will have to wait until later this morning," he said, handing Aaron's papers back to her. "Bring this when you come—eleven sharp."

"Eleven sharp," she said, smiling for the first time since she'd encountered the general.

"Who are you, madam?"

"My name is Louisa Boyd Hudson."

The general raised an eyebrow.

"It's a rather long story, which also can wait until

we meet tomorrow." She extended her hand to the general, and he took it, staring deeply into her tired eyes. "Thank you," she said wearily.

Louisa hardly remembered the quick ride back to Miss Wilson's shop with Alfredo to guide her, nor did she have any recollection of putting herself to bed on the woman's couch in her parlor-waiting room, but she would never forget the horrible nausea that swept over her when she realized she had arrived in San Francisco only hours before Aaron was to be executed for his all-too-convincing impersonation of Marshall Hudson. His skill had almost cost him his life, and whether or not there was any future for them as lovers, Louisa believed she could not have borne his loss through death. In spite of her jealousies, in spite of her anger, in spite of her dreams, she wanted him to be free, even if she could not have him.

Chapter One Hundred Seven

AARON did not expect the treatment he was receiving this morning. He had expected to go the gallows, but instead, without much explanation, he was escorted to the officers' barracks, served a hearty meal, and offered a bath. He was expertly barbered, and given an expensive stack of clothes which fit him almost perfectly. At first he'd hardly been able to believe the eleventh-hour escape from hanging, but as he studied himself in the mirror before being escorted to General Hoffmann's office one last time, he accepted this twist of fate, and smiled deeply at the face reflected in the glass. He looked reassuringly alive.

As he crossed the fort grounds from the barracks to the general's office, the fog-heavy, late-morning air felt incredibly good. But his smile faded the minute he entered Hoffmann's empty office, remembering the treatment he'd received at the general's command: the inquisitions and isolation, the condemning trial he'd experienced in this very room. And what he waited for now was uncertain. He was told he was to be released, yet an armed guard stood with him in the room while he waited.

Aaron speculated about what news had arrived to spare him, what documentary evidence. He thought of a number of possibilities, never once suspecting his exoneration had been arranged by Louisa until the office door opened and she stood before him looking tired and wan, yet, to his eyes, exceptionally beautiful. But she was not smiling, and in his astonishment, he could only stare.

Aaron stood up, not able to take his eyes from her, at first hardly hearing the general's voice. "Mr. Sumner," General Hoffmann repeated. "I regret your treatment. I cannot explain why the government seems not to know you, though this woman has produced seemingly authentic documents verifying your identity. I've listened to you, and I've listened to Mrs. Hudson's corroborating statements. Your stories are remarkably alike; hers a little less detailed than yours, but, similar enough in outline."

The general sat down at his desk, and Louisa sat in the chair Aaron had previously occupied, while he remained standing behind her, facing Hoffmann impassively. "The reason I've been reluctant to accept your evidence, Mr. Sumner, is because, in truth, you have given me no evidence. All the names you name—Melville, Taylor, Brockheim, Anderson, Phillips, and the others are useless." The general looked down at his hands which he folded before him on the desk top. "I could have executed you as an example of the punishment those guilty of treason can look forward to, and few would have risen to defend you. But few of those you name can be dealt with so expediently. The men you've named are far too prominent to convict on your word alone, and Easton burned all the evidence at Monterey. There is nothing left but ashes at Crane's Nest."

Aaron's face registered surprise.

"You were correct in suspecting Easton as the informer," Hoffmann sighed heavily. "Mrs. Hudson says he's on his way to Mexico. And it's of no use to ask Mrs. Hudson to testify, though she's offered to do so. Her oath would never be taken in a judicial proceeding. Regardless of the mitigating circumstances, her word would be easy enough to impugn, and, never fear, in this case, every ounce of soiled linen would be dragged before the court. Your illicit union would overpower any testimony given." He spoke kindly, but truthfully, his eyes resting on Louisa. He paused, then began again.

"While I believe the evidence Mrs. Hudson has presented, I cannot release you finally from custody until I have authorization from Washington. But with Mrs. Hudson's consent, I can release you to her custody," he smiled. "Perhaps this sentence will be more to your liking," he said, not expecting either Aaron or Louisa's startled frowns. "Of course, other arrangements can be made," he suggested immediately, adding his own frown to theirs.

"No, of course, it suits us," Louisa said quickly, sitting forward in her chair.

"You'll remember, Sumner, your friends remain in custody until you are finally exonerated," the general added sternly.

"I know the agreement, General," Aaron replied drily. "You have my word, I will not abandon my friends at this late date."

Hoffmann nodded. "I've given Mrs. Hudson a receipt for your documents. You are free to go."

Louisa stood up, and the general looked at the young couple thoughtfully. What he had thought would be a delightful way for them to wait out word from Washington did not seem to be a cheerful prospect for the young government agent. Nor did the young woman seem very pleased with his solution to the possibly indefinite wait for official acknowledgment of Aaron Sumner's mission. Though it was obvious she cared a great deal for this man who was now, to the general's mind, adequately identified, Hoffmann was certain she had accepted his proposal only to avoid more delay in obtaining the man's release.

Well, the general shrugged his shoulders, it was something the two of them would have to work out between them. They would never know how grateful he was not to have to hang a man he had suspected all along was innocent. At this moment California was such a tinderbox that he had come incredibly close to ordering the execution of Aaron Sumner if only to set an example, and the lifting of the death sentence was nearly as much a relief to General Hoffmann as it was to the condemned man himself.

Chapter One Hundred Eight

LOUISA gave the driver of Hoffmann's carriage the name of a hotel, and then accepted Aaron's hand. It felt warm and she was reassured by the strength of his grip as he assisted her into the carriage. But they said nothing to each other as they rode along.

Finally Aaron broke the silence. "Thank you, señora," he said with a slight nod of his head. "I'm indebted to you, as well as in your custody." He smiled at her slightly.

Louisa acknowledged his words coolly, but she had no smile for him in return, feeling pushed to the edge of exhaustion, and not the least amused by Aaron's assignment to her custody. She found it ludicrous. Louisa did not see herself in the role of jailer, and if there was a more recalcitrant sort of man to deal with than Aaron, she wouldn't know where to look for him. But, she supposed, Hoffmann was only living up to the letter of his responsibilities. If Aaron disappeared, Hoffmann probably didn't care in the least. Nor did she, for that matter. He was free to go, as far as she was concerned. In fact, it would be easier for her if he did take to the wind.

Louisa looked at Aaron steadily. "I've one last errand in San Francisco. And if you would be so kind, I believe I can accomplish it by this evening."

"Whatever you command, señora." The sarcasm was restrained but obvious in his voice.

Louisa glared at him, but otherwise ignored his tone. "I want to leave for home tomorrow. If we can't book passage south, we can go home the way we came."

"And how did you come?"

"By horseback, accompanied by Carmen's nephew, Alfredo—"

"I know him," he interrupted.

Louisa couldn't miss Aaron's astonishment. "You seem surprised, but you forget, again, I've more fortitude than you give me credit for. I'm not as weak as you wish to believe."

"I've never thought of you as weak. Fragile, perhaps. But not weak."

There was a strangely serious note in his voice, but Louisa was too exhausted to pay much attention. "As I started to say, I would like you and Alfredo to make whatever arrangements are necessary. Alfredo's at the hotel now, waiting. I intend to rest this afternoon, then go out later this evening."

"Whatever you say." This time the remark was passed without sarcasm, and the afternoon progressed as Louisa intended. As soon as possible, she collapsed in her bed at the Piedmont Hotel and slept as if she were dead until Aaron disturbed her at the hour she requested.

Then the three of them—Louisa, Aaron, and Alfredo—ate quietly in the hotel's small dining room. "There's no passage available until next week," Aaron informed Louisa. "Therefore, our horses will be ready in the morning, if you want. But you look like you could spend the next week in bed." Louisa shot Aaron a particularly sharp glance. "Sleeping, of course," he added with only a trace of a smile in his eyes.

"Tomorrow will be fine," she replied, and finished her coffee. "Thank you, Alfredo, I think six is a good hour to start out," she said as the man excused himself from their presence. "I've something to do this evening," she began as soon as they were alone. "I've arranged a carriage to take me where I need to go, but perhaps you'd like to accompany me and wait while I conclude my business."

"I've no better plans for the evening, señora."

"Fine," and Louisa gave him the first smile he'd seen on her face that day, but her eyes had a malicious gleam he'd seen on a few other occasions.

Within the hour the hired carriage pulled in front of the Hill house. "What business do you have here, Louisa?" Aaron inquired with obvious curiosity.

"It's personal," she said as she stepped into the night. "I won't be gone long," she promised, turning away from him quickly.

A servant opened the door for her, and as she had suspected from the lights in the house and from the gay noise, Marguerite was entertaining. Tonight the collection of guests was small, but Louisa was not expected to be among them and Marguerite's total surprise was evident, "My dear!" she cried when she turned her attention from a guest to see Louisa.

"Why, Louisa," echoed the colonel. "We'd heard you were in San Francisco!"

She smiled faintly at Colonel Hill. "Good evening, General Hoffmann," she said, nodding to the man standing next to the colonel's wife. The general reached for her hand, and she extended it warmly, as if they were long-term acquaintances.

"I apologize for intruding on your gathering," Louisa continued, standing with her cape still wrapped around her shoulders, "but, before I leave tomorrow, I had to speak with you, Marguerite. This was the last occasion I had to call on you before I left."

Marguerite was flushed. "Why yes," she said pleasantly. "Let's go to my room and talk. You'll excuse us; we promise not to tarry," she said to her guests as she took Louisa's arm and led her to the stairs.

"I'm surprised to see you," Marguerite said in an especially hushed voice as they climbed the stairs to her third-floor room.

"I'm sure you are." Louisa was noncommittal, saying nothing further until Marguerite's door was closed behind them.

"What is it you want, Louisa," she began testily, her politeness vanishing suddenly.

"Not long ago you were given a pearl pendant that belongs to me. I want you to return it."

Marguerite smiled slyly, and there was very real amusement in her voice. "You're referring to a trinket I received from a mutual lover?" she inquired. "I'm not certain which gift you're referring to, but I do remember the man," she added with a wistful note in her voice for Louisa's benefit.

"You remember the gift as well, I'm certain," Louisa said casually. Then her eyes narrowed. "I'm also certain General Hoffmann would be most interested in your 'association' with a number of men."

"What concern could he have with my affairs?" Feeling secure in her position, Marguerite's smile broadened and her voice softened.

"I'm sure you know of Marshall's arrest?" Marguerite nodded. "You're one of the few. As Colonel Hill's wife you often come by information others have yet to hear."

"I also understand your 'husband' was released into your custody, Louisa. That should be interesting—I should have loved to have him released into mine."

Louisa's eyes flickered hatred, and she made an effort to control herself. "Unless you return the necklace to me now, Marguerite, I shall inform General Hoffmann of your many liaisons with the men who have plotted to overthrow the government."

"Really, Louisa!" Marguerite laughed. "I have a fondness for souvenirs, otherwise I'd gladly hand the bauble to you." She obviously enjoyed taunting Louisa. "After all, *you* have so many mementoes of the man, can't you spare me one?"

"If it were a memento from Aaron Sumner, the man you knew, the man with whom we've both shared so many pleasant hours, it would be one thing. But it is a 'trinket' of another sort. And I have every intention of not leaving here without it." Louisa sat down on the bed as if she intended to stay for a while. "Really, Marguerite, you do underestimate General Hoffmann. Not everyone is as tolerant as the colonel, and the

countryside is, as the general described it—a tinderbox. How long do you think your husband would keep
his position if it was known that his wife consorted
with many of the men on the general's list headed
Suspected of Treason? How long would you continue to
flourish in the style you so love if Hoffmann were to
hear those names in connection with yours? These are
very different days than even the last few months have
been. Are you prepared to give up all you have?"
Louisa asked, stroking the satin coverlet on Marguerite's bed. "If you make it necessary, I'm prepared
to tell a very interesting story to your husband's superior officer. And what is more, he will listen. If suspicion is enough to hang a man, as it nearly was in
Aaron's case, surely suspicion is enough to end a man's
military career."

Marguerite was no longer cheerful. Nor did she
doubt Louisa's intention to do just as she said. She
tossed her smoky dark curls, and took a deep breath,
despising the bargain, pouting as she opened her jewel
box and removed Louisa's glittering necklace. "It's
gaudy—I've had little occasion to wear it," she said,
carelessly dropping the necklace into Louisa's outstretched hand.

Louisa caught her precious necklace, cradling it
gently in her hand, watching the diamonds that shimmered about the tear-shaped pearl as they glittered in
the lamplight, and some of her weariness seemed to
ease from her. But it was not enough just to hold the
keepsake in her hand, and Louisa quickly fastened the
pendant securely around her neck where it lay against
her skin. Louisa closed her eyes and touched the pearl
at her throat, then stood to look at herself in Marguerite's mirror. She saw the dark-haired beauty standing behind her and she read the woman's animosity,
the sneer she had for Louisa's fondness for a souvenir
from a man she had loved. "It's something you will
never in your lifetime understand, and I pity you for
it," Louisa whispered.

Then she turned around to face the woman. "Good
evening, Mrs. Hill. The pleasure this evening has been

Chapter One Hundred Nine

THE next morning Aaron expected to find Louisa waiting for him in the hotel's lobby when he came down. But instead he found only Alfredo. There was no sign or word of Louisa. Finally Aaron went to Louisa's room and knocked, and when there was no answer he turned the doorknob to find it locked as he expected. He knocked again, and once more there was no response.

At first the hotel desk clerk was reluctant to disturb her, but a look on Aaron's face made him think better of declining the man's request. As soon as her door was opened, Aaron could see she was still sleeping, and he went to her and sat on the edge of the bed. "I suggested you stay over until the boat sails, but you insisted we leave today, and you named the hour," he said, touching her shoulder as she lay on her stomach with her face turned away from him. But she didn't stir. "Louisa," he said, shaking her gently, and then he felt the incredible temperature of her body and the dampness of her bedclothes from the sweat that poured from her. "Louisa," he said still more loudly, turning her in the bed to face him. She opened her eyes, instantly closing them against what seemed like the morning's blinding brightness. Her mouth was dry and her lips were already cracked with fever. When she tried to speak no sound was heard, and the effort was greater than she seemed able to repeat.

Aaron raised her a little on the pillows. "My God, woman, you're on fire!" he said, wiping glistening perspiration from her face with a handkerchief. "I'll get a doctor." Louisa tried to protest. "This time you've no choice but to do what I say." But he said it with a smile and with worry in his eyes, which in her weakness Louisa failed to see.

The doctor had little to say after Alfredo informed him where they'd come from and the contact she'd had with Luther Dobson's illness. "Keep her from getting chilled and get as much liquid in her as possible, even if she sends it right back," he ordered. "And don't be surprised if she gets to be much worse. I hear a number have died—mostly children and babies though," he concluded without much encouragement.

"I'm an unlikely nurse," Aaron said to Louisa when the doctor left, "but you're stuck with me." And Louisa closed her eyes, vaguely aware of being bundled in blankets and lifted to a chair, while her bed was made fresh and she was assisted into a clean nightgown. She was forced to drink liquids she didn't taste, and it seemed whatever she swallowed reappeared with violent and exhausting regularity. Someone was with her whenever she opened her eyes, yet she seemed not to get any rest. She was far too frequently sick, wishing to be dead quickly and not to die over a prolonged period as she seemed to be doing.

At times Louisa felt she was freezing, and Aaron covered her with blankets, but her teeth still chattered. Sometimes he held her close, not sure she was really cognizant of what was going on. He hoped the warmth of his body, the security of his arms would help her, knowing nothing else he could do, noticing that her frightful shaking was relieved when he held her.

The San Francisco weather was dismal and cold, the dampness pervasive, and Aaron felt it even more than Louisa did. But the chill that settled over him was not only a matter of climate, for in his hours of longing and denial, and occasional regret, there had been some eternal flame of hope flickering in spite of his doubts and uncertainties; some remote confidence.

Now the fever and weakness of Louisa's body made Aaron despair. She was alternately burning with heat, then shaking with cold. Aaron helped her drink broth or water or specially prepared juices from the

hotel kitchen as often as she would allow. He tried
to keep her warm just as the doctor had ordered,
but was frustrated by her temper when she threw
off the blankets, seeming to exhaust herself in fits
of childish tantrums directed at him. Other times
she would huddle beneath those same covers fearing
she would never again be warm, welcoming his arms
when he held her.

Sometimes she slept against him, other times she
stared vacantly about the room having no idea where
she was. Occasionally she would push away from his
grasp and stare at him weakly, his few words, even
his voice, confusing her, but then she would lean
against him once more, sometimes sighing deeply as
she went back to sleep.

That day seemed long and the night interminable.
On the second day, Louisa seemed no better, but no
worse, Aaron reassured himself. Her fever was
still incredibly high, and though she still slept fitfully,
she began to keep down some of the fluids Aaron insisted she consume.

The second night passed even more slowly than the
first. Louisa stared for long hours into the dark moon-
less night. She felt Aaron's presence, his arm around
her, his body providing heat and comfort whenever
she permitted his closeness, and her vanity surfaced.

She wondered how dreadful she must look, feeling herself swim in the sweat of fever, knowing well
how tangled her hair must be from her tormented
thrashing. Yet, when she could see through her haze,
she saw sincere concern on Aaron's face, wondering if
she could read more; she was afraid, praying now
only for recovery, remembering Luther Dobson.

She most feared she would never ever hold Rachel
safely in her arms again. When she thought of her
soft round child, Louisa's eyes would fill with tears,
and she struggled to stop her sobbing, finding her
bouts of crying left her even weaker. She did not
really regret her efforts for Aaron, her regrets lay much
deeper than that. When she found his arms around
her in the night, she hoped it was more than illness
that left her numb and unfeeling, and her conflicting

emotions only made her already confused mind reel.

He was there hour after hour, looking after her needs, as faithful and with a look as worried as any she'd seen on Carmen's face. That night when the the fever finally broke, whenever she stirred in the darkness she would hear her name on his lips. She woke from her distorted dreams, thinking she heard him say he loved her, needed her, never wanted to be without her again, but she could only sigh, unsure enough of reality, especially in the dark, to keep silent.

When she woke in the morning, she was alone, with her head aching, yet reasonably clear. She did not feel strong enough to move, so she lay stiff and uncomfortable, wondering what she had dreamed the last few days, and what had been real. For once, she was terribly thirsty, even hungry.

She was not awake long before Aaron and two women she did not recognize entered the room with armloads of clean linen and pots of steaming water. It was a sight which buoyed Louisa beyond Aaron's expectations, and it was he who remained to assist her, peeling away her ruined nightclothes, covering her with clean linen, bathing her parched, uncomfortable body, little by little, with soothing hot water and fragrant soap, careful to see she did not get chilled. She was embarrassed by her condition, but much too much had passed between them to make the gentle care he now gave her anything but restorative.

When she was clean and dressed in a soft nightgown her tangled hair combed and tied, she lay gratefully in the fresh bed. She smiled at Aaron and closed her eyes and slept, exhausted but confident that she would be well and hold her child again.

Aaron let her sleep, looking after his needs, refreshing himself. He sat with her into the morning, held her in his arms, steadying her shaking hands so she could drink countless cups of tea, beginning to quench her thirst. She ate some fruit and bread, but the strong lemon-laced tea was what she really craved.

Louisa slept most of the day and had no energy to protest their continued stay in San Francisco.

"We'll sail next week," he told her, when she asked about going home, but they said very little to each other. Louisa was still weak and not inclined to speak, and when she was awake she watched him, and he watched back, knowing when the time came, when she was strong enough, Louisa Boyd Hudson would have words enough. What needed to be said could wait.

In the night, he held her again, and his body felt so familiar, his scent wonderfully soothing. She smiled at the hardness of his body he could not conceal, and when he did not advance against her, Louisa turned to face Aaron and put her arms around him in loving welcome. As he began to speak of his love and his regret, Louisa sighed deeply in his arms, letting him take her gently, slowly but eagerly going with him, and as they made love, Louisa knew for certain she had not always been dreaming.

Chapter One Hundred Ten

A week later, Louisa was only just beginning to regain her strength. She could have easily stayed a while longer in San Francisco before traveling south, but Aaron knew when she was able to walk to the hotel-room door without her knees giving way, it was useless to try to persuade her to stay on.

"I'm glad we didn't stay," Louisa said at the ship's railing just before the anchor was weighed. Her cheeks were bright with color, but from the cold wind on the bay, not from fever.

She didn't stay above deck long, retreating to a very confined cabin in a ship more accustomed to modest passengers than those who required luxury. "It'll be all right for the few days we're aboard," Louisa whispered. "It's not like we're going around Cape Horn." She undressed and put on a warm nightgown. "See, I can rest just as well aboard ship as I could in a hotel room. *Better*, since I know I'm going home," and Aaron lifted her into his arms, and into their bunk.

"Get some sleep this afternoon. We'll have dinner with the captain. He rarely has the likes of you at his table," Aaron said, kissing her and seeing the covers pulled around her protectively before he left the cabin.

Aaron knew there remained a great deal to say to Louisa. In the last few days, they had loved each other again, and their encounters had been almost unbearably satisfying. Yet he knew it would only be a matter of time before they would have to meet each other face to face and speak of things that would otherwise always come between them.

At least he knew *he* had a few things to say. He hoped it would be the beginning of a lifelong dialogue with her, and not the end of a short conversation, but he'd sworn to himself during one of those hellishly long nights when she was sick, he would not begin with her again unless he spoke his mind once and for all.

He smiled as he climbed topside: at least aboard ship, there would be nowhere for Louisa to run. She would have to hear him out this time.

The anticipation of at last clearing the air with her could almost be read in his face at dinner. Louisa was for once ravenous, and even the modest meal seemed delightful. She noticed Aaron's edginess, but dismissed it lightly, for he always seemed a bit restless at first when they went to sea.

When they retired to their cabin, she was ready to sleep again, the captain's brandy having had a very mellowing effect.

"Don't go to sleep yet, señora," Aaron insisted.

"Mmmm. Why not? I can barely keep my eyes open," she whispered, snuggling against him. He sat up suddenly, and his movement in the bunk jostled her unpleasantly. "What is it?" she demanded, not concealing her irritation.

"Louisa, we have a number of things to discuss."

"Not now, please," she said, trying to pull him under the covers again. When she realized he was immovable, she opened her eyes and frowned at him, then plumped the pillows behind her head and leaned into them. "What is it, Aaron?"

"I don't intend to go around and around with you again until we have a few things settled." There was a definite determination in his voice which made Louisa's sleepiness disappear all at once.

"You sound so very serious," she offered hesitantly.

"I am. I see very little use in putting any of this off for another day—or another night. The last time we separated, if you'll recall, I never expected there'd be time for us again. If you'll notice, each time we disagree, the fighting is more bitter, and the parting uglier." Louisa nodded. "We're not children, Louisa. Long ago, the quarrels we had were settled and forgotten in minutes. Now it's not so simple." He stopped to watch her stare at him. There were tears beading her lashes, and he reached to brush away one that slipped silently down her cheek. "You're afraid, aren't you?"

"You know me very well," she said, trying to compose herself, sitting a little straighter in the bed. "All right, Aaron. The moment of truth has arrived. No more pretending. No more hoping the unanswered questions will go away, like bad dreams often do," she said, reaching for an embroidered drawstring purse stashed in a rack above the bunk. "Perhaps we can begin with this," she said, opening the bag and removing Juliet's locket and ring suspended on Aaron's thick gold chain. "General Hoffmann gave me your personal effects but you never bothered to ask for them."

Aaron smiled wryly, reaching for the chain. "A mark of how eager I was to be out of the Presidio's walls!"

"Well?" she asked after a few moments of silence during which Aaron stared reflectively at the golden chain and its ornaments.

"It's as good a place to begin as any," he said, lifting the chain over his head. "The reason it never looked right on you is that it was never meant for a woman to wear. These trinkets are all I have left of a young woman I loved desperately, probably as desperately, in my way, as you loved Marshall. And you came by them unfairly."

Louisa's mouth dropped open, and he laughed at her look of astonishment. Then he told her of their first encounter in Jason Russell's house in New Orleans, and how deeply she had affected him. He told her he had loved her even then, and was now ashamed he had used her—not unlike others had, only for needs of his own. "I didn't seem able to stop myself. For a long time I'd dreamed of making love to you, and there you were, so willing in my arms. I never considered whether it was just or unjust to make love to you that way. I thought I had to test my impersonation. But even then I knew my real reasons. I wanted you for myself, however I could have you. And if you'll remember, your consent was for no one but Marshall."

Louisa lay back in the pillows and looked at Aaron as he sat beside her in the dim lamplight. Theirs had been a trauma-filled relationship with few moments of serenity. She looked into his face, into his deep dark eyes, at his lean hard body, which she was sure she would never stop yearning for. And she remembered the encounter he was speaking of. It touched her that he would tell her, that he would humble himself to confess his shame and sadness. She held her hand out to him and took his fingers to her cheek. "At the time, Aaron, I hardly even knew my own face when I saw it in the mirror. I was half crazy. Yet, I remember how different Marshall felt in my arms that night. But I was much too terrified to question ghosts who came to me in the darkness, especially a ghost with Marshall's face, one who spoke with his voice, who seemed not to want to hurt me—only to soothe and love me."

Aaron didn't speak, sensing she had more to say. But Louisa only watched him, staring almost vacantly, drifting through her memories. She knew she'd judged Aaron wrongly—and she had damned herself equally and as mistakenly. Aaron had seen what she had— great misery and sadness, things he had yet only alluded to, and while she had found hope in the depth of Marshall's love and had been able to sustain herself for an incredible length of time, Aaron had seen too little love, doubting love could fulfill even its simplest promises. This courageous, risk-taking man who seemed to fear very little in life—he had been afraid of what she promised: afraid to trust, afraid to feel, afraid to be hurt, afraid to hurt her—afraid of himself.

And Louisa had not been able to trust her instincts. She had been afraid to pursue this man whose wounds and needs were as deep as hers. She had fallen prey to dark superstitions and self-doubt, trusting more in voices from her past than in truth she'd learned from the depths of pain and sorrow.

Louisa now shuddered, realizing how from their separate positions of fear they had each built walls to defend themselves from injury, and how their desperate efforts had nearly damned them to loveless isolation from each other.

"Rachel could be your child just as you've suggested," she said quietly.

Aaron reached out for Louisa, urgently gripping her in his arms, his promising warm mouth close to hers. "I want to hear you say I *am* her father!" he whispered fiercely.

In spite of his intensity, Louisa looked at Aaron calmly, thinking that perhaps she saw for the first time. She thought back to the first occasion she had consciously made love to him—of how she had sensed that, for some unexplainable reason, he was reaching out to her with more than his body, and how odd she had felt it was, because, then, at that moment, in spite of his familiar face, he was a stranger. His need for her, his need for love spoke profoundly even then. He had communicated wordlessly, probably unknowingly—and she had heard—because she had often listened to her own silent voice begging out of the same need. Again she heard him, and this time she could answer.

"Aaron, for me, for the world, you *are* Rachel's father. And," she smiled, hugging him joyfully, "Rachel and I wouldn't have it any other way."

Aaron held Louisa in his arms, overwhelmed by her welcoming responsiveness. Whatever else they had to discuss would wait for another moment, while they filled their senses with the wonderful pleasures of touching each other. "I love you! I love you!" he said as he moved with her. "Hear me. Believe me. Never doubt me again." And when their bodies fused, their joining was intense and love-filled, their love for each other spoken, shared, and never again in doubt between them.